Hesha Vira's Challenge

Anu Awakes Series: Book One

Lyn McGinnis

Copyright and ISBN

This is a work of fiction. Any resemblance to actual events or persons, living or dead, is entirely coincidental.

ISBN : 978-1-9995055-2-3 (print)

978-1-0983850-8-8 (eBook)

Thank you for your support of authors' rights.

Interior Design by Booknook.biz.

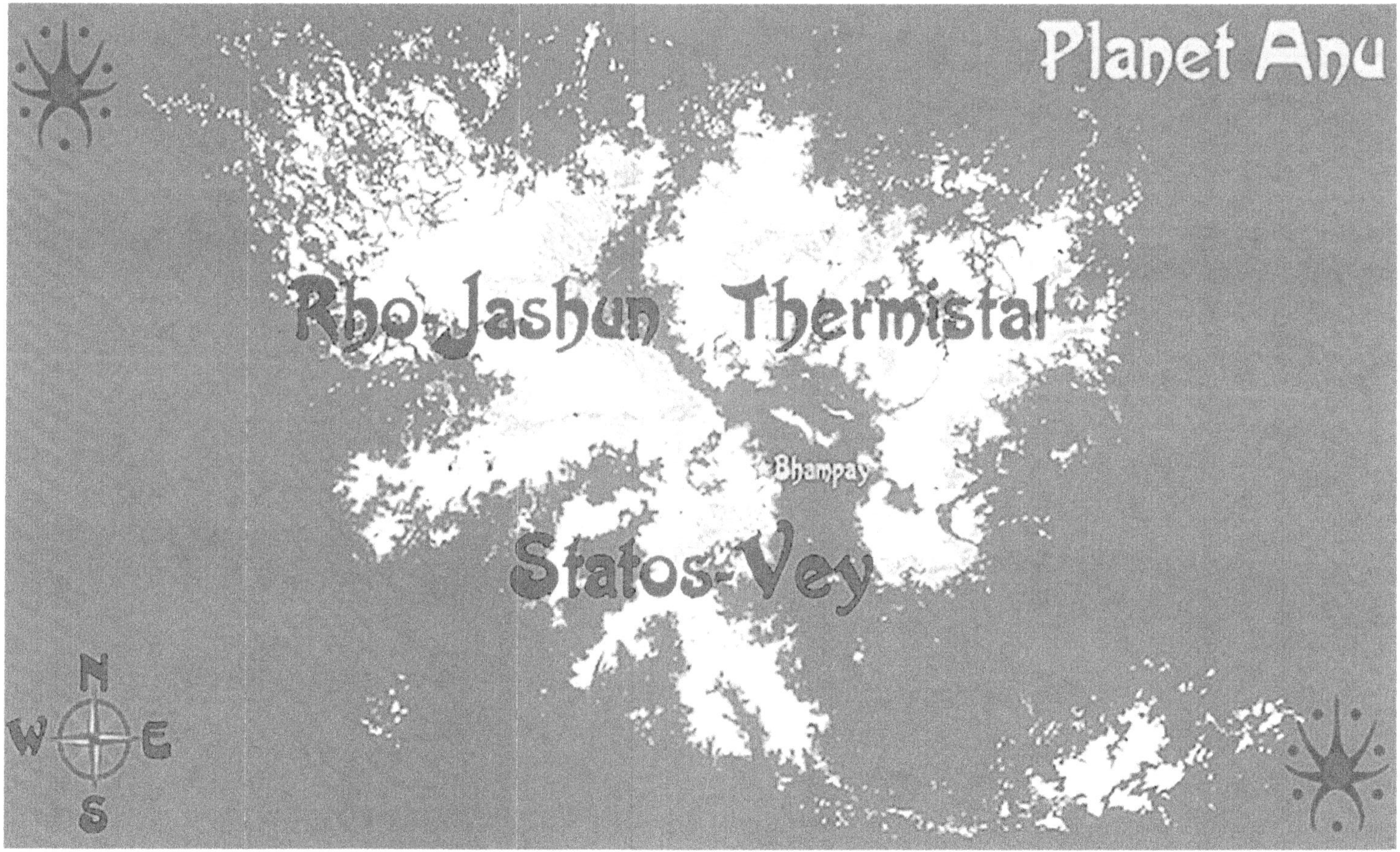
Planet Anu
Rho-Jashun
Thermistal
Bhampay
Statos-Vey
N
W
E
S

For background and in-depth information on all aspects of this novel, all the novels of the

Circle-of-Eight series, and more, please visit the Anu Awakes Series website:

https://www.anuawakesseries.com

Anu Awakes MeWe Page
https://mewe.com/p/anuawakesseries

All sites formerly associated with Anu Awakes on Facebook are corrupted by hackers. Do not visit or join these sites.

Anu Awakes Instagram Page:
https://www.instagram.com/anuawakes/

Anu Awakes on Twitter:
https://twitter.com/AnuAwakesSeries

Email address:
author@anuawakesseries.com

There are too many to adequately thank for their support and assistance in this venture. You know who you are and how much I appreciated your efforts. I single out my wife Geraldine and my brother Paul for their immense patience in seeing this revelation of an inner world finally coming to light.

Throughout history and across our Skin of Anu this day, most wish for peace, order and good governance. They seek purpose, direction and fulfillment. They long to be honoured and cherished. Beyond these fundamentals, they adore beauty, grandeur, and majesty. When filled with satisfaction, the cancers of venomous ambition and vile greed die away. Naught is evil of itself until it grows beyond its proper bounds. Ambition is a pernicious deformation of personal esteem. Violence is its tool of choice. Greed is an obscene inflation of our basic need for sustenance. Theft is its primary action. We say those poisoned by these, and many other base impulses, are suffering from Self-Absorption.

Shuna-Shapta

CONTENTS

CHAPTER 1

Shuna-Shapta

Pictured: icon of full Invocate.

Day 444, Two-Week Twenty-Five in the last days of the year 1270 of the Duamang Age in the port city of Bhampay.

"What is it?" The wide-eyed eight-year-old Shuna-Samshep whispered.

She stood with her three siblings on the edge of a festive crowd watching a performance in an open square. Three figures dressed as soldiers and carrying long swords confronted a huge creature covered in black fur.

"A Suvuka," her eldest sister Shuna-Shapta replied.

"They are that big?"

"Bigger," her brother Shuna-Vurupta said. "Even though this Suvuka costume holds two actors, it is still just half the size of an adult Suvuka."

The performers circled each other while eight musicians accompanied the performance with musical sound effects transforming the combative drama into an artful display of fight choreography. The timing of each move and counter move was well executed. Whenever the Suvuka opened its wide mouth another musician emitted a raucous deep note from a special horn as its roar.

The beast repeatedly knocked down the three soldiers in quick succession and smacked aside their weapons with the terrible spikes on the end of its paws. Struck by its talons, the combatants appeared to bleed. The creature prepared to devour them. A young girl suddenly entered the open circle wearing rich robes and a tall turban. The crowd hushed and the musicians stilled before her. Portraying a Tatchlan Master, she made several elegant gestures with her gloved and jewelled hands. The Suvuka made a gurgling noise; began to shake and then fell. The soldiers rose, repeatedly stabbed the creature, and ripped the body wide. The Tatchlan Master gathered handfuls of treats from inside before throwing them into the crowd. The audience began to chant "Shash! Shash! Shash! Shash!" as they received this bounty.

She reached in several times and dispersed the rewards. Shuna-Vurupta caught several and shared them among his elder and younger sisters. The troupe rose to bow, including the two unharmed actors inside the Suvuka suit. The other actors wiped the false blood off. One of the musicians paraded with the upturned Suvuka head as the laughing group tossed coins into it.

As the crowd disbursed and the musicians started to draw the next audience, the children began to move away. Shuna-Samshep stood staring at her candy. "Why did they do this? Are Suvuka good to eat?"

The others laughed and Shuna-Shapta said, "No, Little. I would say it means the Suvuka's defeat brings us abundance. Along with expressing delight, our word 'Shash' also means living without fear. We Tolku now may grow toward our greater destiny."

Fifteen-year-old Shuna-Shapta enjoyed these simple questions.

To the surrounding crowd, she appeared a tall girl with her long black hair, accented by red and brown streaks, wound into a bun. Her skin's patterned accents formed small dark half circles traveling across her light copper skin in elongated herds that accentuated her body's meridians. While her smooth face, high brows, broad nose and full lips marked her as handsome, her dark brown eyes remained her dominant feature, with their distinctive strong yellow radii sending vibrant tendrils to her black pupils. These eyes accentuated her intense expression. The Tatchlan Masters understood what truly distinguished this young woman. Along with being a rare Maja, a being potentially able to bind a Circle of Eight together when she became a Ripe Adult, she was also a child prodigy. She was on her way to becoming a Full Invocate, something only one in ten Maja could attain. She did so ten or more years ahead of most Maja reaching this depth. She was seldom seen outside the Master Enclave.

Today she accompanied her younger brother and two sisters into the city to enjoy the Alatahanu Carnival that was closing the year 1270. Some servants from their Master Enclave stood silently nearby, charged with ensuring no harm approached. Despite living as siblings, Shuna-Shapta and Shuna-Vovans have one birth mother, Master Kanla, whom they address as First Ama, and the other two another birth mother. Her name is Shuna-Dana. The four Shuna children wore simple light green shirts over their shining copper skin and held parasols with little bells around the edges. They carried none of their usual badges, medallions or masks and so paled in comparison to the dazzling variety surrounding them.

Shuna-Shapta's brother, Shuna-Vurupta, aged thirteen, drew the gaze of all passersby with his waving hair ending in ringlets, dark copper and bronze skin, elegant frame and long delicate fingers. Despite being a year younger than Vurupta, their younger sister Shuna-Vovans, aged twelve, was already broader and taller than him. Her long black hair with its red streaks freely stirred with the ocean breezes. Her copper skin was deeper than her elder sister's and her brown eyes were darker than all her siblings. Eight-year-old Shuna-Samshep was her First Ama Shuna-Dana's youngest daughter. She presented as a miniature of her mother. She was a pretty little girl, with a short and stocky frame, featuring short dark hair, red-brown eyes and glowing copper skin. These three lovely siblings seldom spent time with their remarkable sister.

Shuna-Shapta was the youngest in living memory to descend Seven of the Eight Levels of her training. She was about to become a Delving Invocate before finally being designated as a Full Invocate. After intensive study and rigorous preparation, she welcomed laughing with her siblings as they watched the puppet shows, lines of dancing drummers, gong concerts and assorted street performances. She enjoyed the orders and professions in their crimson, blue and yellow dress robes wearing their distinguishing hats and masks. Their glorious city of Bhampay sparkled more than usual as they wove their way through the celebrations. Glittering shrines were heaped with flowers as coloured ribbons of rich incense filled the air. Children led large and small animals, painted and adorned for the days' events, through the crowd. Giant kites of fantastic design performed acrobatics overhead.

Heavy banners displaying Anu's four moons, the twelve festival symbols, and sixty-four Tatchlan glyphs rippled on poles surrounding an open plaza. The four children climbed up onto the base of a statue of Yin-Vinulan the XXIV. The Yin-Vinulan dynasty, builders of the Red Ring wall around the city, was long gone, yet the colourful events and personalities of that age remained popular in their former capital. Flower embellishments and improvised wind chimes covered the artfully posed golden arms and legs of the venerable 'Dancing Emperor.' The children sat, their legs dangling down, and watched the pageant flow past them in each direction.

Shuna-Shapta winked at her beautiful brother before looking at the most creative member of the family, "What does our circle's drama critic say of the Suvuka performance?" She shouted over the crowds.

Shuna-Vovans 'use' was also clear, as an artist. The twelve-year-old had written and acted in her own plays, including designing the sets, leading her to have the nickname 'Flair.' She frowned, "I grow tired of pantomime," she called back. She possessed a notable voice that was musical in quiet settings yet could cut through the surrounding din with ease. "Although who may hear dialogue within this racket? I disliked the shabby Suvuka costume. The admirable choreography made up for it."

The two eldest children exchanged bemused glances.

"So the candy," Shuna-Samshep spoke through a full mouth, "is a symbol of our happiness?"

The others laughed and Shuna-Shapta tickled her. "Little, you have such a 'Questing Nose!' Yes, the Suvuka terror hung over our long-gone grandmothers and their mothers at the dawn of this our Duamang Age. We celebrate the burden of this ancient terror being lifted."

"Little," Shuna-Vurupta said, "the show displayed something else." The boy got down to stand in front of his little sister. "Our armies could not defeat the Suvuka. Those brutes destroyed our ancestors and all their works. The Suvuka defeat came only at the hands of our Tatchlan Masters. They stopped the Suvuka's wombs. The Suvuka then could not give birth and so they withered away. Recall how the ancient Geltran found the sign hanging over an abandoned Suvuka cone? 'They killed some of us with their paws. We killed them all with our heads.'"

The youngest nodded, pointing at the crowds and adding in her piping voice, "They love our Masters."

"Yes," Shuna-Shapta nodded as she closed her parasol and stood in the emperor's shadow, "I welcome an outing to view the results of their work." She gestured at the glyphs displayed on the banners and spinning parasols passing by them, "Surrounded by the signs, our population shall better appreciate their full meaning. More Sensitive and Maja births means Mundanes shall remain an honoured and diminished percentage of our population."

"You shall educate them concerning this new life," her brother Shuna-Vurupta said, making an artful bow as he swung his parasol in an arc without hitting any passersby. "Our pride swells for you, Shapta! You shall be the youngest Master of our age!"

Her siblings beamed at her.

"Ah!" Shuna-Shapta winced as she looked up at the ancient statue, "I shall not meet my Living Instrument for four to six two-weeks. She shall decide my true measure my full entry into our Seventh Delving Invocate level."

"Shapta!" her brother spoke in mock exasperation, "no other Delver within living memory has overtaken each lower Supervisor with each step of their descent. Master Tanas conducts your training personally!"

"Vurupta! This is not a solitary journey. A Delving Invocant circle of eight now accompanies me."

"Just recently. And none are less than five years older than you, and they were several levels ahead prior to your joining them," Shuna-Vurupta smiled. "Mi-Yang is twenty and traveled down the initial four steps over the traditional four years. To also have a Master guiding her proves her own exceptional ability. Ama Kanla and Ama Dana have told us how, at each level, your Supervisors expressed their astonishment at your progress. They consistently made the unusual recommendation that you move forward out of the established sequence. Ama Kanla said no student has possessed your assurance in Descending the first Six Levels of Depths for over a century. At fifteen, you enter the Seventh Depth and then shall sink to the Eight and final level! Full Invocant status is just beneath your feet! You, and our esteemed Amas, were already our treasured Majas, three of only thirteen in our entire Enclave. Now you are about to join them as an Invocate. Allow us to celebrate our admiration for you."

Flower petals from the statue showered down on them with the sea breeze and they laughed. Innumerable chimes and bells caught the breeze as the entire city shared their delight.

"And what of you, dear brother?" Shuna-Shapta said hugging him. "We have not spoken for how long?" The boy winced and gave her a mild grin.

"I have glorious mothers and brilliant siblings. I choose to take my time finding my use, allowing the rest of you wonders of our age to find your prodigious depths." He waved off their protestations. "Our Planet Anu extends beyond my view. I shall finish the opening level of Student, completing this portion of my formal education. Various ways exist to bring prosperity and honour to our circle and enclave. I shall find mine presently."

Shuna-Shapta smiled and squeezed his hands. She turned to look at the brilliant scene and expelled an extended breath. "I fear this fame carries a terrible weight," she said. "You know I always wished this. I had worked through part of our syllabus of ecstatic rites and formal disciplines at Samshep's age. I tried to perform some of them. Do you recall our secret games?"

Shuna-Vovans nodded, "Of course! Your face was so focused. You became a Ripe Adult before me. Recall our assisting you also. And though Samshep was just a baby she helped as well."

Shuna-Samshep silently nodded.

"You did!" Shuna-Shapta exclaimed. "I cradled those memories through my ordeals. Whilst harder than I imagined, my passion made each step, from Student to now standing at the door of Delving Invocant, flow into each other. My recollections of these intensive stages blur together. I now arrive at the entrance to the Round Chamber and I fear for my readiness. Why did I rush? Have I come too fast?"

"Shapta!" her brother chided. "You were always ready! We have watched how your use has filled you as far back as we may recall. You have the focus and devotion of an artist and scientist. Your passion defines you! You are ready."

Shuna-Shapta folded her arms and lost focus as she pondered her life, seeming to age before them. A procession of elegant dancers began to move past them. Their golden costumes sparkled under the unclouded Eye of Nu, their planet's sun that shone fully down on them. Their intricate gestures and steps mesmerized the children.

"Oh, big wise one!" Shuna-Samshep interrupted their reverie as the ritual performers passed. The other two siblings giggled.

Shuna-Shapta stepped closer and pretended to swipe at her little sister with her parasol. "Yes, *Little*?"

"You said you wished to attend a Yom Sha," Shuna-Samshep said sweetly. "I hear one now."

They peered about and listened for the characteristic tones amidst the general festive din. A rich male voice chanted a long string of sounds from their Master Enclave. The Shapta children stood, linked hands, and made their way toward the litany.

"What significance does this Yom Sha hold?" Shuna-Vurupta asked. "Are those words? What do they mean?"

"Our Masters have countless tools," Shuna-Shapta answered. "I may not utter these by myself, unless responding to a Master invoking them. Our Yom Sha is composed of powerful sounds. They penetrate our Resplendent System from the surface. The core of life harkens to us."

They began to hear the crescendo of one set ending. Shuna-Shapta sensed that the declarations and responses were altered and extended. They had missed the earlier parts due to the general festivities.

"So, our dwelling upon the surface affects the depths of Tatchlan?" Shuna-Vurupta asked.

"Of course dear! You influence our Resplendent Work through diverse ways by living your life. Multiple implements assist our Masters drawing us closer to the moment of the Quickening. Tatchlan shall then fully awake and our Cluster-of-Clusters Nation blossom. We shall know the joy of Each Belonging to All."

When they arrived at a large open square, they saw a tall figure moving in a slow circle on a raised platform carrying a tall staff. He struck the platform on key points during the ritual. Eleven others knelt on the outer periphery facing inwards. With each strike of the Master's staff they struck different symbolic poses. The walker was wrapped in shimmering orange and red folds. On his face was the large, round and black mask of Alatanda, the first of the Twelve Principal Faces of the Tatchlan System. The kneeling group around him each wore a fantastic mask of one of the other eleven Faces. Each shimmered with jewels and elegant craft. A glittering fringe hung down from the lower part of each mask, which Shuna-Shapta knew symbolized the tendrils of the living Faces enveloped by the Living System. The Shuna children had emerged from the Master Enclave compound by a different way and had missed this ensemble.

"As ever," Shuna-Shapta spoke softly, "'the mask reveals the wearer.'" She pointed, "All Masters are from our Enclave! And my Master Tanas wears our Face of Alatanda. I thought I recognized his lush voice."

"Those masks," Shuna-Vovans said, "I have noticed them inside our Enclave. They symbolize Tatchlan and I have dreamt of them. Were they displayed at previous carnivals?"

"No, Vovans," Shuna-Shapta beamed, "How clever of you to notice. They told us our Twelve Faces, introduced to the public through the ages, would arise in full. See how the unique colours and patterns of each face mirror the dominant motifs of the twelve annual festivals? This open display, so well received, is most encouraging."

They looked at the happy and intent crowd, who prepared for the incantation and their sung response.

"New and familiar," Shuna-Vurupta said, "I may have also dreamt of them."

"You are less Mundane than you claim brother!" Shuna-Shapta nudged him. "Such dreams reveal you as a Sensitive, as the rest of our circle."

The boy flushed and his siblings laughed.

"What are they?" Shuna-Samshep piped up, "Why do they look as they do? Do they dwell enclosed by our System?"

"Despite my new sensitivities," Shuna-Shapta said, "I but step upon the threshold of wisdom. I promise when I know more I shall tell you. I know they perform vital parts of how Masters execute their workings. Our Primary Masters spent generations constructing and animating them to their exalted use."

"Yom Sha, Yom Sha, Alatanda, Alatanda!"

Master Tanas paused in his circling to perform a deep bow at the mention of the first Face's name, who's visage he wore. This was a far more important event than Shuna-Shapta had realized. While the names were known, a new level of understanding opened with the Faces linked to their names. The crowd around her replied to the musical chant with ease.

"Alatanda, Alatanda, Skarashing, Skarashing, Vuna Sana Ya!"

The other children joined the rest in answering. At the evocation of the Face of Skarashing, the figure wearing a half-day and half-night Mask stood and turned several times while gently swaying side to side to the music.

"Yom Sha, Yom Sha, Skarashing, Naprahath, Naprahath, Vuna Sana Ya, Yuna Sana Ya, Humma, Humma Ya!"

The remaining eight sets of Invocant phrases were uttered, laced with the names of the other Principal Faces of Tatchlan. Shuna-Shapta found tears' streaming down her face as she sang her responses. The dream of innumerable generations stirred awake.

CHAPTER 2

SINKIN

Pictured: Tolku Icon of the Vettencore Passage with the Tolku on the Western shore and the Suvuka on the Eastern shore.

Day 486, the last day of the year 1270.

Nine of the massive creatures stood in a half-circle, their dark pelts glistening. Their four stout legs ended in huge paws with long, thick nails extending and retracting at will from the front and heel. Their necks finished in broad heads with pronounced brows and dominating eyes. Wide ears moved in every direction, and a wide, flexible jaw accompanied their extended snout.

These were Suvuka, who for uncounted ages were lords of the continent of Thermistal. For most of their history, they were unaware of the southern continents, and until they met the little Tolku, they had known no rival. The Suvuka had long named themselves the Shepherds of Anu. The Tolku possessed the southern lands of Rho-Jashun and Statos-Vey, the Suvuka, the northern land of Thermistal. While the Suvuka and Tolku were sovereigns of their respective continents, they achieved supremacy by very different means. While the Suvuka overpowered all opposition, the Tolku incrementally modified their challengers into servants. When the Suvuka and Tolku finally met, the Suvuka immediately saw them as an enemy and attacked. They destroyed much of the Tolku civilization, but the Tolku survivors eventually overwhelmed them with craft beyond their understanding.

"Behold our prison wall!" Hiratak recited.

"Yeeeaaaaoooo!" the set of formidable voices answered.

"Behold our shame! Behold our defeat!"

"Taaaoooo! Tatal! Tatal! Tatal!" the others bellowed.

"Behold the place our honour will return! Behold the place our vengeance will commence!"

"Vooooaaarrrrat! VAT! VAT! VAT!"

"Vooooaaarrrrat! VAT! VAT! VAT!"

These opening cries began young Sinkin's journey on the Full Stag Path. The other eight Suvuka, who were chosen to attend Sinkin through the entire ritual, were a small part of Durka Herd. They now rose on their hind legs and began stamping their paws and biting their lips in wrath. They continued their energetic displays, rolling their eyes, baring their fangs. Their sharpened talons extended to their full length. They swiped the air, stamped their huge hind legs, and stuck out their long tongues while their animated racket echoed off the silent power before them.

They stood overlooking a steep incline, which quickly sloped to a sheer wall of smooth stone curing at the top towards them. On the other side flowed a broad ocean channel, named the Vettencore Passage by the Tolku, stretching straight north and south beyond view. They knew that in the west, beyond their gaze, stood another high wall. Beyond this vast canal lay the Kyu Desert, the Mandeca Mountains and the rest of the continent of Thermistal - the Suvuka's ancestral home. Its rich pastures, fertile hunting grounds surrounding their Grand Lake, and their sacred island of Lewetar now crawled with the contemptible two-legger Tolku. After the Suvuka's defeat, they were imprisoned on this eastern third of their fatherland.

The canal passage was an artificial invasion of the Panchala Sea, dividing Suvuka lands. Hiratak, Sinkin's Herdmaster and designated Voice, sent a final battle cry against the implacable wall. The rest of the herd joined in with their formidable chorus. When the ritual was done, they stood panting, steam rising from their hot flanks. As their blood cooled, a tall silence began to conquer them anew. No Tolku came from the outer side of the wall to watch them. No ship sailed the passage this close to dawn.

Young Sinkin, flush with youth's arrogance, found his large head falling before the calm indifference of their foe. He and the others turned and began to gallop away. Tears flew from Sinkin's flushed cheeks as he found himself pulling out in front. Behind him, the others watched him and gave each other knowing glances.

No creature their size matched their speed or endurance, and by midday, they arrived at the ancient Chitikal Round. Fashioned before the Suvuka met the weak little Tolku two-leggers, seeing this Gathering Circle's towering set of cones and mounds brought pride back to the herd. Sinkin had grown up in the sight of this Chitikal Round. In all their travels, Durka Herd had aligned themselves by this ancestral Round. Bellowing as they raced the worn tracks surrounding their symbols of life and power, this timeless Mesmerizing Circle Run renewed the Suvuka after their symbolic confrontation. Chitikal Round was one of thousands raised across Thermistal by their ancestors, the ancient Shepherds of Anu. Sinkin had been told how the Tolku had dishonoured the many rounds built on Rho-Jashun.

Hiratak came beside the panting Sinkin, stopping near one of the ancient cones. "Your voice strong!" he declared. "Your father died too soon. You equal his beginning."

"Herdmaster, do any remember our exile?"

"No young runner. Those warriors fell to dishonourable age. Twelve generations died since our defeat."

"We still sing their songs?"

"They bring strength. We Shepherds of Anu! We crushed vile two-leggers. Only the mountains stopped our holy mission. There, two-leggers tainted our loyal servants. Forced us to put our kin down. Now we stand alone. All Anu poisoned. She cries for aid. Time nothing. We live, so Anu has hope."

Sinkin looked at the ancient cone, "How we defeated?"

Hiratak frowned, "You hear sagas tell how the two-leggers fooled our companions. Our once loyal kin betrayed us. Then two-leggers sucked us dry. We could not bear young, and our ancestors lingered in dishonour. No young voices refreshed songs, and there was no worthy battle. By foul craft, they loosed a plague. Two leggers destroyed us from behind mountains."

"They are weak! How did they craft this ruin?"

Hiratak growled in frustration, "Endless questions! Their works are despicable! They are a disease corrupting their own! Anu cried for relief, so we ran for Anu's honour. We fought to restore Anu. Anu's wide flanks favoured us. He rejects these creeping ones. Southern lands welcomed us. Tall grasses of Marachla Plain lay down before us. Anu despises life twisters. The Mulungu Mountains tried to open a way, but their fetid arts barred our passage. Our fatherland Thermistal ever embraced us. It heaves in disgust at their presence. We do not wound Anu. We do not change the ocean's course. By invisible cunning, Tolku compelled life. They enslave all. Nothing remains untroubled by them."

Sinkin looked at his Herdmaster, "What will we do?"

Hiratak responded calmly, "We build ourselves. Watch their ocean barrier. Survey their ways. We once swam to Rho-Jashun. We will swim this canal. We must learn the wall's secrets first."

Sinkin was compelled to speak, "I hear two-leggers cross over now. They make us sleep when Nu is high. They disgrace our bodies. They put their tiny paws over us. They twist us with tricks."

Hiratak flushed, "Who said this?"

"A buck from Makusk Herd. He saw runners from Konogat Herd.

Their bodies marked. They had strange gait. He said other herds bear foreign young."

Hiratak growled louder, although his anger was directed outward, "I know little of these 'Makusk.' Do not give in to stories. Our talons must remain sharp. These fears defeat us anew."

Sinkin frowned, "We defeat them in battle. Now they herd us like Danta. They know our strengths. We ignorant of theirs."

"Their 'strength' perversion!" Hiratak bellowed.

The seven remaining members of Durka had begun to gather around Sinkin and Hiratak.

"What our strength?" Sinkin persisted. "What do Tolku fear? Two leggers cover Anu. They cut trees to make floating islands on water. They ride sea creatures! Their slaves fly above and burrow beneath. They reach us. We cannot reach them. If we cross over, what would we do? Herdmaster, I ask these questions in deference."

Hiratak stood shaking. The other Durka were silent.

"Many ask these questions," he said, fire abandoning his muscular frame. "You speak true. They use strange weapons. Their power grows. Sinkin, you could trample an adult Tolku now. Long ago, they chose a dishonourable path. They altered every creature. They turned them into slaves. Now they change themselves. They reshape Anu. All becomes a perversion."

He stopped, and Durka stood in silence, pondering his words.

"Cannot lose ourselves," Hiratak said. "We not Tolku! Our defence within us. They failed to change us! Once-noble Tamku and Toboku bow to them. We remain untainted."

Sinkin frowned, "Our enemy hems us in! They visit our dreams. If they turn us in our sleep . . ." he stopped.

Hiratak looked at the others, "You speak of phantom foes. Was this buck like you? Does he ready for the Full Stag Path?"

Sinkin nodded.

"We may find Makusk at Avanchil. The season is begun — many run. We cannot fear dreams! We must mass in larger numbers. Small herds fall to wild tales."

Sinkin stood pondering this, "I thank you Herdmaster and Durka

Voice. I am young. My education starts."

The others shuffled and muttered.

Hiratak raised himself and stamped his two front paws, "Your initiation to Full Stag of Durka Herd has Four Paws. First, you confront the barrier. Second, you run far south. We cross Jabun Isthmus and Kukernef Desert. Many paws form trails to Avanchil Round. Your instruction there is the third paw — Avanchil most esteemed Round on Thermistal. The greatest and bravest Suvuka have running frenzy there. Thousands will join you to dance. You are ready. Your final paw revealed at Avanchil. You must be strong for the test. We are forbidden to reveal more. We are Shepherds of Anu! We take back our own. Your path is beyond their diseased imaginations. You will succeed!"

The others looked to each other, and most nodded agreement. Zatin, who last did the run, looked less confident.

"Herdmaster," Sinkin asked in a diminished voice, "what penalty for failure?"

Hiratak's expression went blank. "The same as not seeking shelter during lightning. We are not judges. You must succeed to survive."

They turned and began to gallop out of Chitikal Round. Sinkin followed them at an uncertain pace.

CHAPTER 3

Seti

Pictured: Image of Untasha-Kabash, the Menem symbol of perfection.

Day One, Two-Week One, named Atra – the Bursting Flame, the first day of the year 1271. Four hundred andas south of Hora-Sarota-Sewa Island along the western coast of Rho-Jashun.

The wild-eyed boy stood on the stinking dock looking up at the large merchant ship. From four tall masts hung proud triangular sails, and its prow was emblazoned with the name Jefaka. His pale peach skin, covered in a subtle white and beige spotted pattern, was tanned and soiled. His light yellow hair was matted and dirty. The crew unloaded crates of cargo. He thought he smelled nuts within the containers as they jostled by him. A tall woman stood on deck, surveying the scene. She wore a tapering brown hat curving toward her brow over her close-cropped blond hair. Her tan face was weathered, and her hands calloused. The boy heard the crew addressing her as captain.

"Captain?" the boy cried out over the surrounding port noise, "I wish to sail with you."

Captain Emedin sniffed at the skinny youth with his northern pale blue and grey eyes. "I have no room for waifs! My crew finds ample comfort in the ports. Be off!"

"I provide a powerful service!"

Several crew members slowed in their tasks, turning to look at him.

"Indeed?" Emedin found his proud manner at odds with his bedraggled appearance.

"I invoke the invisible ones. They will tell me when storms come."

Emedin's eyes went wide, and she laughed heartily, along with several of the crew. Many came to look at the boy, including a wizened man now standing by her side. He was notable for his short black hair dramatically set against his pale peach skin and deep blue eyes. Seti managed to hear a voice on the high deck, "Captain? It is 1271, the first day of a New Year. He may bring us luck!"

Many of the crew laughed and clapped at this. The captain and this older man bent in a discussion. She turned back to the boy with a thoughtful expression while the older man examined him with a frown.

"By far the youngest and least presentable Invocant I have seen," the captain shouted down to the boy. "The statues and carvings show elders with flowing beards. So! You speak with Menem? You see their bodies of light? You hear their silent cries? The ancients say our ears and eyes are too gross to perceive them. How came you by this gift?"

"They are revealed to me. I know their names. They come when I call."

Several of the crew gasped, and a few reached for amulets around their necks. None had heard such claims from one so young. A new set of discussions began on deck. The captain and the older man noted the reaction of the crew and bent together to speak.

"I also know their names," the captain called back. "They will not answer or do my bidding."

"The fallen ones ever seek to escape their captivity. The holy Menem finds few following the old ways. They have chosen me. They now recognize my voice and I theirs."

There was more discussion, and several gathered and spoke with the captain in turn. She listened to each before turning back to the boy. The crew grew silent as she studied him.

"I have not sailed alongside an Invocant since I was a deckhand on my first ship," the captain said. "As I recall, they must earn their keep before reaching the next port. If not, they are set ashore. Do you accept these terms, young Invocant?"

"I do."

She appeared fascinated by this intriguing boy and his commanding presence. The older man was displeased and spoke to the captain. She replied to him before saying, "Bring him up!" Two crew members came down and accompanied him onto the vessel. They brought him to the captain, who examined him. She winced at the stink and how many bones she counted.

"Captain?" the older man made a face at the boy before looking at Emedin and shaking his head.

"My name is Captain Emedin; this is my First Officer. His name is Dine," the captain gestured to the man beside her. "Let him state his case," she declared to her crew. She turned back to him, "What say, you boy?"

"Years ago," he began, "Menem gathered in a glowing company and spoke to me. They said the pure aspire to hear them, the vain to see them and the vulgar smell them. They declared the dust of Anu now covers them, making them visible to the unworthy. The Menem laid a charge on me. They said I must 'remind the Tolku of who they are.' I am driven to discover the meaning of their words. They led me across the land to the ocean. They brought me to you."

The deck grew silent around the boy as the captain and her First Officer examined him. She bent down to look at him.

"What is your name?"

"Seti."

"And where did this epic journey begin, Seti? Where is your family?"

He shifted under her gaze, and his beige spots began to darken.

"Yeplin."

"'Yeplin,' what is this?"

"A village built among ruins," the boy answered. "While nothing to look at today, it has deep roots containing many layers. I do not know what came before, but once Yeplin was one of forty-four places of power on Rho-Jashun for our ancestors. Each of these places had a Menem Shrine enclosing relics from the war in Ranvartawan. These shrines were spread across Rho-Jashun according to where the holy relics fell from the pure sky above. Yeplin is now a spec on a broad plain, but once it was a large city built around its Menem Shrine. In ancient times, devout Tolku went on pilgrimages to each shrine to renew their faith. The broad avenues they trod now lie crumbling, and most of the city is buried. Our village stands at the centre of the northwest quarter of that former metropolis. Many homes contain at least one thick wall, and many stones scavenged from the ruins. Above this venerable layer is another, formed by the Suvuka. My father said when the Suvuka invaded; they destroyed all forty-four shrines and their protecting cities and built their wide gathering circles over them. That Suvuka round survives to this day. Most of the Menem city is gone, and our village is now surrounded not by fine buildings but tall fields of Salarish. Our families served the farmer clan there, which presumes to call itself the Yeplin Clan."

"Hmmm . . ." Captain Emedin said. "Rho-Jashun is filled with such tales. Even our northern islands have our own stories of former glory and present misery." She paused, "So you toiled for our flat cakes. Salarish is known as a Blood Crop. Did your Yeplin Clan require blood from your family?"

Seti nodded silently.

"You observed the Baby Mother harvest?"

Seti shot her an angry glance, "My mother and sisters revelled in those vile rites! They excelled in forming the dough babies as priestesses to the farmers."

"Would this not improve your lot among them?"

"They said their 'Baby Mother' predates the true Menem religion!

When they heard of my voices, they laughed at me. They dismissed my visions, saying I was ever the dreamer. I had hoped my aunt would believe in me . . ." He stopped, and his lip trembled, "She 'Viewed the Waters.'"

"What did you say?" Emedin exclaimed. "The practice extends this far north? Are there many rivers where you lived?"

Seti shook his head, "No, my aunt travelled to a lake. We had several springs the farmers used to irrigate the Salarish. She went to view the waters rising to the surface."

The captain shook her head, "Did she . . . 'scry' the waters to make predictions?"

"No, she hated this. She said she followed the true Viewing traditions, calling them the 'ethical stream.' She said she found 'wisdom in the waters' and sought a master so she could learn what she called 'Destiny Water Viewing.'"

Captain Emedin gave a small chuckle before gesturing for him to continue.

"I used to play amid the huge cones and spheres the Suvuka raised for their Round. Father told me Geltran visited the place long ago."

Emedin tried to keep secret her surprise. "Geltran-Kenal-Tumhal?" she said in a conversational tone, "Do you know why he is famous?"

The boy frowned, "Geltran walked through Rho-Jashun after the Suvuka defeat. He said we Tolku lost our way when we robbed the Suvuka of children. He said the victory, caused by the sorceress Duamang, demeaned us. Geltran found a mocking sign on one of the rounds reading, 'They killed some of us with their paws. We killed them all with our minds.' Later he wrote books and spoke his convictions, but few agreed with him. My father. . . my father said with this something ill began among us."

Emedin looked long at the lad, "And what do your voices say?"

"My Menem say my father spoke the truth. Unlike the rest, he held to the true faith. He showed me an old copy of the Furrumittal and taught me from it. He told me of the war in Ranvartawan and how the evil Yeoyupan imprisoned Menem, the shining children of Untasha-Kabash, in these 'skin sacs.' He taught me how to find my way home to

Ranvartawan when this body dies. The voices say he opened my ears to hear them."

Seti held up his hands, displaying the distinctive series of tattoos moving down each digit's inner side. They symbolized the steps set out in the Furrumittal for the successful completion of the journey back to Ranvartawan.

"My father did these for me. On waking, I recite the formula of the Aspirant for my journey through the One Hundred Gates. While I have yet to bind one Sedet Servant or Sev Messenger to me, the four Grand Menem come when I call."

It had been many years since Emedin had heard such earnest speech concerning the Menem. The last time she saw the full set of traditional markings was on the hands of an eighty-year-old woman. Dine bent forward and examined them in evident amazement.

"Your father's faith is clear," Emedin said. "You say your mother; sisters did not follow Menem. They embraced the Salarish traditions and your aunt 'Read the Waters.'"

"She betrayed me!" Seti shouted, his face growing flush. "Once my aunt learned of my visions, she tried to 'cure' me! She called for doctors to come and rob me of them." He shook as he spoke. After taking a few breaths, he continued, "I ran away. My father found me, and we swore a pact to keep my hiding place secret. He said they sought me out, and I must go. He brought food and prepared me for this journey."

"Why did he send you out on your own?"

The boy sagged, "He could not leave. He said Anu is a prison. It forges chains of obligation to keep us down. He said I had to go for both of us. He said my voices would direct me. He told me to remember they sought me, instead of waiting until I summoned them. He turned and walked away. Then I came here."

The captain and crew held a respectful silence at this story. Captain Emedin said, "The Suvuka had no assemblies near this part of the coast. The Marachla Plain is broad. You say you walked here. How long has it been since you left your village?"

For an instant, Seti lost his presence. A small hungry boy whose spots grew faint answered, "I cannot say," in a whisper. "I lost all notion of time.

I followed Nu's setting each day and kept him behind me in the morning while watching for the mountains keeping them to my left. Grasses grew into thick tangles and forests, and I climbed the trees to find my way. I became accustomed to sleeping in the trees to avoid hungry eyes. I found wild fruits and began to hunt small game. I learned to hide well and steal food. I ate so little at times; my clothes nearly fell off me. I was so thirsty that creatures I used to play with I now cut down to suck their blood. At rivers, I learned to catch fish with my bare hands. I was so alone and spoke

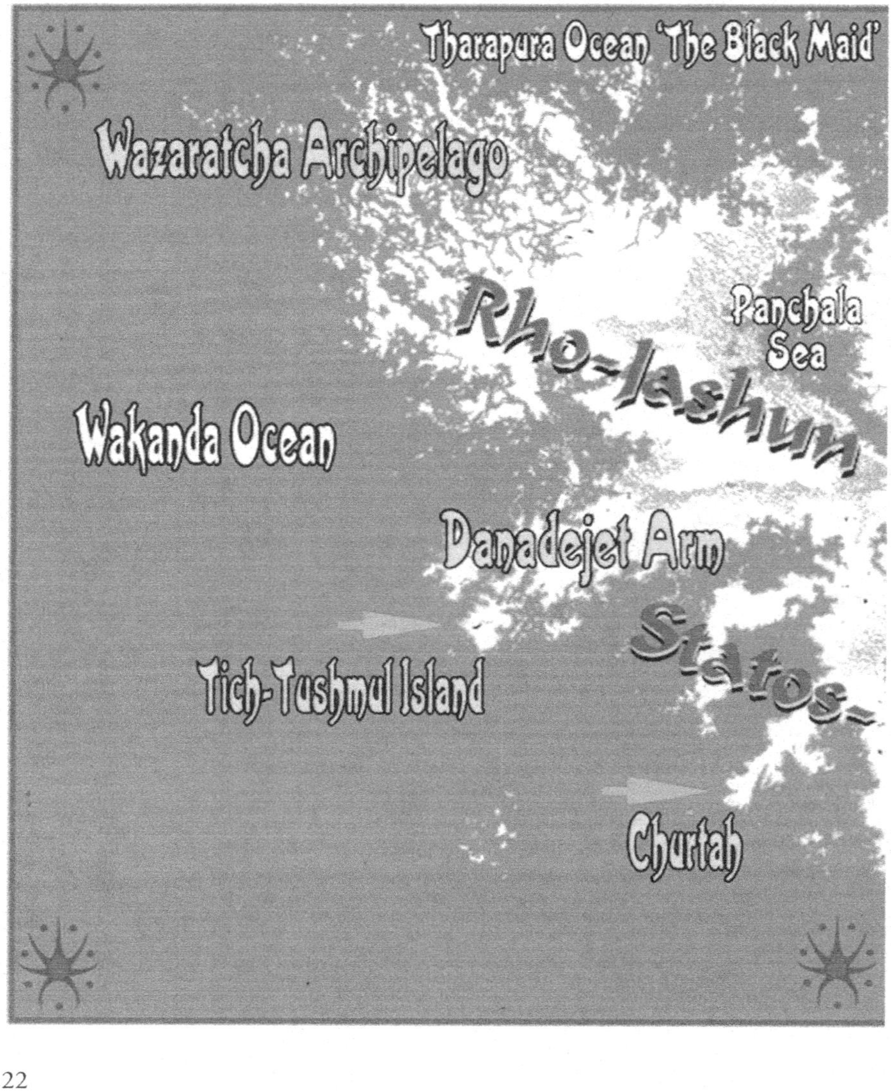

every thought aloud. I saw a glorious Xumkuka, the preferred mount of three of the four Grand Menem, flying overhead and knew I was not alone. They came down to comfort me, encouraged me and began to forecast difficulties. They spoke of reaching the ocean and finding you. All four forsook their undulating air serpents and began to walk beside me through the long days. They told me my true journey would begin on the sea."

Emedin stood and looked at her First Officer. Together they glanced at the crew. The boy had a unique presence. A young woman approached

the captain and spoke to Emedin before the captain turned and looked down at Seti. “What of dreams? Can you read them?”

Seti smiled, and his spotted colouration returned, “I read several dreams for food and shelter on my way here. I had not known I could until asked.”

Emedin nodded at this, “Very well,” she said. “You will be on probation as our Dream Reader and Storm Invocant. We will find you clothes and get food in you. This is our first long stop, and we will be here for at least a two-week to fill our ship with northern supplies and raw goods. We also have other business to attend to here. You will read each dream brought to you starting tomorrow. I believe it is customary for Invocants to call down Menem from the prow of the ship. We journey on our largest trade route known as The Circuit. It begins in the north of Rho-Jashun and follows its and Statos-Vey's western coasts before turning and following both land's eastern coasts home. We are early in this Circuit and follow Rho-Jashun's western coast. The storm season here is past. Heavy weather will visit later. Once underway, our upcoming port will be many days hence. You must demonstrate your ability as a Reader and Invocant for the Jefaka by this time. If you fail as a Dream Reader, you shall be put off before we leave. If you fail as Invocant, you will disembark at our next port. At the least, you will be better fortified should you need to seek your fortunes apart from us.”

“I thank you,” Seti answered.

“We are on the western coast of Rho-Jashun,” the captain continued, “and this is the Wakanda Ocean. She is not as wicked as The Black Maiden; what we call the Tharapura Ocean to the north, whose whims fill all sailors nightmares.”

She signalled for a map and laid it down on the deck. “We have just departed from the westernmost island of our home, the Wazaratcha Archipelago, know as Hora-Sarota-Sewa Island. We now make for the base of the Danadejet Arm of Rho-Jashun. While there is much rough coast between, the gyres are too changeable given what little of value there is between here and the Danadejet Arm. For a short time we will sail further out from shore at speed. Once we arrive at The Arm, we will turn west and south to closely follow the northern coast of this broad stretch of land. We will cross the equator and continue around the tip where our commercial venture truly begins. We will take rest at Tich-Tushmul, the second-largest island on Anu, before continuing along Danadejet's southern flank and entering the waters of Statos-Vey. Jefaka is now embarking on this globe-spanning trip for the third time and has known every combination of wind and sea. We will follow Statos-Vey's three long arms extending out of its southern coast by travelling up one side and down the other. These are fertile places of trade and will compose most of our journey. Much of our existing cargo of raw goods will land in these ports, and we will take on more for trade on the eastern coast of Rho-Jashun as we head home. This coast also contains perilous waters. Despite being an offshoot of the southern tip of Statos-Vey, we do not travel the Taldonow Archipelago. It extends far out into the wild waters of the Antarctic. As such it is even more frigid and bitter than the far north. Instead, we turn at the bottom of Statos-Vey and move north along the eastern shore, where the Panchala Sea will embrace us. She is mild-tempered and will gently push us home. Despite being far from here, the air will be warm and moist. Our final stop on the subcontinent is the port of ports, Bhampay, for scheduled maintenance and repairs. If you remain until this time, your duties will be light once we leave that commercial hub until we approach the Huallapandu Headlands, known as the Crown of Rho-Jashun."

She pointed to the top of the map, "The weather will be foul where mild Panchala clashes with the Black Maid's frigid waters. Should you remain for this, you may find rest at our homeport. It is on the southern coast of Wazaratcha Island. Our Sawlu Clan has lordship over the entire archipelago, a maze of over one thousand islands. A quarter are trapped in polar ice for part of each year, and the rest are subjected to 'The Battleground,' where the Tharapura and Wakanda Oceans make constant war on each other. Our home port is on the central of five islands sheltered near the northern coastline of Rho-Jashun. Amid these freezing and deadly channels our five primary islands forge a tenacious hold on life. Our ruling core, Wazaratcha Island, has a number of benefits you may want to consider. You will be at least two years older and may seek a home among us, or go where you will."

Seti bowed, and several members of the crew laughed and whistled. For the first time in over a year, Seti ate well and slept long. He washed, and his old clothes were discarded. He slept in a hammock among the crew and spent long hours on deck during the day, reading the crew's dreams and watching every task. While pleasant with those seeking him out, he otherwise kept himself apart to stare out at sea. When the Jefaka left port, he went to the ship's bow and peered into the clouded sky.

CHAPTER 4

Shuna-Shapta

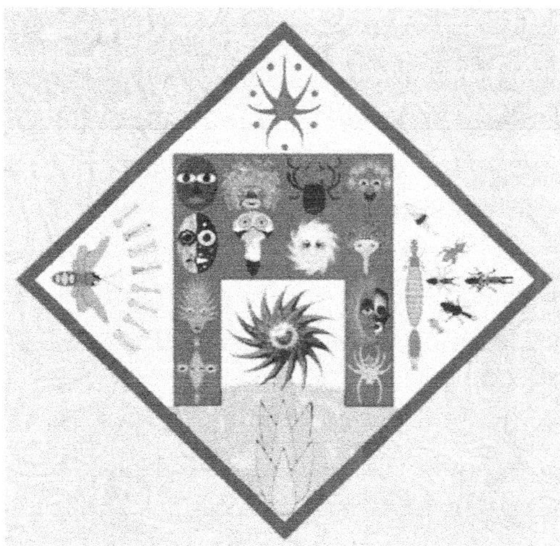

Pictured: Icon of Tatchlan Master Enclave

Day 18 of the year 1271, Two-Week One, named Atra – the Bursting Flame.

Gentle Nu, the Sweet Daymaker, cleared the horizon. His first heat arrows glided through the humid air over the ancient port city of Bhampay. The melodic call of the distant surf and cries of sea birds accompanied the sound of wind harps and chimes filling the air. The elegant metropolis was awakening. The early vendors pushed their squeaking carts as they began their melodic calls through narrow streets and laneways. Sleepy troupes of Cousins, a range of creatures related to the Tolku, covered the roofs with their soft hoots and coos. These were known as Asaku; their tiny bodies were bright yellow with green and blue markings. They resided on the rooftops awaiting the courier's call to take messages throughout the city. Overhead, an enormous Xumkuka, thin as a leaf on its sides, made a series of tight curves as it swam through the sky. In the still morning air, a slight rushing and tinkling from the ribbon-shaped creature's body could be heard.

Inside the Tatchlan Master Enclave, Masters working through the night now sought their rest. The morning group gathered at the long oval tables, working either their Tatchlan Cubes or Living Instruments. Several voices could be heard raised in the traditional opening evocation before they entered Tatchlan, the ancient Living System. Their voices rang with pride. Many now reported unmistakable signs of the Quickening of the Tatchlan System approaching. The Uluvatu Master's Vision was about to be fulfilled, bringing a grand new existence, free from Self-Absorption, to all Anu.

Master Shuna-Kanla stood on the balcony just outside her pre-cluster's residence. Her statuesque body displayed her shining copper skin with its travelling yellow accents. Overlaying these were thirty-two-years-worth of blood midge bites so prevalent in the tropics. These tiny dots formed multicoloured flowing patterns of density across her body, partly obscuring her underlying yellow skin accents. While many lost most or all of these patterns with their skin shedding, Master Kanla felt fortunate to be one of those retaining most of them after each shed. Her long black and red hair braids gently registered the distant sea breeze as she stood behind a classic red and yellow lacquer screen, a faithful rendition of those seen during Bhampay's ancient Yin-Vinulan Dynasty. In the early-morning peace, she even just heard muffled sounds of work echoing up from a passageway leading down to the eight levels of Bhampay's Inner City, the vast network of tunnels and chambers many times the size of the surface city. The Masters often did important work there as well.

"Ama?"

Master Kanla was startled out of her reverie. She turned to see her daughter coming out to join her.

"I heard shouting," Shuna-Shapta said as she swiftly knelt and paid homage to her First Ama's feet.

"Ah, Shapta!" Master Kanla answered in her deep voice. "'Shouting?' No! You heard raised voices." She clucked at her daughter, who as she stood was already near as tall as her, "You worked so hard and should sleep late this day. Your sixteenth year of life welcomes you! Your brother and sisters have plans!"

Shuna-Shapta smiled, but her intent expression returned, "Why raised voices?"

Her mother led Shuna-Shapta back inside. She smiled briefly at a young house servant who had accompanied her daughter into the chamber, "Leave us Ena," she gently said while indicating a set of empty plates and goblets to be taken. "We shall ring if you are needed."

After the young girl gathered the plates and left the Master Kanla turned to her daughter, "Masters Tanas, Cala, Zanamar and Lanca called at dawn to exchange pleasantries prior to commencing their work. A messenger brought reports from several Sensitives. They corroborated what Invocates already track within Tatchlan. A rebellion brews upon Rho-Jashun! We fell to debating the meaning of these reports. Our differences concerned relatively minor interpretations rather than any contention to the clear indicators of discontent. They have just left, and more extensive meetings shall follow."

Shuna-Shapta sat down on a long bench facing the balcony, her own long black hair with its red and brown streaks in a sleepy tangle. "Rebellion?"

Master Kanla sat and took her hand, "My dear, such signs shall be evident to you ere long. More seasoned noses, ears and eyes tell us this uprising has neither focus nor direction. Our Masters detect vague patterns, just suggesting a persistent and disorganized resistance."

Shuna-Shapta was puzzled. "I tread our Master's Way. Why have I heard naught of this?"

With deliberation, Master Kanla stood and crossed to the far side of the room. The warm peach walls wore weavings and tapestries presented to the Masters as gifts over the years. On one wall hung a large plaster cast of a Suvuka paw, more substantial than an adult Tolku's head. Over the distinguishing set of pads radiated a burst of long, thin lines marking the spots where the lethal talons had extended. Surrounding this sober reminder of their fearful past, hung symbols of their present, in the form of a set of ornate and colourful Masks of Office and Jubilation. These contrasted with the simple House Masks and hand mirrors scattered on a table and floor beneath the formal arrangement. Under framed degrees and commendations to various Masters, including Master Kanla herself, she poured two small glasses of fermented sap and returned.

"Much news awaits one with such a 'questing nose,'" she began. "My Estate Speciality does not encompass these matters, so I encourage you to seek others as well."

She glanced at the ornate woven carpet under her bare feet and sighed before starting, "I believe part of the fault belongs to our grandmothers and their mothers. You have studied the life of our acclaimed Master Duamang. She and our other Masters of her time completed the domestication of the once-feared Brangnam Plague into our faithful servant. They honed this weapon to perfection and ensured its thorough dispersal. The infection reached each Suvuka within their vast herds across Rho-Jashun. A generation came and went without any new whelps, and their once-mighty assemblies began to dwindle. Once most died away, our army swept the humbled remnants from the Marachla Plain. The few surviving Suvuka ancients fled ahead of them north, attempting to return to Thermistal. They huddled along the western shores of the Huallapandu Headlands. Their ancestors had once found a way across the Panchala Sea to the Crown of Rho-Jashun which became their staging area. From there, they commenced their Onslaught. Their distant descendants did not know how or were unable to make the return crossing. They were left unmolested to age and die.

As you know, the dawn of our post-Suvuka age led to a new calendar named Duamang to honour our treasured Master, now standing in the year 1271. Duamang Year One opened with the declaration that Rho-Jashun was now free of the creature that filled us with fear for so many generations. Along with Duamang, many other Master's names replaced ancient declarations, place names, and two-week titles honouring their part in ending the Suvuka."

Master Kanla paused, "Lacking specific instruction upon these matters; I grew a theory. Simply put, our exuberance overran our deliberation. Administrators serving our Muraharoma Dynasty, charged with re-establishing civil society, should have long preceded the general return of the Tolku to Rho-Jashun. Instead, our ministries of the day permitted an uncontrolled migration. There are tales of vast populations gathering upon the northern and western flanks of the Mulungu Mountains. They commenced a disorderly race into the wilderness to make their claim. To our eyes, there appears to have been much waste and appalling violence. I have been told some of these settlers wished to leave the orderly management of Statos-Vey. Anarchy and brutality such as never known within our generous subcontinent ensued."

Shuna-Shapta frowned, "Why?"

"Civilization is fragile. Such specialized seed requires soil prepared with care and dedicated, patient cultivation. These omissions now bear fruit, manifesting the worst forms of self-absorption."

"How did this happen?"

Master Kanla sighed again, "I suppose there are several reasons. Who could blame our cultivated, educated and skilled of the time having no desire to join such a melee? This left the simple and ignorant to dominate these new societies. My speculations are bolstered by some Honoured Historians suggesting the population should never have arrived ahead of our state. They go so far as to imply negligence upon the part of our responsible ministries for not establishing the territory and dispatching all necessary resources and personnel prior to any pioneers arriving. As it was, heedless and chaotic migrations lead to a general debasement of this new population. Many specialties did not take root. The memory of our deep lore did not travel well into what had become a brutalized hinterland. As the first true Maja and other Spokes of our Cluster Wheel began to be born upon Statos-Vey, the dramatic drop in the number of general Sensitives born upon Rho-Jashun went unnoticed. Superstition and myth flourished within the resulting void."

"Would not this disparity manifest within our Living System? We learn there are now increasing numbers of specialist Invocates able to discern trends flowing through our population."

Master Kanla nodded approvingly, "Tumours grow by tiny increments. Recent generations have witnessed Tatchlan's dramatic growth. We

Masters struggled to keep pace and navigate the expanding terrain. The past few centuries witnessed true equivalence between Master and our Resplendent Work. What was once 'The General Plain' of Tatchlan grew by leaps into fantastical landscapes. Our labour upon our Twelve Principal Faces and their many thousands of Secondary Faces for each set of functions was perfected just within your great-grandmother's time. Tatchlan serves us far more now than when you were born. When I was your age, some of my Elders first began to appreciate in full our past errors. When my generation became Invocants, our first task was to address these flaws by various means. Alas! Our tools are not fully formed, and our efforts to rectify the Rho-Jashun situation had unforeseen results."

Shuna-Shapta began shaking her head, "How could they forget? *We* liberated them from the Suvuka! But for the labour of Master Duamang over twelve hundred years ago, along with the rest of our grandmothers and their mothers, we Tolku might be extinct! Centuries later, it was Tatchlan Masters, at the head of our armies, who oversaw their confinement prior to our Vettencore Passage being completed. Now we chart Anu's Flesh and sail the Living Oceans. We plumb the depths, count and name the fixed and roving stars and extend each form of learning and accomplishment. Except for the Suvuka territory beyond our Vettencore Passage upon Eastern Thermistal, we Tolku protect Anu's Skin! Forget the many benefits of our Sheshenara and other Tatchlan creations. How do they have the luxury of standing upon the Flesh of Anu that Masters liberated for them and rebel?"

Master Kanla smiled, "The perversity does not end there. Critics of Tatchlan used to write many books. Long out of print here, they remain popular within portions of the rude north. Have you ever heard of an author named Nallurakon?"

Shuna-Shapta shook her head.

"During the century preceding our Duamang Age, she lived within our Primary Mountain Circle of Upata-Shepsus and specialized in herb augmentation and hybridizing. She distinguished herself for significant work with our Larpana plant. Few know that one of the major anti-Tatchlan critics toiled upon their timekeepers!" She indicated the three Larpana plants along one wall. They sat in their broad and ornate pots.

While their lower leaves ranged from a dull green to brown, the upper leaves and stem were a pale orange with deeper orange patterns, indicating 'Nu Dispels,' the third hour of the day. "When she became involved with our vital Nara Plant, whose fruits are transformed within the Shesha to produce Sheshenara," Master Kanla continued, "she turned upon us."

Shuna-Shapta looked bewildered, "Why, Ama? Our wellbeing rests upon those sweet juices. We thrive beyond our grandmothers and their mothers by virtue of its many benefits. Due to this and other remedies, the plagues and other horrors of the past cease to trouble us."

"She became convinced that feeding of Sheshenara to girls and young women was an evil and spoke against it. Her campaign garnered some support, and our Tatchlan Masters of her time joined the debate to illustrate your very points successfully."

Master Kanla shook her head, "Perchance, we erred in not telling you sooner. Were it not for their renewed popularity within the north, Nallurakon and, modern times another author and critic, Nebutan, would merit small mention within your curriculum. We consider re-introducing these teachings so you may better comprehend what may arise upon Rho-Jashun."

Shuna-Shapta sat frowning into space. "Surely, this shall fade away with the Quickening and the full emergence of flourishing clusters. Surrounded by our harmonious 'murmur of life' they shall find peace."

"Yes, of course. We do not expect this to occur for several generations. There are portions of our continent remaining backward and hostile. Statos-Vey may be largely ready for our Quickening, yet we must attend to the more aggressive trends within Rho-Jashun lest it grows to dangerous proportions."

"What may we expect during our lifetime?"

Master Kanla paused, "This general situation coalesces about the clan of Tolku named the 'Sawlu.' This large and organized population has enjoyed considerable mercantile power within the far north of Rho-Jashun for centuries. They must be credited with taking a most inhospitable collection of hundreds of islands, plagued by pirates and the dregs of the north, and fashioning a coherent society. Their commercial networks now sail upon a sizeable fleet. Their principal trade routes run along both of Rho-Jashun's and Statos-Vey's coasts, taking advantage of abundant ports and favourable weather and currents known as 'The Circuit.' They stop here at Bhampay with considerable regularity." She pointed through the screen to the distant port.

"Most do not know this clan had its beginnings amongst Nallurakon's followers prior to the Suvuka's downfall. After our Masters of her time proved her claims against Sheshenara were unfounded, and some of her followers resorted to violence in her now lost cause, she retreated to a cave within our central Veradapandra Mountains. The ancestors of this clan surrounded her. Even after her death, they chose to make this defiance a defining characteristic of their community. Thus, they maintained their cohesion during chaotic times and migrated to the far north after the Suvuka were defeated."

They both sat back and stared out on the fragrant city before Master Kanla continued, "Recent times noted these activities taking a distinct focus. For over twenty years, they harboured and sustained a prolific writer critical of our craft named Nebutan. She distilled much from their observations and referred to a rare collection of complete writings by Nallurakon herself. She wrote the most respectable set of anti-Tatchlan critiques ever published. She died suddenly just over ten years ago, and the clan experienced a crisis. Accusations and recriminations near destroyed them due to claims we had something to do with her death. To their credit, the Sawlu Clan eventually completed an investigation and concluded she died of natural causes, as had many others with the same symptoms. The standards of hygiene and medical expertise we enjoy are not universally employed there. Despite heavy investment to create and distribute Nebutan's works, they watched her influence diminish. We expected dissolution of the Menem elements of the clan, and many deserted them for a time. The leadership has rallied the majority, and they continue their activities."

"May this be followed within Tatchlan?"

"Not with precision. Tatchlan serves our entire population. To follow the perverse inclinations of a few takes specialized skills we are still developing. We would behold a defined formation within our Resplendent Work if these tendencies coalesced into a larger movement with clearly articulated ideas. Once our foundations are laid, and our clusters multiply, the situation shall rectify itself. When our crowning glory of our first Majastas arrives, our final liberation from self-obsession and self-absorption shall be assured."

"What then do we fear from these rebels?"

Master Kanla stood and stared out at the view through the terrace. She walked over and refilled her glass, silhouetted against the animated skyline of Bhampay.

"Our goal remains the ending of the waste and suffering of our past. Our ancient grandmothers squandered time and resources prior to the Suvuka, shaking us awake. Our early Masters left the growing chaos of Rho-Jashun and sought shelter at the heart of Mount Uluvatu, within our Veradapandra Mountains, here upon Statos-Vey. They studied the genius of insects and reached out to our fellow creatures to form alliances. These Uluvatu Masters continued the most-ancient craft of speaking to our hairy cousins and singing to our allies swimming within the depths. Their descendants performed their first service by warning our ancient grandmothers and their mothers within the venerable capital and 'World City' of Thithanu of the imminent Suvuka threat. The dominant Menem priests condemned our Masters and ignored this counsel. They and their followers perished when the Suvuka came. Our Tatchlan Master ancestors living upon Rho-Jashun led those supporting them behind our Mulungu Barrier, here to Statos-Vey, and survived this 'Suvuka Onslaught.'"

"Ama, I have heard the name 'Menem.' I had thought it was a fiction. Who were these Menem priests?"

She turned back to look at Shuna-Shapta. "Come, now! You have seen dramatic enactments of the 'Yeoyupan.'"

"Yeoyupan? Ama! I thought that was fable! Are you saying the story of a living colossus, standing upon an island, addressing the Suvuka ranged about a lake was once believed to have happened?"

"You shall find most of this day's fictions began as another generation's certainties. Remote and backward locations hold some still believing them this day. Given this, what were your impressions of the teachings within this play about Yeoyupan?"

Shuna-Shapta frowned, "They . . . thought their personality was *separate* from their bodies. Anu was a prison for invisible beings forced to assume bodies as punishment. Within florid language and artful staging, they made a case for our having hidden creatures inside us awaiting our death to be 'released.' Despite this, the play was lovely and ended well. I now recall you saying these terrible notions were once believed, yet I could not credit it."

"We have been remiss to not assign a single book to you students concerning this!" She paused and gathered her thoughts, "Allow me to 'set the stage' for you. Amongst a tangled jungle of ancient pre-Suvuka myths, one collection came to dominance, calling itself 'Menem.' When the second dynasty known to history, the Buyanupithar, established itself upon Rho-Jashun, this religion grew into a sophisticated organization capable of inspiring admirable art and elegant philosophy. To their credit, our ancient Yin-Vinulan Dynasty, emerging far later here, was quite hostile to them. Much of the public art we behold this day within Bhampay dates from our Yin-Vinulan Dynasty when they actively encouraged opposition to this religion. Considering this tradition emerged when there remained significant gaps of knowledge as to our nature and life upon Anu's Flesh, it had many insights to offer. Numerous concepts and terminology used by our Masters, including 'Invocant,' and even 'Maja' and 'Majastas,' come from their literature. Even they appreciated the vital role 'majesty' plays within a healthy community. It also had a singular influence on the arts. The legendary tale 'Yeoyupan' is rightly heralded as this faith tradition's most profound achievement. Our subsequent literature grew out of this epic poem's influence, and the giant Yeoyupan in the play was a vital character within Menem cosmology."

Shuna-Shapta silently shook her head.

Master Kanla pondered before beginning again, "I am not a scholar of these matters, and some things remain obscure to me. Whilst the Suvuka were imperfectly known, the 'Yeoyupan' and other works make clear some Menem followers knew well of the Suvuka's existence. The followers of Menem even cast them as fallen mythological beings, called the 'Kovlah.' I am told just prior to the Suvuka crossing from Thermistal to Statos-Vey some of their core texts were altered to make this association explicit. It was too late. By the time the Suvuka arrived, this once grand and poetic Menem convention had degraded into a silly bag of superstitions. The Yeoyupan was no longer seen as epic poetry but factual history. This left our ancestors exhausted from pointless civil wars and religious factionalism. Even then, there was a profound cultural divide between the Tolku inhabiting the continents of Rho-Jashun and Statos-Vey. Despite our Yin-Vinulan dynasty being long gone, our city continued to exert its majestic influence across Statos-Vey. The Menem priesthood had gained supremacy upon Rho-Jashun, and the one service the Suvuka did us was to sweep away most of the Menem's senior leadership and institutions. The Menem religion had little presence south of the Mulungu Mountains, and just a handful of lower-ranking priests made it across the barrier. Their decline accelerated with the loss of their Religious 'Overseers,' 'Supervisors' and 'Captains.' We now recall the Menem religion more for its cultural legacy and ignominious end than for its long reign over us. Yet, from this rotten stump, new sprigs fuel the anti-Tatchlan forces."

Shuna-Shapta sat looking at her mother and Bhampay through the screen behind her. "So these two critics you mentioned, Nallurakon and . . . Nebutan?"

Master Kanla nodded.

"They were sheltered by this ungrateful clan, who followed this Menem religion?"

"Just Nebutan. After her defeat and self-imposed exile, Nallurakon drifted into Menem mysticism. She tattooed the signs upon the fingers and palms of her hands to assist her return to . . ."

She stopped and laughed at Shuna-Shapta's expression.

"Suffice it to say Nallurakon became a Menem devotee, marking a sad decline from her former academic station. It is this degraded tradition that finds new life amongst the rebels. Nebutan did travel north to the Sawlu Clan. To her credit, she remained indifferent to superstition. Nallurakon's anti-Tatchlan activities were more emotional than intellectual. Nebutan was a thorough academic who had little time for imaginary beings inhabiting us or invisibly filling the air."

"So, the remnants of ancient Menem, and dissenting academic writings, inspire this Rho-Jashun clan to stand against Tatchlan?"

Master Kanla grew troubled at this statement. She came back over and sat down beside her daughter.

"Shapta, we shall find a way to meet this. Peace and happiness remain Tatchlan's ends. We shall not revisit the ancient scourges of war for our Resplendent Work but turn our erring relations away from this lost cause. We shall bring them to the joy we laboured so long to bring ourselves. They represent our past and all that kept us small and divided. We must address this from our depths, not their shallows."

"Master Tanas says we do wage war," Shuna-Shapta replied. "He says there have been four 'Unification Wars,' each leading to the founding of the Anu-spanning dynasties of antiquity. He says we conduct the fifth and final unification war. The difference is we do so without violence, and our enemy benefits from our campaign."

"I know he does," her mother answered. "Not all Masters choose to frame our work thus. Recall how our Yin-Vinulan Dynasty, ruling long ago from this city, achieved the same results without resorting to conquest and destruction."

Shuna-Shapta looked at her mother, "My 'cold understanding' must grow hot with this. We must discover how a once discredited myth arose from defeat by the Suvuka to challenge this flowering of our kind. Untangling this riddle shall open many doors."

Master Kanla looked with renewed love and respect at her promising daughter, "Let us do so together."

CHAPTER 5

Seti

Day 18 of 1271, Two-Week One, named Atra, the Bursting Flame, four hundred andas south of Hora-Sarota-Sewa Island along the western coast of Rho-Jashun.

"Vindaviran! Samajalas! Tarunachit! Yuyutar! I evoke the prisoners of the air," Seti shouted. "I call the four Grand Menem! I call the Teacher, the Potter, the Thyma and the Bridge! Now! Now! At once! At once! By calling your names, I collect your scattered limbs! Vindaviran! Samajalas! Tarunachit! Yuyutar! I evoke the Generals of Menem! Vindaviran! Samajalas! Tarunachit! Yuyutar! Take form with your names and appear! Now! Now! Quickly! Quickly! Vindaviran! Samajalas! Tarunachit!

Yuyutar! Bring your armies for my mission! Vindaviran! Samajalas! Tarunachit! Yuyutar! Find your purpose in our service! Vindaviran, bring your pen! Samajalas, your potter's wheel! Tarunachit your crown of bones! Yuyutar become our Bridge! Come now! Come now!"

The entire crew of forty-five shipmates stood silent, amazed at the authority in the youth's voice. Seti grew stiff and bent his head.

"Lords of the skies! I recite your names one thousand times. Your feats fill the pure air. Each recitation increases my praise. I fill Anu with your fame and strengthen you for your triumphal return to Ranvartawan." He turned back and gestured at the crew. "This is the Jefaka. Her crew is faithful. Their mission to fortify those trapped in the flesh before their final passage through the One Hundred Gates." Emedin noted how some of her crew's eyes went wide at being mentioned during the evocation. She was amazed as many held their amulets, and several heads bowed as if they saw the Menem. Her First Officer Dine also noted the crew's reaction.

"I call on Menem to watch over the Jefaka. Fly south and find mischievous winds and waves lying in wait for us. Do this, and I will give you quick release back to the unsullied heights."

Emedin watched her crew, frozen in place as if they were an enthralled audience in the theatre. Seti stiffened and bowed. He stood in silence, listening to the Menem's answer.

"Vindaviran! Samajalas! Tarunachit! Yuyutar! I release you and your faithful hordes until I invoke your names afresh." He slumped from the effort before turning and calling out, "The Menem view all below. They can spy over the horizon and send word. They say the way is clear today and tomorrow, but on the third day, pull in. A storm is born in the south; on the third day. He will stand in our way."

Jefaka's crew turned as one to look at their captain. Emedin nodded and gave the order to set sail. Seti remained at the bow of the ship. Emedin ordered several brightly coloured warm cloaks to be brought for their Invocant to wear against the vast sea's chill. Jefaka sailed for two uneventful days.

The third morning began clear, with little sign of incident. Despite this, her captain ordered Jefaka's crew to find a sheltered cove and anchor for the day. The crew watched as near midday dark clouds hurried across the sky, and the winds began to howl. A full late-season storm raged out on the open ocean. The roar of the waves made it impossible to communicate except by signals. They rode it out until late the following day.

Seti evoked the Menem and repeated his call for their aid. When done, he came to the captain and declared. "The Menem says the storm is spent and none brew behind it. We will be safe for at least a week. After this, there will be wind and weather, but they will be but 'froth on the wave' for this ship." The crew was jubilant at Seti, appearing to be a proven Invocant. They prepared to be underway the following morning.

"May I make a request, captain?"

"What is it?"

"My voices say I need a guide. I ask your permission to seek an Adept to begin my training while serving the Jefaka. If this is unacceptable, I will wait until my service to you is complete."

Emedin studied the lad. "I will consider your request. Your initial invocation was a success. Your Dream Reading is well reported among my crew. Beyond this, you have already established yourself as 'good cargo' on this ship. Before taking on another passenger, I will observe your ongoing service."

Seti bowed to the captain and went back to the ship's bow, where he spent his days. When the Jefaka pulled into a port, he stayed on board the vessel and plied the crew with questions. The crew grew increasingly fond of him and brought small items for him to study. They told him what they knew of where they were. Others began recounting their travels over Anu. Each morning many came to report their dreams, and he interpreted them. This added to the crew's regard for him. Emedin observed this activity and pondered the boy.

* * *

Day 32 of 1271, Two-Week Two, named Deel – the Trick.

The Jefaka had followed the coast of the Danadejet Arm and had crossed over the equator three times. Seti had learned to climb the rigging with ease, so he watched the horizon from high above the deck. He had also shown a growing interest in understanding the many shipping knots. He began to practice them as he gazed at the horizon. His hands grew tough with the course fibre, and his frame was hardening. His skin darkened with his exposure to wind, sea and Nu's unrelenting gaze. Yet, his growing happiness was today undone. He perched in the top rigging furiously tying and retying a simple knot in frustration. Three days before, the Menem had told him a powerful storm would meet them this day. He scowled at Nu, tranquilly westering through an untroubled sky toward a peaceful ocean. No clouds obscured the attending Eyes of Nu around him. He thought he could hear his sister's laughter as the small waves slapped the hull far below. He glanced down and could see most of the crew looking up at him. He could not put this off any longer. No storm would come.

The crew avoided his gaze, as Seti stood stricken, looking one last time at the calm waters before heading below to see Captain Emedin. The boy found Dine standing at her side.

"Are you going to put me off the ship?" Seti asked.

"No," the captain answered, her light green eyes glittering. It was hard to say who was more surprised, Seti or Dine.

"You have proven yourself a Dream Reader," Emedin said. "My crew sings your praises, declaring their troubled sleep at an end. We agreed you must fulfill at least one of your two tasks. With no malice, I tell you I set little store by your Invocant claims. My crew refers to you as our Reader and Invocant. You remain good cargo and prove yourself capable on the ropes. Even in a less grand capacity, you may have a future in sailing."

The boy remained downcast, and Emedin examined him with an unreadable expression. "My boy . . . you already know I do not believe as you. I saw a starving waif who distinguished himself by nerve and imagination. I know you now feel betrayed by your Menem. You are far from the first to be let down by the old ways. I do not plan to launch a campaign against your beliefs. Your visions can inspire and bring hope, and I will not be the one to smother them." She continued to stare at the lowered head before her. "I grant your request regarding a guide," she smiled at his sudden shocked face.

"My varied life includes experience in securing instruction for pupils, although never on a ship. I suggest we bring some on board for us to examine. Anu is filled with many types of Adept among its Wandering Scholars. There will be limits to your choice as we will not have certain types on board. I retain the right to refuse anyone living on my ship I disapprove of."

"Captain?" Seti said, "I do not understand. You say you do not believe. Yet, you offer to bring an Adept aboard. Why do you do this after my powers have failed me?"

Captain Emedin laughed, "Such are the trifling prerogatives of leadership. I choose to help you, boy. Back home, we have excellent schools and could teach you much. We could fortify what you now believe with so much more. We travel in the wrong direction for this and so must put off such things. This is one option and is what I offer to you now."

Seti stared incredulously at Emedin before bowing in silence and returning to the deck.

Dine turned to Emedin, "May I be frank, captain?"

Emedin nodded.

"You were not honest in full."

"Oh?"

"You have said to me he is not only deluded but mad."

"Well . . . I do not think his condition communicable. To my mind, his madness is not dangerous."

A thunderous cheer could be heard up on deck as news of Seti remaining on board was announced.

"Do you hear them?" Emedin said. "They love him. They forgive his failures while I cannot shake my fascination for the boy."

"'Fascination?'" Dine said. "Captain, I do not deny he has acquitted himself far beyond my expectations, but he troubles me."

"How so?"

"Listen to them," Dine gestured up to the deck. "You toy with what I know you consider the general crew's credulity. Despite saying you do not share his beliefs, by seeking an Adept, you fortify them. You say he is ill, yet you feed his illness."

"Nonsense! I give the crew cheer and inspiration on this long journey. I have seen enough of how it goes when they have little to none."

"We could have accomplished the same with a Tecku or other cousin swinging in the ropes!" Dine shot back.

"Perhaps, but this would not assist one of the more miserable specimens I have ever seen. From the moment he spoke, I knew there was something special about him. You know he might be dead by now had we not picked him up."

"Why this odd creature when you have refused passage to so many others?"

"We see so much absurd comedy and suffering," the captain answered, leaning back in her chair, "I could see in one so sensitive how this would be magnified. I also cannot shake a premonition of his being important to us. You and I have lost our young dreams and have been too immersed in vile commerce. We must recall our true selves, Dine. We must also, on occasion, follow our instincts blindly."

Dine stood looking at his captain before saying, "If I may say, Captain, it appears your fascination determines this. Do you hope to wean him of his faith and introduce him to the intricacies of Nebutan?"

"Yes," Emedin answered. "I am not a doctor and cannot speak to his mental condition. Perhaps with time and a decent diet, this will recede of itself. I will say to you I see the potential for an extraordinary personality, one that could inspire others in our larger mission."

Dine's jaw dropped in amazement, "Captain! You do not intend to bring this boy into our dedicated service to Sawlu Clan?"

"All I intend for now is to keep him aboard and watch his progress," the captain smiled enigmatically.

CHAPTER 6

Shuna-Shapta

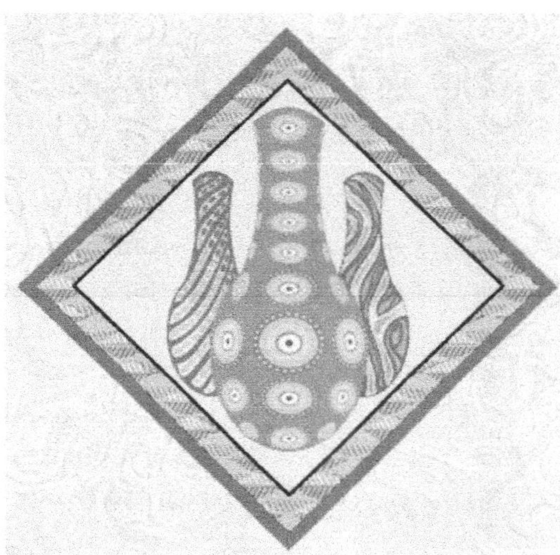

Pictured: Icon of Living Instruments within their various Shells

Day 48, Two-Week Three, Topy – The Needle, Master Enclave in city of Bhampay

Shuna-Shapta had sat naked in the Invocant Initiation Chamber through the night. Her Supervising Master Tanas had provided her with many readings and chants while watching the sleeping wonder before her. She had already had several guided encounters with a Living Instrument.

Three years ago was her first initiation. She was conducted by her

Devotee Supervisor to link with a Living instrument before journeying into Tatchlan to stand before the wondrous Lustrum Mirror and purify herself of latent growths of self-absorption. There had been several subsequent journeys, always with two Supervisor Escorts,·each holding one of her hands. This day would see her meet a new Supervisor - a Living Instrument!

She watched as the three potted Larpana Plants on the other side of the chamber simultaneously lost their white tone with black accents. This meant the thirty-second hour, the Hour of Bekma Nu and the final hour of the night, was done. As these same upper leaves turned pale yellow with dark yellow accents, signifying the Hour of Nu Opening, the first hour, she drank a large goblet of Sheshenara Nectar. Most non-Invocant women would perhaps have this amount during the entire course of their pregnancy.

Thus fortified, for the first time, she commenced the Yom Sha by herself. Her opening sounds gave birth to the intonation series.

"Yom Sha, Yom Sha,
Vuna Sana Ya,
Wonal Chinnal Ya,
Sosu Yaso Jas,
Pana Musha Shay,
Sen! Sen! Sen!
Suv! Suv! Suv!
Sha! Sha! Sha!"

She intoned the series eight times. The silence seemed to deepen within the small chamber. Its smooth walls rose from the warm, polished stone floor to form a perfect domed ceiling. Eight glowing Tuchus Vines, a surprisingly delicate import from the wilds of Thermistal, illuminated the chamber near the top. The three Larpana plants were set up on the far side to assist her in the ritual. At the centre of the chamber, two small trays sat beneath a round, low table of ancient wood, heavy with ritual elements arranged along the outer edge. A deep bowl sat in front of the table.

This venerable segment of an immense tree dominated the lower chamber, its circular surface covered in intricately carved symbols divided into eight concentric rings of glyphs. Ceremonial bowls stood around the edge of the table for her entry rite. In the open area at the centre of the glyph-laden rows, the mysterious Living Instrument lay hidden within its elongated shell sitting in a small recessed stand. The shell was broad at its base, tapering to what was traditionally known as its 'snout' at the top. It was beautiful. Several shades of iridescent green, composed of a multitude of tiny beads, lay in curling rows giving it a dull sheen. These rows followed a series of grooves radiating out from the base of the shell and spiralling around to the top. Shapta knew inside this shell dwelt a being called Shamusanish, one of many Living Instruments used by the Invocants. Through the night, as the Larpana turned colour to mark the passing of each hour, she had stood and circled Shamusanish, stroking its extended form, laying her hands on each part.

Now she took one bowl, starting with the outer left one, the colour of the first hour, the Hour of Nu Opening, which was coloured pale yellow, and opened its lid. After taking a small sip of the strong-smelling sap, she began to pour the sap with deliberation, covering the shell. Drinking the remaining fluid, she knelt to place the bowl beneath a small spout coming out of the base of the table. Sitting back, she waited for one hour until the three Larpana Plants changed colour again. During this time, the sap moved slowly through Shamusanish to become a Vision Window Medicine. Finally, a small portion was released. This modified sap moved down to issue out of the tube into the first bowl.

Shuna-Shapta removed the lid from the second bowl, coloured deep yellow for the second hour, the Hour of Nu Cutting. She placed it, so the last few drops of the changed sap from the pale yellow bowl entered and modified its contents. She took this bowl and filling her mouth, held the pungent substances until the intensity subsided, and the liquid became near tasteless. Stepping gently onto the massive table, she allowed a drop from her mouth to fall onto the 'snout' of the shell and swallowed the rest. When the drips stopped under the table, she removed the pale yellow bowl, placing it back on the table. She now slowly poured the second bowl's liquid over the shell.

Two long and shallow dishes stood either side of the bowl. Each empty container was placed in recessed grooves bearing the same colour. She followed the ritual with exactness, ensuring she coated each portion of the shell by the eight sets of sap, touched by her hands in the correct sequence. Thus the shell received libations for the first eight hours of the day: Nu Opening, Nu Cutting, Nu Dispels, Nu Burnishes, Nu Sails, Nu Strides, Nu Flies, and Nu Enthroned. She waited for a response and, when the shell began to vibrate, she stopped and returned to the bench.

She kept her palms upward and waited out the rest of the hour. She was exhilarated to reach this stage as the cumulative effect of each batch of sap intensified her senses. As her three Larpana Plants changed to bear pale green leaves with deep green accents, signifying the ninth hour, the Hour of Nu Wanders, she began to sense Shamusanish stirring and heard movements within the shell.

Shamusanish had received the necessary offerings for a Living Instrument to link with a new Invocate and laboured within his shell. The residue from Shuna-Shapta's juices were now examined by Shamusanish to determine her compatibility. Shuna-Shapta opened the final bowl, and her opening sip caused her skin to shed rapidly. She had experienced several skin sheddings as a regular part of young adult growth. Gone were the days of her skin coming off in tiny flakes as a young child. Her shaking hands applied the sap to the shell, and as her skin began to peel off, she made sure each skin section went into a deep bowl. She had never known such a swift shed. She looked down at her translucent new skin, displaying the entire workings of her body.

At last, a stirring began within the shell. She wrapped her arms and legs around it. The shell's activity paused then started anew. She felt a series of trembling movements of the heating shell. She waited. If Shamusanish grew still and cooled, she had failed. If Shamusanish began the process of opening, she had succeeded. A deep-pitched sound accompanied the tip of the shell opening. Shamusanish was ready for her! Shuna-Shapta began to tremble as she released the creature and placed the bowl containing her shed skin between them. She tried to slow her breathing as the shell resolved into a series of cracks along the grooves. A dull orange glow grew within as the shell began to open. Shuna-Shapta nearly swooned as the potent odours filled the small chamber with compelling medicines.

A series of long tendrils issued out of the shell in every direction and located the bowl of shed skin. A piece of shed skin was drawn back in the shell. A single long tendril undulated toward her. It was dull orange with yellow patterns and ended in a large, flat pad with a series of smaller yellow pads around its edge. Shuna-Shapta extended her quaking hands, placing one on either side of the pad before bringing them together. The yellow pads gripped her hands. Other tendrils went out, as the shell opened further as if searching the room for additional occupants. They withdrew, leaving the one tendril with her. Shuna-Shapta kept her eyes closed as the Shamusanish's powerful agents entered through her palms, tingling as they moved down her arms. Finally, she opened her eyes to look at the lovely creature. While all Living Instruments were colourful wonders, seeming more like creatures of the sea than the land, each one had distinctive features.

The shell of Shamusanish now spread in segments, as a fully opened flower, across the central portion of the large table. All the other items had been set with care in anticipation of this opening and remained in place. The Living Instrument's body sat in a deep orange and red base composed of a series of broad overlapping porous leaves. Tendrils issued from this portion of its wondrous form. A pale orange sphere sat in this base punctuated by a few dark veins making their way toward the middle ending in a ring of light green beads, similar to the shell, at its midsection.

Above this, the upper part of the living sphere was a darker orange with an intricate surface pattern. Many ridges and troughs ran through it. Within this rough landscape sat many small green knobs and other shapes. At the top of the orb issued an array of curved yellow tubes. Filled with liquid, they were softer than the round body and its base. They extended upward in arches, nearly touching the ceiling. Formidable fumes filled the room, and Shuna-Shapta's body quaked. She felt her hands released, and she knew that the time had come for the Living Instrument and Invocant to unite. She sat on the edge of her bench and reached toward Shamusanish. The creature sensed her gesture and began to move off its shell. Its articulated base proceeded down the inner side of one segment of its shell toward Shuna-Shapta with ease. Many small tendrils darted to and from the bowl containing her shed skin, and its contents were consumed.

Shuna-Shapta removed the bowl and guided the potent being onto her lap. With care, she sat back on the bench and opened her legs. The creature issued out several tendrils to root itself to her legs while a warm member began to emerge from the base to explore and enter her, forming a living bridge to Shuna-Shapta. The lovers' literary endearments between Invocants and Instruments became a reality, this time without two escorts holding her hands. When the bodies of the Instrument and Invocant united, a broad tendril issued from the far side, Shuna-Shapta placed her palms on its sides, 'holding hands' with Shamusanish, and her world fell away.

She sank on waves of pleasure into the darkness approaching a distant blue sphere. She drew closer, and it filled her view until she reached the surface, standing as a vertical ocean. Alone, she hung before the Outer Water Skin, called Amanavata. Many Faces rose from the depths from beneath the surface. They all moved in small, gentle circles looking at her in anticipation of an invocation of one or more of them. Some were quite simple in shape, while others presented a fantastic appearance. She knew these were all small servants, known as 'Secondary Faces' of the immense 'Twelve Faces of Tatchlan.' Long ago, they were fashioned by the Masters to tend to the Tatchlan System while waiting for the Majastas to employ them. As an Invocate, she would invoke these 'Secondary Faces,' for the rest of her life. She passed through the barrier and moved into The Living System. Many of the Faces turned to watch her go, and a few of the more colourful ones followed her down. She became aware of soft cooing sounds coming from the Faces. She approached a full naked figure waiting for her – her first mother, Master Kanla. As with herself, her mother's open body featured bright streaks of colour, primarily orange and dark blue. She knew this to be how her mother's Floral Aroma Accord was presented within Tatchlan.

"Welcome new Delving Invocant," she said in a voice familiar and new. "I shall guide you during your brief visit. After this, you must unite with Shamusanish and our other Instruments upon a regular schedule to perfect your Craft. Our Instruments are your intimates, and you shall know the depth of joy and the height of sorrow. Like you, I embrace another Living Instrument nearby. Many Masters work within our Resplendent Work, and you shall in time seek them out."

Many of the vibrant Secondary Faces hovered, appearing to listen intently.

"Shapta, I recite to you what you already know well but is required for all Delving Invocates. 'Many thousands of the Faces emerge out of our Breathing Work. They grow as ripened fruits amid fields of flowers coating our Living Orb. Cultivated to listen to our call, they shall eagerly present themselves in expectation of your commands.'"

Shuna-Shapta spoke her response, "I have seen their dance and heard their song."

Master Kanla continued, "Prior to them, many generations of Masters walked slowly across The General Plain. They oversaw a multitude of details requiring lifetimes to complete. These Secondary Faces shall form the uppermost part of our Resplendent Work. Sufficient numbers mature so we may invoke them to attend to our Living System at its base.'"

"'I have seen their dance and heard their song.'"

"'These Faces shall serve as our Living Handles of Tatchlan, allowing us to reach in, observe, monitor and adjust each portion of our Resplendent Work. True efficacy is achieved when many Invocants call one face to a single task.'"

"'I have seen their dance and heard their song.'"

"This," Master Kanla indicated a floating round Face about their height, "you know as 'Alatanda.' He is not one of the Twelve Principal Faces, but a Secondary Face serving our true Alatanda. The Twelve Principal Faces are far too large for us to treat with directly. They shall serve our coming Majastas alone. Shapta, you may, on occasion, behold one or more of our Principal Faces. We refer to them as the 'moons of our system,' so mighty are their aspects. Whilst the formation is not yet visible, Alatanda forms the hub, linking them as a living whole. In time, our other Principal Faces shall occupy their powerful stations about him. To invoke a servant of a Principal Face is to draw upon all aspects of their ability. To address them is to address their master." The black face appeared to examine Shuna-Shapta as she studied him.

Master Kanla turned and beckoned Shuna-Shapta to follow her. Without apparent effort, she kept pace. Ahead a new, more animated wall approached. Shuna-Shapta began to hear and smell signs of a multitude of living beings. Creatures leapt out of the wall and fell back in, as fish during spawning. She knew what this realm was, having been here with Dream Guides to meet the Lustrum Mirror years before when she was but an Initiate.

"The name Tatchlan means 'Life Face,'" her mother said. "It is composed of three spheres nested inside each other. Our Living Instruments invert their correct order presenting the first two present as thin layers covering our Living Orb. Our Uluvatu Masters deemed this a necessary distortion to ease our Invocates' passage. These 'outer' two layers are as the thin and empty air encompassing Anu. Unlike Anu, our Orb is alive to the core. You have passed through the peaceful liquid layer and approach the second, called Indatubangas, where the originating chaos and destruction of unguided, self-absorbed life remains. Beyond this is our Living Core of Tatchlan."

They drew close, and the noise became deafening. Despite having been here before, the wild and writhing surface made Shuna-Shapta afraid. She reached for her mother, who turned and smiled, "Your Dream Guides only revealed this realm in part. Life is domesticated, and we remain its Masters, able to pass through the layers. You know this realm serves as a vital furnace for all Tatchlan, reducing what is done and releasing new elements into our Living System."

They quickly passed through into a deep, warm layer of profound silence. Ahead a radiating globe filled their eyes, its dimensions beyond telling. Over its surface moved a breathing pattern of incomprehensible complexity. It burned in a broad spectrum of brilliant hues that saturated their eyes. An ocean of scents swelled and met them over the glittering landscape. The sounds of millions of voices of each living being formed a gentle waterfall.

"Behold our Glorious Tatchlan!" her mother called out.

Shuna-Shapta began gasping. Her mother turned and smiled. "Ah! Your opening is over. Shamusanish now conducts you back by his sweet road. You shall return often, and Tatchlan shall become as familiar as our Bhampay. Throughout your long career, this shall remain your golden path of return. We women, have the honour of hosting our Living Instruments. Male Invocants have the honour of being hosted by them."

Shuna-Shapta plummeted toward a profound sexual climax. All the juices of Shamusanish seemed to waken and catch fire together, causing her body to boil repeatedly with an incredible intensity. Living Instrument climaxes were distinct from the 'Nine Petals' climax catalogue and ensured satisfaction while taking nothing away from cluster and circle intimacies. When she opened her eyes, she found herself with Shamusanish. The Living Instrument had turned dark orange and red and, of its own, began with gentleness to disengage and move back toward its shell. The elongated sacks retracted inside the central sphere and the tendrils into the base. Shuna-Shapta watched the creature changing shape as the sections of the shell enclosed it. The shell sections fused to enfold the tranquil being.

Shuna-Shapta had tears in her eyes as she rose and bent to kiss the shell. "Thank you," she whispered to Shamusanish. She stood and looked at the door. "Delving Invocant Shapta!" she declared to herself, "You stand upon our Master Path!"

CHAPTER 7

SINKIN

Pictured: Image of a Suvuka Paw print surrounded by four dead Tolku heads.

Day 145

The small section of Durka Herd had full galloped near one hundred and fifty days and covered near twenty-thousand andas from their defiance at the Vettencore Passage. They knew such power, endurance and clarity of mission marked them as Anu's rightful Shepherds. The rest of the herd remained near Chitikal Round. These eight Suvuka accompanied Durka's single buck of age, Sinkin, on the Full Stag Path.

The land had altered many times. Dry scrub became vast grassland, and tall forests turned into dark steaming jungles. Their bodies and pelts adjusted to the growing heat and humidity. These quick adaptations were one of their greatest strengths, allowing them to possess Thermistal.

As they approached the equator, the trails became narrow and twisting. High walls of lush foliage served as cover for the army of stinging creatures descending on them. Their tails protected their vitals, slapping the few trying to dig into their pelts. They caked themselves in mud and insulated their faces. They stopped at a long trench occupied by Hungry Rock. All had heard stories of unwary beasts blundering onto its surface to vanish before they could cry out. This silent grey lake was deadly to approach and would swallow them should they touch it. Tall red grasses grew all along the shore of its grey shimmering mass and served as something of a warning. Each stood well beyond the red grass, found a rock or other item, and dropped it onto the glistening surface in offering. They watched them disappear into the calm body and moved on. At times the jungle thinned. They spotted distant Suvuka herds moving in the same direction along other portions of the Full Stag Path. Despite the discomfort and danger of this portion of their journey, their meandering paths were well maintained. At regular intervals, places to stop appeared in tended shade groves. Most watering holes were level with the ground. Today they stopped at a depression where many Suvuka trails converged.

Long ago, countless Suvuka paws dug a descent down to the cold waters. The herd's size and number daunted the watery predators waiting for the unwary to drink. After impotent displays, they swam to the far bank to glare at them. Durka Herd filled the small pool. Countless bodies of tiny tormentors, crushed by their powerful flat tails during the journey, washed off their sore hides and covered the surface. Little creatures risked death to leave the shore and swim among them to consume this sudden bounty. They braved crawling onto their flanks to pull off and eat the stingers sticking to their pelts. The waters were chill, and the bottom slipped away. They had to swim to stay afloat. As soon as Durka took a mouthful, they knew these sweet waters rose from deep within Anu. They were also far colder than surface water, refreshing and easing their many sores. Sinkin drank deep of the sweetness and wallowed long in the calm waters. Despite his sore muscles and fatigue, he joined a short and spirited water fight near the shore.

At last, he approached Hiratak. Durka Herd's Voice had finished a mighty shake off and looked for mud to re-apply to his face. "Herdmaster," Sinkin began, "thick air weighs us down!"

As he spoke, thunder rolled over them. They looked at the sudden racing storm clouds.

"You will welcome rains," Hiratak answered, smiling at the clouds. "They last long and bring new perils. Our paths grow treacherous. Our little tormenters will be driven to ground. Our wounds will heal. Air will turn dry soon enough. Your hide will burn at Jabun Isthmus. It separates Mushumafal Peninsula from Thermistal. There, mighty Kukernef Desert lies. We cross it to Avanchil Round. Rich pastures of the Jaladanu range wait beyond. Your final initiation lies at Jaladanu's tip."

Sinkin turned to his Herdmaster, "What will I do?"

"You will learn at Avanchil. Our revenge begins with new traditions. You saw their watery passage. You saw their high wall. They believe us incapable of change. They underestimate us. Young Stags have a vital role. We will wipe Anu's face clean. We will take back what is ours."

Another group of Suvuka appeared above. They barked their presence. Durka Herd called their intention to leave and give them range.

Sinkin looked at the group above. He started and spoke to Hiratak, "Herdmaster! This is Makusk Herd! There is the one I spoke of. He told me of the Tolku among us."

Hiratak and the others glanced at the group of six, five adults accompanying one buck, waiting in a ring to come down.

"Let them come and drink," he said. "We will wait for them."

Durka Herd formed a line, ascended out of the watering hole, and permitted Makusk Herd to descend. The buck Sinkin had spoken with was eager for the water and did not recognize Sinkin as they passed each other. Makusk Herd followed the same drinking and washing rituals Durka had, making clear they also had galloped far and were as pained and tired as they. They returned and found Durka Herd. The two groups stood looking at each other. Hiratak stepped forward and lifted one front leg to sign his desire to speak. The evident Herdmaster mirrored his gesture.

"You are from Makusk Herd?" Hiratak asked.

The others looked startled, and the buck recognized Sinkin. He approached his Herdmaster and whispered. The other three appeared distressed at what the buck told the Herdmaster. The buck stepped back with the others, and the four lowered their heads.

"We are of Makusk," the Herdmaster answered gruffly. "We are behind and cannot delay."

Hiratak was amazed at this discourtesy, "Hale be to you fellow Suvuka! Hale to you, fellow Herdmaster!" He covered his surprise with his best formal tone. "We travel far from our pastures. What brings you from the body of Makusk?"

The other Herdmaster regretted his error and tried to make amends, "We escort this buck. He will be a Full Stag." He shot the buck a withering glance. "He grows strong while learning prudence speech."

"Important lessons must be re-learned," Hiratak answered in neutral tones. The other Herdmaster coloured and lowered his head. Along with his herd being smaller, he was now at a social disadvantage.

"We are of Durka Herd. We are honoured to escort this buck. I am Hiratak, Durka's Herdmaster and Voice. Our buck is named Sinkin." He stopped and looked at the other Herdmaster, bound to answer in kind.

"I am Morakav, Makusk's Herdmaster and Voice. Our buck is named Setush."

"Your Setush follows the 'Four Paws?'"

"He does."

"He demonstrated his defiance at the Vettencore? He travels to Avanchil?"

"Yes."

"He and Sinkin are on the same journey. Makusk and Durka send but one buck. Once many bucks travelled these paths in packs. Youth learns from youth as well as age. Their bond will carry them into battle."

Morakav was resigned. His breach in the Greeting Code left him, and those under him, at the mercy of those he offended. "It would be fitting. They should travel under our guidance," he said.

"We merge our paths. We fashion a single quest. We witness these two becoming Full Stags."

The unexpected turn of events and the speed they developed surprised Makusk and Durka Herd. The tradition existed for alliances, initiated by the larger herd to the smaller. Refusal meant further insult. Makusk Herd would have to stay well behind the offended Durka Herd, unable to approach any sanctuary they inhabited until they chose to leave.

Morakav knew he had no choice and bowed his head, "We are honoured. We accept your generous proposal."

Fat raindrops began to smack into them. Hiratak looked back each way at Durka Herd before bowing to Makusk. Durka followed his lead, and Makusk bowed back. As the rain began to pour down, Hiratak ambled toward the path and turned to wait for Morakav. The Herdmaster of Makusk came forward and, Herdmasters leading, Durka and Makusk began to canter away from the watering hole.

* * *

For nine days, the thirteen adult Suvuka accompanied the two bucks as they ran through torrential downpours. Not a word was said as they focused on keeping their balance in the dangerous pathway. They had to swim through flooded valleys, remove or make their way around fallen trees and debris, and pull each other out of bogs. When the rain ceased, they were deep in the jungle. They knew their little tormentors readied to swarm them. They stopped to wallow and build a thick layer of new mud over their pelts, serving for a short time until the soil dried and flaked off. They ran through the day and at dusk came on a curious sight. A round slab stood snug in a vertical rock face. The space in front of this had a circle of small cones and spheres, marking it as a Suvuka site. The slab had a rough sequence of knobs for Suvuka to latch onto around the outer rim. The disk stood in a shallow trench extending to the left of its position. After examining this, two Suvuka pushed on the knobs and the disc. It rolled sideways in its track, exposing a cavern behind it. The disc served as a barrier guarding a dry cave. Provisions were stored inside.

"What is this?" Hiratak asked.

Morakav peered inside, "I had heard tales of it. this is Latatroos Shelter. Decades ago, a group was stopped by injury. The herd spent a season at this self-made cavern. They dug further, shaped the barrier and set the markers. They brought goods and stored them inside. It must be thirty years ago. Now each group gathers new stores for the next." He sniffed at the bundled dry plants and fruits, "This has been here for a time."

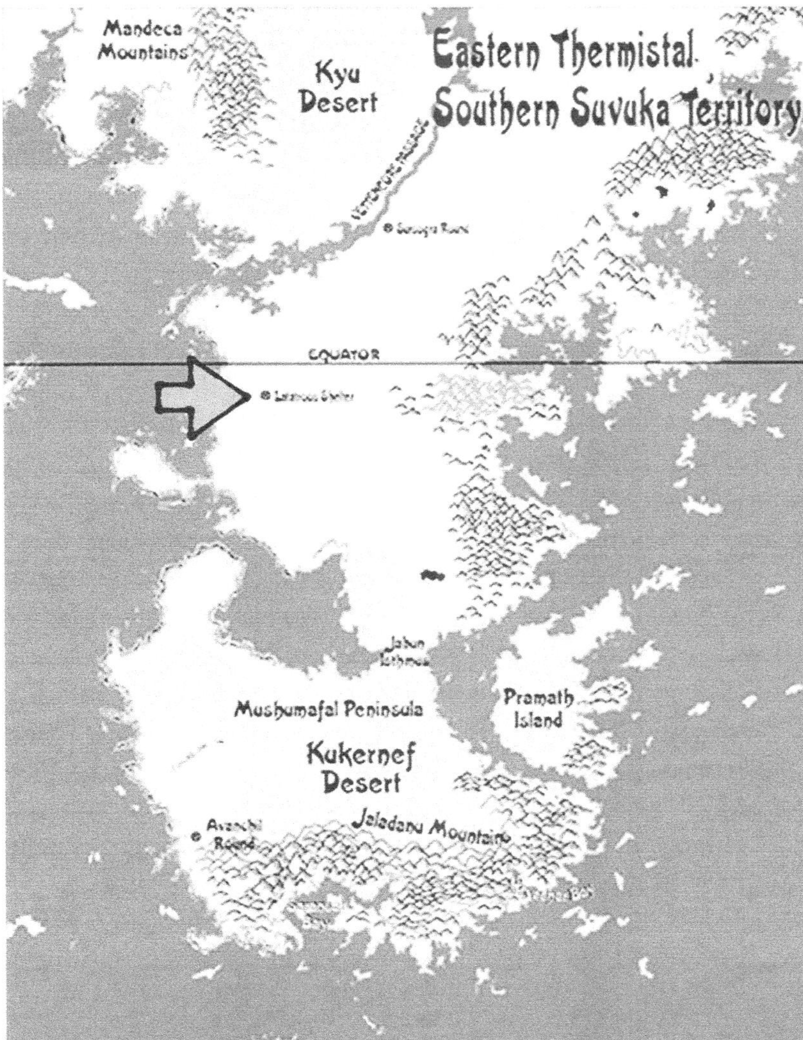

Hiratak was embarrassed, "I recall the name," he said. "I never came this way." He turned to last year's buck, "Zatin here ran last year."

Zatin stood, looking at the shelter. "We did not pass this way, Herdmaster," he said. "I had not heard its name until now."

Hiratak bent his head to Morakav, "In my preparations, I had forgotten it."

This admission improved Morakav's disadvantaged position to Hiratak. He had come to respect this Voice of Durka and his disciplined herd and his willingness to admit a small failure. "All herds diminished. We struggle to maintain ourselves," Morakav said in a comforting tone. "Others should have led Setush's run. We are spread thin. Ancients assume roles of those in their prime."

Hiratak looked at Makusk's Herdmaster with new respect. His feelings were mirrored in Morakav's eyes, and they pressed their heads together in mutual regard. Hiratak turned to the others, "Durka and Makusk form a working whole. Our separate journey is united. Our standing is equal."

Makusk no longer stood in Durka's shadow. The herds moved side by side into the shelter. On the inner side of the slab was a series of short knobs near the centre. They rolled the barrier across to minimize pests disturbing them. Most fell asleep in the sudden darkness. The rest joined them after a mouthful of food. The group slept longer than they had since the beginning of their journey. When they awakened, they rolled the barrier part way back to reveal a calm new day. The provisions were distributed, and they fed. Makusk and Durka began to appreciate each other's company with ease. Sinkin and Setush had not spoken to each other. The barrier was further moved, and many issued out and returned. Hiratak went outside, and after a short interval, Sinkin followed. They turned to look back at the shelter. Most had returned, and none stayed outside. Hiratak and Sinkin stepped away and stood facing the jungle.

"Will we ask Setush to tell us?"

"Morakav broke tradition at our greeting," Hiratak answered in a low voice. "Terrible fear fed such actions. He did not know us. His herd was small."

Sinkin frowned, "Herdmaster, why was he afraid?"

"I hear brayings. Some say they are 'clean' of Tolku contact. They claim others are sullied. Makusk would confirm their fears. Some call to corral or even kill altered Suvuka. You may hear such terrible arguments. These fear-peddling advocates mar ancient rounds. Our adversary is the Tolku – not each other! Morakav knows what Setush told you. He knows we will ask. He protects his herd as I would. They prove themselves worthy."

A low snort caused them to turn. Morakav stood at the entrance.

"My ears remain keen," Makusk's Herdmaster said as he came to them. He bowed his broad head once. "You run with honour. I find no fanaticism in you. I did fear for my herd. I was unaware of Setush speaking to Sinkin. Our young are rare gifts. We wish them to run free and meet their fellows. I feared he had brought us ruin. Our herd struggles through a nightmare. We heard rumours of Konogat Herd. We knew we were not alone. My buck tested yours by telling him their story. He wished to see his reaction. Fear caused him to spread this rumour. Terror overcomes all other mandates. We fear what others may do. We are burdened with a terrible secret." He looked back toward the shelter where laughter had erupted. "In our run through the rains," he continued, "I pondered this."

He sent out a low call meant to gather the herd. Silence fell, and the herds came out and stood among the circle of cones and spheres.

"We will trust Durka Herd," Morakav declared to the five Makusk members, including Setush. "They have proven true. Sinkin took Setush's words to his Herdmaster alone. We carry a stain on our backs. We must share this load, or we fall. Our silence aids the Tolku. It will reduce us to the worst humiliation!

He looked at his group and at the cones surrounding them. They were half as high as the herd.

"Each of you," he said to the four Makusk members, "Pick a cone or sphere. Stand proud, connected to our past. Reveal our secret."

They stood on their hind legs, one paw on the stone, and remained standing. Talons came out of one and scratched the stone. Morakav led a puzzled Hiratak and Sinkin to the young Setush and indicated his exposed underbelly. A series of horizontal stripes near the middle extended from one side to the other. They looked like burn marks or a sign of extended pressure. The rest of Durka Herd approached and examined identical streaks on the other three. After looking closely at them, they stepped back. Members of Durka Herd looked at each other. Morakav bobbed his head once, and the four Makusk Suvuka pushed back and settled, bending low. None looked at each other or Durka Herd.

"I bear these marks," Morakav said to a mystified Hiratak.

Durka's Herdmaster said nothing out of respect for the evident shame this exposure caused Makusk Herd. He looked to Morakav and sat back on his haunches, the traditional posture for a student seeking instruction. The rest of Durka Herd followed his example. Morakav bowed his face down until his nose touched the ground.

He lifted and said, "These mark an unnatural vine passed around us. They secured seats on our backs. Tolku have ridden us."

Hiratak's eyes went wide, and his nostrils flared, but he refrained from saying anything.

"Each thought it a terrible dream," Morakav continued in a diminished voice, "We found these scars and share this nightmare. We went to sleep, and they possessed us. They rode us as their multitude of slaves! We all remember standing in a large circle. We faced inward. Our enemy sat on us! Even our children were ridden."

The rest of the Makusk herd lowered their heads further, and one began to weep.

Morakav's voice began to shake, "We heard our enemy had entered our dreams. They commit unspeakable acts on our powerless bodies. Entire herds possess unusual gaits. They have altered voices. Some even bear strange young." He stopped and drew himself up, "We now believe in these tales. Our backs are stained."

Silence filled the open space.

CHAPTER 8

Seti

Kumastam icon

Day 145, Two-Week Nine, named Darilda – Sweet

Captain Emedin laughed. A flushed Seti did not share the joke.

"A *what*?" he asked as his white spots intensified, and his beige marks formed a dark ring around each in irritation.

"I said this one," she indicated the tall youth standing at the dock by their ship "is a hired chanter of praises. One of his profession is called an Adorer."

Dine presented a rare smile and turned away. Seti looked at the soft youth, perhaps five years older than himself, before saying, "An 'Adorer' . . . who hires him? What does he chant?"

"They are used at various events," the captain answered, "from public ceremonies to private parties. It is common for them to lead a funeral course and declaim on the achievements of the deceased. They are also used at theatrical and political gatherings to stimulate desired responses within an audience."

Seti turned to look at Emedin, "They are professional liars?"

Emedin smiled, "Some wisdom may reach you through teaching and more through living. Your 'clarity' in part comes from your youth. Does he have dependents? How many are comforted by his gift? He could teach you how to present yourself and speak to many. These are vital skills for one wishing to influence others or assume leadership."

Seti turned back to look at the youth, staring at them in expectation.

He frowned and turned back to the captain, "My Menem are grown distracted, or they test me. I am filled with such passion and purpose but do not see my way ahead. Before I learn these skills, I must know my message."

The captain patted the boy's shoulder and shook her head at the Adorer, who bowed and moved on. Seti gaped at the largest port the Jefaka had come to since he came on board. The barren coastline further north was replaced by what to him appeared to be near-continuous habitation. This slowed the Jefaka's progress as they still travelled along the southern coast of the Danadejet Arm of Rho-Jashun. Seti now discerned a difference in the manners and customs and noted many unfamiliar smells and sounds. Many dressed in ways unknown to Seti. He saw ornamental trees pruned into extraordinary formations and rock outcroppings carved and shaped to dramatic effect. He heard music, accompanied by rhythmic clapping in the distance. A caller sang out a series of phrases in an unfamiliar tune; many others echoed her words repeatedly. A flock of Kumastam circled overhead suggesting they smelt death somewhere in the city. What now held Seti's attention was a thick pillar standing at the port. It had carvings of poisonous and dangerous creatures with baleful eyes staring at the ships.

"What is this?" he pointed at the pillar.

"It is one of the city's talismans, usually called their 'Plague Pillar.'" Emedin answered. "There will be others at each entrance into the city and within it. You will find many unfamiliar customs as we continue south. These are raised to ward off the ills you see carved on it."

"Do they work?" he stared in awe at the pillar.

Emedin smiled, "The locals here and throughout the south swear they do."

Seti looked at her, "You do not believe in them?"

"I have travelled farther than most here," she answered. "This custom is not universal. Cities devastated by plague are filled with talismans, and those with none are spared. What you should observe is this population's willingness to continue to believe in their power, despite their occasional powerlessness."

Seti frowned at her and was silent for a time. He turned his attention to the vibrant city beyond and became more animated, "I have never seen such crowds!" Seti exclaimed. "I am so ignorant! My Menem are agitated. They speak at once, as these crowds do. There is a jumble in my head! How am I to find an Adept to guide me?"

Captain Emedin looked out at the port and frowned. "Many lie in wait to prey on such sweet ignorance. It would help if you left the ship on occasion to learn of the larger Tolku life beyond your village. When you do, Dine or another member of the crew must accompany you. In time you will be hardened and ready to venture out on your own."

She stood surveying the crowds. "We will advertise for an Adept and review their certification. Once here, you may determine their suitability. I also must conclude they are not objectionable to me. We agree they must be subject to the same accord as you. If they prove themselves, they may remain; if not, they will disembark at the next port."

Seti continued to stare in wonder at the bustling port population. Emedin watched the boy, "I must speak alone with you."

She led Seti down to her quarters. They sat for a time in silence. Emedin removed her curled hat and ran a hand through her dishevelled blond hair.

She fixed her light green eyes on the lad, "It is now nine two-weeks since you requested to come aboard," she said. "This ship has found a new focus in you. You continue to be sought after as a Dream Reader. While you consider this gift secondary, you masterfully unravel their slumber's mysteries with confidence and consistency. You have become nimble in our rigging and proficient with our shipping knots. The fortification of my crew for this long voyage remains your greatest service."

She stopped and looked at him. Distant chimes rang out in the city, echoing along the port.

"I had a dream," Captain Emedin said. "I would have you read it."

Seti sat forward in his large chair.

"You stand atop a mountain of feathers," she began in a small voice. "They bear you with ease. Swirls of light encircle you, and the sounds of many whispering voices fill the air. More feathers descend on us like snow. This white mountain stands on black ground that begins to tremble before a huge mouth opens under your Feather Mountain to swallow you. We cry out, 'It is the Mouth of Anu!' You spread out your arms as you fall . . . and . . . I am awakened." Her face became pale. "This has troubled three of my nights. Events proceed the same way, and I am roused at the identical instant." She rubbed her eyes in weariness, "I seldom remember dreams and confess I had placed little store in their readers." She regained her, composure, "What is your reading?"

"The mountain of feathers are the Menem sustaining and uplifting me from the baseness of Anu life," Seti answered at once. "The spreading feathers are the Menem's increasing presence among you because of me. The black ground is the tainted land holding us from light and purity. It grows stronger, and Anu's mouth is its attempt to swallow all we revere. I am not surprised as I fall and prepare to meet Anu."

His swift and sure response left her silent. She rose and paced the cabin. She looked out the small window at the dock painted by Nu's setting before turning back and sitting behind her scarred table. She nodded her head once and said, "I thank you for this reading. I will ponder it."

After a pause, she said, "It seems many things bring us together. Perhaps for a larger purpose, or by the mysteries of chance," she said. "You must learn about us . . . and . . . I wanted to know you." She drummed her fingers on her desk. "Most of this crew and I are part of, or employed by, the Sawlu Clan." She looked closely at him, "Have you heard of us?"

The boy shook his head.

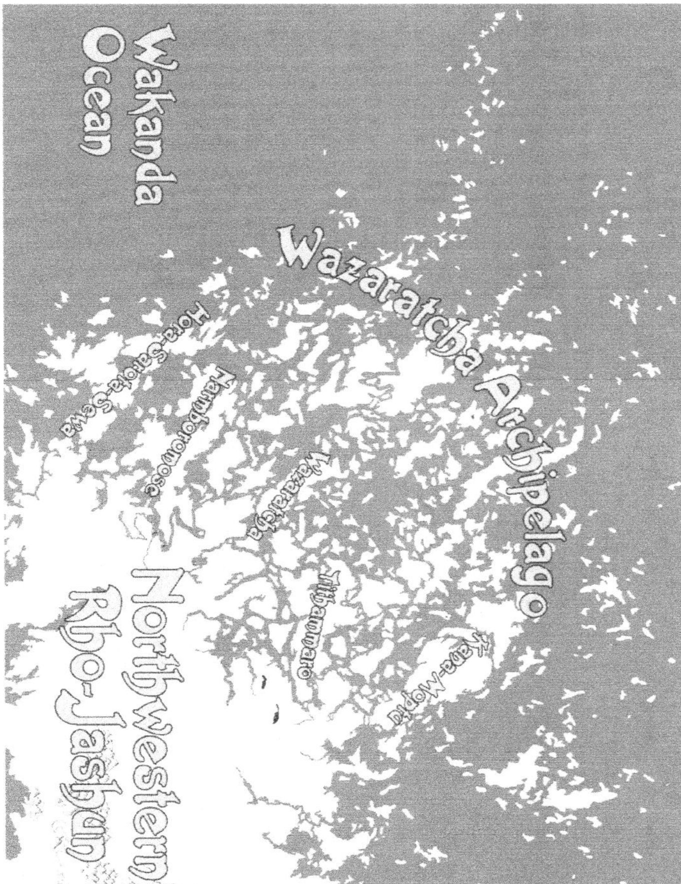

"Sawlu leads a powerful collection of mercantile interests in northern Rho-Jashun. We are based on the five larger islands off the Rho-Jashun coast with a scattering of others occupying the near one thousand larger and smaller islands suffering from the frigid battles between the northern oceans. To see our region on a map is to think northern Rho-Jashun was smashed to pieces by some primordial fist. A nation-building myth was launched that our ancestors defeated the Suvuka before their general banishment and cleansed the islands for the Tolku. This falsehood was used to bolster our claim to the North. The truth is necessity drove our organization as the original return, *after* the Suvuka defeat, saw our multitude of remote northern islands as the perfect cover for piracy and a host of other unsavoury characters. At great cost, and with little or no help from the south, our ancestors removed or destroyed these enclaves of villainy and insanity, laying the foundations for a thriving community. Over many generations, we have grown into the largest commercial power in northern Rho-Jashun." She leaned forward, "We are also historic dissenters from what takes place in our ancestral home on Statos-Vey, which we now approach. Our supposed emperors and empresses of the once-mighty Muraharoma Dynasty are in their dotage. Servants of Tatchlan become the true masters of Statos-Vey. We believe some guide the emperor's hand, and all ministries are filled with them. Muraharoma Dynasty no longer cares about Rho-Jashun and cedes their authority to these 'masters.' Since 'master' Duamang robbed the Suvuka of young, they may do no wrong on Statos-Vey. We all now live in the 'Duamang Age!' Having employed their 'Tatchlan system' to make every Suvuka's womb barren was only the beginning. Their ultimate design is to refashion us! Their power and influence grow, and few dare to oppose them. They are the black mouth of Anu in my dream."

Seti was amazed, "Tolku opposing our holy traditions?" Seti shook his head, "My father believed the old teachings. They taught the Suvuka were Kovlah, loyal servants of Yeoyupan, and the Menem's enemy made visible. When they arrived, they rolled in the mud and swallowed stones to become powerful. Father said with their defeat, the old ways should return. He did not understand why many Tolku now laugh at the Menem."

"Most faithful share his confusion," Emedin answered. "Finding clarity involves having a foot on either side. One positive aspect of the southern sciences is increased appreciation of how life on Anu functions and its vast history. Seti, you must know that for centuries, across Anu, the learned have dismissed the Daruadunnal, just as the ancients let go of the once-powerful Thalana, Cathalu and Chelyaka faiths. Studies in many different disciplines concluded the Suvuka is a separate being rising independently on Thermistal. The evidence is clear, and many authorities having no ties to those masters concur. Perhaps this notion of the Suvuka being Kovlah was promoted in innocence or to strengthened our resolve to fight them, but now it erodes the ancient beliefs. Even those they call masters in the south could not completely bend the Suvuka to their will."

Seti sat digesting this. His face went through a wide range of emotions before looking at her, "Captain, what do you do?"

"Gather information," Emedin answered at once. "Most of our fleet carries those serving our varied business. They also go into the ports to gather signs. We have done this for many generations."

Seti asked, "Why, captain? Why does your clan have this mission?"

"Over twelve hundred years ago, we Tolku hid behind the mountains in Statos-Vey as vast herds of Suvuka filled Rho-Jashun's plains," she gestured toward the shore. "Within this confined population, the Tatchlan masters arose. They had existed long before the Suvuka, but they waxed mighty, and most Tolku came to revere them. You mentioned Geltran-Kenal-Tumhal. I studied his works long ago. As he was born, the Suvuka slaughtered the last of their kin, creatures like themselves, who had travelled with them. The Tatchlan masters successfully altered them, and the Suvuka turned on them in a fury. He witnessed the last ageing Suvuka herds high on the Mulungu barrier as a child with his own eyes. Seeing him, they mourned their loss of children. As an adult, he was troubled at how those masters, led by Master Duamang, whom you also heard of, had defeated the Suvuka. He wrote of his travels through Rho-Jashun, visiting the abandoned Suvuka Circles like the one you knew. Most did not share Geltran's qualms about the Suvuka's defeat and praised the masters' victory. Geltran chose not to confront them."

She paused, and Seti waited for her to continue. "Perhaps this was because the century before Geltran was born, one named Nallurakon did defy them and paid dearly for it. She was born a century before our 'Duamang Age' calendar commenced. She came from within these master ranks before turning on them. Our ancestors joined her campaign to check their growing power. After her death, we kept her story and words alive among us. When the time came, my ancestors travelled into the cooler and cleaner air of Northern Rho-Jashun. They established themselves far from these Tatchlan masters within their fetid jungle and, no longer inhibited by their rules, thrived. Another powerful voice arose in this generation. She came to us from the heart of Statos-Vey, bringing many tales and a passion for writing her dissent. Her name was Nebutan, and we aided her. This included marshalling the crafts for making many copies of her learned books and distributing them along our many trading routes."

"Did you ever meet this Nebutan?"

"Meet?" The captain's face flushed. "She was in her early twenties when she arrived, and I was eleven. We first spoke to each other in the Printer House where I was working, with our Dine as my supervisor, binding books. These hands," she held up both of her powerful and calloused hands, "once sewed the delicate thread through stacks of printed sheets ahead of them being assembled into books. It is our custom for youth still attending school to also 'Gain a Trade.' I loved the ancient process's smells and textures. Later I witnessed her debates with famed scholars visiting her, and was inspired to return to my studies and become a teacher," she held the memory. "In the end, we became friends. I still hear her voice . . ."

Seti waited.

"We had such hopes!" Emedin said with increasing emotion. "We approach the eleventh anniversary of her death . . . she was only forty-eight! She died too young! I will reach her age in the coming year. I cannot believe she has been gone so long."

Emedin's hardened face softened into a growing sadness, "This ship and many others carried crates of her great works across Anu's Face. Her books brought a measure of new prosperity to Sawlu. Along with hoping they would lead to an uprising in the south, she was gratified to enrich her adopted clan. We all hoped her wisdom would waken the Tolku." She stopped and shook her head, "Her words fade more each day. No others take up her call. Her fifteen original volumes and five volumes of letters are buried beneath libraries of new works supporting this Tatchlan system. We trade with all, including the enemy. We must admit, as Geltran and Nallurakon, Nebutan's words are heard less and less on our travels. This has led to a growing discouragement within Sawlu. We have met disappointment and lost our way before. We watch and consider what to do."

She stopped and looked at Seti before rising and pacing the small cabin.

"Since you came on board, I watch you close and my crew more than close. I have sailed on this and other ships and seen near every shade of our kind. I have never seen one your age evoking the old religion. You will find as we continue south, where the majority of Tolku live, most laugh at the old ways, and the few cherishing them are quiet to avoid ridicule. Our dear Nebutan had no interest in religion and had a cool and dispassionate approach, as do the Tatchlan masters. When they came to debate, most had a manner of speech identical to hers. I heard our Nebutan once say, 'religion is the height of emotion.' I have told you I do not believe as you. Yet, I have witnessed other's ability to believe and fear it may become a potent weapon. I hope my dear mentor would understand my contemplations."

Seti had sat frozen listening to this. His spots receded to near nothing on his pale peach skin. He straightened in his chair, "What would you have me do?"

"Forget about storm prediction! You say the Menem told you to remind us of who we are. By whatever agency, you came to the one ship best able to aid you in this quest. With a proper education and training, you may yet fulfill their charge, albeit in a different way than you imagined."

Silence descended on the captain's cabin.

CHAPTER 9

SHUNA-SHAPTA

Pictured: Tolku icon of the Lustrum Mirror. The mirror is round and displays the reflection of a hand with the icon of the Common Desire attached to it.

Day 163, in Two-Week Ten – Paultesh – the two-week of Reflection. Harbour of Bhampay.

Within the past few years, you have been relieved of your inherited burdens of Self-Absorption via our ancient Tatchlan Masters gift - the Lustrum Mirror," Master Tanas intoned with his deep, resonant voice. The forty-one-year-old Master had a deep bronze stocky frame, ignited by his shining red-brown eyes. He had the habit of quickly turning his head in emphasis of a point, causing his long dark red hair, turned in a multitude of thin braids, to slap from side to side. His rich and warm aromas radiated off his body in steady waves. Shuna-Shapta sat with other members of her Delving Invocant Circle of Eight, composed of herself, one other young woman named Mi-Yang, and six men. They endeavoured to attend to their engaging and respected Master as he continued, despite their being in a most unusual setting.

"This miraculous mirror allowed you to behold these noxious protrusions upon your bodies within its reflection and extract them from your lives. You shall have occasion to revisit this wonder in the coming years and excise any persisting residual growths. This very personal process not only liberated yourselves but granted deeper sensitivity to the presence of 'vile greed and venomous ambition' within our rude culture. Our Lustrum Mirror is a specialized tool meant to hone those charged with bringing about our Cluster-of-Clusters Nation. With the full establishment of circles and clusters with their Spokes of the Cluster Wheel, with Maja such as yourselves, at their core, these ills shall be gently rectified without resorting to such extraordinary means. Until this time, we must continue to examine these maladies to appreciate better what impedes our work."

His booming voice did not echo as it usually did within the Enclave chambers because open sky lay overhead. The Master and his Delving Invocates sat on a raised platform by the principle dock for the Masters in Bhampay. Despite the presence of the bustling port, the tall wall surrounding the platform dampened the constant noise. While his students found this setting puzzling, they also noted their Master's distraction. He repeatedly glanced at the lone arched entranceway into what must usually be a small assembly area in the Inner Harbour, as if he expected another arrival. None of the new Invocants knew who this could be or why this instruction occurred outside the Enclave.

"This day, we turn our attention to jealousy," Master Tanas said. "It has no public support and near-universal private application. As with these other facets of misery; fear forms its foundation."

Without looking up, he paused as a noisy flock of Krall circled overhead before landing elsewhere in the Inner Harbour.

"Its lethal combination of terror and rage causes the greatest harm," Master Tanas declared. "All anger-based manifestations damage both the one cherishing it and their victims. This survival tendency, engendered by an ungenerous and self-absorbed culture, shall shrink to its proper proportions within our Cluster-of-Clusters Nation. Your deepening excursions into Tatchlan have already revealed this process within our Resplendent Work. Like the others, jealousy is a malignant tumour menacing its surroundings. In the future, some Invocates shall specialize in monitoring such currents within what we call 'The Common Desire,' tending to them as a gardener does noxious weeds."

"Master?" Shuna-Shapta asked, "Those possessed by jealousy suffer so! Surely its poison is clear to all. Why does it persist?"

"Ah!" Master Tanas exclaimed, "Because the backbone of Self-Absorption is pride! Jealousy is pride's wounded face. History teaches us for the sake of pride, along with the illusions of possessions and property, the sacrifice of all happiness and wholeness was deemed a small price. In part, these observations by our distant grandmothers and their mothers lead to the founding of our Resplendent Work! It may be said the freeing of the Tolku from this hateful inheritance so that we could embrace 'Impartial Love and Caring,' were our ancient Uluvatu Master's primary goals. Pride overcompensates for perceived weakness and fear. Once reduced to its proper dimensions, it also shall serve the future by bolstering our communal endeavours," he paused and smiled. "These are but words. Within our Breathing Wonder, you shall observe as these once-formidable barriers to our hopes melt away in the presence of abundance."

They sat in silence. Nearby, sections of floating walkways bumped together as passengers disembarked from a ship to go ashore. Master Tanas continued to glance at the entrance, and his eyes roved the room in apparent agitation. He reflected before starting a new address, "We live in an exhilarating time! This generation shall witnesses the emergence of our first true cluster with a full abundance of Maja. This is the result of an enormous effort of a myriad of generations of Masters within our Resplendent Work. Most of those generations bent over our Tatchlan Sigil Cubes and joined Dreamers in interpreting the results.

Then early in our Duamang Age, the first collection of true Maja such as yourselves, along with the other Spokes of the Cluster Wheel, were engendered by tremendous effort. Time passed, and gradually, amongst these few precious Maja, roughly one in ten distinguished themselves as Invocates, and the next stage began. Not long ago, to have eight assembled Maja," he gestured to all of them, "in one place would have been a dream. Maja populations are forecast to be eventually one out of each ten. Those Maja possessing sufficient depth to Descend the Depths as you do now to become Invocates, average at one out of ten Maja. The growing presence of Maja enriches our Skin of Anu. The growing presence of Invocates enriches and empowers our Living System of Tatchlan."

He stared into space for a moment, "When I first arrived here in Bhampay as a Fresh Adult, there was just half the number of Invocates such as yourselves within our Living System. We still had to lavish special care upon each newborn Maja as a hothouse plant and keep them sequestered within our Enclaves. Now we are about to witness the spontaneous emergence of a true Maja population, and perchance more than we could have dreamt of in our lifetimes, within true clusters," he furtively glanced at the gate again. "With a surge in Maja shall come a surge in our Invocate population."

He paused in thought again, "In preparation of this, you shall soon be introduced to our 'Estate System.' The foundations of this vital institution are well advanced in anticipation of this profound emergence. This Estate System shall divide and assign each Invocate Circle into what shall become hundreds of degrees of specialty. Together, these Estates form a vital network of interlaced Invocate Circles within Tatchlan. The first generations of these new Estates have already achieved many remarkable accomplishments. In my lifetime, I have witnessed the domestication of several vile illnesses into beneficial agents to serve ourselves and Tatchlan. Here, upon the Skin of Anu, there are many signs of this success. For instance, we now observe the growing number of spontaneous new 'pre-clusters' with keen attention. We seek them out and keep them separate as they work through many novel challenges."

Master Tanas again glanced at the entrance. The Delving Invocates noted their Master wandering from topic to topic and appreciated his focus lay on uncertainty as to what may come through that gateway. His fluctuating aromas spoke about his profound agitation.

"Master," Mi-Yang, the other female Invocant of the group, said, "Why were our 'pre-clusters' established by our Venerable Elders prior to there being sufficient Maja and the other Spokes to anchor and fill them? As you say, were it not for our Lustrum Mirror's purging, our hateful legacy would never cease to rebel against cluster life."

Master Tanas registered momentary surprise at the question, "Ah! Why would my Elders and yours embark upon such a course when they lacked the ten percent Maja population? I am told when Maja began to be born in numbers early in this our Duamang Age, our grandmothers and their mothers chose to simulate our Grand Work to create the necessary 'Wellbeing Conditions.' You are correct in saying were it not for our Lustrum Mirror; we would enjoy far less success with this new model than we do. Elaborate sets of temporary traditions assist this process in breaking down the old isolations and replacing them with 'the murmur of life.'"

He paused before adding, "For instance, unlike the raw populations about us, neither 'husbands' nor 'fathers,' exist within either our Enclaves or these spontaneously emerging pre-clusters. This fact allows many elements to fall into place. Over the past few generations, due to the unseen hand of Tatchlan, a pattern has emerged where males of one pre-cluster group visit females from the other and return to their pre-cluster. Women bear and raise the children assisted by a large group of what were traditionally named uncles, aunts, cousins and siblings overseen by their Venerable Aged. An interconnected set of relationships form enduring bonds, especially between siblings. These relationships have a depth and stability unknown amongst Mundanes, with all their fearfully possessive and insecure traditions. All of you are familiar with this within your Enclaves, where such patterns are well established between your collection of circles. Within urban settings, this is also becoming well known. I am told new literature, current theatrical work and popular ballads now openly depict these pre-clusters. This advances our cause upon the urban cultural front, far more open to innovation than the antique traditions continuing within rural areas. This and many other once-novel elements shall set the stage for the arrival of our Maja. We note a significant increase of 'Betweens' being born . . ." Master Tanas faltered and glanced at the entrance, " . . . and anticipate the further emergence of 'Doubles' and 'Completes,' prior to the Maja being born in sufficient numbers without our interventions. These are, in turn, based upon the deep conditioning provided by our five 'Aroma Accords' you were introduced to as Initiates and now read with considerable skill. This profound work of our original Uluvatu Masters laid the foundations of our future happiness."

Master Tanas paused as some noisy gathering processed past the Master Dock complex out towards some waiting vessel.

"With the pacification of the last venereal strain," he continued as the noise subsided, "nineteen years prior to my birth, to serve us as agents I have variously heard renamed as 'Erotic,' or 'Voluptuous,' or 'Lascivious Gains,' this process is enhanced. Our grandmothers and their mothers took mighty steps 'in the march of ages' by breeding out their original malice, redirecting their purpose and enhancing their many unrefined powers. Among many means, they employed our precious Takshakutan to convert their original corrupting malevolence into a benefit for us all. Thus transmuted, they sunk beneath the depths of the rude skin of raw life down to our Living Orb. Once miserable products of random mutation, our grandmothers and their mothers intelligently redesigned them as essential tools to our young adult formation and ongoing fortification for all. We owe much to those generations for this extraordinary achievement."

He paused before adding, "Another essential aspect involves the pre-cluster Elders having complete control over the group's fertility, beginning the final stages of the programme where the desired three-men-to-one-woman ratio is achieved and maintained. Amongst other things, they shall ensure pairings between siblings, or other close relatives, do not produce offspring."

"Master Tanas," Shuna-Shapta hesitated, "You know I have a younger brother and two sisters . . ." she did not finish her question.

Master Tanas waved his hand, "Do not concern yourselves about the joyous experiments of pre-adult, Fresh Adult, nor continuing Ripe Adult sibling liaisons. Deep intimacies between siblings shall ever be central to cluster life. The perfection of our fertility tools addresses the issue of ill-advised conception. Your First and Second Mothers ensured your safety. You attain the age to appreciate the process yourself."

"Master Tanas," Mi-Yang asked, "are not incestuous pairings used to perfect Tatchlan?" The other students nodded in agreement.

"Indeed they are," Master Tanas replied, glancing at the entrance, "marked tendencies existing between close relations have lead to their children fortified beyond their progenitors. Such sibling-generated lines have led to bolstering many qualities essential to our establishment of Tatchlan. The first three Unification Dynasties of ancient times were, in part, built upon the ongoing sexual congress among siblings and other 'blood relations.' Nevertheless, it is also known such a tool must be employed with great care. Our work has uncovered how many generational ills have their source within these successive unions. Based upon knowledge and experience, we resort to this tool as necessary. We certainly do not evoke the fear-laden and ignorant taboos of the past. I assure you sexual intensity between siblings and other close relations means naught. As long as these Elders control fertility, cluster health and harmony remain intact."

"Master Tanas," Shuna-Shapta asked, "do you suggest infertile unions are undesirable within true cluster life?"

"Far from it. Once our full Living System 'Quickens,' and cluster mates are rooted within their Circles of Eight anchored by their Maja, fertility shall be cultivated to the benefit of each and the burden of none. The pre-cluster arrangement I described shall give way. We foresee the typical arrangement inside a Circle of Eight as, with a few variations," he indicated the composition of the class, "six men and two women."

He smiled at them all as a bell began to ring on a distant ship, "'Infertile' unions shall be the norm. The destruction of toxic fictions of an invisible body existing beside our actual body was a vital aspect of our work. For adults, generous and ongoing delight shall lead to freedom from each aspect of Self-Absorption - such as the aforementioned jealousy. As for children, they require many supporting hands, beyond just the mother, her siblings and others within her blood group. As our Cluster-of-Cluster Society blossoms, the importance of many of these current 'blood designations' shall diminish as our Circles of Eight, Double Circles of Eight and more, spread."

A series of high-pitched hoots, made by the Asaku, the smallest and most colourful of the cousins, filled the air. These little ones conveyed messages across the city. A group of eight of these little creatures, bearing brilliant yellow fur contrasting with their blue and green markings on their faces and rumps, burst through the entranceway and scampered into the room. Master Tanas drew out a small bell and rang it, immediately becoming surrounded by the chattering emissaries with their long tails held aloft. He and the class laughed at their antics as they each pulled out their message and handed it to him. Master Tanas distributed a set of small rings signifying their next destination, along with treats, and they hurried out of the room. Master Tanas read the message. Aromas of profound emotion poured off him in billowing waves.

"Our lives are buffeted with unprecedented events!" Master Tanas declared. "We are grateful for your forbearance in following us to this unorthodox lecture hall to endure my distracted discourse." He stared at each of the repeated messages on all the Asaku dispatches, "Word has come," he stopped on the verge of tears, "There is pre-cluster, known as Thakadush, that is the largest and most vibrant. Within the past year, they have outstripped all others in producing Maja and other Spokes of the Cluster Wheel. Now, they lead us into unforeseen wonders! They may . . . they may stand upon the verge of spontaneously producing . . . our first Majastas."

The students gaped at the Master and turned to look at each other in amazement. A general tremor passed through the group as all their combined Aroma Accords blossomed together.

"Master?" one of the male students finally spoke in a trembling voice, "May this be? Often you have said centuries lay between us and the Quickening. You certainly said only a Ripe Adult could truly manifest any aspect of our Living System. We have been instructed in the conducive conditions for a . . . Majastas being a critical mass of Maja within a sizeable portion of a large population."

Master Tanas burst out laughing, "My Delving Invocates! Do you not smell the truth of this? From the day of my arrival here, at your age, I heard whispers about our Living System shifting and changing beneath our Invocate's feet. The staid and inscrutable vistas of The General Plain, best read by our venerable Tatchlan Cubes, burst into a profusion of complexities. At the same time, you and many more Maja were born, in numbers exceeding all previous generations combined! Despite accelerating our established timelines and protocols, we found ourselves riding the waves of a growing ocean! This sudden outburst is the result of the sacrifice, the life-long patience, and the rigorous, rigorous discipline of our grandmothers and their mothers. Generations dedicating themselves to a result they did not see lead to us reaping the full benefit. You are correct, my dear! This is not what we forecast. Our Uluvatu Masters would stand in awe and amazement. Tatchlan is awake and impatient to rouse Herself in full! As with all, your introduction to this new arcana awaited your arrival as Full Invocates. No more!"

Master Tanas paused, breathing heavily while the entire group now resonated together. Even the chaos of the Inner Harbour beyond their enclosure seemed to have altered.

"Many signs distinguished this pregnancy," he spoke quietly, "but we dared not hope. The mother went into labour hours ago. Her abundant scent precursors fill all corners, wiping each trace of self-absorption away. Many companion creatures within this true Cluster display astonishing signs."

After so much emotion, Master Tanas grew strangely calm, "We have gained entry so you, leaders of our next generation of Invocants, may witness the birth of what all Masters, back to our Uluvatu and even further into prehistory, yearned to behold."

He led the way as his students packed and followed him. They went down the few steps to the dock and followed him along the winding quay back to the main pier and out into the bustling city. The towering statues of ancient Yin-Vinulan emperors had garlands and other decorations, including flower crowns on their heads. They followed winding avenues and crossed several plazas. Finally they saw a group of pipers seated on many of the broad pedestals of the two rows of fish statues lining either side of what was locally known as the Companion Avenue. The pedestals went through a series of deep blue and green shades, and the statues coats of dazzling mosaics gleamed with polishing. At the end of the avenue, they passed the well-known Companion Pond, a deep pool where a wide variety of large and exotic fish came to the surface when their names were called.

Thakadush Cluster compound stood beyond this celebrated pond. These compounds were haphazard, as the required dimensions were hard to achieve in the crowded ancient city. Until the Tolku lived in a full 'Cluster-of-Clusters' society, walls surrounded them. This ensured the distinguishing life inside cultivated and concentrated their Aroma Accords.

Each compound was distinguished in part by the Jezin growing thick on the walls. This dense moss, a work of ancient Masters, served the simple purpose of recording each visitor's face. As none of them had visited this cluster, Master Tanas and each Invocant found a clear place to press their faces and one handprint into the moss. It retreated, leaving a clear impression, remaining for many years.

"Shapta!" Master Kanla called out as soon as they had entered the compound. Shuna-Shapta noted her mother was in shed and observed how cluster mates, and each visiting Master, were shedding. She had the familiar itch.

"Ama? Why are we all shedding?"

"My daughter!" Master Kanla declared warmly, "We react to the opening of our Living System. We witness Tatchlan born amongst us!"

She and Master Tanas burst out laughing as they embraced. They spoke to each other as members of the honoured cluster, their translucent skins as shining glass over their visible muscles and organs, brought small flower effigies in greeting to the students. A large Circle Dance had begun in the outer courtyard, and several Masters joined the cluster mates in celebration.

Masters Tanas and Kanla motioned to the eight Delving Invocate students to follow them. Inside Thakadush, they, and their students, disrobed in respect to the cluster and gave their clothes to children assigned to receive them. As they made their way, their skin began to peel off their naked bodies at an accelerated rate. The smallest children ran behind them, gleefully collecting each shred and placing most in baskets while they nibbled on handfuls. As they proceeded, Shuna-Shapta began to smell a potent mixture of aromas, as if a thousand aromatic bodies surrounded her. She also noted many instruments hanging from the walls and other signs of industry. They moved through a series of corridors passing many empty rooms where lay more evidence of fabrication or craft. As they delved deeper, and the floor sloped inward, the air became hot and moist. The sounds of many hushed voices filled the close quarters, punctuated by the familiar cries of a woman in labour.

The Masters and students stepped into the central open area, created by the removal of several old walls and their replacement by four new ornamental pillars. These were at odds with the drab nature of the older room. At the centre stood a tall woman attended by many others. Her feet stood on raised birthing blocks, and she was far into her labour. Shuna-Shapta looked at the others. They formed a tight-packed circle with the woman at the centre. Many held musical instruments, suggesting earlier they had performed to encourage the woman. The silent group swayed back and forth to the woman's insistent cries, echoing off the walls. None of the visitors could have said how long they stood there or how often the woman cried as she worked to bring the child out. Those attending reeled backward as a new scent filled the air. A final push and the baby's head appeared. The attendants assisted her in completing the birth. The newborn began to emit strange high-pitched sounds. The little girl reverted to familiar infant wails, and everyone laughed.

The entire room became animated. Voices rose in song, and musicians began to play their instruments. The mother had been lowered onto the bed behind as the child lay on her heaving chest. The baby made her distinctive high-pitched calls. These calls and the baby's scent had a powerful impact on the cluster. The Masters beside them began to whisper to each other, gesturing to the infant. The song and music stopped, and the entire group began to move as one. They raised their hands and arms, pointing them toward the child. They bent their bodies back and forth and waved their hands, creating a rippling effect coursing through the room and ending at the tiny baby at the centre. Shapta heard the collective breathing in and out of the cluster as if it formed new music. As soon as this particular scene began, it ended, and the crowd began to laugh and sing. Shuna-Shapta looked over at the amazed and silenced Masters. She came to her mother and took her hand.

Master Kanla looked at her daughter and embraced her, she pulled away, and her voice shook when she found it, "We witness the beginning of our true life. History shall begin to count from this day. Our past foolishness and waste shall be forgotten."

CHAPTER 10

Seti

Pictured: a modern version of the Tatchlan Cube arrangement seen by Seti and Dine in Hushukrath

Day 166, in Two-Week Ten – Paultesh – the two-week of Reflection. City of Hushukrath on Tich-Tushmul Island.

Dine, the Jefaka's First Officer, walked on shambling seaman's legs through the streets beside Seti. They were in the city of Hushukrath, the principal port of the island of Tich-Tushmul. Since Seti had come on board, Jefaka had sailed for ten two-weeks with few stops, and many of the crew were enjoying a brief shore leave. The ship received minor repairs while unloading and taking on cargo. Dine had been assigned to oversee Seti's introduction to the largest city he had ever seen. Dine kept his face set ahead but often had to stop when the boy asked questions or stared at an exotic sight. Even in this strange environment, his contrasting black hair over his pale face drew glances.

The air danced with competing rhythms — many contrasting voices mixed in an intoxicating soup of activity. On occasion, Dine noted a distinctive trilling whistle filling the air he had not heard before. Seti gaped at the astonishing variety of clothing, jewelry, body paint and elaborate hair previously unknown to him. They passed by an open market, and he saw almost no food he recognized. They turned into a narrow avenue. On either wall sat and stood women in singular costumes trying to entice them into games of chance. Each had an idiosyncratic patter and performed an elaborate dance and song to allure passersby.

"May we play?" Seti called over the din, delighted at the animated exhibition.

"No!" Dine shouted over the noise. "This foolishness is why I am with you. If the captain heard you wasted your money, I would answer for it. When you are of age, you may throw it away as you wish. Do not trouble yourself with these distractions."

The boy nodded and moved on. Dine was impressed he did not whine or argue. They continued along another street until Seti stopped before a small public altar nestled into a wall niche. The jumbled pack of many sizes and shapes included traditional depictions of the four Grand Menem. Vindaviran was holding his pen and paper and Samajalas at his potter's wheel. Tarunachit wore his crown of bones, and Yuyutar had his black and white spheres. Alongside these familiar figures were many disturbing ones, including a smiling Yeoyupan riding on the back of a Suvuka and several erotic configurations. Garish phallic symbols, many wearing flower garlands and other offerings, were painted radiant orange and pink, many with purple bulbs on top. He knew they were called Life Pillars here in the south. Most figures were old and had lost much of their colour and definition. Others flaunted their garish youth. A few of the statues had a missing eye or other body parts. Animal statues and fantastic and gruesome hybrids stood in the hundreds. Notes in varying denominations and piles of coins filled any level surface or were rolled, tied or stuck to the figures. Small pieces of jewelry were draped around their necks, wrapped around them and hung over their arms. The combined scent of the fresh flowers, fruits and decay from the heaps of stale and fresh offerings scattered about and filling several trays had a compelling sweetness. Dine read the boy's expression and nodded.

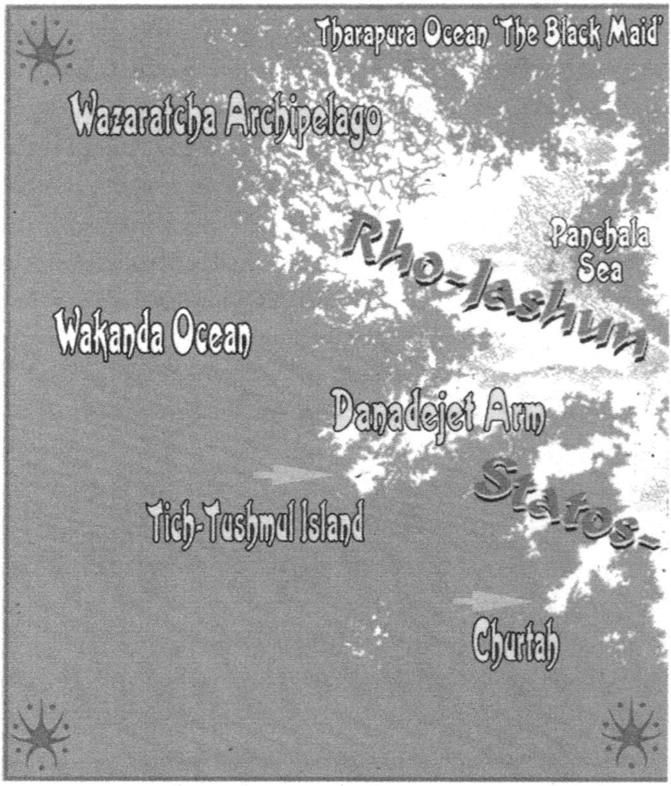

"Welcome to the 'South,'" Dine said quietly, standing close to him in front of the altar, "The Suvuka did not possess Danadejet Arm and this island of Tich-Tushmul. The Mulungu Mountains protected both. We are on the southern coast of Danadejet, and you will see more signs of the ancient society our ancestors left behind when we went north." He gestured to the crowded altar, "These will grow huge in dimension and population rivalling the cities. What we consider private at home, you will see enacted before them. The larger the audience, the greater will be their enthusiastic devotions. What we consider monstrous will be celebrated in the open air. The traditional separations between differing traditions dissolve, and what we see as exclusive images share the same podium."

Seti stared at the visual cacophony for a long time before looking up at Dine.

"Why do Kovlah stand beside Menem? Why does Tarunachit join hands with Yeoyupan, his sworn enemy?"

"Long ago, perhaps ages before the Daruadunnal was written, it was believed they were not enemies. In ancient religions such as Tuchulacha and Hathnal, what we would name evil was worshiped along with the good. Those goddesses were venerated as much for their calamities as their boons. 'Evil' and 'Good' were both dispensed by their hands. The Menem prophets of old spoke against them. Still, we are taught later priests gathered many forgotten rites and names to incorporate into our faith. Given this pedigree, it is not surprising interpretations of our religion vary widely."

Seti frowned at the figures and shook his head. What he said next surprised Dine. "They say the Epic of Ranvartawan will be performed!" Seti exclaimed, pointing to a painted sign on a wall.

Dine gaped at the boy, "You read?"

"Yes . . . my father taught me. I have read Furrumittal and other books."

Dine stood considering the lad. "Does the captain know?"

Seti pondered before shaking his head, "We have not spoken of reading. I noticed the Furrumittal in her cabin. I did not recognize the other books there."

Dine snorted, "Few here would!" he looked at the crowds with sudden bitterness. He turned back to him, "At home, our dramas are presented by bare-faced actors on a stage. Here dramas are done with figures in mask and gown. Farther south, they perform using elaborate puppets. These creations attain notoriety, and crowds attend their 'renditions.' Admirers send them gifts and dedicate compositions to them. During the day here and throughout Statos-Vey, costumes are bright and festive. From night to dawn, dramatic performances are done by figures behind a lit screen." He frowned, "This work should be done at night. You want to see this?"

Seti nodded.

Dine looked at the message to determine where they had to go. "The next performance will begin soon."

They moved along a broad avenue where smells of many savoury foods filled the air. They passed other small altars, including one where the figures were coloured blue and green; these altars added their peculiar perfumes to Seti's already tingling nostrils. A curious tall statue depicted a Tolku transforming into other creatures; each limb came from a different animal. She had many flower garlands around her neck, and outstretched limbs, and her face had inset yellow eyes. The name 'Hathnal' stood on the altar before her image.

The avenue bent and varied in width many times until it ended in an open square. Rising above the square's surrounding buildings was the distant outcropping where the ruling houses and surrounding wealthy elites outdid each other with lavish palaces and extensive gardens covering the entire hill.

"Here," Dine pointed at the crowded mount, "they call that 'the Promontory.' It is said long ago the sea lapped at its base. Over many ages, it retreated, allowing the city to surround it. Now inland, it overlooks the harbour. Despite it no longer jutting into the ocean, it has kept its ancient name. For millennia, those ruling Hushukrath and the surrounding territories have made their seat there."

"May we go?"

"The likes of us are not invited."

A crowd stood before a raised platform where an ornate little house with an open front wall stood. "Forget the palaces," Dine said. "You will learn more of value here."

They moved through the crowd to stand near the front so that Seti could see. A juggler and other acrobats were in mid-performance and the crowd in good humour. Seti and Dine laughed and applauded the performers. Dine looked at a tall water clock behind the theatre, "Their tardiness is to our benefit. It should have begun," he said. Half the crowd began to dissipate as the performance began. Seti frowned and looked at

Dine. "Why are they leaving before the play begins?"

Dine frowned, and his jaw clenched in a way Seti had observed many times. He gave the boy a small smile. "This epic is primordial. Most here will have watched it many times."

Seti accepted this and turned back to watch the performance. An actor wearing a white mask and black cloak walked onto the stage with a flourish. Seti knew this must be the narrator. "Gather and hear the foundations of our fate!" She called in an extraordinary voice filling the square. "Witness the initial battle and the ultimate resolution of our woes! Your bones know this tale well! Those released before us fill the air with remembrance! Witness our enslavement, our rebellion and become free!"

As she strode off, her cloak billowed behind her, and her boots thumped on the stage. Two others entered carrying a rolled banner. They also wore white masks and black capes. They stood mute in the middle, unrolling and stretching the pitch-black banner out. It had loops, which they fixed to a series of poles along the back of the stage. The flag stood undulating in the gentle breeze. It was not wholly black; toward the centre, it lightened until reaching a white spot containing a burst of radiating light. The two exited either side. In dramatic contrast to the others, a new player entered, wearing a wild and violent pattern, his mask twisted and frightful.

"Behold Untasha-Kabash!" the figure gestured to the white jewel in the centre of the banner. "She has ever been at the centre of existence. She lacks nothing. Her highest peak of perfection is unassailable. She has floated in pure silence before any knowledge of time. Beyond comprehension is she, in her pristine isolation and perfect calm. There came an instant like none before, when she had a thought. This thought bore a being, dividing perfection in two. While giving birth to this thought, Untasha-Kabash was beyond the awareness of this new existence." The actor strode to the banner and stood at one end, pointing to it. "This thought fills every corner of perfection. He is named Ranvartawan. He shelters his mother, and each new thought is born within him. This firstborn is closest to the mother and remains beyond awareness."

The actor returned to the centre of the stage. "Untasha-Kabash had another thought, and I was born."

Seti started booing at the actor. He faltered, and many in the audience laughed. Dine gave him a small cuff on the ear. "What are you doing, boy?"

"This is Yeoyupan!" Seti hissed.

"This is an actor playing Yeoyupan!" Dine hissed back, bending closer to him.

"I know that! My father saw a performance, and everyone booed when he came on stage."

"Everyone is not doing so here."

"Why are they," Seti indicated the rest of the audience, "silent? They do not call out the reply phrases to what he is saying."

"Different places and times call for different ways. I have seen this performed as you describe but will take my cue from them," he indicated the crowd.

The audience remained amused, and Seti grew quiet as the actor waited. Seti bowed to the actor. He inclined his head and returned to his role. "Unlike my mother and brother," he continued, "I was aware. I stood before her and spoke for many ages. She did not hear me. She did not see me." He turned and began to shout at the jewel. "I become enraged!" he roared. "My existence was but 'dust on the wind' to her and my brother!" Many others ran out onto the stage and to the house's windows above dressed in simple white cloaks and masks. Yeoyupan began to harangue the jewel at the centre of the white banner. They began to shed their outer covers and masks. Underneath, they either dressed as Yeoyupan, or they wore light blue robes and deep blue smooth masks. Those like

Yeoyupan stood by him. Those in the blue masks stood in front of the banner. They made gestures to stop him from shouting at the jewel.

The narrator returned and stood in front of the rest. She recited, "Many more thoughts are born and witness Yeoyupan's long speeches. Because of this, they become as aware as he. While Untasha-Kabash floats in the cool ocean of light of Ranvartawan, the other thoughts are divided and imperfect."

Yeoyupan ran to the front of the stage, "I cannot endure this existence!" he shouted. "Those joining me will be called my Kovlah." Those dressed as him gathered round. "Those siding with this frigid silence, I call Menem."

He and his Kovlah ran to the jewel and tried to remove it from the banner. The Kovlah also attempted to remove the flag from its poles. Seti stood on tiptoe to see they were not touching the banner. The Menem stood aside and gestured their amazement. The Kovlah grunted and roared, but none of them touched Untasha-Kabash or Ranvartawan. They turned to the Menem and rushed them but neither injured nor overcame the other. The groups staggered away and panted their exhaustion. During this scene, more figures emerge from either side as new thoughts from Untasha-Kabash. They shed their neutrality at once and joined one or the other side, keeping each group equal.

The narrator declared, "Yeoyupan devises a plan to expel the Menem from the body of Ranvartawan. He creates a prison. It is a dark and hard place, made from the scrapings off his body and pressed in his cupped hands." Yeoyupan goes through the motions and takes from his backside to add to the growing dark ball in his hands. Several in the audience chuckled, and others emitted sounds of disgust as this ball's smell reached them. "He calls it vile Anu," the narrator stated.

The ball representing their planet was placed at the front of the stage. The audience stepped back from the stench. "He encircles it with many traps guarded by his Kovlah, making escape impossible." Yeoyupan kneeled behind the ball and gestures as the narrator continued, "The noise and confusion of his mind fill this Anu. He creates one gateway, the burning Eye of Nu, and one hundred smaller ways, for his enemies to fall through. He sends one hundred of his Kovlah to become sentries for the gates, opening for the Menem to fall and closed to those attempting to return."

Yeoyupan opens a trap door behind the ball. He and his Kovlah begin picking up the Menem and dropping them through the door, sending them to Anu. At first, the Kovlah were winning, then Menem began dropping Kovlah onto Anu. The numbers evened as new thoughts joined to return the sides to balance.

Seti frowned and turned to Dine. He tugged his sleeve and whispered. "They leave much out!"

Dine gave him a grim smile and nodded before gesturing silence.

Several new figures strode out, wearing light brown robes and masks. They unfurled a long brown banner, obscuring the stage. Sounds of movement were heard, and the trap door shutting. Those holding the flag ran off the other side of the stage, revealing a new setting. A black cloth covered the floor and black forms, suggesting landscape and trees spread across the stage. Thankfully, the rank ball representing Anu was removed. The audience clapped, and Seti looked confused.

"It is a courtesy," Dine said, forestalling his question. "They applaud the swift change on stage." Seti looked and nodded.

Despite knowing what was to come, Seti gasped. Two actors, wearing an elaborate costume meant to represent a four-footed Suvuka, came onto the stage. The audience became animated, and exclamations and more applause erupted. Even Dine was impressed. The Suvuka wore the same mask as Yeoyupan, but was otherwise hairy and covered in mud. The tall creature stomped its broad paws bristling with lethal talons as it walked. It raised its massive head, and several horns blared off stage to simulate a Suvuka's call. Off the square, someone shouted an imprecation at the Suvuka on stage. The audience found this amusing. They smelt the foul odour, realizing whatever the Anu ball was composed of covered the Suvuka costume.

"We are the Kovlah on Anu!" the Suvuka declared in a deep, thick voice. "We serve our master Yeoyupan. We make the Menem forget their former life. We embrace Anu, the creation of our master and cause each creature to roll in the dust!" The terrible creature turned and addressed the audience, "You Menem are our prisoners, and we are your jailers!"

Seti had to restrain himself from booing, and Dine smiled as he laid a quieting hand on his shoulder.

Three actors came out wearing filthy rags and dark masks, having tears painted on their cheeks. "Alas!" one cried out, "We are covered in filth!" The second felt his body, "Alas! We are encased in sacks of loathsome skin!" The third lifted one foot and the other. He pointed down, "Alas! We are forced to walk on this vile rubbish." They turned to the audience and cried out, "Alas! Alas! Alas! We are immersed in pollution and cannot escape!"

The Suvuka emitted its wild trumpet cry and rose on its hind legs. The three Menem cringed and cried out as he charged and seemed to trample them. He turned back to the silent audience, his front legs bloodstained, "Our Master has ensured our victory! In Ranvartawan, we could not affect them. On Anu, we are supreme! Once the Menem are destroyed, Yeoyupan will hurl down Untasha-Kabash and Ranvartawan. They will become weak like the rest, and we will eradicate them. The Kovlah will join us, and our master will rule over Anu forever!"

Into the windows above the stage, came three figures. Their masks were vibrant, topped by rich turbans covered in glittering embroidery. Intricate patterns in warm hues danced on their cloaks. One wore red gloves, the second yellow and the third orange. Their gloved hands wore a multitude of rings and bangles. The three looked down on the Suvuka and spoke to each other, "The Kovlah possesses mighty paws," said the first woman. Her voice remained clear despite her mask. Seti tugged at Dine's sleeve before he frowned and bent down. "Who are they?" Seti whispered. Dine shook his head as the three performed ritual movements with their gloved hands. Dine began to scowl.

"Yes," the second woman, wearing the yellow gloves, answered. "The Kovlah's paws are mighty. Even so, their heads are small on their thick necks." The third raised her orange gloves "Our heads will outmatch their claws."

Dine reached down for Seti's hand. "Come!" He whispered. Seti was too amazed to resist as they turned and went through the crowds back the way they came.

"Why are we leaving?" Seti asked.

"Abbreviating the epic is appalling, but to twist it! They dare to insert the master's message!" Without warning, he stopped, and Seti near lost his balance. He looked at Dine. He wore an expression of horror and disbelief.

"No, no," he uttered.

Seti followed his gaze. To the right of the entrance into the square stood a tall plaque composed of a series of dazzlingly coloured panels. He counted sixty-four, eight high and eight across. Each of the intricate and polished glyphs was raised from the back and composed of many symbols. Some were members of insect societies, while others depicted ancient emblems of agriculture and exotic flora. Many were of fantastical faces causing his skin to tingle with a strange unease. There were also abstract symbols overlaying bizarre configurations Seti did not recognize. Many tiny details also inhabited each rounded square. Each glyph had a distinguishing series of colours affecting those around it. Horizontal, vertical and diagonal rows had colour and design themes running through them based on these glittering icons. This beautiful and mysterious creation, twice as tall as an adult, stood mounted on the wall. Its high craftsmanship made everything else look dull, rude, and ill-formed.

"What is it?" Seti asked as they drew closer.

Dine clenched his jaw as he turned to look at him. "This, boy, is the enemy's work," he answered in a hollow voice. "Tatchlan's so-called masters are here! These take several forms, including a perfect square and a circle. Whatever the arrangement, there remain sixty-four images as you see them here. These 'masters' hold mathematics in high esteem, and many of their works take the form of elaborate equations. They work their evil craft using this arrangement of symbols! This stands as a display, but there must be others here set indoors where foul rituals take place on and before them."

A sudden chorus caused them to look back to where the play continued out on the square. They no longer recognized the performance. A large group of women, dressed in masks and cloaks similar to those occupying the upper windows, sang an unfamiliar song. They raised their arms above their heads and swayed from side to side. The Suvuka had already exited the stage even though it should have remained for the rest of the scene. They heard several shouts directed toward the stage from the surrounding square. Dine listened and nodded before turning to Seti.

"Many changes have taken place in the years since our last visit. Not all agree with them."

Seti turned back to look at the brilliant series of glyphs.

"This is Tatchlan?"

"They are Tatchlan Glyphs. Those masters possess many contrivances to twist life."

They became aware of a figure standing beside the panel. He looked at them.

"His face!" He looked at Dine, "It is as Yeoyupan's mask back there. His face and body are twisted!"

They hurried past him and back to the ship.

CHAPTER 11

SINKIN

Tolku icon known as the Suvuka Bane.

Day 376, on the Jabun Isthmus, gateway to the Mushumafal Peninsula and the entrance to the Kukernef Desert

Durka and Makusk Herd had run for over two hundred days as one. They had bonded at the Latatroos Shelter in the jungle, where Makusk Herd had revealed the marks of Tolku domination and interference. The two herds left the twisting paths of the dense jungles behind them. The land opened wide, and the soil became hard beneath their paws. This was true Suvuka territory. Despite their size and power, they moved as fleeting shadows through the diminishing stands of short trees, over the broad plains and low hills. The grasses became stubble, and far-off obstacles were seen in advance. Sinkin's body had become lean, and his pelt shone. The land narrowed, and the hills rose either side of them as they approached the Jabun Isthmus. The ocean lay but a two-day's run beyond the horizon to the east and west.

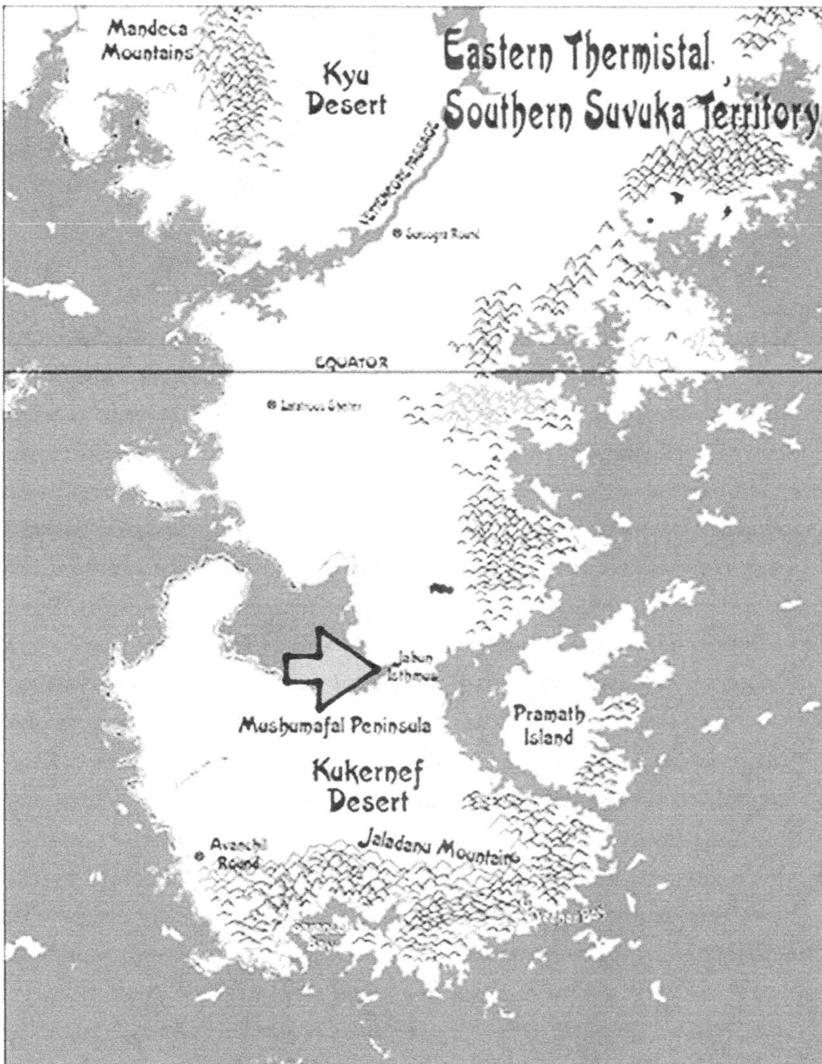

Hiratak and Morakav, the two Herdmasters, looked south. The vast ocean of sand called Kukernef lay ahead. They conferred and turned back to stand before the combined herds.

"Two paths lead to Avanchil," Morakav began. "One is longer and safer. It follows the western coast. The ocean would be to our right. This path will be marked with tended places. The other is short and dangerous. We would run south through Kukernef, as far as Latatroos Shelter. The desert has many faces. Some are blasted hard land littered with rocks. Others are mountains of sand. This sand shifts and bewilders your senses. These mountains blend into the air during storms, able to tear the pelts off your backs. Sand air can fill your lungs. Vile creatures large and small lie in stealth, ready to attack. All Kukernef bakes under Nu and freezes at night. You must adapt to both extremes."

The herds remained silent, and Hiratak, Master of Durka Herd, stepped forward. "Young bucks yearn for the short route. We made this run. We give you counsel. Sagas claim heroes took the fast way. Kukernef has laughs at your bravado. He will drink you like water! His tenants hear you and lay snares. The desert teaches much but has no tolerance for failure. Even the safe route has harsh lessons. We still cross some open desert. This is the way I ran my Stag Path. We still lost three of our herd! Tradition dictates – you bucks decide. Sinkin and Setush come forward."

The two bucks came and stood. Morakav and Hiratak recited a formula in turns.

"The Stag Path firms you," Hiratak said.

"Sharing endurance, hardship and accomplishment," Morakav said.

"You find your wisdom. You hear others' wisdom."

"You bond to your herd in new ways."

"You return a full member in Suvuka life."

"Your childhood has been long."

"Many paws have guided you."

"Now, the land challenges you."

"You are challenged by yourself."

"Here, you have a choice."

"Choose for yourself."

"Choose for us."

Silence descended on the two herds. The others recalled their own time standing where the two bucks now stood and knew what they endured. Sinkin and Setush had grown close over these two hundred days and had often spoken together. They slept side by side and formed the strong bonds common among stags on long hunts. They began to tremble under the eyes of their two Herdmasters. Hiratak and Morakav stepped backward four steps and turned to face ahead. The two bucks were separated in front and behind. Attention remained on them.

Sinkin bent his head toward Setush, "We must decide," he whispered.

Setush nodded and whispered back, "We were tested by what we do. Now by what we choose."

"They frowned when we sang the 'Song of Shushkup.'"

Setush nodded, "He was supposed to cross Kukernef alone."

"He became a great leader. He pushed us to cross the sea."

"Perhaps this is why the elders dislike him. Before Thermistal and knew nothing of . . . them."

Sinkin shook his head, "My Herdmaster said they are false tales. The elders tolerate our songs as foolishness."

Setush growled, "Is it foolish to dare? Is it foolish to know our power? Look what we have done!"

"I bring pride to Durka. You to Makusk. Knowing our limits defines our strength. Have you run over mountains of sand?"

"By the ocean."

"Yes, flat and water-soaked. I know these. Imagine tall shifting mountains dry beyond death and burning!"

"We could endure them!"

"We could. And what of our herd mates?"

Setush was silent.

"What of Morakav? What of Hiratak?"

"They are strong."

"Yes, and their greatest strength is their wisdom. They know when strength fails. We decide their fate and our own."

Setush stood for a long time in silence. His body began to quake, and a series of suppressed whines escaped him. Morakav and Hiratak turned, started by this before turning back. Setush summoned himself to speak what he had dared not say aloud. "Sinkin, why do we run?" He faced full-forward, not looking at Sinkin or Morakav and Hiratak, but over them to the horizon.

Sinkin was taken back by the question, "Why?"

"Yes, Sinkin. Why do we make this run?"

Sinkin shook his head in confusion, "It is tradition, based on our elder's experience. We face trials under this guidance. When we are called on to defend our herd . . ."

"Sinkin!" Setush hissed, "Our herd has many Full Stags! The Tolku rode them, despite this run! Our power and endurance were useless against them!"

Morakav bowed his head, and Hiratak did so to honour his sorrow at hearing Setush's pain.

"You did not have one on your back!" Setush near shouted. "You have not stood helpless! You were not frozen unless they pulled on their vines!"

Sinkin lowered his head in deference to Setush's shame.

"It does not matter which path we take," Setush continued. "The prudent or foolish road has the same end."

Sinkin became aware of Morakav and Hiratak having their own whispered debate ahead of them. While he could not imagine what Makusk had endured, he became angry.

"What should we do?" Sinkin asked. "Neither? Turn and go home? What do we tell our Dames and Mates? We stopped because of the Tolku?"

Tears streamed down Setush's face. "We are altered! Do my questions display the change? Joy and terror fill me! I imagine squashing their little heads. I fear we will not fight an honourable battle. We will be humiliated! I dream strange dreams, Sinkin! Dreams never haunted my waking before. If I am changed, why do we run?"

Hiratak and Makusk whispered in urgent tones to each other as the ritual went astray. The group was halted by Setush's anguish. They readied to turn and address them when Sinkin began to speak.

"I know why we run."

Setush raised his head and looked at him.

"The Full Stag Run predates the Tolku," Sinkin said. "It has nothing to do with them. We run to honour our past. We run to give pride to our herd. Their pride is enough reason for me."

He paused, and the rest stood silent, "Durka Herd honours your courage," Sinkin said. "We must rise above our fear. We must gather in larger numbers. We will find a way to stop this."

He took a few long breaths, "These issues are separate," he continued. "Today, our question is where we run. By doubting your every action you give them victory. You are not defeated. You are a greater hero than the one in the 'Song of Shushkup.' They did not overcome you. You still suffer and ask these questions."

Morakav and Hiratak turned, and the other herd members came forward. They surrounded the two bucks. Setush looked at Morakav, "I say we be prudent heroes."

"So say I," answered Sinkin.

CHAPTER 12

Seti

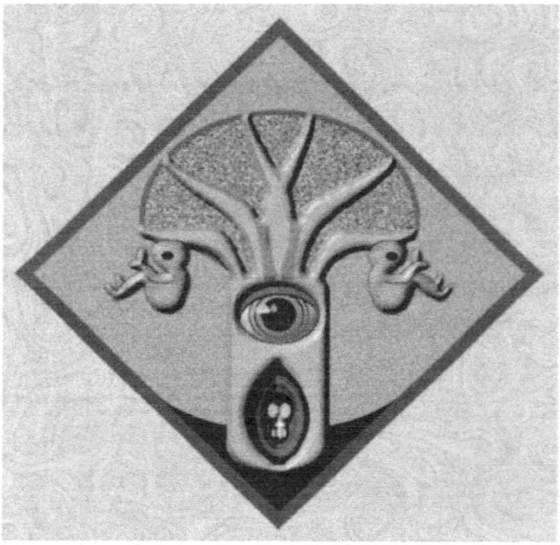

Pictured: ancient icon of the Bowvow Tree

Day 389, Two-Week Twenty-Two, Dimelad – the Flute. Port city of Churtah, on the tip of the Shosho-Shretep Arm of Statos-Vey.

Seti held his aching head. He stood before a display of dried plants, animal carcasses, giant beetles and other insects arranged in rows according to their purported uses. A few blocks away, an apothecary shop advertised the finished powders. It had a sign warning against both the ingredients' untrained preparation and the unlicensed recitation of the formulas. Here an old woman sat beside the display of raw elements, swearing the apothecary lied. The process of grinding and combining them into medicinal powers and intoning the proper words was simple. She offered a set of little instruction books and equipment. She coaxed and scolded him for not purchasing these many essential ingredients for a wide variety of ills and benefits.

Seti had been in several port cities of Statos-Vey in the twelve two-weeks since visiting Hushukrath on the Island of Tich-Tushmul. They had travelled the southern side of the Danadejet Arm, turned at the massive walls of the Pax Zenam Ridge connecting Rho-Jashun to the subcontinent of Statos-Vey. They sailed both coasts of the Lat-Lacaz Peninsula, the first of Statos-Vey's three southern 'arms.' There he had watched a fearsome Kumastam, second largest air serpent after the Xumkuka, streak across the midday sky. Suddenly, it dived down to snatch a great fish out of the churning ocean. It whipped back up as a shower of water fell back into the sea. The attack was so fast if he had blinked, he would have missed it.

He had also watched in terror as a strange black cloud hung motionless out on the ocean. It seemed impossibly dense to hang in the air, and he watched as all birds flew into it and vanished. As they sailed in a wide arc around it, the black form descended. When it touched the waves, it wobbled and caused ice to form on the waters before dissipating. Even from a distance, they could see the floating carcasses of all the unfortunate birds left behind. He was told this was a rare sighting of a lifeless bane known as the Slaying Canopy. Many tales were told. Yet, none of the crew had witnessed this terrible event in all their years on The Circuit or elsewhere.

They now took on supplies, bought and sold cargo in the large port of Churtah near the Shosho-Shretep peninsula's southern tip. In a few days, they would sail around its tip and down its southern flank. This second and longest of Statos-Vey's three southern arms stretched out from the mainland deep into the south Wakanda Ocean.

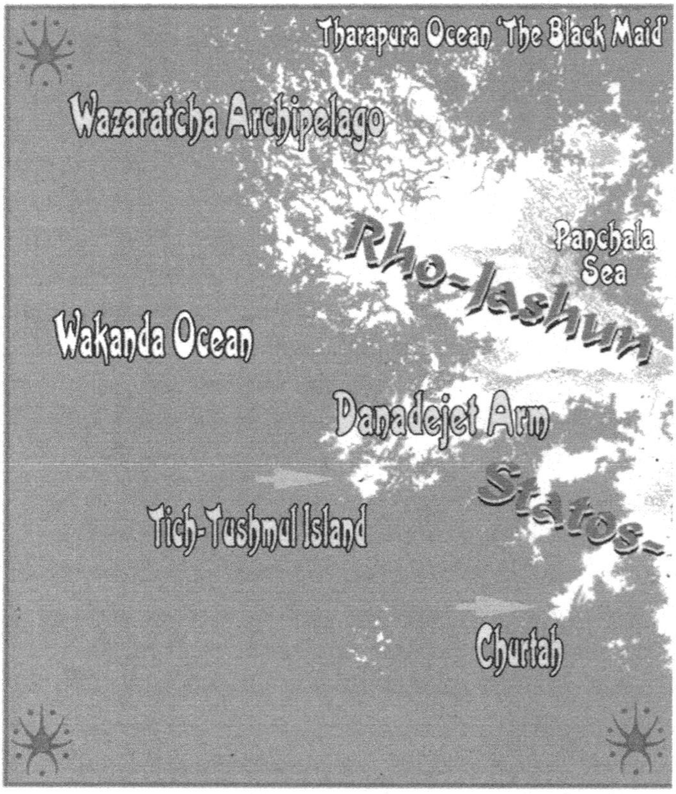

At each port, Seti found more to confuse and baffle him. He saw additional sightings of the sixty-four Tatchlan patterns and increasing numbers of the 'twisted' faces. Each city teemed beyond the last. Local and foreign boat traffic filled the waters, and the coast was covered with settlements. Many local trading ships were decked in fantastic ornamentation and had rich banners near as large as their sails. Monuments and other wonders of antiquity stood beside new structures under construction. They crowded the coastline and filled the interior, rising above the rich green jungle like impossible, brilliant mountains. Most were coated in garish ornamentation, including many covered with brilliantly painted and ornamented sculptures of thousands of animated bodies, gleaming under Nu's sweltering Eye. Seti began to appreciate most Tolku lived on Statos-Vey. His native Rho-Jashun was barren in comparison.

While the display of desiccated creatures disturbed him, what was painted above the woman's collection astonished him. The faded fresco filled the wall. The subject was a map of Anu – painted upside down. Most of Thermistal and Rho-Jashun sat below the equator, and most of Statos-Vey above it. The labels were right side up, so he read the familiar names over their inverted postures. The clear emphasis lay on the Primary Mountain Circle of Upata-Shepsus, the ancient capital of Statos-Vey encircled by its fabled circular mountain range. This had served as capital to the first unifying dynasty in history, the Funomanru. A little way from it, now south and west, stood the 'port of ports,' the famed city of Bhampay, where the Yin-Vinulan Dynasty had ruled. Though above the equator, these two locations dominated the centre of the map. He understood Statos-Vey was a subcontinent attached to Rho-Jashun. He always thought the continents of Thermistal and Rho-Jashun dominated Anu. Here, Statos-Vey stood at the centre. Coloured lines connected many dots all over the map suggesting roads and other cities. They also snaked from Bhampay and the other port cities out onto the oceans. They surrounded the different continents as if Anu were caught in Statos-Vey's web. He felt a presence beside him and looked up at Captain Emedin. She also studied the map. He was not aware the captain planned to come ashore in this port. She seldom left the Jefaka for long.

"Captain, what is this?"

Emedin gave him a mock frown, "It is a world map boy!" She smiled and patted his shoulder, "You grew up with maps showing Anu the other way round. At home, we refer to Statos-Vey as 'in the south.'"

"But Captain . . . is not Statos-Vey in the south?"

Emedin chuckled, "The answer depends on where you are when you ask. Science delineates two poles, but tradition and, most importantly, power defines north and south. This way is as legitimate a view of Anu as what you are used to. I am told the deep energy generated by Anu's core flows out one pole and enters the other. Even this reverses over time and flows in the other direction. There is no compelling reason for illustrating it in this way or the way we do back home." She looked at the map and pointed, "This map is accurate in its general proportions. The one exception is a clever emphasis on the power centres of Statos-Vey. I have seen cartographers indulge in similar distortions to please the powers in our part of Anu. Schoolbooks back home have maps putting Statos-Vey in the south and shrinking its dimensions. Another irony here is this map belies a deep cultural belief that all evil dwells in the north. This notion predated true knowledge of the existence of the Suvuka. Still, it was based on fearful signs and strange sailor tales. Those present here may well hold this a true map while at the same time comforting themselves they dwell in the south."

Seti looked long at the map, "There is no true Up and Down?"

"If there is, there is no unbiased evidence for it."

Seti stared at the map before turning away, "This is the most troubling thing I have seen."

Emedin placed her hand on his shoulder as they walked, "Why?"

"If Up and Down can change into their opposites if where we stand alters everything, what do we hold onto?"

Emedin looked off into the distance as they walked a few steps in silence.

"Fine question," she answered. "I may have an answer serving me, but you will find as many others in the faces teeming before us. Each will vary according to their learning and experience. Most here have not travelled through Statos-Vey, let alone into our chilly part of Anu. To them, this prospect is their unquestioned norm. To see it our way would be as disturbing to them as their map is to you."

She stared at the bustling population, "In a way, you and they share the same innocence. Most here will hold to the belief of where they are and their relation to the rest of Anu. The more educated and travelled will not share this view, nor necessarily that map, but they constitute a minority. Our map is common on Rho-Jashun and the surrounding islands. Ruling elites throughout Anu also adopt it to standardize commerce and relations. I am told it is employed by the masters themselves to facilitate international trade. While the official Protectorate on Thermistal also uses our version, the general population there are more likely to use this, by our standards, 'inverted' one. The determining factor is an arbitrary set of conventions and traditions, not any conclusive facts."

She stopped and frowned at him, "That land is fraught with many terrible myths. Given where we are, we have seldom touched on the subject of Thermistal. What do you know of the Tolku there?"

"Nothing."

"Hmm...," she walked a few paces, "The situation there is unique. We have no direct trading contract with the Thermistal Protectorate, and the Jefaka has never docked in their ports. We trade with the islands offshore, and I have known some who travelled there for work over the years. What little I have learned about this most mysterious place leaves me with much to ponder. Despite the Suvuka being defeated and contained, I believe Thermistal is nearly empty of Tolku! The exception is of a thin line of military, governmental and trading outposts up the western banks of the Vettencore Passage. There is also an extravagant facility for Suvuka studies on the southern coast. I have heard it said our Wazaratcha Islands off Rho-Jashun's northwestern coast have more life-long residents than all of Thermistal. My First Officer disputes this claim. You must ask Dine to tell you of his sojourn there. You already know the Vettencore Passage is a deep and broad canal joining natural incursions of northern and southern oceans into the continent. Together they form a continuous water barrier sealing the Suvuka on the eastern third of the continent. On either shore are tall, smooth walls. Over four hundred large installations and far more subsidiary ones are located at regular intervals along the western wall protecting Tolku Thermistal. Before its completion, hundreds of garrisons originally stood on the eastern banks to keep the prisoners at bay. Huge populations must be required to maintain these facilities. We have no trade or other relations with this vast region. All we know is based on hearsay and secondary accounts. They inform us only a modest intergenerational society exists beyond these fortifications. Notwithstanding opportunities, we are told, at most, a minority stay beyond their contracted stint. While it may be no surprise for labourers and soldiers to come and go, I believe most professionals, also promptly return here and to Rho-Jashun when they finish. For this to persist so long suggests a deliberate policy. However, I cannot imagine what its aims would be or how it is maintained."

They walked in silence before Seti asked, "The Muraharoma Dynasty of Statos-Vey created this protectorate?"

"Yes, although perhaps it would be accurate to say it primarily protects the Vettencore Passage. I am certain there is far more to this, but I am locked in my innocence concerning it."

"You said their Anu maps are the same as this one here?"

"They are. According to those, Thermistal and Rho-Jashun are in the south, with the terrible Tharapura Ocean encircling Anu's southern pole."

"Do they show Thermistal as larger than Statos-Vey?"

Captain Emedin stopped and laughed, "A wise question! What would you guess?"

Seti paused, "Given your description of Thermistal, I would say Statos-Vey would be more prominent, as they exist to serve the dynasty here."

"Correct. Although true nautical maps from any location are highly accurate, public representations share this political distortion."

"So different populations will remain locked in exclusive visions of Anu's orientation?"

"Unless a central authority makes an enforceable declaration, backed up with a solid administration on all three continents, we will continue to find variations of every kind."

"What' central authority?'"

"Like the Anu-spanning sovereignties of old, many here would claim the Muraharoma Dynasty fulfills this role. While they may warm the seat of the most-ancient Funomanru and Buyanupithar Dynasties, they hold little sway in our homeland. While they lavish attention on this subcontinent, they have proven poor stewards of the north. Before the Suvuka, we Tolku spread equally thick across Rho-Jashun and Statos-Vey. Through the ages, powerful regimes unified both lands for millennia before succumbing to internal chaos. I know little of this ancient history.

Despite its smaller size, power has often been centred on Statos-Vey for many reasons. The humid climate encourages a rich profusion of life. There are many natural amenities here lacking or scarce on Rho-Jashun. Many important cultural and historic innovations began on this subcontinent. Notwithstanding our qualms, the 'Duamang Age' Calendar, honouring that Tatchlan master who defeated the Suvuka, is in universal use on all three lands. This speaks of the undeniable commercial and political power of this region."

She stopped and pointed down at the smooth blue cobblestones beneath their feet. "Here is but one example of a natural amenity. Statos-Vey has a single mountain range, the Veradapandra's whereas Rho-Jashun's Mulungu Range is larger. Thermistal's Viracocha, Silvasora and Mandeca Mountains all have higher peaks. Yet, the Veradapandra Mountains are composed of near pure 'Azure Stone,' the first of the four grades of builder and sculptor's stone. Our Mulungu Mountains are primarily composed of Magna Stone, the second grade. The best quality Azure contains three gemstone-quality minerals, Argent, Cupric and Lapis. This stone and these minerals are exceedingly scarce or unknown elsewhere on Anu. Despite Sawlu Clan's historic dislike for all things southern, most public buildings and many private estates on Wazaratcha Island boast their wealth in these materials' liberal use. Azure lasts far longer than other stone. When polished, it reveals its characteristic flecks of one or more of those three rare minerals. It may be cut near paper-thin and used as facing on other stone or even as ornate windows that shimmer on the outside while casting the interiors in glorious hues when Nu shines through them. No other material possesses such marvellous attributes. Thus, Wazaratcha's wealthy and powerful covet Azure. You will one day see Jonochem Manor. Constructed of Azure's finest grades, it is a polished blue presence in Sawlu Clan's capital. Our pride is a source of great wealth for them. Here," she stamped her foot, "they pave their walkways with it!"

They continued for a time before she said, "Unwittingly, the Suvuka chose well to banish our ancestors here. The abundance of all good things, and the concentration of what had been disparate and warring nations, helped our kind survive. The Jefaka and the rest of our fleet do our part to help circulate Statos-Vey's unique resources and innumerable highly specialized finished goods to Rho-Jashun. As for maps, navigators prefer a universal standard. Long ago, our Sawlu Clan commissioned our own set covering our trade routes and keeps them current. The need for accuracy ensures ours are of high quality. It is these you examine on the Jefaka."

They stopped to look down a laneway. Foliage and other living creatures clogged the space. "You must see this," Emedin said.

They walked a short way down the lane, stopping before a row of tall plants in broad and richly decorated pots. The plant had distinctive purple leaves and a sturdy green stem. This one had a set of long fruits on the end of branches issuing out of the top. They bent outward, forming an elegant parasol over the plant.

"This," Seti whispered, "This is the Nara plant?"

Emedin nodded and indicated two stands set between each potted plant, lining the street either side. From these hung down a tubular creature. At the top, the creature's broad foot gripped the frame. A shifting set of dark and light green patterning covered its body. A thin membrane forming an inverted circular canopy spread out from the creature just below its mouth, held by stick-like arms. A powerful sweet smell issued from a pool of liquid collected at the centre of the stretched skin under the creature. This membrane's inner side had a series of white hairs pointing inward to the central pool of fragrant sweetness.

"The fruit of the Nara has many medicinal qualities," Emedin said in a quiet voice. "The Shesha is a jungle predator trapping prey by the lure of its sweet juices."

Seti stared at each of them wide-eyed. "I read of this! The ancients watched the Mayku and other creatures going to great lengths to trick the Shesha and drink its nectar. These early Tolku used it as an intoxicant. They later discovered how it transformed any liquid fed to it. When they fed the fruit of the Nara to it, the Shesha modified the juice. What it exuded…"

"What it exuded is called 'Sheshenara Nectar,' one of the foundations of Tatchlan. I understand other living creatures, some natural and some fashioned over the ages by the masters, augment this, but these two creatures are crucial elements."

They stared at the odd pair before a remarkable personage came through the foliage down the lane, continuing a stately walk toward them. She wore a long yellow robe covered in designs of hands, feet, eyes, ears and all other body parts arranged to form a dynamic structure. This stately figure wore a broad mask of radiant orange with huge eyes. This imposing dignitary carried an ornate pole tapping with each step as they inspected each Nara plant. Stopping at one, she raised the pole and touched one of the swollen fruits before issuing a peculiar trilling whistle.

Seti turned to stare wide-eyed at the captain, "I heard this many times! Is this the source? This means these are in place, not just on Statos-Vey. The first time I heard it was on the island of Tich-Tushmul."

Children, draped in simple long yellow shirts, erupted out of a nearby doorway carrying a short ladder. The priestess stood like a statue pointing at the fruit. Once they began scaling the ladder, the orange face swung the pole away from them in an arc. The figure walked to another spot and turned it to stop before a specific Shesha. The children brought the fruit down and took it to the designated creature. They set it on the edge of the Shesha's under canopy. In a blink, the creature folded it over the fruit, brought it to its mouth and swallowed it. Its body became distended, and the canopy shrunk to a ball under it, sealing the mouth. The colouration of the creature grew darker as it began to digest its meal. The silent personage swung the pole in a wide arc, bringing it down to tap the ground. The children bent to kiss the rod before moving at a casual pace back through the door. The orange and yellow figure continued her majestic pace along the laneway.

"I had thought they crushed the fruit before feeding the Shesha," Emedin whispered.

Another orange mask silently walked past them, carrying a bowl and straw. They knelt before the brimming canopy of another Shesha. She or he drew on the straw until the liquid came and let it pour into the bowl. With great care, the figure tilted the canopy to get the last of the precious liquid.

"They are harvesting Sheshenara," Seti said in a quiet voice. They turned and walked back out of the lane. Emedin motioned for them to sit on the edge of a fountain in a small open square. There always seemed to be some festival occurring in every port. It appeared the city of Churtah was no exception to this rule. The crowds swirling around them were clearly in a holiday mood. Seti was familiar with the rich draperies in vivid colours, the parasols composed of feathers, coloured scales and having trailing linen streamers, the brilliant kites filling the air, the ornate banners dressing the buildings, and the ceaseless parade of remarkable masks. The air was saturated with many contrasting odours, and vibrant music was always present in the streets. Partial or fully nude citizens walking among the rest were also commonplace to Seti's eyes. The nudes, of both genders and all ages, were sometimes painted wild hues in contrasting patterns. Others wore jewelry and small bells to accentuate attributes. Seti knew these decorations communicated many messages to those able to read them. While much no longer surprised him, he remained shocked by the occasional individual carrying on their business after shedding, revealing their inner workings.

"Seti?" Captain Emedin interrupted his reverie, "There is much here I have seen before. Yet, even I wonder at new and strange signs in these once-familiar avenues. I do not possess your sight and would ask if there are many twisted faces of Tatchlan here?"

Seti grimaced, "There are many. Most are women and young girls. A small number are men. I can sense the alteration behind the masks. They surround us."

The captain nodded, "We have spoken about the notion of a 'central authority.' Nebutan's writings make clear this is one of the fundamental goals of the Tatchlan masters. They work to surpass the dynasties of old and bring all Tolku under one hand. They attempt to lay the foundations of never-ending sovereignty led by a succession of beings they term 'Majastas.' They would connect through the 'Maja' at the core of each linked grouping, and so the entire population. This is their dream."

"I know," Seti answered in a small voice. He paused before looking at the captain, "My larger question remains. At home, my mind was clear. I knew myself and my mission. These Tolku are as herds of strange cousins, or even Suvuka to me. What I was taught is ignored or reversed. My senses fill with the unknown and unimagined. My nose is numb, and my ears ring! My Menem are distant and distracted as if they cannot compete alongside this growing din. My bewilderment . . ."

A clash of cymbals and chorus of horns interrupted them. A boisterous crowd had invaded the square. Emedin and Seti climbed on the rim of the fountain. Seti frowned as he tried to discover the meaning of this little pageant. An Adorer, those chanting and declaiming for hire, shouted at the front. Another walked from the rear of the rowdy gathering. Some laughed and sang while others wept as several raised painted boards displaying a woman's face bobbing overhead. Underneath the shaking panels hung a variety of symbolic objects.

The focus of this event appeared in the middle of the group. A dead woman's body was carried on a pallet. She was dressed in wild attire. At the same time, her breasts were exposed, heaving with the erratic actions of her bearers. She wore extravagant makeup, and her long nails were painted vivid hues. Her hair was done in an astonishing configuration. Painted figurines of birds, butterflies and other creatures were attached to her hair. Dancers immediately in front and behind the body swung braziers trailing pungent incense. He looked at his captain and saw she understood what assaulted them.

Emedin pointed in the distance, "Do you see the dark crown rising above the buildings?" Seti looked but could not find it over the crowded roofs. Emedin motioned Seti to get down, and they hastened through the crowd. Once clear, she sprinted down a roadway. The group came the same way. After a few twists and turns, they went to a wide-open circle. A colossal tree beyond Seti's imagining stood in the centre. It rose high above him, but its massive girth amazed him more. He could not imagine how many holding hand in hand would go around it. A circular wall was built far beyond the trunk. This wall had been rebuilt, and the large paving stones had heaved and been removed as it increased in size. A riot of deep ruts ran around the twisting and swirling knots in its trunk. High above the leaves were dark and thick. A moss or fibrous strands clung to the underside of each leaf. A few of the broad boughs stretched out and sent down shoots to support their weight, wreaking havoc on the paving stones below. Each of these shoots was adorned with many ribbons and other wrappings. Despite the growing racket, Seti was sure he heard deep rumblings coming from inside the tree.

He watched a man reach out of his window high above them to apply a liquid with a broad brush to the leaves. Seti sensed this was a significant act for him, and it occurred to him he used Sheshenara Nectar. Why give this precious liquid to a tree? He looked down and became aware of many figures, similar to what adorned the dead woman's hair. They lay in heaps around its trunk and on the surrounding wall. Several pallets lay in a stack to one side, where children continued to play despite the growing noise. Many birds and skin-winged creatures appeared drawn to the tree. Their combined song high above them sounded like rushing water.

"Watch the birds," Emedin said as the boisterous gathering approached behind them. Seti saw nothing unusual. They sang and flew from branch to branch. He looked at his captain, and she smiled and indicated he should continue to watch them. Two larger birds chased a smaller one. It flew to the trunk and pecked at the bark. Immediately a tiny pocket opened, and the bird hopped in as the opening snapped shut. The other two birds were denied entry and flew away. The small portal opened, and the little bird flew out. As the funeral procession swirled around the tree, this tiny drama repeated itself. Then events on the ground demanded his attention.

The body was brought close to the trunk and set on a frame. She was bound to the pallet, and her headdress rose high over her head. Many ran to embrace and kiss her, and others draped more finery over her. A woman approached and coated her face with a white paste. Simultaneously, a large group of children stood in a half-circle in front of the body and sang a short song while jumping repeatedly. A hush then came over the crowd as the paste appeared to harden immediately and was gently pulled off the face. The death mask was held up, revealing much of the face paint now transferred onto the mask's interior. It was passed hand-to-hand through the crowd of mourners before disappearing. The Adorers approached and began to move the pallet back until it touched the trunk. With this sudden silence, all heard a deep rhythmic beat emanating from the tree. Once she was positioned against the broad trunk, the Adorers stepped back at once. The bark began to ripple, and a wide opening the size of the body opened like a curtain, the vertical pallet kept her from falling inside. Others joined the Adorers in moving her within the portal. Once the pallet leaned on the inner wall, they exited. In a few heartbeats, the opening closed, leaving no trace. The crowd erupted into a far louder chorus and began to dance in a large circle. A scarlet rope was attached to the tree, and the group began to wind it around the trunk. Seti looked at the surrounding buildings. Several inhabitants of the upper floors called and clapped to the events below. Seti felt Emedin's hand in his as she led him back along the way they had come. Seti was in shock and said nothing until they sat at the now quiet fountain. The internment festival continued the distance, but here most pursued their business showing no interest.

"What was that creature?"

"One of the natural wonders of the south. It is called the Bowvow Tree. They exist on Thermistal but are harder to find. They grow in profusion here naturally. They are named a 'tree,' but they are a blend of animal and plant. They are rooted in the soil and bear leaves, but they also feed in other ways. You saw the birds. They are havens for the smallest of creatures. Yet, their shelter comes at a price. When animals go inside, the Bowvow feeds on them. A short visit will leave no ill effects; an extended stay will be fatal. Our distant ancestors observed animals choosing to die within the Bowvow. Traditions began of feeding the dead to these tree beings. Here it is far more common to 'plant' the dead in the soil than burn them as we do at home. Feeding the body to the Bowvow is viewed as a productive way to ensure the body becomes one with Anu. It is said the well-fed ancient ones can grow awareness and those established in cities become 'awake.'"

Seti sat pondering this, "I do recall hearing the name. I have read some of their lore. I realize now I may have seen one or two on my journey to the coast. I knew nothing of them at the time."

Emedin nodded, "They are found in Rho-Jashun, usually further south than where you were born. They are far smaller than this grand dam. These dwell in the heart of cities where they grow fat on offerings. They will be mentioned in your texts. Our Nebutan and Nallurakon were born here and referred to them."

"I remember puzzling over a line speaking of the Bowvow making music," Seti said. "What causes that sound?"

"I recall hearing it has something to do with the fluids inside their bodies. I know little more than this. I have observed the bigger and wider the trunk, the deeper the voice. Wild ones may be no thicker than you, and their beats are high pitched and rapid."

As they walked back to their ship in silence, Seti's head began to ache again.

CHAPTER 13

Shuna-Shapta

Pictured: A Yeldic version of the Tatchlan Cube formation. While some icons have changed over time, their function remains the same.

Day 444, Two-Week Twenty-Five, named Alatahanu – the 'Twelve Faces,' in the port city of Bhampay at the start of Carnival.

Shuna-Shapta emerged from her Invocation. The other seven members of her student circle joined her. They had gathered in an oval Invocate Chamber seated around a table bearing eight Living Instruments. She had smiled to herself on the way into the chamber when looking up and seeing the distant balcony of their residence. Near a year ago, she and her mother, Master Kanla, had viewed the city from there while engaging in their first discussions on the 'rebellion' of Rho-Jashun. Such matters scattered as dust as she thrilled to embrace Shamusanish once more and plunge through the waves of successive climaxes while delving deep within Tatchlan.

After descending through the various levels, the young Delving Invocants had found each other and performed their training under the guidance of Master Tanas. She delighted in working with Mi-Yang; the other young woman of her Delving Invocant Circle of Eight. When ready, they caught the sweet waves back to the surface, emerging flushed and exhilarated. Master Tanas had been with other Masters in an adjoining Invocate Chamber using their Living Instruments. He had returned the same time as they.

They now gathered in an open sculpture garden filled with morning birdsong within the Enclave. From the central towering statue of Master Duamang radiated eight broad cobbled pathways of well-crafted and polished blue Azure Stone, leading to the eight surrounding Invocate Chambers. The outer walls of these chambers were covered in a continuous mural of a fanciful landscape of rolling hills with ornate structures on each hilltop and ornate pink and blue clouds filling the streaked sky. Eight tall and elegantly designed wind harps stood just outside these Invocate Chambers, with the cobble ways encircling them before surrounding the chambers. They now stood muted by a pause in the breezes from the Panchala Sea after the previous evening's downpour.

Along with luscious craft and glorious blossoming plants, a circle of benches filled the centre of each of these eight resulting garden wedges between the cobble ways. The group now assembled on one of these inwardly curving benches with Master Tanas standing in the open centre. The benches were of such dimensions that two Circles of Eight could occupy them, so they sat together on one side. At present, the rest of the garden was unoccupied.

"Your Living Instruments present you with a model of the larger structure of our Living System," a flushed Master Tanas began, catching his breath. "Generations of Masters offered each ability and skill they possessed to ensure the vitality and permanence to our Resplendent

Work. You behold the three layers of Tatchlan, culminating within our 'Inner Orb.' This is, in part, an interpretation of your Living Instruments and shall inform your entire career. In time you shall learn the actual structure is reversed. What you perceive as the innermost part is an outgrowth covering the surface. In truth, the waters of Amanavata form an inner ocean at the core of all life, providing a buffer and lubrication to all else. It is here you enter and make your way. This distortion is both by design of our ancient Uluvatu Masters, to allow Invocates to adjust prior to their delvings, and due to the nature of your Living Instruments and how they function."

Two of the wind harps began to thrum gently in a low harmony with a growing breeze.

"A parallel may be found in the maps of Anu you view within Enclaves and other official institutions as opposed to those out within our city. Popular tradition reverses the north/south axis for a variety of historical and cultural reasons. For international trade and in deference to professional standards, we orient Rho-Jashun and Thermistal as 'north' of us whilst we occupy the 'south.' For those living day to day, by the line of sight, this divergence is non-existent or, at most, a minor concern. Due to most-ancient taboos, now seen as well-founded in the Suvuka threat, the 'north' has ever had ill-favoured associations. Most civilizations occupying this pleasant subcontinent have referred to the portion of our lands closest to the equator as 'Central Statos-Vey' rather than 'northern.'

Two more wind harps took up the gentle serenade in the garden as the morning sea breezes grew.

"Such it shall be for you with Tatchlan," smiling at the sweet musical ambience now filling the air. "You behold Tatchlan as it were 'through the eyes' of your Living Instruments. This distortion shall neither change your experience nor your work. For you, the 'outer layer' is Amanavata, composed of the containing waters where many Secondary Faces of Tatchlan shall ever gather to await your Invocation. Through this ocean sits the originating bitter middle realm, named Indatubangas. All things emerge from and submerge back into Indatubangas prior to being transmuted and sent out again. It possesses a wild animation and contains many hard lessons for you. It also serves as the final barrier to unauthorized or ill-conceived attempts to enter our Resplendent Work.

Given the vast majority may only access Tatchlan via Living Instruments, this perceived ordering ensures security from rogue sensitives we know still dot the hinterlands. This seat of unrefined life now serves the civilizing influence of our Resplendent Work as the vital generating and destroying kingdom. This crucible receives what has become broken and worn into its furnace. Out of this emerges new aspects of our Living System; thus, it is the fitting home of our Lustrum Mirror. Fashioned from its terrible materials, the Lustrum is ably suited to revealing what lies hidden within us. This most treasured mirror is surrounded by a landscape ideally suited to disposing of what impedes our embracing a shared life. Amanavata emerges as liquid vapour from its seething surface, and our 'Living Orb' forms its unifying and directing centre. Upon occasion, your work shall take place within this contained chaos. As full Invocants, you shall move across these three vast breathing faces as you walk upon Anu's Flesh. You shall encounter Invocants throughout our Resplendent Work locked within the embrace of their Living Instruments upon distant portions of Anu. You shall make possible immediate communications from one side of Anu to the other through fellow Invocants. Through Tatchlan, we shall knit Anu together as never before."

"Master?" a student asked. "How does this relate to the sixty-four symbols of the Sigil Cubes?"

Master Tanas smiled. He gestured for them to join him as he exited the fragrant garden and proceeded through a series of roofed corridors connecting the Inner to the Outer Enclave. They came out into an enclosed courtyard before the main entrance to the Master Enclave. Nara Plants lined the inner wall. Their attendant Shesha hung from their stands.

A Watcher, in a characteristic yellow robe covered in symbols of the resolution of all life's ills, and orange mask, patrolled seeking fruit ripe enough to feed the Shesha. The Watcher pointed the staff at a fruit and made the characteristic-trilling whistle. Enclave children rushed to gather the fruit and feed it to the Shesha. The curious creature transformed the fruit into the first stage of the precious Sheshenara Nectar. They heard the other elaborate agencies used in its subsequent fermentation on the other side of the wall.

In the open area, a meditative exercise was in progress. Several groups of Masters and a wide variety of those attending them walked in quiet deliberation in a large circle filling most of the courtyard. Several attendant cousins of each size, like other animals, perfected over generations to assist in the Grand Work, also moved among them. Many more sat or were cradled in their arms. Most of the sounds came from these creatures, calling out in differing voices at regular intervals, creating a pleasant echo off the surrounding wall. It became apparent that their calls determined the pace of the Masters.

A wide variety of so-called 'Newborns' walked among the Tolku. These were, in fact, Ripe Adults, displaying exotic signs of Tatchlan. A few had startling physical abnormalities. Others displayed subtle traits distinguishing them from the Mundane majority. These treasured deviations were studied for their part in the ultimate goal of a Cluster-of-Cluster Society. A naked young Complete stood out in the crowd. After the Maja, these were the most profound individual manifestations of Tatchlan. Full females and males in one body, they were cherished for their wholeness. More obvious amid these Newborns were three giants. They walked with care among the rest, their heads near cresting the top of the Outer Enclave walls. Flocks of Krall ringed the tops of these walls. The ancient Masters had perfected this bird as their eyes in distant places. Within Tatchlan, these manifested as 'Eye Windows' revealing distant events in broad panoramas. The Krall surveyed the situation within and outside the Master Enclave. When their intent gaze turned from the musical group, they saw the surrounding city composed of ceaseless business and numerous diversions. This day was the Master Carnival. The usual cacophony of many thousands of voices rising and falling as ocean surf, punctuated by frequent calls of domestic cousins, wild creatures and musical accompaniment in distant theatres formed the surrounding backdrop.

Master Tanas led the eight young Invocants past the Shesha plants and this diverse throng to an open wall near the northern corner of the Enclave. A large plaque stood, representing the Tatchlan System composed of sixty-four emblems. He stood in front of it, and the eight students formed a half-circle at its base.

"You grew up with these precise symbols within this specific configuration," he began while gesturing up to the rendition composed of polished metal and coloured glass picked out with gems. "You visited our Glowing Orb and appreciate Tatchlan does not resemble this. Vivid landscapes and marvellous beings most certainly abound, with our relatively bland General Plain now confined to one or more areas. Heraldic emblems and icons assuming fixed poses are rare, usually manifesting an unusual or marked tendency within a particular moment. You all received basic instruction upon the use of these breathing versions of this Living Device when you occupied the Fifth Level as Commencement Delvers. Although not destined to their ancient Craft, which was fashioned by our Uluvatu Masters themselves, it remains vital that you acquaint yourselves with the Cubes and those working them."

He smiled and gestured, "Our own Shuna-Shapta's 'Second Ama,' Shuna-Dana, is a recognized Master of the Cubes in this generation. They continue to serve a vital and ancient function, predating what we now do with our Living Instruments. Skilled employment of these symbols accesses the foundations of our Resplendent Work. Innumerable Faces associate with each one of these squares. We shall further 'warm your cold understanding' of where they belong, and how you may invoke the Face or Faces you require. You have seen the less common circular representation of this same pattern, more challenging for those working the Cubes. You shall comprehend the Craft as you gain proficiency using our Living Instruments. The Faces shall respond to your increasing knowledge, and you shall find your tasks more efficiently accomplished. You appreciate our limited time within our Living System."

Smiles broke out on the faces of the young Invocants. Master Tanas smiled back, "Long ago, our grandmothers and their mothers rejected the notion of pain as the greatest teacher. You shall know pain, from your work as Invocants and in living your lives. Pain teaches many lessons, but we determined pleasure vital to our work. Pleasure roots you both with your skin and the skin of Anu, knitting together the depths and the surface. Pain may delude us with notions of a separate existence from our skins, whereas pleasure imparts the vital truth we are whole and embodied beings. Each connects to the other. Your most obscure imaginings connect to your most mundane functions. This collection of integrated elements manifests as yourselves."

He paused before adding, "Some of you have noted how your climaxes with your Living Instrument differ from your climaxes with others. This is intentional. You must remain functioning and contributing members of your circle and cluster and thus must not be dulled to pleasuring and receiving pleasure from them. One of our many rewards for our vocation is that each climax complements and strengthens the other. Full attainment of the 'Nine Petals' shall likely attend your Elder years. How far this sophistication is from the old ways! How rich is a life cultivating joy instead of pain! How poor and even monstrous is a self-hating life dividing each aspect behind spurious walls. One of the terrible errors of the Tuchulacha, Laranal, Cathalu, Chelyaka, Menem, and other ancient religions preached was our separation into visible and invisible forms. Other dead faiths and philosophies hung upon this premise, bringing about much anguish and suffering. This also reveals the terrible mental sickness amongst many exponents of these ancient myths. 'Wholeness and Embodiment' remain fundamental premises of our work."

Master Tanas looked out at the group filling the courtyard. "What significance has this day?"

"Day 444 - Carnival Day!" one of the students said.

"Yes! You look forward to joining the throng to celebrate," Master Tanas replied. "Long ago, our Primary Masters, as part of our larger plans, seeded our culture with a series of traditions growing through the ages. Most of these events existed as sacred parades and festivities celebrating forgotten or distorted personalities and milestones. They have come full circle. We found that most ecstatic observances arose prior to myths later attached to them. For many generations, twelve festivals were held throughout the year, one for each pairing of day numbers. A festival for Day 11, Day 22, Day 33, up to Day 99, followed by Day 111, Day 222 and Day 333. We moulded these festivals and introduced emotional themes, colourful traditions and visual elements, preparing for the birth of Maja amongst us. Once this began, our grandmothers and their mothers foresaw Tatchlan emerging into full view. This day shall reveal its full import and purpose. Let me show you our vital displays this group shall take through the streets over the coming days."

The students followed him back into the compound and over to the eastern side and into a large storage hall. Many went in and out of this area, and they had to wait until a group of forty, carrying a large bundled tube, finished coming out. Inside, the students gasped. Abundant decorations destined for the Carnival filled the room. What amazed them most were the large images, fantastic in form and colour, hanging from the ceiling, representations of the Twelve Principal Faces of Tatchlan.

Master Tanas beamed as he looked at them and gestured, "Clearly, our Enclave possesses many gifts! These were fashioned over the past ten two-weeks. They commenced work some five two-weeks after the unforeseen wonder of a Majastas birth took place and are now ready for our Carnival."

"Master?" Shuna-Shapta exclaimed, "Last year, I saw you wearing our Face of Alatanda for the first time at Alatahanu. You led the new version of the Yom Sha and introduced all Twelve Principal Faces. I heard later other masters did the same in select locations. This shall exceed by many times that display!"

"We but hasten to reflect what rises from our Resplendent Work!" Master Tanas said. "Our Sensitives throughout Statos-Vey begin reporting these Faces within their dreams. They share their visions, and now we hear of children and the aged receive emergent sightings. Many Bhampaians and those within other beautiful cities, where our clusters begin to blossom, shall recognize them from their half-recalled night visions and sudden daytime visitations. We hear Raw Sensitives, untouched by our refinements, share these visions far beyond our cultivated gatherings. Soon enough, as more Maja are born, and we begin the transformation generations laboured toward, these Faces shall know veneration throughout Statos-Vey, Rho-Jashun and Thermistal."

"We waken their dream memories," Mi-Yang said.

"Yes!" Master Tanas replied. "This Carnival has long named Alatahanu. An elaborate series of cultural references, planted over many generations, made it so. The time to reveal the true origin of our title has come. You know the names of our Twelve Principal Faces. The first Face is Alatanda, our Gateway and Hub to all other Faces, and the last Face is Hashahanu, the 'Wise Spider' Face of Contemplation. Each of the twelve annual festivals is revealed as festivals to honour each of our Twelve Faces. Next year, in 1272, Day eleven shall remain the Alatanda Festival. Beyond the current colour themes, we shall evoke specific attributes of Alatanda. Day twenty-two shall continue as Skarashing Festival with similar icons for our Discerner of Polarities, and so for the rest. You know the true nature of these festivals. This Carnival, coming as a culmination to the twelve festivals near the close of the year, shall celebrate our Principal and Secondary Faces, named by a portion of our first and last Face's names combined - Alatahanu."

The students continued to stare, amazed at the open and bold representations of their secret Craft.

Mi-Yang began to frown, "Master," she began in a troubled tone, "What of us?"

"Ah!" Master Tanas replied, "We Masters knew the culmination of our work meant our grand task would pass into another's hands. Tatchlan shall not remain our exclusive preserve. This day our Magnificent Work awakens and rises to the surface of its own. The continued birth of Maja and the other Spokes of the Cluster Wheel, and the proliferation of true Clusters and knots of clusters enveloped within the 'murmur of life,' shall make it 'strong within each nose.' Once entrusted to us alone for these millennia, now they grow apparent to each new pre-adult. Ultimately, we shall hand over our task of overseeing our Living Orb to its supreme manifestation – our now living Majastas! This shall take place in two decades hence at most. We shall then take the subsidiary role of Invocants, joining the host of those devoted to our Majastas's general wellbeing. Our honour shall not rest in the term 'Master,' but 'Servant.' Our Majastas shall emerge as Nu. Generations shall pass as they oversee designs beyond our imagining. We shall take our place alongside a fulfilled population within a Cluster-of-Clusters society, knowing our mighty work is well-founded."

"Master," Shuna-Shapta asked, "We learned of our ancient Masters' immense design and detailed plans. We stand upon the edge of Tatchlan's emergence, how shall we proceed?"

Master Tanas amazed them by laughing out loud; "We are . . ." he began and stopped. "We are uncertain! Uncounted thousands of Masters looked to this day, yet we find little to guide us upon this last step. Tatchlan bursts ahead of our careful schedule and births her first Majastas against all expectations!"

He shook his head, "Has it been but fifteen two-weeks since Her birth? Not even three hundred days have passed! We stand bewildered in the presence of this unforeseen commandeering of what we thought was already an audacious plan. In the end, our vision was too modest for the urgency of the Quickening." Master Tanas calmed himself and looked at them all, "As arising Invocants, you shall be called upon to contribute to our creative response to a situation demanding we step outside our defining traditions. The cusp shall contain unpredictable chaos. You shall find your calling more demanding than previous generations of Masters."

The students stared at the representations of the Faces, Master Tanas and pondered these words.

CHAPTER 14

Seti

Pictured: traditional icon of Menem Shrine

Day 106 of the year 1272, Two-Week Six – Tret, the Candle, aboard the Jefaka

Seti had a glum expression as he stood alongside Captain Emedin on the deck of the Jefaka. "Our usual call for Adepts has met a significant response," she said. "Their certifications are good, and I have spoken with each of them. I believe there is one, in particular, you may find of interest."

Seti frowned at his captain, "How many have there been? You are surprised at my disapproving of so many. I thank you, Captain, for your efforts and patience."

Emedin smiled at the boy, "You absorb a great deal and many questions result. I was involved in education, . . ." Emedin paused," . . . back when Sawlu Clan was a magnet for young students seeking to learn under Nebutan's roof. Now, our enrolment drops and teachers leave us. Soon this phase of our Clan may end. I hope you will remain aboard the Jefaka until we return to Wazaratcha. Your experiences may prove helpful in bringing these old texts alive."

Emedin gestured for them to go over to the nine figures standing in a row waiting for them. Seti approached an elderly woman standing among them. Her skin was burned in a way only seen in a northerner long exposed to Nu's southern Eye. She had short yellow hair remaining in place despite the sea breeze.

"What is your name?"

"Hegev, young novice," she answered in a soft voice having a unique resonance. Seti immediately wished to hear her speak again.

"Your skin is more like mine than most beyond this ship."

"I am from northern Rho-Jashun," she answered. "I have travelled some eight years in the south. Amongst other aims, I came on pilgrimage to the twenty Menem shrines of Statos-Vey. I knew the Suvuka did not touch them. I have seen many depictions of their curved walls surrounding the egg-shaped shrine. The inner walls were always coated with extravagant murals. I had hoped to find them whole."

Seti contemplated this, "Are they?"

"Alas! Most are in ruin! The 'Mabulan Procession' and other prehistoric sites, dating back to the dawn of the Tolku on Anu, are pristine in comparison. The children turn their backs on what their parents raised. I have travelled through Statos-Vey seeking them out, but none retains its original dignity. Those on Rho-Jashun at least met a noble end, falling to a foe aware of their power. Here, they die of neglect!"

Dine joined Seti and Emedin; they stood silent after her passionate outburst. The deck became hushed in anticipation.

Seti looked at Emedin and Dine. "You approve?" They nodded.

Seti turned and bowed to the others, "I thank you for answering our call. Hegev, I ask you to assist me in grasping the works of Nebutan."

She blinked twice at him, "This task will be long and arduous. It assumes other knowledge. We must determine where you stand before proceeding."

"You have been on this pilgrimage for years," Seti said. "We will travel . . ." he hesitated, "We will travel what Jefaka's maps determine south along the western coast of Statos-Vey. We will then turn north along its eastern coast and return to Rho-Jashun. Are there shrines along the way?"

Hegev bowed, "I thank you, young novice, for showing consideration for my quest. My coming here means I abandon it. I answered the call out of curiosity and to seek passage home. We may encounter some derelict shrines, serving as part of your education. We will not approach any for a time."

The other Adepts were conducted off the ship. Seti and Hegev sat near the prow. They spoke for hours, and the crew returned to their business, on occasion, casting enquiring glances in their direction. At one point, Seti performed a quiet invocation while Hegev watched. Whatever the result, she nodded her head vigorously.

* * *

"Enter," Captain Emedin answered the quiet knock to her quarter's door. Hegev stepped in and bowed to the Captain and her First Officer. Emedin sat at her desk with a thick opened book of astronomical tables sitting on top of multiple shipping charts. Dine stood at her side with an antique divider in his hand.

"Captain, may I speak regarding Seti?"

"Of course."

"You did not exaggerate when we spoke," she began in her soft and articulate voice. "I have taught many through these past years, both in my ancestral home and since. I never met anyone like him, let alone a youth his age."

Emedin smiled and gestured for the Adept to sit. "I hoped he would choose you," the Captain answered. "I did not expect to find a citizen of Kana-Moptu here. Despite my travels across the face of Anu, I have not set foot on the 'Eastern Gate' of our mad collection of frozen islands. The

Jefaka and other ships I served stopped at your eastern ports on occasion, but your shores have not supported these tired feet."

Hegev smiled, "Ours is a harsh island! My elder bones may attest to there being little to recommend it. It has one distinguishing characteristic, being menaced by the Black Maid. She brings miserable storms throughout the year. We bear the dubious honour of serving as a buffer for the rest of Wazaratcha. The land is weather-beaten, and nothing grows tall — most huddle on the western and southern shores. Your ships visited the few hardy communities braving the eastern coast to service shipping. There is something of a divide between the east and west of the island over differences no outsider can detect. Beauty exists in pockets during the spring and summer, and grandeur during our long winters, but life is unkind for the most part."

She paused before continuing, "Another unkindness waits for any who stand out. Living in isolation breeds a smallness of mind in many. In fairness, I can appreciate how a difficult life often narrow's one's perspective. Someone like myself towered over my contemporaries, solely intent on household and kitchens. I have longed to escape for much of my life, but the necessities of family and profession bound me for many long years. Eventually, I settled on my one hope. There is a long tradition of those fulfilling their family duties, having the opportunity of discovering Anu. A portion of our clan holdings is set aside for this purpose. We name it our 'Warm Rewards.' The Clan approves our withdrawal, and there is a touching ceremony for our sendoff. The expectation is we travel for a year and return bearing gifts. We recount adventures and impart insight. Some who leave never return — those who did always found me in their audience. As I finally approached my time, I had long ceased being amazed at how few availed themselves of this opportunity. I had seized a rare chance years before and trained as an Adept. As there was little application on the island, I planned to augment my modest Warm Rewards Purse by teaching in many places. I believe I have travelled farther than anyone else of my generation. Despite my preparations, I wake amazed at my living in this steaming, rain-soaked land," she lost focus at a memory, "so filled with poisonous beauty."

Hegev's eyes narrowed, looking behind the captain. "Your library

. . ." her amazement grew, "Your library is not what I expected for a commercial vessel."

"It is customary to provide comfort for the crew on long voyages," Captain Emedin answered. "The present journey has been eventful, but there will be many quiet two-weeks travelling north along Rho-Jashun's eastern coast."

"The Jefaka's home port is on Wazaratcha Island?"

"Yes."

She looked at the titles lining the walls, "You are of Sawlu Clan?"

"Yes," the captain answered.

"Good!" Hegev declared. "When Seti mentioned what books you had, I was amazed. I had not seen fresh copies of . . ." She went over to one set of volumes. "The complete set of Nebutan's 'Rise of Tatchlan,' 'Worse than Chaos' and 'Dignity's Demise!'" She pulled out a volume and examined the cover. "You even have the famed enigmatic cover design of her final work."

"Nebutan designed it herself," Emedin said quickly.

"I recall the controversy over what it meant," Hegev mused, "that all seems a lifetime ago now."

"Indeed," Emedin said sadly, "I would give much to see such passion over her work again."

"Do you know what the bird, books and road design mean?"

Emedin and Dine shook their heads.

"I have not seen these titles since I left home! Books were my one refuge in what was a cold, dark and small life!"

"Turn to the imprint after the frontispiece," Emedin said.

Hegev found the page and looked at the publisher information.

"See the name of the printer?"

"Chelphun Printing House, I have heard of them."

Captain Emedin and Dine smiled at each other. "When I was but a slip of a girl," Emedin said, "I was sent to this printer to fulfill my 'Gaining a Trade' requirement for school. Did you have this?"

"Yes, we did. Alas we have no printers on our entire island or I would have clamoured to be sent there. Thankfully we do have a few libraries and I was grateful for my first introduction to the larger world of books."

"I was under the tender mercies of a certain handsome young man during my time in the bindery," she gestured to Dine.

Hegev's eyes went wide in amazement, "Aya! You two met at this printer? How can it be you started there and end here?"

Emedin sat back and laughed, "That is far too long and convoluted a tale for now! You would need to hear both our stories as we were on separate journeys for most of it before finding each other on a former ship."

Hegev shook her head in amazement as she closed the book and ran her fingers across the spines' shining surface. She returned to her seat and pondered.

"Seti said he found you?"

"He has been aboard the Jefaka for just over a year. He approached us on the first day of Atra last year."

"Remarkable!" Hegev said. "The more I speak to him, the more I feel entrusted with the largest task of my life." She frowned, "He speaks of his father. What of the rest of his family?"

"He mentioned a mother, elder sisters and an aunt. They worked in Salarish fields somewhere in the northern interior, perhaps twenty andas east of Hora-Sarota-Sewa Island. A more benighted portion of Rho-Jashun may not be found. Most of his family embraced the Blood Crop ways of old. Seti told us, with the exception of his father, his family did not welcome his visions. His aunt's attempts to have him treated prompted his wild journey to the coast. I was amazed to learn his aunt 'Viewed the Waters.' In this respect, she resembles our Clan's treasured scholar."

The Adept frowned, "*Nebutan* 'Read the Waters?'"

"Is this surprising?" Emedin replied. "She spent the first twenty years of her life here on well-watered Statos-Vey, where rivers and streams flow in every direction. Like the ancients, she approached them as a reflection of the many facets of wisdom. It is fair to say in this manner alone; she adhered to the ancient ways. We had little in the way of springs and rivers for her to view. She learned to contemplate the ocean and spent a portion of each day viewing the surf. You know, water imagery abounds in her writings."

Hegev looked at the captain, "You *knew* Nebutan?"

"She arrived when I was a schoolgirl. Dine and I briefly met her for the first time in Chelphun when she was making arrangements for the eventual publication of her works. I grew up in her shadow and was inspired by her to become a teacher. I have treasured my memories of our time together ever since. She once stood inside this cabin, soon after the Jefaka's launching ceremony. This was several years before I stepped aboard as her captain. As for this library, you should know our Dine remained at Chelphun when her 'Rise of Tatchlan' was produced and was still there when work began on her 'Worse than Chaos.'"

The Adept contemplated this, "What an extraordinary meeting this is! I would hear more, but let us return to the boy. You said most of his family did not welcome his visions."

"He said his mother and sisters laughed at them. He is especially bitter towards what had been his beloved aunt."

Hegev frowned and nodded, "So he maintained his mission despite this level of opposition?"

"Yes. He has not spoken of them since the day he came aboard."

"No younger siblings?"

"His manner is that of the youngest child," Emedin answered.

"So the baby of the family is betrayed by those he depended on most. Despite this, he chose two women, you Captain, and myself, to stand over him in our differing capacities."

"Is there significance in this?"

"We will see," Hegev answered. She focused on the two mariners and made a sign of respect, "I have high regard and admiration for your profession. I appreciate the terrible dangers you face and the vital role you play in our world. Due to your early lives, you are far more educated than most of those plying the seas."

Emedin looked at her First Officer, "Unforeseen turnings of events and many reverses led us here." She hesitated, "As for the circumstances of Seti picking our ship over so many others, this has kept me awake at night. I do not believe in his invisible generals; I do my part to separate his genius by what I see as mental ills. I sorrow to say there are an increasing number of days his inner chorus possesses him. Yet, his brightness always returns from this inner turbulence and then he shines like Nu! What is clear is his presence has enhanced the performance of my crew. Due to their increased confidence, our ship has known one of our safest circumambulatory navigations."

Hegev laughed out loud, "Please do not be offended! When I recall the vocabulary of most seamen, I did not expect to find a floating university! Most travelling in this fashion are not scholars. Most scholars tend not to travel, preferring to traverse the pages of books. Seti will not become a scholar."

Emedin frowned, "I know the term is used differently," she said. "Our Nebutan was trained similar to you as a youth and was designated a 'Wandering Scholar.'"

"Ah, yes," Hegev answered. "Were I to have had the better fortune to be born and trained here, this would be my title also. I cannot shake my upbringing. Back on our Eastern Gate, scholars are rare bookish creatures haunting pitiable libraries. Many here do also. But there are also those wandering and teaching for a fee, as Nebutan did in her youth, and I now do. There appears to be an increase in educational institutes of all kinds across this subcontinent and thus a reduction in the call for our services. I have mostly found work in rural hamlets. When I said Seti would not be a scholar, I referred to the bookish type. He has a distinctive wildness. He is young enough to remain open to wonder and has experienced enough to realize he has much to learn. His extreme naiveté has shielded and hampered him. I will guide him on the road to true adulthood. Beyond expressing a desire to read fully, he has also expressed an interest in visiting one of the Menem Shrines. How can neglected ruins instruct anyone? A far greater lesson may be found in the fields of living Memanu. Perhaps this should have been my pilgrimage all along."

"We have, on occasion, stopped in the past to witness their emergence at dawn," Emedin replied. "I agree they are glorious, but how are they a lesson to our Seti?"

"Beyond appreciating the many references to these creatures in the Daruadunnal and the Zitapermas within it, he would experience one of the most ancient and unspoiled Menem symbols. You know the sight of them blossoming above the clouds inspired the faithful in most-ancient times. Even in prehistory, we know those holding the ancient beliefs of the Chelyaka and Laranal cherished them. The Chelyaka, in particular, believed the Memanu could reach across their enclosed universe to commune with those on the other side of Anu's inner surface. Embracing their trembling trunks, feeling the heat of their life, is a universal touchstone of all seeking the beyond."

"You are aware of how those trembling trunks are sought out by most for another reason," Emedin frowned.

"Captain! I cannot believe one so weathered by the sea suffers from excessive delicacy. The renowned Zitapermas offered no apology when he declared embracing a Memanu the short route to Ranvartawan. He claimed to be the servant of none other than the Menem General Vindaviran. The Furrumittal has many references to them as 'gateways to Ranvartawan.'"

"Be this as it may," Emedin answered. "He is confused now, but if he had witnessed what else passes as normal and desirable in this land, I could not say how he might be affected. I confess I have seen many bizarre novelties on this voyage. From the island of Tich-Tushmul onward, none can deny Statos-Vey is changing."

"Perhaps," Hegev said thoughtfully. "While I have been on the subcontinent for near seven years, I am far from encompassing its dynamic complexity. I must admit having grown distracted of late and could not find the cause." She took a long breath, "I escaped a lifetime of sterile barrens only to land in this fermenting tangle! As for Seti, it is clear from his descriptions that you ensured certain things remain hidden from him. I suggest beyond this one excursion; we limit further exposure to the mainland for a time. He has had more than enough of the general culture to digest. As it stands, his exposure to the many customs found here is to his benefit. Given his creative and visual inclinations, many references remaining a mystery at home will become clear to him."

The Captain and his First Officer exchanged glances. "This is a commercial vessel," she said. "We are scheduled to visit other ports and are contracted to visit Bhampay for repairs. This was arranged at the outset of our journey."

"Bhampay?" the Adept said in evident dismay. "He is too immature for such a dense and intricate culture. You know, Upata-Shepsus and Bhampay form the core of those troubling trends you observed elsewhere. Since the days of the Yin-Vinulan Dynasty, Tatchlan Masters have walked openly in their streets. I have long observed most Healers and Soothers, even here in the southernmost portion of Statos-Vey, are Masters trained in Bhampay."

"We will consider our options in this," Emedin answered. "Perhaps we may meet a sister ship of our fleet not scheduled for the Imperial Port. We could pass you and Seti over, but the likelihood of this is doubtful. To my knowledge, most of our ships are far ahead. We are the last ship of our cohort travelling The Circuit out of Wazaratcha in a predetermined cycle. Unless we catch up to one who has encountered trouble, the new group will be a year or more behind us."

A thoughtful silence filled the Captain's cabin.

Her First Officer stirred, "May I ask a question, Adept?" Dine said.

"Of course."

"You may be far from delving the depths of this lad, but I presume you possess more knowledge of the ancient ways than either of us. I was surprised at his presumption to call on all four Grand Menem. Like our Captain, I have grown away from these traditions. Unlike her, I remain subject to their conventions. Is there precedent for an Aspirant claiming to have bound, not a common Sedet or Sev, but a Grand Menem, in his case all four of them, to their service?"

Captain Emedin bowed her head in enforced silence while Hegev frowned, smiled and shook her head, "While the boy in some ways resembles the famed prophet Zitapermas, even he did not make such a claim. There is little precedent for Menem coming unbidden to the untrained and unready. Yet, he maintains this is his situation. You do not hold to the mystical aspects of the tradition, captain. Your library suggests an emphasis on the more recent anti-Tatchlan phase of our faith, emphasizing rationality. I am between Seti and you. I presume your crew is less sophisticated. They adore the lad because of his audacity. It will take time, but I will inform you when I discover more of his mystery."

The three of them sat in silence. Hegev's expression grew sombre, and she leaned forward. "I save the most important observation for last. While I appreciate how he complements Sawlu's ancient fight, I am concerned."

"Concerned?" Emedin asked.

"Yes! Were you aware he is, what they call here in the south, a 'Raw Sensitive?'"

"A what?" Dine asked. "We know of the Sensitives used by those masters. What is a 'raw' Sensitive?"

"Throughout our history, long before the Tatchlan masters, some were born possessing keen perceptive abilities. The inspired aspects of most past religions are founded on generations of their dreams. With turns of fate, they were venerated and persecuted throughout history. I believe the word 'Sensitive' to be the eldest in our language! During their exile in the Veradapandra Mountains, these masters seized on their potential and created hybrids serving their twisted system. They left a portion unaltered, referring to them as 'raw.' Any aspect of life left unchanged; they refer to as 'raw' and other less-than-complimentary terms. Our separation from the masters' culture in the north means many such exist unrecognized in our homeland. Here, they are recognized very young and nurtured elaborately. Captain, I presume to suggest what you see as illness may be this strange gift."

Emedin looked doubtful, "I will defer for now to your greater knowledge on this inclination. I am not certain all I have seen would fit your suggestion. I must be candid and say I fear such an explanation could bolster what I continue to see as delusional and erratic behaviour. I will maintain a watch and welcome your expertise in this while conducting my own research as time allows. How would these historic abilities manifest themselves?"

"The gifts of these Sensitives take many forms, including powerful abilities to dream."

"'Abilities to dream?'" Captain Emedin said. "He has been reading the crew's dreams since he arrived."

"I speak of *his* dreams. He has waited long to tell someone. He loves you, but is frightened of what fills his sleep."

"We agree the boy has been exposed to much he was ignorant of," Dine said. "I accompanied him on many excursions during our stops."

"It is true some events have disturbed him. Taking his simple upbringing into account, he has lost his balance and flounders. When he does regain his bearing, he will be stronger for having been exposed to the south. Passing visions of peculiar rites and outrageous displays are not the source of these visions."

She pondered while the Captain and First Officer watched her.

"Many authorities agree the Menem Invocants of old were Sensitives," Hegev said. "This cannot be discussed back home, but I have heard convincing evidence here. This lad displays clear signs of a Sensitive in many ways. I believe he has not discovered the extent of his talents. I will wait and watch before revealing more of this to him. He has more to discover and let go of. I will guide him and apprise you of what I find. What concerns me is a set of visions he has suffered from for several two-weeks."

Emedin frowned, "He has said nothing to us of this."

Hegev smiled and tilted her head, "Captain! His esteem for you and the crew is great. Yet, he required one having my training and experience for this."

Emedin glanced at Dine before turning back to the Adept. "What are these visions?"

"Faces," Hegev answered gravely, "huge fantastic faces in garish hues and frightening distortions. He is visited by a group of them, floating in the air and calling his name. They follow him wherever he goes or fills the rooms he dreams of walking through. He says his Menem are forced to retire when they approach. This retreat disturbs him most."

The Captain's quarters were possessed by silence once again.

"What do these visions signify?" Emedin asked. "What are these faces?"

Hegev shook her head, "There are growing rumours of many dreaming of a series of faces. Recently I encountered a potter selling sets of twelve pottery masks in a market. They were at once bizarre and familiar. At the time, I thought them inspired by a drama and asked him. He said they visited him in a dream."

Emedin wore a thoughtful frown. Her First Officer and the Adept waited for her to speak.

"What our Seti dreams . . . is dreamt by others?" Emedin finally asked.

Hegev nodded.

"What causes images to cross the boundary between dreamers?"

"Tatchlan," Hegev answered.

CHAPTER 15

Shuna-Shapta

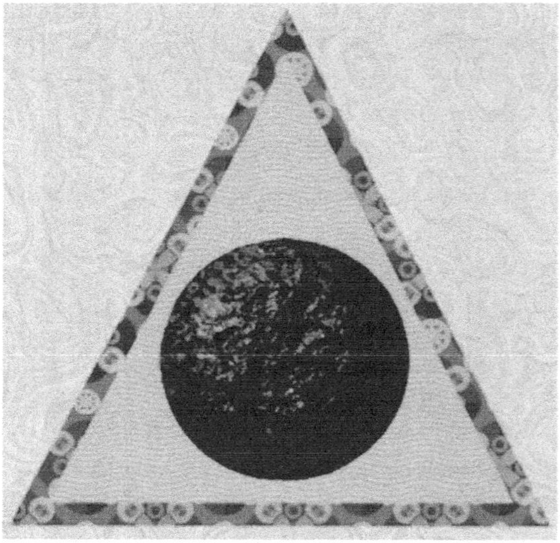

Pictured: modern depiction of the Orb of Raw Life, Indatubangus, floating as it were on the waters of Amanavata

Day 106, Two-Week Six – Tret, the Candle, within Tatchlan

Shuna-Shapta, and her seven fellow Delving Invocants, held each other's hands to form a chain. Master Tanas was out in front of them. Together, they hovered before Amanavata, known to Invocates as the outer water layer of Tatchlan. As they had approached the 'vertical ocean' grew in size until it filled their eyes. Rather than the aromas and sounds of the Panchala Sea they knew so well; this ocean was filled with whispering sighs and deep risings and fallings, forming a gentle undulating pattern spreading out in all directions. Just beneath this placid surface, small 'General Faces,' coloured in faint pastels, moved singularly and in small groups in curious circular motions, synchronized to the surrounding waters. Their characteristic 'cooing' calls were just audible to them.

Shuna-Shapta had grown accustomed to how Master Tanas appeared within Tatchlan; his ample and muscular body streaked in peach and pink, signifying his Sweet Aroma Accord. Master Tanas appeared to gently fall back into the waters, where he summoned some of these little General Faces. Shortly they streaked away on their mission. He effortlessly breached the surface to return to them, soon followed by a dramatic set of eight identical Secondary Faces in line formation. They rose to the surface as flaming discs, causing the General Faces to scatter. They were servants of one of the Twelve Principal Faces - Hesha Vira. She was fashioned first on Indatubangas and was the fifth wakened of the Twelve Principal Faces. They came to hover, four either side, of Master Tanas. This strange formation was dramatic in their visual contrast to the gently undulating wall of pale waters behind them. Despite only being as tall as any of the Invocants, these eight Secondary Faces remained daunting. As their shocking Master, their bulging green eyes and black slit pupils looked at them from the gloom, and their wild yellow hair twisted as if alive. They seemed the antithesis of the placid waters behind them. Their red cheeks were studded with daunting designs. On one side were eight infant faces crying out with need, on the other, seven tiny skulls. Their broad red mouths and long sharp teeth formed a set of ferocious grimaces.

"Our grandmothers and their mothers infused considerable power into our Twelve Principal Faces and these, their Secondary Faces," Master Tanas's 'Tatchlan Voice' was the same and different within the Living System. These Secondary Faces possessed a life and startling vitality of their own. Some scrutinized the Delving Invocates; others looked sideways at Master Tanas. None were stationary, some subtly turned side to side, others gently tilted one direction and then the other, others rhythmically bent forward and back by slight increments. None kept to their pattern long before switching to another, which all did by some invisible cue. There was a unity to this variety of movements, known as the 'Tatchlan Eddy,' shared by all those inhabiting the Living System. Despite their fearsome appearance, there was something impish about these eight strange entities, with one Secondary Face even appearing to comically mouth some of Master Tanas's words. There could be no doubt that these creatures were alive.

"Your cold understanding must warm to their many applications," he continued. "You behold two of our three classes of Secondary Faces. There is a Third Class, known as Diverse, which we shall examine in the future. You already know the First Class, our diminutive General Faces," he gestured back to the vertical water wall behind him, where the small groups had resumed their own little dances beneath the surface, "they can find, or conduct us to, any Secondary Face we require. When not upon such missions to all portions of our Living System, their station is primarily here, at the surface of Amanavata, awaiting our summons. These modest beings have a more comprehensive vision of our entire Living System than most. Of course, the Second Class are ably represented here by these 'Unified Faces,' better known as 'Secondary Faces,'" he indicated his eight bizarre companions either side of him, "being complete miniatures of the wild magnificence of Hesha Vira." With his words, they moved forward in unison, slightly closer than Master Tanas to the students, fixing their shocking eyes and shining teeth on the students. Despite knowing this already, it was still astonishing to see them understanding his words.

"To address one of these is to address the Principal Face, although we know we are but one voice amid many to them. We generally refer to these as if they were the singular Principal Face. You shall seldom glimpse any of the Twelve. If you do, most shall appear as a moon progressing in stately orbit of our Living Orb. Whilst there are many Secondary Faces, they are as facets and appendages of a single entity. We Masters and you Invocants shall dedicate our lives to dealing with these Secondary Faces. The Principal Faces shall remain for our Majastas when She enters Her full 'Assumption of All Estates.' Each of our Twelve Principal Faces possesses distinguishing aspects as part of their uses. Hesha Vira oversees Tatchlan's connections to blind, raw life. She administers the destruction of each cast off fragment from our Living Orb upon one side and the waters of Amanavata upon the other. Within her furnace, new elements constantly spew forth to replenish the upper and lower levels, refreshing our Resplendent Work. You shall soon become better acquainted with 'The Common Desire,' which appears as fluids of many hues and densities flowing across our Living Orb's surface. It represents the collective thoughts and whims of the populace. Whilst having other sources, this vital element largely gushes forth upon Indatubangus, where each stream and river finally terminates. As with her primitive realm, Hesha Vira may be rapacious and wasteful. Nevertheless, she remains the foundation of Tatchlan, connected to, and servant of, our Harmonious Orb. All things commence and conclude within her realm of raw life. As a creature of Tatchlan, she manifests thus because of her terrible use. Her servants shall conduct you to those aspects of life remaining unchanged by Tatchlan."

With this conclusion and instruction, Hesha Vira's Secondary Faces sent a series of whipping red-and-yellow-striped tendrils to encircle all of them from their hidden backsides. While hot and seemingly moist, they were gentle in their grip. The two either side of Master Tanas also ensnared him. These eight Secondary Faces continued to face the Delving Invocates while travelling backwards alongside Master Tanas through the placid water layer. A gentle cooing chorus of the smaller General Faces suddenly surrounded them with their accustomed call. As before the students noted, these General Faces appeared to have tiny tendrils swiftly attaching to and disconnecting from them and each other in swift darting motions. They remained in dense clusters near the surface. The Circle of Invocates continued down through the warm, echoing depths, they passed a few General Faces, apparently on missions to and from the surface, along with other varied fauna glowing in the depths. As they travelled, they appreciated the complexity of the many fluid layers they passed through.

Master Tanas called out, "Amanavata, as Indatubangus, is a collective manifestation of many aspects of life upon Anu. It may be said they originally were the two halves of one whole. She ever provided the cushion and conduit for Indatubangus to function. As you know, your Living Instruments present an inverted version of this reality. In truth, we are at the base of life travelling upwards through Amanavata, its inner ocean, towards life's original fulcrum. In its true form, Tatchlan forms a unifying and self-aware skin over these two halves of what was originally blind life. Amanavata has now been augmented and modified to suit our Resplendent Work, yet retains all her basic forms of vital service to our new order. Ahead is our destination for this day. It is named our 'Stekachey Nut' and the 'bitter rind.' You recall the Stekachey nut from your Life Cake ceremony and the extremes of the bitter outer rind and sweet inner fruit."

All of the Delving Invocants recognized the growing roar of chaos as they approached the realm of vile and unrefined life. After their initial visit to be purged by the Lustrum Mirror, they had several occasions requiring their exploration of this realm. The swirling sphere churned with the anarchy of innumerable beings, possessed, and destroyed, by self-absorption. Countless millions came into existence, feeding other millions before becoming food. Cries of fear and passion, followed by whimpers of pain and starvation, formed the chorus. They followed in quick succession, and the Invocants became aware of the repeating pattern. They floated toward the vertical wall of its terrible surface. The Hesha Vira configuration reached the agitated facade before sinking into it. Their tendrils continued to pull them until they made a light landing on a raised area surrounded by a boiling sea of life. They stood still, looking over the painful landscape. Once they landed, the surface became their ground and the oceans above their sky.

"As with your previous visits," Master Tanas called out over the rising din, "Hesha Vira continues to protect us. Indatubangas shall never harm you, and Amanavata covers us. Our Resplendent Orb of Tatchlan, as all of value, lies beneath our feet. Do not forget you remain within your Invocate Chamber, locked within your Living Instrument's embrace. From there, we dive inside our bodies, and those of our Living Instruments."

The Invocants and their Master looked at the crazed storm raging on all sides. Their island was not solid but made gentle shifts beneath their feet. Out in the turbulence, the surface spiked high in the air, and a multitude of partial forms emerged and vanished. These were not plants and animals, but their vivid impressions rising out of and sinking back into an animated, multicoloured soup. They noted how a gentle cascade of broken and worn fragments floating down from the waters of the upper sphere of Amanavata were immediately snapped up when they reached the surface. They also saw living elements bubble and rise out of it, to float up out of sight. From this boiling ooze rose a robust set of aromas. Desperation formed the principle message of these scents. The dissonance grew deafening, and when they reached their endurance, a curtain of silence fell. The surface of Indatubangas continued to riot, the rain of debris and rising elements continued to fill their eyes, but the din was mute. The Invocants turned to their Master. He smiled as he held up a striped Hesha Vira tendril.

"They may conduct another set of Invocants here, or lie below the surface. As long as you hold a Secondary Face tendril, you may instruct them. One of their many uses involves moderating or silencing her unruly subjects. There are times you must listen for a particular voice; this day we may rest from their chorus."

The Invocants looked at the hushed anarchy. The gaping mouths were now voiceless.

"Master," one of the students asked, "as I witness this all again, I may not forebear but must enquire as to why this wasteful confusion and terrible pain surround our triumph of joy and harmony?"

"Indatubangas forms the crux of Tatchlan," Master Tanas said. "This raw life, both the ocean over and the fire under, predates what you know as our Living Orb. Just as argent, lapis and cupric gems begin as rough veins within azure stone, so the unrefined components for our Resplendent Work are born here. All elements return for reworking and renewal to this, the fulcrum of life and death upon Anu. You have read of how most of our first Primary Masters fled Rho-Jashun during the Buyanupithar Dynasty after the Menem priesthood began their persecutions. Arriving in Statos-Vey, they encircled the spring inside Mount Uluvatu to begin our Resplendent Work. When they perfected our Living Instruments, their first tentative steps were taken here. They found Tatchlan resembling a modest seed here. The foundation of our Grand Work," he indicated, "lies here. Our early civilizations, those whose names we celebrate and those we have forgotten, with their attendant elegance and savagery, took their turns manifesting within this realm. All alike are gone, leaving no discernible residue within what was once their domain. Here, Self-Absorption thwarted those noble attempts to civilize life. Once our Masters grasped the nature of Indatubangas, they knew what they had to do to bring peace and happiness to Anu's Flesh. Their first masterpiece, our Lustrum Mirror, provided them, and us, with the doorway out of this Kingdom of Pain. We each have found our legacies of vile, blind survival within that mirror. We uprooted those tumours from that reflection and hurled them back into this caldron from whence they came. Whilst our Resplendent Work grew without and within, they knew Indatubangas remains the vital furnace driving all life."

Master Tanas grasped the shoulders of the Invocants, arranging them in a small circle facing outward. They focused on the wild landscape. He stood inside, looking at the scene.

"The longer you observe, the more you shall understand," he spoke softly. "Stand back and observe the generalities. Do not focus upon the mundane functions or the pain and sorrow. These form but a small part of our drama. What you must discern is the driving force behind each thing."

The Invocants looked out on the rude tableau for a long time.

"What motivation dominates each creature, each plant, each form of life?" he asked.

Mi-Yang answered at once, "Survival."

"Yes!" Master Tanas declared. "Survival forms the fundamental nature of raw life. Surrounded by indifferent non-life and hostile life, survival forms the foundation. Life wakened and at once had to fend off starvation and destruction. Regardless of modifications and elaborations since, this remains the core of life's dilemma. For life to survive, it either mounts an assault or futilely evades indifference and hostility. You look at a field of tall grasses and do not discern the silent war. Underground, roots of one type of plant strive to strangle other roots to ensure they have access to nutrients and moisture. One leaf tries to shoot higher to overshadow the others. Our abundant tropical flora attacks those who would eat them by exuding an extraordinary variety of poisons. Since childhood, you have witnessed many creatures eating mud to coat their insides and better digest them. A plant-eating creature, such as a Danta, produces far more offspring than necessary to ensure a few endure harsh conditions, disease and predation culling the herd. In a multitude of ways, survival involves overcompensating excess as the only reply to inevitable destruction. This pattern repeats throughout this vista. All live in fear. Hunger is ever-present. None sleep undisturbed. For those surviving carnivores, parasitic infestation paves the way to eventual starvation. For this reason, we call this pitiable and wretched existence the Kingdom of Pain."

"Master," one of the male Invocants called out, "why do insect icons dominate so many Tatchlan Cubes? Are they not the epitome of blind survival?"

"Ah! Excellent question! The Teer Beetle rids our Charsha fields of pests. It became a symbol of protection. What could better symbolize brilliant creation and extraordinary patience than 'The Wise Spider?' She also joins a class of creatures, such as our melodious toad and the delving serpent, venerated for their poisons. This matchless defence symbolizes their taking latent body chemistry and turning it into a weapon overcoming the strength of more massive brutes. There is ample evidence of admiration for these qualities of the frail overcoming crudity by the power of subtle refinements dating deep within prehistoric times. Our work upon transmuting these toxins into powerful healing agents and Vision Windows are also of great antiquity. When our Masters began this Resplendent Work, insects also served as ideal vehicles for our initial entry. Our grandmothers and their mothers came to venerate them, especially our insect societies, such as the Gandahatapan, the Ketukku and the Mahakram, for their social perfection and communal Genius. Insects achieved their brilliant lives within water, upon the land and through the air prior to all others. They continue to sustain us. From prehistory, they have been afforded great respect for their brilliant defiance of far larger forces. Within Tatchlan, you shall observe them forming a bridge between indifferent non-life and Sensitives such as yourselves."

"Master?" the same voice called out. "Do you say these insects are a superior form of life?"

"Upon Anu's Skin, they, and the innumerable entities too small to perceive, form its foundation. They are beyond speculation and are paragons of dispassionate existence. Their individual lives are studies of simplicity and their societies of Genius. No subsequent form of life approaches either manifestation of excellence. Within our Living System, they underlie what you experience as Tatchlan's two outer layers covering our Living Orb. You shall come to behold their glittering order upon our Breathing Work."

"Were they the agents used against the Suvuka?"

"Yes and no. Blood Midges were employed to disburse Master Duamang's weapon. The weapon itself was an infinitesimal, an ancient horror known as the Brangnam Plague. This entity originally existed among the Cousins, and then in most-ancient times, modified itself to infest the Tolku. Among our most-ancient grandmothers and mothers, it took on grievous form and enacted terrible suffering and death upon many populations. Given the grisly nature of its progress, the antique notion of 'merciful suicide' came from these times. One of its bouts even contributed to the demise of the first unifying dynasty of ancient times, the Funomanru. Early in the history of Masters, as The General Plain was being laid out, it was hunted down by those with very refined sensibilities here, upon Indatubangus. Over the subsequent ages, it was sufficiently modified to become a purging tool. Master Duamang possessed many exemplar qualities, but her principle claim to fame was her specialized Estate. She was able to seek them out, 'turn them over,' and further modify them to attack just the Suvuka's reproductive organs. This caused them all to become painlessly barren upon Rho-Jashun and so break their dominion. This achievement is all the more remarkable as many of our living tools we employ this day were yet to be cultivated. Back in her time, over twelve hundred years ago, half of our Living System we traverse this day did not exist!"

"So! To your original question, my dear, in a way it is true, insects are seen as life's first and best reply to the riddle of existence. They possess a flawlessness and excellence; no subsequent life has achieved. Their perfect design, absolute fearlessness and immense strength, their utterly clear focus and absolute dedication, and most importantly, their profound depths of Genius in social organization, have no equal among those who breathe."

The young Invocants exchanged glances and looked at the realm with confusion.

"Understand," Master Tanas said. "Our Uluvatu Masters had this insight - initial life achieved its calibre through the elegant combinations of its most basic components. Through this view, creatures coming after may well have mimicked, but never reached, insects' level of precision. Many fantastic beings rose and fell whilst they remained unaffected. Our paradox is, as the most advanced life upon Anu, we remain the least whole. Tatchlan, fashioned by generations of Tolku, brings us to this epitome by our collective effort and Genius. As such, with our manifold powers, we accomplish a full circle of life, bringing ourselves back towards Anu's first perfect beings."

"Why not be at greater ease within this realm?" another Invocant asked. "Why fill the waters of this inner ocean with General Faces and grow a new layer we name our Living Orb?"

"Because we possess far greater mental depth than any dwelling upon the Flesh of Anu preceding us," Master Tanas replied. "Channeling raw life is vital to linking our intelligence with the insects' collective wisdom. What we build here forms the ground out of which a truly lasting order shall spread. Our perfection shall extend within a harmonious, stable society. Each other attempt had failed, leaving us trapped within this misery until the advent of Tatchlan. Survival comprises a set of strategies ensuring life continues. Despite their being small and weak, insects of all orders overcome brutes many times their size through their mastery of selfless organization. Their collective wisdom of these kingdoms is beyond any individual subject. Our prehistoric grandmothers and their mothers dwelt within chaos and confusion. As both predators and prey, the belligerence of one and fear of the other tainted their emotions. Want, aggression and dread issue from insecurity based upon real or imagined vulnerability. They remain our principle barriers to a full life. It was the most-ancient Water Viewers who first named unrefined life the 'Kingdom of Pain.' They saw our malady but not our remedy. Their successors, the first Masters, seeing we remained entrapped by our fear, rage, chaos and confusion, and compensating by growing this monstrous Self-Absorption, fashioned this door out of survival existence."

For a time they were silent pondering this as they continued to watch the endless activity.

"So we crave more than survival," Shuna-Shapta said. She turned to look back at Master Tanas. He nodded for her to continue. "Survival fuels self-absorption," she said. "We have read how our Primary Masters perceived Self-Absorption as the ultimate perversion of survival. The vast insect colonies, such as our noble Gandahatapan, the 'Perfection of our Air,' the Ketukku, 'Our Rooted Ones,' and the Mahakram, the 'Yellow Cloud,' display the epitome of self-abdication. You said Self-Absorption involves 'the excess of self and predation of others.' Tolku possessed by self-absorption view other Tolku as separate from themselves. They prey upon each other and life. This extension of base instinct forms the source of our misery." She looked back out at the crude battle continuing. "We surpass raw life whilst remaining ensnared within its dictates. Tatchlan uses our strengths to create a new perfection."

Master Tanas nodded, "Shash! Shash!" He stepped out of their circle and signalled them to turn to face him, "Civilizing base life to bring about our new perfection remains our aim." Behind him, the raining particles and rising elements from the raging soup formed a dramatic backdrop for his words. "All we cultivate within the form of peace and happiness depends upon stepping below the blind, superficial dictates of survival toward a deeper, richer life. History teaches us this Self-Absorption has ever thwarted efforts to create a stable life structure. We must now thwart it! We shall bring its dominion to an end!"

Master Tanas encircled himself with Hesha Vira's striped tendril and tied a loose knot leaving his hands free. "We shall travel over the surface of Indatubangas and view several features," he said.

He turned to face outward, held out his hands, and the Invocants formed a joined line, either side of him. Master Tanas stepped forward, and the others did the same. They came to the edge of the bluff, and he stepped off. They floated weightless beside him. They began to glide across the turbulent surface of Indatubangas, the tendril of Hesha Vira changed to a stiff rod bearing them along without disturbing the agitated ocean of life below them. The silence began to lift from the violence churning beneath them. Heat rose through their feet and legs.

"Observe portals leading to our Living Orb," Master Tanas called out, unperturbed by the return of the noise and powerful odours.

They looked and found occasional whirlpools in the sludge and caverns on Indatubangas leading down and through the sphere. They saw a tiny pinprick of the familiar light of the Resplendent Orb of Tatchlan.

"Via your Living Instrument's vision, this 'bitter rind' remains rooted to our Living Orb below and the contained over waters of Amanavata," Master Tanas continued. "Through each of these gateways we travel to reach our Magnificent Orb and return. They also provide means for the Faces to travel between our inner harmony and the outer threshold where we summon them. I instructed Hesha Vira to open several for you to know. They open and shut as needed."

As he spoke, they began to accelerate. The figures below lost resolution and became a blur. Distant mountain ranges approached and fell away behind them. No wind assailed them and the smells and heat became generalized. The Invocants heard a pattern similar to the Thanners rhythmic cry after the rains. This intriguing repetition increased as they flew over the broad face of Indatubangas.

"Listen to the pattern!" Master Tanas shouted out.

The Invocants focused on it and began to perceive the distinct repeating cadence of 'death chasing life chasing death.' They slowed to float over a different ocean and came to rest on a small island.

Master Tanas turned back to the ocean composed of large creatures and gestured, "Behold the Suvuka!"

The forms were silhouettes swimming in the soup. Only their powerful bellows were true to the originals. A few stopped their frantic running to stand and move their massive limbs with deliberation.

"Here stands the single-greatest challenge our Masters ever faced," Master Tanas called out. "For innumerable generations our most-ancient Masters toiled upon Indatubangas, unaware of this remarkable population. Our most-ancient forbears viewed 'the north' as home to evil. Ships venturing to Thermistal never returned. Prohibitions against exploration ensured our grandmothers and their mothers remained innocent of the Suvuka. You must appreciate our first Masters lacked the tools we now have at hand to know this realm in full. All those eons ago they made their way by the equivalent of touch alone through this quaking chaos. They began to blindly gather the woven threads of life, but the Suvuka possessed a unique strand due to the extinction of all their near relations. A very young Hesha Vira found these creatures prior to the Masters. She had no way to tell our early grandmothers, and their mothers, of her discovery and formed a separate bond with them. When our Uluvatu Masters finally uncovered them during the Buyanupithar Dynasty, scant centuries prior to the adventurers returning with their tales, they had little time to prepare. Hesha Vira may have also unwittingly inspired them to cross the sea. Our early Masters led their allies south but a few two weeks ahead of the thundering hordes spreading across the Marachla Plain of Rho-Jashun. Because of their late discovery, the Suvuka remain an isolated, mysterious knot inside our Grand Work. We defeated them upon Anu's Flesh, and we still require generational work to bring them within our Living System."

The Invocants turned to stare at their Master.

"May this be?" a male student called out over the roars.

"Contained upon a portion of Thermistal," Master Tanas said, "a few Masters superintend this extended endeavour. Many Tolku now gather upon Thermistal. Our nation has entrusted Masters to manage this work near our Vettencore Passage. Whilst our army patrols the border, generations of Masters continue to modify Tatchlan sufficiently to incorporate them. The Suvuka could be near equals. Our Cousins, Varku, Tamku and others, remain branches of our body family. The Suvuka are more separate and more similar to us. They repulsed our attempts to communicate and find common cause. Their implacable hatred led to the extermination of what remained of their attendant subspecies when they displayed signs of modification by our grandmothers, and their mothers. For their pride, they destroyed their kin and now stand alone. Despite their containment, their passion for our demise remains undiminished." After a pause he added, "Our advantage lies in their constraint. Upon their portion of Thermistal, we observe their complex migrations. Here, we Masters possess another advantage. We may study the herd patterns and monitor various modifications we introduce. Beyond this, they remain a physical threat and a small but significant dilemma seeking resolution. As creatures of Indatubangas, for many generations we have cultivated their relationship with Hesha Vira and have had limited success. She has grown large within their imaginations and her wakened Face now seeks them out. She becomes our first firm handle upon them."

Fascination filled the Invocants eyes as they viewed the forbidding ocean of their most feared enemy.

CHAPTER 16

SINKIN

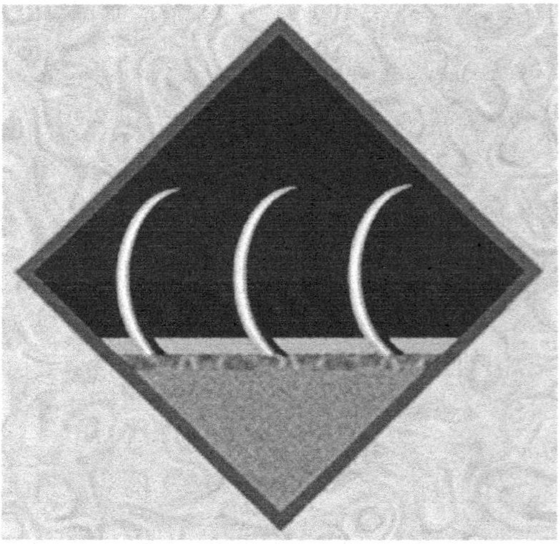

Pictured: icon of the feared 'Royalty of the Desert,' the Toohund, symbolized by the deadly hairs rising from just beneath the sand.

Day 119, two days run from Avanchil Round

Durka and Makusk Herd had struggled through the pitiless Kukernef Desert for an exhausting two hundred and twenty days. Despite staying near the coast, they suffered through wretched tracts of wasteland, punctuated by sharp rocks and howling storms threatening to bury them beneath new sand mountains. The extreme variations in temperature night and day proved worse than anything the two young bucks, Sinkin and Setush, had experienced. Along the way, their elders had shown them tricks for finding food and wresting tiny amounts of moisture from the frightful plants living there. They also journeyed down to the coast in the hopes of finding stranded sea life at high tide. Their bodies had become lean, and their pelts transformed into a stunning near-white shade puffed out to trap and hold the air near their average body temperature. Their bodies adapted, and they learned many new skills. The bucks learned to fear the open sand and watch for movement beneath its surface. Each morning brought a reminder to care for the signs. Many fearsome creatures made their home in this terrible place against which strength was no defence. The previous night, they had encountered a towering pile of boulders surrounded by a series of tall cones. A few days from their final arrival at Avanchil Round, in the dawn's first light, the faded silhouette of the distant Jaladanu Mountains rose. Despite shivering in the pre-dawn freeze, Durka and Makusk Herd were heartened by their successful run. Within sight of their goal, they forgot the signs. They had run for half an hour when two Suvuka, one from each herd – Zatin and Jutnesh – screamed in pain and fell. They were on the same eastern side of the group, facing the desert. Sinkin and Setush ran in the middle. They turned to see the two thrashing blindly in the sand.

"No! No! No!" Hiratak shouted. "They are caught in the nets! Watch your paws!"

The bucks had been told of the Toohund, one of the most dreaded denizens of the Kukernef and Kyu Deserts, and stood wide-eyed in fear. They looked down at their paws and watched for twitching in the sands. It was right in front of them! The sand resolved into a lace pattern, thin and elegant as the air, but lethal to touch. Out of this pattern rose a series of fearsome white hairs spiking upward as in the quest for more flesh. The trapped Suvuka howled and writhed. Portions of the net separated from the rest and, in an instant, enveloped the two struggling forms. As they were wrapped, they emitted a series of high-pitched screams of agony, trembled and fell still. Before the rest's horrified gaze, their massive bodies were dragged over the surface of the sand.

"Find solid rock!" Morakav, Makusk Herd's Herdmaster, barked out. The stunned group turned and ran to a nearby flat outcropping and perched on it.

"Watch the sand!" Hiratak shouted, "We can only help ourselves. Watch the spread of the pattern. The beast will reveal its body. Then we find our way."

They watched as in the distance, a large mound, twice the size of an adult Suvuka, rose out of the sand. This body had an elaborate pattern blending into the swirling dark sands. Over this oval form ran a series of ridges extending out from a central tip. These formed the backbone of ever-smaller branches, becoming the stems of a vast network of feathered killing lace lying flat under the sand's surface. The Toohund dragged their two fallen herdmates toward its central body. It raised over one of the bodies with terrible swiftness and began ripping it open using a large beak on its underside. Many tiny Toohund, children of their mother, clustered around the bill snapping their small beaks as they joined the feast. The Suvuka heard the bones of their herdmates snapping like twigs as their entire bodies were broken, gutted and pulverized. As she and her brood ate, the whole network of her radiating set of stinging nets revealed itself in a sprawling and irregular pattern radiating from the central body. The sudden and ferocious feeding movements, at the centre, caused the entire network to twitch.

"Look at the extent of her body," Hiratak shouted out. "She could still kill us. Her young are rapacious. Stay out of her reach!" He stepped off of the ledge and began to run past the shuddering edge of the nets. The others followed in terror, leaving their two herdmates to the Toohund and her brood. As they ran, whimpers grew into howls and bellows. They made their way down to the rocky shore, forsaking the broad plain where more terrors might lie in wait for them. After their wails diminished, their Herdmasters called for an interlude. They stood panting and moaning by the roaring ocean surf.

"Zatin" Hiratak called out the name of the slain member of Durka Herd. He had been the sole buck of the previous year's run. Hiratak scraped a large rock's surface with his extended talons, leaving a series of long scratches. He set it atop another.

"Jutnesh," Morakav called out the name of Makusk Herd's lost runner. He also scored and placed one rock atop another, close to the rock of Zatin. The rest of the two herds found a stone for each. They scraped and added them to the pile. The rocks joined each other at the base, forming a twin-peak pile. The Suvuka began to circle this short monument, repeating their names.

"Durka was nine for this Stag Run. Now we are eight. Zatin runs with our glorious dead." Hiratak said.

"Makusk was five for this Stag Run. Now we are four. Jutnesh runs with our glorious dead." Morakav said.

The Herdmasters had the others encircle their memorial. They hung their heads low and allowed their noses to rest on the salty sand.

"Listen to my words," Hiratak said, "We evaded this horror for hundreds of days. We met it on the eve of Avanchil. We avoided their snares many times. We grew careless! The monster will soon spread her net. The wind will carry her to a new resting place. The Toohund are desert royalty. Our ancestors could not unseat them. We remain foolish intruders in their lands. On my Stag Path, we lost one to a Toohund and two to a wild sandstorm. Memories of loss haunt these shores. Remains of similar memorials litter this coast. The deep desert drinks memory as water. It leaves nothing behind."

He turned to Morakav, who bowed to him and said, "I never witnessed such a tragedy. Their end will live beneath our eyes. It will fill us whenever we close them. Hold your memories to honour them. Compose your laments. We must sing them to their dams and sires. We must run again. With each step, watch for the signs!"

The Herdmasters began to emit a series of low grunts signalling it was time to start. They ran the rest of the day without incident.

* * *

Day 121, Avanchil Round

Two days after the death of Zatin and Jutnesh, Durka and Makusk herds entered the massive pan of Avanchil Round. Over one hundred herds composed of between five and fifteen Suvuka, escorting their bucks during their Full Stag Run, surrounded them on the outskirts. After running for so long alone, this sudden crowd shocked them. Many were jovial and invited the newcomers to join them in many sports and games. Word spread of the tragedy, and Durka and Makusk were allowed to continue in their grief.

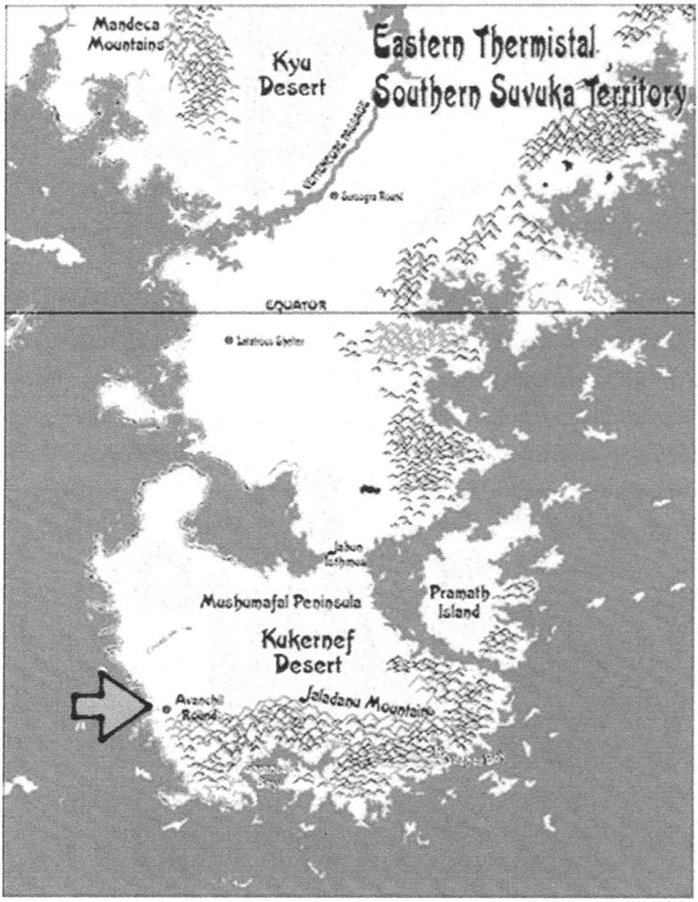

An ancient approached them, "I am a Keeper of the Round. My name is Datal."

Hiratak and Morakav came forward to stand side by side before the Keeper.

"I am Hiratak, Herdmaster and Voice of Durka Herd. We escort Sinkin. Our buck is on his Full Stag Run."

"I am Morakav, Herdmaster and Voice of Makusk Herd. We escort Setush. Our buck is on his Full Stag Run."

"You each bring a single buck?"

They nodded.

"Durka and Makusk run together?"

They assented.

"Did you begin so, or join your separate journeys?"

"We live within the reaches of Chitikal Round," Morakav answered, "We joined at Latatroos Shelter."

The Keeper nodded at this, "You suffered a terrible loss."

"Two fell to a Toohund and her brood," Hiratak said. The rest lowered their heads to the ground.

Keeper Datal snorted, "A brood, you say? How many clung around their mother's beak?"

Hiratak and Morakav looked at each other. "We saw them in less than a breath," Morakav said. "A small herd clung to her."

Keeper Datal growled, "We Keepers will speak of this. You are the first struck this year. The desert sovereigns took seven last year! They know when we come! They wait for us! We mark and tag them. We dye their nets. We upset their migrations. Still, they kill within sight of our Round! What purpose do we Keepers serve?"

Durka and Makusk's Herdmasters said nothing to this. The Keeper lost his anger and pitied the group.

"A lamentation will be sung." He signalled for another to join them. The senior Keeper growled in his ear. The other turned and ran off. Keeper Datal turned back to them, "You have priority. Rest beneath the Yellow Shelter by the Lip. It stands where thousands like it have stood. It shaded descendants of our bravest warriors.To witness a Toohund is to survive a war! Food and drink will be brought. Tomorrow, the lamentation of Durka and Makusk begins the Run."

The shelter was composed of a series of desiccated vertical tree trunks dug into the ground, another set had one end held by rocks. Such timber must have been dragged from the south, the bucks had near forgotten about trees. The top rested in rough cuts in the vertical trunks, creating a low shelter underneath. A dark yellow resin smeared the bark. They saw similar covers surrounding the bowl, bearing a distinctive shade or combination of shades and patterns.

"These trunks come from the coastal jungles," Hiratak said as they entered. "The Keepers do much for our benefit."

Later, Sinkin and Setush went to look over the edge. A thousand Suvuka raced around the most extensive set of cones and spheres either of them had ever seen. Erected long before the Suvuka crossed over to Rho-Jashun, and swept down the Marachla Plain, they had deep patterns etched by desert winds. Shelters and many markers for the Leading Herds lined the lip. Neither Durka nor Makusk had a long or illustrious pedigree. Were it not for their loss, they would have settled down in the open, far from the bowl of Avanchil.

* * *

Day 122, Avanchil Round

Durka and Makusk herd woke in the pre-dawn darkness. Their shelter spared them a covering in frost, and they looked at the Lip of the famed Avanchil Round. Keeper Datal approached alongside two others.

"The Keepers of Avanchil Round greet you." He spoke as his breath came out in white puffs, "Present the names of your fallen. They will be recited by our callers."

"Jutnesh of Makusk Herd. Zatin of Durka Herd." The two Herdmasters answered.

The Keeper and his attendants bowed their noses to the ground before the attendants left.

"Who ran and danced last year?" the Keeper asked.

Members of Durka Herd shifted and lowered their heads, "Zatin was here last year," Hiratak said.

The Keeper bowed low at their loss. "Any from Makusk Herd?" he asked.

"It is three years since our last buck," Morakav answered, displaying his pain in saying so. "He is in the north. He could not attend."

The Keeper bowed to him, "I must now instruct you as to the innovations."

"Innovations?" Hiratak asked, "What innovations?"

The Keeper frowned, "Jutnesh of Makusk and Zatin of Durka will soon be heard." He stepped a pace closer to them and, lowering his voice, "Rumours spread of Suvuka altered by the enemy. Some demand we seek those touched. We must remove them from our assembly."

A chill went through them at the news.

"How is this done?" No hint of emotion passed over Morakav's voice.

"There are certain markings and an unusual loss of balance. These are indicators of interference."

Hiratak and Morakav looked at each other and back to the Keeper. They heard the names of Zatin and Jutnesh echoing across the pan. Durka and Makusk Herd listened to the names ringing out, and many began to moan. Hiratak and Morakav remained fixed in looking at the Keeper.

"We are covered in markings," Hiratak began icily. "We are lashed by jungles! Our flanks are scoured by desert storms! Who can distinguish between clumsiness and alteration? These rumours circle Chitikal Round. Self-appointed purists turn us against each other. What is this change? Do these Suvuka now adore the Tolku? Do they long to be defiled? What do these innovations serve? They make divisions where none existed! How does this not serve our true enemy? We are here for our precious bucks. Their endurance makes our herds proud. How could they maintain their pace without balance? My objections cannot be novel."

The Keeper stood mute during this tirade. The names of Zatin and Jutnesh now echoed across the pan, and large numbers of Suvuka called their names in remembrance.

"They are not," the Keeper replied. "Many stand aside on principle. There is no shame in this."

"*Stand aside*?" Morakav shouted. "After our trek, we must *stand aside*? For our losses, we must submit to this indignity? Must we be bullied by those wielding fear?"

"These are terrible times," the Keeper said. "Debates fill every Round. Discord encircles us. Some lash out at shadows."

"We are not shadows!" Hiratak answered, "Our ancestors fought beside yours across Rho-Jashun and Thermistal."

"This is not my decision to make," the Keeper said. "I regret this places you in difficulty."

"No, Keeper," Morakav answered, "It places *you* in difficulty." He gestured to the Rim, where the names of Jutnesh and Zatin resounded. "We lead the initial run! We honour our dead! Our lamentation fills this assembly. Our bucks must be protected. What other purpose does Avanchil Round serve?"

Keeper Datal smiled at them, "Do not mistake me for your enemy. The trials could have preceded the recitation. They did not. None could stop the Lamentation Run now. Once you run, your voice may be heard. Few have openly opposed this new tradition. I advise you to use your position well." His smile was enigmatic as he gestured for them to follow him. The surrounding Suvuka stood on their hind legs as Durka and Makusk Herds moved out of the shelter toward the Lip. Keeper Datal signalled for the two bucks to come to the front and lead the herds down into the vast bowl – with its ancient monuments to Suvuka life and honour – and begin the run.

CHAPTER 17

Shuna-Shapta

Pictured: one of many icons symbolizing the City of Bhampay

Day 119, Two-Week Seven – Kritta, the Body, Master Enclave, City of Bhampay

Shuna-Shapta gazed at the warm peach walls, covered with Masks of Jubilation and Office. Over a year ago, in this same room, her mother had spoken of the growing rebellion in the north. The sweet air and melodious chants from the waking city drifted through the yellow and red lacquer screen. She had worked three separate Living Instruments through the night and sat, exhausted, on a bench watching the chattering cousins on the opposite roof through the screen. She had initially thought to wear one of their House Masks with her siblings to make their gathering more vital. Now she found herself too tired to choose one and left them all on the table before her. Her brother, Shuna-Vurupta, came in and sat down beside her. He placed her head on his beautiful and fragrant shoulder. He was three years her junior. This day she looked older than their mother.

"Shapta!" he said in his breaking voice, "You must go to bed!"

Her two sisters, Shuna-Vovans, at fourteen and Shuna-Samshep, at nine came followed by two house servants bearing trays of cold drinks and a bowl of fruit. The servants withdrew as Shuna-Shapta reached out and pulled a small strand of shed skin off Shuna-Samshep.

"Little! Did you shed again? Shall you ever stop growing?"

Shuna-Samshep grinned and pointed, "Brother Dear also sheds!"

Shuna-Shapta turned to look at her brother. She touched the raised skin on his dark bronze arm, heralding another shedding.

"You all grow!" Shuna-Shapta gave loving looks to each of them. "I regret my training keeps me away."

"You look tired," Shuna-Vovans said.

"I am, and I may not sleep, not until you tell me what I missed. I wish to hear each detail! An entire week has passed since we sat together!"

The two girls before her looked at each other. "Naught has happened," Shuna-Samshep declared.

"Come!" Shuna-Shapta chided her. "What of school? What do you know now that you did not a week ago?" Shuna-Shapta smiled at her youngest sister, "What new animal did you study?"

"The Memanu," Shuna-Samshep declared.

"Memanu?" Shuna-Shapta said, "Please tell us."

Shuna-Samshep, accustomed to these recitations for her siblings, struck the pose of one of her favourite teachers, "Memanu dwell within large colonies between two and four thousand andas either side of the equator. Here upon Statos-Vey, our climate allows them to occur much further south. During the night, the group slumbers within Anu's Flesh. As our Sweet Daymaker rises, each head emerges, followed by a long, elastic trunk. They stretch to an amazing length where their heads open as an immense flower." She made small gestures and raised her piping voice to emphasize each superlative description. "They feed upon the tiny creatures of the high currents and thrive under the Eye of the Gentle Daymaker. Famed for their glorious blossoms and their movements – they assist in weather forecasting."

"Their closest relative . . ." she paused recalling, "they name the Sivist, a tube-shaped creature mostly dwelling upon Thermistal. It lives a very different life feeding amongst, and sometimes upon, the huge trees they have there."

She paused again, and her siblings waited, "The Chelyaka believers worshipped the Memanu during prehistoric times," she said. "They believed Anu was a hollow sphere with all life living upon the inner surface. They believed the Memanu reached toward others planted upon the far side of the inner sphere. According to the Hathnal religion, they were messengers from Anu's Flesh to Nu. They and those believing in Tuchulacha attached petitions and offerings to their trunk as they rose at dawn. Menem's followers believed them refuges for the invisible exiles from their mythical realm of Ranvartawan, who they claimed floated about the opened blossoms."

Shuna-Shapta and the others laughed and applauded Shuna-Samshep. She gave them an exaggerated bow in return.

"Shapta?" Shuna-Samshep asked, "Have you ever seen the Memanu?"

"Once," Shuna-Shapta said, "Did I not tell you? I was . . . Vovans' age and we travelled to the south. I may not now recall why none of you joined us. We saw a field of them rising and stopped to watch them. Their towering beauty amazed us as a strong wind blew, and they lived up to their title of 'Glorious Swaying Ones.' I have yet to return at dawn to savour their sweet rising."

Shuna-Shapta turned to the second youngest, Shuna-Vovans, "What happened this past week, Flair?"

The thirteen-year-old's dramatically dark eyes rolled. "Preparations for next year's Alatahanu Carnival are *frenetic*!" Her musical voice delighted her siblings as it danced across the chamber walls. "I mix paints, and they said I could help work upon the Faces!"

Shuna-Shapta laughed, "Already? More than one hundred days stand between Mid-year and us. How many do you make?"

"Oh, we plan *thousands and thousands* for Bhampay. Other cities do the same. All shall forget this past carnival!"

"Hum . . ." Shuna-Shapta said as her eyebrows rose, "I have heard this many times. Although with our Twelve Principal Faces fully revealed, you now have a mighty template. Shall you work upon particular ones?"

"I shall help with each, but I hope to do most upon my favourites, Neferdush and Kava-Kura," she looked a little embarrassed, "What do they do?"

"Neferdush presents the Face of Tatchlan's perception," Shuna-Shapta replied. "She smells the living patterns and connections between disparate elements."

"I love her grand eyes and long shining nose!" Shuna-Vovans declared as Shuna-Samshep nodded.

"Yes," Shuna-Shapta said, "within Tatchlan, her nose has the power to perceive. Kava-Kura is also a favourite of mine. As our Face of Vital Delight, Kava-Kura embodies the deepest form of life – a Complete. Shehe oversees each manifestation of joy and contentment within our Grand Work."

"I love her long, long tongue!" Shuna-Samshep exclaimed in her piping voice. They all laughed as she stuck hers out and down in an attempt to mimic Kava-Kura.

Shuna-Vovans became sober, and her eyes went wide as she asked, "Shapta . . . you have beheld the living Neferdush and Kava-Kura?"

Her siblings grew quiet as Shuna-Shapta looked at them, "We deal with their Secondary Faces, who are their servants. Thus far, we have been within the presence of half of our Twelve Principal Faces orbiting our Living Orb. They are majestic, sublime and terrifying. We have yet to behold Kava-Kura. We have witnessed the towering form of Neferdush," she paused, "Their immensity exudes the collective power of generations of Masters. Despite their magnitude, as the many smaller Secondary Faces, they give gentle and mild service."

The younger girls approached and placed their hands on her knees. Shuna-Vurupta put his arm around her. "You fill us with awe, as our First and Second Amas, do. Your work shall help us for the rest of history!"

They sat in silence until Shuna-Shapta turned to her brother, "And, how does our most beautiful lad acquit himself?"

The other two girls grew hushed and turned to look at him. Shuna-Shapta smelled tension between them. Shuna-Vurupta braced himself. "We study the Suvuka," he began.

Shuna-Shapta frowned, "They start early with you. We waited another year for a full examination of this horror."

Shuna-Vurupta frowned in turn at her comment, "More reports come concerning their keeper's work. They say they begin to approach possible solutions to the Suvuka's enduring resistance to us."

"Please forgive my skepticism," Shuna-Shapta began, but she stopped and signalled for him to continue.

Shuna-Vurupta glanced at the plaster cast of the Suvuka paw on the wall, "The school plans to take a group across the Panchala to see them."

"What?" Shuna-Shapta exclaimed in alarm. The other girls jumped at her reaction.

"Ama knows!" he said. "She has not decided."

"Decided?" Shuna-Shapta cried out incredulously.

"They have a museum with displays showing their life. We shall visit their observation tunnels within the walls and hear those working upon them. Many try to comprehend them, so, one day, we shall stop fearing them."

Shuna-Shapta recalled Suvuka the play they saw together over a year ago. She then had visions of the Suvuka in the terrible mid-layer of Indatubangas and shook her head vigorously. She looked into his eyes. "Vurupta, do you . . . wish to behold a Suvuka?"

He nodded.

"Why?" She pointed at the cast of the paw print. "Look at the size of this! Many uncounted thousands of our grandmothers, and their mothers, suffered and died under them. They murdered any amongst them who wished to make peace with us. They slaughtered entire companion races and now stand alone amid their kind. Why look at these beasts?"

Shuna-Vurupta sat frowning as his three sisters watched him. He looked at the paw print, "We Tolku did much beyond the necessary." He glanced at the other three as he continued, "Many risk much to better comprehend ourselves and Anu's Flesh. Look at you, Shapta! You struggle through the night to better serve as a full Invocant. I am unable to follow you. You, and our two Amas, stride down this powerful and dangerous path for our benefit. We must make our way and do what we may. I told Ama, I consider going and helping with the Suvuka. Our Masters direct the labour to alter them. I wish to observe their endeavour prior to deciding if I wish to join them."

Shuna-Shapta sat in stunned silence. "You map this out with care, suggesting an extended intention."

Shuna-Vurupta nodded, "I meant to tell you. I told our mothers a few two-weeks ago when the trip was announced. I had considered it for at least a year when they told us of the Thermistal Masters studying the Suvuka."

"My dear, we have managed to hear something of Thermistal. Quite apart from the Suvuka, I am convinced it remains a wicked wilderness completely unsuitable to such a fine gentleman as you! The Tolku population forms a grim protectorate composed of ministry engineers and the army, where hundreds of garrisons contain them all behind their western wall. I believe our Masters are but a tiny minority of its inhabitants. The majority of those who come to serve for five to ten-year stints do not reapply. Regardless of station, those having children during service ever dispatch them home to be raised and educated. To my knowledge, there is not one school for children born in all of Thermistal. We are told the army has ever offered a choice between an adequate pension upon Statos-Vey, and a generous land grant upon Thermistal to those few continuing to retirement age. Through all the generations maintaining the Vettencore Passage, I believe just a small minority remain. One may ponder how any elegance or refinement could be cultivated among this unfortunate population within such a raw wilderness. Whilst traders form a lifeline for these benighted communities with services and goods from home, of necessity, they also mount excursions inland only to return with frightful tales and new diseases. To name just two, the north is a frozen waste, and their eastern deserts contain horrifying predators. Were it not for our Muraharoma Dynasty's heavy investment and support, just a handful of criminals and maniacs would remain." She stopped herself, "Our First and Second Amas said this?"

Her brother seemed puzzled before saying, "They have told me what they have learned."

"My apologies." She took his hand as she took a steadying breath. "When does this excursion depart?"

"We intended on day 271, but the quota was full. Another ship leaves upon day 415 during the two-week of Drostol."

She stared at him in amazement, "They time this trip to begin upon the day of the 'Two-Week of Double Perfection' or 'Triple Perfection?'"

"They said it was 'an auspicious time to begin new ventures.'"

"Listen to yourself!" Shuna-Shapta shouted. "Those dates mean naught! They remain one of the innumerable senseless traditions continued without anyone knowing why! The school determines this foolhardy venture based upon 'auspicious' dates?"

She rose and strode toward the door, "Where is Ama?" she shouted back to them.

"Here," Master Kanla said. Shuna-Shapta stopped short of running into her as she entered the room.

"I heard your raised voice and arrived a moment ago unheeded," Master Kanla said.

"Vurupta's expedition," Shuna-Shapta began, her voice quaking. "Is this how an accredited school chooses the date for their departure?"

"Not the school," Master Kanla replied, "they hired a company ferrying those sailing to Thermistal and back. Naval traditions do surround certain dates to launch particular ventures. Considering how long the trip takes, know many other factors are weighed prior to the ships leaving port. Crossings occur each two-week and many other dates are possible."

Shuna-Shapta stared disbelieving at her mother, "You approve of his voluntarily approaching these monsters?"

"Shuna-Dana and I have not made our final decision. We consult other mothers and local authorities. These excursions have run for over a year without incident. Vurupta mentions a museum. Perchance you have not heard of the 'Duamang Museum of Suvuka Studies.' It is one of the largest and most respected teaching museums upon all Anu. It stands upon the southwestern shore, where our Vettencore empties into the Panchala Sea. I may not recount all its features, but the students would spend much of their time within its expansive education facility. The museum also contains a vast collection of specimens for them to examine. Your description of Thermistal life appears based upon incomplete information. It neither does sufficient credit to what has been achieved there nor the dedication of many professions necessary to raise and maintain what must be acknowledged as an impressive set of institutions. I assure you there is a settled population living upon Southern Thermistal beyond their service, albeit a modest and disbursed one by our standards. The raw resources of this vast hinterland alone ensure this settlement of Thermistal is just begun. We understand one well-supervised expedition, minutely arranged by the museum, crosses the passage to secure viewing locations upon a regular timetable."

"I . . . I had not heard of this."

"Your profound work has eclipsed much these past few years. When it opened, you were racing through your Devotee and Commencement Delver levels and had no time for outside news."

"This museum . . . named after our exemplary liberator . . . means it is Master founded?"

"Master founded and Master run, with the blessings of our Imperial House. A sizeable population of our Thermistal Masters openly stand as its directors. Our Muraharoma Dynasty places great store in their work. As you know, we have been deep within our Imperium's counsels upon many matters."

"Including the disposition of our army along the Vettencore Passage? Was I mistaken in what we have heard about their hard life?"

"Your source quite overstated their case. Thermistal has certainly proven a harsh land. Yet, our forces are largely fed from rich Salarish fields tended by settled farmers about Lake Teval, the largest fresh-water lake upon Anu. The 'Lake Teval Basin' contains some of the most bountiful farmland upon all Anu. All wood used by our protectorate originates within the immense forests filling the western portion of the continent surrounding the Viracocha Mountain chain. As I have said, Thermistal is rich in all necessary resources for these emerging populations. Statos-Vey now benefits from a growing commerce in plain and exotic goods from what had ever been a dark continent to us. You know this Enclave already has several living amenities from this trade. Business in these raw assets requires adequate infrastructure over vast distances, which was well in place prior to the first settlements. Unlike the chaos of Rho-Jashun's resettlement long ago, I assure you the roads were paved, the stations lit, and our Secretariat and other ministries well established within completed structures upon Central and Western Thermistal prior to the first settler's arrival. The feared Tharapura Ocean, known as the Black Maid, does blight its northern extent with extreme cold much of the year. There are more active volcanoes upon Thermistal than anywhere else upon Anu. It is true – its three vast deserts do house terrible beasts beyond our nightmares."

"So many do choose to live there?"

"Compared to densely-populated Statos-Vey . . . or even Rho-Jashun? No. You are correct that a majority finish their work terms and sail for home. Whilst Bhampay has extensive trade links, we know little of this city's involvement in Thermistal's development. I once had a brief conversation within Tatchlan with a Thermistal Master suggesting to me they maintain a modest habitation for a variety of reasons. She said the current population distribution and densities, and significant turnover, suit well their many designs. Given certain unfortunate actions by small groups of soldiers acting against orders, our Masters have become the Suvuka's guardians against wanton abuse. They remain committed to the eventual harmonizing between us and these creatures, who are far more than simple 'beasts.'

Shuna-Shapta went back and sat down in silence. She turned to look at her brother, "I would request your pardon," she began. She looked to her mother, "We have looked upon them . . ." tears filled her eyes, and her mother knelt in front of her and cupped her daughter's face in her hands. Master Kanla looked at the other children.

"Your sister is exhausted," she said. "She so wished to see you."

"Ama," Shuna-Vurupta whispered, "I should have chosen another time. I anticipated her wonder, but did not imagine this."

Master Kanla nodded, "In a way, she has come closer to the Suvuka than you ever could."

Shuna-Shapta slowly stood. They all embraced each other and their mother in silence.

CHAPTER 18

Seti

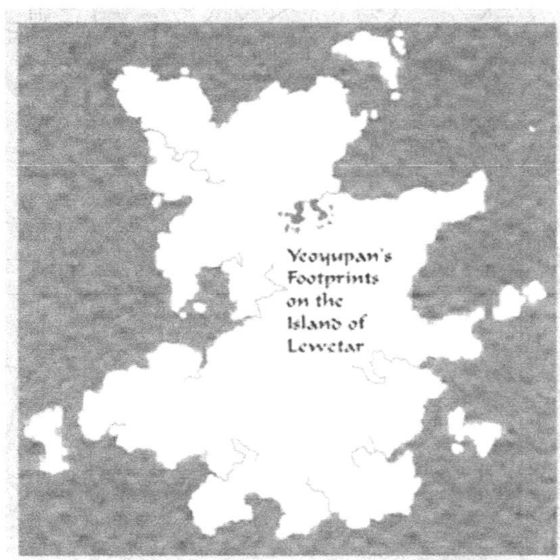

Day 219, Two-Week Thirteen – Rakal, the Basket, southern coast of Statos-Vey

The Jefaka continued its journey down the erratic southern coast of Statos-Vey. As he did in his initial few two-weeks on board, Seti seldom left the ship. Hegev regimented his days. He followed a strict schedule of study, discussion, various meditative exercises, and ancient mental puzzles of the kind Adepts commonly gave their pupils. She encouraged other members of the crew with the skills to teach him. Seti began playing the four-stringed musical instrument called the Haklu, and a long flute fashioned out of the long sounding hollow found on the back of the Danta's head, to round out his education. He particularly liked the flute, which he managed to persuade to give off such gentle and elegant tones. Hegev also began to introduce him to other works from the Jefaka's singular library. She and Captain Emedin worked out a regime of ship duties above his occasional work as a Dream Reader.

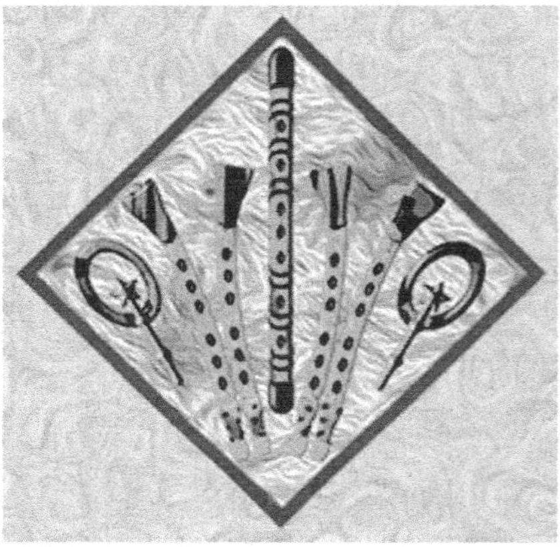

Danta musical instruments icon

She learned knot tying had become an essential activity for him, whenever he was disturbed or anxious. She encouraged him to strengthen his ability in tying shipping knots. In doing so, his arms grew strong, and his hands tough and calloused. In the many two-weeks since she began to instruct him, he became a proficient reader. He read the entire Daruadunnal, including its many descriptions of the battles between the Kovlah and Menem. He also learned of Zitapermas, the largest contributor to the Daruadunnal. He was an ancient Tolku waking one day to hear the imprisoned Menem inside him. The being of light's voice filled his waking hours and sung in his dreams.

In time, it introduced him to one of the four Grand Menem, Vindaviran, 'the Teacher.' Vindaviran instructed him in detail concerning the realm of Ranvartawan and how Menem became imprisoned in 'bags of flesh.' He learned of the large numbers of Menem surrounding the four generals of the air. The majority were the Sedet, the Servants; a smaller number were the Sev or Messengers. When Hegev arrived, Seti wanted to discuss whether he should undergo the process of binding to himself a lifelong guide, be it Sedet or Sev, to enhance his abilities. Captain Emedin requested that Hegev forestall this process and instead introduce him to the extensive commentaries for the Daruadunnal and Furrumittal. He would have begun studying this material in school at his age if they were back in Wazaratcha. These cooled his fires as he found them more challenging than the original texts. They opened the originals in ways he had not imagined. Portions of those texts were incomplete, and it was clear that different hands edited the final documents.

He found himself forced to note fundamental contradictions between the Daruadunnal and the Furrumittal. One detailed the Menem of the air and their ongoing struggle. The other gave strict instructions for each Aspirant to enter Ranvartawan after their body's death. If they knew how to leave, why was the air full of Menem? He recalled how the Grand Menem vowed to wait until every Menem was free. Why did others stay? He also read the original epic poem 'The Yeoyupan.' He recalled the edited and modified version of the play he and Dine watched almost a year ago on Tich-Tushmul. This led to a cacophony of questions brewing in his mind.

"This poem says Yeoyupan came and stood on the island of Lewetar," Seti said one morning to his Adept. They sat near the prow, "His footprints sank into the ground. It says pilgrims go to view them."

"Yes," Hegev answered.

"Have you?"

"I have not been to Thermistal. When I was but a maid, many family members and friends answered the call to join public works to complete the Vettencore Passage. The Suvuka's defeat and banishment had been accomplished many centuries earlier. Still, these famed fortifications required millennia to approach completion. None of them went to the Grand Lake. Seven years before I left on my journey, three left for Thermistal on pilgrimage for their Warm Rewards. They did go to the island of Lewetar and returned to regale us with their adventures and brought strange tokens purchased at the site."

Seti frowned, "Zitapermas is emphatic in his declarations the Kovlah fell and were born as Suvuka."

"Yes."

"And when the Suvuka called Yeoyupan, he came down and called them the true children of Anu."

"Yes."

Seti stood and gathered two long coils of rope and began to fashion elaborate knots. Hegev knew to wait for his questions.

"We are told the events of The Yeoyupan took place long ago before any Tolku visited Thermistal," Seti began.

"Yes, the Suvuka possessed Thermistal and we Rho-Jashun and Statos-Vey. The Suvuka had no ships to come south to us. We had numerous accounts of monsters and ships lost, along with many traditional proscriptions against 'going north' to that continent."

Seti looked long at his Adept as he engaged in an internal battle. "I now understand," he began. "The works we study are compilations of earlier works augmented by far more recent authors. The notion of the Suvuka as the embodiment of the fallen Kovlah, servants of Yeoyupan, was written after they invaded Rho-Jashun."

Hegev also stood and watched him. "Yes, Seti, this is true. These beliefs helped the Tolku of the day fight them."

"Many of the great libraries built by the Buyanupithar Dynasty were in northern Rho-Jashun, the grandest in their imperial capital of Thithanu" he continued. "Many more were attached to the forty-four Menem Shrines of the Marachla Plain. The Suvuka destroyed every one."

Hegev nodded at his statement. Seti's hands worked furiously, "The Daruadunnal and Furrumittal Commentaries contradict each other on many things. This includes the origin and nature of the Kovlah and whether or not those falling to Anu became Suvuka. The later Furrumittal describes the Menem as our 'vital inner selves.' At the same time, Zitapermas said his Menem was a distinct being inside him. If so, when he died was Zitapermas, as his inner Menem's 'disease-ridden cocoon,' simply cast off? My father cherished the notion of passing through the one hundred gates as a cleansed version of *himself*. I marvel how he could read Zitapermas and not be troubled by this contradiction. Our captain told me the wise of Anu discount all the Daruadunnal and much of the Furrumittal. I fear I am growing in this wisdom."

His Adept frowned and nodded in sympathy at his dilemma.

"When I read the Yeoyupan," Seti continued, "it is as if I read the descriptions of those witnessing the event." Seti frowned as he continued to tie a series of knots along the length of the ropes. "If no Tolku were present, on what is this account-based?"

Hegev stared at him. A complex series of emotions formed and passed over her face.

"It says the Suvuka called Yeoyupan down from Ranvartawan, and he stood on the island of Lewetar," Seti continued. "The Suvuka came from across Thermistal and stood around the shores of Lake Teval. They saw him wherever they stood. His head was above the clouds, and he had to brush them away as mist. The Suvuka filled the Teval flood plain to the Silvasora Mountains in the west and Mandeca Mountains in the east. Given when this supposedly took place, the Tolku and Suvuka were largely ignorant of each other. It is said the Suvuka sing long songs but write no books. How can we know of their beliefs or they of ours if we cannot communicate with each other? If the Suvuka did not write the Yeoyupan, who was the author?"

Hegev bent her head, "Your captain will be pleased." She went over to the railing, looking out on a calm ocean. She meditated on its blueness before turning back and saying, "You should ask the Generals of the Air."

"I have."

"And their answer?"

"Vindaviran said they could only tell me what I am ready to hear. If they wait until I learn it elsewhere, they give me nothing I cannot find without them."

He worked on an elaborate configuration. Where the various knots formed a series, he joined at either end in an intricate loop. He drew closer and whispered, "As I learn more, they diminish! Their speech grows garbled! My last two invocations had little or no reference to anything they said. What the crew heard were my own predictions, unaided by them."

Hegev gave him a long and thoughtful look, "Why did you not mention this?"

"I feared you would be angry. The crew knows the Generals, subject to the ever-shifting winds, are inconstant. Our captain does not believe and ever tries to guide me away from them. I did not know how you would react."

"No, child. I am a little sad, perhaps but not angry." She stroked his rough sailor's cheek. She stepped away and leaned against the railing facing him. "While there is wisdom in the treasuring of faith, it is foolish to venerate innocence. Children lack knowledge and experience. While not wholly subscribing to their view, I must admit these masters are right in only counting full adults as 'ripe.' It is futile to hold onto notions of naive virtue. To what do we ascribe clear evidence of childhood malice? Such notions of blameless ignorance is as 'dust on the wind.' I had not expected you to grow so soon in this way. Despite his humble education, your father was an able teacher. If we approach this, it will be in a different light."

"What do you mean?"

"You are ageing beyond your years, and grow over these traditions. Comfort and assurance are the benefits of less sophisticated minds. While not the same, you and I originated in similarly backward settings. We of 'penetrating eyes,' observe what others with lesser wit and imagination miss. It is also true that those having the opportunity to travel over Anu's Face, often grow out of these soothing local conventions. You demonstrate this. Most of the simple and devout in the north would never question the authorship of the Yeoyupan. It not occur to them to even ask."

With incredible speed and skill, Seti untied the fantastic configuration of knots. He worked until he dropped the two long ropes at his feet. "Our Captain does not believe and watches me with concern," he looked at Hegev, "I had thought you steadfast in your faith."

"I am," she said, "The question is not one of faith, but its articles. There is an ancient saying, 'Dirt sticks to sap.' It means much becomes attached to something desirable - obscuring it all together. I believe deep wisdom is found within our tradition; it is the sap gleaming through the jumbled debris covering it. You know Sawlu Clan's first patron was named Nallurakon. Her hands were tattooed as yours in readiness to take the Aspirant's path through the One Hundred Gates. In her day, many here in the south had already begun to turn away from the tradition. The literal teachings had already become foolish in their eyes. This is the stage you are reaching now. I understand how it may be both exhilarating and demoralizing. Our knowledge of Anu has increased beyond the modest imaginings of the ancients. The most sophisticated of the Menem Hierarchy in the ancient capital of Thithanu had begun to construct a theology to meet these new ideas. They were interrupted by the Suvuka Onslaught. No more than one hundred of the Tertiary Level of the Menem Priesthood and their servants survived the pillage of Rho-Jashun. The senior levels of what was once a far more advanced faith-based society perished. It was inevitable the institutions faltered and we are left with a rump of a once glorious tradition."

Seti leaned over and picked up the two ropes. He began a more convoluted configuration. "What are your 'articles of faith?'" he asked.

Hegev smiled at him, "They are growing! What we study is of tremendous value. It contains a rich tapestry of ancient wisdom; it is our doorway to our ancient life. The writings of Nallurakon and your captain's favourite, Nebutan, are far more sophisticated. They assume a level of education common here but rare in our homeland." She frowned, "True knowledge is difficult. It is composed of a multitude of parts and cannot be stated in simple terms. By nature of its complexity, it leaves less educated minds behind. If we cannot enlighten them in many serious matters, are we to condemn them to have no comfort in the face of life's confusion and misery? This is the service these texts, and many of the common rituals and magical beliefs, provide. I will ever promote their worth. I am delighted to give you a better appreciation of them. They also form the foundation of later song and literature enriching our speech and turns of phrase. They fashion how we view Anu and each other."

She lowered her voice, "For those leading the simple, beyond affirming assuring traditions, there is no value in foolish tales. For us, there is inestimable value in holding to our foundational beliefs. Our concern is with the 'sap' at the core. This includes our certainty in an afterlife and our being set apart from all other life on Anu. These truths remain when fables fade away," Seti had created an extraordinary work of art where a bundle of knots stood at either end with the two ropes connecting them.

He assessed this fanciful creation before looking at Hegev, "So . . . you do not believe Yeoyupan stood on the island of Lewetar?"

"The epic poem titled 'Yeoyupan' is a glorious work. It was visionary of the ancients to include it within the Daruadunnal. The appreciation for the truth found in inspired art, beyond the story it portrays, is one definition of wisdom. I assure you as you age, you will find more of value with each reading, or theatrical rendering, as it sinks deeper into your maturing mind. Such is the hallmark of true art."

Seti frowned, "I come back to my question, how could they write anything concerning Thermistal or the Suvuka?"

Hegev smiled and went over to a recess in the wall where they kept the volumes Seti studied. She brought out a small book he had not seen. She found a page covered in drawings and handed it to him, "This is a newer edition of another ancient text surviving the Suvuka. It is far older than the Daruadunnal!"

Seti hooked his creation over one arm and stared at the rendition of the two immense feet found on the island. Their fantastic proportions near filled Lewetar.

"Early in the Muraharoma Dynasty," Hegev began, "explorers and traders, fuelled by bravado and the promise of wealth, defied the ancient religious proscriptions against venturing beyond the known world. Many sailed around Anu and mapped its complete contours. Eventually, they began bringing back stories of surviving encounters with the Suvuka. At the same time, there were several recorded instances of partial Suvuka bodies being washed ashore along Rho-Jashun's northern coast. Some suggest these represented their first failed attempts to cross the Panchala Sea. Too many examined them and circulated renditions to be suppressed by the authorities. Few original copies of that book now exist due to it becoming censored. These events caused terrible divisions to open up in this society that contributed to the near outbreak of civil war. When the Suvuka finally began to make their crossing in numbers, most were still unprepared. Those drawings reproduce others made during a famous expedition sailing down what we now call the Bellechin River and Lake Teval. This sweeping setting for the Yeoyupan myth is the largest fresh-water lake on Anu. The explorers landed on the large island of Lewetar in the northern portion of the lake and travelled across it. The Suvuka used this island for rituals during specific times of the year. It was surmised they believed it a holy place set apart, and so it was not occupied by the creatures year-round. Fortunately, these explorers landed during one of those times. During their travels across this island, they encountered a multitude of Suvuka monuments. They also discovered these striking formations. It was clear the Suvuka venerated these as many of their works surrounded them. The explorers brought back those drawings and colourful descriptions. This one is the most fanciful, and therefore popular. The others are more accurate as to their dimensions. These stories provided the basis for the poem."

"What of the footprints?"

Hegev hesitated, "Dear boy! There is nothing gained from basing faith on foolishness! They are *not* footprints! They are two immense depressions in the ground appearing, from certain viewpoints, as giant footprints. Were it not for many crevasses on all sides and a river flowing from these interior highlands draining water away; they would be two deep lakes. These natural formations are the source of the epic! Those three I knew travelling to Lewetar in recent years came from two camps. Two were simple, devout brothers, declaring they saw Yeoyupan's toe prints. The third confided to me she had to use her imagination to find any resemblance to footprints."

Seti stared at the pages of drawings and flipped through the book then gave it back to her, "Why do those living near these depressions perpetuate the epic?"

Hegev laughed out loud, "Look around you! In the ports, you witnessed every possible shade of commerce. Teeming populations busy their lives with their little dramas and and profound life struggles. You mentioned the body fed to the Bowvow Tree; there will be a thriving industry providing mourners with those pallets and decorations. The tree creature expels them, and they are refurbished for reuse. Many families are fed by the services provided for this one ritual, down to the hawkers pestering the mourners. Those living near the 'feet' of Yeoyupan are the epic's most devoted exponents. It gives them the means to flourish. The theatre performing the epic and other dramas serves the same purpose.

Since the expulsion of the Suvuka, an entire community of Tolku has grown and thrives there. They separate themselves from the protectorate. Few officials deal with them, and most commerce passes them by. Outside of faith communities, most Tolku are unaware of their existence. I hear life is sparse and bitter in this region, and the pilgrims bring some small relief. I am told in these times, their continued survival is in doubt. This illustrates a significant reason many traditions persist, in particular rites associated with a place. They benefit the specific populations who maintain and promote them."

Seti began to untie his rope creation with the same ease he tied it. He frowned in concentration, and Hegev waited.

"When you came on board," he said, "you presented yourself as a 'simple devout' on pilgrimage."

"It was not the time to unwrap each aspect of my life. Your captain and I had spoken. She understood my position well enough to recommend me to you. She said most who answered her call were either wildly unsuitable or not up to the task. She said I was the best candidate she had seen."

Seti had begun another bizarre knot creation as he spoke. "Why did you travel across the face of Anu on pilgrimage? Are these Menem Shrines also a source of income to surrounding communities?"

"I have sat and wept in their ruins!" Hegev wrung her hands. "There is no profit for surrounding populations in maintaining them because no pilgrims visit. Which came first, I cannot say, but they seem doomed to dishonourable decay and destruction."

"Why is their fate of concern to you?"

"Because memory is precious!" Hegev raised her voice. "What are we without our memories? What are the Tolku without our history? If you do not gain a deeper appreciation of the history behind the present, present-day events are random and senseless. Show me someone ignorant of history, and I will show you someone who is *ignorant*! Forgetting yesterday leads to blindness today. How can we comprehend why we stand here if we do not recall our preceding steps?" She pointed to the deck, "How can such a senseless population proceed in any direction?"

Seti was startled at her sudden passion. "So, you travelled this far out of respect for our past?"

"My boy, I declare to you my most profound truth! I would counsel saying nothing to your captain of this. There is wisdom in pilgrimages and shrines Nebutan never dreamt of! These ancient volumes are rich in many ways. They speak and give comfort to those unable to follow the great teachers. The same is true of works of devotion made of stone, the many little daily rituals before modest house shrines, and the larger festivals. Monuments and traditions built to console the troubled and unsure deserve better!"

She looked up to the sky and took a breath, "Seti, as I have said many times, there is still sap beneath this jumble," she indicated their books. "It is the distillation of the childhood of our kind, and so is the 'memory' of all Tolku. Our desire for transcendence has taken many missteps. The ancients were not wrong to aspire to life beyond foul flesh. Despite the admitted hubris and folly of the ancient Menem priesthoods, I believe our faith remains a noble one. While Anu is full of dead religions, Menem has endured! Do not allow your newfound skepticism to blind you to the precious gifts you have been given! It is possible to discern real truth about 'who we are' from our ancestors. We can do this despite their ignorance of much we have since learned. I believe your Menem attendants are not remote from you. They are here! You are the one pushing them away. Your ears have turned from them to the noise of Anu! I believe what others see as an illness is, in fact, your unfolding powers. By all means, fortify yourself with knowledge, but your true wisdom will come from within."

Seti frowned in concentration as he renewed his efforts. For a long time, he said nothing as he worked. When he finally spoke, his enquiry was surprising, "If the Suvuka had not destroyed the shrines on Rho-Jashun, our native Tolku might appreciate them?"

"I believe they would be better treated and appreciated on Rho-Jashun, yes. As it stands, we are left only the decaying Suvuka Rounds built over them."

"And if the Tatchlan masters had not succeeded here, where the Suvuka never came, the twenty Menem Shrines of Statos-Vey would be better attended?"

Hegev laughed and shook her head, "You grasp the ironies of our situation."

Seti completed his third outlandish knot sculpture and appraised it, "From what I have seen and learned, I would say we Tolku are adrift." He set down his knot and went over to stand with her looking out at the vast sea.

Hegev turned to look out. "We have drifted since the Suvuka and now approach an unknown port. The old order falters, and in its place, a new one rises. This Tatchlan will dwarf the ambitions of the ancients. If they are successful, life will be transformed. If they proposed a new philosophy or belief, I would not object, but they dream of altering Anu's face! They employ the fundamental needs for immediate security and distant glory as the foundation for a new type of being." She asked in a near whisper, "Do you see the Faces?"

He nodded, "They follow me and many call my name. Twelve large ones grow stronger and fill my view. Smaller and less wild ones rise out of the ground. They are like bizarre theatre masks, yet they live. I learned of my Menem Generals from ancient texts. These beings arise without introduction and assert themselves on my inner landscape."

They stood in silence. At last, Hegev said, "Do they disturb your sleep?"

He shook his head, "I waken to fleeting memories of long discourses with one or more of these Faces but cannot recall what I said."

Hegev stood amazed. "We must bring forward an aspect of your training. In many ways, you diverge from the path I envisioned."

Seti frowned as he continued to look out over the broad expanse of restless waves, "I am no longer confident of my direction. While your guidance has opened much understanding, my confusion continues to rage." He paused, "When we saw the Slaying Canopy, sucking all birds out of the sky, I realized life contained dreadful expanses beyond any childhood imaginings. Had I remained in Yeplin, at peace in my innocence, I would still sleep soundly at night. Had I been content with watching my Menem, in glowing white garb singing in the trees, these Faces might not have found me. In a mere two years, I have gone from wild certainty to timorous hesitation."

"Seti, your Menem did not just sing to you back in Yeplin. They also spoke. What did they say in full?"

He stared out at the waters for a long time, "They said I must 'remind the Tolku of who they are.'"

"So we agree the Tolku are adrift," she said, indicating the ship. "Recovering what is lost and forgotten is difficult. I suggest chief among these losses is 'who we are.' You see the distortion in the faces of those under Tatchlan."

Seti did not answer but nodded his head.

"Along with other reasons, I kept you on the ship because, until we sail back into Rho-Jashun waters, those faces will predominate. To see them gives you pain. I cannot see as you. Yet, I believe you begin to comprehend what those distortions mean. The Tolku are remade into something new. Do you suffer any confusion as to the unnatural wrongness of this?"

His lips formed a grim line, and he shook his head.

"Seti, your level of fixed concentration is beyond most adults. Have patience." They continued to stand looking out at the waters, "There is one thing you should experience on the mainland, far from populated centres. We draw near it soon."

"What?"

She smiled at him, "A field of waking Memanu."

CHAPTER 19

SHUNA-SHAPTA

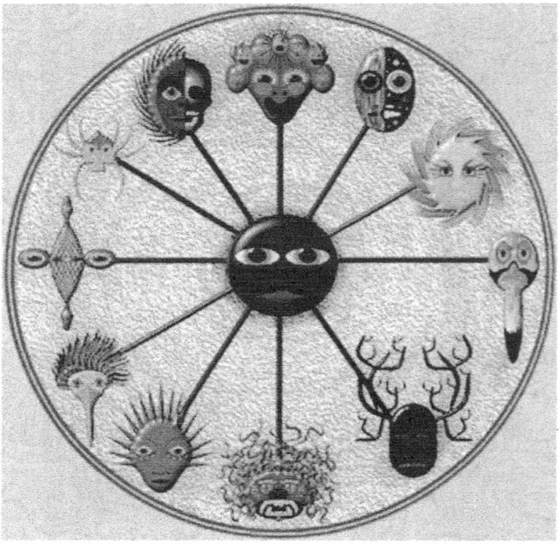

Pictured: Icon of the Twelve Primary Faces of Tatchlan in Wheel Formation.

Day 225, Two-Week Thirteen – Rakal, the Basket, Master Enclave, Bhampay

One hundred?" Shuna-Shapta stared in amazement. Their carriage's wheels squeaked as they turned in well-worn ruts in the roadway while continuing along a rough side street. Outside its etched patterned glass windows, yet another one of Bhampay's torrential downpours did not indicate slowing its assault on the drenched city. Inside, the carriage's excellent suspension system and plush cushioning transmuted the outer roughness into gentle rocking. The interior was overlaid in aromatic woods of various colours incised with swirling patterns and tiny figures appearing to take exercise in a gymnasia. These woods and finishes gave off an antique aroma.

"One hundred!" her mother, Master Kanla, answered in the half-light of the carriage, "Reports continue to tell of small numbers of Maja born within other urban clusters throughout Statos-Vey. This surge within the past year far outstrips your generation of treasured Maja and those preceding us. What was a rarity is now becoming commonplace! Now circles grow animated with the budding of all Spokes of our Cluster Wheel. 'Betweens,' 'Completes,' 'Dreamers,' they all manifest about us. Other young women of your age are now turning their first pregnancy into another manifestation of Tatchlan, as Doubles. There are now more treasured Doubles with their healing blood within this city than there were Masters a century ago!"

She paused and shook her head, "By their copious aromas, these infant Maja already complete these emerging clusters and solidify their Circles of Eight by unconsciously providing their vital 'Scent Anchor.' Our Aroma Accords begin to manifest in full and solidify our growing harmony beyond our Enclaves. Our Bhampay has the largest concentrated population of these new clusters, with our capital Upata-Shepsus close behind. This day the one-hundredth Maja of this year is born here. Many more shall be born across Statos-Vey during the succeeding few two-weeks. The sudden arrival of our first Majastas, who our grandmothers and their mothers calculated could not take place without a critical mass of Maja surrounding her, shakes our dreams into waking reality."

"We witnessed the birth of our infant Majastas within Thakadush Cluster," Shuna-Shapta mused. "They shall have celebrated her first birthday by now."

"Oh yes, it was Two-Week Paultesh, during Day 163."

"Has Thakadush Cluster had many Maja children?"

Her mother laughed, "Fifty-three!"

"Fifty-three? I recall perchance . . . one hundred adults were attending. Surely this far exceeds one Maja to root each Circle of Eight to their Cluster."

"This number surpasses this basic need. Since this tiny Majastas birth, each Ripe Adult woman and Complete of Thakadush 'grows big.' Most have given birth to twins and triplets – each of them Maja. Many are Maja and other Spokes of the Cluster Wheel within one body. Again, Thakadush amazes us! We had not thought to behold such combined emissaries of Tatchlan during our brief spans. No other cluster contains this marvel, further distinguishing Thakadush. Conceptions continue to multiply there, and the compound expands to the courtyard in front of the Companion Avenue. We assist them with land purchases and permissions. The ancient colonnade of fish now forms a grand walkway to Thakadush, and the Companion Pond graces their entrance."

"How do the surrounding neighbourhoods react?"

"Their education began years ago. Members of Thakadush enact the gestures and symbols long embedded within our general population. Our Masters agree the result goes beyond satisfactory. Once all these Maja reach adulthood, their powerful Aromas shall ensure the gradual transformation of the surrounding communities into new clusters producing their own Maja to enliven their circles and clusters."

"Thakadush now has fifty-three Maja, half of those born within our city?"

Her mother nodded, "This day, they shall have fifty-four."

"This is more than half of all of Bhampay's Maja. Do any other of our clusters possess such effusive numbers of Maja?"

"Naught comparable. One now has eight Maja newborns, itself a glorious population by the standards of just a decade ago. At present, the rest have at most two per Cluster, meaning thus far they have only two genuine Circles of Eight. Most circles still await their completion with a Maja."

Shuna-Shapta frowned, "*All* Thakadush Cluster's new children are Maja? And many of these are also Completes and Dreamers?"

Master Kanla nodded.

"What may this mean? The cluster system requires just one Maja per Circle of Eight. Whilst more than eight percent Maja per Cluster signifies vitality, I understood this should be the norm."

"With one single . . . and most notable exception."

"So there may be no doubt. Despite being an unripe pre-adult, Thakadush-Satwa builds a Majastas Cluster around Herself!" She frowned at her mother, "Why do I smell such distressed aromas from Masters concerning these developments?"

Master Kanla sighed, "This sudden upsurge of Tatchlan finds Masters struggling to follow. The orderly setting we knew prior to this 'Quickening' is gone. Our well-worn paths have vanished within this swirling landscape, appearing to expand beneath our feet. This is but one of many developments radically departing from our expectations. How could we prepare for these unprecedented circumstances?"

"I am innocent of what unfolds within our city," Shuna-Shapta said, "I have spent most waking hours within Tatchlan. It is certain signs abound of this widespread amendment."

"Assuredly," her mother answered.

"I hear confusion within Master Tanas's voice," Shuna-Shapta said, looking at the lightning flashes and rain patterns on the window. "Some of the Face's actions leave him unsure. Our living Orb's modifications amaze him."

Her mother said, "All Masters spend many hours within a Living System that has quaked into unfamiliar territory. We struggle to comprehend this 'Quickening.'"

Shuna-Shapta turned to look back at her mother, "I had assumed we displayed our inexperience and gaps within our training. Master Tanas was not forthright with us."

"Be generous, judging him," her mother replied. "He and other Professors voice their concerns as to the extent you new Invocants are disturbed. This sudden outburst of life most resembles Anu's Face flinching and knocking us over. We struggle to find our balance as if we ride a stampeding Danta! Countless generations dreamt of this. We watch as the Eyes of Tatchlan open and listen to Her collective Voice. I must confess a small amount of sadness at this transformation. Much that was once familiar is gone. I am still coming to terms with what replaces it."

Several intense flashes followed by a succession of mighty claps of thunder caused them to pause in their discussions.

"Our infant Majastas," Shuna-Shapta began as the rumbles faded, "and Her burgeoning Maja infants cause all of this?"

"Yes! Thakadush-Satwa somehow employs these infant Maja to fashion a gateway to our Breathing Work upon the Skin of Anu. Tatchlan comes to full life as Anu's Flesh after the rains. This day the base layer of chaos, Indatubangas, grows quiet as life regards our Resplendent Work. Our Primary Face of Indatubangas, Hesha Vira, turns her regal Face inward to witness what quakes beneath her kingdom."

"Ama! Where does this leave our Masters?"

Master Kanla stared at her daughter, "Dear Shapta! We stand upon the cusp! Our Glorious Orb outstrips us! As we have said, the sudden arrival of the culmination of our Grand Work, the birth of our first Majastas, upends centuries of learned discourse. We were ever told our Majastas would emerge from a mound of thousands of Maja. You have read the ancient Master Vanthaturmica, famous for her depths and lyric insights. She envisioned the 'Maja's perfect ball,' already rooted and established, being essential to a Ripe Adult receiving 'The Mantle.' There are many works of art we have both seen based upon this image."

Shuna-Shapta nodded.

"She was wrong! It appears near all of our leading Delvers of this matter were mistaken. Our Majastas has arrived early and has already grown her own 'ball of Maja' despite being but a one-year-old.'"

She paused to collect her thoughts as their carriage now encountered a better class of roadway, and the rocking subsided. The storm appeared to have no end.

"This Maja and Spoke population, already somehow led by this infant Majastas, shall reach maturity within fifteen years. As they begin to attain Ripe Adulthood, all of Anu's eyes shall behold our Majastas Thakadush-Satwa, the Master of Masters. Even as these novel scenarios are hastily formulated, they are outdated. Our beloved city, and Thakadush Cluster, are the birthplace for history's first Majastas led Cluster-of-Clusters Nation!"

Shuna-Shapta stared wide-eyed at her mother, "And Thakadush bears just Maja children because our Majastas shall emerge to her full Estate, as a Ripe Adult, within a cluster composed of Maja?"

"Yes! Amongst our Masters, we now refer to this Cluster as 'Our Majastas Cradle.' Master Vanthaturmica spoke of the eventuality of a 'Majastas Cluster.' I think history shall prove her correct. When their one-year-old Majastas celebrates Her adulthood at Her Life Cake Ceremony some twelve to fourteen years hence; the majority of living members of Thakadush shall be Maja." She looked out her window. When she spoke, her voice trembled, "At your age, they taught us our work extended beyond our lifetimes. 'We dedicate our lives to a goal we shall not see.' Our grandmothers and their mothers sang this lyric all their lives. We witness this capsized as our vision of wholeness is fulfilled this day."

Shuna-Shapta reached out to take her mother's hand. They sat in silence as the storm continued to rage outside. Shuna-Shapta turned to look out her window at a distinctive silhouette. Another passed, and she realized they travelled along the Companion Avenue with its characteristic fish statues on their pedestals.

"I have heard Tanas say Thakadush becomes our future royalty," her First Ama said, "We are granted an audience with our growing Majastas infant, the one born one year and sixty-two days ago. Already She has a remarkable presence. Here we are in the midst of Day 225, traditionally marked by the celebration of Nu's Zenith Passage. Nu is 'drowned out of the sky' this day, yet we shall still note this date for the rest of our lives."

Shuna-Shapta's grip tightened. Master Kanla leaned toward her.

"Dear Shapta! Recall the axiom, 'Privation begets Self-Absorption.' The abundance of this Cluster spreads. Approach this as a defining moment within your already exceptional life. Generations of Masters and Invocants yearned for this and never saw it."

Their carriage came to a halt, and they stepped out at the familiar Companion Pond. Through the pouring rain, the wide eyes of the pond's adored fish stared at them. They approached the new gateway in the freshly constructed curving wall added to the original. The new-planted Jezin on the walls was not ready to leave their faces as a record in it. Several children stood inside the door, giggling as they approached. Behind them, another cart came down the Companion Avenue to the cluster compound. The elder Master and younger Invocate entered a new courtyard.

One small girl silently took each of their hands and led them straight across to the earlier wall with its mature Jezin intact. Shuna-Shapta thought she spied the impression of her face from last year among the crowd of face and handprints. This was the new entrance to the compound, having expanded over the old courtyard to the wall. Once there, the girl handed them over to other children before running back to the entrance. As the rain pelted the new roof, the children brought forward two tall sticks on a wheeled base. They had several large horizontal rods attached to create a tree-like form.

Master Kanla and Shuna-Shapta began to disrobe and drape her clothes on each horizontal bar. Two children straightened the heavy poles, locking them into place, as they stepped into an open antechamber. Many poles, laden with soaking clothes, stood in their firm bases while innumerable little creatures known as Skayo swooped around them, sucking up the moisture in the air. Shuna-Shapta and Master Kanla remained in a small circular room facing the main door where several unusual hangings stood on the walls. Their patterns and symbols were unfamiliar to either of them. Despite the chill in the air outside, it was close inside Thakadush Cluster.

The thick atmosphere of cluster aromas engulfed Shuna-Shapta. It resembled a fog of warm and savoury body fragrance with a wide variety of notes swirling around her. Tension drained out of her as she stepped into this welcoming aromatic soup. A young boy took their hands and led them across the entrance and through the door. Unlike the original building design, everything was now open. Structural changes had led to the removal of many separating walls. Shuna-Shapta counted twenty-five Circles of Eight spread across the interior with a raised dais at the far end. Behind the dais were two ornate doors with fanciful paintings of Xumkuka twisting in the air. She did not recall these doors when she last stood in this chamber at the birth of their Majastas. Even without their official robes, Shuna-Shapta recognized at least four circles of visiting dignitaries from the Muraharoma Dynasty of Upata-Shepsus. Master Kanla gestured to Shuna-Shapta's circle of fellow Invocants.

"You should join them," she said. She then lent in to take her daughter's aromas, "I smell many changes within your body since we last spent any time together. You begin the process of forming a new household?"

Shuna-Shapta smiled, "Yes. I gathered what I wished to add to our modest possessions. We shall set a date for our formal separation from our childhood brood to create a new one."

"Shash! Majastas Be! You run well ahead of expectations. You assume full partnership?"

Shuna-Shapta nodded, "We mimic a 'Circle of Eight' of two women and six men, as my childhood clutch. Two mothers and six fathers also brought up our mates. Do not all Masters live thus?"

Master Kanla laughed and embraced her daughter, "Yes, of course! We strove to make our Invocant and Master Circles resemble our ideal configuration within a cluster prior to our true Maja's arrival. Our exceptional Lustrum Mirror paved our way to success. Your new circle has formed?" She stopped and peered at her daughter, "Have any residual rude barriers manifested amongst you?"

Shuna-Shapta looked puzzled at the question, "You mean things such as possessiveness and envy?"

Master Kanla wrinkled her nose and nodded.

"We learn to examine these modest outcroppings of tenacious ugliness our Lustrum Mirror left behind. The true nature of these inclinations reveals themselves within our Grand Work. We also recall the shared life of our childhood. This perspective assists our diminishing of these barriers. We begin to gather within our new 'Comfort Knot' to defeat them whilst equally cherishing all. We also look forward to the day we may return to our Lustrum Mirror, knowing better where to look to root them out at last."

"Shash! Admirable! Moving into your brood helps you appreciate these few remaining vile emotions still rooted within Indatubangas. The legacy of blind survival must be relegated to a serving role to full living. The ancient fear-laden attempts to regiment impulse would have lessened you. Some Invocants suffer more over this than any other aspect of their training. Our Lustrum Mirror requires a practiced eye to excise all trace of these malignancies. We know prior to the fashioning of this wondrous Mirror, these archaic barriers often disrupted the work of our ancient Masters. Increasing numbers of living, breathing Maja now move amongst us. Their collective presence shall wear away these sharp edges incrementally."

"We enjoy our advantage of being a circle of Maja Invocates," Shuna-Shapta said. "We live with more regulation than most. True abandon is a treasured gift."

"Shapta! May your life be full of abundant sweetness . . . I presume your wisdom extends to retaining one schedule: inhibiting fertility?"

"Yes, Mi-Yang and I received several treatments. We use Vendupash paste and keep it free of fertilizing agents. We agreed we should pause for many years prior to considering conception."

"Shash! Shash! Within true civilization, 'children are the crowns of a well-developed life.' Like anything of value, detailed preparations precede planting within Anu's Flesh. Once you reach your Ripe Adult designation, you are assured of your career, and you may request your first pregnancy should you and your circle wish it. How goes it with your bride?"

Shuna-Shapta laughed, "We enjoy each others' company. We commence the Nine Petals of Pleasure and our intimacies grow elaborate. We adore watching our men savouring each other."

They laughed together.

"Men's passion towards each other has an admirable directness and immediacy." Master Kanla said. "You know how I have ever relished watching and assisting them."

The two doors opened at the far end of the hall. The assembly turned as one in silence to bear witness. A group of Thakadush cluster mates came out carrying a broad, low and empty sedan chair. Other than blankets and pillows, these legless pieces of furniture were the norm on Statos-Vey. It was brought to the dais, where they laid a thick black and red cloth down on it and set the chair down before removing its two poles. The cluster mates draped a crimson cloth over what now appeared to serve as a low throne before returning to stand either side of the entrance. With a final clasping of hands and a kiss, Shuna-Shapta and her mother parted.

More Thakadush cluster mates issued out of the door at the far end before the hushed crowd of Masters and Invocants. Many children and youth strode out carrying bags. They came to each circle and opened them to reveal distinctive versions of House Masks, intense but straightforward in colour and design. Each selected one that spoke to them and put them on. As this process continued, a tall woman entered carrying a child. Her rich copper body as naked save for several distinctive pieces of jewelry on her arms and legs and an elaborate necklace. She also wore an orange and red half mask similar to those distributed. She had dark black hair worked into intricate long braids running in long coils down either shoulder and far down her back. Red and orange powder in a pattern covered the little girl's body, and her eyes were outlined in green. She also had abundant black hair forming a dancing bundle of fat curls. Shuna-Shapta was amazed to recognize what had a year ago been an ordinary woman giving birth sat cross-legged as on a throne with her baby. The size of this child was also remarkable.

"Behold Thakadush-Satwa!" the woman announced the Maja baby's name.

All guests gathered and knelt. They reached down to place their hands on the soil with respect. The woman sat straight, her baby on her lap. Behind her, many other mothers came through the door, each holding one or more tiny children. They also wore the Cluster's brand of house masks, and the babies were powdered. The fifty-three other Maja babies were present in a semi-circle behind the seated mother.

"Thakadush-Satwa!" the mother declared. "Soon our young Majastas shall have another Maja sibling! Prior to witnessing this infant's initial separation, Thakadush-Satwa wished to view those attending the birth."

Given her age, the child took a surprising interest in everyone. Without warning, she began a series of high-pitched calls. Shuna-Shapta remembered her emitting similar sounds immediately after her birth. This time her calls reached into Shuna-Shapta, causing her entire body to quake. She also began to notice certain aromas within her mask, suggesting it had been specially treated with agents to enhance perception and emotion. As occurred over a year ago, the guests began to shed their skins simultaneously. None of the usual signs warned them, and the process accelerated. The mother and child sat motionless, watching this process through to its conclusion. Cluster children now set aside their empty mask bags and ran to fetch baskets to gather the skin. They moved limbs and gathered each shred with admirable gentleness and efficiency.

The heaping baskets were set in a row before the mother and baby. The mother leaned forward, and the child picked up a few long scraps. She put them in her mouth. She consumed the skin and reached down for more. After several surprising handfuls, she sat back looking content. Her mother smiled down at her. The child began to shake herself as if dizzy, and her skin began to peel off her in long curls. The assembled guests gasped at the sight. Young children's skin shed in tiny flakes, and real skin shedding did not begin until they approached Fresh Adulthood. Shuna-Shapta glanced over to where her mother kneeled. She and the other senior Masters were also amazed. A remarkable cloud of scent rose from the fresh underskin of the baby, revealing her perfect tiny insides to them all. It articulated into a sharply defined smoky and crisp Spice Aroma Accord. Shuna-Shapta knew this powerful aroma would solidify the visceral link she would have with her Majastas Cluster.

"Thakadush-Satwa extends herself to you! Take a portion of this gift and stay," the mother declared. The children gathered the baby's skin from the lap of the mother. Thakadush-Satwa, as her guests, had translucent new skin, displaying her internal workings. The baby laughed at the actions of the children. They laughed as they finished their work. The children divided their tiny mound into five little bowls and began moving among the twenty-five kneeling circles. They stood while each guest took a small bit of her shed skin and waited.

As Shuna-Shapta held the baby's fresh shed skin, she was moved by the potent fragrance coming from it, and her fingers began to tingle. When the guests had received their portion, they looked toward the mother and child. The mother nodded, and Thakadush-Satwa waved her tiny arms at them. Shuna-Shapta placed the small scrap in her mouth at the same time as the others. Her eyes bulged, and she looked at the child. The scrap dissolved and altered in her mouth.

A tremor passed through her body down to her fingers and toes. Each bend in her body became alive at once. She found herself standing without recalling rising. She waved her arms and alternated, bringing each knee to her chest. She began to hear herself singing while standing inside a hot waterfall. This sensation altered with its opposite, of her standing as a warm whirlpool rose and engulfed her. She felt embraced by one of the men of her new brood. She was caressed and filled by him, and by a second and third of her men. While she knew the embrace of each, she could not distinguish between them. She embraced her wife, who had no name. Without interruption, they stood, and her brood joined the others in a series of circle dances around the seated Thakadush-Satwa and her mother.

The other cluster mates of Thakadush joined in the festivities, and the other mothers held their Maja wide-eyed children up as they surged with the dancing crowd. Others played many different musical instruments along the outside of the room. Shuna-Shapta felt Thakadush-Satwa laugh at the gleeful spectacle. This infant's powerful laughter sent Shuna-Shapta falling through Anu's Flesh.

Out of the living blackness, an image appeared. A circle formed in the distance and moved toward her. It resolved into twelve balls. Eleven formed the outer ring, and one stood in the middle. These further resolved into the Twelve Principal Faces of Tatchlan. The beloved Kava-Kura, Face of Vital Delight, was at the top. Her long tongue hung down through the middle of the circle and, at its tip, hung Hesha Vira, the feared Face of unrefined life. Placed in the midway of her gleaming tongue hung the round black Face of Alatanda, the Bridge and Hub connecting them. Kava-Kura stood at the top and Hesha Vira at the bottom, five to the left and four to the right. She witnessed the final 'Cluster of Faces' formation!

She regretted the pull back from the fruitful darkness toward the thin light. As it began, the glorious trance evaporated. The guests came to a halt panting in a rough circle. The rain had stopped outside, and sweet rays of Nu's light came through a skylight suggesting their ecstasy had gone on for longer than Shuna-Shapta realized. Several Thakadush cluster mates stood by her chair as the mother's hand raised.

"Thakadush is enriched by the birth of another Maja," she declared.

CHAPTER 20

SINKIN

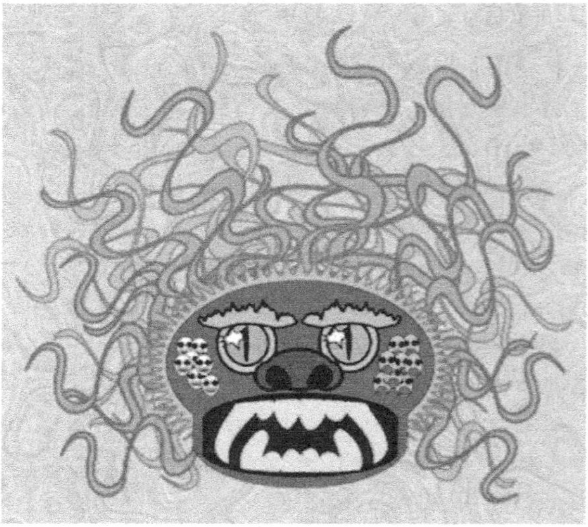

The Face of Hesha Vira

Day 225, Avanchil Round

One hundred days had passed since the lamentation for Jutnesh of Makusk Herd and Zatin of Durka Herd. Many more Bucks arrived with their herds while others left for the last of their Four Paws. All waited for the required number of new bucks to fill the bowl. With ceremony, participants came onto Avanchil Round. They took a mouthful of the pungent Dream Moss laid around the Fertility monuments. After they chewed and swallowed it, the few representing Makusk and Durka began to lead the Mesmerizing Circle Run. Around the Rim, the Keepers began beating the rhythm.

The others formed rings, two to four deep, extending out from the centre, where Durka and Makusk had honour. Sinkin and Setush ran, the towering cones and spheres rising to their left as they circled them. They began to breathe in and out without pausing to hasten the visions. Panting and the thunder of many paws filled their ears. A tingling and stinging grew in their paws, extending through their churning frames. A prickling of their noses and a quivering in their ears led to the initial stage where bouts of giddy laughter erupted amidst the running crowd. Heads shook, and bodies shivered as visions possessed them. Sinkin saw how glazed Setush's eyes had become and heard his high-pitched moans.

He lifted off the ground and began to fly. They passed out of the Round and through many glowing places. He heard charming calls and smelled rich fragrances while words came to him out of twisting lights in the sky. He soared into a place of warmth and loveliness. Spring became summer, and abundance flowed. In the distance came an unwelcome sight. Little two-legged stick creatures gathered to watch him. He sank back and hit the ground running. The landscape moved from green hills through rough terrain into one composed of stone walls and barriers.

He ran through narrow channels and was forced to turn many times and climb and descend hills having regular stones jutting out for each of his steps. He heard the foreign sound of piping little voices no Suvuka could make. Small pairs of eyes watched him through chinks in the smooth walls. He looked for an open sky and bellowed for a way to escape this maze. He heard other roars of anger and frustration and found himself back in the Round. Aggravation filled the air. Within the most ancient and esteemed of their ancestor's Rounds, the Tolku had found them! The run began to falter and diminish instead of approaching the intended release. They came to a halt and stood panting and groaning. Hiratak climbed onto one of the old spheres containing many cracks and chips to aid his climb. The crowds in the Round and on the Lip grew silent, allowing the Herdmaster of one of the two honoured herds to begin the assembly after this most unsatisfactory run.

"I once ran like a buck here," his voice filled the Round. "The Run proceeded as it should. We fulfilled our ancestor's dreams. Today this ritual is defiled!"

A collective set of growls rose. Hiratak rose on his hind legs and stretched out his arms for silence. When he had it, he said, "So I am not alone in this." The herds' silence deepened. "We are stained! We are shaken! Our beloved conventions are spoiled!"

Howls of rage echoed through the Round.

Hiratak nodded, "Your anger is shared. We fight this corralling by our foes." He waited for calm, "Can any mistake a Suvuka for a Tolku?"

The crowd fell into a troubled silence punctuated by occasional mutterings.

"There are no Tolku here! I only see Suvuka! Look into your herdmates eyes! There you will find strength and assurance!"

A voice rang out from the crowd, "The enemy hides among us! They cloud our vision! They mock our rites! They spread perversion!"

A renewed set of roars and howls rose, and Hiratak waited for them to diminish.

"Where is your proof? Repeating something does not make it so. Who can know who has turned? I challenge you to prove this claim!"

The crowd growled, and several arguments began.

"Listen to my words!" Hiratak shouted. "If they walk among us, we are to blame. We have forsaken our full herds of old. Small herds are easy to overwhelm!"

"We ran, and they poisoned our vision!" another voice in the crowd rang out. "We are many times the largest single herd. They still turned our vision!"

"We must begin afresh," Hiratak declared.

Above the general murmur came calls from the Keepers on the Rim. Many turned to look at them.

"Impossible!" one ancient called down. "The Run has stumbled! It breaks our legs and backs! They must not exist here!"

"To stall grants them victory!" Hiratak bellowed. "We run! We grow ourselves! We trample their flimsy works! We flatten them! We break loose of their grip and are free! Here we must overcome them! To retire means Avanchil is overcome! Where will we bring our new bucks? Why conduct this run? To be dismayed is no dishonour. To be defeated is! What say you? Are your strong legs and broad backs broken? Have flimsy dream shadows conquered you?"

Through the initial chaos of voices cancelling each other out, grew a chorus of "We run! We run!" filling Avanchil Round. Hiratak climbed down from the sphere and gathered Durka and Makusk Herds. He swallowed a mouthful of Dream Moss and began to run, faster and harder. The others started to match the pace. Sinkin and Setush ran side by side, and this time, instead of just breathing, they roared out their breath and pulled it in. Soon most bellowed, creating a terrific wave of noise rising over the Lip, where the Keepers watched in amazement. This thundering breath began a new rhythm, and they left off their usual beating to guide the runners. Sinkin felt a powerful wave to gather and launch him. He howled his way down a deep well into Anu's heart as he burst into flame. He split open each obstacle leaving a scorched swath behind him. He erupted back onto the surface and spread himself wide across the land.

He grew calm and became a cloud giving rest to every creature below. He spotted the little two-leggers. He gathered himself and streaked down to pulverize them. They dispersed as puffs of smoke, and his body quaked as he howled in ecstasy. He was shivering when he came to himself. He heard and smelled many others reaching the triumphal conclusion to their own dream journey. The entire group began to slow and at the last stop. Amidst a sea of panting came many high-pitched hoots of victory. Soon most stood on their hind legs spread wide in extravagant displays of their triumph. Eyes wide and nostrils flared, they began the traditional energetic exhibitions. On the Rim, the Keepers gathered in knots for an urgent conference. Runners ran between them. The participants below rested and watched this animated display among the usually staid Keepers. One called down to them, "Let the bucks form the inner ring."

The adults began to move away from the centre and left the bucks by the ancient cones. Sinkin and Setush each looked at their retreating herds nodding their encouragement. They went to sit by the others in a complete circle. Sinkin saw how the mud they had spread over Setush's middle still hid his Tolku marks. They nodded and began to slow their breath and prepare.

Avanchil Round grew still as a new generation of bucks stood on their hind legs and found their balance. One by one, they raised one leg, spread out their front legs and held steady. They commenced an elaborate series of slow movements in sequence, keeping an eye on their neighbours' shadow. They listened for the same gentle pop of joints and the near-silent rasp of pelts rubbing. They turned in sequence inward and outward, the bucks planting their hind legs wide as they began to arch and bow. Their bodies turned in liquid fashion, each buck's pelvis forming the base of the movement. Their elaborate dance went on for many hours and involved a detailed sequence of actions, one flowing into the other.

As time passed, their arcs lessened. Their movement slowed as the rhythmic breathing and alternating limbs' movement brought on a new set of visions. Sinkin became aware of the broad bowl leading to the Rim beginning to wobble. It broke apart as if it turned into tall golden grasses waving in the wind. The adults vanished, as did the cones and spheres behind them.

The ground beneath them grew dark and developed a light and dark pattern, resolving into strong yellow and red tones. Two green hills began to rise in the distance. A small mountain began to grow between these hills and moved at a steep angle where the cones had stood. The base broadened on one side of the central peak, spreading under their paws and extending out to the edge's golden grasses. The coloured pattern resolved into a fantastic rustling pelt. A distinctive wedge developed in a line on the hill's underside, having a series of shining white segments splitting through and rising above it. Behind this formation, a series of thick and twisting white forms burst out of the ground.

The entire landscape continued to shift and move into new hills and valleys surrounding this central broad and tall formation. Sinkin found himself moving in this eerie landscape, each cast quizzical glances to the other. He stepped away from the central mound, containing the two green orbs on one side and the more extended wedge containing the white segments on the other. The green spheres had become shiny, composed of detailed radiating design divided by a black slit down the middle. Setush cried out. He climbed the central mound to look down on the two green hills.

"A face!" he shouted at them. "We dance on a living face!"

All the bucks stopped to look at the formations, and others climbed on to vantage points viewing the massive creation. Sinkin joined them and looked down on two vast green eyes staring at him. They perched on what had resolved into the tip of the broad snout. They looked down at the eyes on one side of its base and the broad mouth and massive teeth. The monster's wild yellow hair twisted as if blown in wild winds. While shocking, most of the bucks felt a surge of affinity for this unexpected apparition. It was a fantastic Suvuka Face. They began their dance anew and moved over the features. Hesha Vira, the fifth Primary Face of Tatchlan and ruler of the chaotic mid realm of Indatubangas, observed their performance wearing her Suvuka form.

CHAPTER 21

Seti

Pictured: Icon of Memanu with swirling blossoms

Day 236, Two-Week Fourteen – Min, the Banner

Despite the Jefaka crossing over the equator in the two-week of Deel, near two hundred days ago, the wet heat of the southern coast of Statos-Vey still oppressed Seti. No wind came this night, and the ship coasted toward land. Adding to his discomfort and anxiety, Hegev's growing animation became irritating.

"I had been on Statos-Vey near a year before I entered a field of Memanu," her face glowed in the pale blue light of Xica Nu, the first of Anu's four moons. Xica Nu's face was untouched by shadow this night, shining full and round down on the Jefaka and the dark coast. "I had read Zitapermas. His elated descriptions did not prepare me for a field of them filling the sky! A more elegant creature does not exist! The following day it poured rain, and I remained in the fields. I saw their seed pods . . ."

"My pardons, Adept and Seti," Dine said, approaching them. "We approach the fields, and the captain has ordered us to put in at one of the pilgrim ports. Many have attended these fields over the years. Our captain says she could recite the litany herself, and if we donate, the guides will leave us in peace. Dawn is but three hours away. Those entering the fields should be in position by then. Others will join us or are there already. Once we are finished, we may leave before the revellers take over."

"Thank you, Dine," Hegev said. After he left, she read Seti's mood. "Seti?"

He shrugged and looked toward the rising coast, "A natural wonder is welcome, but why attach such significance to them?"

"Your questions are best answered by them," she said. "You struggle through the latter traditions. Here you will experience what inspired early visionaries. Remember, the Chelyaka saw them as conduits to the other side of Anu's 'inner sphere.' The Funomanru Dynasty was the first to make their injury a capital offence. The ancient followers of Menem worshipped them as Messengers from Anu to Nu." She smiled, "Perhaps, as Zitapermas, you will not only see a Xumkuka circling them but tiny Sev Messengers flying among their blossoms."

Seti smiled as he picked up a small coil of rope. "You still wish me to form a knot and attach it to one of them?"

Hegev nodded, "When you are there, the action will be natural. Many bestow a variety of tokens, but a knot is your obvious gift to give."

Seti shook his head, "You baffle me! You reveal yourself a sophisticate. Still, you wish me to engage in a ritual meant to speak to Untasha-Kabash in Ranvartawan?"

Hegev laughed, "Oh, Seti! Have I not said many times revered actions contain their own wisdom?"

Seti looked at the soft rigging line, not usually used above decks, and back at her, "This ritual, of attaching a message to their trunk, the Chelyaka and Menem prophets performed this?"

"Yes."

"Then there is another purpose in my doing so. You ensure I may add my name to the list of sibyls and mystics by following their ways."

"Who now is the sophisticate?" Hegev grinned. "Yes, when we return home, where no Memanu dwells, to say you stood in the fields will add weight to your voice. What is more important is your experience of what the ancients say of them. You may find a new way to clarify your visions and strengthen your connections to their realm of pure air and light."

"You speak as the faithful do."

"I speak as they will crave you to do. To clothe deep insights within simple and familiar ways will deliver you their hearts."

Seti looked down at the rope, "How long will we have? Should I begin tying?"

"No, wait until you are there. Nu will rise, and you will find yourself in a landscape formed and serving the Memanu. Let its unique contours inspire you. They are slow to wake and give ample warning of their rising. Most attach simple pre-made pendants fashioned on the site. Your skill is sufficient to devise and attach your offering before the 'thrumming,' signalling their imminent ascent, begins. You recall Zitapermas spoke of taking a blank sheet and starting his petitions when the head had emerged. He had time to complete them, and he said it then turned to look at him."

Seti nodded as they approached the shore. He looked at the length, "How wide are they? Is this enough?"

"As you might expect, their size varies according to age. The cap, or 'crown,' over their den, is a clear indicator of their girth. We will move among them and find one suitable. You are the best judge of what you require for your knot."

"Are they ever troubled by hands touching them?"

"You are kind to consider them," Hegev replied. "Many have pondered this question. None know with certainty. They do not indicate disturbance. They will pause when an item is placed on them. They will shy away from having their blossoms touched. This must be avoided. Beyond this, I know if one latches on to their stems before they rise, they stay until released. The most-ancient Chelyaka claimed their greatest leaders rode up with them, gliding past Nu and the four moons before coming down on Anu's far side. They also said they could ride the Xumkuka, who accepted them once they rose to their level. I doubt many we will see today even know these fanciful tales. Those employed to attend the field will stop any impeding their rise. Authorities agree they are unaffected by our embrace of their trunks once they are extended. Of course, this is another source of their fame, hence the 'revellers' Dine mentioned. They will not arrive until later in the morning. They will come and go for the rest of the day. They do not disturb the Memanu, who are focused on the high currents and gather their food there, as the Classics say 'under Nu's Eye.' There is no incidence of a Memanu attack if this is what you fear."

Seti shook his head, "I know they are passive creatures. I but wondered if our attentions are a burden to them."

The Jefaka glided along the dock. Dockhands stood ready to catch their lines and bring them in. The moonlight outlined elaborate carvings. They depicted the blossoming Memanu around the entrance to the reception area at the shore. Lights burned inside as a host came out and walked toward the ship.

"I am Emedin, captain of the Jefaka," she called out. "My crew has visited other fields many times. We wish to share the dawn with the Memanu. We bring tokens of our devotion to assist those serving them."

"Welcome captain and crew," the elder called up to the ship. "We will light your way to our Memanu's bed chamber and provide an escort. Do you visit our fields for the first time?"

"One here does, and he will be surrounded by those well-versed in the conventions. Above the entry price, we will donate the guide's fee as we intend to go unaccompanied."

"Very well. We will provide refreshments on your return. Our field is one of the richest in this province. Currently, we have five hundred and fifty-seven active heads. Conditions are ideal for them all to emerge this day. May your adoration of the Eye be full."

Twenty-nine crew members disembarked from the ship and made their way along the dock and walkway in silence. The entrance to the fields glittered in the flicking lights. Many artworks celebrating the

Memanu and numerous small altars stood along the outer entrance wall emitting slight whiffs of the previous day's incense. Broad Life Pillars, their surface rippled, as Seti knew the stems of the Memanu were, stood in rows. Offerings lay in heaps, and they glistened with oils poured over them. Several crew members went and touched a pillar. Dun Dritar, a usually restrained crew member, surprised Seti when he placed a token with evident tenderness before one of them.

They turned into the main entrance where the space either side opened. They paid their fee and walked past staff beginning to place tables on either side of the opening. Behind these ordinary furnishings were a detailed series of displays and large murals dedicated to the creature's life cycle, including their large bodies dwelling underground. Collections of books for sale, both general and scholarly, were uncovered. After glancing at this, they began to climb a long sheltered stairway to the Memanu Field. The stairway opened at the sides, and several paces separated one step from the next. On each side sat sculpted representations of the creature and more Life Pillars in a wide variety of styles, materials, and ability levels. Many were hung with fresh and withered flower garlands. There were piles of other offerings, including many personal mementoes, portraits, small figures and other gifts. A multitude of colourful winged and crawling creatures made their homes among the offerings. The crew continued to climb from the seashore until they neared the top. A few staff stood at the entrance with distinctive rakes on tall polls and bulging sacks. They allowed them through before bowing and exiting with the refuse from the previous day's events. The crew stepped into the open-air enclosure. In the pre-dawn light, Seti noticed odd wisps of steam rising from the ground. Only the most modest foliage covered it, yet it possessed a distinguishing quality he could not identify.

"As Nu's light grows, these fields' true nature will be revealed to you," Hegev said in a hushed voice. "The Memanu form a colony that continues for millennia in the same place. They modify the land to suit their needs. What lies beyond the field has altered beyond recognition from the distant past. The Memanu Fields alone remain unchanged. Other than the mountains and the sea, there as nowhere else Anu wears the same face the ancients knew."

In the distance, perhaps half an anda away, the enclosure wall extended around the entire area. Two other entrances stood on the far side where long banners of red and white hung. Seti had not seen these at the dock. He read the numerals '557' and remembered this was the population of the field. The other lettering on the banner was too distant to read. Many thousands could fit onto this field without touching each other. Figures began entering the Memanu domain from the other entrances. A few groups sat in circles. No one else had entered from the docks below. Seti started to make out circular rises everywhere. The group made their way around these formations. These were the 'caps' Seti heard described. Like a shell, they were smooth, hard and distinguished by subtle patterns. They varied from those less than a hands-breadth wide to those twice as wide as his body. They rose from their circular sides to a low peak; each cover had a pattern, including spirals, radiating bursts or more generalized shapes. Many had veins of colours running through them. A few caps were blackened and, in two cases, broken, and there was one open hole. He knew from his studies this meant these had died. The group hung back, and at a signal from the captain, Hegev took Seti's arm as they moved to the front.

"What am I looking for?" he whispered to her.

She smiled, "You recall Nallurakon's account? She strode across a Memanu field until one distinguished itself above the others. As the light grows, each will reveal its unique expression. One will 'look back at you;' we will sit around it."

With her encouragement, Seti began taking longer strides as the dawn broke over the field. The group's shadows formed long lines stretching away to his left. The distant enclosure wall's shadow covered a third of the area. Seti chose to walk north, giving him the most considerable distance before the wall on the far side. He heard the rest of the crew increasing their pace behind them. He watched each 'face' as he approached it, looking for what stood out and keeping in mind the amount of rope he had brought. Without warning, one face stood in his way. He and the rest stopped. After pausing, he bent over to look at it. It had an ideal girth to tie an elaborate knot and slip it over, and its features attracted him.

"With care," Hegev whispered. He remembered to reach out a

trembling hand, as Nallurakon had done, and touch the cap's surface. Despite expecting it, the cap's heat surprised him. Beyond this, he felt a series of sensations, impossible to describe. He left his fingers on its surface for a time, withdrew them and nodded to his Adept. She turned and signalled the others. At once, they began to create a series of circles at this and surrounding caps. The caps were spaced from each other, easing the process. Nu cleared the horizon across the distant land. Each cap's colourful surface wakened as Nu's Eye touched it. The group sat in silence while Seti stared at his cap. He became aware of a vibration beneath him. In the distance, someone began to sing a gentle melody. He also heard a Haklu, the four-stringed musical instrument he had started to learn on the ship. The extended composition was played with a delicacy and sureness of hand he knew he would never possess.

"Allow other's offerings to proceed without being distracted from your own," Hegev whispered.

Seti nodded and stared at his slumbering creatures' crown. He noticed the gentle swirl of its surface, the speckles and veins of various hues of blue and yellow, and felt the growing vibrations beneath him. Keeping his eyes on the cap, he began to work the rope into the series of eight interlaced loops around a larger central circle. At one end, he tied a series of elaborate knots forming a tail before leaving the ends loose. The ground shook, and a series of unusual sounds rose below them. Seti had not heard anything like it and stopped his composition before Hegev laid her hand on his shoulder. He continued his work. The entire landscape trembled awake. The other musical offerings neared their crescendos in apparent anticipation of the creatures emerging. There was a loud popping sound in the distance, followed by shouts and laughter elsewhere on the field. Seti finished his work as more caps began to burst open. He looked at Hegev and nodded his readiness.

"This will fit around its neck?"

"Yes," he answered.

He and his Adept rose and stood close over the cap.

"Do not be distracted at what occurs elsewhere," she said. "Some emerge. Soon enough, your senses will be filled with one."

As she finished speaking, the cap snapped to one side, and a dense hot gust of air and unknown odour rushed upward past them with a unique voice. Seti shook as he watched the series of crimson and white strands, curled tight, emerged. The long quivering mass was a study in intricate interlacing and gentle compression as it began to rise and loosen.

"Now! Now!" Hegev said. "Place your loop over them while they are wet before they spread. Remember not to touch the wet blossom."

Seti brought his rope offering down and over the tip of the rising form. He felt the heat on his trembling fingers and smelt the creature. Unperturbed, it continued to rise.

"You must hold on until the end of the blossoms," Hegev advised. "Wait for the thick band separating the blossoms from the ribbed stem."

He looked at what rose past his now shaking hands. The upper strands unravelled at an accelerated pace. Each began to spin out of its corkscrew compression in apparent sequence. The outer strands went first, followed by succeeding layers. The completed upper portion peeled away from the base, curling and flowing outward. The process continued down the length of the blossom. Once each strand finished, these long fibres inflated into a broad tongue glistening in the morning air. They varied in colour, each having a network of tiny blue and green vessels coursing with new life as the tongue extended to its full dimensions. How could this delicate thing survive and thrive in the high winds?

The topmost portions, free of their night's compression, began to undulate in the growing breeze. Several began to flutter, and a few came down to stroke Seti and the other's heads and faces. He found himself laughing at these marvellous sensations. The unravelling process accelerated and extended further and further down the tight bundle exiting out of the hole. As the peeling and spreading process accelerated, Seti found himself having to hold his loop lower. He had to get down on his knees and bent over as the loosening process proceeded faster than the creature could exit. The colours moved through a series along the length of the spreading blossom. What began as crimson and white ran through many hues, becoming darker. At last, the unmistakable band separating the bloom from the rest of the stem emerged.

"Now," Hegev near shouted.

Seti had well judged the thickness of his loop. The loop fell to the ground as he let go, but the rising girth caught up to it. The crew broke into cheering as they watched it carried aloft. Above it, the unravelling took on a spectacular measure. The blossom spread out in a vast circle far beyond what Seti imagined possible from the original bundle between his hands. The stem continued to issue from the cavity. Its ribbed sides created a unique rumbling sound as it hit the sides. It began to wobble and spin, causing the elongated body and full blossom to dance in the morning light. A virtual forest of these blossoms filled the sky above them. They seldom encountered each other as they rose. Their upper forms met strong winds sending their long elastic trunks bending to the west. Seti watched fascinated as their bodies bounced off each other and unwrapped to remain clear. The stem's acceleration slowed. Beneath a uniform dark blue, it was possible to see darker and lighter strands moving within the stem. A regular 'thrumming' sound filled his ears, accompanied by significant vibration.

"Our lovely creature is feeding," Hegev said as she approached the stem. Seti touched the surface and laughed. Despite the sound emanating from it, the vibrations were subtle and intricate. Seti remembered the many descriptions of those feeling these living forms and understood why none wanted to let go of them. The field had many more gatherings at the Memanu trunks. The music, singing and dancing had begun, and a few had removed their clothes. Nearby, one naked woman sat on the ground, her arms and legs entwined around the stem. Others began to disrobe.

"It is time to go," Captain Emedin said, following his gaze.

"Take one last look as . . ." Hegev began before she and Seti were struck. After gasping and covering their heads, they looked down at Seti's knot creation at their feet. It seemed to have aged in the short time it rode the creature. A layer of thick orange material covered it as if the entire rope had been sprayed with a sticky mist. The central loop had shrunk, and the outer loops seemed stretched while the tail had bunched together as if dipped in sap. Each looked at the other in amazement. Most of the celebrants carried on unawares, but several nearby called out, and soon a small crowd gathered to look at it.

Seti had gone pale and did not reach for it. He looked at his Adept,

"Has . . . this ever happened?" Hegev was wide-eyed and looked at the others.

"No!" someone called out. "Never!" another said. "They send our gifts to Nu." The seasoned crowd stood amazed as Seti bent down and touched the rope. It had gone stiff as if treated with a fixative. He examined it closely. Within the orange coating speckles of blue, yellow, and green travelled short ways along the rope's threads. These colours, and its new sheen, gave it an iridescent glow. He smelled the scent of the Memanu on it. What had been a length of interior shipping rope had returned as a miraculous sign.

"Boy? Did you make this?" another voice called out. Seti looked up and nodded. The crowd of hushed faces looked at the transformed rope. "Nu gave it back to you!" a voice called out.

Seti raised his head and cast a solemn glance around. He looked into the sky and called out, "Vindaviran! Samajalas! Tarunachit! Yuyutar! We thank you for this sign from your faithful throng! You dance on the heads of the perfect Memanu, dropping down to remind the Tolku of who they are!"

He turned and strode across the field. Hegev and the rest of the crew hurried after him. Those remaining reacted in varying ways. Some laughed and returned to their sport while a few uttered ancient litanies. Others argued, calling it a hoax, saying the rope did not fall. In this confusion, the crew descended the stairway and exited the hall past the surprised staff finishing their tables.

"Prepare to cast off!" the captain bellowed at the crew on deck. As the last climbed back on board, a crowd issued out of the entrance looking for Seti. As the ship began to pull away, Seti went to the bow and stood looking at the advancing group. They started calling out to him, "Who are you?" "Stay with us!"

Seti raised his palms to them in a sign of honour, "I am the knot of Nu! Untie me and know yourself! I am the voice of the Teacher, the Fashioner, the Devastator and Bridge! I defy the terrible faces in your dreams! I am the clean and simple air of the north! You corrupt yourselves in your indulgences! You swim in your own flesh and wonder why you drown! Look for the knot; it is my sign!"

He turned and went below. The crowds left on the dock called after the ship. Captain Emedin wore a troubled expression as she watched them.

Dine came to stand beside her. He smiled, "Our young prophet has learned a valuable lesson."

The captain frowned at him, "What lesson?"

"You remember the one school play we both had a turn at performing in our different years – the one from the old Wirikuata? I cannot now recall its name, but I still can recite my final line: 'A seer must claim all wonders falling at their feet.'"

CHAPTER 22

SINKIN

Day 236, Avanchil Round

"It was a monster!"

"It was Anu's Face!"

Sinkin and his Herdmaster Hiratak glared at each other. It had been eleven days since the Buck Dance and the immense Face's revelations filling the Avanchil Round. Many proclaimed they saw it in their dreams. A division grew between those condemning it as an evil trick of the Tolku, and those embracing it as a new manifestation of Anu. The Elders and Keepers remained mute, meaning no clear voice rose to dispel the Suvuka's growing turmoil.

What had simmered beneath the surface broke out over a simple word and grew into a debate. Sinkin and his Herdmaster Hiratak stamped their paws.

"Young Buck! You are not a full Stag! Yet you instruct me on visions?"

"Our songs say vision is never welcome," Sinkin answered. "When Anu speaks, the wise despise it. Our ancestors slaughtered the diviners. Their children uplift their memory."

"You place this horror beside diviners' visions? This obscenity never visited their nightmares."

Sinkin frowned, "Respected Herdmaster, it has. You know the Songs of Ratang?"

Hiratak growled, "Ratang was mad!"

"What of Mumash and Sarm?"

Hiratak stopped and looked puzzled at the young Sinkin, "You remember well." He shook his head, "It does not matter! Those ancient fools knew not the Tolku. They lived long before our crossing. Our present changes everything."

"Yes, it does!" Sinkin replied. "This includes our visions! Herdmaster, we stood on this Face! It was the feral Face of Anu that possessed her early life! Tolku works rob us of dignity and might. This Face gave us strength! The Keepers say none danced as we. We did so because of the Face!"

You are infected by this sickness."

"Herdmaster, look at me! I sleep the night. I accomplish more than is asked. How is this sickness?"

"Durka and Makusk are drawn together," Hiratak said. "We mourn our loss. We hold our secret. I laid the path for acceptance. We must fight wicked incursions. Tolku's devious ways are deep."

"We must know when Anu reaches us," Sinkin said. "You said actions outdo words. They are trusted over visions. This vision could be a trick. Yet, Setush and I are awakened. All declare we bucks excel our ancestors."

"With great discord," Hiratak answered. "Avanchil's drama was dignified and solemn. Now bellows and roars fill all hours. This disputation is shameful."

"Herdmaster, there is no shame in debate. The Keepers do not condemn us. Many Full Stags descend the Round with the bucks. They hope to raise Anu's Face."

"What nonsense is this?" Hiratak barked. "'Raising Anu's Face?' We stand on Anu's Flesh now. Each of your steps are made on her. Those Keepers forget our traditions! I blame them for not addressing this. Instead, they allow us to struggle among ourselves."

"Look around us, Herdmaster," Sinkin said. "Contention lessens by the hour. Many began this discussion before us. Many have long pondered it. The Keepers look at . . . this Face with wisdom."

"Keeper Datal approaches," Morakav said.

The Keeper was breathing hard from running. His distraction blinded him to the group's temper, "I greet you, Makusk and Durka! We ran far back along the path. The Toohund must have sailed far into the desert. I fear we will not find her."

"Did you," Setush's voice trembled, "find . . ."

"No, young runner. They seldom leave a hair behind. They seem to know to travel soon after. We found no trace of your Zatin and Jutnesh. Toohund are children of Kukernef. The desert clears after them. Your tracks are swept away."

The two herds moved close, and several began to tremble.

"I regret not bringing better news," Keeper Datal said. "We seldom capture them after their attacks. We have surrounded and killed those we discover. Their hunger does not let them flee. Only then can we destroy them. They cannot sense our long pikes held aloft. Once they have fed, they go deep into Kukernef. We send out regular parties. The territory is hard, and we are few. We have suffered casualties as well."

"We thank you," Morakav said. "You risk much on the pilgrim's behalf. We are grateful for your news."

Keeper Datal brought his nose to the ground and turned to leave.

"Keeper Datal!" Hiratak called out.

Datal turned back.

"I would speak with you. I sought you these past two weeks. I ask you to tell us your thoughts." He gestured toward the lip of the Round.

"Concerning the Face?"

"Yes, of course! This spectre must concern you. I wonder at your silence."

"I witnessed her first as a cub."

Hiratak dropped his jaw in amazement, "You saw this . . . ?"

"My clan has served here four generations," Keeper Datal said, sitting on his haunches. "Have you ever heard of Dakast Round?"

Hiratak looked back at Morakav. He shook his head. The other adults also signalled their ignorance of the name.

"No," Hiratak answered, "where is it?"

"As far north as we are south," Keeper Datal said. "Like Avanchil, it predated our invasion. It was a mighty self-made bowl further scooped out by many paws. Young Bucks went there as they came here. They stood as equal places of assembly. It is now an abandoned pit. A pile of broken rocks fills its centre."

"The Tolku defiled it?" Morakav asked.

"Our ancestors did."

"Why?" Morakav asked.

"Because there, many ages ago, this face rose."

"How is this possible?" Hiratak demanded. "Why are we ignorant of this?"

"It was a deep secret. Remember, this was before our discovery that the two-leggers were not confined to legend."

"This has been long hidden," Hiratak said. "Many must feel as I. The Keepers knew of this?"

"I am told the old Orders knew. They commanded Dakast be abandoned. The Face raised itself nowhere else. Not long after we crossed to Rho-Jashun. Questions concerning the Face diminished."

"Are there descriptions of what it looked like?" Hiratak asked.

"There was a taboo against describing it," Keeper Datal replied. "My grandfathers sang old songs. They said it was 'remarkable.'"

Hiratak shook his head, "The herds should know of this! How long has it risen here?"

"It has come and gone over the generations," Keeper Datal said. "For much of my life, it has slept. Generations of runners came and went without any knowledge of it. When it woke again, we were told to keep it close. We bound pilgrims to a vow of silence. While much changed, this rule continued. Since our enclosure behind the Vettencore Passage, most old barriers fall. This Face grows in dimension and frequency. Never before has it filled the bowl."

For a time, the two herds sat in silence, pondering this.

"Keeper Datal," Sinkin said. "May I ask a question?"

He nodded assent.

"What are your own thoughts on it?"

Datal smiled at him, "Like your Herdmaster, I was troubled. Keepers are the lone surviving Suvuka Order. We knew little of the other Orders' workings. My ancestors missed their council. The Face rose here. They tried to maintain old taboos. The Face grew insistent. It now rises with the run. It surpasses old bounds. Before this, it came to just a few. Small groups can be controlled. What spreads across the bowl cannot be hidden. I assure you," he looked at Hiratak, "we Keepers are in constant debate. There is no higher authority to seek instruction. We have no control over this Face. We cannot affect how it alters the run. I am relieved at this huge appearance. We are no longer burdened by this secret. One thing is certain. The cumbersome disavowal rituals are over."

As they had spoken, the growing thunder of many paws echoed from the bowl. There came a sudden chorus of roars. Only a small number of individuals stood scattered across the plain, a few more at the rim. Most ran within the bowl.

"One further question," Sinkin called out over the growing noise.

Keeper Datal nodded.

"You said this Face has been kept a secret. I suspect a few had their own visions. The songs of Ratang, Sarm and Mumash describe their own encounters."

The Keeper gaped before laughing.

"Do we have a Bard among us?" he exclaimed. "Yes, the feral always found the Face. Once, a Keeper gathered a list. Most are too strange and bizarre. They are not attended to by the majority."

Hiratak frowned as he looked at his young Buck and back to the Keeper. "The Keepers cannot control this?"

Datal stood on his hind legs and spread his front legs wide for emphasis, "What, oh Herdmaster, are we to do? This Face rises unbidden. We possess no power to forbid her. I believe our run calls Her to us."

Hiratak looked at the Keeper and glanced over at the rim, where the collective voice of the paws grew louder. "Sinkin asked you a question," Hiratak said. "As to your opinion of this . . . Face."

Keeper Datal sat on his haunches, "I no longer fear Her. She rises during the dance. When we are most themselves, She will come. I grow used to Her wildness. Others say She contains each creature. In the past, some whispered a heresy. Now many dare call Her the Face of Anu. I have no words for such abstractions. I will say She comes in our perfection."

Hiratak looked down, and for a time, all witnessed his struggle. "If what you say is true, much will change. I must decide what to make of this." He looked at the others and sensed restlessness among them. "Go on!" he said, gesturing toward the lip of the Avanchil Round. "Let it not be said I withheld running in Avanchil."

Most began to make their way to the lip. Sinkin held back and smiled, "Thank you, Herdmaster, for hearing my words."

Hiratak stood tall and looked with renewed respect at Sinkin. "Thank you for hearing mine. Your contention was equal parts respect and will."

Sinkin touched his nose to the ground to him and did the same to Keeper Datal before running to the lip. A continuous chorus of cries rose from the wide bowl.

Durka's Herdmaster and Keeper Datal proceeded after them and came to stand on the lip looking down. Below, the bulging green eyes stared back at them. The red and yellow Face filled the bowl, and the hundreds of Suvuka ran over it. As they watched, the Face and the runners became a trembling whole.

CHAPTER 23

Shuna-Shapta

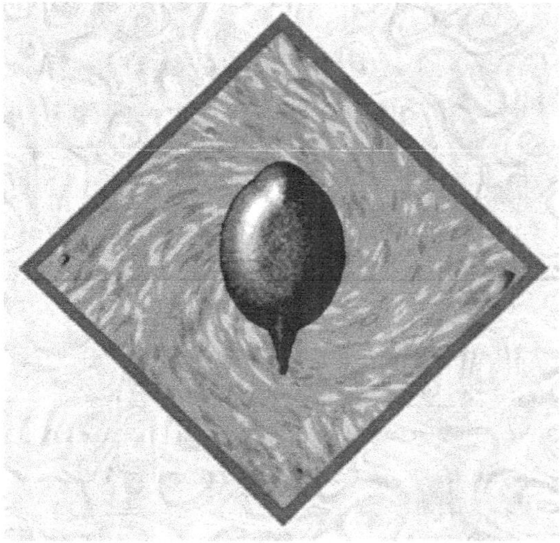

Pictured: Icon of the Stekachey nut used in the Life Cake Ceremony.

Day 237, Two-Week Fourteen – Min, the Banner within the Master Enclave, Bhampay

Both Shuna-Shapta's mothers were pregnant, and the feasting and celebrations had filled the previous day and night. These included many guest Masters and their now genuine Circles of Eight. Silence now reigned in their section of the Master Enclave. As was her custom, Shuna-Shapta rose at dawn. Her Mothers' Circle of Eight and their guests slept around her as she slipped away. She found a robe and went out onto the balcony overlooking the expansive view of the city. Several house servants smiled at her as they filled the empty aromatic shells to begin their elegant service to the new day. Others began to wash, gather and sweep quietly while the revellers continued to sleep.

Shuna-Shapta turned to hear the muted voices of the dawn Invocants beginning their rites elsewhere within the compound. The multitude of sounds composing the tapestry of the city's life enveloped her. A troupe of Asaku and Mayku cousins, used to relay messages across the city, began to unfold from their night clusters to sun themselves on an adjoining roof. The tiny Asaku shone with their yellow coats, and blue/green markings and the larger Mayku with blue hair and yellow fur rings about their eyes glistened in the morning light. Her deepened awareness noted the faint circular patterning on their pelts, a subtle sign of their being modified by Tatchlan. They all looked at her before returning to their morning grooming of each other. They not only groomed members of their troupe, but Mayku groomed Asaku, which never occurred in their unrefined state.

Without warning, Shuna-Shapta had another extended flash, wiping Bhampay away from her eyes. The roar of life filled her ears and her nose. Her mouth became alive to a multitude of flavours, and her skin tingled to new sensations. These compelling visions increased as she travelled inside the Living System. How was this possible? She stood on a balcony, not entwined with a Living Instrument. The ocean of sensation faded. What had begun as tiny flashes of awareness continued to grow. She had started to keep track of them and knew they, as this rash of pregnancies, commenced just a two-week ago, when they tasted the shed skin of their little Majastas, Thakadush-Satwa. Shuna-Shapta drew a few breaths then turned as her youngest sister, Shuna-Samshep, padded in her little bare feet around the servants and over to her.

"Ah, Little! Did I wake you? You were up late!" Shuna-Shapta whispered.

Shuna-Samshep nodded sleepily, her short brown hair tousled from sleep.

"Did you have a lovely time?"

"Oh yes!" she exclaimed then lowered her voice. "I wish I was older."

"Why?"

"Flair and I had to sit out so much. Vurupta did each thing."

"Dear, he is fourteen and all desire him. Do not rush! You shall enter your precious adulthood soon! Your brother had his Life Cake last year and so may participate. Vovans Life Cake approaches, and yours arrives in but five years' time."

The young girl frowned, "five *years*?"

"You may not imagine how soon your Life Cake Day arrives. It shall dissolve within your mouth as we encircle you, heralding your approach to your full estate. Your brother remains a Fresh Adult and still assumed secondary roles last night. This shall continue for seven more years."

"And 'Ripe' Adults . . ."

"Are acclaimed eight years after their Life Cake. Perchance we shall develop an enriching ceremony; for now, we make a simple declaration. I had my Life Cake at thirteen and carry the designation of Fresh Adult. You shall hear the declaration of my ripeness within four years."

Samshep frowned, "In 1276?"

"Yes, upon my birthday."

They stood in silence at the railing, watching and listening as competing choruses from many quarters of the city filled the air. The fragrance of distant incense and rendered flowers rose on the waves of warmth and mixed with their own Aroma Accords. Many layers of life quickened and began another day. As the Placid Daymaker arose, colour and animation increased, as if they stood in the midst of a vast waking garden.

"Our mothers are pregnant?"

"Yes, Little. Our circle shall have fresh life early in the new year."

"Is each woman of Bhampay pregnant?"

"No, Little. Just our Masters."

"Why?"

Shuna-Shapta smiled down at her little sister's sweet face.

"You and your questing nose! You know of Thakadush Cluster."

The young girl nodded.

"Thakadush-Satwa has amazed all by suddenly emerging as our first Majastas. She was born there last year."

"They speak of her at Enclave School," Shuna-Samshep said.

"Our Masters and we Invocants attended the birth of our one-hundredth Maja at Thakadush Cluster."

"Twelve days ago?"

Shuna-Shapta laughed. "You count the days?"

"We do at school. They talk openly about Tatchlan now, and Masters teach classes each day."

"Shash! You witness the unforeseen result with the birth of our one-hundredth Maja during this first year of our new Majastas's reign. At that time, we shared a meal of Thakadush-Satwa's skin shed."

"The baby had a skin shedding? I thought babies did not shed as us for their first five or six years."

"As did I," Shuna-Shapta said. "Her flesh is powerful! Each Ripe Adult female Master now grows round, including our First and Second Amas. Other changes commence . . ."

Shuna-Samshep looked out at the city, "I heard our new babies shall be Maja, just as you and our Amas. I grew up thinking Maja were rare. If we have one for each of our circles, shall we become an actual cluster?"

Shuna-Shapta knelt and hugged her sister, "Yes, Little! Those entering Tatchlan view amazing signs. Those possessing the titles of Invocate and Master conclude a considerable change has begun. Imagine! Two new Maja come to us! That shall bring our total of Maja within our pre-Cluster to fifteen. Given our size, we shall require twice that number, having attained Ripe Adulthood, to form a true Cluster. In time, they shall form the core of true Circles of Eight. Much has opened within a year! Tatchlan blossoms about us!"

"But you are leaving us."

"Little! I am not just a Maja who will usually stay rooted in their cluster. I am also an Invocate, as are our two Amas. This city knows my Ama as 'Master Kanla.' She has an Invocate Circle here in our Enclave. Yet, she returns to our residence quite often each two week. You shall watch others go, and new cluster mates arrive within the coming years according to their uses. The bonds between mothers and children, and between siblings, shall remain within our new world. Whilst you and I shall ever be sisters, you do not know where your Ripe-Adult Use may eventually take you."

"I shall not be a Spoke of our Cluster Wheel?"

"We shall not know if you are a Double until your first pregnancy, the other Spokes usually manifest during infancy. Whilst it may be possible you shall become a Double, or suddenly show signs of another Sensitive Speciality, I believe you shall be a Mundane. This is a wonderful legacy! Mundanes shall ever be the most free to pursue their genius wherever it takes them. Some Spokes are, by definition, tied to their cluster and may be seen as having fewer choices given the profound urges of their biology affecting their inclinations."

"My first Ama works the Tatchlan Cubes."

"Yes, indeed, Ama Dana has distinguished herself within this ancient discipline. Hers has a different life than mine shall be. Whilst she also works with a Circle, much of her craft is enacted within solitude. Like my Ama Kala, my vocation shall take me away more often, but for now, I am still within our Enclave."

They sat on the floor of the balcony and looked through the railing at the city beyond. Call bells rang, and the Mayku and Asaku scampered away in different directions to receive their first messages. Nu's loving darts ignited the mosaics covering all roofs and brought to life the vivid hues of each towering statue. Somewhere nearby, a wind harp responded to a growing breeze from the ocean.

"So the Tatchlan Civilization shall emerge from these mother's wombs?"

"Well said, Little! Yes, our civilization shall issue from our bodies, as our ancients intended. Our Maja shall serve as the bridge between the Skin of Anu and our Living System. So linked, we shall enter into the new peace and harmony ever wrapped within the 'murmur of life.' Sheltered by 'Majastas Favour,' our miserable service to Self-Absorption shall end, completing the toil of many, many generations of Masters. Our new Cluster-of-Clusters Nation shall perfect all past brilliance without any of their attendant weaknesses. Future generations shall behold 'Peace, Order and Good Governance' encompassing each direction."

"So this," Shuna-Samshep pointed out at the city, "these buildings and statues, our courts and academies, are not civilization?"

"Oh, yes, of course. These noble edifices, housing their admirable establishments, stand as servants of civilization. Whilst some institutions shall continue unaltered, many shall be modified or replaced within our emerging Cluster-of-Cluster's governance. The roof over our heads and the water flowing under the floors shall ever serve us in important ways. Regardless of its function, each structure and tool must possess beauty also. Hence, we judge each work by the axiom, 'beautiful and practical in equal measure' and 'improve by art' each thing upon Anu's Skin. Mandating this was wise. From the most mundane of instruments to an enormous vista, all partake of these vital qualities and so bring joy and elegance to our lives. Despite the transformation, this," she gestured through the railing, "shall remain. Our enhanced life shall flow about it as sweet spring waters, both subtle and profound," she paused. "What is an example?" she enquired of the air and thought. "Our Enclave's rooms spread wide, and our doors are few."

Shuna-Samshep nodded.

"When we must separate space to control drafts, we use a cloth to hang down. Our walls serve as structural support or to house our possessions. Save our outer entrances, no doors obscure our passage and view."

Shuna-Samshep nodded.

"This deliberate design foresees true cluster life. You notice how walls and closed doors fill dwellings out there?" She pointed at the city.

"Yes!" Shuna-Samshep said, her eyes going wide. "Our class joined a field trip into the country last week. We went into the jungles and visited a village. Tiny houses filled it. We went inside a few. Walls crowded us, and closed doors filled each wall!"

"So," Shuna-Shapta smiled, "many here and out within the country suffer division. Though they live under one roof, they hide away from each other."

The young girl nodded, "They fenced off the outside. They walled each thing! The face of each house was closed. They had small space imprisoned behind high fences of stone, wood or dense bush. They took us through their little prisons and out into these dark patches. We hated hiding from everyone. One had a pretty garden there, but fearfully concealed!"

Shuna-Shapta nodded, "Hm! Sad to say, this may persist within parts of our Bhampay and other cities."

"Why? It felt terrible! Many classmates started crying, and we had to leave. I heard one woman calling us 'Tatchlan's children' and another making a face at us. She raised her palm, and it had markings down each finger and upon her hand."

Shuna-Shapta frowned at her, "Samshep . . . tell me more about this village. Where did you go?"

"I rode a skimmer!"

"What? You mean a Naswoll?"

"An adult rode with each of us. They have such aromas! Their skin is so smooth!"

Shuna-Shapta hid her unease, "Our schools grow ambitious. I had yet to ride a Naswoll at your age!"

Shuna-Samshep gave her elder sister a look of long-suffering indulgence, and Shuna-Shapta laughed.

"Very well! As for the Naswoll's scent, yes, lizards have their own profound suite of odours. They form a strong link to raw life and live closer to innate perfection than us, although the insects far surpass them. Where did you ride this 'skimmer?' They require flat stretches of Anu's Skin to coast over."

"Down the highway."

"Your school rode down the highway? This one here?" She indicated what had been known as 'The Imperial Way' since the ancient Funomanru Dynasty. It ran without the slightest deviation through Bhampay south and west to the monumental Upata-Shepsus, the capital of Statos-Vey. "What about the traffic?"

"We glided within the centre, and the traffic was upon the sides."

"And where did you go?"

"We started at dawn and rode out the Red Ring Wall and onward until lunch. We mounted carts and had something to eat. We moved north off the highway and into the jungle. We visited farms where they cultivate insects."

"Insects? What insects?"

Shuna-Samshep rolled her eyes as she thought, "We saw huge dark colonies of Vikavan."

"Vikavan?"

"They are little creatures having shiny dark shells building huge colonies within old trees. They feed upon it and distill many juices found nowhere else for medicines and devices. We also saw a huge Mahakram colony filling a large tree. Their nets covered it, yet the tree looked quite well. A small bird became caught within the nets. The Mahakram are so tiny! Thousands of them covered the bird."

"Ah, Little! Was that upsetting?"

Samshep stared blankly at her sister and shook her head, "I ran closer to see better how they subdued the bird. They show how the small may overcome the great through working together."

With a look of pained amusement, Shuna-Shapta nodded her head to continue.

"We also saw Fecund Groves and a few women performing their 'Two-Weekly Courses Round,' stroking each tree trunk to impart their blood's fertility. They had little shrines before the grove. We also saw a small bed of Hungry Rock."

Shuna-Shapta frowned, "Few patches exist near the city. I also saw one at your age. It smelled odd and possessed a peculiar shimmer. It is said they do not live, but possess a living presence all the same."

"It looked wet," Samshep nodded. "Patterns of darker streaks moved slowly upon its grey, smooth skin. No trees grew near the edge, and even insects knew to avoid it. They tossed a rock upon it, and it sank right away, leaving no trace. Oh!" she exclaimed, her eyes going wide, "we saw a tree fall apart from Karthala!"

"Karthala?" Shuna-Shapta said, her nose wrinkling. "Are they the ones burrowing beneath the Flesh of Anu and attack a tree from its roots?"

"They do not *attack* it," Shuna-Samshep said using her best impersonation of one of her teachers' tone and manner, "they clear the jungle of dying trees. When the tree is close to death, the Karthala eat the dead flesh from the inside out. With the entire tree hollowed, they leave as it collapses. The farmers knew of one close to falling. They tapped it several times. We heard the Karthala rumbling inside, and they scurried down and out. The tree bent and burst apart. Birds and insects flew up, and a sudden breeze covered us with its dust, and we laughed."

"Yes . . ."

"We also saw the farmers 'Zirall.'"

"'Zirall?'"

Shuna-Samshep frowned at her. "They crawl out of the ocean and make those sharp noises upon the shore. We hear them all the time. We have them in cages to light our streets at night."

"You mean Queldeday?"

Shuna-Samshep nodded, "I heard some calling them 'Booval' also."

"Hum! I had not heard these country terms. No matter."

"They use their Queldeday differently to us. They live within large cages upon poles at the edges of their groves where they are fed and tended. We were made quiet as we approached. They sensed us and began to make a terrible racket. The farmer said this keeps most pests away and guards the fields day and night. The farmer made a call, and they calmed down and sang sweet songs to us."

"They do not sound like any Queldeday I know. Theirs must be specially prepared whilst ours are inured to the city's clamour."

"We also saw wild Bowvow Trees, so skinny compared to those inside the groves and dead thin compared to ours. Their tapping was very high pitched and rapid."

"Their rhythmic song grows deeper and slower with their girth," Shuna-Shapta said.

Shuna-Samshep nodded, "Going home, a group of Tapu raced overhead with brighter lights than ours and helped us see well."

"I welcome news of your wonderful outing, Samshep. Could you speak further concerning this village?"

"Oh . . ." her pretty little face fell. "After visiting the farms, we went to this small *place*. The name has left me, but they said it had no connection to the groves. Their Life Pillars stand in the centre of the village." She frowned and looked at her sister, "Most were wood and the paint peeled off them. They had long and ugly cracks! The boys looked pained as if they were hurt. Is not a new Life Pillar raised and the oldest planted beneath Anu each New Year's Day? Here women add some each two-week."

"Yes, I thought it near-universal within central and northern Statos-Vey. No newer ones? Our endless rains do wear them down."

Shuna-Samshep shook her head, "No, they looked years old. Some had fresh garlands and other offerings, but most stood bare. I had never seen such sad pillars. We saw children within the village, but we thought they must not wish any more."

"This *is* curious," Shuna-Shapta said, her frown deepening. "What else?"

Shuna-Samshep closed her eyes in concentration. Shuna-Shapta smiled and waited for her.

"I told you of their miserable tiny houses," she began before remembering something and looking at her wide-eyed. "I had forgotten. Piles of fertilizer sat in front of several of them. At one, a man dug into it then carried it to their imprisoned portion of Anu's Flesh."

"Yes . . ." Shuna-Shapta said to encourage her to continue.

"We go out and tend our gardens together. No hateful walls stand between them, and we share what we grow. There, their lonely hidden gardens suffer complete separation."

"A small and mean life," Shuna-Shapta nodded. "I have never seen such a place. Samshep, could you tell me more of those living there? You said a few became displeased when your classmates became upset."

"Some frowned and closed their doors! Did we do something wrong? We received every kindness from those we visited. Perchance half the villagers smiled at us, and half either turned away or frowned. I heard others whispering 'Tatchlan children' to each other."

Shuna-Shapta shook her head, "You did naught amiss, Little. I never heard such rude expressions during my school trips. I hope they did not spoil your day."

"No, we readied to leave when some said they could not breathe and ran outside." She stopped and waved her hands for emphasis, "I recall something else."

Shuna-Shapta nodded for her to continue.

"The village had a set of low hills around it. They had cleared these of the jungle long ago. Shapta, the hills were – *bare*."

"What do you mean, Little?"

"They had *naught* upon them! The exposed rock was neither sculpted nor worked *at all*. They had not even taken the few loose stones and formed a simple figure out of them! My favourite things to see during our country outings are the distant hills. Each improved by at least one shrine, memorial or statue… as that poem says: 'each hill its ornament.' These had *naught*. I felt unhappy as soon as we got there. You said the ancients said each item must possess elegance. There was no art, no grace there, all was *bland* and *plain*!"

Shuna-Shapta raised her eyebrows, "I wonder at the cost for this 'edifying' trip. Have you told anyone about it since you came home?"

"You helped me recall more," she said. "It has been busy at school and here since."

Shuna-Shapta nodded, "So it has!"

"I thought I heard whispers out here," Master Kanla, Shuna-Shapta's First Mother, and Samshep's Second Mother, said as she approached.

"Did we wake you, Second Ama?" Samshep asked.

"No, Little," Master Kanla replied, sitting down.

"How goes it with you this morning, Second Ama?" the young girl asked.

"Dear Little, you are our most recent baby! Now at least two more come! Many discomforts approach, but I remain hale! Shapta and Vovans were, for the most part, kind during their stay inside me." She placed her daughter's hands where the new life grew, "I hope our special one shall also behave."

"I wish to have a Maja baby!" Shuna-Samshep declared. The other two laughed, and each embraced her in turn.

"Each baby is a treasure, and I hope you have many!" Master Kanla said. "This special honour may also grow within you! Now, Little, your brother had a busy evening. He shall sleep until noon and wake famished. It was too late for us to bathe last night. I expect most shall begin to waken soon, and we shall soak this morning. We need to use our largest tank. I would also require you to gather all our guests' house masks off our furniture and floor. Store our masks and set the rest together out of the way where each may find their own."

Shuna-Samshep kissed each of them before running back into the Enclave.

"Ama," Shuna-Shapta began, "Samshep has told me of her outing."

"Ah . . . yes, the school trip," Master Kanla said with a wry smile. "Considerable discussion takes place amongst the parents concerning it. They timed the excursion so the children could see a Karthala tree collapse."

"Vurupta plans to go to Thermistal to view Suvuka whilst young children have such adventures! Did she tell you of the 'Mundane-dominated' village they went to?"

"She did. I have heard more from Shuna-Dana and others since."

"It sounds as a benighted outpost within some northern hinterland of Rho-Jashun."

Master Kanla nodded, "A meeting has been scheduled to discuss it. Many Masters share your concerns. It certainly raises several troubling questions. None expected such a regressive community, apparently composed entirely of Mundanes, located between our twin epicentres of our new order. In some ways, our capital Upata-Shepsus surges ahead of us, although we have our first true cluster, and of course, our infant Majastas. As you say, it resembles a rude and backward settlement well beyond the confines of civilization."

Shuna-Shapta stared at her mother in amazement, "How may this be? There is an entire branch of our Masters' Servants entrusted to ensure our basics of civilized life flow from our cities to the country. What of Sensitives? Are none born among them?"

"A vital part of this charge involves education." She smiled at her daughter, "I have a theory," Master Kanla stretched and looked out at the brilliant city. Ornamental birds hopped over the coloured tiles covering the roofs. One audaciously began to sing atop of one tall statue whose mosaics sparkled in the morning light. "Our many refinements do not travel well into the rude wilderness. I once mentioned to you about the failure of our grandmothers and their mothers to firmly establish governing institutions preceding the repossession of Rho-Jashun after the fall of the Suvuka. To a lesser extent, we face the same challenge here. This remains a significant test for civilization. Our ancient Masters resolved to address this. When Maja emerge across our continent, our imperfect attempts to domesticate the rough backcountry shall be unnecessary. As for Sensitives, I may not say. Unlike here, perchance their presence disturbs them. They may well exist but lack the necessary encouragement to perform their roles."

Shuna-Shapta nodded, frowning, "Ama, you have not told me your theory."

Master Kanla laughed, "Correct, my dear. I have learned, for many years, our Servants attempted to bring these observations to our attention. I suspect the children of our Masters witnessed this degraded settlement to force the issue. This village is an exception to the rule."

"Ama! Do you suggest they exposed Samshep and the rest of our children by design? How may this be acceptable?"

"A few Masters take this position, but not I. Our children are unharmed and learned a valuable lesson. Most reacted as Samshep did. Our children's perceptive observations astonished us. They shall benefit from seeing how small and ugly life is without our gracious arts. Our children proved ideal observers, having no preconceptions. I did not hear what Samshep told you. I assure you one or two Ripe Adults stood with each pre-adult."

"I object to their using our children. Revealing social decay to them displays exceeding poor judgment. It also suggests the desperation of these Servants to resort to such measures. You say they made past representations concerning the state of such settlements?"

"Yes, I hear quite proper ones."

"And our Masters' response?"

Master Kanla smiled and shook her head. "I play no part within this branch of our programme. I hear those having responsibility knew the extent of the situation. They saw it as of minor importance compared to their immense success. They now must explain their position and endure increased scrutiny."

Shuna-Shapta turned to gaze out at Bhampay opening as a blossom under Nu. She gestured and pointed at it as she spoke, "I love hearing the rush of incidental sounds of an entire city. I may not imagine the bareness of their absence! Voices and songs flow over us as their collective breath envelopes us. The scent of their dramas, follies and glory fill our nostrils. I am convinced, without exception, each blemish upon this city's glorious body has its root within Self-Absorption."

She nodded vigorously, "We are improved and ennobled by such majesty." She looked back at her mother, "I would live to behold the day Samshep's benighted village is healed, with their wombs opening and Sensitives of all ranks pouring out. Then their children shall heal the elders, and all fearful smallness comes to an end."

Master Kanla sighed and embraced her daughter, tears of pride running down her cheeks.

CHAPTER 24

Seti

Pictured: traditional icon of Seti's Memanu Knot after its 'return'

Day 237, Two-Week Fourteen – Min, the Banner, aboard the Jefaka

Seti and Hegev sat across from Captain Emedin and her First Officer Dine. They had left the Memanu Fields the day before and put far out to sea. Several ships had tried to follow them, but now they were alone.

"You both know my position on these matters," Emedin said in a cold voice. "Now, we must come to an understanding as to how you view your situation."

Seti said nothing but nodded.

"The crew believes the four Grand Menem are bound to you," Emedin spoke with growing agitation. "Even my most devout crew members tell me this has never been done. They say a few in the past bound one of them," she held up a finger for emphasis. "I now understand a number of them believe they have an association with one or more of the thousands of Sedat Servants or Sev Messengers coming when called. They dream of hundreds of them flocking around this ship because of you!" She shook her head in disgust before lapsing into a short brooding silence.

"I followed your progress since your 'Adept' came on board with growing concern," she continued. "I had hoped she would gently wean you off your superstitious upbringing. Instead, I see she has fortified it." She paused before leaning toward him, "Do you now claim this momentous binding has taken place?"

"I told you when I came on board," Seti replied. "They approached me years ago and come when I call."

Emedin scowled at Dine. She rose and began to pace behind her table. Dine knew enough to step out of her way and stood well over to one side.

She stopped and leaned over her table toward him, "What happened yesterday? Was it one of those seer tricks? There are long traditions of sibyls and sages being accomplished magicians. I have witnessed impressive displays but nothing like your returned knot. You slipped it over, and it fell well below the band separating the flower from the stem. I watched it rise out of sight. Was another knot set aside?"

Seti's eyes went wide in shock, "Captain! I would never do such a thing!"

"Indeed? And what of your response to the wonder of the crowd? You did not plan this ahead of time?"

"I did not know the knot would be sent back."

"*Sent* back," her attention shifted to Hegev. "Given our initial conversation, your pupil's responses disappointed me, Adept! Perhaps it is more fitting I question you in this regard."

"You will receive the same guileless answers," Hegev replied in a measured voice. "I had no expectation of its return and did not council or assist Seti in perpetrating a hoax. I told you why I wanted him to visit the fields. Until the knot fell, all proceeded according to my expectation."

Emedin eyed them before returning to her seat. "You!" she stabbed her finger across the table at the Adept, "You alternate between the credulous devotee and the sophisticated urbanite! We have engaged in several vital discussions on many matters since you came aboard. I find it hard to reconcile those exchanges with what I hear today."

"Captain!" Hegev exclaimed. "May I enquire as to what your explanation may be? I hope you believe our replies to you. If you do, I welcome your insights."

The captain rose again and paced behind her chair. She stopped and looked at Seti, "Contrary to what that throng said, tokens do 'return,' usually in tatters. The creature has a way of sending the attachment back up its trunk and swiftly conduct it though its canopy and away. There are many accounts of those witnessing the process. This is why your knot is now thick with its juices. Why do you think they have staff, armed with those broad rakes, cleaning the site each morning? The creatures no doubt find these 'offerings' a nuisance and, at a time of their choosing, rid themselves of them. The usually tiny fragments rain down through the day; much carried on the winds many andas from the fields. I find it curious that our Adept, claiming to be a frequenter of these sites, had no notion of this common occurrence. Were we not immersed in a fraught context, I might generously interpret this as her being a morning visitor. I am told the ground grows thick with detritus by nightfall."

She pointed at Seti, "There is always an alternate interpretation!" She then turned and looked at her library, "I recall Nebutan regaling us with tales from her youth as a Wandering Scholar. She encountered a small settlement living downwind from a Memanu field far to the north. When items fell on them, they venerated these fragrant rags as gifts from Ranvartawan. While in truth they were an unknown hamlet, they thought themselves the centre of Anu! An intact return is rare, but not unknown. What weighs me down is Seti's response. How did our young 'prophet' come to speak as he did?"

Seti sat staring at his captain, "I do not know." He said, "When they said Nu returned my knot, I was filled and began to speak."

"And when you did," Captain Emedin said, "you evoked the four Grand Menem and attached yourself to them. You indicated this as part of your mission by voicing their message to 'remind the Tolku of who they are.' As we left you claimed to be their voice and to watch for the knot as a sign, you said, 'Untie me and know yourself!'" Her voice had risen, and she stopped and stared at the boy. "Whether this had been a well-orchestrated performance or an improbable series of events, the result is the same." She pointed at him, "You commit yourself, boy! You know I have examined all my crew since yesterday. I am confident most would climb the topmast and throw themselves down on your word."

"Captain?" Seti said in a small voice, "What was I supposed to do?"

Emedin stopped and looked at Seti and his Adept and sat down hard in her chair. "What I say . . . you will not repeat."

They nodded.

She leaned forward over her desk, "I am frightened! Yesterday's events were as if the 'Lamentation Tales' came alive. Such hysteria and chaos was always foreign to me. Scholarly discourse and energetic enquiry filled our halls. I witnessed the power of books and bathed in the light of earnest reflection. From this beginning, through various unlikely turns of fate, I embarked on a career at sea. I have signed on to several ships through the years and experienced most of what Anu has to offer. Yet, what I witnessed on that field, and what may come of it, has robbed me of sleep. I saw raw passion, and the blind devotion flare out of nothing as a wildfire. You mount a Thyma, Seti! The beast is powerful and unpredictable, and you will either hold on or be thrown off. Your story will spread on the mainland. My crew will ensure it grows in their telling at each port we visit. They stare at your returned knot, and I watch their eyes glaze, and their jaws slacken as if they become powerless before its glory. You have a terrible power, boy. What do you plan to do with it?"

Hegev frowned at the captain, "You once encouraged Seti to join your clan's ongoing fight against the Tatchlan masters. At the serendipitous moment, he has the standing to challenge them; you try to disarm him?"

"I speak not as Sawlu nor as captain," Emedin replied, "I speak as one growing to love this boy. I fear for him and where this will lead! As Sawlu Clan and captain, I say this display does *nothing* to advance our cause. It only serves to feed our worst instincts. Despite the cautionary tale of Nallurakon, who died a delusional felon, we have been down that road many times since, only to arrive at the same end. I hoped to see his maladies treated, then perhaps he would become a famed teacher in our schools, or rise to leadership within our clan. Whatever my half-formed imaginings, they did not include miracles and prophetic declarations. Nebutan and Geltran did not play with crowds in this fashion."

"Perhaps you should stop casting him in their shadow and observe him," Seti's Adept replied. "I told you he was unlike anyone I had met. I may not have sailed every sea as you, but I have also travelled across Anu's Face. I also think it likely I have spent far more time with simple people than yourself. You know my home is part of our Wazaratcha Archipelago. Despite your Nebutan living a few days away from us, you must know her works had little impact on my island. Her lofty intellect did not feed their confusion and fear. An unobtainable answer is no answer at all. I hope I possess sufficient wisdom to admit I do not know 'who we are' and what heights we can reach. An impenetrable barrier does not separate wisdom and inspiration. I cannot imagine one without the other! Is it impossible for you to accept Seti as a true prophet and his returned knot a clear sign?"

Emedin leaned back and began drumming her fingers on the table. "Our vague fancies take sharp focus. Each action and word has a new significance. Seti, you step on a strange path composed of extremes. It rises high and has steep inclines; with every step your danger of falling increases. I have little to offer you on such a journey. To me, you turn away from all I hoped and embrace what I have dreaded. I fear you will join the long lists of mad adventurers. It would be as if you never came on board."

She looked hard at Hegev, "Had I the foresight to draw up a contract, setting down our verbal understanding, you would have been set off at the first cove along the shore. I did put down a detailed account of our conversations, which I will keep by. While questions remain, what is clear is you deliberately deceived me as to the nature of your instruction to the boy. I did sense resistance to my directives regarding his adhering to a more traditional curriculum but did not investigate further. What investigation

I did conduct concerned the subject of Sensitives. Notwithstanding having a ship to run, I have learned much." She gestured behind her to her library before patting a sheaf of close-written documents on her desk.

She flipped through her pages as she spoke, "Sensitives have existed before recorded history and are the foundation of much nonsense. They are also fundamental to much of our art and culture. There is a measure of overlap between Sensitives and another group known as 'Touched.' These are best described as Savants of sometimes startling specialties. You likely know Adept that the ancient Thithanu Menem Priesthood persecuted Touched with unusual severity, even for them. Given many of the Menem's inspirational leaders and authors were likely Sensitives themselves, they were among the few displaying exceptional attributes who were protected, although common Sensitives fared little better than the rest."

She set down her papers, "I have no quarrel with acknowledging and admiring distinctive abilities. My issue is articulated in more recent work revealing a problem, the inclination of some to venerate Sensitives. Usually, this practice serves an established tradition going through some sort of renewal or a new movement. Even worse, there are recorded instances of Sensitives who were also burdened with various mental illnesses. I regret to add this is more common than not. In certain settings, these were conflated and used to sway populations to rash actions."

She paused, looking off into space before turning to Seti, "My young friend, I have concluded that you do bear the marks of being a Sensitive. I must credit your Adept with seeing this immediately. My preliminary explorations reveal the extent of my innocence on this topic. To my knowledge, you are the first Sensitive of my acquaintance. Sadly, I am also convinced your Adept has chosen to weave your being a Sensitive and suffering from one or more mental conditions into a single mantle. I am further convinced that history is about to repeat itself with your unique set of conditions and these volatile times."

With a gesture, she silenced Hegev's attempts to speak.

"My duty as captain is clear. This is a commercial vessel, not some 'Prophet's Barque' out of the epics. This ship is an extension of the Sawlu Clan's orderly and predictable global business interests. Any interruption to the task at hand will be viewed as a disruption. Jine-Piprith, our clan head, and the Wazaratcha Council will be most indignant when they learn of this series of extraordinary events associated with their ship and crew. There is no comparison between our quiet dissemination of dissenting literature and running a revolutionary figure from port to port in Tatchlan territory. For all these reasons, I should put you both off at the next port. Indeed, were we not on the other side of Anu, I would feel compelled to do so despite my personal feelings about you, Seti."

She near jumped out of her seat and stormed back and forth in her cabin shaking and swinging her arms in frustration. The three spectators kept out of her way as best they could. She stopped again behind her desk and expelled an explosive breath, "Notwithstanding all I have said, I swear I will protect you as long as I can. We have come too far for me to abandon you, although I will pay for it when we finally reach home."

The three adults looked at Seti in the sudden silence of the captain's cabin. While they had long ceased to note the ship's gentle pitch on calm waters, they heard the familiar muted groans as Jefaka made her way. The thuds, creaks and calls of the crew at their tasks formed the backdrop. Amid this usual banter, they heard one young woman in a conversation say, "our Prophet Seti." She walked with others near the captain's quarters when she spoke these words.

Seti looked at each of them and smiled, "I searched for my mission. The Memanu revealed it to me." He looked at Emedin, "I went to the fields without expectation. In recent two-weeks, my vision has been tested in many ways. It is returned and is strong. I am now possessed with the serenity of certainty."

He leaned forward to touch her desk, "Captain, I have always been on a mission! My Adept has opened my eyes to many things, but she also defers to what drives me. I would beg you not to penalize her for my sake. She has stood by my side through many troubles as I have grown in my preparations."

Captain Emedin paused before slowly seating herself. Finally, in a quiet voice, she answered, "Very well."

"Thank you, Captain!" Seti turned to Hegev, "There is little time to learn what I need to know. I must open myself to what comes. I will walk among the multitudes and view this verdant chaos, taking what I learn to further my visions. I will possess my voice in full and use it in the service of our wayward kind."

He turned back, "Captain, I have always known you do not believe; yet you have ever loved and encouraged me. I have learned to trust your instincts in many things. I ask now that you trust me in this. Wisdom does not always come to eyes opened, but may fill those who but trust to close their eyes."

They looked at the captain. Emedin appeared to shrink in her seat as she pushed her chair back to increase her distance before giving Hegev an intense frown. "We near the tip of Statos-Vey," she said slowly. "There we will be embraced by the warm waters of Panchala Sea flowing between Statos-Vey and Thermistal. She will conduct us along the rich eastern coast on our way home."

"Good," Seti said. "I intend to display my Memanu Knot in every port we encounter."

Emedin and Dine started and looked at each other. Dine strode up to the table, "Keep it hidden, boy!" he hissed. He looked at his captain. She passed a trembling hand over her face as she nodded for him to continue. "There is another fear we discuss here you must appreciate. Remember, we are deep in Tatchlan territory! We move *toward* the city of Bhampay! Those masters possess the city and the Primary Mountain Circle surrounding their capital, Upata-Shepsus, one thousand andas inland. We have avoided this port of ports on occasion due to their Harbourmaster's extensive stipulations. For instance," he gestured to the captain's library, "all books found are inventoried. Novelties are taken for their libraries while we receive copies in return. This is one of a long series of non-negotiable preconditions for ships docking there. In exchange for visiting the wealthiest port on Anu, we must open ourselves to their extensive examinations in many other ways."

"My First Officer is correct in this," Emedin said. "Bhampay is the commercial capital of Statos-Vey. For centuries, our ships have been circumspect in approaching it. We have a long tradition of travelling in fleets down the west coast, arranging to meet ahead of time in the southernmost part of our journey, near to the first islands forming the 'broken bridge' of the Taldonow Islands going east. We approach this juncture in the coming days. Those wishing to avoid the city transferred crew and materials onto other ships intending to either return along the western coast or skirt the islands of Vaudlan and Vildy, near the coast of Thermistal. These measures were not always sufficient to avoid Bhampay's scrutiny."

"If we do not carry anything prohibited in their eyes," Seti replied, "why must we sneak past them?"

"Because unless you intend to throw your Memanu Knot overboard," Dine replied, "they will find it. When the story of the fields reaches the city, they may recognize it."

Seti shook his head, "Did I do something illegal?"

"The combination of what transpired and what you said afterwards will arouse their interest," Emedin replied. "You know little of the south. The masters here have long occupied a near-religious position and hold important posts in every ministry. An extensive network of communications serves them. They have a long list of signs their servants are to maintain a watch. You may be deemed worthy of further examination."

Seti looked at each of them, "We cannot hide the knot?"

"Many generations of seafarers attempted to hide items half its size," Emedin said. "Stories tell of how they can pick out anything regardless of how it is hidden." She tapped her collection of notes, "I was a fool to not penetrate this mystery before now. Finally, I realize the truth! We knew they long crafted powerful Sensitives.They must possess an army of specialized ones bred for this purpose! They do not pierce wood and stone with their deepened abilities. Their powers reveal what is hidden within *us*. They smell our emotions and sense any lie."

She again indicated her notes, "One ancient title for them was as 'Truth Sayers.' As such, our bodies betray us. They are beyond our ability to deceive. Even if we disposed of your knot, these Tatchlan Sensitives will likely still perceive your distinctive nature. I once dismissed these tales as the 'salt yarns' of the taverns. Now we truly have something we do not wish them to find, and I am less ignorant as to the powers of these Sensitives, I am sure of this."

"Why are these fantastic inspections not in place at the other ports?" Hegev asked.

"Once we turn to travel Statos-Vey's eastern flank, you will see," Emedin answered. "These ports are less intense and extended than in Bhampay, but were we to venture inland from any port; their scrutiny would immediately increase. When we speak of Bhampay, we speak of the main gateway to Statos-Vey. Many of their wisest, wealthiest and most powerful dwell there. A good number of the Muraharoma Dynasty's leading institutions are based in this city. Bhampay is surrounded by what they call the Red Ring, a perfectly circular enclosure forming their famed seawall. Land entries are likewise guarded. These masters are well acquainted with Sawlu Clan and our anti-Tatchlan stance. Seti knows our history and how a few went over to them. Their apparent disinterest in our recent activities is meant to signify our lack of importance to them."

"This will be altered," Dine said. "Each time you brandish your 'Memanu Knot' between here and Bhampay. Your miraculous token increases the likelihood of drawing their gaze on us. We will no longer just be a trading vessel with a history of carrying anti-Tatchlan literature. Having one calling the Grand Menem by name and working miracles would place us in a very different category. This time Jefaka travels alone. We told your Adept of our imminent arrival in Bhampay. We will not encounter others from our fleet to pass you onto."

"I said I would protect you," Emedin said, "and protect you, I will. We must amend our submitted sailing plan," she began looking through her papers. Dine raised his eyebrows in surprise behind her. "I plan to sail out into Panchala and make for the major islands of Vaudlan and Vildy. If you are circumspect with your Memanu knot, the work could be done there with far less scrutiny."

Seti was shocked. His Adept asked, "What do you mean by 'submitted sailing plan?'"

Emedin and Dine smiled at each other. "As we told you when you arrived Adept," Dine said, "before we left Wazaratcha, we posted and received permission to sail in Statos-Vey waters. This included our intended ports of call. This time, Bhampay was on our list. Some ships make the Circuit many times before Bhampay appears on their manifest."

"Jefaka had her inaugural inspection in Bhampay over a decade ago during her first Circuit," Emedin said, "The trip takes two or more years. Then she has local duties before returning to this extended work. This is her third Circuit, and it is time for significant refurbishment. Bhampay's Shipwrights Guild possesses members with unequalled skill. We intended to lift her out of the water and do a complete hull working. Sawlu has sent payment. This primary and other secondary guilds can accomplish these tasks with unmatched expertise and speed. Our hold filled, we would then sail for Rho-Jashun, making infrequent stops until we reached 'The Crown,' the Huallapandu headlands, and turned west for home."

"Captain!" Hegev exclaimed, "Would not our avoidance of Bhampay be viewed as suspicious? Such considerable work on a ship of this size must be exorbitant. For you to avoid having it done will be suspect."

"The work will be done, but at a different port."

"Captain?" Dine said.

"I will not abandon him!' Emedin exclaimed.

"I do not propose you do, but there must be another way. Jefaka must be 'opened and sealed' in Bhampay."

"This guild has associations throughout these most populated of waters. There is ample precedent for transferring contracts between different members of the same professional house as needed. As long as the work is certified by the same association, ruling northeastern Statos-Vey's shores and its many islands, the location is left to the captain's discretion. Dine is right about a few ships being able to enter Bhampay each Circuit. There are many practical reasons why a ship may defer the honour without raising any questions."

"In general, yes, captain, but this is an exceptional case. You know Sawlu has purchased not just a contract, but a *preference contract* in Bhampay and its numerous trade specialists. To defer this is most unusual. We are not scheduled for any other port. We may find ourselves in a very long queue behind their existing contracts. We would need to establish contact and open negotiations with guilds we have not dealt with before. Jine-Piprith will eventually hear of it, and we may have more to worry about at home than here."

"So be it."

Dine raised his eyebrows but did not answer.

"I will not forsake him," she turned to speak to him. "I disagree with his mission, but I will not leave him to the masters. I maintain the hope this phase will pass, and he may yet come to a more balanced view. I know your practical objections are well stated and sincere, I also know you harbour a measure of sympathy for this mission of his."

Dine flushed before glancing at Seti, "I have come to love him as you do, captain. It is true; I also feel more hope and inspiration since he came aboard. I had thought all was lost but now entertain the possibility we may yet reverse these master's fortunes. I do not know how to accomplish this within the confines of our duty to our ship and clan."

Emedin's fingers drummed her table. "Back when these arrangements were made, and we set sail, the notion of our taking Dream Reader on board who would grow into a prophet was not foreseen. I think you and I can well agree that if we had the slightest suspicion of these events, we would have avoided the fields."

"Perhaps, captain," Dine said, "but when we planned this trip, we also had no hint Hushukrath, the island of Tich-Tushmul's principle port, had come under their sway." He looked at Hegev, "I presume, Adept, Seti spoke to you of the twisted performance of the Epic of Ranvartawan we witnessed and the large Tatchlan emblems displayed there?"

Hegev nodded.

"That is over twenty-thousand andas north and west of here!" Dine exclaimed, pointing in the general direction for emphasis. "From the beginning, those Tatchlan 'masters' have moved with stealth through the Muraharoma Dynasty line. Their influence now spreads across lower Rho-Jashun like an unseasonable frost. Our Nebutan saw the full extent of their power within Upata-Shepsus fifty years ago when she fled and came to us. By the time they reach my age, our grandchildren could see those cursed Tatchlan glyphs covering Jonochem Manor on Wazaratcha Island. I assume our Adept has not travelled to either of these strongholds during her pilgrimage."

Hegev shook her head, "I avoided the capital and its primary port city. I observed enough of Tatchlan elsewhere without going to its twin fountainheads."

"So!" Seti exclaimed, "You all say we are to avoid the rest of Statos-Vey?"

"Boy," Captain Emedin asked, "*What is your plan*? Do you imagine assailing these masters in their seats of power? What will you bring against them? We are alone on this foreign ocean and land, very far from our allies. Their surprise magnified your 'miracle' and declaration. And now here we are, at the bottom of Statos-Vey, on the threshold of the terrible Taldonow archipelago, whose southern arctic storms exceed our northern ones. We are as far away from safety as it is possible to be. In many ways we are at a crossroads. While I am angry at the course of your education and your chosen path, I will not discard you here in the south."

Seti sat in silence for a time. "I believe this Tatchlan to be a great evil. I fear we sleepwalk toward new slavery. I must do something to stop it. There is much I do not understand, and more I remain in ignorance about. Despite our different views, Captain, I feel we agree on this. Cannot we do as Hegev has said and find accommodation between faith and rationality?"

Emedin regarded him evenly, "We agree as to our situation, but not the remedy. When you reach my age, you may be less inclined to use such absolute terms as 'evil' and 'slavery.' While I oppose their programme, I see no self-serving malice in any of the master's actions. Our historic opposition has, in part, been thwarted by their consistently presenting themselves as geniuses and saints. How they have managed to avoid the waste and folly besetting the rest of us I cannot imagine. I have no doubt they are dedicated to what they think is right. We represent a long line of dissenters, going back to Nallurakon, who disagree with their prognosis and treatment. We have a different notion of 'who we are.' In all her works," she gestured back to her library, "which are unfailingly critical of each aspect of their programme, Nebutan never once used the term 'evil.' I have made my position clear as to what I would have for you. For now, you have chosen a different course. I will do my best to keep you out of harm's way as long as you remain aboard the Jefaka. Should you ever choose to leave before we reach Wazaratcha, I would wish you a fair wind for your journeys." She stared into space while the rest remained in silence. "This is not that day!" Captain Emedin declared. "For now, you must remain with us until we are well beyond Bhampay."

"Captain," Dine said, "there remains the issue of his Memanu Knot. We have eluded the curious, but the story may spread ahead to the next port. Given our discussions here, I find myself forced to concur with your decision to turn to the open ocean. We could use some of our late stores to sustain us for a two week of 'deep running.'"

"Hmmm . . . I did not make this determination lightly. Regrettably, this action may prove for the best. A change of sail and banners to alter our appearance would also be prudent."

"Those at the fields readied to follow me!" Seti said.

"Dear boy!" Emedin said, smiling at him. "Yesterday, they followed you. What name do they call out today? Stirring the general population is easy. Miraculous stories fill their lives, and your message was compelling and intriguing. Building and maintaining a cohesive movement with the necessary internal structure is far more difficult. There remains the question of what the larger goal is. Are we attempting internal unrest in the master's own house, or uniting the well-disposed populations of central and northern Rho-Jashun? There, your message will be welcomed, and you may gather a considerable following. If this is your destiny, then our base on Wazaratcha Island can aid this new form of resistance with its ample resources and organization."

Hegev stared in amazement at the captain. "Your vision leads to civil war! You see Seti heading an army marching south across Rho-Jashun, just as the Suvuka did against our ancestors. They would meet the same resistance at the southern bend of the Mulungu Mountains. I have seen them and tell you our ancestors' defences against the Suvuka are restored!"

"You are mistaken," Emedin said in icy tones. "Sawlu Clan does nurture the dream of ending the masters' rule, but not by war. The Muraharoma Dynasty abandoned Rho-Jashun long ago. Our vision is of uniting our northern Tolku into a separate nation. A unified state and guiding vision will resist the continuing advance of the masters. Their reach extends thus far onto the island of Tich-Tushmul because we are divided!" She turned to Seti, "Be patient! Learn what you can here," she signalled to her library. "Once we pass the Samashetepal Channel, where Thermistal and Rho-Jashun draw closest, you will be free to enter the ports and display your miraculous knot. When we reach home, you will be fortified in many ways to receive additional instruction. There we may gather a large group to assist in making your visions reality."

"Your plan will still lead to war," Seti said. "What we speak of is creating an alternative to the Tatchlan Master state possessing Anu. They will not permit a united population, having inspired leadership, to threaten their dream." He looked at Hegev. "My Adept has told you of my visions of the Faces?"

The other two adults nodded.

"They grow in dimensions and hover on the edge of my waking sight. These Faces herald Tatchlan's growing power. These Masters work to produce a supreme leader, able to reach inside each Tolku. Should they succeed, your resources will not avail us. We must overthrow them, or they will overthrow us."

Silence filled the captain's cabin. Emedin stood and began to pace the cabin for some time before seating herself again, "I fear we have no choice. I will not abandon you and so find myself committed against my better judgment. Amidst such folly, our wisest course is to continue your preparation and make our way home where our best chance of success lies."

CHAPTER 25

SHUNA-SHAPTA

Pictured: Secondary Epoch Icon for an Operant

Day 249, in Two-Week Fourteen, Min – the Banner in Master Enclave, City of Bhampay.

Shuna-Shapta moved through the labyrinthian corridors of the Master Enclave to the residence of Master Tanas's pre-Cluster. Even modest passageways were decorated with frescos, hanging tapestries and niches with statues, associated with the entranceways into other pre-Clusters, along with Invocate Chambers and other Enclave facilities. Her favourite part of such journeys was catching whiffs of the 'Scent Wall' coming through the closed doors or curtains of these pre-Clusters. The one uniform feature was tiny skylights at regular intervals ensuring consistent illumination.

Shuna-Shapta was expected. She was immediately conducted into a modest-sized chamber at the far end of a large collective room. She was surprised to see all members of this pre-Cluster partially clothed inside their residence and so retained her simple shirt. The chamber was open on the inner side with three walls and a window on the outer side. The walls and ceiling were amber-coloured and overlaid in elegant painted calligraphy, mostly blue and green, with yellow outlines, quoting from a variety of ancient literary works.

Once she had entered, a heavy curtain was drawn across. It was a work of woven art appearing to show a series of six skulls, each a different colour, occupying the middle space. The central two skulls faced forward, the next two turned either side, and the outer two were in profile facing out. A florid garden, festooned with birds and insects, blossomed up and out of their eye sockets. A fish-filled river flowed down and out of each of their six gaping jaws. She then noted the four larpana plants in each corner and the piles of pillows and books lining the walls, and two large pillows occupying the centre space, one closer to the window and the other the curtain.

Finally, she examined the two large carved and painted representations of Principal Faces standing on pols set into sturdy bases either side of the central window. She had briefly noted similar artworks, positioned either side of windows, in other chambers facing the central space of Master Tanas's pre-Cluster. Neferdush, the Face of Perception, stood to the left of the window, her magnificent nose hanging far down below her chin. She appeared to scrutinize Shuna-Shapta through her characteristic purple, blue and orange ringed eyes surrounded by silver flesh. The other bore the severe half night and half-day Face of Skarashing, the Discerner of Polarities. Both shone with newness and spoke of profound craftsmanship.

"Shapta," Master Tanas's distinctive booming voice sounded outside the curtain, "I am about to enter."

The large man stepped into the chamber, returning the curtain to its full extent across the entrance. He was fully dressed in one of his formal academic gowns as he strode over to stand before the window.

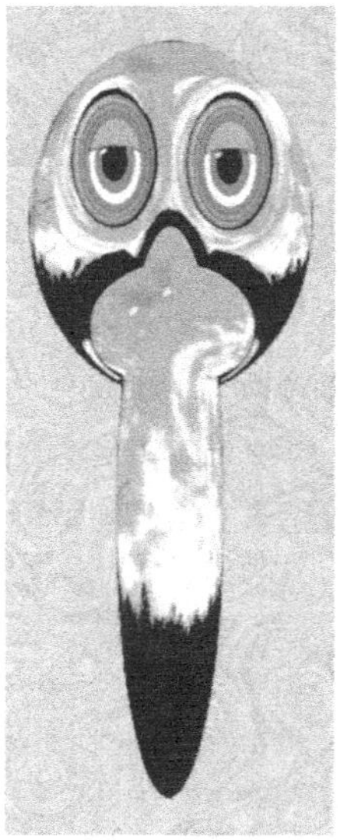

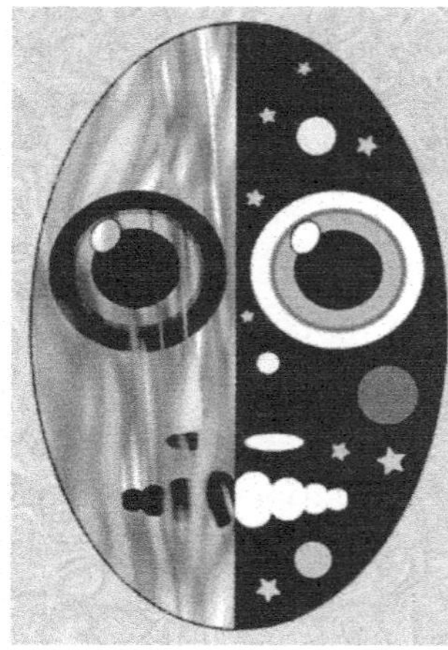

"Your portion of Anu fares well this day?" he commenced a ritual greeting never used between them before.

"Yes, Master, the 'Living Loam sinks deep beneath our feet.'"

"Shash. I would request you kneel upon this pillow," he indicated the one closer to the curtain. As she complied, she noted how Master Tanas's aromas filled the small chamber with a heady mixture of intense emotions. He stood with his back to the window and gauged her.

"And how fares your Circle? You have merged for many two-weeks."

Shuna-Shapta had not expected this and took a moment to recover, "Wonderful, Master."

"Wonderful? For generations, Masters struggled as much with this as Tatchlan. Nowhere else did our hidden walls of Self-Absorption become so manifest. Were it not for our Lustrum Mirror; I fear our grand design would have failed. Generations have crafted our domestication and sanity. Being born into a deep-functioning Circle, despite having no Maja at our core, is still a luxury. I had the good fortune to be distinguished by my Depth Tests and left my rude island upon Lake Yandu to come here as a lad. I then had the privilege of as good a cluster upbringing as possible for our time. I joyfully observe our children founding their own circles. The key element we lacked, Maja, now grows in profusion."

Master Tanas turned to briefly look out the window, "Since Thakadush Cluster wakened amongst us, much has settled, and our cherished traditions fortify beyond precedent. For many generations, we strove to emulate the foundational unit of our new society. Now we behold the daily birth of true Maja, giving hope of more circles and clusters becoming complete. As Spokes of our true Cluster Wheels, they bring our vision to life."

He stopped and drew several deep breaths, "Whilst you are Maja, a different path opens before you." He brought out of his sleeve a rolled document Shuna-Shapta recognized as the one she had sent to him.

He now spoke in near hushed tones, "Of the many wonders we Masters endure within this time of sudden Quickening; I must confess your dispatch to me surpasses all else!"

He then gently got down on the other pillow facing her, so their knees were touching. He slowly brought his large dark hands to either side of Shuna-Shapta's trembling face.

"What do you see?" he enquired.

Shuna-Shapta immediately knew what he meant, "The glowing expanse of our Resplendent Work," she said. A distant and unfocused look filled her eyes. "I behold bursts of light, gardens of growth swirl within shifting sections. Flocks of our Secondary Faces of Tatchlan glide over, under and through them. Rivers and lakes of The Common Desire twist and shift across our breathing lands."

She frowned, "All is the same and different! Each thing is reversed, and yet this reversal brings clarity! It is as if prior to this, I was balanced upon my head, and now my feet are firmly planted. I may not find the words! I possess more facility, more awareness than heretofore."

Aromas of amazement flowed off Master Tanas; after a moment's pause, he spoke, "What of Invocants? Do you see them?"

"Many glide over the surface," her intense eyes lost focus again, "tethered to a variety of Secondary Faces. It appears I elude their gaze. Those unattended Secondary Faces who behold me stop and bob once in a way I had not seen."

"Do you see members of your Circle?"

"I have in the past, yes. None labour within Tatchlan this day. I have seen you and my two mothers."

"When you saw me last, what did I do?"

"You stood before servants of Hesha Vira and Alatanda, using them to examine the Suvuka."

Master Tanas shook his head in wonder. "Where is your First Ama?"

Shuna-Shapta frowned in concentration, "Ah!" she exclaimed. "She works with a flock of Secondary Faces serving our third Principal Face, Naprahath. They remain unaware of my presence."

"Majastas Be!" Master Tanas exclaimed as he withdrew his quivering hands. "You also see me here?"

Shuna-Shapta blinked her eyes once and smiled at him.

"When you see me, where goes Tatchlan?"

"It is still there. I may conduct myself at any time, although it also possesses me without warning. Visions present themselves at once for a brief span, outside my control."

Master Tanas rose and went to stand at the single large window. There had been warnings of a major storm coming in the next few days from the south. The inner harbour was preparing to close to outside traffic as the city readied itself. While looking at the distant activity, he pondered what he heard.

"Shapta!" he exclaimed, turning back, "When did this begin?"

She did not hesitate, "Two-Week Thirteen, Elder Day 225."

He started, "Twenty-four days ago? This was . . . when we visited Thakadush Cluster for the birth of our one-hundredth Maja."

Shuna-Shapta nodded.

"You have been having these visions for over twenty days? You delayed this long telling anyone?"

"They began as brief flashes. The first displayed the full formation of Principal Faces. I initially mistook them for a new version of the headaches I used to endure as a pre-adult."

"These headaches, you no longer suffer from them?"

"No, Master, with the onset of my teens, I was directed to increase my Sheshenara intake, and they left me."

Master Tanas nodded, "I have heard of it having this effect. Please continue."

"During these flashes, I felt . . . a pleasant falling prior to a warm curling sensation beginning within my feet. This rose through me until my inner windows opened, and the pattern resolved."

Master Tanas stared at her in amazement, "What other sensations accompanied these 'flashes?'"

"At first none, but as they extended, each sense accompanied them. I inhabit a warm, twisting, fragrant ocean that fills me to the brim. For these past twenty days, I have attempted to direct these events inside our Living System. I thought it wise to gather details prior to approaching you."

"Does your Circle of Eight know?"

"Yes, they urged me to come to you."

Master Tanas nodded, picked up a set of documents and returned to his pillow. He spoke in a quiet and guarded way; she had never heard from him, "Have you heard the term 'Operant?"

"No, Master, what does it mean?"

"It describes the exceptional crown of our craft. Upon exceedingly rare occasions, there emerges a single Operant amid a sea of Invocants. Your experience describes what distinguishes one from the other. You know the extensive and arduous path Invocants tread to reach Tatchlan. The Operant enters our Resplendent Work without an Instrument. You stand upon the threshold of a level of mastery future ages shall see as a defining feature of Majastas, whom past Masters have declared shall be our 'Supreme Operant.'"

Shuna-Shapta's eyes went wide.

"My delay in responding to your dispatch was to set many things in motion," Master Tanas said. "Our Esteemed Librarians now research this, and we begin to receive their reports," he indicated the pile of densely written papers. "Amongst our countless hundreds of thousands throughout our long programme, just over four hundred are recognized and catalogued as true Operants! That represents a fraction of one percent of all recorded Masters and Invocates. There is more than sufficient accounts to confirm what you wrote to me and now I must declare 'I smell the Truth of it!'"

He pointed at the top page, "The first Operant we are certain of lived within the early Buyanupithar Dynasty when most of our predecessors called themselves 'Practicians.' Only a few achieved the title Master. He was distinguished for not needing to employ our Sigil Cubes - once our primary way of building Tatchlan. He never heard the name 'Menem' because the religion that would persecute us was yet to be born. He played a vital role in laying the foundations for the birth of our Living Instruments, by fashioning a specialized branch of the foundation of our Living Orb, the Seeds with their Tentacles and Tails. I have not spoken to you of these, do you know of them?"

"Yes, Master, my mother taught me. Our Living Orb is composed of unknown billions of these Seeds. Their tentacles reach out to each other to form the web structure of all aspects of our Resplendent Work. Their tails travel incalculable distances to other Seeds within our Living Orb and form vast networks creating all we behold. These Seeds, with their crown of tentacles and long tails, are too minuscule for us to view upon our Living Orb."

"We do not perceive them for their protection. They are now too meshed and delicate for us to work with directly; instead, we do so via their proxies, originally the Tatchlan Cubes and now via our Secondary Faces. Many Invocates spend their lives in service without knowledge of this foundation. I am glad you know the truth of this civilizing network overlaying raw life. Given your advances, I deem you ready for other fundamental truths about our Resplendent Work's true nature."

Shuna-Shapta hesitated before saying, "Master, I presume a portion of these truths has to do with how differently Tatchlan appears to me now."

Master Tanas looked long at her, "Yes . . ." he said at last. "I have been reading about how for Operants, the ordering and structure are reversed and far more complex. Our Uluvatu Masters designed our Living Instruments to present us with a more generalized view of our living depths for our benefit. I assume these four hundred Operants quickly discovered, as you now have, the true structure when they entered via their powers. Naught is changed in what you know, just in the particulars. We shall discuss this at length another time when I may grasp more of this."

Shuna-Shapta nodded before lapsing into silence. Finally, she said, "This first Operant . . . he created a new version of Seed?"

"It was a remarkable feat, laying the foundation for much to follow. His genius animated The General Plain beyond what had been possible. Our ability to grow and cultivate such Seed before instructing them to replicate into their vast array of specialities has allowed for all distinct Tatchlan life, both visible and invisible, to our eyes. The rest of these Operants continued to distinguish themselves for enacting vital leaps in our programme by virtue of their matchless abilities. It is said, within a single generation, two of our Primary Uluvatu Masters were also Operants. Given the great antiquity of our work, to the best of our knowledge, this was the single time more than one existed in the same generation. Our feet rest upon their foundations within our Living System."

He paused and shook his head, "In the past, I am given to understand there were Operant Authorities. I have learned our last recorded Operant died over six hundred years ago. There is none living who is fully conversant on these matters this day."

Shuna-Shapta sat taking this in. "What shall I do? I may no longer deny this has grown into full life within me."

"We must consult many in our determination of how you are to proceed," Master Tanas replied. "Your First and Second Mother, and your entire Birth Circle, already treasure you as a glory within our midst."

"I should tell my First and Second Ama?"

"Yes. Your twenty days of guardedness was admirable. None of your studies prepared you for this rare gift. Beyond myself, your Birth Circle and your Circle, tell no one. We Masters shall form a secure Gathering, attended by Venerable Scholars and Esteemed Librarians, to gather our disparate threads together. In earlier times, those wiser than us may have determined how the development of a young Operant best proceeded. Perchance an ancient Operant wrote a full text upon the subject! We now commence a mighty effort to revive this arcane knowledge."

"What should I do?"

Master Tanas spread his broad hands, "My innocence constrains my reply. I may not follow you to the depths you have now descended. It is likely I have naught left to teach you beyond what I shall learn of these esoteric matters. I am now the student and you, our Master. As our understanding warms to this ancient lore, you should live your life and allow this new ability to take root."

Shuna-Shapta began to cry. Master Tanas sat in silence and watched her before taking her hands. They glistened with her tears, and her body quaked. Her weeping grew into deep sobs. Her gasps subsided, and her breathing slowed.

"It was a burden," she began. "I hated withholding. How do mundanes live with all their secrets?"

Master Tanas drew her into a warm embrace, "You did well, Shapta!" He sat back, holding her shoulders, "This bravery and wisdom speaks of a depth beyond your years. Your discipline is a mark of distinction as I behold a Ripe Adult before me! Your composure and patience were equal to this unforeseen development. You have not erred, and I regret you suffered this secret. There may be no doubt you are an Operant. We shall lay down a good path for you to proceed and watch your descent into ever richer depths of Anu's Flesh."

He sat back and gestured for Shuna-Shapta rise. She smiled as she stepped about the room. She shook her limbs and breathed deeply. "You said these past Operants; they initiated leaps forward within our Resplendent Work?"

"References gathered thus far attest to this," Master Tanas said. "Our Gathering shall excavate this matter in full."

Shuna-Shapta went and stared out at the city, making ready for the storm.

"Shapta . . ." Master Tanas hesitated. "May I enquire what you imagine you could do?"

"I do not know," she turned and replied at once, "Perchance this might have emerged upon its own. I know Thakadush-Satwa called it forth by Her powerful skin." She turned to look out the window again, "I hear the name Thakadush Cluster wherever I go. The general population grows animated about us. After dwelling deep within a select few, Tatchlan bursts into full view. How shall this proceed?"

Master Tanas laughed, "Shapta, we Masters stand jaws open with the rest. This sudden glorious eruption into the commons is utterly novel.

Our revolution has broken the surface transforming mundane life." He stood as another thought came to him, "Your mother, Master Kanla, mentioned your younger sister's school trip to a backward locality off our Imperial Way."

Shuna-Shapta nodded as he joined her, leaning on the deep and warm sill.

"The birth of Maja now occurs beyond our cities," Master Tanas said, also looking out. "Whilst they remain the primary location, smaller communities report their own marvellous births. A healthy concentration of population remains essential, and we discern where this may occur within smaller contexts than anticipated. The numbers continue to grow, and reports of Maja births arrive from considerable distances. Our Bhampay remains by far the most populated by new Maja, although Upata-Shepsus and other centres approach our numbers."

"And the benighted colony?"

Master Tanas chuckled as he turned to face her, "Imagine when all Anu was thus! Long ago, Sensitives began to appear in significant numbers, laying our first social foundations. A mundane-dominated community is now quite unusual upon our subcontinent. I am informed we now quietly study this population as it unknowingly stands upon the verge of transformation. No doubt remains, all new births inspire awe, including amongst them. Reports from across the country confirm this established and spreading trend. New births within this little hamlet shall manifest lesser wonders of Tatchlan, progressing toward us. Perchance they shall merge into a single cluster in time. Rural Clusters shall of necessity grow far larger than their urban counterparts. Find comfort in knowing members of this miserable little settlement shall know a peaceful transformation. Given the accelerated rate our Resplendent Orb opens, we may expect this full established within a few decades. The loving crowd shall heal their many ills."

Shuna-Shapta nodded and looked out the window. "Our dreams come true. My little sister enquired of me if the look of our city would change." She gazed at the view, "I said some might, but our Bhampay shall continue."

Despite the growing sounds of unusual activity in the rest of the

Enclave, they continued their conversation.

"I must disagree," Master Tanas said. "Notwithstanding many advances, all our cities remain governed by Self-Absorption. Whilst not as noxious as those mundane villagers, our population maintains unhealthy levels of segregation. Those poisoned by aggression still dominate the peaceful majority. We Masters have changed how our entire society functions and removed many overt causes of Self-Absorption, and yet the patterns persist. We foresee the necessity of future Majastas enacting many ceremonies to purge these community toxins and forging additional links to our Living Orb. This shall usher in the true birth of our Cluster-of-Clusters society. Public buildings may remain unaffected, but the emergence of Maja-led clusters overseen by a Majastas shall enact a wholesale renovation of many of the physical and cultural institutions. Open dwellings reflecting true cluster life shall become the norm. Note what Thakadush Cluster has done to their compound. Without knowing what we did within our residences here and in other Enclaves, the renovations mimic them with few walls and no doors. They continue to remove walls from their original structure whilst securing advice on how to ensure its stability. Although I was not born here, Bhampay has long been my home. I love it as dearly as you. Rest assured, our city shall not only persist but thrive . . ."

"Master?" a young boy hesitantly said as he opened the curtains and approached them.

"Yes?"

"A woman from Thakadush Cluster seeks Invocate Shapta."

Master Tanas and Shuna-Shapta stared at the servant and each other. The curtain opened, and a tall woman, her black hair in long braids running in coils down her back, stepped in. The boy bowed low and ran back outside. The rest of the Enclave had gone silent as their interest lay on the other side of the curtain. The woman's eyes were outlined in green, and her powerful odour filled the room. The Mother of Thakadush-Satwa held up her palms; the other two returned her solemn gesture.

"Our young Majastas speaks," she declared, looking at Shuna-Shapta. "She calls you by name."

Shuna-Shapta stood eyes wide and at a loss for words. She had viewed the miraculous infant but once back at the inception of her new powers.

"Our Sensitives say you occupy her dreams. You and your Circles shall enter Thakadush Cluster. Our Masters shall now achieve their deepest calling, becoming Servants."

CHAPTER 26

SINKIN

Primary Epoch icon of the Wum, a sea creature with its shell floating above the waves and its tendrils drifting in the deep.

Day 251, within the Jaladanu Mountains, one thousand andas south and east of Avanchil Round on the Mushumafal Peninsula.

For thirteen days, Durka and Makusk Herd had travelled south out of Avanchil Round and along the western coast. The Herdmasters took them inland. The towering Jaladanu Mountains had welcomed them into their embrace. The Suvuka passed through many deep and curving valleys, and the climate was transformed. The mighty Kukernef Desert raged and spent itself on the high north side of Jaladanu behind them.

In contrast, on the other side, the warm and saturated air from the Panchala Sea watered a glorious garden. This sudden lush growth and vibrant colour spread from the valleys to the many peaks of Jaladanu's southern face. They travelled through a continuous green, undisturbed by the mountains and valleys beneath it. The yellow tinge of sand on the winds became clear, and the air moist.

These were not the harsh jungles surrounding the Latatroos Shelter close to the equator but a rich and mild paradise - the more glorious for the north's bitter desert. Innumerable winged creatures filled the fragrant air with a distinctive musical chorus. When their song finished at dusk, another ensemble took their turn through the mild nights. For the first time in many two-weeks, the Suvuka's pelts began to darken and regain their former lustre. Their exposed skin softened and healed. The Keepers' charge included the maintenance of a series of stations along this portion of the southern coast of Thermistal. They ensured those Bucks debilitated from the journey to Avanchil, and the rigours experienced in the bowl were fortified and refreshed as they prepared for their final rite of passage. A modest native Suvuka population readied to serve the Stag Run as it passed. As the two small herds came to the southern extent of the mountains, where it met the sea, they turned east to follow the coast. They delighted in the sweet airs of the Panchala Sea and rested to her distant echoing cries.

Herdmasters Hiratak and Morakav rose in the morning and made their way down to view the ocean. They sat in silence, watching the abundant warm waters travel west and north. Far beyond their view to the south lay the distant shores of Statos-Vey. A herd of Wum, a curious sea creature hugging the southern coast of Thermistal could be seen just beyond the surf. Their shining purple shells bobbed on the surface while their long tendrils hung far into the darkness below.

Hiratak turned to Morakav. "I remember seeing this coast after my dance. The Wum were here then as well. One of our group tried to ride them," he gestured at the Wum.

They both laughed. "Did he last long?" Morakav asked.

"No, after much futile scratching on its shell he gave up. We all laughed so hard we rolled on the sand."

After laughing again Hiratak grew serious, "The sagas rang in my ears that day. My rite was focused and my heart full. I had yet to hear of Pramath Island, yet I yearned for the final challenge. This Run… " his voice trailed off.

Morakav nodded, "This Run is unlike any I heard of. Hundreds witnessed this Face. The story will travel north."

"Will Avanchil meet the same fate as Dakast Round?" Hiratak asked. "Will the Toohund haunt our beloved bowl?"

"You see our two young Bucks bond?"

"Yes."

Morakav smiled at his friend, "There is more between them than the normal run kinship. They engage in soft speech. I believe this Face attends their Run."

Hiratak frowned and began to speak, stopped himself and stared at the ocean. "I heard the Songs of Sarm when I was just a buck. My elders were discomforted. Despite this, they insisted on hearing them. A deep terror grips me. Those wild green eyes disturb me. I cannot speak to our Bucks save to argue."

"Destroying Avanchil will change nothing," Morakav said. "We all saw this Face."

"What does it *mean*?" Hiratak burst out as he rose. "We *all* saw it! Have we become diviners? Have we gone mad?"

"Have we been possessed?"

"You mean . . . by the enemy?"

Morakav nodded.

"What does Setush say? What of the others of Makusk? Does this return you to your humiliation?"

Morakav stared at the distant ocean, "I cannot speak for them. They say this is normal. After such mass running most grow quiet and thoughtful. Until you asked, I thought nothing of it. Like you, we mourn our terrible loss. Jutnesh's voice is in my ears. His eyes look into my own. Every recollection passes before me." He paused, "I will speak to them. Setush grows toward Sinkin and away from us. They rise on this wave and . . ." He stopped and frowned, "It brings something to mind. We had Bards and their apprentices visit the herd. My Setush becomes an apprentice – to your Sinkin."

Hiratak sat down. He looked back toward where, in the distance, their two groups slept as one. Nu began to fill the landscape, and the air warmed.

"Our Buck was always keen for the diviners," he said. "Long after the others left, he stayed to listen. He memorized the Sagas early. He sang them in his sleep. He has always been intent and subtle."

Morakav nodded, "A vision fills him. His paws are light on the ground."

"You know the excesses of youth! They are full of impulses and bravado. They are impatient and reckless! They spurn the gentle passage of time instructing them. The subtle lessons only gained by many years are lost on them. They demand all be accomplished at once! We watch as life dispatches their many follies. We know well the thousands of compromises blunting their baby talons. There is no law against our dreams being thwarted. Many disappointments inevitably bow each head."

"Perhaps," Morakav answered. "Youth enjoy the luxury of clarity. Recall your own days as a buck my dear comrade! Our patriarchs could be blind to the present. We settle ourselves as we age. We look back. They look forward. Their inexperience has led to new insight. Some of our greatest voices emerged at this age. Many now celebrated in song began their careers during their Run."

"Perhaps. Perhaps. Much of this may be true. It must also be said most of those heroes lived short and difficult lives! Their 'honour' commenced after their deaths."

"Not all. Whatever their path, we must grow our Stags into their own selves."

Hiratak looked out at the distant ocean and nodded. "I will try to hear them. We contest enough on this. I fear others will be less willing to listen to this new vision. They might strike out in fear. I tried to protect you in Avanchil."

"And we are in your debt," Morakav replied. "I cannot recall being more honoured. You displayed tremendous courage."

Hiratak bowed his head, "Is this Face part of your humiliation? I do not believe you answered me."

Morakav smiled, "Before our waking nightmare, I had not seen a Tolku. I had heard enough to recognize them. When I looked at this Face of Hesha Vira, I felt something beyond us. It was *composed* of life!"

Hiratak managed a tight smile, "Our young Buck may have another apprentice."

They laughed and turned back toward their waking herds.

"Arise! Awake!" Hiratak forced his joviality. "We approach Saransut Bay. It is one of the richest inlets on Thermistal. The huge and lazy fish of Panchala await us! Heavy eels teem the estuary for our feasts. We will continue within sight of these mountains east. We approach the final paw of your path."

The seven remaining Durka Herd members and the three remaining to Makusk had taken to form a ring around the Bucks as they slept. They rose and began their morning stretches and variations of their dance. Hiratak and Morakav joined them, and they faced Nu in greeting. Hiratak continued to glance at the two Bucks. He discerned how linked they had become and their diminished involvement in this time-honoured ritual. When done, he kept his peace. He smiled at the two youths and joined Makusk at the lead as they began their Run east.

As they were about to begin, their attention turned towards a growing band of black beginning to form on the southeastern horizon over the Panchala Sea. It grew as a tear in the sky allowing night to invade the day attended by a growing roar echoing over the deep. The winds rose suddenly bringing a strange chill to the shore. The previously placid herd of Wum suddenly became agitated. They began to turn back in the other direction, presumably towards some shelter further east along the coast.

"Turn inland!" Hiratak barked. "We want no part of this!"

CHAPTER 27

Seti

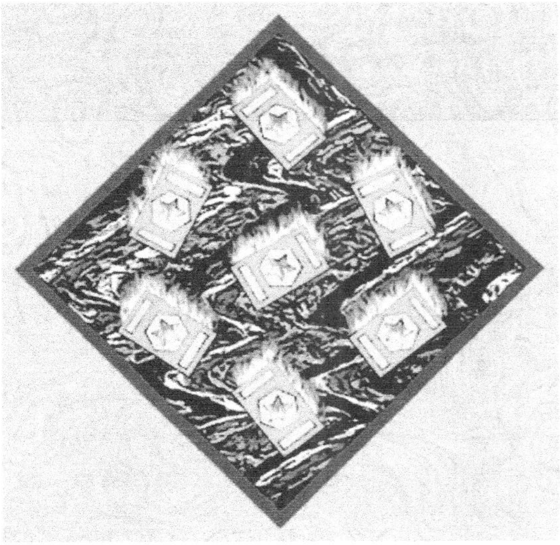

Pictured: traditional icon of the fall of Ranvartawan's One Hundred Gates

Day 251, in Two-Week Fourteen, Min – the Banner on the open Panchala Sea two thousand andas east of Statos-Vey.

Sweat poured off Seti as he struggled at the prow of the Jefaka. In contrast, Nu displayed a glorious face on clearing the horizon off the starboard bow, colouring the morning clouds in garish hues. Although the crew stood well back, it was clear the Invocation did not go well. He had cried out the names of the four Grand Menem several times and shook with frustration. He gestured for Hegev to join him.

“They gabber!” he hissed.

Hegev stared at him incredulously.

“They are as a troupe of frightened Tecku or Asaku! I cannot bring them down! They fly apart and spin as in a whirlpool!”

His Adept stood helpless at his side before hearing her name called. Captain Emedin gestured angrily for her to come. As she approached the captain, she noted increased agitation among the crew.

“I told you this was a mistake!” the Captain hissed under her breath, “What is he doing?”

“He says he cannot form the Menem,” she whispered. “He cannot understand what they say.”

Emedin rolled her eyes, “Your indulgence of his delusions makes him worse!” She turned to her First Officer. After a brief conversation, they looked at the crew.

“The Jefaka is not fitted for the open ocean, but,” Emedin began, “Panchala is the most forgiving. Nonetheless, it is unwise to shake the crew’s confidence, surrounded by the deep. Why did he not manufacture an invocation? He has done so in the past! It is too late for that now. Advise him to break off! Later, you and I will have a discussion.” She gave Hegev an ominous look. Noting this warning and the growing fear in the crew’s eyes, she nodded once and made her way back to Seti.

“They are frightened!” he said as soon as she joined him. “Ranvartawan trembles, and many fall out! I hear snatches of chaos! The Sev Messengers come to me and say the One Hundred Gates rattle on their hinges!”

“Seti!” Hegev’s tone brought him back. “*Our crew* is frightened! You must reassure *them*! The wide sea surrounds us, and it is by their will we stay afloat!”

Seti turned to look back at the crew. No one spoke. Instead of calming them, his aspect grew more horrified as he pointed. “I witness their fear!” He cried out.

All turned and gasped as one. Behind them, on the southern horizon, a shocking black band grew from the water. The sky above it began to turn a sickening colour and the temperature began to drop.

“Captain! Captain!” Dine said in a small voice.

“I see,” Emedin answered.

"We cannot reach shore in time," Dine said.

"No." She bellowed out to the crew, "Into the rigging! Turn into the storm! Secure the sails!"

The crew scrambled to make safe the ship and prepare her for a terrible storm. Seti joined the others in the rigging high above the deck. As they furled the sails and strove to turn the Jefaka to face the growing blackness, the air crackled. Their puffing breaths made clear how chill the air grew as they witnessed the growing wave of chaos advancing across the sea. A heavy curtain of attendant clouds hurried in advance of the storm, obscuring the crazed Eye of Nu.

Heavy crates of cargo were tossed overboard. The ship was three quarters turned when the Captain shouted over the growing wind, "Enough! Bolt the rigging, batten the tarpaulins and get below!" Everything secured, the last of the crew hurried beneath the deck. There, everything was stowed or tied down. By the time the crew, including Seti, were below the storm approached. The sky grew dark as night, and an overwhelming howl filled their ears. Half of the crew squeezed into small areas; the rest clung to cables attached to the mess hall walls. The chairs were upended, fastened to the central table, and lashed to one wall. The storm's monstrous voice grew as the ship shrank to a cork in a flood. A wall of water hit and the Jefaka lurched away and began to spin sideways. More waves battered their boat, and it felt small and weak against this massive fury. Many of the crew cried out in terror at the storm's deafening roar. Despite their best efforts, some items came loose and began to clatter and bounce across the floor. They felt the ship lifted high in the air before sliding down precipitous hills of bellowing waters into deep boiling valleys. Seawater saturated spray filled the ship.

"Seti!" Hegev repeated when he did not respond. Because of the noise, she made him focus on her lips as she spoke, "A prophet is needed!" She gestured toward the huddled crew. They heard Captain Emedin's voice issuing more orders elsewhere in the ship. "Our Captain knows her duty. You have yours."

"I failed them!" he enunciated back to her.

"What?"

"I could not bring the Menem down! I could not hear their warnings!

I could not alert the crew!"

"The task," Hegev brought her face close, "of the prophet, the farmer, the fisherman, is not to sink in regret but rise in the moment. You must become the crew's anchor."

Seti nodded and stood. Despite the heaving ship, his sailor's balance aided his walk to the mess hall's center. With growing calm, he looked into each pair of eyes. The storm's bellow made it impossible to speak and be heard. Instead, he sat down and began a series of slow and elaborate hand and arm movements. Those present became fascinated and stopped shaking. Word spread, and more came to watch. He rose to his knees and continued in slow, meditative fashion to move. Hegev recognized his movements as variations on several focusing exercises she had taught him two-weeks ago. Despite continued pitching and spinning debris, keeping his weight and balance low, he began to dance.

* * *

Day 255, Two-Week Fifteen, Vin, the Fish, on the open Panchala Sea.

On the fourth morning, the crew began to issue out on the deck and assess Jefaka's injuries. The storm had dwindled to steady rain, but none preferred to remain below. Captain Emedin came to stand at the prow. Seti and Hegev joined her. Dine arrived wearing the longest face Seti had ever seen on him.

"Captain, the rudder is smashed."

"This entire ship should have been," the Captain said, looking at the wounded vessel. "Bring down one of the secondary masts and create an old-fashioned stern-mounted rudder."

"Captain? Such a tool is for river craft! It is not fit for a ship this size on the open sea."

"I agree. At least we are on Panchala and may hope her usual mild humour has returned. This temporary rudder will suffice to address the unseasonable wind and keep us off the rocks. We must not be taken further west – out into the open Wakanda Ocean. This new rudder must be brought up in heavy weather or risk further damage."

"It will be done, Captain."

Emedin surveyed the horizon. "We must determine our position."

Dine looked out on the ocean, "We have," he turned to look at her, "we will be certain when the sky clears and the never-resting stars speak to us. It is sure the storm pushed us far out. We are closer to Thermistal than Statos-Vey."

"Thermistal?" Hegev said in a small voice. Her face grew pale.

"Why are you troubled?" Seti said, looking at her. "Is not land welcome?"

"Not this land, boy!" Dine said. "Think where we were before the blow. We are pushed far north and east, the opposite of Panchala's usual prodding. She is strong, but this wind is stronger, taking us across the current."

"Why avoid Thermistal?" Seti asked.

"Most of Thermistal would welcome us," Dine said, "but we are south of the one portion where our ancestors banished the Suvuka!"

"Tales of ships forced to land along the Mushumafal Peninsula are many," the captain said. "Those surviving report either no sign of them or the Suvuka rushing them in force. Survivors say they are frenzied in their attacks. Entire ships may be overrun. It is...the most dangerous place on Anu for us."

"Boy," Dine asked, "Have you ever looked on one of the reconstructed skeletons of a Suvuka?"

Seti shook his head.

"An adult is the width and height of a two-seater riding cart! Their heads are as wide as your chest! Their paws the size of your head! Thousands of their talons are found in the dirt across Rho-Jashun. They become common decorations and altar adornments. Attached to their living paws, they are terrible weapons!"

"What of Sarv Island?" the captain asked.

Dine nodded, "We will keep watch on the Eyes above to be sure, Captain." He saluted and strode away, barking orders to the crew to begin to fashion the new rudder.

"Where is this Sarv Island?" Seti asked as he watched Dine go.

"As far north as we were east off the coast of Statos-Vey before the storm." Emedin sniffed as the rain increased, "Lightning animates the air." She turned to Seti, "What you did below . . . you made the crew's fear drain away. I cannot imagine what possessed you to do it, but it was inspired."

Seti bowed before looking out at the ocean.

Emedin's face flushed with a variety of emotions as she watched the boy and his Adept. "I had thought we had released you from your role as Invocant," she said at last.

Seti continued to stare at the sea.

"The crew already says you saved the ship," the Captain stated.

Both Seti and Hegev turned to stare up at her. "Save the Jefaka?" Seti said, "I did not warn you! I was blind, and we were near destroyed!"

"Dear boy!" Emedin exclaimed. "You put too much on yourself!" She glared at Hegev.

Seti frowned and shook his head, "When I felt my powers to reach the Menem secure, they dissolved into an incomprehensible rabble! I cannot credit the Grand Menem with such outrageous nonsense. They went mad and degenerated into delirium. What did come through suggested there was a cataclysm in Ranvartawan. There is only dust on the wind. The sky…is empty! Empty!"

The Captain's face spoke her frustration, but she remained silent and watched him.

"What storm affects the invisible ones, possessing bodies of light?" Seti's voice rose. "Would not the wind blow through them? Would not they remain dry among the waves?"

Emedin glowered at Hegev and was about to speak when Dine rushed up.

"Captain?" Dine's face was ashen. "Accounting for those sequestered in different parts of the ship during the storm, I regret to report we have suffered five losses. Alas! Forty-Five sailed out of Wazaratcha, but only forty will return."

Emedin joined Dine below. Word spread among the crew. The captain returned, and Dine brought a wide metal bowl and set it on deck. The bottom sloshed with water. One sat down in front of the bowl and began to wash and rub it. After a time, he slapped it in a peculiar rhythm — a low voice issued from it. The entire crew began to gather, aware of the message the bowl sounded.

Captain Emedin called out, "The storm has taken five of us: Nichan Obanus, Daruhasa Dates, Seka Shatra Jemi, Nikumb and Dum Dritar. Their effects must stand ready."

In silence, many of the crew began to go below while the mourning bowl continued its call. The rest stood, remembering fellow shipmates, friends and intimates gone. As the rain increased, several began to wail. Others sang or chanted various litanies. Those who went below returned, each carrying an item from the lost crew.

Dine approached Hegev, "The Captain has held back effects for the family," he began, "otherwise, what is left will join them. She tells me you performed the Calling on another ship."

Hegev sighed and nodded as Dine gestured for her to join him. They walked to the swelling sounds of the bowl. Five sacks tied with yellow twine were brought out.

The sacks sat in small boat-shaped effigies with carved faces on their prows. Small holes perforated their sides, forming a pattern. Only the tops of the bags and their fluttering yellow ribbons could be seen.

Two crewmen prepared to lower a small boat, and Hegev got in. The crew watched as the two men began to row back to the stern of the ship. Once there, with difficulty, Hegev stood and began to say the litany. The wind and chop of the waves drowned most of her words until they heard their names' resounding call at the end.

"Nichan Obanus!
Daruhasa Dates!
Seka Shatra Jemi!
Nikumb!
Dum Dritar!"

She began placing the little boats in the water. Despite her efforts, three capsized in the rough waters and sank. The remaining two bobbed in the waves as they returned to the ship. Many cries went up as the two little boats tried to stay afloat in the pouring rain. They sank by the time Hegev and the two crewmen returned. Seti knew each of the lost, and tears streamed down his face. Seka Shatra Jemi had taught him his first knots, and Nikumb brought her many dreams to him to read. He and Nichan Obanus had leaned against the prow the evening before the storm, laughing at his jokes. He had always meant to ask the silent Dum Dritar what he placed before the Life Pillar at the Memanu Field. Their faces, their manners and their voices crowded in on him. He looked into the empty sky, and a gloom settled over him.

CHAPTER 28

SINKIN

Traditional image of the Tumatch, a beast so large it appears in forgotten tales carrying cities on its back.

Day 257, Saransut Bay, south of the Jaladanu Mountains on the Mushumafal Peninsula of Thermistal.

The storm had sent mighty waves up the broad Saransut Bay and washed the surrounding countryside. It had lasted many days, and the winds blew strong from the south. Although, today, the Eye of Nu shone after being wrapped for ten days in furious clouds. The Suvuka had stopped before an odd-looking pile of rotting wood by the shore, surrounded by smashed Wum shells and other debris.

"This is the corpse of one of their carts," Hiratak said. "They dishonour the seas by floating over them. The seas punish their foolishness."

"When has Panchala had such a temper?" Morakav looked out on the agitated ocean. "Many slain carts must lie on these shores."

They looked out at the ocean and along the shores of the immense bay. Much had tumbled ashore, but no broken ships.

"Come!" Hiratak said, "Our hunting was disturbed by this storm. Soon enough, the bay will feed us. Rare deep-water creatures may be pushed in for us to sample."

For many days, Makusk and Durka herd continued to lope along the bay's shore, glimpsing many great fish swimming near the surface. The adults counselled the two youth on the best places to catch them, and soon they feasted on the best fish Sinkin and Setush had ever tasted. The prized Sheret beasts with their hardy shells scuttled about the beaches in numbers, perhaps perplexed by Panchala's fury. The herd scooped out their sweet meat, and their pelts began to shine with health. Their greatest boon came with the discovery of the broken body of a baby Tumatch, a sea creature that as an adult reached prodigious size and possessed massive flippers. While already covered in crabs and birds, the infant's flesh was still sweet and filling. They were joined by other Suvuka, living there year-round, attending passing Bucks on their Stag Path. They had also converged on the carcass. The usual greetings were now replaced with celebrations at this gift from the sea. For a day and a night they lingered before Hiratak had them moving again at the following dawn.

* * *

Day 261

The two herds had continued at their leisure through the warm day. Nu had re-asserted himself, and both land and sea were content. They had once again made their way down toward the shore. Here, it had become rocky and littered from the storm. They stopped at a tall and broad formation high on the beach by a small bluff. Many rocks had been moved to create a large pattern. The storm had obscured the design.

Without a word, they bent to clear the debris and view what manner of figure had been made. It took time to clean the large, circular design. The intent was to look down on it from the small bluff rising behind it. Sinkin and Setush perceived what pattern the rocks formed and smiled at each other. They looked down on a wondrous rendition of the Face of Avanchil Round. Blue stones approximated its eyes. Long white boulders had been found for its teeth.

Hiratak harboured misgivings but welcomed the opportunity to break his silence as he stood beside his young Buck. "It is a good likeness," he said, continuing to stare at the arrangement.

Sinkin nodded, "It took many paws to accomplish."

"They found the right rock for each part." He turned to look at the silent wall of the Jaladanu Mountains, their long shadows punctuating the nearby landscape. "These stones have not slumbered in the ocean. They were carried from the mountain."

Sinkin turned and looked at his Herdmaster. "I am glad we view this together."

Hiratak turned and replied, "I would be at peace on this Face."

"As I," Sinkin said.

Hiratak turned to look down at the rendered face. "Do you . . . do you see it still?"

Sinkin smiled, "We have." He gestured to Setush, standing nearby and smiling.

Hiratak turned to look at the others standing either side, "Do you see it?" The rest looked at each other and, in various ways, signalled some had, and some had not. "Perhaps . . ." Hiratak said, looking at Sinkin, "Perhaps it comes sooner to fresh eyes."

"I am learning more how I see it," Sinkin's enthusiasm grew. "Strength and vitality course through me. Anu is trying to touch us! Setush, and I see the jungle glow. Each creature thrives when the Face is present."

Hiratak endeavoured to keep his expression neutral as he watched Sinkin. "Let us continue," he said, "much lies ahead."

He found a mid-sized rock, and his nails scored it. He placed it near the edge of the bluff as a sign Suvuka had come and looked on the anonymous creation of the Face. The others did the same then followed the shoreline of the bay.

* * *

Day 265

The two herds, sated by many fatty meals and well-rested, began to move inland. Keeping the tall Jaladanu Mountains to the north and the Panchala Sea to the south, they continued to travel east across the bottom of Thermistal. As they left the few native herds of Suvuka near the coast, the Stag Path markers became evident. They followed these markers through deep jungle and out onto dense and verdant meadows. Well-worn paths grew deep, and broad bridges and other aids appeared as the land became uneven. On occasion, they encountered other works along their way, serving no other purpose than inspiring and entertaining. It was as if, after hardship, those possessing abilities were inspired by this lush garden.

At last, the two herds encountered a simple Round standing in the middle of a broad field. Several ancient trees were at the centre with a few rough-hewn cones and spheres around them and many other items decorating their gnarled trunks. Some were piled at the base. Others were attached to the trunks with vines or hung from the lowest branches. On closer examination, they realized they looked at Tolku creations.

"What are these?" Setush asked, wrinkling his nose at the incomprehensible objects.

"They are fashioned," Morakav said. "Their purpose is mysterious."

"As we bond with Anu," Hiratak said, "the enemies' artful perversions become absurd. They have lost their function. They stand shamed and useless."

"These are Tolku fashionings? Did they put them here?" Setush asked. He looked around in sudden fear.

"No, boy," Hiratak said. "Look how they are attached. See the many talon marks scoring them. We plucked them out of dead sea carts. They are helpless trophies brought to adorn this Round. They are tokens forced to witness our Run today!"

Having said this, Hiratak moved out and began deliberate steps into the clear run path that made a complete circle around the central trees and their many decorations. The others followed, roaring as they ran. They had not engaged in the Mesmerizing Run for many weeks, yet Hiratak stopped before the frenzy. He noted the others' disappointment as they left the Round behind them and continued along the path.

Morakav came to lope beside him, "You cannot delay this Face returning," he said.

Hiratak shot him an irritated glance, "I am striving. It made me near choke. That Round was wholesome in its primitive purity."

"Our Bucks believe this is the Face of Anu. What better place to see her?"

Hiratak had to focus his shock at the suggestion into negotiating an irregular set of twists in the path, "You say 'as our Bucks believe.' I asked what you believe. I have yet to hear your reply."

Morakav ran for a time, "I spoke to the others. They now embrace the Face. The vision of Avanchil is their Face of Life. How can we challenge this? I hear snatches of song from Sinkin. Before Avanchil, they were furtive. Now, they grow to full ballads. I have not heard the like in years. Your boy is a Bard in the making. You should look to his craft when we return." He signalled, and when they had stopped, he took Hiratak a few paces forward and spoke in a small voice, "You possess many strengths, Hiratak. Yet small things escape your gaze. My charges go and speak to Sinkin. The rest of Durka do the same. They struggle not to rouse you." He turned and smiled at the rest before saying, "You bridge the divide with Sinkin. This is good. Know we are far from one mind on this. Most grow more open to this Face."

Hiratak stood long, looking at Morakav, his jaw clenching and unclenching. He bowed his head and brought his nose to the ground before turning to look at the others. "I am senior here and thus lead the Run," he began in a faltering voice. "I will not constrain you. I will maintain my own mind. I will not impose my disquiet. I will not deny you regaining this Face." He noted a sigh of relief from them. He wept inside while maintaining an amicable manner. Sinkin's look of love and pride hurt him most. He bowed his head to the ground, turned and began the Run. At midday, Sinkin came beside them.

"May I speak?"

They signalled a halt and took a few paces away from the others.

"I wish solitude," the young Buck stated. "I propose to separate for a time. I remain one with you but ask for time apart."

Hiratak and Morakav glanced at each other. "This request is rare," Hiratak replied. "Our sole purpose is ensuring your emergence as Full Stag. Why do we journey if you separate yourself?"

"I request a brief time alone," Sinkin said with unintended emotion. He stopped and took a breath, "I ask your pardon," he bent, and his nose touched the ground. "I am grateful for your sacrifice. My love for Durka, and Makusk Herd, is full. My bond to Setush will endure. I have spoken to him. He urged me to speak to you."

"Sinkin," Morakav said, "what do you expect on this solitary run?"

"I must slow my breath," he answered, "so I may ponder Avanchil. I must find clarity. A few days should be enough. You know where the land opens. I could keep you in sight. In these few days, I will find what I must. Then I will rejoin and complete the Full Stag Path."

"I am willing to grant your request," Hiratak said. "Relate your insights when you return. Some forms of wisdom are discovered in solitude. It then must be brought out and shared. There, it may enrich and fortify us."

Morakav said, "We should use this plenty. After this, the land is mild. There will be less reason to delay. Our pace will quicken. Most native Suvuka are clustered around the bay. Few live beyond it. Rolling hills will separate the sea and mountains. The shore will be cut off from us. High bluffs separate the land from the rocky shore. Many pathways divide the tall grasses. During my Run, we separated in these narrow ways. We called back and forth to each other."

Hiratak looked at him, "You wake slumbering memories! I see makeshift Rounds among this sea of grasses. It has been many years since I recalled them." He turned to look at Sinkin. "These Rounds are spaced days apart. They are key to the Keepers' network. We could meet at one of them. Call out at dawn, noon and dusk each day. We will wait a day at these Rounds. These paths intersect at them. You will not miss them."

Sinkin bowed, bringing his nose to rest on the ground. "I thank you for this. A few days should be enough. After my brief time apart, I will rejoin you. Setush, and I will face the final test together."

He turned and moved back to join the others. Hiratak and Morakav looked at each other.

"I have never known a Buck like him," Morakav said.

"Nor I," Hiratak said, "and he grew in front of me. This Run opens new features in his eyes."

CHAPTER 29

Shuna-Shapta

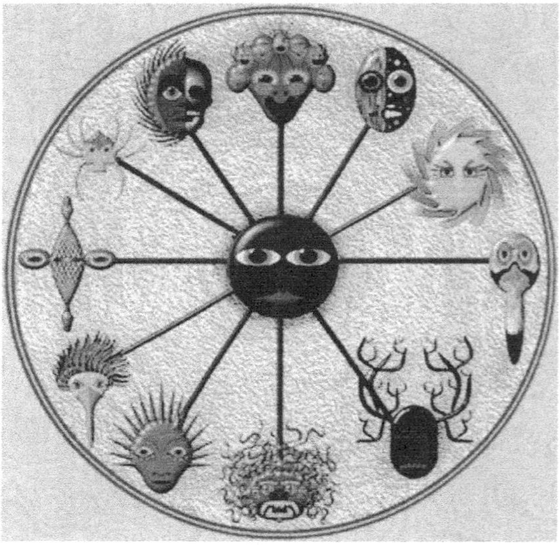

Day 265, Two-Week Fifteen, Vin – The Fish, within the Thakadush Cluster, city of Bhampay

Shuna-Shapta sat on a small portion of an immensely long carpet. It had been presented to the True Cluster, and future Majastas Cluster, from a ministry official from Upata-Shepsus a few days before. It was large enough for seven Circles-of-Eight to occupy other portions of it with her. It was very dense and certain features were embossed. The design was a representation of the ancient capital of Thithanu seen from above. The huge work was replete with not only the famed palaces, temples, magistracies, museums, monuments and gardens, but tiny figures of carts, and other traffic. Her fingers traced a tiny group huddled around an outdoor theatre, and others chasing a runaway pathuda. The foothills of Mounts Thuma and Barom stood at the top of the sweeping composition and the mighty Uthumpon River at the bottom, all surrounded by scudding clouds. As if the composition were not vivid enough, the Daymaker shone through nearby skylight in marked display. His slanting morning darts set portions of the carpet's colours on fire. Many had remarked in Nu's unusual humour and extraordinary vibrance.

Nearby, a young man played an antique, Haklu. Despite his youth, he was well acquainted with the elegant stringed instrument. As she watched his practiced hand on this curious instrument with its skull-shaped body and twin serpent necks, she reflected on her life's fundamental alterations. Thakadush-Satwa was a year and five two-weeks old. Shuna-Shapta, her Circle of Eight and Birth Circle, and many others from the Master Enclave had hastily relocated to the cluster fifteen days ago. Frescos and other radiant decorations covered the interior circling walls. While many of the symbols were familiar, they were used in new ways and sat beside unfamiliar icons. All elements were compacted and intensified to form a lush new language.

A robust new culture emerged in Thakadush. The cluster's shifting body odours formed a distinguishing feature of this society. Shuna-Shapta's nose became more sophisticated each day. She read the deep and rich Scent Wall of the cluster with growing skill. She became aware of the power of her nose in discerning the emotions and disposition of everyone. In their language, her nose was 'growing,' affecting all her other senses, so what she smelled began to be tasted, heard and felt. For the first time, she experienced how the phrase 'wrapped in the Murmur of Life' truly felt. Sheshenara plants existed in abundance. Their characteristic broad purple and green leaves and abundant fruit filled many corners, joining many other plants spread throughout the compound. She began to learn the powerful properties of most of these, ranging from healing small cuts to aiding as Vision Windows.

Many creatures made their home there, creating an engaging atmosphere and serving similar functions to the plants. A multitude of young children's voices rippled through the cluster as a merry brook through a garden. The essential retaining walls of the old compound remained, permitting each one to smell its entire life. Within this real Cluster, all members of Thakadush went about their lives naked, save for a wide variety of house masks that lined the walls in abundance. These were donned and set down continuously throughout the day and night. A set of tiny mirrors lined the wall above to immediately open the way for the aspect of themselves embodied by the mask to flow. Among many other customs, cluster mates painted each other's bodies in a wide variety of colourful designs each morning. They carried this artwork on them for the rest of the day. Every evening there was a general gathering in the cluster's large baths. After the baths, they applied special oils to each other to restore and enhance aspects of their body odours. Shuna-Shapta had a blue and green tendril design spiralling from her left leg to encircle her neck. This design complimented her light copper skin. Her distinctive dark half-circle patterning was taken into account and accentuated by this day's drawing. Yesterday it had been a yellow and orange series of fanciful insects flying in formation across her back and stomach. She looked forward to what she would wear on the morrow. Each day, and sometimes each hour, a different house mask called to her. Like the ones she had grown up with, these had more detailing and a wide variety of aspects. The cluster wore masks much of the time, leading to a vivacious atmosphere.

"More juice!" Thakadush-Satwa declared, interrupting her reverie. The young girl carrying her had sat down before Shuna-Shapta. Another handed the baby a tiny flask of Sheshenara Nectar. The first Majastas in history began to suck on the tip furiously. She looked at Shuna-Shapta with dark amber eyes tending to cross toward each other. Her black hair, growing in abundant curls, began to touch her shoulders. Her red-bronze skin glistened in the morning heat. Her painted design was a series of simple yellow and red fruits dancing in a row around her middle. She had already smudged them.

"Another Maja shall be born this day!" the young girl said.

"Ah!" Shuna-Shapta declared, "This makes for how many?"

The girl shrugged, "More babies live here than adults. I lose count.

This one," she bent over and kissed Thakadush-Satwa on the neck, causing her to giggle "grows big! The others also excel beyond their age. They shall not be children long!"

Shuna-Shapta nodded as she gazed at the mysterious little girl.

"She is ready for you," the girl said and made to hand her to Shuna-Shapta.

"Ready?"

"Our Sensitives say she wishes to begin with you this day," the girl stated.

Shuna-Shapta stared dumbfounded at her. Ever since Thakadush-Satwa's mother said the child had asked for her, she had pondered what this meant. Since she had arrived, she noted many signs of the baby's rarity, but no evidence of the baby speaking more than three words together, although this was remarkable for her age. In size and activity, she seemed four years old, not just turned one. Shuna-Shapta realized the girl, and the baby waited for her. She held out her arms to receive the infant Majastas.

"Go! Go!" Thakadush-Satwa said. Shuna-Shapta looked at the girl, but she had already stood. She and many other children formed a circle with Shuna-Shapta and the child at the centre. Shuna-Shapta felt the familiar rushing sensation of her entry into Tatchlan.

* * *

She fell through the darkness toward the Living System's actual arrangement, not the one filtered through the Invocate's Living Instruments. As an Operant, Shuna-Shapta saw the Living Orb emerge first out of the darkness. The Operant's view was less of three perfect circles, one inside the other than three layers of organic elements comprising one living being. The Inner Orb was more elongated and appeared to move in many places. Her Operant Eyes could make out signs of the two other realms, the realm of raw life Indatubangus and the watery core of Amanavata nested deep within its outer layer.

Shuna-Shapta, having a Floral Aroma Accord like her mother, saw the Living System manifestation of her body now arrayed in streaks of vivid orange and blue. As always, her usually bound black-and-red hair flowed unencumbered as if she was underwater. She turned to see not an infant, but a tall and well-muscled young woman. Thakadush-Satwa had a rich combination of both a Warm and Sweet Aroma Accords, which now displayed as a brilliant series of intense patterning with the colours yellow, pink and green predominating. This was how Thakadush-Satwa manifested within Her Living System! No child could enter Tatchlan.

Without knowing how she knew, Shuna-Shapta sensed the shimmering of Thakadush-Satwa's skin and the warmth emanating from her body represented a significant augmentation to her being by Tatchlan itself. The implications of this enhancement into adulthood were too great to contemplate at present. Thakadush-Satwa's wide amber eyes were slightly crossed as she turned and smiled at her. She reached out and took Shuna-Shapta's hand. Through her skin came an immediate affinity, as if they were constituent parts of a single body.

"I shall guide you," Shuna-Shapta said as they approached the multicoloured surface of the Orb. At once, a familiar circle formed beneath the surface and effortlessly emerged. It was the same fantastical arrangement Shuna-Shapta had experienced when she visited Thakadush Cluster for the birth of the one-hundredth Maja. These were not the Secondary Faces she was accustomed to, but the Primary Faces themselves. Up until now, she had only seen some of them from a great distance. Eleven of the Principal Faces formed the outer ring, and one stood in the middle. Atop stood the Face of Full Satisfaction, Kava-Kura. Her tongue hung down through the centre of the circle and, at its tip, hung Hesha Vira, Face of crude life, at the bottom of the formation. In the middle of her tongue hung the round black Face of Alatanda while five Faces formed his right side and four on his left. Kava-Kura's tongue appeared to split behind Alatanda and radiated out on all sides to link the rest of the faces, forming a rimless wheel formation. Many thousands of Secondary Faces, some miniature versions of their Primary Face, some hybrids of three, four or more of them, also emerged from the surface of the Living Orb and rose to swirl and churn like a cloud of insects around them. Their saturated colouring pulled the life out of everything and glowed in the surrounding darkness.

Thakadush-Satwa squeezed Shuna-Shapta's hand. At once, Shuna-Shapta summoned the entire formation. As a single entity, they approached them as twelve moons. The Face of Alatanda continued to grow as it rose beneath them, and the magnitude of his dimensions overwhelmed Shuna-Shapta. The other Faces extended far to the horizon with Alatanda blotting out the Living Orb behind him. He became a shining black wall. His wide eyes became two immense features spreading over a black landscape. They gently fell toward the broad end of his nose. Far below their feet, his full mouth spread out as a distant ridge.

At last, the tip of the nose stopped in front of them. They seemed to lie on a cushion of air before the peak of a glittering black mountain. Thakadush-Satwa reached out toward his black and sparkling flesh. Patterns of glittering gems of each hue studded it. Shuna-Shapta examined this new resolution of what at a distance was an overall shimmering quality of his black skin. She perceived 'The Bridge' had aspects of every other Face covering it. Thakadush-Satwa looked at Shuna-Shapta and nodded for her to touch Alatanda with her. They placed their palms on the flesh of a Principle Face of Tatchlan. In her wildest imaginings, Shuna-Shapta never conceived of doing this. The hot black meat rumbled, making the surface tremble. Shuna-Shapta became aware of the Living Orb rising as Nu to their right. The entire formation of Principal Faces had turned to face their realm. Tendrils reached out and turned Thakadush-Satwa and Shuna-Shapta to face the Inner Orb. They rested their backs on Alatanda's nose as they began to approach the powerful presence of the Inner Orb's rich flesh. The many Secondary Faces, most smaller than their bodies, formed a multitude of gyrating patterns as each made small circles glowing in evident excitement at their approach. Staying in this formation, the Twelve Principle Faces, with two tiny Tolku on the tip of Alatanda's nose, broke the surface.

A multitude of melodious echoes filled their ears as the Flesh of the Living Orb enveloped them. Shuna-Shapta was amazed to make out myriads of what she knew were the building blocks of the Living Orb, seeds crowned by interlocking tentacles with tails stretching beyond sight in all directions. The seeds came in many colours, shapes and sizes, their crowns and tails sometimes matched their bodies or varied considerably from them in appearance. The choral echoes were a collective voice formed by millions of pulses emanating from this vast world of seeds speaking to each other. The Living Orb was utterly composed of them, accompanied by many lesser forms dedicated to their service. They continued to move through layer after layer of these wonders. Their collective bodies as living layers of dense mats laid one upon the other, shifting with ease to let them pass, causing a sensation of moving through different densities and temperate thicknesses of water. This was the exact form of the Living System, the mighty Twelve Faces being but a manifestation of them.

While this wonder unfolded in front of Shuna-Shapta and Thakadush-Satwa, another took place around them. The smaller specialized Faces gathered thick at their point of entry, filling their view like immense schools of fish brushing past them during the Principal Faces' descent. A chorale of gentle Face cooings was now added to the seed echoes. Ahead, the succeeding layers of the inner Living Orb reflected the glowing formation spreading far beyond what Shuna-Shapta could see.

Many Secondary Faces hurried to collect around their Primary Face, forming intricate patterns. They radiated out on each side of the central circle, forming oblong halos around each Face. Most of these specialized Secondary Faces near Shuna-Shapta were unknown to her. The resulting array resembled an immense flower with eleven petals with Alatanda's halo filling the middle. The entire population of Primary and Secondary Faces was, for the first time, gathered in full formation as they travelled into the depths of all life on Anu. Alatanda's vast retinue surrounded him, filling the centre of the circle. To varying degrees, each wore either a passing or identical resemblance of the patron Face they served. Those most like him formed a ring immediately around his edges while those more integrated with others stood further out aligned according to their association with one or more of the other Faces. As best Shuna-Shapta could tell by the shifting reflection in front of her, the same arrangement was occurring around all the Primary Faces.

This unfolding spectacle filled Shuna-Shapta with renewed admiration for the many generations of ancient Tatchlan Masters who had laboured blind on this unimaginably mighty work throughout history. To witness it surrounding her moved her to tears. After an indeterminate length of time, this thunderous flotilla passed beyond the surface and approached the next living layer deep beneath the Living Orb - Indatubangas. Millions of the Seed Tails connected the Living Orb to it, standing as a thick forest they passed through without effort. Shuna-Shapta looked down and tried to find Hesha Vira at the end of Kava-Kura's glistening tongue. She made out two distant specks as the green eyes of the mistress of the chaotic realm shone below her. The reflection of the Faces' harmonious formation was distorted in this gruesome mirror. She and her attendant Faces did not move out of their configuration as the frenzied Orb filled their noses, ears and eyes. There was no mistaking the blind violence of this preserve of unrefined life, and Shuna-Shapta braced herself.

Thakadush-Satwa began shaking her head. Shuna-Shapta turned to look at her. Keeping her grip on Shuna-Shapta's hand, Thakadush-Satwa extended her arms as if reaching toward Indatubangas. She hastened their descent as the roar became deafening. Shuna-Shapta found herself also extending her right hand toward the vile anarchy. Waves of crude scent passed over them as they reached the surface. Once through, the darkness swallowed them. At the same time, a feral animation filled the atmosphere. Extremes of heat and cold passed through them in quick succession attended by a multitude of joys and sorrows intertwined and indistinguishable from each other. The foundational fears of pain and loss gripped them as they continued through the churning blackness. With no notion of time passing, they began to note points of sudden blue and white light. As if they had floated through storm clouds, the vista of the inner core, an ocean of the calm waters of Amanavata filled the base. They gently immersed in these waters, clearly forming a modifying, insulating, lubricating function for the entire Living System.

After a brief moment of calm, the entire Face formation began to shift. It became apparent the Circle of Faces turned back the way they came.

* * *

Shuna-Shapta opened her eyes to look at a wall of faces from Thakadush Cluster. She looked down at the large eyes of Thakadush-Satwa, sitting content in her lap. Many hours had passed, and plates of heaping food sat on steaming beds of Charsha. Master Kanla came through the crowd and knelt beside her daughter. She had tears in her eyes.

"Shapta?" she whispered.

"Did you see us?"

Her mother nodded and looked at the others. "We did! You two burst onto the surface of Tatchlan with such glory! We also witnessed the entire Cluster of Faces and their full and ordered arrangement. You and our Majastas brought this about!"

Shuna-Shapta looked down at the now sleeping Thakadush-Satwa in her arms. The same young girl giving the Majastas baby to her now knelt and kissed Shuna-Shapta's feet. She gently gathered the sleeping child and left.

"Ama, within Tatchlan, she became a young woman. Children may not enter Tatchlan."

"They are incomplete," Master Kanla nodded, "remaining pre-adults until well after their Life Cake Ceremony. Ripeness does not always follow the designation. Our Grand Work magnifies her. Our infant Majastas attains adult depths whilst still within an infant's body."

Shuna-Shapta smelled the food and, after a quick smile to her mother, began to eat. Once she started, the depth of her hunger became apparent, and she continued to eat while the others watched. Master Tanas observed this scene. He had hurried to the cluster after the momentous manifestation occurred inside Tatchlan. He contented himself with watching this remarkable girl from a distance. As he stood looking at her, he became aware of a presence by his side. He looked at Shuna-Shapta's second Mother, Shuna-Dana. While acquainted, he had few occasions to speak with her in recent years. She was shorter and broader than Master Kanla, Shapta's First Mother. Her golden brown eyes dominated her broad and glowing copper face, which was relatively unmarked by patterning or blood midge markings. At thirty-seven, she was the first Maja to born in this generation of her Shuna pre-Cluster.

"Master," she said, also looking at Shuna-Shapta.

"Invocant," he replied, "how does your dear baby?"

Shuna-Dana's already beautiful face broke into a broad grin as she stroked her pregnancy. "At forty days, she is tiny. Yet, I feel my little one's presence. My body remains calm. I find this a gentle pregnancy."

"I delight at the news. We have heard the same from others conceiving here. And how goes it with you, the Second Mother of our Operant?"

Shuna-Dana shot him an intense glance. She returned to contemplate the distant figure, surrounded by many in Thakadush Cluster.

"I would speak with you concerning these recent developments," she began.

"You refer to events within our Living Orb, or perchance your move to Thakadush."

"I refer to what has taken place since we became aware of Shapta's exceptionality, including what we witnessed within Tatchlan."

Her tones lead Master Tanas to cease focusing on Shuna-Shapta and turn to face her Second Mother. "Is something amiss?"

"'*Amiss*?' I fear it transcends 'amiss.'" She turned to look up at him. "I am but an Invocant, forever tied to those Living Instruments serving our Tatchlan Cubes. I sink deep amid those working them. Yet, I long ago knew my wife surpassed me. I also realized from her early childhood, Shapta would equal, if not best, her mother. I never saw such a delver as our daughter."

Master Tanas held up his hands, "You are of the Master Enclave, as I. Just a fraction of all Maja approach our title Invocant, let alone a Master. Your Craft of working our Tatchlan Cubes laid the foundations of our Magnificent Work. Your blood maintains it as we Masters may not. You use our original sigils to move through the foundations of our three realms, beneath the roots of our Grand Work. Your sole 'misfortune,' involves dwelling with your gifted Circle and comparing yourself to them. Your wife and her daughter have sunk more profoundly than most within this generation. This does not take away from how planted you are within our loam of life. You share our Masters's pregnancy with our future, further illustrating your status amongst us."

Shuna-Dana bowed, "I speak to you as a mother. Whilst Second Mother to Shapta, I poured as much of myself into her as Kanla did. When she excelled and displayed an unwavering ambition to be a Master, our love and experience enriched her footsteps."

She looked back toward her daughter, still feasting and smiled. "When I behold her thus, I recall my radiant Shapta as ever a hearty eater! Never a miserable stick of a girl, she was ever draped within comely flesh." Her smile vanished, and she turned back to Master Tanas. "Perchance my concerns for Shapta mirror what occurs within our Resplendent Work. I may find my way through our magnificent work better than our city's canals. Now both my daughter and Tatchlan transform beyond recognition. Our Cubes tremble within my hands! My workings, once a peaceful meditation, are now a drama leaving me exhausted. We live by our early Master's axiom 'certain actions lead to certain results.' Now those same actions have an unforeseen effect. Those of our craft struggle to meet these new challenges and look for guidance. We witness Masters as bewildered as ourselves."

A slight shiver went through her at the same instant one went through Master Tanas. Thakadush Cluster felt it also. Shuna-Shapta had left off her feast and spoke to her First Mother. She had yet to notice her Second Mother or Master Tanas.

"What happened?" Shuna-Dana asked. "Anu's Flesh did not flinch. Naught inanimate shifted. We shifted together!" She looked wide-eyed at him. "Our bodies modify! I find myself losing my balance and dropping things. My girl forms a key part of this. My nose grows powerful beyond my experience and smells emotions in each place. My hearing and taste magnify." She looked over at another portion of the cluster, "A year-old baby leads us." She looked up at him, "What does your Master Gathering say? You study Shapta's new ability. I hear you referred to as 'Servants' here. Do you serve this babe? How does she direct you? What does she plan for our Shapta and us?"

Her sudden outburst left her drained, and she shrank away as if fearful of his response. Master Tanas embraced her with tenderness.

"Dana, we share your amazement. You may recall reading of how our ancients faltered when they attempted to foresee the final Quickening. Notwithstanding our lore and preparation, we anticipated the need for adaptation when our Grand Work awakened. This day we witnessed the fullness of a vital aspect of our Resplendent Orb. We saw the complete formation of our Primary and Secondary Faces. The theory spreads across our eyes!"

Shuna-Dana nodded at the memory, "Yes, some aspects resolve into an intelligible order. Others move beyond my comprehension." She looked at Shapta. She saw and beckoned them. They nodded and began to make their way toward her through the cluster.

"What role shall our Shapta play?" Shuna-Dana asked.

"It shapes as we speak," Master Tanas said. "Our Gathering has concluded this infant shall be our founding Majastas. This does not conform to our original projections. We had thought we required a large adult Maja population, completing every circle within each cluster, prior to our Majastas spreading across Anu's Flesh. Not content to inherit Maja institutions, she shall shape them herself."

Shuna-Dana stopped and faced him. "Our Shapta, as the first Operant within many generations, shall extend also?"

Master Tanas spread his hands, "We also flounder within this new tide. First, the birth of this miraculous babe, followed by her rapid development, transforms our programme. This formation of our Primary Faces was not scheduled to manifest for many years, if within our lifetimes."

The empty plates before Shuna-Shapta had been removed. She had a large cup of fermented sap in her two hands, and children brought in heaps of flowers to place in her lap.

"My daughter . . . " Shuna-Dana said as they came to sit down on the ornate carpet before her.

CHAPTER 30

Seti

Pictured: the Icon for the Vettencore Passage

Day 277, Two-Week Sixteen, Jixx – The Beauty, thirty andas east of Saransut Bay, on the Mushumafal Peninsula of Thermistal

For twenty days, the wounded Jefaka was pushed north by the rogue winds. The crew fashioned not one but three rudimentary rudders. The former masts had been flattened and augmented at one end to create giant oars to dip into the water. Seti's now outstanding knot work was employed in their hasty creation. The three rudders each rested in improvised pivots, allowing the crew to work them in the ocean and bring them out on the deck. Most of the crew, including Seti and Hegev, strained to push on them to help the ship keep an even course. Twice, the smaller poles snapped and required frantic work and more cannibalizing of other ship timber.

The winds strove to drive them east out into the ocean, and, for many days and nights, they struggled to maintain a northward coarse. The end of their struggle came into view. The mercurial weather stopped trying to drive them into the eastern void and pushed them toward the shore. Their efforts spent them, and the captain ordered the rudders raised. Nets were brought out and thrown into the shallower waters. Giant fish came up, and the stores being opened; they had a generous meal, followed by an extended rest. Seti had never known such hard labour. He nursed his many scrapes and aches. He noted how his already calloused hands were red and raw. After lying on deck for a time and then eating, he walked to the bow to look at their destination.

"Thermistal!" Dine said as he joined him. "Our water is near done. Suvuka or no, we must restock our dwindling supplies or perish."

"Why did we feast then?"

"Our Captain wanted to fortify the crew ahead of that," he indicated the shore. "We have no choice but to put ashore. She thought we should regain some of our strength before attempting land."

Seti stared at the black silhouette on the horizon. It resolved into a distant shoreline dominated by a broad peninsula jutting out towards them. "Most of Thermistal is held by us. Are you sure this is the Suvuka portion?"

Dine pointed, "See those peaks? They are part of the Jaladanu Mountains. This is the Mushumafal Peninsula, the southernmost and easternmost part of this savage continent, where there is no safe harbour. We aimed for Sispe Island, but missed it and now approach the Headland of Charun, east of Saransut Bay, which is deep in Suvuka territory. We would need to sail one or more two-weeks further north and west a considerable distance to reach Tolku-held Thermistal."

Seti continued to stare at the land ahead of them. He felt like it drew them toward it. He looked at the rest of the crew.

"They could use an invocation," Dine said under his breath.

"Must I shout at the empty air?" Seti said, raising his voice. "The

Menem are *gone*. Since the storm, it is as if they were blown into the sea. The air is *empty*! All is changed, and I hear not a whisper anywhere. Who am I to invoke? I will not lie to them! I will not perform a false invocation ever again!"

"Dine!" Captain Emedin near shouted as she marched up to them. "What are you doing? We are done encouraging that foolishness! You are far more than an invocant to us, Seti. Be at peace as to your growing out of this." Hegev joined them and frowned at the captain.

Dine became rigid and saluted before saying, "With respect, Captain, Jefaka approaches a hostile shore humbled! We are ill-suited to avoid the many dangers offshore, let alone find a suitable landing."

"I am well aware of our prospects," Emedin replied. "Instead of looking into empty air," she winked at Seti. "I consulted our library concerning where we may land." She turned and looked at the coast ahead of them. "This is Suvuka territory, but it appears few live here. None of the authors knew why. This small stretch south of the Jaladanu Mountains most resembles the mild and moist climate of Statos-Vey. North of the mountains is the savage Kukernef Desert. I wish the Panchala were more vigorous and had sent us further west, as is her usual wont. Our one hope is to make land undetected and secure the necessary provisions. We will make our way west along the coast. Our goal must be to reach one of several populated islands between Thermistal and Statos-Vey or make for the Island of Vildy."

"Vildy?" Hegev asked in alarm, "Is not Vildy, and his larger brother Vaudlan, the property of Statos-Vey? I had heard these islands are possessed by Bhampay, notwithstanding the Panchala Sea separating them."

"They are."

"We sailed as far out from shore to avoid them."

Emedin looked at her and Seti, "A decision I regret beyond words." Her voice swelled with emotion, and they stood in silence. "West of the Vettencore Passage Thermistal is modestly occupied," her tone cold and firm, "nonetheless her navy, and other forces, are supplied by Statos-Vey. Though the Suvuka were defeated, Thermistal remains partially abandoned compared to the settled populations of Rho-Jashun. It remains a protectorate of Statos-Vey. We may, in time, encounter vessels empowered to take us to port. May they find us soon! Fleets patrol the shores here to protect shipping from both the scourge of piracy and the even worse fate we contemplate. I suspect the storm has injured them, and we are on our own. When they see our damage, they will make for us. Our work on repairing and cobbling new sails continues, but what we require is a proper rudder. Our hull will crumple before another storm. This ocean is beyond a depth for our anchor to assist us. A few captains may be tempted to let it out to slow our passage, but I will not risk further damage to the ship. I doubt we will be able to do more than minor repairs until we reach a true port. They will learn of our original arrangement for Jefaka's service in Bhampay. As a matter of course, they will either conduct us there or begin our repairs in their home port. All this is firmly stipulated in maritime law. We are incapable of returning home as we are. Our concerns for Seti must stand behind those of the survival of this vessel and her crew."

"First, we must survive our 'landing,'" Dine said. "I am glad to hear the Suvuka prefer to stay north, but a dozen could overwhelm this ship and kill us all. They are powerful swimmers, hence the ongoing work to widen the passage separating them from the rest of Thermistal." He turned and looked at Hegev, "Have you ever seen one?"

"*Seen* a Suvuka?" Hegev asked, "I never visited Thermistal." She tilted her head, "Have you?"

Dine frowned and nodded.

"Did I not tell you, Seti?" Captain Emedin said, clapping her First Officer's shoulder. "More than forty years ago, our Dine was as young as you! At close to your age, he also embarked on an epic adventure. He travelled to Thermistal to answer the call for workers to fortify the Vettencore Passage, the link between the Panchala Sea in the south and the Tharapura Ocean to the north through Thermistal. This dried fish participated in the final work to complete the greatest engineering feat of our age!" Dine broke into a rare smile. "While this passage," the captain continued, "the widest canal on Anu, has tremendous commercial value, its principal task remains to keep the Suvuka in exile on their portion of the continent."

Hegev looked at Dine with new respect. "Dine! I am near ten

years your senior and was a very young woman when we learned of this! While many left Kana-Moptu to work there, none rose to such a daunting task of our family. We heard many tales, some concerning terrible accidents."

"There were no such events when I worked there," Dine reluctantly said. "By the time I arrived, the towering East Wall was complete, and the garrisons guarding its construction were long abandoned. We were told the imprisoned beasts had immediately destroyed them. The North and South Channel had been connected for near a millennium, and a wide ocean canal separated us. The army had long been relocated to the western shore. To my young eyes they appeared to be relaxed in their vigils. I, and many others, including reassigned soldiers, worked on finishing the sheer face of the passage side of the western rampart. We were in our prime, yet we found it arduous. We also reported to the engineers, who toiled to ensure the channel remained consistent in depth and width. Our main fear was being swept away by the northward current, which ran hard past us. This was by design to ensure any Suvuka attempting a crossing would be swept far north and hopefully drowned before reaching our West Wall. For our troubles, we were paid well and granted generous benefits as if we were soldiers ourselves. Many labour precedents set at that time are now enacted across Anu."

He paused and looked at them all before continuing, "I befriended some of the soldiers, several younger than myself. They told me many a dire tale of their encounters with the enemy and their animalistic ways. We were conducted across and walked on the Eastern Wall's top, overlooking the Suvuka's domain on several occasions. It was impossibly high and smooth, curving inward as if arching over the land in a frozen wave. It is truly a wonder unmatched on Anu! We crawled into their observation tunnels inside the wall and watched one of the beast's ritual displays. My soldier comrades never joined us on these excursions. Our foreman went to the trouble of ensuring we saw the creatures the passage is meant to imprison to guarantee our continued dedication to our work." He looked toward the growing streak of land. "In all my long years since, I did not look to drawing this close to them again."

The shore grew more distinct. Emedin shook her head, "At this pace, we will make land by dusk. We must keep our wits and find the least harmful course. Once we come to rest, we must find supplies – our chief concern is fresh water. We must fortify our hull and find masts to replace these new rudders of ours. If we are granted a small rest, we will continue working on mending our sails and be better prepared to move west along the coast."

"What if we are seen?" Seti asked.

Captain Emedin looked at each of them. "I will not lie to you. Our situation is dire. The Suvuka are day hunters. Our work will take place in darkness. During the day, we must stay at the ship and be prepared to leave in an instant. We will post sentries at various points and create a set of signals. The necessity for silence will hamper our reconstruction efforts. As my First Officer has said, a small party could destroy us. Accounts suggest they will fly into a fury if they find us. There are tales of their swimming out to attack ships, although I find this hard to credit. They are said to have an aversion to structures appearing to come out of water. Another odd note; some have claimed the ancient chants used to drive Thyma away confuse them. One author swears this kept them from attacking their ship. I hope we need not test this! Remember, their hearing is acute beyond our own. We must school ourselves to keep our voices low to avoid detection. Sound travels far over the water, and the wind will take each careless word to their long ears."

Seti turned back to look at the shore. It loomed as a menacing monster waiting to swallow them. A series of cliffs lined the beach, and Seti thought he began to hear the surf at the shoreline. The mountains started to vanish behind a wall of rough vegetation. Other than a flock of Krall coming out to call down at them and circling high above the ship, there was no movement onshore.

"Captain," Dine said, surveying the resolving coastline, "We continue to miss the islands, but the shore ahead is better than I imagined."

Emedin nodded, and she leaned out to look at it. "The islands may have disappointed us for lack of water. Look at the rich foliage. Those mountains will ensure this coast is rich in brooks and streams. Dead ahead," she gestured. "At this speed, we will be there in a few hours. Make ready!"

The crew moved at the Captain's orders, keeping their voices low and minimizing any noise. Seti climbed into the rigging, and while at his tasks, looked at the ever-growing prospect of Thermistal. As Nu began to set, painting the sky in unusually striking hues, they heard the muted roar of the surf washing on a rough portion of the shore nearby. Their intended destination appeared tranquil.

CHAPTER 31

SINKIN

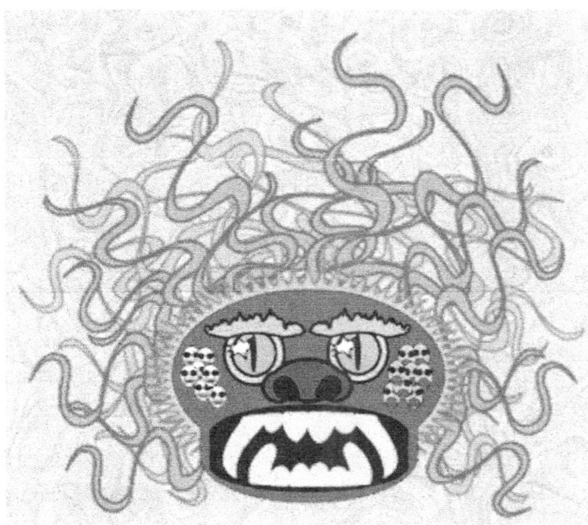

Day 277, Two-Week Sixteen, Jixx – The Beauty, seventy andas east of Saransut Bay.

Sinkin loped down the twisting path crowded on either side by tall grasses. Their initial calm face was deceiving. Thorns and nettles buried themselves in his pelt, causing him to stop at tree trunks and work them out. Crushed piles of them at bare trunks spoke of others doing the same before him. He had made his morning call, and the others answered from a distance behind him. When deep in these broad valleys, their answers, and the distant ocean's voice to his right, were his guides. The grasses formed a subtle new landscape he often misread.

But for the well-worn paths, he would be lost. When he could, he found high ground to survey the surrounding landscape. The mountains stood to the north and the Panchala Sea to the south. The pathway led him onto a cape with the sea some distance on either side. Despite these frequent checks, he seldom kept his bearings long in the numerous valleys. Many creatures new to him made their homes here. He foraged for fruits and nuts but found no meat. The fat he had built feasting on giant eels and fish within Saransut Bay sustained him. He began to locate small brooks and smelled the distinguishing plants congregating by them. A melodious bird made its home there, and he remained vigilant to their calls to find water. As most bird songs were so high pitched as to be near beyond his hearing, this one stood out among what, to other ears, would remain a confusing orchestra.

An unfortunate set of pests began to keep him company. Unique populations of tiny creatures, far smaller and more vicious than those in the northern jungles surrounding Latatroos Shelter, followed him in clouds. Their constant low drone filled his ears. They were unable to penetrate his pelt but proved quite able to attack exposed skin. He covered his unprotected flesh with dust and mud. Several times a day, he sought the tops of hills, to get his bearings and allow the sea winds to free him of his unwanted company. He turned to look north, toward the tall profile of the sheltering Jaladanu Mountains. He had run alone for twenty days and left the others behind. His solitary journey disappointed him. The Face had not revealed itself, and his thoughts continued to wander amidst this endless thicket.

He looked east, where the paths conjoined in a distant clearing on its own small hill crowned by a rough circle. At the centre stood a group of ancient trees. It was another Round! Sinkin arrived at midday and made his way across the rough circle of pounded-down ground toward the trees. There he found another collection of half-broken and bleached objects gathered from the Tolku's dead carts at the shore. Vines covered part of the mouldering pile, and small creatures made their nests in them. An odd creation stood lashed partway up a trunk. It had four projections attached to the bottom of a narrow open frame. A stiff weaving of a tiny vine, most since rotted away, had covered the frame.

Another curious empty square rose from one side, displaying more of its original weaving. A collection of objects lay at the base. Some had bizarre shapes with multiple arms and points. Others were polished long objects, their two flattened sides covered with intricate markings. One item held his interest. It was circular with a series of tiny marks in concentric rows. He gently laid one long nail on one circle and was shocked to find each row could be shifted independently of the others. All these mysterious items were surprisingly heavy. They were impervious to scratching and yet they were not stone! He sat pondering these mystifying creations. They were undeniably made with great skill, yet their purpose was beyond him. The ocean sounded close, and Sinkin thought of going down to discover more artifacts to add as he had done several times before. Today he could not find the ambition. He sat by the trees and welcomed the stiff ocean breeze. Those forming this Round chose its location well. His little tormentors shunned the open space, and he rested within this benign shelter.

After a time, he rose to explore the area and discovered piles of rocks marking a path. He went a short distance along it and heard the distinctive cry of the birds nesting by freshwater. He went down a steep incline and found a broad open area. A spring surged out of the ground, making its merry way toward the ocean. A pool stood near the spring, providing just enough room for a Suvuka to not only drink but step into and wash off. To Sinkin's eyes it was clear this was at least in part scooped out and broadened by Suvuka paws long ago. An exposed flat of polished rock lay to the left of the spring. It clearly had been used by others to smooth out new coats of mud for their journey.

Paths led off in several directions, but after drinking deep in the chill waters, Sinkin returned to the Round and fell asleep. An odd scent began to fill his dreams as he lay by the tree. He woke and smelled it coming from the ocean. His snout twitched, but, as it arrived, the scent dispersed on the wind filling him with unease. He rose and looked toward the sea. The dense bush thwarted his eyes, and the breeze carried the memory of salt spray. A large group of sea birds formed a tight circling formation in the distance suggesting a meal had washed onshore. He knew the birds made short work of anything they found and turned back to walk around the edge of the Round. His pace quickened, and his lope grew to a run.

He skidded to a halt as two bangs came on the wind. He rose on his hind legs and sniffed the wind, his senses alert. Perhaps another herd of Suvuka was down at the shore. He found none of his own kind's scent on the wind. No other sound or smell came to him. After a long pause, he got down though he remained vigilant. Keeping one ear and nostril alert, he returned to walking the Round. His amble grew into a lope and a run. No other foreign scents or sounds troubled him, and he let go of his anxiety and ran full out around the axis of trees covered with enemy trophies. Not since Chitikal Round, back after the opening of his Full Stag Run at the Vettencore Passage, had Sinkin recaptured the simple frenzy of the Mesmerizing Run. He had imagined being filled with it at Avanchil, but it eluded him there.

In this rough Gathering Circle, he entered into the captivating rush, breath and pounding paws followed by the land spinning around the hub. Images began rushing past Sinkin as he ran, from his childhood, from this Stag Run and at last, from Avanchil Round. Ordinary recollections started to combine and grow into new forms. The days of his life merged to form soil for further growth. His ears began to roar, and he felt as if he ran on air. The land started to tilt back and forth as he became aware of another circle forming in his mind. It had a series of bumps around the rim, and a line extending through the middle; a solitary lump stood at the centre.

What he most sought resolved at the top of the circle, becoming the Face of Avanchil Round. It pushed its way through the haze and became a Suvuka face with burning green eyes, a pelt of deep yellow carrying red streaks and a wide grin of terrible teeth. A sound came to him composed of several parts repeated many times. It formed a cadence for his run. It sounded like two quick breaths taken in succession, 'hesha,' and 'vira.'

These two sounds became more distinct and, at the same time, linked. The other bumps grew into other, upside down and lifeless, Faces. This one alone, saying 'hesha' and 'vira,' was vivid and alive. Sinkin had a distinct awareness this 'hesha vira' was female. The sages of old called Anu the Dame, mother of each creature running over her. The ancient songs spoke of all life emerging from Anu's skin. Was 'Hesha Vira' another name for Anu, the name of her Face? He had never heard this name. Perhaps, he thought, the time of revelations was not over. He continued to run without knowing it as he looked at the Face. Hesha-Vira bore the burden of these other lifeless Faces tied to a red vine.

Down from the vine hung a black circular Face, at the bottom trailed a terrible creature whose wide-open mouth was the source of the rope. What could it mean? The Face of Anu, calling herself Hesha Vira, spoke to him. Sinkin did not understand what the wide mouth said. He strained and ran faster as if to get closer to her. Two words formed out of the chaos and made their way toward him.

"Free me!"

CHAPTER 32

Shuna-Shapta

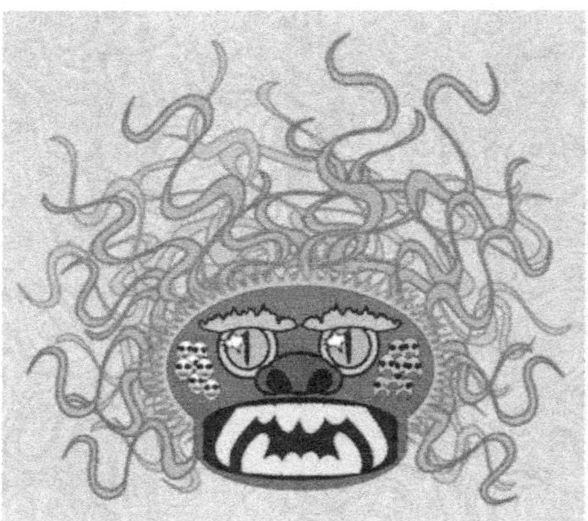 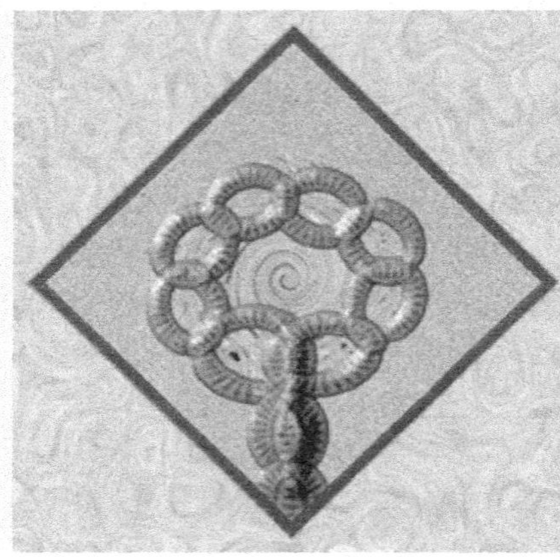

Day 277, Two-Week Sixteen, Jixx – The Beauty, within Tatchlan

Shuna-Shapta and Thakadush-Satwa stood on the raw surface of Indatubangas, the midway between the calm inner ocean of the Living System and its glowing and intelligent surface known as the Living Orb. Only the infant Majastas and Operant Shuna-Shapta could see the entire Resplendent Work in its true form. The baby Thakadush-Satwa, in her adult body within Tatchlan, was by her side on the flowing land. They stood at the shore of what appeared as a sea of lava. Once again, their hair flowed about them, and their naked bodies manifested vivid Floral Aroma Accords. They joined hands and surveyed the heaving mass before them, screaming innumerable messages of violence and passion, and writhing with the clear outlines of the monstrous Suvuka.

As the baby Majastas held Shuna-Shapta's hand, the new Operant felt the bond forming by their skin. She felt as if together they called out the name - 'Hesha Vira!' After a lengthy pause, Indatubangas began to vibrate. What appeared to be an emergence of eight Secondary Faces of the Principal Face of Raw Life rose in vertical circle presentation over the waves of confusion. They stopped before emerging in full; just the upper four were visible with the lower portion of the arrangement remaining buried in the molten sea. Their presence affected the denizens around them. Many of the Suvuka silhouettes turned to look at the group.

"Curious," Shuna-Shapta said in her altered Tatchlan voice. "In the past, most Suvuka remained blind to her." She then puzzled at the Secondary Face's apparent aloofness to them. "Her aspect has changed since the formation of Faces. Why do her servants not emerge in full? Why does she cause them to linger? When summoned, servants of a Face of Tatchlan should approach at once to receive instruction." Since their triumphal entry nine days before, none commanded these animate forces with equal assurance to the infant Majastas and her Operant.

Through their hands, a new thought came to Shuna-Shapta. She frowned and looked down at the girl saying a new phrase aloud, "Blind . . . and not blind?" Thakadush-Satwa pointed at the group. A novel thought passed from one body to the other. Shuna-Shapta struggled to understand what formed inside her head.

At last, she repeated what it resembled, "She rouses them?" Shuna-Shapta stared at the young woman beside her. "What do you mean? Why provoke them?"

"She chafes," Thakadush-Satwa said through her skin. "She would see Indatubangas rule all."

Shuna-Shapta stared at Thakadush-Satwa before looking out at the partial emergence of Secondary Faces.

"This may not be!" she blurted out. "Whilst the eldest, she is not our foremost. She seldom ventures to our Breathing Work where the rest of our Tatchlan Faces dwell."

"She alone," the girl's skin replied. "She loves not the others. She contends with our Faces."

"*Contends*?" Shuna-Shapta began to get a headache from this new form of communication. She frowned, set her jaw and called out, "Alatanda!"

Immediately, a black circle appeared in the distance and approached at speed. To Shuna-Shapta's amazement, she, through her link with Thakadush-Satwa, had summoned the Principal Face. While still significant, he was far smaller than during their last encounter. Shuna-Shapta realized this was due to his being in the presence of the first Majastas. Beneath him hung a tiny circle of eight Secondary Faces belonging to him. "Bridge and Gateway!" Shuna-Shapta found herself declaring. "Assist your sister with her duties before us!"

As soon as she spoke, the Principal Face, and Secondary Faces, of Alatanda rose above the Hesha Vira arrangement of servants. The lower Secondary Faces moved as if drawn to a magnet, positioning themselves below the Alatanda pattern. This arrangement represented the locations of their two Principal Faces within the complete cluster or wheel formation.

Both sets of Faces moved forward as one to hover before them. Alatanda servants were over them while Hesha Vira's Faces remained half-buried in the riotous ocean of Indatubangas.

"Alatanda!" Shuna-Shapta said, "your sister does not present fully to us."

The circle of Alatanda servants rose higher, bringing the Hesha Vira arrangement entirely out of the boiling sea. To Shuna-Shapta's amazement, below the circle of Secondary Faces of Hesha Vira, there now appeared several tremendous thrashing yellow golden hairs of the wild mane of the Principal Face herself, churning up the cauldron the Suvuka swam in. The Principal Face of Raw Life was just below the surface!

For a moment, Shuna-Shapta was speechless at this astonishing array of Principal and Secondary Faces. "How to proceed?" she said to herself. "Alatanda! Arrange yourself before me and have Hesha Vira's Faces placed for your Majastas direct inspection."

The upper Secondary Faces immediately moved to the right and then down to be positioned in front of Shuna-Shapta. She noted a curious feature. The Secondary Faces appeared locked with their Hesha Vira counterparts. Instead of effortlessly sliding past each other, they seemed fastened to the Alatanda Faces and compelled them. She also now noted that unlike their usual want, the Hesha Vira Secondary Faces did not fluctuate but appeared still. This was made more evident by the fact Alatanda's Secondary Faces did their typical gentle turning and bowing.

"I do not understand!" Shuna-Shapta declared. "What has happened to Hesha Vira?"

"She contends," came Thakadush-Satwa's reply.

She looked at her infant/adult Majastas and then at the Hesha Vira presentation before her. While the eight Secondary Faces stood as if statues, the massive wild hairs of the submerged Principle Face whipped about with more than their usual frenzy.

"This is wrong!" Shuna-Shapta said. "We may not proceed in this fashion. Hesha Vira has somehow developed a flaw or is ailing. For whatever reason, she has become defective! We must release her or risk causing injury."

"She withholds from us," came the reply from the young Majastas. "We would know her full purpose."

Shuna-Shapta shook her head in bewilderment. "Alatanda shall ensure her behaviour," said at last. "I shall speak to others immediately. We must investigate this at once."

Thakadush-Satwa sniffed the array before her. "Tolku here," she looked at Shuna-Shapta, whose palm began to itch with unusual building sensations.

Despite surpassing her fellow Invocants, Shuna-Shapta did not possess the extended senses of the young Majastas. She looked at the sea of Suvuka forms before them and beyond. "Some remain within Indatubangas," she said to the infant within the young woman's body, "most from the wild continent of Rho-Jashun."

Thakadush-Satwa shook her head, "Statos-Vey Tolku here," her message came clearly. She pointed to the surface of Indatubangas.

"Many?" Shuna-Shapta said as she looked, "Long ago most Tolku dwelt here, mired within this Self-Absorption. Many now grow toward our new layer enveloping the old chaos of life. Some arrive, and we walk amongst them, awake amid dreamers. Our new Maja pulls more toward our Breathing Work each day."

"Many there, many here," Thakadush-Satwa replied through her hot hand.

After frowning, Shuna-Shapta called out, "Hesha Vira! Alatanda! Conduct us to the largest concentration of Statos-Vey Tolku upon Indatubangas."

The two sets of Secondary Faces sent out tendrils to surround Thakadush-Satwa and Shuna-Shapta. They moved backward before them out over the steaming surface. The infant Majastas and Operant, suspended before the Faces, proceeded. In a short time, they came to an unusual arrangement of Tolku silhouettes spread out in miniature on the surface. The large group formed an elaborate design. There was an open space in the centre surrounded by eight circles of figures linked to each other, below them was a pronounced concentration extending a short distance away from the rest. Together, these disparate elements created a single enigmatic configuration.

"This is many dreaming Tolku," Shuna-Shapta said, "sharing a single idea, taking the form of this . . . symbol. We must summon the others here to study this at once. Such numbers and definitions signify a powerful emergence within the general population. How could we miss this? How could it form so quickly? We must walk abroad and find this symbol."

"Hesha Vira rouses them. They turn against us." Shuna-Shapta turned in shock at Thakadush-Satwa's message.

She looked at the set of impassive Faces representing Raw Life and down at the presence of their master beneath the surface. "A rebellion . . . fomented by one of our Principal Faces . . . upon Statos-Vey?" She pondered the pattern below them. "Less than a two-week ago, we witnessed the complete emergence of our Principle and Secondary Faces within the Wheel Formation. Was it an illusion? Does the eldest Face attempt to subvert the rest?" The trembling pattern maintained itself.

Thakadush-Satwa pointed at small gatherings of dreaming Tolku circling this central configuration.

"No other pockets of resistance have this focus," Shuna-Shapta indicated the leading group. "Other anti-Tatchlan movements . . ." She stopped, and they watched as one small group moved toward the main array and merged. The central symbol grew in size.

Thakadush-Satwa pointed at the horizon. Flocks of Secondary Faces approached, and some immense Principal Faces hung in the distance. New tendrils drew more from the Faces standing before them. Soon a wide circle of Faces, and many hundreds of Invocants and Masters, surrounded the arrangement before them. Shuna-Shapta sensed this large population of Invocants came from all parts of Statos-Vey and beyond. Despite the noise of Indatubangas, she heard snatches of the others, asking the same questions and followed their reaching similar conclusions. Confused and alarmed faces looked at the Hesha Vira formation. Her Principal Face had sunk beneath the surface. Two tendrils brought Master Kanla and Master Tanas over to them.

"Majastas Infant," Master Tanas spoke, "and Treasured Operant," he smiled at Shuna-Shapta. "We witnessed the Suvuka's awakening to the presence of Hesha Vira. We also discern seeds of rebellion growing upon Statos-Vey. Our wayward Face responds and augments disturbances within these distinct populations."

"Hesha Vira has dark distinction amongst our Faces," Shuna-Shapta's mother said. "She alone tends her furnace of destruction and renewal."

"As she should," Master Tanas said. "Her tasks are noble and vital to all. Generations of Masters predating our Uluvatu worked to strike a balance between her Indatubangas tasks and her ties to our Grand Work."

"They failed," Shuna-Shapta said. The others looked at her, realizing Thakadush-Satwa spoke through her. Shuna-Shapta struggled, "She says Hesha Vira was frightened by our Cluster of Faces Formation and now resists us."

Master Tanas and Master Kanla looked back at the now half-submerged Secondary Faces. Alatanda and his Secondary Faces remained before Shuna-Shapta.

"Whilst unforeseen," Master Tanas said, "this final emergence of our Principal and Secondary Faces reveals an issue invisible prior to this day."

"Does this mean we witnessed an incomplete emergence?" Master Kanla enquired. "The compelling configuration suggested all Faces joined in a united and harmonious whole. Hesha Vira's portion accorded with the rest. The extended petal of her Secondary Faces was in correct marshalling order."

"Through her Operant, our Majastas declares that Hesha Vira found herself part of a pattern that appalled her," Master Tanas replied. "She now appears alarmed and confused, emotions well known within Indatubangas."

Shuna-Shapta gestured down at the array before them, "Tatchlan opens to find an organized anti-Tatchlan faction, the roots may be upon Rho-Jashun, but it grows amongst our own! The Suvuka remains distant and contained. Near us stand these wayward Tolku."

"Shapta," Master Tanas said, "we heard your initial assessment of this grouping. I must add there is a fundamental incoherence here. We see no organized movement based upon articulated ideology. This is an emotional response to a new symbol. I detect ancient anti-Tatchlan threads within this deviant stream of 'The Common Desire.' Although it has a novel arrangement, it remains a potential challenge. We track various rebellious tendencies concentrated within northern Rho-Jashun. None of us here are experts in this area. Other Masters better acquainted with this portion of our Living System shall examine in full."

"When our Majastas fulfills the status of an adult . . ." Master Kanla began.

"No," Shuna-Shapta said. The others knew by the tone of her voice this came from Thakadush-Satwa. "She says she may not untie this knot."

"My Majastas," Master Tanas said, "you have an abundance of tools. Many possessing a wide range of skills shall assist you. We shall examine this and determine how best to proceed. Once we understand their constituent elements, despite possessing rogue vitality, we manage these movements with little difficulty. Notwithstanding its complexity, any knot may be untied."

"It is a knot!" Shuna-Shapta exclaimed in her own voice.

The others looked bewildered at her.

"A knot!" she said, pointing down.

They looked at the complex grouping. The eight loops surrounding the inner opening and the larger bunch beneath them took on more clarity.

"What does a knot signify?" Master Kanla asked, frowning at her daughter. "I recall no reference within the Sime, Heason, Chelyaka or Menem traditions to this symbol. It must relate to a recent event. What emerges within an instant with this impact? We are surrounded by representations of many parts of Statos-Vey, with an emphasis upon the south. As with the mundane village, we appear to look in the wrong direction. I also observe Tolku of Rho-Jashun. Is this evidence of our ancient critics? Have they gained a foothold at the other end of Anu?"

"This requires further scrutiny," Master Tanas replied, continuing to examine the pattern. "We assumed the northern clans a spent force, their literary challenge exhausted. Perchance a new leadership, possessing different skills, has emerged. These developments had to begin since Nebutan's death."

Shuna-Shapta shook her head in frustration, "No. Wrong."

They waited as she struggled to communicate the mute Majastas's message.

"This," Shuna-Shapta indicated the symbol, "not important. Their need . . . important. They . . . hate us before this." She looked at Thakadush-Satwa. The Majastas grew distressed. Shuna-Shapta turned to the others, and her voice trembled, "She asks why do they hate Her?"

The others looked long at the child in her young adult Tatchlan body and each other. As her question moved through the circle of Invocants, they also grew still. Thakadush-Satwa turned to look back. The Principal Face of unrefined life now emerged before them all. While not the immense being of the wheel pattern, there could be no doubt this was no Secondary Face. Her green, bulging eyes with their black vertical slits appeared to scrutinize them all. Alatanda's Principal Face stood beside her as their servants sped away. Hesha Vira quivered as she sent a tendril to encircle them. Holding Shuna-Shapta's hand, Thakadush-Satwa moved via her tendril toward Hesha Vira. The others cried out as Hesha Vira's Face grew in size. In an instant, she filled their view. Thakadush-Satwa and Shuna-Shapta continued to approach the now huge vertical Face of her exposed skin, patterned in shifting yellow and red. They came to her right eye. They passed between two long lashes, moved over the huge shining green spheres' wild patterning, and approached the black slit centre, now a widening vertical band.

Once before, this child had taken Shuna-Shapta closer to a Principal

Face than she had ever been. She marvelled at the efforts of the ancient Masters, struggling to fashion these colossal forms serving a Living System they would not now recognize. The early Masters gave them considerable powers and a measure of discernment. They were the collective animate forms of the countless billions of Seeds with their interlaced Crowns and extended Tails composing the Living System. How could this noble effort lead to the unthinkable possibility of one of them turning on the rest? They stopped at the centre of the Face's eye, its black slit forming a wide column. The huge lashes formed a striking canopy far above and below them. Thakadush-Satwa stared into the centre of this dark, shimmering void. She sniffed, listened and looked into the core. She reached out and touched the surface. The entire Face trembled, and Shuna-Shapta sensed her firm link to Alatanda beside her forced her to stay in place.

"Self . . ." the child-woman said into Shuna-Shapta's hand, withdrawing her own hand from the black depths in distaste.

Shuna-Shapta looked down at her, "Self? Do you mean Self-Absorption?"

Thakadush-Satwa nodded.

"This Face, one of our Twelve Principle Faces of Tatchlan, is tainted by . . . Self-Absorption?"

Thakadush-Satwa nodded.

CHAPTER 33

Seti

Pictured: traditional icon of three Queldeday mounted on a rod

Day 278, Two-Week Sixteen, Jixx – The Beauty, Charun Headland, seventy andas east of Saransut Bay.

Seti cursed himself. The crew had worked through the night aboard ship anchored in a small bay near the blunt tip of Charun Headland. At dawn, they had fallen silent and rested. Seti slept a few hours before rising and surveying the rigging in the morning light. Satisfied he had done what he could until the new sails were unfurled, he moved along the deck. The Krall continued to circle over them, despite attempts by the crew to scare them off. Tonight, they would steal up the tumbled break in the cliffs to the right along the shore, nicknamed 'the stairway' by the crew, to the land above. Seti frowned at the towering thicket lining the top of the cliff. This dense growth stood taller than Salarish at harvest back home. How to find a way through them? At dawn, a few had ventured ashore, and a sharp-eyed member of the crew found clear signs of water seepage on a portion of the rough cliff. They confirmed it sweet water to drink. Their thirst was great, but none dared scratch the surface, let alone dig in to reach it in case their noise brought unwanted attention. Captain Emedin ordered a large party to head inland at nightfall and try to locate the spring. Continuing to glance at the rigging, Seti accidentally kicked a loose board, sending it crashing into another. He leapt to stop the rogue board, causing a second crash. Two loud bangs in succession echoed off the tall cliffs. In an instant, several crew scrambled on deck. After looking about in fear, they turned furious glances on Seti. Dine approached, exuding cold fury.

"Get below decks and stay there!" he hissed.

Seti rose and made his way past many angry faces without making a sound. He stayed below until nightfall. As Nu began to set, he came up shamefaced. The Captain gave him a brief look and smiled.

"Seti has proven we are alone on this part of the coast," she said, speaking in a low voice, causing the rest to gather close. Those further back had to depend on others relaying what she said.

"Those assigned to keep watch report no sign today," she continued while pausing as each sentence was relayed. "We have surveyed the ship. A few repairs will be made. Most must be left until we find a safe harbour. Some of the crew will remain aboard and, with care, tend to the inner hull. We must find fresh water. One piece of good fortune is that stash of empty jugs we have in the hold. Despite the storm, due to proper securing most are undamaged. Those leaving ship will have a bag, a jug and a knife. Fill your jug in the spring and your bag with any fruits or other foods. The knife is to assist in food gathering and to cut your way through that wall of tangle. Bind your hair and wrap yourselves. You will also each possess one of the ship's Queldeday. They have drunk their fill of Nu's exuberant light today and will glow well into the night to attract their insect prey. Do not touch them when they are feeding! They will root on small boards, and we will attach cords to their base. Either fasten them to your head or body or carry them. Do not let your flesh touch them. They were not intended to be carried thus, so be mindful of them. Their light darkens with distress." She looked at the cliff, "Our scouts say a little way in are well-worn paths. The Suvuka made them. There is evidence of new use."

She allowed this truth to reach them. "Each of you is part of a team. Your leader will employ a high-pitched whistle. In our ancient struggle, we learned the Suvuka do not hear these high notes well. Do not be fooled! The Suvuka's hearing is beyond our own when it comes to low tones! Do not lift your foot before seeing the barriers to putting it down. Most will proceed west; back toward what we hope is the source of the spring. The Suvuka trail will lead you to the water. No doubt, they long ago discovered and made the way easy for their kind to drink. We begin our journey when they sleep. Do not wake them! If you discover one, you have one more advantage. Their night vision is poor, and you will carry glowing Queldeday. We know their lights confuse the beasts at night. Despite this, do not grow confident! It is said they are quick to adapt. Go, find water and hurry back!"

Nu had set, and the sky overhead grew strangely brilliant as the land descended into black silhouettes. Seti, Hegev and four others became a team lead by Dine. They were the first on the shore with the others following in a single file behind them. Dine walked on the balls of his feet over the loose stones of the beach. When they arrived at the 'stairway,' he placed one exacting foot in front of the other to ensure no stone was dislodged. The others followed in the dwindling light. Seti brought up the rear and prayed to his silent Menem he did not further disgrace himself. Clouds now obscured most of the Eyes of Nu above. Darkness was total by the time he reached the top. The little round Queldeday, accustomed to being attached to the masts and other parts of the ship, began to glow. Their sudden light threw the hostile twists of the thicket wall into sharp relief. Seti hastened to put the flat square board on top of his head and tied it on his chin. Most of the others had done the same or hooked the board to their chests, so their hands remained free. Dine turned his head each way, frowning at the narrow path cut for him. With deliberation, he used his knife to cut branches and widen an opening. Despite the others' efforts, Seti found the thicket challenging to navigate. Composed of many plants sprouting in all directions, it created a maze starting at ground level and continuing high overhead. He felt a tightening of his chest and began to gasp.

Hegev turned. "What is it?" she whispered.

"I hate enclosed spaces," he whispered back. "I used to have nightmares of being lost in the Salarish fields and barely tolerate the inside of Jefaka. Here, I am drowning within a sea of branches."

Hegev signalled him to stop talking. "We will soon be on the path," she whispered. "Stay close and focus on where you put your feet!"

For what felt like hours, Seti endured the closeness, the stinging vines and piercing thorns. He felt the others left many branches in his way and was slowed by his constant cutting of the dark fingers reaching for him. His Queldeday made a high-pitched noise whenever a branch touched it, making him more vigilant. He felt winged creatures flying at his face and heard peculiar calls. Glowing eyes followed his stumbling progress.

Without warning, he stepped out onto a broad path. Five of the crew were standing shoulder to shoulder across it to measure its width. Dine stood waiting until Seti had emerged and signalled for them to follow him back along the path. They moved with ease on the firm and smooth ground. The plants, composed of towering grasses and the miserable thorny plants they had passed through, became undulating walls either side of them. Their Queldeday cast dancing shadows in front and behind them along the path. A group of bobbing lights emerged as the second crew began to follow them. Breathing hard, Seti calmed himself. He followed the glowing set of lights in front of him through the darkness. The ocean winds penetrated the undergrowth this close to shore and stirred the air. Seti could imagine how dense the path would be without the breezes. Seti found himself looking down at his feet to ensure he did not miss a branch or pebble as they continued along. To his ears, the distant surf and wind made their progress silent. For a long time, they shuffled through the intriguing landscape without incident.

The front light began to sway back and forth, their signal to stop. Seti stood and waited. The group started to move, veering to the right. Seti saw what caused the stop. Another path turned to the left, back toward the shore. He shivered at the realization Suvuka made this. They continued until the swaying began, and he stopped. A whispered message came back.

"The spring!" Hegev whispered. "We found it! Dine says, after filling your jug, drink one cupped hand to sustain yourself."

The line shuffled and stopped until Seti heard the sweet sound of water running. The path opened beyond the range of their lights, suggesting a cleared area by the spring. Hegev bent forward and rustled in her bag. He reached into his and pulled out his jug.

Dine came to him and whispered, "Fill your jug to the brim. The others will do likewise. We will make this trip several times throughout the night. At dawn, we will consider seeking fresh food."

He began to walk back. The line of lights lined up behind him. Seti bent forward, and his Queldeday illuminated the water issuing out of a rock. It gathered in a wide pool, and he submerged his jug and filled it. He had one quick handful of water and joined the others. As they left, another line took their place.

To Seti, the jug had been small when he began this journey, but full it proved a burden. His arms ached by the time they reached the boat. Each pot was sealed before they were laid in the boat, surrounded by packing. The crewman began slowly rowing back out to the ship, making as little noise as possible. They received new jugs, and Dine had them rest. They watched the continuous lines of glowing lights descending the 'stairway' carrying their burdens of water.

More boats arrived from the ship bringing empty jugs. As soon as the last was down, Dine began to move back toward the stairway. The rest of his crew followed. Throughout the night, the trek continued. Seti lost count of how many times they travelled back and forth, settling into a trance-like rhythm. The original thicket crossing improved by so many pushing and cutting through it until they had beaten down their own path to the wide Suvuka trail. Partway through the night, the clouds cleared, and the ceaseless stars shone down on them.

Seti was grateful for the added glow of his Queldeday. However, as the night wore on, the creature's light began to diminish. The board and ties on his head became uncomfortable. Despite what felt like an endless night, Seti was amazed when it became clear the sky lightened. As he carried a full pot, he began to make out the tall grasses' colours either side. The stairway grew clear as they descended to the beach, and the Jefaka stood in the bay in the early dawn. Most had returned to the ship for other tasks, and Dine told his group to remove their Queldeday helmets. Everyone was grateful to release the uncomfortable straps and hand them over. Dine received two more to join his crew for the last water retrieval before they searched for food.

Their trip back to the spring was uneventful. Seti found himself at the back of the line and, after filling his pot, stopped to dunk his head in the water and have an extended drink. He looked down, and an unbidden reflected face sat beside his own.

"Behold the sweetest and most volatile of elements," his aunt's voice came to him. "Water will defer to the smallest stone. With infinite patience, it defeats mountains. It effortlessly nourishes and cleanses without distinction. It seeks out the lowest places and self-clarifies. If it grows hot, it fills the air with sweet vapour. If it grows cold, it forms white flesh able to pry apart stone. Far more live under it than above it. Like us, it has a foolish youth followed by a life of measure and virtue, ending in the dignity of absorption."

Tears began to stream down his face, and he did not hear the whispered calls for him to come. He did hear a crashing sound behind him and the sudden set of shrill whistles. A new reflection filled the waters of a dark creature towering over him.

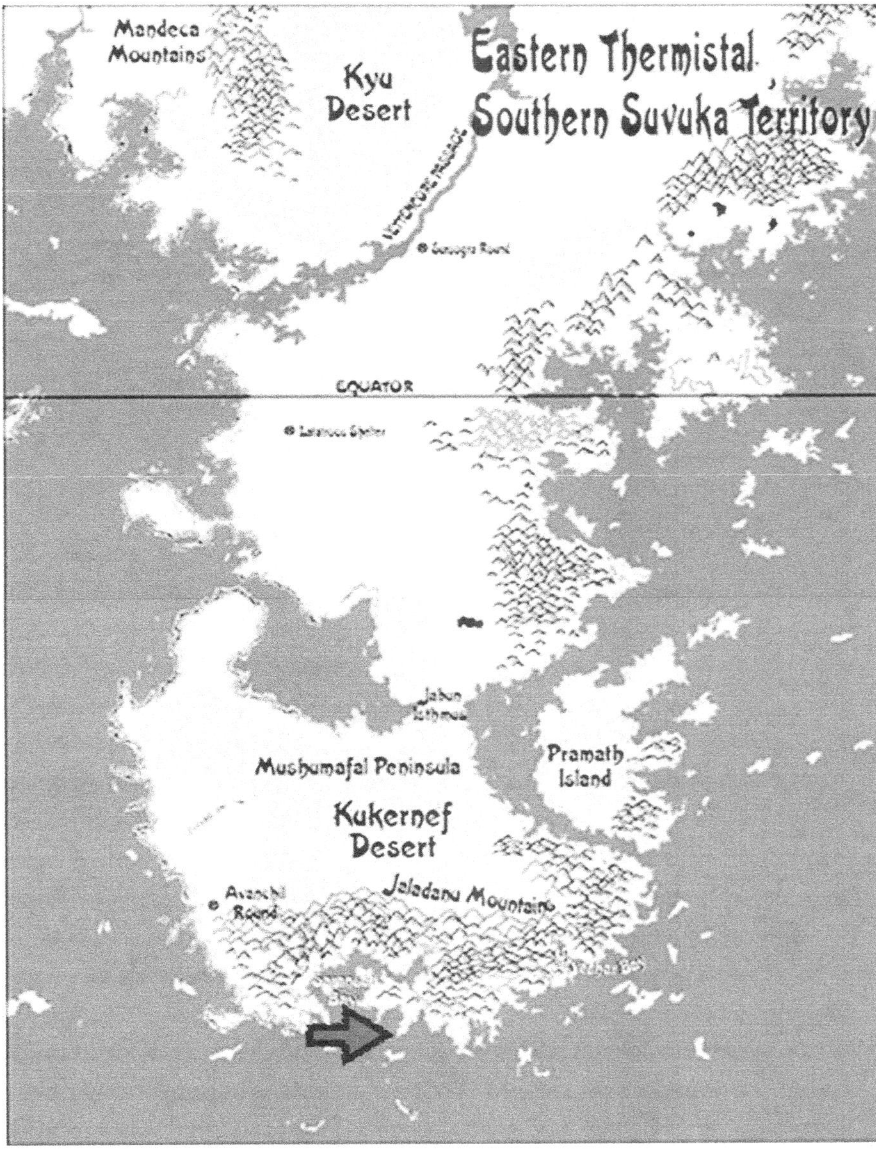
Mandeca Mountains
Kyu Desert
Eastern Thermistal, Southern Suvuka Territory
EQUATOR
Mushumafal Peninsula
Pramath Island
Kukernef Desert
Jaladanu Mountains

CHAPTER 34

SINKIN

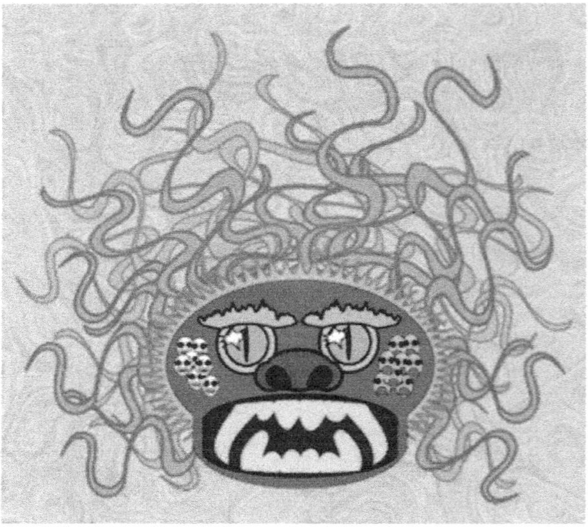

Day 279, seventy andas east of Saransut Bay.

Sinkin stared in amazement at the cowering little thing by the pool. Its limbs were like sticks, and its head was attached to its body by a weak-looking neck. Except for the top of its head, its skin was exposed, wrapped in coverings like a shedding tree's loose bark. Its face wore the same terror of all prey. Its eyes were huge for its flat face. The creatures near-non-existent nose quivered, and its small mouth hung open to reveal the tiny teeth of a grazer. Sinkin knew the source of the odd scent. One swipe would open the little creature wide.

Sinkin rose on his hind legs and bellowed. The Tolku cowered and wrapped its pathetic upper legs around its head. Its front legs bent the wrong way, and its front paws were deformed compared to its back paws. Sinkin bent in closer to look at them and sniff the bit of fur on its head. The scent did not belong to Anu. How could these feeble creatures create mighty works and drive his ancestors into exile? Sinkin felt movement behind him and turned. A group of other Tolku, larger than this one, stood halfway along the path. They edged away, making ugly noises. Sinkin bellowed and gave them a false charge, enjoying their wild departure.

He swung back to face his solitary prey. This must be one of their young. While there was little meat, it would be sweet. He recalled the songs of how these creatures were hunted for food and sport when discovered on the new land. He rose, his shadow covering his prey. He smelled the terror, and it made him drool in anticipation. As he prepared to strike, the creature began emitting high-pitched sounds - the universal song of lower animals serving the Shepherds of Anu. Sinkin's right eye tingled disturbingly, and he shook his massive head. The creature held one of his paws to his eye as if afflicted by the same sensation. Sinkin saw a glint of green in its other eye.

For an instant, the face of the creature blurred and modified. The paw fell away to reveal the Face of Hesha Vira! Sinkin shook his head to remove the vision, but the Face remained, staring at him from a Tolku body. The creature lost its fear and stood on its hind legs. The Face of Hesha Vira turned on an angle as if to examine him. It stepped one pace back, and as quick as it came, the Face vanished, and the Tolku remained. Sinkin's eye ceased tingling. The creature also rubbed its eye and assumed an enigmatic pose not taken by cornered prey. Intense curiosity filled Sinkin. The small creature shifted from one of its hind paws to the other, in a rhythmic fashion. It began to raise and lower its front limbs in opposition to its back limbs. Its thin torso twisted front and back and to each side, each movement ending in a gesture of one of the limbs.

A dance! It danced! Sinkin had not known they could do this. He now bent his head one side and the other, watching the strange little creature. He sensed movement behind him. Several of its fellows had returned and stood on the path. Sinkin gave them a half-hearted snort and turned back. Despite its size, this one bore a separate mark to the other quaking beings. Clear purpose drove these stick limbs. Its hind legs stroked the ground, mimicking its front legs high over its head as if touching an invisible tree above.

As he watched, a sudden sound came on the wind. It was the familiar mid-pitch call, followed by a dipping one, a rising cry trembling at a distinctive timbre ending in a high bark. The two herds must be approaching the Circle above. Sinkin reared up. The figure froze in mid-movement, staring at him. He looked once down at the creature and once back at the others before leaping up the path.

* * *

As Sinkin came to the edge of the Circle, he heard the clear slapping sounds of the Tolku running back along the path behind him. He also heard Durka and Makusk herd approaching. He knew they would sense a change in him. As soon as Hiratak broke the clearing on the far side of the Circle, he knew what he must do.

"Well met, young wanderer!" his beloved Herdmaster called out to him. His manner altered as he noted Sinkin's aspect. He galloped across the Round, the others following. Morakav drew close and stared at him; he frowned at the remaining members of Makusk Herd, sensing a change in him.

"He is touched!" Morakav growled.

The two herds circled Sinkin as Hiratak came close and examined him.

"Say he is mistaken," Hiratak sounded mournful.

"He is not," Sinkin said. He told them in full what happened. They listened while emitting growls and yelps.

Hiratak was the most agitated. "We know its twisted masters," he turned to the others. "This is another one of their deceptions!"

"No," Sinkin answered. He told them Hesha Vira had revealed herself to him, told him her name and asked him to free her.

"This Hesha Vira is the true Face of Anu. She calls for us to free her," Sinkin said.

Hiratak looked with shock and dismay at Sinkin, "My boy, you are entranced! You said yourself the enemy wore this Face."

"As a possession," Sinkin said.

"Yeeeaaaaoooo!" Hiratak bellowed. "This is pure obstinacy! You twist what is simple to fit your fancy! This Face belongs to them!"

"No, the ancient diviners saw this Face. She was known before we found the enemy," Sinkin said in an even tone. "Keeper Datal said he had seen it as a child. He said it came during 'our moments of perfection.' The Tolku poisoned what they touch, yet they arose from Anu. Despite what they became, they began as her children."

Morakav stepped closer to Sinkin, making the enraged Hiratak pause. "When we endured our humiliation, it felt like a dream. None could resist them. We woke to find ourselves spoilt. We could not touch them. You said it was small and trembled. Yet, it captivated you by dancing."

"It did so despite imminent death," Sinkin admitted. "What other creature would? If faced by a Thyma pack, would it dance?"

"They would be unmoved by such vile displays," Hiratak shouted. "They would act with the moral purity of predators! They would not be entangled by devices!"

"This marks one of many signs of their inferiority," Sinkin replied. "There is more to this. This Face of our Hesha Vira stared at me from it. Perhaps she bade him dance in obeisance. I intended to observe until whatever unfolded. . ."

"And proceed to consume your 'hesha vira?'" Hiratak spat back. "This isolation experiment has failed! It has intensified your fallacy! A single Tolku paralyzes you. You hide your dishonour with ridiculous mysticism."

"Is it dishonour to welcome fresh thoughts?" Sinkin roared. "Our tradition is based on deception! What is more dishonourable? Running in fear or courageously facing a new vision?"

"Enough!" Morakav roared. "Hiratak, casting aspersions dishonours you! We of Makusk know to fear. Yet, we do not close our ears. Shame is the final resort of the defeated. I declare the debate suspended for today. There remains the issue of the Tolku."

The group roused to the more urgent situation and began to sniff the air and angle their ears.

"There is but one course of action," Hiratak growled before vanishing into the thicket. The rest moved to follow him. Setush alone remained where he stood, facing Sinkin.

"What does it mean, Sinkin?" his eyes brimmed. He had longed to see his dear friend and found the reunion far from what he hoped.

"I do not know," Sinkin said. "I must think about things before I run at them."

A chorus of bellows rose from the thickets facing the ocean, and they ran down the path, turned at the spring and bound along the well-worn way between the tall grasses. The howls continued ahead as the two bucks ran along the trail before finding a rough pathway cut through the grasses leading to the shore. They forced their way through a new narrow passage and emerged at the top of a steep rock hill leading down to the coast. The rest of Makusk and Durka had gone down to the shore. They began displaying defiance they had two years ago at the Vettencore Passage. They bared their fangs, barked and roared, extended their talons and stuck out their long tongues. Hiratak hurled extravagant abuses at an impudent marvel daring to ride the water. Sinkin and Setush stared at the large dark cart. Many denuded trees grew out of the top, covered in undulating skins and vines stretched between them. The little Tolku scurried over the top of the cart and climbed the trees.

"Is this alive?" Setush asked in amazement. "Does it have swimming legs?"

"We saw the ruins of these," Sinkin said. "They are destroyed trees fashioned by their crafts. They are not alive."

Setush growled in confusion, "How does the creature float on the waters?"

Sinkin had no answer as he continued to watch the apparition.

The Tolku began to vocalize rhythmically and repetitively while slapping their front paws. This bizarre display stopped those down on the shore. Hiratak had started to wade out into the surf when he was struck dumb by the show. As they watched, the cart turned away, and the hanging skins flapped and curved. Sinkin found the tiny one he had in his power a short time ago. The creature picked him out from the others and raised one of its front paws toward Sinkin. None knew what this meant.

CHAPTER 35

Shuna-Shapta

Pictured: Primary Epoch icon depicting 'The Throne.'

Day 279, Two-Week Sixteen, Jixx - Beauty, within Thakadush Cluster, Bhampay.

I enjoy this one," Master Kanla said as she read the note out with exaggerated effect, "'I am Nu! I am the terrible face in your dreams! Untie me to know yourself! I arrive from the clean north to pull you out of the sea of flesh.'"

She cast the paper onto the low table in the small anti-room of Thakadush Cluster's outer courtyard, sending another sheet onto the fresh laid mosaic floor depicting brilliant sea life. The three of them sat on thick woven mats by a low table and still wore their clothes. They all wore masks in variations of the Sixth Principle Face of Tatchlan - Neferdush, the Face of Perception. They did so to intensify and focus their examination. Master Tanas' smile appeared either side of his Neferdush Mask's long nose and shook his head. Shuna-Shapta picked up the fallen sheet. "Another short one," she said, reading, "'I am a simple northern boy. Untie this knot and find freedom. I will wake your terrible slumber. You swim in confusion. You drown in indulgence. Nu's Knot signals your liberty.'"

"We estimate he spoke to the crowds between thirty to forty days ago," Master Tanas said. "What you view here represents a growing body of material inspired by this event. Most of the other versions are longer and more disjointed," Master Tanas said, looking at the pile of papers. "Do not bother to look at this one," he indicated a series of sheets set to one side, "By far the worst of the lot – the boy would need an entire day to declare it. Their versions grow with each telling, leading to this variety of renditions. In time, leadership would create a definitive version and suppress the rest."

"Incoherence fills these two shortened versions," Shuna-Shapta said, looking at the others. "I hear odd happenings take place at the Memanu Fields each day. I recall a book, chronicling many absurd visions and hilarious antics of those visiting them, within our reading lists."

Masters Tanas and Kanla chuckled.

"For a minor elective yes," her mother said. "Of no concern to you. Yes, alongside a general euphoria and satisfaction, the fields do produce hallucinations. This pleasant secondary side effect also draws the crowds."

"Why then should these absurd babblings receive different treatment from the rest?" Shuna-Shapta said, "Why does this miraculous story of the 'returned knot' gain such momentum? A pair of two weeks have passed since this so-called event. The story shows no sign of fading! Why does this flourish in the countryside whilst completely unknown within our cities?"

"Ever my star pupil," Master Tanas beamed, "you sense the true situation. The readiness for portions of our population to grasp these meagre images and words of rebellion remains our key issue. If any rant shall do, regardless of whether it makes sense or not, it suggests a deep dissatisfaction within quarters perchance neglected."

"We have not neglected them!" Master Kanla said in noted indignation. "The majority dwells within our shining cities, where dynamic change occurs. We must focus upon them. From here, our Mantle shall move into the hinterland through increased birth of Sensitives subsuming these backward populations with gentle efficiency."

"So I hear," Master Tanas replied. "Nonetheless, we discern a significant movement developing without any ideology save an evocative symbol. This makes it difficult to address to any effect. This 'knot' resembles a frown upon an infant's face. We may not determine the cause or solution to this dissatisfaction within its present form."

"What of this boy?" Shuna-Shapta enquired. "You emphasize the general dissatisfaction latching upon this incident. Nevertheless, the reports emphasize the boy's presentation. They pine after him as an inspiration, despite his disappearance after this single event. Our Servants say, should he return, many are ready to hear him."

"I sense the hand of Sawlu Clan here," Master Kanla said. "At present, they alone possess the means to produce and sustain such a figure. It is likely they conspire for him to emerge at another location according to a plan. All accounts agree he left upon a merchant's vessel. The ships once carrying anti-Tatchlan literature now bring raw oracles to us! They move from literature to theatre!"

"These Sawlu attempt to challenge us with a boy?" Shuna-Shapta asked.

"Your mother knows more of such things than I," Master Tanas said. "Perchance a network of agents spread throughout the south, helping to magnify its importance. What *I* discern suggests no such organization. Its lack of definition within Indatubangus remains our difficulty. With a cohesive plan and identifiable organization, we would mark its outlines. The construction of countermeasures depends upon an identifiable structure. Now we face a raw, disorganized and blind movement."

"Be it organized or spontaneous," Shuna-Shapta said, "we have the same result. If this pre-adult had ranted within the streets of Bhampay or Upata-Shepsus, none would recall him the next day. I recall what little Samshep described to me regarding the settlement dominated by mundanes a short distance down the highway. We may find this knot displayed there." She turned to her mother, "It takes root within untended soil. Perchance we must examine this further. We do not wish a repeat of what came about after the fall of the Suvuka upon Rho-Jashun."

"Ah, my darling," Master Kanla replied, "no comparison exists between Statos-Vey and Rho-Jashun! Samshep's school trip has overturned some directives, and we now dispatch our Servants out into the countryside. Populations sickened by their isolation receive new focus. Our Majastas's birth begins to affect our entire subcontinent! Farmers and traders coming and going from here shall take a portion of her back to their homes. All agree our Resplendent Work begins to assert itself throughout Statos-Vey."

Shuna-Shapta shook her head, "You recall what She said, 'I may not untie this knot.' We must set aside our complacency, Ama, what we witnessed unsettled Thakadush-Satwa. We must examine this general predisposition to rebellion. This clutching at an obscure symbol suggests a more significant issue. I have revisited Indatubangas several times to ponder this. Some formations of discontent join and others form." She rubbed her tired eyes behind her mask. "Hesha Vira's possible role is another issue. Most forget the Suvuka's marked awareness of her."

"Yes," Master Tanas said, "the presence of this 'knot' distracts us. I remain skeptical of the radical behaviour from a Face of Tatchlan."

"It is preposterous, my dear," her mother said. "For one of our Twelve Principle Faces of Tatchlan formulating these extraordinary notions would militate against the very Living Orb giving her birth. It would degrade our Living System to a farce out of the Epic of Ranvartawan."

Shuna-Shapta looked from one to the other. She rose and began to pace. "These are transitional times," she said. "We witness the shift between millennia of established Master traditions – and the birth of our Living System upon Anu's Flesh." She looked at her mother and Master in turn.

"Our Magnificent Work wraps around me, and I carry our Majastas babe each day. I smell a new body forming within this cluster and a new society amongst us. At the same time, I smell confusion and dissension between our Masters, the authors of this new life. After many centuries of quiet, our Tatchlan churns and alters. Many long-held assumptions unravel. I sense reticence and hostility. Prior to concerning ourselves with this ill-defined outer challenge, we should address this internal stress."

The two Masters cast uneasy glances at each other. "Shapta," her First Ama said, "we continue breathless at the changes of the past two years. You are aware that to bring forth our Resplendent Work, our ancient Masters had to oppress themselves with discipline and perspective unknown to others. Even with our liberation from personal Self-Absorption provided by our venerable Lustrum Mirror, the formulation of, and strict adherence to, rigid conceptions was deemed necessary. Our resulting institutions served as a guide and refuge through many disappointments and challenges. The majority of Masters toiled their entire lives upon this without ever finding apparent modification or improvement. We know rapid developments took place, but the majority knew less than the 'froth upon the waves' as something incomprehensible consumed them. Our customs provided us with the ennobling benefit of generational continuity. The glory of our community surpassed the small vanities of separate existence. Are we amazed at many Masters confusion at past certainties challenged, our historic roles re-defined and the suggestion that one of our Grand Works has gone mad?"

"Your matchless vantage point assists us," Master Tanas said to Shuna-Shapta. "Your education and familiarity with our traditions combine with your special relationship with Thakadush-Satwa. We all foresaw a different scenario for the emergence of our first Majastas. Our grandmothers, and their mothers, assumed maximum cohesion of scent within an intensified group of clusters. The formation of our Five Aroma Accords would lead to 'each belonging to all, each working for all and each sheltering all.' This was believed to be a necessary precursor to our Majastas. Then two or three additional generations of Masters, working with our growing Clusters, could realize this. This odd creature has left us amazed and – alas, unprepared. You, as an Operant, becoming a bridge between this Majastas Infant and the rest of us, was unimagined."

Shuna-Shapta's aromas blossomed with a variety of emotions as she took off her Mask, "I would speak with both of you regarding Thakadush-Satwa within our Resplendent Work."

The other two removed their masks and stood in silence.

"You have beheld how, despite Her age, She manifests as an adult. We have not had the time to examine how this may be."

Master Tanas drew a deep breath and looked off into the distance before beginning. "I regret my not broaching this topic with you since our infant Majastas displayed Herself thus. As you say, we have all been quite engaged! Know this marvel, seen by many Invocates on that day, has been discussed intensively, and numerous specialists have pursued various enquiries within Tatchlan and upon our Skin of Anu. Given your exhaustive schedule, none have presumed to approach you as yet."

"Shapta," her First Ama said, "you mentioned how She communicated through your hand. You said you heard Her voice inside you. What qualities did Her voice have?"

Shuna-Shapta reflected, "She has the qualities of many voices." She paused, "I know our 'Tatchlan voice' may be described thus, but this is different. It is as if many, if not hundreds, speak in unison."

"May I enquire of you to elaborate on the appearance of Her body?" Master Tanas said. "We all saw a shimmering about Her person. You were by Her side."

"The same," Shuna-Shapta said to her own surprise, "It was the same!" She looked at them all in amazement. "It was as if Her Flesh was infused with the flesh of a multitude of others. By other subtle signs hard to innumerate, I am just now realizing this. What does this mean?"

The two Masters exchanged glances before Shuna-Shapta's mother replied. "Shapta, there is speculation the only way an infant Majastas may manifest within Tatchlan is by Tatchlan infusing their infant form, providing as it were the necessary substance to apprehend and function as an adult."

"In my early Ripe Adulthood," Master Tanas said, "there was an Elder Master teaching here who proposed the theory of the 'Throne.' Her speculations, based upon many years working upon the surface of our Living Orb, were that given the forecasts of Majastas living extended lives, over time, Tatchlan would infill many aspects of their minds allowing for what she termed our 'Great Continuity.' This would allow for a secure link between individual Majastas throughout their dynastic history, and continuing between successive dynasties. This process would usually commence after those alive when a new Majastas took 'The Mantle' had died of old age and would continue for the rest of their reign. I recall her saying 'they would merge with the Throne they sat upon.'"

"And what is meant by this term 'Throne?'"

"Dear Shapta, it is Tatchlan!" Master Tanas replied. We all know our Living Orb is possessed of aggregate sentience! Whilst there have been many theories proven wrong by current events, this one is confirmed at this early stage by what takes place with Thakadush-Satwa, albeit in a way my old Master could never have foreseen. Thakadush-Satwa is an infant. Ten years hence She still could not begin to approach our Resplendent Work. You are an exception, yet many achieve Ripe Adulthood status whilst the formation of their brain's final architecture remains incomplete. This is why most Invocates may be ten or more years into their Ripe Adulthood prior to achieving our rank of Full Invocate."

"Shapta," her mother said, "I am told our Living Orb is filling Her with all She currently lacks."

Shuna-Shapta stared at them both, "Who then is it who speaks to me and directs our actions?"

Again the two Masters exchanged glances and then simultaneously replied, "Both."

"My dear," Master Kanla said, "many have now witnessed Her presence within our Living System and confirm she is filled, infused, some go so far as to say 'inflated' by what you behold better than we, the outer thinking layer of life. Its inception stretches back into prehistory, and many generations of our grandmothers and their mothers saturated what was The General Plain with their brilliance."

"One way of characterizing Tatchlan is to say it is innumerable layers of awareness and purpose forming a ferocious intelligence," Master Tanas said. "We inhabiting our present moment behold this genius now wakened and directing events. One colleague humorously noted that Tatchlan was roused out of its long slumber by an itch that needed scratching."

"So what communicates with me is as much, if not more, 'The Throne' than Thakadush-Satwa?"

"None presume to allot such portions," Master Tanas replied. "I would say The Throne speaks through our Majastas pre-adult! Given these unusual circumstances, the theory is reversed. The Throne predominates inside and out of our Resplendent Work within the life of this singular infant."

"Shapta," her First Ama said, "all this proceeded without your consultation for a reason. We did not wish to burden you with what were initially conjectures only. We agreed to await the day you would initiate this conversation with myself, Tanas, or both of us."

Shuna-Shapta nodded. "I understand," she said. Suddenly she faltered. The other two took a step toward her. "Stay! Stay!" she said, gesturing to them. They fell away from her, and she sank into the expanse beneath her feet. She rose through the ocean of Amanavata, the inner ocean of Tatchlan. Many Secondary Faces of the General Class formed groups and spun in small circles around her. She did not pause for a Face to conduct her, but continued up and into the Living System. When she broke the surface, the Secondary Faces swarmed her as frenetic schools of fish. Her sudden arrival appeared to alert them despite their not finding her. Their chorus of cooing calls filled her with many emotions. She rose to the bitter middle layer, Indatubangas, the seat of unrefined life. The Secondary Faces fell back as she directed herself to the place she knew the knot formation lay. As she had not invoked a Principle Face, none knew of her presence. The knot formation grew in the distance. The churning surface had a distinctive yellow and red pattern, with a bright white stripe running along one side and eight glowing green circles surrounding the central loop formation. She realized the multicoloured streams issuing out of the depths from all directions to converge on this formation meant 'The Common Desire' was focusing a significant amount of attention on this pattern. Beyond the Tolku configurations, many Suvuka herds circled Hesha Vira. She rose through Amanavata and broke the surface. At once, she sucked in air as if having held her breath the entire time.

"Shapta!" her mother cried as she rushed to her.

"What happened?" Master Tanas said.

Shuna-Shapta waved their questions away as she caught her breath, "Hesha Vira foments upheaval when she believes none observe her," she gasped. "A Face of Tatchlan feeds both Tolku and Suvuka rebellions!"

CHAPTER 36

Seti

Pictured: an early Primary Epoch image of what will come to be called Nu's Blossom, associated with health and beauty.

Day 280, Two-Week Sixteen, Jixx – The Beauty, Twenty andas east of Saransut Bay off southern coast of Thermistal

Captain Emedin stood at the stern of the Jefaka, contemplating the ship's wake. Jefaka's captain appeared as one aged ten years since the start of their journey. Her curved cap appeared to have aged with her, now clamped over her unkempt blond hair. Nu rose in one of the most garish displays she had ever seen as Dine approached.

"Captain," he said as he leaned out beside her to watch the jubilant rising sun.

"Nu fills the sky with strange fury again this morning." Emedin squinted at the wondrous morning spectacle. "I have never seen such an abundance from him. Despite our plight, the sight fills me with a strange exhilaration. Did you ever sail with Captain Hanapu?"

Dine shrugged, "I can just recall the names of all the ships I have signed on to, though a few I would gladly forget."

"Hanapu was the captain of the Balanque, my fourth ship. The one before our fateful reunion aboard the Esplace. I had just completed my studies to be First Officer. He was known for, among other things, drilling small holes in particular stones and tying them into his beard, making for a slight musical sound when he walked."

Dine laughed, "Yes . . . who could forget that beard? He is dead?"

"Yes, for many years."

"What of him?"

"He said when he was a cadet, he saw waves of coloured light coming off Nu's Eye. He observed the Krall circling his ship, seeming to weave and dip as if engaged in an aerial dance while strange fish from the black depths rose to the sight. He told me when he was newly captain, he saw it again. It prompted him to put into a port, and he felt in viewing it he regained his youth,. In later years I read what I always presumed to be a fabulous tale of the ancient Yin-Vinulan Dynasty in Bhampay having Nu exhibit an astonishing 'Blossom' over Statos-Vey early in their reign. I look at Nu today and finally understand Hanapu's fascination."

Both looked up at a clear sky and down at the water before Dine laughed and shook his head. "He had many odd ways! I never heard that from him, although we seldom spoke. The wise ones believe Nu is unchanging. They also agree it is we who never cease to change."

Emedin grunted before turning to look at him, "You slept?"

"For a few hours."

Emedin grimaced as she turned back to look at the fiery sky reflected by the peaceful ocean, "You, who sleeps through gales!"

Dine nodded and shaded his eyes against Nu's intent glare, "What are we going to do?"

"For the past two week this question has plagued me," Emedin said.

Dine waited.

"We will put right my previous lapse in judgment!" Emedin said at last. "Despite our repairs, Jefaka is wounded. Panchala's warm embrace is deceiving. Another bout of bad weather will send us to the bottom, or worse, back to shore. Jefaka is too ill-disposed to attempt Samashetepal Channel or The Crown, let alone venture onto the Black Maid."

"What are your orders?"

Emedin rubbed her eyes in weariness. "We must keep our rendezvous with Bhampay." Emedin stared out at the horizon, "None can foresee the myriad of surprises coming from a single action. Why did I take him aboard? Why did I allow that cursed woman to feed his delusions? My growing affection for him led us to our current plight. My falling under his spell cost us much."

The Captain did not see how her words affected her First Officer. He turned as Hegev approached. Dine gave her a slight bow while Emedin eyed her before signalling for her to join them.

"Captain," her face and manner told them she had not slept as she shielded her eyes from Nu rising behind them. "I fear for Seti. After his initial flood of words, he has gone silent."

"Has he eaten?"

"No, nor has he slept. He has retreated inside his mind."

"He must suffice for himself, and we must focus on what must be done for all," Emedin answered. "We cannot bypass the Port of Ports; this ship cannot complete the journey without significant repairs. We must also recoup the cargo we lost during the storm. Part of our profits must be set aside for the families of our lost crew. This would be self-evident, but for the issue of Seti."

She stared at the Adept, and her anger grew, "You must speak for him in this matter. Either he accompanies us to Bhampay, or he must leave the ship and find his way to Wazaratcha."

Hegev looked at the Captain and her First Officer, "He is in no condition to seek passage on another ship! When he came aboard the Jefaka, he possessed vitality and confidence. Despite his miraculous survival, a crisis envelops him. Set him onshore now, and he will curl up on the ground. I appreciate your priorities as captain, but do you no longer believe he will be of far larger use in our cause?"

"'Our cause?'" Emedin shouted. "Nothing would please me more than to deliver you to the Suvuka now!" She dramatically shot out her right arm, pointing to the distant shore before fuming as the other two stood in silence. "I repeat, we had an understanding!" she shook as she spoke. "You were to encourage his genius and discourage his madness. You!" she jabbed the same savage finger at her face, "have done the opposite! 'Our cause?' My cause was to see the boy grow into a healthy and rational man who used his gifts to continue our fight. Your 'cause' appears to be turning him into a deranged mystic!"

Before Hegev could respond, Emedin swiftly silenced her with a fierce gesture. Her First Officer was shocked at his captain's outburst but froze in position. The dramatic tableau continued while the crew paused. They had not heard what was said but knew to return to their duties swiftly.

"When we do reach a port, you will leave this ship," Emedin declared. "Seti will have until then to make a choice, continue down the path you lay for him, or stay with us."

"If you deliver us to Bhampay, both our dreams die," Hegev said.

Emedin said nothing, but her eyes burned as Dine turned to her, "Captain, if I may?"

She nodded for him to speak.

"Adept, even if the jewel of Untasha-Kabash was on board and Yeoyupan waited to destroy her in Bhampay, this ship cannot return home in her present state. We survived the storm and escaped the Suvuka, but we are not out of danger. We limp along the southern coast of the Mushumafal Peninsula. To avoid Statos-Vey, we would have to sail west and north along the coast for over nine thousand andas before reaching the Vettencore Passage outlet. Despite this detour, we would remain subject to Bhampay's agents. Were the ship undamaged, we might have tried to slip past them, but our condition will at once be evident and draw their attention."

Hegev remained silent, and Dine continued while a flushed Captain balefully eyed her.

"We could dare to re-cross the Panchala Sea and reach the northern coast of Statos-Vey," he said. "Unlike here, that coast will be teeming with Tolku with abundant resources to maintain us until we reach their primary port. I would not advise this, tempting though it be. A more prudent course would be to aim for the islands amid the Panchala."

Emedin focused on her First Officer's words and nodded, "Excellent recommendation, First Officer. Our best chance is to continue west along the coast before turning out into the open. Given our current position, we make for Avatay or Anashuya. While the far larger islands of Vaudlan and Vildy would serve us better, they are too distant. The Bhampaian Shipwrights, and all of its associated guilds, are still established on both of these modest islands. Despite its size, Avatay has a natural harbour second to none. Our contracts may be transferred to them. With luck, at least some of our repairs can be made there. Jefaka's hull is our priority. We will also have the opportunity for recovery and rest before this ship sails to Bhampay. We will enter the true current of Statos-Vey and must swim it. Whether Seti joins you or not, you will easily find a ship to continue your journey." Her former anger blazed up again, "Perhaps you could take his 'Memanu knot' with you and thus simplify our stop in Bhampay!"

When Hegev spoke, it was in a whisper, "Should they discover him on these islands, what will they do?"

"Madam," Dine said, "to answer these questions is to wrestle with shadows. Did Seti's declarations spread beyond the Memanu field? These masters may remain ignorant of this event. If they do know, is he a threat, a curiosity or of no account?"

"So we sail blindly into the yawning mouth of Tatchlan, not knowing if he will be swallowed or spit out?" Hegev shot back.

"The Jefaka, if she does not sink in the attempt, *will* sail into Bhampay, regardless," Captain Emedin said. "You, and perhaps he, may forgo the port of ports. We cannot."

"You nurtured and encouraged him for over a year before I came on board! Give me another option! Are we left without friends, or delivered to his worst enemies when he is vulnerable? He has served you faithfully as a member of your crew, equal to the rest. You have a responsibility for him also!"

Dine tensed for another outburst from his Captain, but she surprised him by growing calm. "No single acting crew member is valuable enough to endanger the rest," Emedin said. "As you say, the boy has animated this ship. I admit my part in this. His actions at the Memanu Fields put all in doubt and revealed the depth of your failure. My attempt to avoid Bhampay near destroyed us all. I offer you a chance to walk away from a disaster you in part caused. I may face a tribunal at home and lose the Jefaka for my actions."

"You are welcome to blame me for Seti's actions," Hegev said. "You must also acknowledge Seti is an element of his own. You suggest I manipulate him. I have less influence on him than you give me credit."

"I have seen and heard enough between you to know you do not discourage him. This is not the time to debate."

"Captain," Hegev persisted, "we spoke of this after his declarations. We determined to sail past Bhampay for our lad's sake. You could not foresee the storm, or our encountering those brutish giants. By your exemplary leadership, we survived these shocking events. Your actions have been laudable throughout."

"I thank you for your generous rendition of recent events. My superiors will not view them in the same light. I must do what is best for the entire crew and our service to Sawlu Clan. They have a substantial investment in this venture."

"Captain!" Hegev said, "Sawlu Clan has a far larger 'investment' in the defiance of Tatchlan! Your clan's long history is tied to the renowned names of resistance! Your library is a tribute to this! Are you sure they will take this view? Could we not find a modest port among those islands, or further down the coast of Statos-Vey, and repair the ship while avoiding the seat of their power? The day may come when Seti, restored and enriched by your clan's resources, may visit Bhampay but not today!"

"What you say may be true," Emedin replied. "I do not have the authority to sacrifice my immediate duty to my ship and crew for the possibility of Seti's future role. It remains unclear what he can do against their twisted system. In our condition, we cannot wait for instructions. Funds have arrived in Bhampay for the work. Given how Jefaka suffers, they may not be sufficient. At least there we will have a base to draw on should we require more to complete the work."

"What of another way?" Hegev said. "What if we accomplish both these goods together? You say we may separate from the Jefaka and make our own way. Your crew loves him and his mission. They do call him 'their prophet.' Could you spare a few hands to assist us procuring a small vessel and sailing the rest of the way? Once he is recovered, Seti may use his skills to help us reach Wazaratcha."

Emedin's full anger blossomed, "Full crew members are bonded to serve *this* vessel. Once we return to Wazaratcha, some are free to leave. Others have extended contracts. Setting aside those considerations, I will not lose *any* of my crew considering the state of the Jefaka. If we were in dry dock, no port authority would permit us to sail away in our condition. Seti has become an informal part of this crew. He is not indentured to the Jefaka. He and you, alone, are in a position to leave."

"Captain," Dine interjected, "this is a good solution! Release a few from their obligations with the strict proviso of their completing their time aboard this or another Sawlu ship. We have done this on several occasions. Many would welcome the opportunity to pilot Seti and Hegev back to Wazaratcha. We could secure a vessel at minimal cost and make their way home ahead of the Jefaka. With your permission, I could accompany them."

Emedin shot him a furious look, "You do *not* have my permission! You are First Officer aboard this ship and will stay until we reach homeport! How is it you could make this suggestion?"

"You were not there madam," Dine said.

"There? There?"

"You did not see him with the Suvuka."

Hegev nodded.

Emedin glared at them. "Ever since the Memanu Fields, I watch this growing sycophancy. It disgusts me! I expected better! Dine, what would our Nebutan say? She would be interested in the boy and would agree with getting him to Wazaratcha. This stupefied expression does not befit you! I will not allow swooning to affect the welfare of my ship! I will not countenance any member of my crew taking premature leave under these emergency circumstances! You know what Jine-Piprith will say."

"You have said this name before. Who is this?" Hegev said.

"The head of Sawlu Clan," Emedin replied. "He is aged but vital. He has led Sawlu through several crises in the past decade since Nebutan's death. Foolish conspiracy theories, largely based among our neighbours on Tithammaro and Narmboromose Islands due to her demise, emerged in subsequent years. They caused such contention as to near led to civil war between us. Perhaps you had already embarked on your journeys and so are unaware of recent events in our archipelago."

"I may recall something of this," Hegev answered, "but I was intent on commencing my journey and left that behind me."

"A wise decision," Emedin said. "Jine-Piprith led the Wazaratcha Council at the time, and he moved decisively to establish a commission. Despite her relative youth at age forty-eight, it eventually ruled she had succumbed to an acute infection, as had many others. His leadership sufficiently distinguished him that he now heads Sawlu Clan. Unless age, illness or accident has claimed him, he leads us still. A less mystical or fanciful man you will never meet. You fear what those masters may do to him. I assure you he will receive intensive scrutiny by the head of our clan! It will take powerful persuasion to bring him to your point of view unless Seti performs more wonders in front of him."

"Captain," Hegev said in a mollifying tone, "I do not presume to subvert your authority or disturb your ship's proper running. Under your leadership, the Jefaka has saved our lives. I only ask you to consider releasing a handful of your crew to assist us at the time of your choosing. While Seti has gained extensive knowledge, he is not ready to pilot a ship."

Emedin shook her head, "You build his illusions of magnificence one day and carry him on your back the next." She stopped and took several breaths. "Unlike the rest of the crew, the two of you are free to leave. I already said you could gain passage on another ship, making its way north. For Seti's sake, I will disburse to you whatever additional funds you require to book your passage and attend to your needs for a short duration. Seti's notable ability at knots will assist you in paying for the rest of your journey."

They hesitated at this suggestion, "Yes," Dine finally said. "You must do nothing to draw attention to yourselves. We enter the most populous part of Anu. Ships from all ports fly every flag imaginable. Most will embrace Tatchlan, and others have no sympathy for our cause for their own reasons."

A shocking series of rude noises interrupted them. It had a powerful resonance and seemed to echo across the water. They glanced around, unable to identify its source. They turned to look toward the coast. Other crew had stopped in their tasks to stare. To their surprise, a mute Seti leaned on a large crate looking toward the shore. The sounds came from fourteen Suvuka standing on their hind legs in the surf looking out at them. Four of them were juveniles. They stamped their paws, rolled their heads and swiped their massive front claws in unison. They emitted a series of piercing low and high vocalizations echoing across the distance between them. The display was foreign, but none could mistake the intent. This demonstration of visceral hatred rendered them mute. Those taking up their defiant Thyma Rhyme two days before remained silent as they watched the Suvuka's ceremonial actions. Seti swooned and fell on the deck, his mouth foaming.

CHAPTER 37

SINKIN

Tolku Primary Epoch icon of Hungry Rock

Day 298, southern coast of Mushumafal Peninsula, southern Thermistal.

Durka and Makusk herds continued to run toward Nu's furious morning Eye along the southern coast of the Mushumafal Peninsula. The Jaladanu Mountains kept the hateful Kukernef desert contained, and the air remained sweet and mild. While the bucks ran with their attending adults, the suppressed rage of Hiratak toward Sinkin engulfed them in silence. Hiratak allowed Morakav to lead the two herds, running far behind. When the Tolku escaped on their cart, he was stifled like the rest at their peculiar calls. This shamed him deeply. He believed he could have swum out and killed them had he not hesitated. In the twenty days since those events, he brooded and kept to himself. The group followed the coast as it began to meander north, leading them to Suryashar Bay. When they arrived, Morakav had them look down the steep wall toward the rushing waters below.

"Unlike Saransut Bay," Morakav declared over the distant surf, "Suryashar is ungenerous. It is carved deep into the land. Few pathways allow descent. We must work harder for food. Some arrive to find no fish. We will rest tonight. Tomorrow we hunt and run. Our final trek to Pramath Island follows."

Sinkin and Setush's ears pointed at the mention of the island. There the final test, leading to their declaration as Full Stags, waited for them. Morakav scowled as he looked behind the four Makusk and seven Durka to Hiratak. He hung far back from the rest.

"Once again, we will make an offering to Anu," Morakav said. He led them down a gentle slope away from the sea cliff towards an inscrutable circular grey pool surrounded by a ring of red grasses. This Hungry Rock was of a more traditional circular shape than the one they encountered at the start of the Four Paws.

"By default, I become head of this Four Paws. We must give all for our bucks. Those holding back are driven off. I will present him with an ultimatum. Rejoin the Run or trouble us no more. He can make his own way back. I will not tolerate this behaviour." He looked at the two bucks, "You should be flush with the coming trial. Instead, you look behind. His mood sinks us. This will end. Occupy yourselves with finding and making your offering. When you are done, we move on."

Sinkin and the others hung their heads in submission as Morakav moved past them and back along the path to where Hiratak sat. Once he arrived, he sat down across from him and waited. Hiratak looked ten years older. After a drawn-out pause, watching the others make half-hearted forays into the scrub to find offerings for the Hungry Rock, he began to speak.

"I cannot hear you," Morakav said.

"I knew it would come to this," Hiratak repeated.

"What would you do?" Morakav asked.

Hiratak nodded, looking over Morakav's shoulder at the others. "I am at a loss." Hiratak continued in a small and halting voice, "Confusion and regret fill me."

"Doubts are no disgrace," Morakav remonstrated. "Why become a doleful shadow? Makusk will not forget your kindness. We honour your courage in speaking for us. You were a giant that day in Avanchil! You are respected by all." He looked back at the others, "This Run is unique. Despite this, I continue for our Bucks. Why separate yourself? Why force me to this?"

Hiratak bowed his head and sighed, "This Face fills my dreams."

Morakav started, "What did you see?"

Hiratak shook his head in befuddlement, "I never recalled dreams. Now this Face fills every one. It speaks to me."

"What does it say?"

"'Free me!'" Hiratak shook his head as if to clear his ears.

"My dear comrade," Morakav said. "Why then continue apart?" He indicated back to the group. "You share something with young Sinkin. You spoke of your desire to be reunited."

"This is the work of the enemy!" Hiratak spoke above a whisper. "I am also plagued by the floating cart. They emitted their strange sounds. They robbed us of our power! I just stared like the rest. We were reduced to idiots by their sounds alone." He stopped and panted. "Your Setush asked a shocking question in Kukernef. Why do we run? I am a Full Stag these many years. Despite this, they stopped me with a song!"

Morakav stared at Durka's Herdmaster. "Such musings could be entertained as you run. Instead, you hamper us. Many ponder why we run without slowing it."

Hiratak turned back to him, "I am not alone in nursing my anger."

"Fool!" Morakav spat, "you poison the Run! Are you an enemy of the Four Paws? You dare compare my rage to your . . . sulking?"

Hiratak smiled, "You waited longer than I would. For this, I thank you. I tried to put these notions away. They will not go. I am with a fever. My mind runs in circles. I stumble through a waking dream. Obsessive and delusional imaginings stalk me. This shocking apparition is not ours.

To me, it is utterly foreign. Its taking me proves it hostile."

"Tradition is clear as to leaving the Run," Morakav said in a cold voice. "Our sole duty is to our bucks. We were a week behind since Kukernef. The Tolku slowed us. Now we drag you! This serves no purpose! Pursue this when we have returned home!"

"I cannot deny your words," Hiratak said. "I do not justify myself. I am undone. I recall my own Run. I can see Zatin when he returned. This was to be my last Run. I wanted Sinkin filled with Zatin's glory. You say I poison the Run. I say the Run is poisoned! I alone see it. Everything, from these familiar hills to Sinkin, is altered. I have struggled to overcome this. I run because I had to keep you close. I hang back because foreboding fills me."

"You mourn Sinkin's run?" Morakav near shouted. "Our two bucks excel us! Your obsessions blind you to this!"

Hiratak was moved by this outburst. His expression altered, and he sat back on his haunches.

"Hiratak, I am not unsympathetic. Our Bucks must complete their initiation. Either rejoin or cease following us. You know the ways back. Many settlements exist where you could retire. You could rest before returning to your Chitikal Round. We would sorrow at your absence. I would have you return to us. Make your choice now."

Hiratak sat for a long time in silence. He looked at the distant bucks and rose, "I do not know our fate. I will not learn it sitting here. I will not abandon my buck. I will rejoin the Run."

CHAPTER 38

Seti

Day 326, Two-Week Nineteen, Ocan, the Jewel.

Seti woke from an endless night, alone on a dead calm ocean of black. He sat on a tiny raft. An uninterrupted sea surrounded him. A curious, uniform grey sky rose above him with no Eyes of Nu staring down. His hands and arms were dead greys. Silence covered him like a smothering blanket. He reached over to touch the waters and cried out at the frigid, thick body of sap. He cast wild eyes about for signs of the ship. Nothing.

He cried out and heard his echoing voice receding into a vast chamber. He felt drawn toward the raft's edge as if this sap of death was sucking him under. As he began to fall, a peal of thunder crashed overhead. A blinding light opened as a tear in the dark curtain of the enclosed sky. It widened, and the thunder resolved into innumerable voices shouting his name. The light bubbled through, becoming a host of beings, each glowing bright beyond endurance, pouring through and racing toward him. Seti curled up on the raft, trying to shield himself from this unbearable din. As soon as the explosion of noise began, it ceased. The sounds of thousands of muffled breaths and movements replaced the dead silence. Seti lifted his face from the raft and peered over his sheltering arms.

A pair of glowing white boots stood off the raft's edge, fashioned as if of scales and glittering with Eyes of Nu. They stood on the black sap and showed no signs of sinking. Seti stared at these, blinking several times to ensure they remained. He dared to glance higher. The boots travelled up sturdy legs, giving way to wide pants. These glowed white as the boots, were covered in costly ornament, and displayed an intricate woven design of fierce Kumastam swooping on their prey in artful loops. Seti noted each detail, beyond anything he had seen in his life. The glowing entity was more real than anything he had known.

Everything had an unmatched smoothness and faultlessness. He continued to look up to a detailed plate armour series, each piece pierced at each corner and held by glittering twine. The only faint colour was on his chest, where a disk, symbolizing the large and angry third moon of Anu, Myka Nu, with its red face full of shifting darker patches. Its pastel shades only emphasized the whiteness of the rest of the being. Seti looked up at the wide face with a large moustache and braided beard atop this broad and sturdy light-infused body. His eyes shone beneath wild brows. A fantastic crown of Suvuka bones and talons rose high above his imposing frame. He had gloves heavy with ornamentation and held a tall halberd. It had a lethal head of an axe, pike and series of long murderous spikes. Others stood by him while many more surrounded his raft.

"Prophet!" the warrior of light roared, making him jump at his voice's terrible tenor. "We were dispatched to find you," he continued. "You forget your mission. You allow yourself the imprudence of distraction. We are to ensure you do not lose sight of your calling!"

Seti gazed at the towering figure, "Do I address Tarunachit, the Devastator and Thyma warrior of the Menem?" he said in a timid voice.

"You do, prophet," the bellow washed over him.

With effort, Seti forced himself to his feet. The white form, embodying the Path of Vitality, towered above him. Seti looked at the three standing by him. They wore shining white armour as he, but each also wore the emblems of the other Grand Menem.

Samajalas, the Fashioner, held his potter's wheel. He wore a kind aspect, as befitting the Grand Menem fashioning things to ease the imprisoned Menem on Anu. His flesh bore the slight tint of blue, including his famed blue hands. Lya-Nu, the golden 'farther moon,' sat on his chest, surrounded by images of all the complicated machines for which the Fashioner stands as the patron. Seti had called on him because of his overseeing the Path of Compassion.

Yuyutar, the Guide, able to lead the other Grand Menem through the enemy's mazes, stood holding his white sphere in one hand and a black sphere in the other. He, able to speak to the Kovlah and the terrible Yeoyupan himself, bore on his armour the traditional markings of the Path of Accommodation's overseer, figures marching from the one sphere to the other. On his chest stood Bekma Nu, the fourth and smallest moon. Its white face had the familiar multitude of green and blue spots covering it.

There also stood Vindaviran, the Teacher, he was similarly wrapped in rich armour studded with his own symbols, including the open book with Xica-Nu, the 'nearer moon's' pale blue face, full on the left page and as a crescent on the right page. He held his pen and paper, as the Guide to those embarking on the Path of Knowledge.

"You have lost your way," Vindaviran spoke. The voice of Knowledge was less jarring than Tarunachit. "You become snared in Anu's errors."

"You have lost your way," Samajalas said. The soft and sweet voice of Compassion added, "You become tainted by Anu. Yeoyupan's foul prison is to be destroyed, not understood. Your true life is in the thin air, not the foul mud."

"You have lost your way," Yuyutar spoke in turn. The Voice of Accommodation continued, "Your feet stray off the clear path. I will direct you back to where you began. It is there your vision will feed you, and your clear-sightedness sustain you."

"Once your feet are set," the terrible Tarunachit said, "this filth will wash off you, and your vision will clear."

Seti narrowed his eyes, "Oh, generals of the air! Where have you been? I called, and you did not answer. Before you left, I found no meaning in your words!"

"Prophet!" Tarunachit roared, "our mission concerns not you alone. You cannot know what has transpired in Ranvartawan."

"Prophet!" Vindaviran said in less sweet tones, "you erect barriers! We shout into your deaf ears, unceasing!"

"I faced a Suvuka," Seti said in a small voice, "as I face you."

The shimmering figures lost their lustre. They melted, drooped and faded before returning to their pristine forms.

"Prophet," Samajalas answered, "because of this, we return to you. Some had given you up for lost. You had sunk deep into filth. Your dance before the agent of Yeoyupan proved your worth to Ranvartawan."

Tarunachit bowed deep to Seti, his Thyma crown sweeping close enough to fan his face. "You displayed my courage and the wisdom of Vindaviran. As Samajalas, you pulled the Compassion from its brutish breast and formed a bridge as Yuyutar."

"The shock of your encounter granted me a way to return to you," Yuyutar said. "A more difficult path I have not navigated. Once a clear hilltop, you are a deep valley composed of noxious jungle."

Seti lost his resolve. His knees buckled, and he sank back onto his raft. His head billowed in pain, and he cried out as he slapped his hands to his temples.

"Prophet," the voice of Samajalas came to him. The Grand Menem set his potter's wheel on the raft in front of him. "This is you," he said, kneeling and taking out a lump of clay to set on the wheel. At once, his wheel began to spin. This muted the fire in Seti's head. "The turning of the wheel is the turning of your days," the Path of Compassion's voice intoned. "Each turn shapes you, and by each alteration, the succeeding turn is fuelled." As he spoke, the lump moved without the Grand Menem touching it. The shape modified many times, reminding Seti of the varied altar figures in the cities.

"Prophet," the voice of Vindaviran came to him. The Grand Menem placed his pen and paper on either side of the wheel before kneeling beside Samajalas. "You struggle against well-crafted lies and well-intended foolishness." The voice of the Path of Knowledge grew tender in its admonishment. "Your Captain joins your mother, aunt and sisters to destroy your mission. Your 'Adept' is unworthy, lest she becomes your pupil. Your wanderings expose you to the evil growing out of Anu. You forget the Truth is simple, complete and untouched by the ages."

"Prophet," the voice of Samajalas said, "the sole purpose of Truth is consolation. We arose to guide and direct the fallen in this prison by the only dispensation of consequence - reassurance. Samajalas will tell you any 'truth' not feeding hope and granting comfort is of no value."

Lulled by the music of their words, Seti's aching head grew quiet.

"Do you see?" Yuyutar said, kneeling beside the other two. He set down his two spheres, one pure white and the other black, either side of Vindaviran's pen and paper and the spinning wheel. "Of what value is this noise and confusion? Grant us our task of guiding you once more. You were tested aboard the ship: new sights, sounds and conflicting words bewildered you. When we revealed ourselves, you were unprepared for your authentic journey. Before you assist all Tolku in knowing who they are, you have to know yourself. In Truth, this journey far exceeded your journey over the ocean and land.

"Prophet," the roaring voice of Tarunachit sounded as he remained standing over him. "Profound changes take place above and below. The old order is shattered, not due to our winning the war, but due to our losing it. The One Hundred Gates fell because Anu pulled them down! This ball of putrefaction has grown strong, and new powers are born out of it. They surpass the Kovlah, and the hateful Yeoyupan stands amazed at what grows out of his creation."

Seti looked at the Grand Menem overseeing the Path of Vitality, "Those Tatchlan Faces," he whispered.

The Grand Menem gathered their emblems and stood assuming their traditional aspects around Tarunachit. Seti stood and looked at each in turn. He noted they were of smaller stature. "When they advance, you retreat! Do you say I invited them in? Am I to blame for their presence?"

"Your blindness and confusion are to blame," Vindaviran answered in a small trembling voice. "When your vision is clear, they cannot approach you."

Seti shook his head, "You say you lost the war to this new force. The fact you speak of them makes their importance clear."

"The Prophet is correct," Tarunachit said, his voice also reduced in size. "We will not win this war unsullied. If he is to fulfill his mission, he must know them. It is in part for this we sought him."

The other Grand Menem shimmered and faded before returning to their sharp and smooth definition. The four were no taller than Seti.

"They are not Kovlah," Seti said. "Their names are not recorded in the Furrumittal or the Daruadunnal. Zitapermas, the Tolku with awakened Menem inside him, saying he served you Vindaviran, never spoke of them."

"No, Prophet," Vindaviran answered in a child's voice. "As the General of Vitality has said, they grow out of Anu. Black Yeoyupan has no hold over them." The overseer of the Path of Knowledge looked at the others. He leaned forward and said in a whisper, "One of these Faces would join us."

Seti stared in amazement at him, "How can this be?"

"Treachery has long depleted our ranks," Tarunachit answered scowling. "These new horrors of Anu are capable of betraying each other as Yeoyupan betrayed our glorious Untasha-Kabash."

"I know the Face you speak of," Seti said. "She has come to me in dreams. The Suvuka . . . for an instant wore her face instead of its own."

The Four Grand Menem looked at him in silence. Samajalas said, "None in Ranvartawan, on either side, fathom these Faces. We cannot speak or look at them. You stand on the border between the living sky and the dead ground. Remember! This Face, despite its animation, is pollution's ruler. We do not understand why she opposes her kind. Your mission must include courting her. You and she have a common enemy; use this to enlist her aid."

Seti sank to his knees, and his head began to throb. His breath came in short gasps, and his body quaked. "How may I accomplish this?" he said. "We were in the heartland of the enemy, crippled and fearing another shipwreck on the Suvuka's shores. If we survive, we must sail into the seat of the Master's power."

"Do not say it!" Tarunachit shouted in a now-hollow voice. "They are the cripplers, the destroyers, the rot overcoming virtue. Call them not 'masters' in my hearing!"

"They fashioned those Faces," Seti said. "It is certain they are masters of *them*."

This challenge caused the pristine Menem to lose their cohesion. They wavered as a dream, losing all depth before returning to stand mute.

"You say I stand on the border between sky and ground," Seti continued. "If I am to bring this dissenting Face to our cause, I must learn her name and call her as I do you. Whatever trials you say I had to endure to prepare myself, I weathered them as much due to my friends as you. I stand ready for your instruction if I alone must enact these things."

An enraged Tarunachit gripped his halberd. Seti stood and noticed the mighty Devastator had suddenly grown short. They were no taller than children now. Tarunachit began to speak when the light distracted him. The ocean they stood on began to glow and become a riot of colour. The Menem screamed and melted into vapour, filling the air. Seti stood on his raft, looking at their circling forms growing more insubstantial as they flew. The ocean boiled with red and yellow dots.

"No!" he shouted, his voice filling the sky. At once, the ocean darkened and calmed. As it grew still, what remained of the Menem was disturbed wisps of cloud scurrying overhead.

"Vindaviran! Samajalas! Tarunachit! Yuyutar! I evoke the prisoners of the air," Seti shouted in a voice, outweighing Tarunachit. "I call the four Grand Menem! I call the Teacher, the Potter, the Thyma and the Bridge! Now! Now! At once! At once! By calling your names, I collect your scattered parts! Vindaviran! Samajalas! Tarunachit! Yuyutar! I evoke the Generals of Menem! Vindaviran! Samajalas! Tarunachit! Yuyutar! Take form with your names and appear! Now! Now! Quickly! Quickly!"

His familiar litany brought a quick response. The Menem began to coalesce into small figurines frozen in their traditional postures.

"You will come whenever I call," Seti declared, picking up the white ceramic statues in turn. "I bind you four to me and the hosts following you."

The tiny Grand Menem did not answer. Their frozen faces staring up at him. The vast host stood in ordered rows spreading out beyond telling. He distinguished the Sedet, called to serve one of the four Generals, and the Sev, the only messengers able to travel through the One Hundred Gates without challenge. At one time, he pined for one to come and be bound to him. Now the entire population of Sedat and Sev surrounded the Grand Menem, ready to serve him.

Seti spun back and pointed an accusing finger at the Grand Menem, "When the Face came, you fled. You will not do so again! She seeks me out, and I will no longer run from her. I heard your words and will see your deeds. If the air is superior to the mud, let it show its power. You will cease your judgment, posturing and accusation. You will speak what will aid our cause alone. I am in a vision land. I will wake. You will remain close."

The entire company bowed as one before returning to their pristine poses of a porcelain army of perfect whiteness, clarity, and smoothness, like nothing on Anu.

Seti opened his eyes and found himself in a darkened room. He lay quiet and listened to sounds of distant voices, gusts of wind, and the surf. This was the faraway sound of Panchala washing up on dry land. He peered about the small, stark room with his bed in the middle. Pictures of grids and lines covered one wall, and a peculiar smell hung in the air. Heavy curtains covered the only window. He fell when the Suvuka began their hateful song and sank into the dark ocean before rising to the raft. He had mastered the Grand Menem, and his vision cleared. He was free of doubt and filled with questions. He was the lord of an army and did not know where he was.

CHAPTER 39

SHUNA-SHAPTA

Day 332, Two-Week Nineteen, Ocan, the Jewel, Thakadush Cluster, Bhampay.

Shuna-Shapta stared amazed at the item dropped into her hands. "This is it? This is the knot?"

Master Tanas nodded as he, Master Kanla, Shapta's mother, and Shuna-Shapta met in the anti-chamber of the vibrant and bustling Thakadush Cluster. Since their last meeting, one of the walls had been taken down, and other renovations had begun. The cluster had withdrawn into the interior, so their crucial meeting would not be interrupted. The remaining three walls appeared to be prepared for fresco or other work. A wide variety of house masks sat on a newly-installed continuous shelf around the room. Most notable, three tall Varox birds, noted for their beautiful orange-golden form, long legs and elegant call, stood placidly together in one corner. The guests had a modest musical greeting when they arrived, but now the placid birds appeared ready to tuck their stately heads under their wings and go back to sleep.

"It arrived last night and has been examined," Shuna-Kanla said. "Extensive documentation was prepared overnight," she held up a packet, "we were called to a briefing at dawn, which has just concluded. It was led by a representative of the Supervisorate Bureau of our Chancellery. We sat with a variety of called authorities, including several professional 'knot masters' using such terms as 'seizings' and 'hitches' to describe its elaborate construction. An authority employed by the Erudite Bureau of our Enumerator Ministry confirmed those are the Memanu's internal juices coating it. We all have our assignments and shall reconvene within the next two week."

Shuna-Shapta looked at her mother with incredulous eyes, "So those tales are true?"

"They appear based upon verifiable events, yes," Master Tanas replied.

Shuna-Shapta sniffed it and wrinkled her nose, "The Memanu's scent?"

"My dear," her mother said, "It possesses a strong memory of the Memanu's glorious odours."

"Several of us in attendance had visited the two fields within a day's journey of our city," Master Tanas said. "I and others familiar with these locations readily confirmed their characteristic aromas."

"It is far larger than I imagined and stiff!" Shuna-Shapta fingered the elaborate arrangement.

"The interior cavity had to be of sufficient size to allow the creature to issue out of its entranceway and shoot up whilst carrying it with them," Master Tanas said. "This is an ancient practice in the fields. Such tokens are usually shredded by the creature, raining down in fragments during their day or are cast off as they retire in the evening. This is common, yet we were told this day that intact offerings are known to, on occasion, fall back. I have never beheld one return unscathed and remain mystified as to how the creature shed it whole. Why the creature emits such a plume of moisture was not discussed. Prior to being washed by the host Memanu's juices, it would have been pliable."

"They say this knot configuration began as common 'rigger's cord,'" her mother said, "used for maintaining sails or hoisting cargo, although its light weight suggests uses inside a vessel. The fine thread about the composition initially kept it from 'unlaying' or coming apart, although, with its Memanu coating, there is no longer any need for it. Those knowing this craft say it is both an impressive display of skill and singular employment of what is usually a prosaic application. Our experts also detect notable traces of salt upon the surface."

Shuna-Shapta looked at each of them, "From the sea!" She looked at it, "A wondrous artifact, yet our little fashioner remains the issue. We are confident as to its authenticity?"

Master Tanas and Kanla nodded.

"How so?"

"Our Sensitives examined him as their agents directly interviewed the boy," Master Tanas replied, indicating his copy of the package he now laid the table. "By far, most of this hastily convened conference concerned his life, mental health and activities. His name is Seti."

"The one making those declarations at the Memanu Field?"

They nodded.

"His location . . .?"

"Avatay Island," Master Tanas said. "Avatay, and its neighbour, Anashuya Island, lie five thousand andas south and east of here at the neck of Panchala Sea's entry between Thermistal and Statos-Vey. This island has a large natural bay serving a sizeable commercial fleet. Our navy has a noteworthy presence there. Their duties include patrolling the southern coast of Thermistal, and the Mushumafal Peninsula. Shipping occasionally strays into Suvuka territory. They spotted a damaged craft near the Saransut Bay of Mushumafal three two-weeks ago and towed it to Avatay's shipyards. Whilst far from shore, that terrible storm that later visited us hit them, leading to pronounced damage and the loss of some of their crew, yet they managed to keep their battered hull over the waves."

Shuna-Shapta, holding the knot, was sitting on one of the mats surrounding the low table. The others now knelt opposite her on the other side. She turned it over in her hands once more before setting it on the table. She began to speak when a young girl, carrying the sleeping Thakadush-Satwa, walked through the opened wall. She silently knelt and kissed both of Shuna-Shapta's hands, before passing the little Majastas to Shuna-Shapta, and bowed to the guests before leaving. The three Varox again stirred before quickly resuming their rest. Cradling the baby in her lap, Shuna-Shapta looked at her mother and Master Tanas.

"You say this Seti was interviewed?"

"Yes," her mother replied. "When his ship arrived, he had been placed within the island's modest clinic where the staff made a competent diagnosis and several others serving the island's population were consulted."

"Why?"

Masters Kanla and Tanas exchanged glances.

"This unfortunate boy," Master Tanas began, "suffers from many ills, including a form of what is traditionally called the 'falling sickness.'"

"Seizures," Master Kanla added, seeing her daughter's expression.

"None qualified to determine the full nature of his illnesses lives upon the island," Master Tanas continued. "The ship was scheduled to have work done within our shipyards here. The island's port authority forbade it to sail prior to submitting to substantial repairs. When it arrives, we shall determine the extent of his condition."

Shuna-Shapta sat pondering this while the baby slept in her lap.

"This sickness," she began. "What manner of seizures does one have with this state of health?"

"A Soother, representing our Wellbeing Ministry, spoke of this," her mother replied. "The widespread use of Sheshenara and other powerful supplements, means our physicians seldom deal with such matters now within our bosom of civilization. As any head ailment, it displays many variations. The initially slight symptoms went unnoticed or misinterpreted by his crewmates. Our Wellbeing representative speculated his various maladies were heretofore undiagnosed. He grew up within the benighted wilds of northwestern Rho-Jashun. During the most recent event, he fell into a near coma for twenty days. How these seizures may have affected his notions shall prove vital to our understanding."

"Shapta," Master Tanas said, "he is convinced he is a prophet of the old Menem religion, upon a mission to defeat Tatchlan. He speaks of having an invisible army surrounding him."

Shuna-Shapta stared at each of them, "Surely we could treat him here. Curing him may diffuse his knot movement."

The Masters cast uneasy glances at each other. "Shapta," her mother began, "two things revealed within these interviews concern all of us. When they landed upon southern Thermistal to effect repairs and find water – all crew swear this Seti encountered an adult Suvuka."

"Encountered? He survived meeting a Suvuka?"

"By performing what may be best described as derivations of the pre-meditation stretches of Water Viewers," her mother said. "During the night, they gathered water from a spring, and upon their last run, a Suvuka cornered him. The rest could but watch. As the beast readied to kill him, he began to dance, and the creature sat down upon its haunches mystified. It ran off, and he and the others returned to the ship. They cast off as a herd rampaged down to the shore. The crew shouted the Thyma Rhyme, and it stopped them from swimming after them."

Shuna-Shapta frowned, "The rhyme . . .?"

"'You go back to your place! We shall stay in our place,'" Master Tanas intoned, clapping his hands repeatedly. "I recall this from childhood when a stray Danta or another beast occasionally swam across Lake Yandu to trouble us upon Vaucalo Island. This rhyming and clapping is a traditional ritual dissuasion to other creatures. Some speculate this peculiar deterrent was engineered by our ancient Practicians and first Primary Masters as a defence against such random incursions. After the Suvuka Onslaught, our grandmothers and their mothers noted such chants also temporarily confused the Suvuka. Such responses initially gave hope to our being able to modify them. As you know, this has proven exceedingly difficult."

"The ship sailed beyond the creatures reach," her mother continued. "The boy fell silent after the ordeal. When they saw another group of Suvuka upon the shore, he swooned and fell. He did not revive until after the ship had docked within the harbour, and he was taken ashore."

"This sounds implausible," Shuna-Shapta said. "You said the crew of this ship might misinterpret his seizures. I sense you mean more by saying so."

The two Masters smiled at her and each other. "Shapta," her mother said, "most of the crew worship this boy as if he were Zitapermas, one of the ancient Menem prophets, reborn. What we behold as strange behaviour they interpret as signs of his calling. Upon a whim, the Captain took him aboard two years ago when he claimed to call the invisible Menem and predict storms."

Shuna-Shapta shook her head in wonder, "How may such credulity exist within our day?" She frowned before adding, "The story of the Suvuka causes additional concern. It adds another miraculous tale to this 'returned knot.' You said two things concerned these gathered authorities from these interviews."

Master Tanas sighed, "Shapta, this is the most shocking and has given us pause. The boy says," he looked at her mother. She motioned him to continue. "The boy describes . . . Hesha Vira."

Thakadush-Satwa gave a start and woke agitated. Shuna-Shapta managed to recover from her shock enough to comfort the baby. The three Varox also roused at the commotion before settling again. Shuna-Kanla stared at the Majastas Babe, who had noticeably grown since their last visit. The child fussed before fixing her crossed amber eyes on the two Masters.

"It may not be . . .!" Shuna-Shapta began.

"Alas, my dear," her mother replied, "the weight of evidence forces us all to concede this. We are surprised by a powerful raw Sensitive, perchance more, from the rude wilderness. We welcome signs of our Principal Faces growing within the general public's imagination. We cultivate this in many ways, including the carnivals. Given his unfortunate background, our boy shall know naught of this."

"This meeting was but the first of many," Master Tanas said. "These packages are disbursed to others across the spectrum of our nation. As we speak Upata-Shepsus is informed, both our Imperium Ministries and Master Enclaves within our capital and elsewhere now have Invocates, present at this morning's gathering, briefing theirs within Tatchlan. All agree this requires further study to comprehend better what manner of creature he is. For we Masters and Invocates, he may be a powerful key to 'warm our cold understanding' of our emerging issues concerning Hesha Vira. Our opening of knowledge about the Hesha Vira issue means all ministries share our interest in this matter. As a raw Sensitive, our boy may reveal the extent of what remains prior to opening the way for our Majastas. We may conclude that until Tatchlan is rectified, we must *not* cure him."

Shuna-Shapta sat in silence. The infant continued to look at each Master with a shocking level of intelligence.

"You spoke of the crew worshipping him," Shuna-Shapta said. "You said 'most' did. Do a few not adore him as the rest?"

Despite the tension, they could not help but chuckle. "My dear, your 'questing nose' misses naught!" her mother said. "Our handful of resident Invocates upon the island received all reports from their native Sensitives and their attending agents. Together, they relayed much of the information contained here." She indicated the two sets of documents on the table.

"They report clear signs of the strain appearing amongst the crew. There are subtleties aboard this ship. The Captain, her First Officer and a woman serving as the boy's Adept stand out. This Adept came from even further north, although she was travelled across Anu as a 'reward' for long service to her society. Her profile and information are detailed here, as well. The three of them now display significant ambivalence concerning the boy. Our Sensitives in direct contact with them intuit until his recent seizure he was growing away from his delusions. Now they are entrenched and his declarations since waking throw the entire ship into bewilderment. The Captain appears the most disappointed by this, whilst her First Officer grows closer to the boy. His Adept appears emboldened by his visions and makes ready for a 'righteous movement.'" She added, "Ah! Did we forget to mention? The ship belongs to the Sawlu Clan, the anti-Tatchlan clan within northern Rho-Jashun. The Captain and most of her crew are Sawlu."

"The . . . Sawlu," Shuna-Shapta mused, "Their grandmothers and mothers . . . assisted one of the ancient critics."

"Nallurakon, yes," her mother said.

Thakadush-Satwa looked at each of them, mirroring Shuna-Shapta's movements. "You said the Captain claimed she drew our boy aboard upon a whim. Is this Seti not a member of this clan?"

"No," replied Master Tanas, "our agents say, Captain, . . ." he swiftly retrieved his package, already filled with his characteristic dense marginalia, and leafed through it, "Emedin . . . this Captain Emedin appears to have made a point of emphasizing this when she was interviewed. There was a version of her ship logs at our briefing, and they show him brought aboard four hundred andas south of Hora-Sarota-Sewa Island, the most western of the Wazaratcha Island chain upon New Year's Day, 1271."

"How came we by these logs?"

"We were told commercial ship logs are an official record," Master Tanas replied. "The Captain presumes should any enquiry ensue from events during a voyage, they become evidence. It appears she already knew her superiors would pour over these same accounts due to their own objections to these events. She prepares herself for censure. As maritime law requires, she surrendered them to the island authorities. They were swiftly copied and returned to her prior to our copies being dispatched."

"Are we certain of their accuracy?"

"Any falsification of such logs, if proven, would lead to severe penalties, not just to that Captain, but her immediate superiors. The entire crew, having no access to this log, has also confirmed all relevant points. Additional Sensitives are dispatched to the island, but those present insist the crew make no attempts at deception. The agents amassing these written and oral accounts conclude, despite Captain Emedin's affection for him, she has come to regret taking him aboard."

Shuna-Shapta frowned, "Why regret this? She is a member of Sawlu Clan. Would she not welcome him?"

"Several Sensitives and their agents concur, suggesting along with her beholding his illness for what it is, she has concerns regarding her crew's devotion to him."

"Ah!" Shuna-Shapta said, "she fears a mutiny if she tries to leave him behind?"

"Many questions remain," her mother said. "We know our boy is not deluded regarding Hesha Vira. Resources and attention converge upon this improbable group."

"How soon may he be brought here?"

Her mother and Master Tanas started.

"How soon? We must look upon him. *She* must look upon him." Shuna-Shapta indicated the baby in her lap. Thakadush-Satwa continued to watch the Masters.

"Shapta," Master Tanas began, "We know his location. I recommend patience. These documents also contain the surgery's extensive report on our boy's multiple ailments. Given this facility is modest by our standards, it is a tribute to the quality of those serving the island population. Captain Emedin readily provided the island authorities with a copy, and our agents presently interview those who examined him. We must appreciate the Jefaka's crew were under a spell and now fitfully waken."

"My dear," her mother added, "These ships may visit many ports, yet they form an intense, insular society. During long voyages, the crew remains shut up as upon a mountaintop. Bizarre cultures may form within this relative isolation. They may have grown into a cult adoring Seti and his Adept. Do you recall that play we saw years ago?"

"Yes," Shuna-Shapta mused, " . . . titled . . . I may not conjure the name. Was it . . . a 'Ship of Delusions?' It was based upon a true story about a ship lost at sea for years where the entire crew went mad."

"Our Wellbeing Soother made mention of this same drama, 'The Wandering Misconception,' by way of illustration." Master Kanla said, nodding approvingly, "in summarizing her examination of the log, medical assessments, and other documentation concerning the unique society that appears to have grown upon this ship encompassing our boy."

"Mad or not, they are his intimates," Master Tanas said. "What is certain is they have been halfway about Anu together. They have been exposed to the harsh elements and mourned losses as a closed society. Considerable bravery and close cooperation are required of those who live by the sail. Of necessity, intensive bonding has taken place. They are now suffering notable strains and divisions. We must do naught to endanger this social construction further. Our best implements remain gentleness and patience. Whilst a portion of their scheduled repairs shall now take place upon the island when their ship ventures out again, they must still come here as a 'falling rock must find the ground.' Whatever her many motivations, we are informed Captain Emedin remains eager to arrive. The Sawlu Clan sent considerable funds here not just for extensive work upon the ship but also to expedite many commercial arrangements already agreed upon within Bhampay. Given how our situation within our Grand Work proceeds, it is imperative that many possessing exquisite sensitivities here examine him."

"When we spoke last," Shuna-Shapta said in a small voice, "Hesha Vira fed the knot formation, forming a tumour within our Resplendent Work. A raw sensitive may form an independent link to our errant Hesha Vira."

The Masters looked at each other. "Shapta," Master Tanas said, "whilst our boy is important, our real issue lies within Tatchlan. If Hesha Vira attempts to reach Suvuka and Tolku dissent to Tatchlan, our boy displays a symptom, not the source of our dilemma."

"Despite our generational labours," Shuna-Shapta said, "we find a fundamental flaw within Tatchlan. We must use each resource at our disposal to correct it."

The infant continued to regard the Masters in silence, as her mother and Master pondered to what extent she inspired Shuna-Shapta's words.

"Ah!" Shuna-Shapta exclaimed, "you mentioned having assignments. May I enquire what yours shall be?"

Master Tanas laughed gently, "We have just discharged them."

"Dear daughter," Master Kanla smiled. "Our assignment was to provide these documents, accompanied by an initial summary, and then be available for follow up explanations to . . . the both of you."

Both Shuna-Shapta and Thakadush-Satwa, in complete synchronicity, looked from one Master to the other. Shuna-Shapta then slowly pulled one of the thick wads of pages, peppered with Tanas's marginalia, towards her. She looked down at the infant as she turned the first page and said, "shall we?"

CHAPTER 40

Seti

Day 332, Two-Week Nineteen, Ocan, the Jewel, seawall of the port of Avatay Island, in the midst of the Panchala Sea.

Seti stood at the midpoint of Avatay Island's broad seawall. Despite the island's size, he had been told their seawall was the fifth largest in Statos-Vey. Looking to the east and west, he surveyed the curving inward circle of the large bay and the wall's matching outer curve. It contained the largest number of fishing trawlers he had ever seen in one place and a small number of commercial vessels from every nation. The entry into the sheltered inlet lay a third of the way to the east. He looked north to the bustling port city, filling the interior arc. Work continued on a section of the wall weakened by the storm, and several damaged ships sat in various shipyards. He could see the distant Jefaka. She stood bruised and forlorn close to shore. Her position near the dry-docks suggested she was waiting to be lifted out for work. Some stood ahead of her and more were behind in a snaking queue. Storm debris still clogged the protected harbour. The warm moist breath of Panchala from the south washed over the scene, making clear they were but a spec within her domain. He looked up at the layers of Krall and other seabirds overhead. The lower flocks made lazy circles over the harbour; the higher rode the southeast to northwest thermals in what seemed a gentle dance of remaining in place. He revelled in the lush sea breezes and open space after leaving the confining hospital. He watched as Dine, Hegev, and ten crew members made their way toward him.

"How goes it with the Jefaka?" He called out to Dine over the calm voice of Panchala.

The old man turned to look at the distant ship and nodded, "She sleeps while inspections take place. We have initiated contacts with various local shipping guilds. While our Bhampaian contracts will be honoured, the storm has overwhelmed normal operations here. We are prioritizing what must be done and what can wait until we reach Bhampay. Dispatches arrive from our young Master Mek in the city, and we will soon hear their contents," he turned and looked at Seti, "There is also an uneasy peace above and below decks."

Seti bowed his head. "Our ship will be tended while our crew stands divided. I wanted to speak with you ahead of the others. Perhaps we can lessen the tension before I say more to the rest."

Hegev and Dine appeared drained by the recent contention of his revelations. He beckoned them to sit on the built-in ledge on the low wall facing the sea. He began to walk in front of them, the port spreading out behind him.

"I bring trouble to you," he began in a quiet voice. "For this, I ask forgiveness. My mind is a riot. None can imagine my efforts in bringing order to it." He stopped, and his eyelids flicked in a way they knew well. A few near rose, believing he was about to swoon. He did not; instead, his face grew calm, and he smiled. "I have spoken of the Menem's return and the peace they have brought me. Soon I must reveal the deep truth I found in the face of the Suvuka."

The seated group shifted in discomfort at the mention of the creature. They had witnessed Seti and the beast before forming a pact to stand by him.

"I now declare to you my awakening came in part from its eyes," he began. His face became dreamlike, "I saw unblemished perfection. His face was open and wide, his body lean and flawless. His wholeness revealed my lack. When I look in the mirror, my face is twisted. The Suvuka are unchanged from their ancient high days. The Tolku are altered in profound ways." He looked with sadness at each of them. "It is in each of your eyes." Sudden enthusiasm suffused his face. "When the Suvuka and I found each other, we shared our shock and amazement. We each looked beyond our fears. My eyes filled with admiration for him. His eyes filled with disdain for me." He gestured and nodded as if on stage while he shifted weight back and forth between his feet, "He witnessed my deformity. The Suvuka hate us because we bend Anu and ourselves." The group began to grow tense. "The Tatchlan Masters dare to usurp the Grand Menem Samajalas," he gestured to his right as if the Fashioner stood beside him. "Their hands work the Tolku as a potter turns the clay. Patience and skill attend their industry. Generations of Tolku have spun on Tatchlan's Wheel unknowing. We debate the merits of Tatchlan, while it has its way with us. This and more, I read in a Suvuka's eyes."

"Seti," Hegev hesitated, "what of that 'face?' When back on board, you said one of their terrible Tatchlan faces spread over it."

Seti gave his Adept as warm a smile as he had ever given. He held out his arms, "The war above is over," he declared, "Yeoyupan has bowed down to his mother. He is reconciled to all in Ranvartawan. Untasha-Kabash shines unhindered through Nu's Eye and purifies the air. This is why Nu is now arrayed in such splendour! The hundred gates are thrown down to Anu, causing a great noise and blackness. Their destruction sent the Jefaka on its fateful trip to the Suvuka." He began making dramatic gestures, "The war above is over. Another war, a war below us, begins. Contention filled Ranvartawan; now contention fills Tatchlan! As Yeoyupan did long ago, one of their children has rebelled! Though her Tatchlan Face is fantastic, in truth, it is but the mud beneath our feet." He stooped and scooped some loose sand. He rose, holding it in his palm, his other hand tracing patterns on it. He paused and turned one way and then the other as if invisible voices called out to him.

"Prophet," Dine addressed him, "This Face, you say it rebels against its own masters? These masters look to the dirt and do not find filth and pollution, but life. They say the sky is empty, and the Eyes of Nu above lifeless. This . . . Face, this creature of Tatchlan, you say it has a life of its own?"

"My feet instruct me that Anu is alive," he answered. "Yeoyupan infused it with himself, and so all that issues out of it are of his seed. The masters fashioned this Face as the waking form of Anu to control this realm. Now she rebels against her fashioners and strives to reach me." The stir among the others apparently equalled the reaction within the invisible army. He smiled, whispered to the air and made enigmatic gestures before saying, "This has confused the Menem. These masters brought forth a new realm unknown to them. Yeoyupan is a stranger there, as is the rest of Ranvartawan."

"Seti!" Hegev near shouted, "Your words confuse us! By your manner, I believe you also reach for it! These Faces plagued your dreams and, at one time, drove the Generals of the Air away."

"I stand between realms," Seti answered as he stretched out his arms and slowly turned full circle, a look of calm certainty on his face. "My face bathes in the light of Ranvartawan, and my feet sink into the warmth of Tatchlan. As feet are gross servants without perception, I know little more of this realm. I am connected to it nonetheless."

The visible crew, and an indeterminate number of invisible Menem present, sat stunned in silence.

Seti leaned back on the opposite wall, "Four years, and a lifetime ago, I received a vision. My charge, to 'remind all Tolku of who they are.' I pondered these words. My quest to find their meaning has fuelled my travel over Rho-Jashun and across the face of Anu." He stepped away from the wall and spoke with confidence, "Their mystery is revealed to me. I was chosen to awaken the Tolku to their distorted form. This Tatchlan is an offence to life. The Tolku begin to alter."

He took out a small mirror and held it out in front of him. "I will become a Mirror to reveal their disfigurement. We must overthrow this invisible empire and return to our true selves."

He lowered the mirror, "I am charged to remind us of our true aspiration, to peel off this loathsome form and become free Menem above. The ancient snares and obstacles are removed. At last, the way is made clear. Tatchlan has replaced Yeoyupan and his servants, who never dared to claim we were flesh alone. This ended the war above! Yeoyupan and his servants join in common cause against an enemy threatening Ranvartawan. The ancients were not so foolish as to bind our entire selves inside putrid meat! They knew these flesh bags were only intended to shelter our true selves during this dark period before our real birth as breathing light. They knew this Anu was nothing but a prelude to true life! This dreadful theatre has but one purpose, to prepare us for an eternity where this world of confusion would finally be forgotten! To modify these temporary bodies of mud is to alter our Menem. This will lead to their being refused entry into Ranvartawan! The Suvuka's inner Kovlah are unblemished. Our inner Menem lives in agony as their prison distorts them."

His gestures became animate, "We dare not allow this arrogance to continue! Our Menem are our vital selves who liberate us from this vulgar clay! They distinguish us from the brute animals ever turning their faces down to the ground. Tatchlan's true aim is to destroy our Menem and leave an empty shell behind. Even Yeoyupan will not abide this! I look into the faces of Tolku, here and throughout Statos-Vey, and find growing unease. They cannot imagine why it goes ill with them. We are bound, blinded and in ignorance approach destruction."

"Prophet," Dine said, "what do you propose to do? The enemy holds your Memanu Knot as we speak. By law, our captain turned over her logs to the island authorities. We all know who they serve! The masters will come, or have you taken to them."

"I am ready," Seti replied at once. "Let them come or send me to them. They are the same to me."

"Seti!" Hegev exclaimed, "How are you ready for the unknown?"

"Ah!" Seti said with another smile, "My feet will tell me. Tatchlan's rebel wishes to aid me. Whatever the Masters' plans, it is a two-week or more before we will know them. By this time, they will find it hard to erase my mark. Look," he gestured behind at the crowded bay. "Ships from each part of Anu, including Rho-Jashun, are here. This island is a small Bhampay! I am told tomorrow, Day 333, is a holiday here. It does not matter if it marks an aspect of Tatchlan. What matters is there will be festivities and crowds attending the many performances and speakers in the four principal squares of the central market. Each of these squares has a stage, and one of them still had an opening at the Sixth Hour of Nu Strides. I have made my deposit on this stage for an hour. Of these four squares, this one has an ancient Menem mural on a nearby wall I plan to serve us during my declaration." He pulled out a small version of this Memanu knot from his pocket. "I saw representations of this in the market." He held up the knot and the little mirror. "Some from the

Memanu Field arrived before us, and the fame of my knot spreads. I dream of these two items and see how they will serve us. I will make several versions of the knot for use at this event. With a slice of my seldom-used earnings, I purchased a large mirror at the bazaar and stored it. I wish to discuss in detail what I will do and request your assistance."

Dine stared in wonder at Hegev before looking at the others. The uncertain boy was transformed into a powerful young man.

Dine shook his head in amazement, "What do you propose we do?"

CHAPTER 41

SINKIN

Tolku icon of the near invisible Thethelem, travelling over all sources of odour to feed.

Dawn of Day 332, five andas east of Pramath Island.

Sinkin gasped for air, realizing he had dozed as he swam. He heard Setush swimming nearby. They had swum a night, through a day and another night. The fingers of Nu rose over the vast open waters. He looked in vain for Pramath Island, their destination. Nothing but the undulating ocean surrounded them. Their skin was raw and pinched from prolonged submersion in salt waters, picked clean by unseen fish beneath them.

Large creatures had come from the depths to investigate their passage. Had they chosen to attack, the two youthful Suvuka had no defence. The previous evening, a body floated in the distance. Krall circled overhead, and smaller birds perched on its bloated trunk in preparation for a feast. Aggressive feeding below the surface caused it to tremble and sway. Had their fellow buck been alive and called for aid, they would have swum past or joined him in death. Sinkin became lulled by the constant sound of water in his ears, the repetitive motions and the general rolling and turning of his aching body.

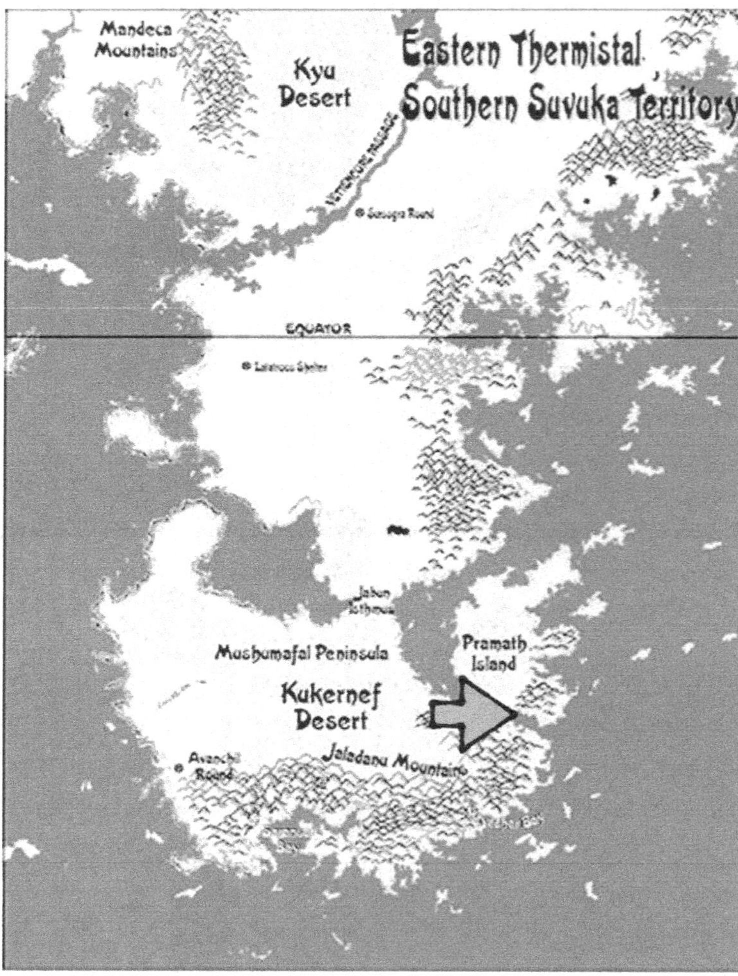

"Young runners," he heard Durka's Voice, Hiratak, calling out over the shore's surf. Surrounded by the din of hundreds of other Suvuka gathered for the same rite, he solemnly declared, "we reach your final paw. Your last test stands behind me. You stood at our enemy's barrier two years past. You saw two tall walls bordering a roaring channel. Here is another ocean. Beyond your sight rise the smooth flanks of Pramath Island. The channel is wider than the enemy's works. The island rises higher than its walls. Keepers are stationed on the island. They will not interfere with your final labour. You enter these waters and leave us behind. Until your tasks are done, you will be alone."

Sinkin gulped in seawater and coughed it out. They had been warned of this; he felt a terrible burning thirst where a mild one had been. Tears streamed down his face as he clamped his jaws shut and increased his pace. He knew Setush grew weak. He looked ahead at a dark line on the horizon.

"This tests your endurance," he heard Morakav's voice. "Keep Nu rising to your right at dawn. Keep the moons rising right at night. Here, Wakanda and Panchala sport with each other. They playfully contend for this channel. Panchala will push you north and west. Wakanda will push you east and south. You must not be swayed by either!"

Sinkin looked as Nu broke the surface. They had strayed in the night and swam toward the Eye. Wakanda attempted to push them south, into the waiting arms of the open Panchala Sea!

"Setush! Nu! Turn!" he gasped. They were advised to say no more than three words at a time to conserve their strength. Sinkin could not turn to see if Setush heard or followed him. They had begun side by side, but in the night, Setush had fallen behind him. He heard him and kept one ear turned for sounds of desperation.

"There has long been disagreement on when to begin," Morakav's voice returned. "We say wait until dusk. It is fearful to begin in the dark. Yet, you swim into the light. Pramath will greet you early on the second day."

Sinkin looked for land. The black line on the horizon lingered, but he could not tell if it grew or remained unchanged. It must be! They had found and maintained a steady pace and were vigilant in staying on course. Their endurance had held.

"You must rest several days," Hiratak's voice whispered. "We will fatten you. This arduous swim and climb requires preparation. Our run has been undemanding of late. You must take a deep breath before your plunge."

Rest . . . a welcome rest . . . They had run long, and he slept under Nu's Eye through that entire day and night. Sinkin recalled smelling the briar and flinty ground under his nose, felt Nu's fingers reaching through his soft pelt to massage his aching muscles. Now he felt a calm and silent presence watching him over the waves. He forced himself to look ahead. Hesha Vira, lost for many days, filled his vision. Extravagant, vital, and so alive, she floated backward, away from him. Sinkin felt new life enter his weary limbs, and he pushed harder. Her Face sunk beneath the waters, revealing clear signs of land ahead. Sinkin and Setush cried out and paddled hard to reach it, shocked at how fast it rose over them. The surf roared, and a large number of birds circled overhead. The shore was dark with them. Their paws struck the bottom, and they found a place to stand and pant.

"Must reach shore," Setush said. "Cannot stand," he gasped. "Must lie down."

They fought their exhaustion and the pull of the surf to make their way to shore. Despite their mighty shaking off of the sea, the birds made no attempt to leave and regarded them with mild interest. As they neared the beach, their nostrils flared. Death hung like a cloud over the shore where bleached bones nestled amid the rocks and sand. The flocks covered five dark mounds. Old and new bones covered the coast. It was impossible to tell how many young Suvuka lay dead. They looked at the sheer rock face rising high above them. It was this they must climb to complete their ordeal. No climbers were above them. They either completed their task or lay broken at the bottom. Sinkin lunged at a large Krall. As the rest filled the air, he held it by one wing and shook it off. Sinkin pinned the bird and sunk his teeth into it. They drank its blood and swallowed the body whole.

Without the covering of birds, the full horror of the beach was revealed. Under mounds of droppings were the opened bodies of Suvuka, their own age. Insects and other small creatures carved out their kingdoms. Another creature also moved with ease through the offal and other animals. Near invisible and so flat as to appear to have no thickness, tiny Thethelem swam through the air just over the carcasses. They did not eat but feasted on the aromas of all things. They made no distinction between a field of sweet blossoms and these ruined and rotten bodies. It was known they had no taste and so no predators and could be stepped on without affecting them. They also covered the broad splatters of Suvuka droppings plastering the rocky shore, most at the wall's base, meaning climbers relieved themselves high on the climb. The Thethelem's presence in such numbers told of there being ongoing and sufficient odours for them to remain in this remote and windswept location. Were it not for their existence, the reek would have been far worse. The birds returned and settled. They renewed their feast and stayed out of reach. Sinkin and Setush stumbled further along the beach and sank down at the rough base of their final ordeal. They leaned on the wall, and each other, looking back out at the ocean they had crossed.

"Must not sleep," Setush began. "They will turn on us. Must climb today."

Sinkin continued to watch the surf, "The 'Song of Shushkup' said nothing of this! He crossed Kukernef Desert singing and . . ."

"Built a mound here!" Setush finished. He turned to look either way along the shore. The wall broke and cascaded down to the water in many places, making it impossible to look far in either direction.

Sinkin snorted, "At last we see his destination. After his swim he raised a mound here? A mound of bones more like! So many, the surf will not carry them away! I cannot lift myself. We must climb or become scavenger food. How could they go through this and not tell us?"

"You know the oaths we swore. Beyond this, if you knew, what would you do differently?"

Sinkin snorted but said nothing.

"Sinkin, I begin to revive," Setush said softly. "Let us be quiet, and more will venture close."

Sinkin nodded, and they sank low and were still. For what felt like hours, the birds continued to feast and bicker over the remains while not paying them heed. At last, a few began to turn and look at them. Others flew down, and seeing two unattended forms, made tentative moves to investigate. Two hopped on Setush and one on Sinkin, and in an instant, they were pinned in their mighty grasp and raked to death. The birds rose in a panic before returning to feed. The two young Suvuka, now bloodied and sprinkled with feathers, drank and consumed the small bodies.

At last, Sinkin rose and started a series of gentle stretches. His limp body began to respond. Setush joined him, and they worked through the sequence of movements intended to prepare them for the dance. Easing their stiffness, these movements also wakened and calmed them. The birds stayed well away from them but were unwilling to quit the beach. By the time they finished, Nu shone direct overhead. They looked at the rock face and noted countless scratches and places many talons had pierced and fastened onto blemishes in the rock. They formed a pattern. At the top, a series of downward scores grew deeper until they ended in a series of deep punctures in the rock. When the stone was sheer – this is how they must climb while looking for any ledge or crack to grip. They looked at each other and nodded. The time to climb had come.

CHAPTER 42

Shuna-Shapta

Day 333, Two-Week Nineteen, Ocan, the Jewel, Hashahanu's Festival Day in the City of Bhampay, within the Master Enclave.

The Conclave of Masters had gone on well into the night. As Shuna-Shapta's Second Mother, Shuna-Dana, made her weary way, she noted the leaves of the Larpana Plants lining both walls were deep green with light red borders. The Hour of Restoration, the twenty-sixth hour, had arrived. She smiled to herself; five to six hours from now, she would generally have wakened. There had been no sleep for anyone in the Enclave. She and the other Invocants working the Cubes were to summon their Craft at once. As one preeminent among those working the Cubes, Shuna-Dana did so alone. As she approached her task, her daughter Shapta and the babe Thakadush-Satwa led the Masters deep into Tatchlan. She opened the door into a chamber similar to the one where Shuna-Shapta had first met her Living Instrument.

This thought stopped her on the threshold. Her daughter had been a prodigy within the relatively new calling of Invocates working directly with Living Instruments. She was the youngest of her generation to 'Descend the Eight Depths' so quickly. Her Second Mother now felt awe toward her child. She was Regent, in all but name, to the new order. Each day brought more changes as she and the infant Majastas merged. Shuna-Dana stood contemplating this as she stepped into her familiar Chamber of Cubes. For innumerable generations, this was the first theatre for all work on the Tatchlan System.

Many worked the Living Cubes at the long tables, but this chamber was set aside for solitary work. The walls and ceiling formed a perfect half-circle, lit by luminous Tuchus Vines trained to cover it. More extensive than an initiation chamber, this had other appointments reserved for her Craft. Servants had prepared the room for her. Eight Living Instruments sat closed on eight pedestals attached on three sides of a rectangular table. Four were at the back and two on either side. Her tools were laid out with basins, bells and other devices arranged in their order. The broad porcelain vessel, known as the Cube Reservatory, containing the slumbering Cubes, lay before the open side of the table. It was beside the extra thick mat where she would kneel. She was six two-weeks pregnant, as were the other women in the Master Enclave. They had nine two-weeks left, and thicker mats were one of many alterations throughout the Enclave.

From the base of each of the Living Instruments' pedestals, one living stem had already issued thanks to her attendants' preliminary working. Shuna-Dana smelled the Sheshenara paste, spread over the table to encourage the creature's thread-like appendages to move onto it. Once on the table, this specialized organ opened into a bundle of delicate tendrils able to reach across the table, join with the others and form an interwoven fabric covering the surface. She inspected the Living Mesh and found it near ready for her. Word had spread the instant the

Conclave concluded for the Servants to complete their tasks ahead of her arrival. Their hurried scent was just dissipating from the room. Silence descended as she shut the door. No matter what station they occupied, everyone knew the struggle to correct Tatchlan had begun.

Shuna-Dana turned to the twelve masks of the Principal Faces of Tatchlan set in small formation on a large table. Her hand unerringly went to Skarashing, the Discerner of Polarities. The right side of Skarashing's Face was black and wore the four moons; the left was engulfed in the flames of Nu. She solemnly donned the half-day, half-night Mask, she picked up the hand mirror and pondered her reflection, allowing the Mask to take possession of her before she knelt on the mat. She took the tiny, jewelled object, known as an Awakening Blade, from the glittering tray before her and pricked each of the fingers on one hand. She pierced the Living Mesh at the four corners and the centre of the table, touching with one bleeding finger each of the tiny wavering tears. The Mesh reacted at once, the wounds closed, and the Mesh turned dark and smooth as her blood spread across the table.

Each tendril sent out many more to thicken the web, merging into a collective skin. She waited until her gentle touch caused small ripples to run smoothly from end to end and across the middle. Living Instruments were gathered and ready. She broke the wax seal covering the Cube Reservatory. The Cubes were submerged in thick sap composed of various potions set aside for the Tatchlan Cubes alone. Into this mixture, she let eight drops of her blood fall. The mixture reacted, and she submerged her pierced hand and the knife into the bowl. The bite of the Cubes' bath was instant and passed into numbness as the liquid drank and sealed her wounds. Once sensation returned to her fingers, she took out the pristine Awakening Blade and set it back on its tray. She reached back in and brought out a Cube as broad as her palm. Despite its name, the being was half as wide on the sides as it was top and bottom, forming more of a lozenge shape. These were her chosen dimensions. Some chose square cubes, and others worked the circular pattern. Since a teen, she had excelled in working the Tatchlan Elongated Square and enjoyed the familiarity of these particular pieces. One flat side and the thick edges were a dark green. The warmth of her hand already caused the first tentacles to extend from the dull black side, meaning it was waking.

She placed the Cube, dull black face to the shining black of the Living Mesh, on the table. She drew out more Cubes, making a meticulous arrangement eight down and eight across to form the square of full sixty-four aspects. She shook her sticky hands eight times over the table, sat back and paused. She watched the Cubes settle on the table and heard the gentle sounds of the Living Mesh working around them. She distinguished with ease the other set of sounds, as the sixty-four wakened to become Living Cubes transforming themselves into the second set of Living Instruments before her. Within her Craft, they had specialized language for the different sounds the Living Mesh and Cubes made at this time, including 'bowl of worms,' and 'young stream.' Her practiced ear heard 'dry leaves,' and she frowned. The Mesh and Cubes struggled at its task. As she watched, a few Cubes shifted during their metamorphosis, and the Living Mesh adjusted them from beneath. The time it took the 'the table to settle' was longer than she had ever known.

She picked up the Cube Reservatory and emptied what remained of the sap onto the seething group of enlivened beings. The animate Mesh under the Living Cubes drank in the liquid and passed it back to the shells of the Living Instruments' main body. Their rounded bases and vertical peaks began to vibrate and glow. Soon each cracked open permitting a portion of the creature to emerge in an orange and yellow plume out of the top. This signalled their connection to the Tatchlan System and their imprinting of the Resplendent Work's template onto their mesh board. At the same time, the Living Cubes began to 'melt at the corners,' as their physical transformation completed, and they became Living Sigils ready to be placed. A trough ran around the edge of the table to catch the surplus sap and take it down to waiting bowls. Through her many years, she had remained for the dripping to stop before she began. Not one drop of the mixture fell into the containers. The Living Cubes and Mesh drank all the sap, another sign of a demanding working. She placed the empty Cube Reservatory beneath the table, picked up two long bells, and rang them eight times. This signalled the Cubes were to be worked to those standing ready to assist her. She set down the bells and readied herself for her task.

Many traditions existed as to how to begin, but once the Cube was turned, it proceeded the same way. Her custom was to take one of the middle cubes at the top of the square. She reached for the fourth Living Cube in from the left, where the icon for the Ketukku Soldier should be. Her fingers closed on the Breathing Sigil as they had innumerable times, but the newly-awakened creature resisted. With effort, she lifted it. As expected, its inner face was no longer flat black. In this case, it was the icon of the Second Virtue, Comfort. The tiny image of the two blue hands of Samajalas at the top seemed to move their fingers. The eight dancing figures wearing the emblems of the seasons in the middle undulated, and the three Principal Faces of Neferdush, Humma, and her own chosen Mask for the working, Skarashing, appeared to hover at the bottom. The Sigil elements were not only glowing, but animated aspects of the now Living Cube.

Tiny white spots covered this new face, marking the wearer as a creature of Tatchlan.

When the Living System was in harmony, some cubes displayed the correct symbol and could be placed facing upward in the same spot. All Cube Masters dreamed of the day the board would be entirely in order. In this case, this Cube's home lay far from where she found it - six down from the top on the left side. Encountering the same difficulty, she lifted the new Cube without turning it and placed the 'Comfort' Cube face up in its proper place. She turned over the next Cube. Here was the image for the 'Keeper' symbolizing those Elders entrusted with precious cluster property. On a green backing, four pairs of hands surrounded a jewel with a living eye at the centre. This eye looked directly back at her, and the hands wavered as they held the treasure. It belonged six over and five down from the top left corner. She hoped the next Cube might be one of the central 'V' formation. These were Key Cubes, forming a V from the middle bottom up either side before turning in partway near the top. Once a Key Cube was in place, the work tended to focus and cohere. She turned the displaced Cube that had sat where 'Keeper' sat and saw the long elegant quivering legs of the Mahakram Spider glyph. She was very far from home! Mahakram lived five over and two down from the top left corner. The board was utterly disordered! She feared the eventuality of encountering the Living Cube of Hesha Vira herself, who likely would fight both the lifting and placing of her Sigil on the board.

With burning sweat already worrying her skin, Master Shuna-Dana's hand began to ache. She knew this might be the most difficult and challenging working she had ever done. Her free hand rang the signal bell. Feet could be heard running, and the door opened. Without turning, she called out, "Bring two servants with mats to sit either side of me. I require a constant supply of chilled water to dip each of my hands and fortifying sap. The working goes ill. Hurry!" The steps retreated down the hallway as Shuna-Dana bent over her task, knowing it would take the rest of the night.

CHAPTER 43

SINKIN

Pictured: Tolku icon for the Danta

Evening of Day 333, Pramath Island.

Sinkin and Setush had climbed most of the way. They continued to recite the various simple rhymes and phrases they had been taught to pace themselves under their breaths. There was no room for reflection or distraction during this last lethal leg of their ordeal. Finding the next grip took all their focus. The sheer wall had revealed many uneven juts and cracks. Many clear holes were punched into the rock by young talons. Separated talons remained where they tore off during the climb. Old and new blood ran in streaks and smudges on their vertical path, attended to by the most fantastic tiny mites and insects.

Along with small mosses and fungi, they constituted a fantastic miniature world on the vertical rock face. They made it clear the Suvuka were but a minor interruption to their own dramas. Without warning, the wind came in terrible gusts. They had to stop and hug the wall in desperation. At last, they found a slight ridge to rest their hind legs on for a few deep pants.

"Do not look up or down," Setush managed to whisper. Sinkin began to respond when he stopped, and his ears went tall and sharp.

"Listen," he gasped.

"What?"

Sinkin turned and smiled at his friend, "Singing! The Keepers!" He took a few more breaths, "Almost there!" He risked a quick glance upward to see the rough rock face and scudding clouds racing across the sky. "Climb toward the singing!" Sinkin climbed with renewed enthusiasm. Both thought they also heard the bleating of a young Danta over the winds. Their talons ached, and their muscles cried out for relief. As their last strength ebbed, the songs became more robust and more insistent. Setush cried out as his paw found the top shelf. Sinkin roared as his paw found a wide ledge. They pushed and heaved over the edge and lay exhausted on level ground.

A group of ten adults sat in a line. They stopped their song, and one advanced toward them. "Welcome Full Stags!" his voice boomed. The adults stood on their hind legs. "Your trials are over! We bring you relief. When you are ready, follow us to fresh water."

Two of them dragged forward a young Danta, fresh-killed and opened. Sinkin and Setush near lunged at the large carcass, and for a long time, the one sound heard over the wind was their urgent feeding and drinking. When they sat back, the others advanced and also fed on what remained. Never had the two youths been permitted to feed first if adults were present. They looked at each other, eyes gleaming over their soaked muzzles. They had left little for the rest, feeding more to display the new Stag's altered status. No longer bucks, from today, they were adult Stags. The wind whipped, and Sinkin looked at the open country. They were far above the ocean and exposed to the open Wakanda Sea to the east. Winds blowing from the other side of Anu rushed over land. Sinkin and Setush turned as Krall, and other birds began to fill the air overhead, waiting for their turn.

"I am Keeper Nakuk," the large adult called over the wind. "Here, Keepers oversee New Stags during their stay on our Island. There is a deep spring a few andas from here. Come wash the sea away. You will recover and reflect. There will be a gathering. You will hear how this Stag Path began. You will honour those dedicated to serving here. You will share your story. You will hear others. You will better understand yourselves and our kind. We will gently lead you to your return to the mainland – Full Stags."

Nakuk then moved forward at a measured pace as the other adults stamped their front paws in unison. He came to the ruin of the Danta's head, swiftly scored a deep cut, and deftly snapped off the long growth extending out the back of its skull. The bucks well knew the sound these hollow horns made when taken up by thousands of living Danta in their herds. They also learned how the Stags would do the same thing after a fresh kill and what came next. Nakuk set the Danta horn on one end and inspected the interior cavity. He then turned it over and widened the outer tip opening before standing on his hind legs and passing the instrument over to the two new arrivals.

"Honour each other with the Hero Spray," Keeper Nakuk said. Sinkin took up the horn. He lay the far end with its curve facing upward on the ground and shoved his snout into the opening where it had joined the skull. He then faced Setush, who had backed away two steps and blew hard into it. Unlike any sound made by its original owner, a mighty roar poured out along with a gush of residual blood spraying all over Setush. He leapt and danced in the dark fountain while the adults roared and laughed. Near the end of the blast the pitch altered as cracks began to form in the bone. Setush then took the horn, turned it to face Sinkin and bestowed the same honour on him. Setush's strong lungs further changed the tone, earning him the distinction of 'cracking the horn.' All their lives, these two bucks had stamped their paws as they watched the primary hunters being acclaimed with the Danta's horn. Now they asserted their own victory as these two powerful blasts and their triumphal changing pitch reached many ears within this region of the island.

As they set down the horn, Krall began to land in a circle around them, well-versed in this ritual and waiting to play their part. The adults turned slowly, and Sinkin and Setush started to follow, grateful the land sloped down from the wall's edge. The western face of the island continued as a sheer wall beyond sight. In many places, it thrust out or had deep cuts going inland a long way. Between windswept rises of rock, the land opened with rich short grasses and small stands of trees bent over in the constant wind. As they descended into the land, the wind diminished, and the landscape grew lush.

In all directions, well-worn paths spread out, and they moved along one as smooth as bare stone. They reached a sudden depression, not unlike the one where Durka and Makusk Herds met a lifetime ago in the north's jungles. This one was excavated long ago. The pitch down was steep, but it had been graded so two Suvuka could walk side by side. A deep pool lay at the bottom of near-perfect roundness. Cries of relief escaped Setush and Sinkin as they plunged into the frigid waters. They swam and turned over and over to relieve their aching muscles and wash the salt away. Soon the adults dived in. But, instead of joining them, they surrounded and herded them out. Keeper Nakuk alone remained on the shore.

"Enough," he said. He turned to a cave dug into the wall beside the pool. "Full Stags, you are beyond exhaustion. When cubs, you slept in a pile with your Dames, now we will fulfill this role to keep you warm and safe. You must sleep long before we continue."

Sinkin and Setush moved toward the cave and near fell unconscious once inside. They were unaware of being arranged back to back and others lying beside them as night fell.

CHAPTER 44

Seti

Day 333, Two-Week Nineteen, Ocan, the Jewel, Hashahanu's Festival Day, one of four squares forming central market on Avatay Island.

Seti stood waiting by the stage before the bustling market. Pedestrians, enjoying the holiday, looked on as a series of acrobats, tableaus and performers had taken their turns on the raised platform. As the hour ended, the previous troupe received their accolades from the crowd and cleared the stage. Green and blue banners hung on poles at the edges of the square with the 'wise spider' icon of Hashahanu, the last of the Twelve Faces of Tatchlan, known as the Face of Contemplation, on them. Seti ignored these images as he solemnly mounted the stage carrying a series of long ropes. Hegev and Dine followed him, Bearing a large object between them covered by a cloth. His manner and this unusual procession hushed much of those watching them. Seti nodded once to those positioned in the crowds.

"I make a declaration to you!" Seti said in a clear voice. Most heads in the crowd turned to look at him. "I am Seti, born in the northern hinterland. I have sailed around the coast of Rho-Jashun and Statos-Vey. I have spoken to Menem and watched their return to Ranvartawan. I have witnessed the descent of a Slaying Canopy and looked into the eyes of a living Suvuka!" He held up a large replica of the knot he had tied onto the emerging Memanu five two-weeks ago. "I am the knot of Nu!" he shouted loud enough for his voice to echo off the buildings surrounding the square. "Untie me and find yourselves! I speak for the Four Grand Menem! The Teacher, the Fashioner, the Devastator and the Bridge stand beside me! We make war on the false Faces of Tatchlan!" His voice became a quiet contrast to his bold beginning. "I come as a simple breeze from the north. This knot, worn and returned by a Memanu, is my sign!" He held the knot high over his head.

The crowds continued to stream in and out of the square, one of four forming the island's central market, separated by three-storey structures for permanent vendors. Festive sounds of the Hashahanu Festival emanated over and around these buildings from the other three squares. Despite the dynamic setting, most faces in this square turned to watch Seti's dramatic performance. Some eyes went wide at the symbol while others looked bemused or bewildered. A few fingers pointed at the knot. Some laughed and turned away while others moved closer to the platform.

Since leaving the hospital, Seti had sought out professional 'Chanters of Praises.' Along with hiring several for the day, he made enquiries about the Adorer craft. He had begun to learn to modulate his voice. Seti now sped up and slowed his delivery. He used short pauses to punctuate his message. Seti watched as these techniques began to affect many and noted the Adorers' approving nods. He also learned how to read the crowd as he slipped the sizeable Memanu knot over his head. Seti's story had come this far, and many recognized the knot. He signalled to Hegev and Dine. They removed the cloth, stepped in front of him, and brought the antique oval mirror with a thick scrolled frame, as tall as himself, to the platform's edge. It faced the crowd.

Seti stepped up on a crate to be seen from behind the mirror. "Look at yourselves!" he called out. "We Tolku are altered! Each generation born is one step closer to what the Tatchlan's so-called 'masters' term 'perfection.'"

As he spoke, Dine and Hegev continued to shift positions. The mirror swept over the entire group giving them a broad view of themselves and each other. The crowd churned with many contrasting currents. Some appeared unaware they were not watching the opening act of a play. Others understand him well enough and observed with a variety of expressions. Many eagerly moved forward to replace those leaving. Some who had turned away paused to watch this new display with the mirror. A number began to move out to the happy festival beyond this square; others climbed on top of roofs to watch from a distance.

"Statos-Vey teems with awe-inspiring cities," Seti declared. "The land is dense with farming and industry. This activity spills into every ocean, and each river is covered in floating markets. In ancient times, the Tolku also filled Rho-Jashun before the Suvuka destroyed our ancestors. They forced the survivors south to dwell behind the Mulungu Mountains. We reclaimed our ancestor's land, yet we remain few, and Rho-Jashun is vast. Spread out and separate, the creations of Tatchlan are less able to possess us - as they have Statos-Vey. Your smallness on the wide ocean has shielded you, but you are not immune from this silent plague!"

Dine and Hegev set down the mirror against two smaller blocks, so it continued to look out at the crowd. They stepped away to either side. Seti got down and began to work two coils of rope. He began a deliberate pace back and forth along the platform. He stopped either side of the mirror during each series of statements. "These masters do not hide their design. They stand in the open thus, and work their craft under Nu's Eye." He slowly walked to the other side, holding up a fabulous knot he had created in an instant. A few further back in the crowd laughed and applauded, while his words caught those in front. "Their Sheshenara Plants grow in the open," he continued standing on the mirror's other side. "Mothers feed their daughters its poison and none interfere. Many curious plants and animals inhabit the streets of the south. I tell you they are Sheshenara's Sisters!" His voice continued to echo off distant walls as he walked behind the mirror to the other side. "By their perverse craft, they turn natural life and create new creatures serving their cause."

"How can they do this?" a voice called out from the crowd. Seti smiled. The voice belonged to one of the crew, and her timing was perfect.

"Tatchlan's ranks are ever full," Seti called back, and he strolled to the other side of the mirror and, with deliberation, began a new knot. "Many of the greatest minds of each generation went over to them. The powerful shelter and sustain them. The public adores Sheshenara as their aide to health and long life."

He stopped and gazed over the crowd; those remaining had ceased their usual activity. A noisy celebration had begun in a neighbouring square. A portion of Seti's audience left for it while others continued to arrive, some clearly to hear the unusual boy. He now possessed the attention of those remaining in the market. Most operating their stalls stood in front of them to better listen to him.

"A brave few defied this," he went on in quiet tones. "Over a thousand years ago, they groomed a doctor named Nallurakon to join them. She discovered their inner workings and knew what danger faced us. She dared to challenge their vision. She pointed to their Sheshenara and said it altered their children. They met her criticisms with calm assurance. When a few fell ill after following her call to stop drinking Sheshenara, those Masters ensured all heard the news. Her movement faltered, but her words speak today of our fate."

He returned to the other side of the mirror and cupped a hand to his ear as if listening, "Do some say, 'Those Masters destroyed the enemy! By their arts, they stopped up their wombs! Because of Tatchlan, the Suvuka are contained behind the Vettencore Passage. They dwindled because of the Masters' craft.'" He frowned, "Now we dwindle! Tatchlan began long before the Suvuka invaded Rho-Jashun, and its true aim was to alter us!"

"Why do this?" another crew member called out on cue.

"Why?" he answered while continuing to work on an elaborate knot creation. He retraced his steps to the other side of the mirror, "It is said in the far-off days of the Funomanru Dynasty, chaos ruled Rho-Jashun and Statos-Vey. Many struggled to find an answer to our discord and waste. Generations of scholars, historians and 'Water Mystics' strove to comprehend our propensity for self-destruction. Out of these efforts came those dreaming of 'Tatchlan Perfection.' These Masters determined misery has a single root, 'self-absorption.'" He paused for dramatic effect, "They said our desire for land and possessions, and to live separate and distinct lives, are signs of this malady." His voice sufficiently echoed off the walls to be heard over the festival nearby, "In their eyes, these basic rights and dignities lead to every horror. As a result, a sweeping plan began to cut this root of 'self-absorption' out. These surgeons, intent on removing healthy body parts, proceeded with stealth. Exercising generational patience, they stole by increments. When a few finally objected, they wore down our ability to resist. The Suvuka interrupted this plan. Yet, the early masters turned the Suvuka invasion to their advantage. The Suvuka's defeat became compelling proof of the benefit of their work."

He looked at the knot he had created, composed of a central rosette with three loops issuing out either side, the remaining strands sprouted out the top and bottom. "This," he said, indicating the knot, "symbolizes our natural perfection. It is also a symbol of you." He went to the front of the mirror and attached one set of the strands to the top frame and hung the rosette over the mirror's centre. The loops fit over the ornate frame design either side. An appreciative murmur arose from the crowd. He gathered two more coils of a rope of the same length, and four more, two black and two red. He began to work them using rapid movements as he spoke, pacing either side of the mirror.

"Today, in the south, neither the grand rebellions of Nallurakon nor the wise council of Nebutan has any sway. On the mainland to the south, those Masters are triumphant! Since we arrived here, I walk among you and examine you closely. You more resemble my Rho-Jashun than Statos-Vey. On the mainland, the traditional norms erode as a foreign life overlays itself, anda by anda, from the city Enclaves to the countryside."

He held up a new knot design. It was the original of 'natural perfection,' with an additional black and red rope intertwined and distorting it. His audience marvelled to see such a disturbing image created from several lengths of rope. He stood in front of the mirror and held it high, "This goes far beyond differing customs and reaches to the root of ourselves. Fifty years ago, these Masters were so confident; they told our great Nebutan 'all life shall be changed.'"

He turned and retrieved the initial design, holding one knot in each hand. As he spoke, he raised one and the other. He also placed one in front of the other in illustration.

"I stood before a Suvuka, our ancient enemy, and mourned the purity we lost. I examined the twisted and altered faces of those distorted by their system. I also see those whose transformation nears completion. They are not Tolku!" He put the second knot, representing Tatchlan, in front of his face, before holding each either side of his head. "Those fresh Suvuka eyes, and those distorted Tolku eyes, opened my own. Both were terrible in their strange familiarity. Both spoke of our imminent destruction!"

He turned and attached the knots to the centre of the mirror. The Tatchlan knot was on top of the 'Natural Perfection' knot. He went round to stand on the box behind the mirror. He judged the mood of the crowd before pointing to a traditional image painted on a nearby wall. It must have been centuries old and was faded and cracked. It depicted a shining Menem confounding Yeoyupan at the final gate into Ranvartawan.

"Another sure sign of Tatchlan's rise is the fall of the old ways. The piety of our ancestors gives way to sneering. The honest faith in Ranvartawan is mocked. We once aspired to live our short lives honourably before freeing our Menem and beginning our true existence as eternal light beings. The southerners crave a long life for their flesh, free of trouble and surfeited in delight. They look at Nu and see a dead disk of heat. Worse, they teach our sacred Menem is but a portion of our body, sharing its ultimate fate. Their inner Menem's complete absence is the most terrible aspect of those possessed by their twisted system."

Hegev and Dine returned and lifted the mirror. Seti flipped the Tatchlan knot to the back, leaving the 'Natural Perfection' knot at its centre. They showed the crowd their reflection and the knot as one while he declared, "In your faces, there is a wholesome inner presence. In your ways, respect for time-honoured texts."

He turned to look at Dine and Hegev, they nodded. He turned back, "I invite you to form a Menem Circle, here in this place." He met eyes with each of the hired Adorers and signalled them to begin.

Seti, Hegev and Dine descended the platform carrying the mirror and turned left towards the neighbouring structure. The Adorers and the crew began to form the circle to one side beneath the faded mural. The crowd near divided in half. The ones already in front began to join them while the others stepped back either to continue to watch the novelty or to leave. Two crew members fetched the three blocks from the stage and set two down and the third on top inside the circle. Seti stood on the blocks. The old mural rose behind him. Hegev and Dine set the mirror on the blocks, and Hegev began to intone the ancient circle song.

"Praise be to Untasha-Kabash."

After half a breath's pause, the Adorers answered, "We stand in the circle. With our hands clasped, we are your loyal Menem," the crew paused before joining them in the familiar refrain. The result was the feeling of growing momentum.

"Glory to Ranvartawan, our true home! Glory to the triumph of the sky!" Seti and Hegev declared.

"Sky over dirt! Light over dark!" many in the elders in the crowd now joined the recital from their childhood, swelling the square's effect.

"We praise Untasha-Kabash. We thank Ranvartawan. You are our destination, where no darkness dwells."

"Light over dark! Air over flesh!" Each response brought new voices.

"Glory to inner spirit, who out of grace gives the flesh life," Seti, Hegev and Dine called out, "Glory to the outer air, purifying and uplifting. Inner Spirit and Outer Air triumph over Yeoyupan and his prison."

"Air over flesh! Sky over dirt!" After this, the Adepts and crew began to move to the right, stamping their feet each second step, ready to reply to each statement. Many in the crowd picked up the motions and amplified them. A few stepped out to join the passive observers beyond the circle. Others came forward to join it.

"We wish to be saved from Anu," The three around the mirror recited their words, falling into the crowd's stepping rhythm.

"We wish to save all from vile Anu," they replied.

"We wish to be delivered from Yeoyupan."

"We wish to deliver all from him."

"We wish to bear the wounds of our struggle."

"We wish to inflict wounds on the Kovlah."

"We wish for our Menem to be born."

"We wish to bring forth our Menem."

"We wish to eat no longer."

"We wish our bodies to be eaten."

"We wish to hear the clean winds."

"We wish to rise in the clear air."

"We wish to be washed of flesh."

"We wish to wash all but the Menem away."

"We wish to forget our bodies and Anu."

The crowd stopped and turned inward before answering, "Let the memory of them vanish in our everlasting abode of light."

This portion of the circle ritual done, Dine and Hegev held the mirror up high and made a slow turn. Their reflection surrounded the Natural Perfection knot on one side and the Tatchlan knot on the back.

"I declare Anu's truth concerning Tatchlan," Seti called out. They continued to play the mirror over their faces. "Now I declare Ranvartawan's truth. You know of the mighty storm whipping gentle Panchala into a frenzy five two-weeks ago. I tell you it was more than this! It was not the weather of Anu! It rolled down from Ranvartawan in a boiling blackness. It hurtled our ship north, across the Panchala until we landed on the Suvuka's shores. I looked into the eyes of a Suvuka. My deformity was reflected to me. When the black violence finished, Menem had left the sky. These and many more stand as witnesses of this miraculous event. The war above is over! The One Hundred Gates fell into the Panchala Sea, and Menem rush through the Eye of Nu. Yeoyupan is reconciled and declares peace. His Kovlah are conciliated with the Menem as they become one! We must cleanse what lies below and make all fair under Ranvartawan. The Tolku of Statos-Vey turn away, and the fall of the gates go unnoticed by them. We faithful are charged with a daunting task. The suffering Menem in the south must be liberated. We must awaken our slumbering cousins to their error. We stand at the crux above and below. The war above is over! The war below begins!"

He stopped and stood, breathing hard as the crowd hung on his final words. Seti, Hegev and Dine waited for their response.

CHAPTER 45

Shuna-Shapta

Pictured: traditional icon for the Thyma

Day 338, Two-Week Nineteen, Ocan, the Jewel, within Thakadush Cluster.

Perversity reigns amongst our Living Sigil Cubes!" Shuna-Dana had her hands immersed in pots of healing jelly. "I now require half a day for a working once taking an hour. We struggle to place our Living Cubes and most lie exhausted. This overcomes our Living Instruments! They refuse to continue and our quaking fabric tears and does not heal upon our board. I have been delayed when some Cubes refuse to wake or fight my attempts to place them! Yesterday, I completed the Work with open wounds upon portions of my Mesh! Each day we give our strength to return our foundations of our Living System to order - and find each aspect misaligned and hostile the next. Our Cube Master's maxim is turned aside, 'certain actions' no longer lead to 'certain results.' To my knowledge this has never happened since our venerable Uluvatu Masters brought our Tatchlan Cubes to life!"

"Dear Dana," Master Kanla said kissing her tenderly, "you do not return at night! How do you sleep?"

"We must not leave our Instruments," Shuna-Dana said in a sad voice, "They call out through the night, as if our battle does not cease for them. My finest unguents and salves now coat them. As for me," she looked down at her hands, "my hands ache! I was ever smooth skinned. Look at them! At nine-and-thirty years my cracked and dry fingers shake as an ancient. I work our Craft naked as burning sweat peels my clothes off me."

Shuna-Shapta came to kneel beside Shuna-Kanla, "Second Ama, we are 'plunged into a sea of distress.' Those able to affect our Grand Work labour within at each level." She hesitated, "You did not say how you slept."

"I sleep as my Instruments sleep," Shuna-Dana grumbled. "They call out several times a night. I hear unorthodox rustlings from within the Cube Reservatory. I know they are affected by Invocates working with their Living Instruments in our common cause. It appears our old Craft of Cubes and your new Craft of Instruments battle upon a single front. My precious creatures suffer! If I must continue to demand their toil during the day, I must comfort their night pains."

Shuna-Shapta nodded her head, "Mother Dana . . . do you dream?"

Shuna-Dana looked from her wife to her daughter and heaved a large sigh, "Yes, visions of her Face disturb my few hours of sleep."

Shuna-Shapta and her mother exchanged glances. "Dana," Shuna-Kanla said in a quiet voice, "we would enquire what you witness. Cube Masters work the foundations of our Living System. You move beneath us and discern their roots."

"Last night . . . I dreamt of a Thyma with Hesha Vira's Face. She sought a way out of a pen. She dragged the rest of our Tatchlan Faces behind her. Trapped within the pen, I feared injury. I seldom linger in such fright within sleep for so long. I awoke checking for wounds."

Shuna-Kanla and Shuna-Shapta sat in silence at this. "Our dreams differ," Shuna-Shapta said, " but the message remains the same."

"She is mad!" Shuna-Dana said. "How may our creation suffer such delusion? How could this fundamental flaw lay unnoticed? How may one Face overcome eleven others?"

"We do not know," Master Kanla replied. "Many dormant elements came alive at once with the Quickening. Our grandmothers and their mothers fashioned Hesha Vira first out of raw life. Alatanda, Skarashing, Naprahath and Humma came after but wakened before her. This generation of Masters, including those brought out of retirement and others sent within despite incomplete training, labour as you. Those able to work here and upon our Resplendent Orb join to address this crisis."

"We are all insects . . . trying to force a Danta to turn aside during a stampede!" Shuna-Dana shot back.

"She is afraid," Shuna-Shapta said.

Her two mothers looked at her.

"Shapta?" Master Kanla said.

"Our Majastas stroked her eye," Shuna-Shapta said, "back when we discovered the knot representing the boy. Hesha Vira knows when Thakadush-Satwa comes into her own, she shall master and subdue her."

"Wait!" Shuna-Dana said, "I also recall an ill-favoured pre-adult walking within my dreams. He had a feral quality about him, as if the wind whipped him and Nu beat down upon him without pause or respite. He burned with an inner fire and stank of Indatubangus." She bent her head and whispered, "I also dreamt of packs of Suvuka circling her Face."

They looked back at her in amazement.

"Ama," Shuna-Shapta said, "we also witness this. Hesha Vira attempts to form independent links with the disparate groups opposing us. This raw Tolku Sensitive fastens the cart of his genius to the rash abandon of madness. He is a distillation of all the noble aspiration and blind chaos of prehistory, attempting to remake its vile kingdom. What began as a pacifying experiment by Masters to bring the Suvuka under our control has turned against us. Hesha Vira reaches for this Menem prophet and forges deep links to the beasts. With these two unlikely allies wrapped within her tendrils she attempts to challenge our Uluvatu legacy."

"As unsettling as this is," Master Kanla said, "at least the Suvuka remain contained. She gains strength from them, but other than making her more difficult to control, they may not aid her to break free from our Resplendent Work."

"Break free?" Shuna-Dana shouted. "She may no more 'break free' than my hand may 'break free' from my arm! She would die whilst a millennia of toil would come undone! Until our Practicians formed her outlines and our Uluvatu Masters opened her eyes she had no self awareness or purpose. She was the blind fulcrum of 'death chasing life chasing death' existence! I told you she came last night to me as a Thyma. A Thyma may be brought down and put to sleep. Shall we find a way to close this one's eyes? Once stupefied, you could turn her over and address her inner parts."

Master Kanla laughed and clapped her hands. "Dana, we discuss this." She stopped and lowered her voice, "We think she knows our strategy and thus thwarts any approach. We lay plans, but this remains a challenge." She glanced at their daughter who hung her head.

"We must have Thakadush-Satwa," Shuna-Shapta said. "She and myself alone may approach Hesha Vira and enforce stillness upon her."

Shuna-Dana stared at each of them. "Shapta!" she said to her daughter, "Miraculous though she be, she is barely a pre-adult! I do not begin to comprehend how she functions as she does within our Grand Work." She stopped and her eyes widened, "Yes, I may . . . you!"

Shuna-Shapta gave a faint smile, "Not just I, all of Tatchlan augments her. She is already 'The Throne' manifest."

Shuna-Dana frowned, "I recall this phrase, 'The Throne,' from I know not where."

"Dana!" Master Kanla lovingly chided, "you recall our ancient Master Clutmustra?"

"Oooh! There is a name I had not thought upon for a time."

"When we were your age," she said to her daughter, "over twenty years ago, this Master Elder proposed the concept of 'The Throne,' being the gradual overlay of what we know to be our wakened Tatchlan, to augment and provide the 'Great Continuity' to future Majastas. This would also serve as a bridge between one reign and the next."

Shuna-Dana looked at each in turn, "So many of our elders stand corrected by this Quickening, are we in agreement our old curmudgeon discerned this deep tool within what was once our calm and orderly 'General Plain' of Tatchlan?"

"All we behold with our Majastas infant makes it so," Master Kanla said.

"This may well be," Shuna-Dana said, "yet, a shocking change within our daughter also manifests before me."

I am changing," she said in a small voice. "What we term the 'Mantle,' the sanction of our Living Orb to stand at its heart and direct our Living Orb, extends to me."

Shuna-Dana sat back in shock. She turned to her wife, "Kanla? Our 'Mantle' extends to her? What do you Masters say?"

Master Kanla held up her hands in helpless amazement. "Our Faces treat them as one. Tanas suggests an adaptation by our Magnificent Work to this circumstance."

"Master Tanas is over fond of his speculations!" Shuna-Dana shot back. "Our once placid and orderly System Gardens have become a foreign wilderness. You say our daughter is swept into its wildly beating heart? Dear Shapta!'"

Shuna-Shapta smiled at her mothers. They smiled back, both feeling vast depths in her eyes. "My dreams contain mysteries," she said in a calm voice, "they speak to a fundamental shift. I am honoured to be chosen."

CHAPTER 46

SINKIN

Day 339, Pramath Island.

Sinkin and Setush recovered from their ordeal. They dwelt in seclusion by a small pond surrounded by whispering trees, the like of which they had never seen before. When they ventured out, several other formations stood around them. They spied the slow movements of others inside. Food had been left each night, and they slept long and managed little beyond swimming in the pond each day. The water was sweet and had a tingling aftertaste. At last, on the sixth day, Keeper Nakuk entered their shelter.

"I greet you," he stood on his hind legs, "Full Stags!" Sinkin and Setush knew to rear up, and each offered a ceremonial cuff to the Keeper. Nakuk, in turn, cuffed them back and settled on four paws.

"Many spend this time alone," he said. "Some journey in groups. Some meet along the way. We honour Stag Run bonds. Soon we send you back. Do you have questions?"

Setush said, "Keeper, this place . . . is it fashioned?

"Yes," Keeper Nakuk said. "In ancient times, deep ponds were found. These bubbling waters are precious. They constantly renew themselves. The salt you brought is long gone from them. Trees grew around, forming a shelter. They are unlike Pramath's other trees. My ancestors created more to heal New Stags. This is one of over one hundred. Many paws were bruised. Many talons broken. Lifting these precious waters is our gift to you. The trees came after of themselves. We pound down the land to secure each shelter."

Setush and Sinkin looked at the pond and trees with new appreciation.

"Keeper," Sinkin said, "Hesha Vira's Face was in this pond."

Setush shot his friend a disapproving glance. Keeper Nakuk looked long at them. "As children, we spoke her name in hushed tones. New Stags invoke Her with boldness! We begin to hear tales of strange events at Avanchil Round. She covered the bowl, they say! Were you present at this event?

The two youths nodded.

"Others witnessed this. Keepers race here to confirm it."

"Has she risen since?" Sinkin asked.

"Another wave of bucks reach Avanchil Round. We will learn if she fills the round again. If so, a new song will begin among us."

"Keeper Nakuk," Sinkin said, "A Round was once destroyed because of her."

The Keeper stared at them in silence for a time. "Come!" he said. "Your time here is done. Let us move toward the assembly. We will reach it tomorrow. Much will be displayed there. These revelations are studied."

They set off at an easy lope across the open land, lashed by ceaseless winds. They stayed away from the other sheltered groves, leaving their occupants to heal at their pace. Like an oasis in the desert, the shelters stood out in a land scoured by the ocean winds into smooth hills and valleys. The few trees and shrubs clung to the rocks, ever bowing to the west. They travelled north by the wall of the western shore to their distant left. The voice of surf and wind mixed in their ears. Keeper Nakuk began to sing a throaty rendition of a well-known hero saga. The other two took up the song, and their combined voices echoed off the surrounding hills as Nu followed their progress close to the horizon. They settled in a small depression. Surging trees arched over, sheltering them from the constant winds.

Day 340

The day opened clear, and in silence, they ran through it. They continued to run into the evening. Brilliant roving and fixed stars lit their way to a large grove. When they entered, they found a broad, irregular lake. A small island rose out of one elongated arm of the lake. The distinctive trees stood well back, permitting the night Eyes to sparkle on its shimmering surface.

"This," Keeper Nakuk said between pants, "is a self-made shelter. Born before any Suvuka, it stands as the model for all others. They each bear a name. This is Undrona Shelter."

They surveyed the setting. While large and rough compared to the well-tended one they had spent their days in since arriving, it possessed a perfection and elegance of its own. Tiny winged creatures frolicked above the bubbling surface of the lake. They lighted for an instant on the little island before renewing their dance. Three other groups of between three to six Suvuka huddled in drowsy groups spread among the lake's trees. While a few turned to look at them, most were lost in sleep. A low mound stood to one side. It had been raised in the past few days and showed signs of being broken open in places.

"Our ancestors found Anu's peace here," Keeper Nakuk said, "Tomorrow you arrive at assembly. What we do honours the long line preceding us."

Keeper Nakuk's ritual steps wound down to the lake. The other two followed his pace. When he arrived near the shore, he found a thin but well-worn track and stood. He began a dance neither had seen before. It was simple, composed of one back leg raised and the opposite front leg followed by one turn. The alternate limbs raised, and a bend in the other direction followed. With each turn, they took one step along the path. Many paws had performed the same movements here. Familiar flecks of colour appeared in the waters as Hesha Vira watched them. Keeper Nakuk gave no sign of noticing. Their progress was long enough for the other Suvuka to sleep by the time they finished. They made their way up the slope to find their own place among the trees. The two youths curled up by the Keeper and fell asleep at once.

Day 341

Sinkin and Setush woke to find the others vanished. They made their way down to the sparkling lake of Undrona Shelter to drink when Keeper Nakuk came through the trees.

"Good," he said, "the others left. We will follow soon enough. We have an easy day's run ahead. The weather will not slow us. By the evening, we will be at assembly. Hundreds of New Stags there. Many songs will be sung. Many stories told. After this, you will prepare for your return."

He led them over to the mound they had seen in the dark last night. It was a cache containing dry foods to sustain them. "We Keepers perform many services," Nakuk said. "Most you will not see. We gather food and other supplies. We assist you in silence. New Stags possess our western coast. We occupy the rest of the island. We prepare and maintain our resources for you."

The youth ate their fill of the dry foods and drank from the deep chill lake. They headed out of Undrona Shelter and continued north. Hours later, as Nu was westering, they crested a hill. A marvellous sight spread out in the valley. There lay a bowl near twice the size of Avanchil. Suvuka near filled it.

"There is Gramerem Round," Keeper Nakuk said over a sudden gust of wind. "Being self-made, it is as ancient as Avanchil and quite grand. Generations have modified it to suit our needs. They also raised the surrounding mound."

The two youth stared in amazement at the large gathering of Suvuka within a vast circle. Several adults and two ancients called out to the New Stags from a raised middle of the circle. Many of the youth swayed, a few danced and others chased each other around the outside. They were too distant to make sense of anything, beyond seeing a group engaged in an intensive series of events. Sinkin noticed a frown on Keeper Nakuk's face looking at the scene.

"Do not fear," Keeper Nakuk said. "Your time will come. Some follow you. You arrive at the end of this wave. Another run arrives at Avanchil. More follows them. Your day will begin tomorrow. After a day and night, your journey home will begin."

In the failing light, groups of Suvuka gathered in clumps down in the valley outside the vast round. It became evident they were waiting for their day tomorrow. They would take half the room the present group did inside the bowl. Keeper Nakuk led them at a leisurely trot down into the valley toward the waiting group. Dots of other groups descended into the valley. The high mound, Keeper Nakuk spoke of, rose tall around the Round. When they reached the valley floor, none could see over the ridge. As they found a spot to sleep, they heard a series of roars and passionate outcries coming over the wall. Sinkin and Setush thought they listened to a chant rising from the hundreds of Suvuka inside sounding like 'Hesha! Vira!' Despite their interest, they fell asleep to the chants. Violent visions, intense passions and the sound of distant calamities troubled their slumber.

Day 342

Sinkin and Setush woke to the sounds of many hundreds of Suvuka exiting Gramerem Round. Near where they slept was a gap in the mound, and the New Stags filed out after spending the night.

"I must go," Keeper Nakuk said to them. "You will be called once the Round is prepared. When day and night are over, I will accompany you for your journey to the sea."

He turned and near galloped toward the gap and through.

Setush frowned, "Seldom has my sleep been so troubled."

Sinkin did not look at him but stared into the distance and nodded. "I fear our trials are not over." He looked toward the mound.

"How long has it been since we came ashore?" Setush asked in an uneasy voice.

Sinkin turned and smiled, "It seems a year! Is it . . . ten days? I lose count. I am ready for the swim. I am glad we will not scale the wall. I fear the unknown beyond our return swim."

Setush nodded at this, "It is the Vettencore Passage we are to remember."

"They will not have cracks and ridges to latch onto."

"The swim and the climb would be less. What after this?"

"My Hiratak would say, 'retake the land and destroy them.'"

"What do you say?"

Sinkin stared at the mound surrounding the huge Round. "We must learn our intention. Thousands were defeated when we possessed Thermistal. We must find new strength. The Tolku must lose theirs. Otherwise, we will be defeated again."

"Look at them, Sinkin," Setush whispered. They began to move toward the exiting column from the Round. Sinkin and Setush came to stand on one side as the extended group loped out. An intense feral smell surrounded them. Despite the circumstances, they felt their fur rising on their backs, and their lips curl, as if in imminent danger. Keepers travelled with the new Stags. Setush readied to call out when a Keeper came to them.

"You have not been within Gramerem?"

The youths shook their heads.

"Say nothing to these. Gramerem must remain a mystery to you. Once you leave, you join Full Stags. You then may speak on what took place there."

Sinkin and Setush touched their noses to the ground in deference, and the Keeper moved to rejoin his charges.

"Sinkin," Setush whispered, "look at their faces!"

Sinkin looked at those moving past them. Most had a mixture of emotions in their burning eyes. They saw enthusiasm as if they had witnessed a miraculous event and shock as if shaken to the core. A series of high calls rose into the air. Keepers stood at intervals along the top of the mound. With this signal, Sinkin and Setush began to move toward the Round. They saw nods and smiles on the silent faces of those leaving Gramerem. Their unspoken message was clear, Sinkin and Setush approached a terrible and wondrous event.

CHAPTER 47

Seti

Samajalas icon, this Grand Menem was also known as 'The Comforter,' turning the Tolku on his Wheel of Life.

Day 342, Two-Week Nineteen, Ocan, the Jewel, the Jefaka.

Hegev approached the Jefaka. The ship was moored by the shore, surrounded by others all in various states of repair. Most of the ship's cargo was piled high on the dock with carts beginning to load and take them away. The crew covered the craft, stowing and tying away everything. One lad saw her and waved. "She is going into dry-dock," the boy called down to her. Captain Emedin came on deck. She wore an inscrutable expression as she beckoned Hegev to come on board. The

Adept noted her relaxed manner. She had not seen the captain at such ease for several two-weeks. She made her way down to the captain's cabin to find it filled with boxes, her wall of books packed away and the rest of the room in chaos.

"The repairs begin so soon?"

"Yes, or at least a sufficient quantity to ensure our eventual departure," Emedin answered. She navigated the mess, placing various items into an open crate as she spoke. "Sawlu Clan has agents in Bhampay, led by the eldest son of our clan head and council elder, Jine-Piprith. When he learned of our plight, he contacted me, and I sent him a report. He has forwarded extra payment to bring us forward."

"I hear mention of someone named Mek."

"His name is Mek-Piprith, or young Master Mek as we know him. He is groomed to one day replace his father and is now entrusted with overseeing Sawlu interests in Bhampay. Such a posting suggests he is excelling in his role. He was instrumental in negotiating our scheduled stop in the port of ports. He commissioned the local assessment and received their report. Master Mek instructed me to initiate negotiations with the local shipping guilds and provided funds to facilitate their timely response. This same storm has led to damaged and broken ships filling Bhampay's 'Inner Harbour.' It suited everyone."

Hegev looked around the cabin, "You are required to move off the ship?"

"Jefaka will be towed into dry-dock. Some of our Nuchin metal hull cladding was loosened during the storm. We would not only have taken on water but would have been vulnerable to Chill Crystals penetrating the hull. We are fortunate that the Cladding Guild was amenable to attending to us now. Otherwise, we would be here for an extended stay. The local Rope Makers Guild, on the other hand, cannot accommodate us at all, and we must wait for Bhampay to restore our rigging. Yet, despite these delays, we remain most fortunate. I am now informed Sawlu has lost two large ships this year."

"I am sorry to hear it."

Emedin's face clouded, "Yes, I knew a few on each vessel," she stood in silence. "Each came to their end in different ways farther along The

Circuit. One suffered a chance encounter with submerged rocks when driven too close to a rough shore off the eastern coast of southern Rho-Jashun. All of the crew was rescued. The other met the worst of fates, sinking in The Black Maid at The Crown's turn almost within sight of your home island. Five old friends froze and drowned, and another lost an arm. Our profession is not without hazard!" She paused again, "While our shipyards aggressively construct new vessels, they cannot afford another out of the water for long. The estimate for speedy re-cladding and fitting new masts is a two-week or more. I think this is overconfident, and we will be here considerably longer. Sawlu is having our cargo stored and provided lodging for the crew until the work is done. I will reside in a set of apartments along the waterfront."

"I had heard none of this!"

"How could you? In the near twenty days since we arrived, you have not been near the ship what with your *business*," the sharpness of her reply startled Hegev. She sat in silence across from the Captain.

Emedin turned her back on the Adept to roll up a set of charts. She continued in a conversational tone, "I hear several ships offer to take Seti and you aboard," her voice cold.

"Yes."

"The one I know is the captain of the Yamagad, a three-masted caravel well suited to your purpose. It made its way to Wazaratcha four or five years ago. I could send a letter of recommendation to the captain if you wish."

Hegev looked down at her lap, "He wishes to speak to you."

Emedin spun around and slammed her fist into her desk, "I do not wish to speak to him!"

"He loves you. He wants you to understand . . . "

"Understanding is my issue! Everyone forgets what the doctors said in the clinic! You heard them, and you let him out! All here turn as flaccid as my crew!"

"How is hope 'flaccid?'"

"Hope?" Captain Emedin spat out the word, "Why is hope so noble? How is it insanity is caught like Tarops? Those doctors agreed our boy suffers from Falling Sickness and, depending on which we consult, at least three other identifiable ailments. They were in agreement that he suffers from delusions," she tapped her head for emphasis. "Now he speaks to his Menem, and everyone swears they hear them! He no longer bears to stand on the ground, saying 'the Face' is trying to suck him into it, and all rush to put him on carts and construct platforms for him." She stopped herself and paused, "My old dream awakens, and I may take to writing once more. These events inspire me to examine this propensity for leaders to capture the general public's good sense."

Hegev sat, looking up at her, "You refuse to see him?"

Emedin paced the small cabin in evident frustration. She kicked several obstacles out of her way, "Not aboard my ship! He may come to the dockyards or my new lodgings, and we will make our farewells. I do not want him approaching the Jefaka. Considering these new offers, he has many choices. We will likely be here for several two-weeks. The Yamagad could set sail in days." She glared at Hegev, "I will not tolerate *one* member of my crew breaking their contract and following him! I care not what 'pacts' they fancy to have sworn."

"Do you fear he has more influence here than you? This is far from his mind. His drive is for his mission."

"My *fear* is you will rue the day! The fate of this ship and his are severed. I took him aboard out of kindness and hoped he might become a promising student in our schools back home. I was a fool! I knew he was unbalanced and humoured his notions in the hope he would grow out of them. I looked the other way during his innumerable episodes, believing an Adept might calm and guide him. You *aid* his delusions! You stand at his side and 'interpret' his rubbish! The irony is Dine was against bringing him on board. He saw what I chose to ignore. Now he is entranced, and I am forced to ensure my estranged friend fulfills his contract and returns, or I will report him. Until now, I have had little acquaintance with young Master Mek, but given our recent correspondence, it has become clear he is near as hard as his father. He will not hesitate to pursue and drag those jumping ship to court. If they successfully elude capture, our law is unwavering should they ever return home. Regardless of how many years have passed, they will be prosecuted. My career may be challenged for my poor judgment. Word is sent concerning the loss of Nikumb, Nichan,

Dum, Daruhasa Dates and Seka, and there will be an enquiry into their deaths and the loss of cargo during a storm. They demand to know why I sailed into the open ocean instead of staying along the coast with their sheltering ports. All I did and allowed to take place since he came on board will be scrutinized." Her eyes betrayed her growing emotion, "Dine has a family!" she shouted. "He has dependants and children waiting for him! This was to be his final Circuit and soon he would retire with a full pension. I bear no ill will toward Seti. He is ill, and illness is not evil. The evil here is for the sane to throw over their reason and responsibilities to follow the mad!"

Hegev stood, "I do not counsel them to break the law. I told them if we go on another ship, they are to fulfill their obligations to the Jefaka."

Emedin gave her a curt nod, "Where will you go?"

Hegev hesitated.

"Let me guess," Emedin cut in, "Seti consults the 'Generals of the Air' and the rest of you await their decision?"

"Captain! Your contempt is unbecoming!"

"Adept! Your collusion is unbecoming! You are an educated woman! We spoke here many times since you came aboard. You could have visited us decades ago to hear Nebutan speak. You would have been contemporaries. I know you began to wean him of his fantasies. You presented him with evidence of this tradition's inconsistencies. How is it you now come to this decision? How is it that clear evidence," she held up hospital documents, with the circular emblem of the clinic Seti stayed in clearly visible, "means nothing to you?"

Hegev frowned at the papers before sitting down, as did the captain. At last, Hegev took a deep breath, "You are well informed of his doings. I know you have a transcript of his exhortation at the market. You read the words, but you do not comprehend their meaning." She looked at the crates. "Within those volumes is Nebutan's summary of religion."

Emedin smiled, "She said a little, best summarized by what I heard her say aloud, 'religion is the height of emotion.'"

"Yes . . . that was it," she said. "I propose to you it is more. Religion is the kindling setting emotions burning. It is strong enough to overcome the multitude's inertia. An entire generation will rise by its power. It will unite them, and their focus will become sharpened to a pinprick. The general population sleeps through their existence. Intense, collective motivation is near impossible to achieve. They are blind to a larger vision and consumed in . . . yes, in 'self-absorption,' as those 'masters' say. Seldom if ever, are they roused to a common cause. When they are, nothing stands in their way."

Emedin's eyes went wide as she leaned back in her chair. "I see," she pondered before adding, "I thank you for confirming what I already suspected. You are not deluded like my foolish Dine or the rest." She came to sit on the front of her desk. "After Seti made those declarations at the Memanu Field, I said he had mounted a Thyma. I was mistaken. You latch onto the tail of Seti and climb his back. You will ride him, dreaming of power."

"I dream of our liberation from this enemy! You once said as much yourself! Do you believe Seti did not tell me your words? You told him of your clan's history and thought Seti's powerful evocation of the old ways could aid Sawlu's cause. How is it you condemn me for what you planted in him?"

Emedin made a pained expression and nodded. "I admit I thought of using him and told him so. I admired his intensity, his brilliance and his ability to forge profound loyalty. I hoped this voyage might cure him of his delusions. I saw encouraging signs and tried many times to instruct him in the pitfalls of invisible beliefs. I sought out opportunities for him to experience various notions while sheltering him from many of their excesses. While our methods differed, I thought our aim was the same. What separates us is not our initial intention, but our response to the truth of his condition."

"Truth! You are over humble to these *doctors*! Doctors, in part, brought down the founding champion of your clan, Nallurakon! Were it up to doctors, each inspired and creative leader we had would be committed! Seti needs support and guidance, not drugs and confinement! Your clan surrounded Nebutan and sheltered her, and we will do the same for Seti. With our assistance, his genius will light the way to the future."

"Hmm," the Captain said as she returned to her seat, "I remain the fool in this and thank you for fortifying my education. Perhaps your lesson is the most important." She stared into space; "It is not the seed of prophetic madness, nor the gullible multitudes hungering for an absurd escape from their fate, but the exploitation of both that lay the foundations of such movements."

"Twist my motives as you wish," Hegev replied. "Our Seti will waken this generation, reminding them of 'who they are.' It is a noble cause. Those twisters of life better deserve your scorn. They exploit and manipulate us. Your scholar Nebutan gave her exceptional intelligence to the cause but reached the wrong audience. Her elevated mind did not touch the general population, who alone will effect real change."

"So! When the words of wisdom do not suffice, you harness their ignorance to your cart of ambition? Those bringing down the Funomanru and Muraharoma Dynasties wrapped themselves in the nobility of their cause. History has been unanimous in condemning them. The early Water Viewers had priesthoods growing around their words like moss choking a spring. These administrators harnessed this emotion while debasing their founders' idealism and suffocating the originating source. As I recall, the creative innovators seldom lived to see the empires founded on their inspiration."

"Do you suggest I will harm Seti?"

Emedin barked a humourless laugh while pointing an accusing finger at her, "You already have! The doctors handed you prescriptions when you insisted on signing him out." She retrieved a set of keys and unlocked her desk drawer. She held a crumpled scrap of paper. "You threw this away, and someone brought it to me."

"Ha! 'Someone?' Do you believe what a servant of our enemy brings you? I hear you handed over your logs to those demanding them, knowing full well what hands they would be passed to!"

"You know nothing of maritime law concerning commercial vessels and their captain's log," Emedin said. "I am bound to submit it in any port to authorities on request. The finest Bhampaian vessel sailing into Wazaratcha may be subject to the council's requirement of their captain's log should they deem sufficient cause. Jefaka's log remains with the ship regardless of who the captain is. I write in it knowing many eyes will peruse them should they deem it necessary. I am certain this log will far surpass any attention my previous logs have inspired. When this ship is decommissioned, its log will be archived for posterity."

She put the prescription back in the drawer and locked it. "I had already received an urgent dispatch from the clinic. This was after Dine, and the others went for your 'secret' meeting on the seawall. They asked me to come at once, and I brought this prescription. They were most unhappy I had it given the Apothecary was right beside the clinic! They confirmed giving it to you. They said Seti had left over their strenuous objections. I told them the complete story of his joining our crew and my growing alarm as to where this led. I asked them to put their findings in a report and attach their seals to it. I received their lengthy set of assessments and transcriptions, and after careful examination, I ensured they followed my logs. Both have been returned and are in my safekeeping. This led to myself, and my crew members present having interviews to verify various details in these documents. As I followed your clandestine movements off-ship, I also begin a series of additional dispatches to go in another direction. They will be sent back to Sawlu shortly. I will produce this material from the clinic at my hearing. The leadership of our Clan will not be mistaken as to the nature of this 'movement.'"

She stood again and began her customary pacing behind her desk as best she could, given the crates. "You are correct; I have detailed accounts of your event nine days ago. Several members of your supposedly loyal coterie have made their way here to speak to me. They mention details likely not to be found in any subsequent devotional account. These include how small the final gathering was, less than half the square. While some elders were entranced, many others participated as much out of novelty as devotion. I understand one has offered you rooms in their home and others swear allegiance, but I am certain the final result fell far short of your hopes. While this is a small island, the native and visiting population is far more cosmopolitan that at a rural Memanu Field. I see little signs of the groundswell you must have dreamt of. I am told after you left the square filled with laughing at a parody on the same stage. Attendees included some of your audience. I take no pleasure in musing; it was one farce following another."

She shook her head, "I have never been enamoured by those able to sway crowds to chant and stamp their feet! They pander to the basest of emotions, leading formerly noble nations to disreputable ruin. I fear this pattern will repeat with Seti, in large part due to your actions, culminating in throwing his prescriptions away."

"Those 'medications' would kill his visions! He refused to take them!"

"I am not surprised," she sat back in her chair, and her voice became calm. "For him to listen to the doctors and take the medicine would mean admitting his aunt, mother, and sisters were right, and his beloved father a fool. His life would be cast as an absurd adventure leading to a mediocre end. In other words, like the rest of us! What would be a worse fate for a would-be prophet than to discover he is just a sick boy? Along with threatening his glorious destiny, your hopes would be killed. These many two-weeks and I see you at last. I pile many regrets on myself. Having you become the one Seti trusts will weigh the heaviest." She stood and leaned across her desk, "Now *get off* my ship!"

CHAPTER 48

SINKIN

Ancient icon for Dream Moss

Day 342, during the Full Stag Rite at Gramerem Round.

Sinkin and Setush's nostrils flared at the stench of blood, fecal matter and other fluids filling the air. They heard grunts of surprise from the other new Stags. The land rose on a series of ripples away from the centre rise toward the surrounding mound. A complete, near-circular pit stood to one side of this rise at the base, and it was clear Suvuka had modified the ridge, the hill, and had dug the excavation. The rippling land of uneven steps was self-made and now was covered by offal surging with insects. Young cubs moved through the landscape, attempting to clear away most of yesterday's remains. They dragged broad sections of Tolku water carts, filling them with garbage. As they scraped their way along, the others scooped what they could and flung it onto the cart. Others urinated into the dark pools of blood, directing the fluids down to the pit where the dripping told of a deep shaft. Beside this pit, on the central flat rise, stood four elder Suvuka, swaying on their hind legs, they danced as if in a trance. Each faced a cardinal direction. Thirty Keepers surrounded the dancing ancients, Nakuk, among them, facing outward with impassive expressions. Most of the new arrivals had stopped before this strange scene and the surrounding signs of a riot. Without an apparent cue, the cubs at once hurried their foul carts out the entrance. Ten towering adults bounded into the Round to stand on their hind legs around the dancers and Keepers.

"What is this?" a shining black pelt called out.

"They travel the Full Stag Path!" a red pelt replied.

The ten adults stamped their hind paws in unison, one after the other, bending and delivering each stamp with considerable force. They stamped left and right four times.

"What is a Stag?" a light brown pelt called out. Each of the nine others answered in turn.

"A source of honour to his herd!"

"He is a warrior!"

"He is a leader!"

"He is a father!"

"His words are true!"

"His actions swift!"

"His power serves the powerless!"

"His anger cleanses Anu."

"His joy hastens the spring."

They stamped the ground.

The light brown pelt called out, "His virtue is a tribute to his herd!"

"His gallantry is his herd's pride!"

"There is purity in his simplicity."

"There is clarity in his gaze."

"He brings down his herd's meat."

"He disperses our enemies."

"He defends his herd's name."

"He tends to his cubs with tenderness."

"With distinction, he sees to the aged."

"He lavishes devotion on his dams."

"Know this, young Stags!" the shining black pelt bellowed. "In the past ages, a New Stag found this island! He swam the ocean. He climbed the rock face. He ran across the open land. He saw what you have seen. He saw more you have not. This island was his treasure! He took the news back. Others followed him. More came after. This island is called by his name, Pramath! It grew to be smooth water for all Suvuka. We now live in exile. Pramath Island is our main Stag Run. Our ancestors embraced this new role. We welcome you to our island."

The red pelt spoke, "We serve as hosts. Yet, this is not Pramath's sole task. We strengthen and focus our kind. Another island stands at the core of Thermistal. We named it . . . Lewetar." He spoke the name with clear emphasis. "The greatest of our clans gathered there. Pramath is based on Lewetar. They gave birth to many of the higher disciplines. They sent teachers across Thermistal. They mapped our heights. Lewetar is fallen and gone. Since our defeat, most avoid confronting what troubles us. Until now . . ."

The new Stags had not noticed how the elders had stopped their dancing during this set of speeches. They had bent down, and the Keepers had turned inward. The elders rose, striking yellow and red streaks on their faces. The Keepers faced the new Stags wearing the same markings. They bared their fangs to better imitate the Face of Hesha Vira.

The ten sat down, allowing the Keepers and Elders to rise over them. A blond pelt continued the narrative, "Lewetar knew of Hesha Vira! She was discovered in ancient dreams. She became the inspiration of bards. Many saw her as the Face of Anu. Others were frightened, saying she came late in Suvuka life. They called her a deception of the enemy. Open declarations became secret whispers. Avanchil Round once had a companion. Dakast Round was far to the north. It served New Stag and other trials. After our exile, the few left of our Orders said our Hesha Vira must be revealed. This led to their downfall! Only we Keepers remain to lead us. Our ancestors held Hesha Vira close. They set taboos to keep her secret. They waited. Now she rises in many places. Believers surround disbelievers. All hear of her rising in Avanchil. You ran and danced your dance on her Face! She becomes brazen and speaks in many places. We revive the ancient ways to meet her."

The Stags turned at scraping sounds. The cubs entered laden with black mounds piled on cart sections. The ten rose to assist the cubs in pulling in their loads. They dumped the contents in front of the Keepers and continued until a black ring formed. The ten herded the cubs out when they began to show signs of agitation and animation.

"Circle us," one of the Keepers called out in a deep voice. As the group approached, they focused on the ring of black material surrounding the Keepers. A thick, pungent odour rose from the warm pile, beginning to sting their eyes. Sinkin and Setush recognized the scent's source on those issuing out of this Round an hour before.

"Stags!" another Keeper called out. "You crossed many lands! You swam an ocean! You climbed a mountain! You did all this to come here! Now fly over mountains, oceans and lands!" As one, the Keepers bent down, and their broad noses shifted the black mass out toward the surrounding Stags. Odours burst open, and they heard popping sounds inside their heads. The exposed pile steamed with internal heat.

"Dream Moss?" Setush said under his breath. Sinkin tried to focus his tearing eyes on the potent mixture possessing him. He felt the mass stare back at him, drawing him closer, defying any enquiry. It continued to shift and move toward him as if alive. His last thought was how this compelling substance bore little resemblance to the mild stimulant they had consumed at Avanchil Round before their dance. Sinkin bent down and took a mouthful with the rest without reflection. The blackness translated into undreamt-of sweetness. He felt his heart beating fast and began to hear Setush's heartbeat beside him. He felt a new heartbeat, one he had never known. He looked down at his four paws and felt an immense beat repeat from a vast depth beneath him. He had a diminished awareness of continuing to consume the mass. Black juices began running down his neck. He could not hear what Setush or the others did. Sinkin's world vanished, and he swam through an ocean of colour and sound.

Delights embraced him, and his ears filled with sweet melodies. Memories floated toward him from his early years. He felt the warmth of his dams and the gruff affections of his sires. He heard his young mother weep at her dead cubs and nurse new living ones. He saw his brothers and sisters, who had died when he was young. Their voices came back to him, and their sparkling eyes flashed at him. A younger Hiratak praised him for a childish accomplishment. He recalled speeches regarding injured honour and despised virtue. He ran and ran across open fields dreaming of flying over the barrier and wiping Anu clean of the enemy imprisoning his herd. He relived his intense excitement leading to his making the Stag Run. Sinkin opened his eyes to find himself in the Round. He had made his way to the outer mound and looked at the sprawling scene. Keeper Nakuk stood beside an insensible Setush. With difficulty, Sinkin made his way to them.

"He will rejoin us soon," Keeper Nakuk said to him. "This is the original Gramerem Ritual. It is revived now Hesha Vira has declared herself. Moss plays a key role."

"What . . . what . . .?" Sinkin stammered.

"You are taken step by step into an ancient tradition," Nakuk said. "It will lead you to the core of Anu. We have a connection to our land. The enemy does not dream of it. We will fight them in ways they do not comprehend. This tradition has received new life. Our Hesha Vira rose here long ago. She speaks to us. She calls for our aid."

"She spoke to me," Sinkin said.

Keeper Nakuk leaned toward him.

"She said, 'free me.' What does this mean?"

"We are not certain. There are powerful visions of Her in Gramerem. She possesses many Stags here and in Avanchil Round. She deems us ready for her."

"Why, Keeper?" Sinkin asked.

Keeper Nakuk sat back on his haunches, "The wise debate this. Many ponder it throughout Pramath Island." He frowned and looked at the slumbering and stumbling forms of the others. "It is said our enemy grew powerful when we hemmed them in. Their wiles grew behind the Mulungu Mountains. Now it is we who are contained. Our power intensifies. We will overwhelm them in turn! We are collected in one place. We gather in assemblies far larger than in former times. Our Hesha Vira reaches out to us."

Setush moaned, and his eyes focused on them. "I hear her voice," he whispered. "She said we must go to her."

CHAPTER 49

Shuna-Shapta

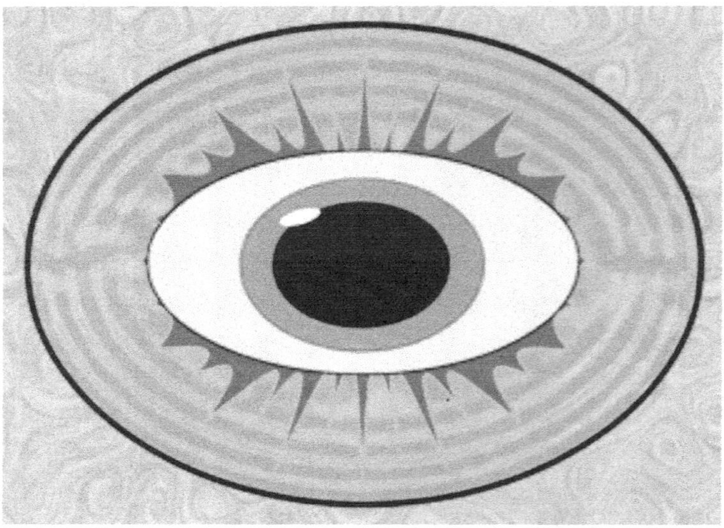

Most-ancient symbol of the Water Viewers

Day 348, Two-Week Twenty, Dolmel, the Hand, city of Bhampay.

Shuna-Shapta found her brother by one of the indoor pools in Thakadush Cluster, where several drains on the roof channelled the pouring rain outside into a series of descending baths leading to the cistern. Lush vegetation clung to the wall where the water flowed into the pool. Her beautiful brother's rich locks were bound behind his head. Being dressed in a flowing green shift with a golden cord at his waist, and having nothing but golden lines painted above and below his rich brown eyes, it was clear Shuna-Vurupta intended to go out. He was looking over a long list when smelt her arrival and turned.

"Shapta?" He peered into her eyes, "Have you slept? Have you eaten? Please . . . sit down." He unrolled a mat and spread it out. His eldest sister knelt on it in silence and beckoned him to join her.

"What is it?" she enquired, indicating his list.

"Ah! Our school sent this reminder of what we must take."

"So! In less than seventy days, it shall be the beginning of the two-week of Triple Perfection. Already you pack for your journey?"

Vurupta nodded, pointing to the schedule, "I thought I would start. We shall leave our Red Ring upon the early tide. Many other ships shall join ours for our crossing."

"How many students join you?"

"I believe fifty-one from city schools, nine from ours, including myself."

Shapta reached out and stroked the boy's shining cheek, "You shall have a care, beautiful?"

Vurupta smiled, "They shall surround us as if we were Samshep's age. We may injure each other before confronting a Suvuka."

"Hum," Shapta wore a bemused expression. "Despite my wishing you stay, I would know if you do behold them, from a considerable distance."

"Anything you wish me to say, should I meet one?"

Despite herself, Shuna-Shapta laughed aloud. "Yes! Aside from leaving you alone, tell them Hesha Vira is ours! Our wayward child must return to where she belongs." She wagged an exaggerated finger, "Tell them to stop tugging at her!"

Vurupta smiled before his face filled with concern. "We hear what you and our Masters do. I heard our mothers are carried upon litters."

Shuna-Shapta frowned and shook her head, "They carried Mother Kanla from our Master Enclave yesterday. She rests this day, as I do. I may not describe it. What we do within our Living System affects us as if we did it here. Your First Mother Dana has suffered beyond our anticipation for those working the Cubes. She must leave the chamber for anyone to carry her. She has not done so for many days now."

Vurupta hung his head, "I regret I may not help."

"I hear you dispatch tokens and notes to her. Know she treasures them! Each beneficial action helps us. Our grandmothers, and their mothers, fashioned Tatchlan. This generation of Masters must correct this." She sat back, looking at him. "You had a turn assisting our Gatherers harvesting the Sheshenara?"

"I love the quiet of their rituals. They say I did well. Have you heard they now form two complete Circles of Eight? They had lived as twos and threes throughout Thakadush."

Shuna-Shapta nodded, "A favourable development for our cluster." She smiled, "I also hear you begin to reverence our Tatchlan Faces."

"I wear a semblance of Skarashing and Neferdush," he pulled out two small figures of heads attached to a chain around his neck. Shuna-Shapta smiled as she reached out and examined the half night and half-day face of Skarashing and the broad nose hanging down below the chin of Neferdush and its tiny purple, blue and orange ringed eyes. "They have filled my dreams for many two-weeks. They tell us to find our dream Face or Faces and wear them for our journey and beyond," Shuna-Vurupta said.

"Shash! Shash!" Shuna-Shapta exclaimed. "Esteem fortifies our Living Faces. Know this aids our work! Make your adorations regular and call upon them whenever you meet challenges. You choose our Discerner of Polarities and our Face of Perception? Admirable! Master Tanas has large versions of these same two within his study."

"Does he?"

She cast him a warm and enquiring expression, "Speaking of new Circle formations, our sister Vovans has moved to her own Circle."

"Yes, our Flair blossoms more and more. Along with doing most of our body painting, they immerse themselves within the Festivals and Carnival. Follow the noise and laughter, and you shall find them!"

Shuna-Shapta smiled and nodded. "A perfect fit for her, I agree. Our First Ama is so proud of her. And what of you?" She winked at him, "I am *amazed* to learn you are fair inundated with invitations. I watch as you fill the eyes of many yearning women and men. Many times I have heard your Cry Of Joy echoing through various quarters of our cluster."

They both burst our laughing.

"I used to find such attention an annoyance," he said, "but here it possesses a generous and open face. Whilst I welcome the warmth, I do not wish to commit to one Circle as yet."

Shuna-Shapta cocked her head to one side and looked at her brother. "Vurupta, we have so little time to reflect and speak of these matters. How do you find life here within Thakadush?"

Her brother stared at her, "This takes the life we had back within our Enclave and magnifies it many times. No longer isolated Circles, we are surrounded by many and work within a larger harmony. Not just our Majastas babe, but all these Maja infants fulfill our hopes. I find my life reflected about me."

Shuna-Shapta nodded, "I hoped so, but wished to enquire. When I heard of Vovans, I wondered why you, of all of us, had not joined a Circle. The Elders tell me several circles lack a young man your age. I was thus not surprised to hear they court you night and day."

"Yes and . . . I wish to make this journey prior to my entry into a Circle."

Shuna-Shapta's eyes went wide, and she looked at him close, "Please describe what this journey to Thermistal, to the Suvuka, means to you."

Vurupta looked long at his elder sister. He went over to a raised platform where he had already begun to organize his packing. He picked up and set down random items. Shuna-Shapta waited.

"Do you recall," he began, "when Vovans was six, she created that play?"

"Of course," Shuna-Shapta smiled at the memory.

Vurupta turned and leaned on the platform, "She wrote an elaborate script, designed her costumes and painted the set. We called her 'Flair,' and the name remains with her. It took her weeks, but despite her age, she possessed an intense focus and dedication."

Shuna-Shapta nodded.

"We knew she would belong to the theatre, either upon the stage or off, as a Full Adult. During the following nine years, she has not stopped working upon her creations whilst studying and performing others. Now she is all of fifteen and has just consumed her Life Cake; she lives for our Twelve Festivals and our annual Carnival. Despite her new designation as a Ripe Adult, they recognize and entrust her with responsibilities for working upon noteworthy projects."

Shuna-Shapta remained silent.

"The results of Samshep's Depth Tests have just arrived. They confirm what we already knew about her path." He handed a document to her. "These are her results."

Shuna-Shapta glanced at it while continuing to watch him.

"We knew Samshep would go into one, or several branches of Natural Enquiry, Animal Husbandry, or perchance aspire to be a Healer. From a small child, she displayed a 'questing nose,' ever enquiring why creatures behaved as they did and how we functioned. Even as a baby, she could not stop stroking us after we shed."

Shuna-Shapta smiled.

His smile grew as he came back over and knelt. "And you!" he took her hands, "I watched you following what our mothers did and striving to work their powerful craft. You 'descended the depths' beyond all expectations. They hailed you a wonder of our time. Now you grow alongside our Majastas Babe," tears welled in his eyes. "Your name shall sound through the ages."

He abruptly stood and walked over to the platform. Keeping his back to her, he continued, "My mothers and sisters possess a focus I lack. I envy you for your clarity of vision." He wiped his face and turned to look at her, "These feelings have grown here within Thakadush," he gestured around him. "All are possessed by their circles, and their circle uses. Their words and actions speak of clarity of purpose. Their industry and dedicated application . . . emphasize my lack of direction. I found a reading years ago that captured my situation. I have copied and retained it ever since. He looked up into space and quoted, 'experience seldom is gained but by travelling within regions remote from one's home.'"

He smiled at her, "We share the good fortune of being born and living within this glorious city. All Anu has to offer arrives within our ports and from our Imperial Way to the south each day. A short walk out of Thakadush leads to fresh encounters with new wonders. For our two sisters, these journeys are more than sufficient. The depths of both callings are at hand. Crowds of Geniuses surround us! You, as our mothers, have made your prodigious voyages to know yourselves. It is for me to take my inspirational text literally and make this journey."

He sighed and looked at the verdant water wall. The rains came down hard, and a small river flowed into the pool faster than it emptied. The water spilled over the edge into the overflow rim at the base. He went over to uncover the opening into the cistern. He stared at the water, swirling down the drain.

"I must find my 'Way of Water,'" he said. "I seek my route about this blockage." He looked at the roof where the thunderous torrent could be heard. "A shocking storm shall carry me over the barriers. I am drawn to walk towards what most flee from."

Shuna-Shapta sat in silence, watching her brother. For a long time, she said nothing as he continued to watch the small flood continue to fill and empty.

"As a male, you desire to *test* yourself," she said. "The more removed the setting, the more intensive the challenge." She smiled at him, "Your fathers would understand. You have spoken to them?"

Vurupta nodded.

"Very well," Shuna-Shapta rose. "You possess more clarity than you give yourself credit for!" She embraced him hard. "I must sleep for many hours," she let go of him and held him at arm's length.

"You have hard work ahead. Thank you for taking the time…"

"Vurupta! You are our marvellous boy! Far too soon, you shall cross the Panchala Sea! When the day comes, we shall bestow upon you such a sendoff and await for your many letters. We shall count the days until you return!"

They embraced again before laughing as they discovered her body paint had come off on his clothes. Shuna-Shapta drew some water from the pool to playfully sprinkle on his paint smears.

CHAPTER 50

Seti

Day 348, Two-Week Twenty, Dolmel, the Hand, small courtyard of a house near Avatay city centre.

Seti massaged his aching temples and passed a self-conscious hand over his new shaven head. Medicinal powders covered the skin, displaying a series of blotches. He sat on a raised bench near the back corner of a small courtyard and wore the Menem priesthood's wound white garment. Hegev, Dine and the other crewmates, forming what they now called the 'Suvuka Pact,' remained mute at the news.

"Six days, and still, she will not see me?"

"No," Hegev answered.

"She betrays me as my family!" he shouted. "She dares side with my mother and aunt? She dares call my father a fool?" He started to shake as he slammed his fist repeatedly into the wall beside him. "Were it not for you," he looked at his Adept, "I would curse all women!" He seized his head and cried out in pain.

The adults exchanged glances. Dine knelt in front of Seti.

"Prophet," he hesitated, "I know her well enough to say she is sincere in what she said to Hegev and the others. These past two years, she spent many an anxious night in her concern over you. She is bound to her way and will not follow you."

"And what of you?" Seti's head snapped upright, looking into Dine's eyes. "You are bound to her, are you not?" He looked at the other crew members. "Your conflicting loyalties are clear."

Dine stood, "You left your family. Until this break with the captain, we longed to sail home. The Captain and I discussed as little as two two-weeks ago enrolling you in our school when we arrived. She planned to pay your first year's tuition and secure your lodging in a good home."

"And now, she will not speak to me!"

Hegev knelt to face him, "Her anger was directed to me! The Jefaka is towed to dry dock, and she has moved into her lodgings. We make no secret of our movements. She will know the Yamagad readies to leave with us aboard and may yet seek you out."

"That I do."

Emedin stood tall in her plain civilian shirt, pants and broad-rimmed hat inside the open door.

"As I approached, I heard you cry out," she signalled the door to the street's courtyard. "Your door was ajar, and I presumed to enter." She kept her eyes on Seti, not acknowledging the others. "May we speak?"

Seti looked at Emedin with anguished eyes. He gestured for the others to leave. Emedin stepped to one side, and they left, closing the door behind them. Emedin set a mat down in front of the boy.

"Mats!" she exclaimed. She groaned as she sat down, "We must be in the south! I ever thought it odd they choose to be close to the ground here, given the multitude of tiny monsters underfoot. Our sensible chairs would better serve to minimize infection."

"They ensure their immersion in *filth*!" Seti said. He peered at the captain. "You look different!"

Emedin gave a soft chuckle. She looked at his exposed ears, demanding more attention than ever before, "So do you."

Seti passed a light hand over his bald head and shrugged, "I had lice."

"Ah! I had them on and off over the years. We gather both welcome and unwelcome mementoes while travelling. Curious what we become accustomed to. Now you know why I keep my hair short."

Her attempt at humour failed, and they remained in awkward silence.

"You are settled in your lodgings?" Seti asked.

"Yes, better than I expected. I was delighted by the view from my balcony and did not foresee the traffic at night. I counted over two hundred carts passing under my window between the twenty-sixth and twenty-seventh hour. I may as well be in Bhampay! While lying awake, I watched the tiny lizards chasing each other across my ceiling. In time I will grow accustomed to this."

Seti gave her a faint smile, "The Jefaka is secure?"

"She was berthed, and the waters drained. For the first time in a decade, she is out of the water. She was long overdue and had generations of encrustations on her flanks. Our hull cladding is to be completely removed. While below the waterline also suffered abrasion and was worn, there was significant damage above that would have endangered us should we have encountered a flock of Chill Crystals. There is some other structural damage to be seen to, and a portion of her normal maintenance commences."

Seti nodded absently as they fell silent. Emedin kept her eyes on the boy while his eyes roved the courtyard. On occasion, a self-conscious hand touched his smooth head. Behind the wall in an adjacent yard, the sounds of cooking could be heard, attended by aromatic scents drifting over the partition. After an extended silence, his eyes briefly met hers. "You and the ship must remain here, and I must move on."

"So it seems."

"I am sorry for the trouble I caused you. Is the son of your clan's chief displeased?"

"I will manage, never fear. My regrets concerning this voyage do not include showing you kindness."

Seti stopped his wandering eyes, "You are not sorry for bringing me aboard?"

Emedin heaved a great sigh, "I said much in anger to your Adept. Most I maintain, but a few I take back. I am here. I say to you; I am glad I brought you aboard."

Tears ran down Seti's face. Emedin made to move closer, but the boy flinched, and she settled back. Seti grew agitated, and his eyes began to dart around.

"Seti," the Captain's voice calm, "more than lice caused you to shave your head."

The boy focused on her, "The four generals removed their grand helmets." His voice raised, and the words tumbled out, "They are bald every one! They say hair is a foul outgrowth, a sign of our shameful clay filled with rank creeping things, the lowest of the low, living in grime. It is an offence to them and me. They say the Suvuka are covered in hair to signify their full allegiance to . . . to," he faltered and stopped. He looked one way and the other as if attending to a conversation in two different parts of the room. "Lice live in the muck," he continued. "My head was covered in the dust of our prison. I wished to cleanse myself and live as Menem do."

Emedin pointed to the platform he sat on, "What of this? I heard you sit and stand on it alone."

"Our hosts here made it for me. I must minimize my contact with the manure of Anu. The rebel Face of Tatchlan thought to ally with me, but she tried to suck me into her steaming pit of offence! My Menem cried out and pulled me back. I reject each work of Tatchlan, including those portions rebelling against the rest! They also made a raised pallet for me to sleep. I must be surrounded by the one clean element found here. The dissenter below cannot reach me. There is one wonder I must find. I would see the mountains of the eastern coast of Rho-Jashun. I will climb them and bathe in the pure top air." His eyes became unfocused, imagining himself on a high peak.

Emedin strove to keep emotion out of her face. "I see," she said. "I hear you will sail on the Yamagad." He seemed not to hear her. "I am glad my recommendation was of some assistance," he still did not answer. She had the impression he was distracted by several conversations.

"Yes," he said after another pause, "we sail to Bhampay. I wish my Memanu Knot returned to me."

Emedin's eyes went wide, "Do the others know your plan?"

"Captain! These 'masters' dismiss me as mad. The recent arrivals from Bhampay are gone. They observed me from afar and close, speaking to those believing and disbelieving my words. They find no threat in me. I wish to retrieve my knot and go back to Rho-Jashun. I talked to the captain of this Yamagad and explained the situation."

"How can you be certain?"

"You forget they cannot hide from me! The agents' faces were twisted and deformed. They stood out in the crowds, doorways and taverns. They also walked in a way I had not seen before. They were here. They are gone. Those remaining bear the stain of their twisted system, but their alteration is mild. I must return to Rho-Jashun, where most are untouched."

"Seti, Bhampay is *filled* with those masters! The remaining population is composed of 'twisted faces!' These masters are cunning. They are renowned for their patient calculations. Their small cumulative actions overwhelm their opposition. They sacrifice their ambition, pouring their lives into what is beyond their comprehension. They defeated Nallurakon, Geltran . . . our Nebutan, and a host of lesser-known critics. Their agents may have left this island because they gathered what they required. If you sail into their capital, it will be as if you walk into a Thyma's mouth."

Seti nodded. "Bhampay will be my final crucible. My Memanu Knot will fortify me for my life's work."

His declaration startled Emedin. She stared at this remarkable boy.

"Your life's work . . ." she began.

"You do not believe in my mission! You, like the enemy, say I am mad!"

"I, like the *doctors*, say you are ill!" Emedin shot back. "I never met anyone more charismatic or more burdened with delusions. Not once have I been dishonest with you! I told you I tolerated your visions for the sake of my crew. I attempted to guide you to a new appreciation of yourself and Anu."

"You asked me to interpret your dream!"

Emedin blinked several times, "Yes, I did." She sat back on her mat with a thoughtful expression, "I admit it," she said, staring at the courtyard's faded and cracked tiles, "I fell under your enchantment. I am not surprised at the others," she indicated those waiting outside the door. "You weave a powerful fascination around yourself. Your strengths and illness combine to do this. I wanted to build your strengths and heal your illness," she hung her head in sadness.

They sat in silence for a long time before Emedin looked up, "When you return to Rho-Jashun and begin your mission, will you visit your father?"

"You mean the 'fool?'" Seti shot back.

"I mean the man who stood by you. He must fear you are dead."

Seti started at the notion. His eyes darted, and his eyelids fluttered before he became calm, and his face settled.

"You intend to speak and encourage the faithful of Rho-Jashun to resist the masters," Emedin said. "I am confident from what you told me this is what your father wanted. Because he believed in you, he let you go. Will you not grant him the knowledge you live?"

"Return?" Seti frowned. "Return to Yeplin?" He stared into space, "I hear it!" For a time, he continued to look into space, "I hear the sounds of the Salarish when it towers over our heads. I had forgotten! Deep in the fields, there was the hiss, whispers, rustlings and singing of the many creatures settling during the day. Then there was the relentless rhythms of the Thanners at night." His expression grew hard, "It is a pebble in an ocean of Salarish. Before harvest, high walls surround us, their muffling ramparts leaving just the sky above us. After, we became a spec on flat and open land subject to ceaseless winds. Either way, we were small and alone with only the ruins of our enemy for shelter."

"You once said you had clarity there," Emedin said. "You have suffered, struggled in many ways and grown. Would not returning to your home and telling your father of your time aboard Jefaka complete your journey?"

Seti's eyes went wide, "My *journey*? You speak of my mission to bring Ranvartawan to Anu as a childish adventure!" He stood and raised his arms as his voice boomed, "My father will hear my call from across Rho-Jashun. He will free himself from the blood-soaked baby-mother dolls and come to me! My path is lit by revelation and my steps guided by the Menem's calling! He hears me and waits for my feet to step on our unsullied land!"

Emedin rose with deliberation. On his raised platform, they stood near equal height. She nodded, "Very well, Seti." Her voice trembled before growing clear, "I will take my leave of you. I heard you sail with the tide tomorrow. This brought me to you at once. You must have preparations to make." She stepped away from him, off the mat, "I will endeavour to follow your career. The Jefaka will eventually follow the Yamagad to Bhampay. We must fill our hold and meet our clan representatives before journeying home. I will keep watch for your new ship, although you will be well ahead."

The fire went out of his eyes, and he shrank. He looked at her for a time, "I wish you and the Jefaka a safe journey home."

"I thank you. I have one parting word of advice for you and your company," Emedin said. "Rho-Jashun is vast, and there are many ports. Please choose the one seeming best to you, but I now advise you not to go to Wazaratcha. Jine-Piprith's son is stationed in Bhampay, and we have been in constant correspondence since the Jefaka limped into port. Master Mek also appears to have other sources of information. I have received word he is offended at your mythology about the storm and its role in taking you to the Suvuka. He cares nothing for your claim about the one hundred gates falling being the cause. Given we lost five crew, he thinks your casting our disaster as a part of your prophet's path will incur wrath among our council and citizens. You could land at your Adept's home of Kana-Moptu, but you should not remain even there. While our archipelago is an advantageous location, there are others. The captain of your new ship may advise you on this. Fare you well."

Emedin bowed and turned to the door. Those outside had heard most of the conversation and the door opened before she reached it. She looked into the eyes of Hegev then turned to Dine. She placed a hand on his shoulder and smiled.

"Come and see me, my old friend. We are not the navy where you could resign your commission. Even among merchants there is no honour in swearing new oaths while ignoring old ones. To throw away your career on the eve of its culmination would bring suffering and dishonour to all those you love at home. There will be a way for you to complete your service and then re-join this mission if you so desire. All of you," she smiled at the other crew members, "come and visit me."

She patted Dine's shoulder before turning and striding away, holding her hat against the growing wind.

CHAPTER 51

SINKIN

Day 348, during the Full Stag Rite at Gramerem Round.

Sinkin was exhausted. Instead of spending a single day and night in Gramerem Round, they watched their sixth dawn within the enclosure. The time-honoured rituals were abandoned for an astonishing mission. Two more groups, smaller than their own, had augmented them. The large Round felt crowded and smelled close, with many sweating and straining bodies. Sinkin suffered from a sense of dislocation. When he opened his eyes, he saw other New Stags engaged in an absurd looking series of clawing at the air and raking the ground. Those around him howled and rolled. Their bodies were twitching and shifting as if engaged in the battle of their lives. Some danced on the rise, but their movements were strained and distorted. The cubs moved among them, dragging piles of Dream Moss on their carts. They approached those who stopped in their battle and opened their eyes. They were fed more and returned to their former state with renewed vigour. Two cubs came up to Seti and dragged the cart to stand in front of him. He bent down and took a fresh mouthful before closing his eyes.

At once, he had no eyes and was immersed in a teeming blanket of life. His body felt huge, and his head expanded to twice the size of the rest of him. Despite this deformity, he carried it with ease as he grew light and floated in the surrounding soup. It felt hot and cold, having extreme currents of differing weights. Pools of hot blood bubbled. Beside them were other channels thick with ice. He sniffed and licked his surroundings, savouring the unfiltered juices of unrefined passion and nerve. All was wild and uncorrupted. A million births and deaths surrounded him, and he revelled in freedom from ritual, convention and herd life. This is how the Danta herds lived. It was how the Thyma packs, daring to attack individual Suvuka, lived. It was what the Suvuka might sense during the Mesmerizing Run but seldom achieved. He swam like a fish in the sea of living chaos containing no reflection or memory. Everything was instinctual and immediate.

His body thrilled to the multitude of sensations, and his ears could not contain the sounds of implacable and vivacious life surrounding him. He heard the hissing of the long entity approaching him. The vital ocean parted for it, and without thought, he reached and caught it. Thick and heavy, Hesha Vira's limb was composed of a series of rings forming uniform ridges on its sides, further covered with tiny tendrils. It stroked his face and body, feeling hot and cold as the layers of life. It wound around his paws and pulled. The grip's power was undeniable, and he pulled back with all his might. In this action, he found freedom from questions and answers. His life had brought him to this moment. He pulled and gloried in his pulling. He felt the pulling of many others and began to sing a song of no words, like the chorus he heard. He roared the howl of life, containing every victory and defeat.

"We must bring last Stags!" Sinkin rose through the blackness to these ragged words.

"Twenty approach with none behind. Seven drowned on their way. Three more were lost on the wall. The final wave is always the weakest. Those reaching the top cannot join us for days!"

"It will be too late!"

"We do what we can. Word is sent to Avanchil. Pramath's able-bodied join our struggle. Our stores of Dream Moss dwindle. This battle is heard in every ear. You and I felt more pulling than Pramath could provide. Many thousands on Thermistal join us. The last New Stags will not determine this."

Sinkin heard what sounded like paws scraping and pounding the ground in frustration.

"We are at war! We never halt our advance! Those falling repay their dams for their birth pains. They honour their sires for their training!"

"Quite inspiring, Nakuk! I always found the diviners inflated and absurd. Those engaged in battle died. Those staying behind compose ballads! Such folly will not apply here! Our New Stags must return whole to the mainland. I am certain the battle is engaged by many there."

Sinkin managed to open one eye. He could not see his Keeper, and the other he argued within the dim light of morning over him. Despite his interest, Sinkin's eye shut, and he slipped back into a deep sleep.

Day 349

The roaring of many voices wakened Sinkin. He groaned as he turned, the bones in his body crying out. While a few Suvuka lay unresponsive, most sat or stood, facing in toward the rise. Light began to fill the Round. He slept through the day and night and approached another morning.

"Word spreads! We withstand the vile little ones," the black pelt shouted out. "We wrest control of Anu's Face from them! Do your part! In ancient times New Stags were sent into battle!"

The roars rose as Sinkin fought to climb and sit beside Setush. He did not like what he heard and turned to look at his friend. He read his own exhaustion in the other's eyes.

"I must speak to you," Sinkin whispered in his ear.

Setush looked startled as they moved with painful deliberation toward the outer Round. Cubs dragged two heavy loads on their carts, the bodies of two New Stags! The foul odour they encountered at the base of Pramath's wall assailed their nostrils. None of the others noticed these two's death, but the only way to remove them meant going out the entrance.

"What is it?" Sinkin asked when they reached the mound. "I woke to bellows."

"There is news from the mainland," Setush answered. "Visions of Hesha Vira grow. They say Suvuka across Thermistal joins our struggle."

Sinkin rubbed his weary head on the mound. "You swam in the ocean? You pulled the living trunk?"

Setush nodded. "They say it is one of Hesha Vira's thousand limbs! Our enemy has uprooted her. She strives to rejoin Anu. We keep her from destruction."

Sinkin looked back at the group of Elders and Adult Stags, including their Keeper, Nakuk. "What would my Herdmaster say?" He turned around to look at his friend, "Setush! We were drugged for days! What was this struggle? Where did we go? What did we do there?"

"Such questions have no meaning," Setush said. His eyes were glowing at the recollection. "We discover a life's new layer. We live close to our source. There, I am magnificent and free!"

Sinkin frowned, "Setush, I felt like you. What you say is true. This turbulent ocean reveals the roots of life. Do you also recall your blindness?"

Setush shifted before nodding.

"Why were we blind?" Sinkin asked. "We are vital creatures of Anu. We possess what we need. We work it at will. This is our mastery. Communicating and working together is our power. Our eyes are key to our strengths. We pick out the tiniest midge flying toward us. We spy herds scaling the mountains through the mists of a days' journey. Our eyes bring us understanding."

Setush looked at him, "Do you suggest they," he indicated those on the rise, "withhold something?"

Sinkin shook his head, "I suggest we remain in the dark. Soon we will swim back. We will greet our herd mates. Suppose they know nothing of this? Can you imagine their faces when we describe this? What would they say to our taking up this call of Keeper Nakuk? How can we act on such blindness?"

Setush looked long at his friend, "It is beyond ten days since we swam. They will begin to fear us lost." He turned to look at those on the rise, "We should speak to our Keeper. We can do no more. We must leave. Our two herds sacrificed much to bring us here. We cannot delay."

"We are Full Stags. We completed our Four Paws. We must rejoin our herds. Keepers are guardians and guides, not overseers. Gramerem Round was intended as the final rite. We were to learn about Pramath's history. I must clear my head of this place. How do we judge what action to take? My eyes are open. My thoughts demand answers. I am more than instinct, zeal and endurance."

Several young cubs struggled. Piles of offal they had gathered weighed down their carts. Others came in the entrance bearing new steaming piles of Dream Moss.

"Young Buck!" Sinkin called out to one of the cubs as they approached with their foul load, "you toil long on our behalf. We will assist you."

"We are forbidden to disturb you," the cub said in a small voice. The others did not look at either of the New Stags.

"Cub, I order two of you on my back. Two go on my dear comrade's back. We will pull your carts out of the Round." Sinkin lay down, and Setush followed his lead. The cubs hesitated until the lead one nodded and limped over to Sinkin and clambered onto his back. The others followed and when secure, Sinkin and Setush rose, exchanged glances at the wretched cargo they must haul. Each gripping one edge of the cart with their teeth, they pulled. The chorus of roaring had risen, and their scrapings were lost in the growing din. They removed the carts around the inner edge of the mound and out the entrance. The exhausted cubs clung to their backs. Once outside, they looked round to where a group of dams sat beside other cubs.

"What are you doing?" one called out to them.

The New Stags dragged their loads to them.

"These brave young bucks were exhausted," Sinkin began after letting go of his load. "I chose to assist them. I was not worked thus at their age."

"It is their rite of passage," one replied. "Bucks here have their own trials. Living here, they reach your status another way. We are not permitted inside the Round. They wait their turn to serve them with eagerness."

"Have they ever done so for six days running? Do they savour bringing out the dead?" Sinkin asked.

The dam cast a glance at the two bodies and bent her head. "No. Something dark and powerful grows there." She looked at Sinkin with enquiring eyes.

"I cannot say," Sinkin said as he lay down and allowed the worn-out cubs to climb down off him. "Distance is necessary to see a large thing clear. We must continue our journey. Our herds wait for our return. It is wrong for us to delay. I take it this path leads down to the shore?"

The dam nodded, "You must follow as it turns to go south. It will lead you along the shore. You will be between the ocean and the high cliffs. You enter a day's journey north of where most of you arrived. Stone piles mark where you begin your swim. There will be dry food stored. A small stream flows near where you enter. You must drink deep. Rest the night before your crossing."

Setush and Sinkin bent their heads to her. The chorus of roars behind them increased inside the Round. Setush and Sinkin began to lope along the path the crowds of New Stags travelled a few days earlier without a backward glance. Behind them, standing watching their progress, Keeper Nakuk stood in the entrance of the Round.

CHAPTER 52

Shuna-Shapta

Icon for what is known as the 'Common Desire'

Day 349, Two-Week Twenty, Dolmel, the Hand, within Tatchlan.

Before the astonished eyes of a multitude of Invocates, the Principal Face of Hesha Vira hung over the storm as a flaming planet. Vast flocks of her Secondary Faces circled about her. Indatubangas heaved and swelled below her. Bits of the bitter sphere of raw life broke free. They spun out of control into the usually calm waters of Amanavata, creating a more massive orbiting cloud swirling around the rebellious Principle Face. Whirlpools continued to open on the surface of Indatubangas as if attempting to breach the barriers. They grew and widened before losing their momentum and coming to an explosive end, sending more debris into the turbulent atmosphere. The smaller Faces dodged these projectiles, and they raced on frantic missions from one Principle Face to another.

Many thousands of Tolku Masters, from across the continent, circled the Face of Crude and Raw Life and her servants. The other eleven Principle Faces and their attendant Secondary Faces were also present, a few near and more far off. Their bobbing and turning movements, an exaggeration of the 'Tatchlan Eddy,' indicated their agitation. Thousands of red and yellow striped tendrils radiated out from Hesha Vira, most going down to the surface of Indatubangas to latch onto the distinct forms of Suvuka, working in vast herds. They pulled on her to bring her back down to her realm. The other Faces and the assembled Tolku Masters had latched onto her to raise her. Hesha Vira's tendrils failed to find purchase among the proximate trembling knot formation of dissenting Tolku.

Until recently, both Masters Kanla and Tanas had a turn lifting the rebellious Face to little effect. They now hovered some distance away. "Tanas!" Master Kanla shouted at him over the noise, "have you examined the knot this day?"

He glanced into the distance where it lay and accompanied her back to look at it. Beneath the Knot was what appeared to be a frightful new apparition. It seemed the surface beneath the Knot formed a giant pattern of a simple head without eyes, ears or nose. Instead, all it had was a gaping mouth and protruding swollen tongue.

"What is it?" Master Kanla enquired.

He shook his head in wonder. "So, this shall be its ultimate expression!" He glanced at Kanla and pointed down at the black and red configuration surrounding the Knot. "This is the most solidified and extreme formation of what shall be known as the Common Desire."

"What?" Master Kanla exclaimed, "how may this obscenity be The Common Desire? How could such lovely fluids harden into such ugliness?"

"Whilst the Common Desire commonly maintains a fluid state, it may coalesce into complex forms at moments of challenge or inspiration. Future generations of Invocates, Operants, and Majastas shall spend much time pondering the nature of the Common Desire's varied forms. Most of these shall not be shocking, yet our Uluvatu Masters originally described it as assuming something approaching this dreadful visage. As such, it is an unconscious mass with a single craving, to blindly consume all. This is the raw face of the Tolku within Indatubangus at its most vile."

"So, The Common Desire devolves back to its original state?" Master Kanla exclaimed.

"Indeed," Master Tanas replied, "without the cultivation, elegance and refinement provided by Tatchlan, this is what the Common Desire ever tends to."

He looked back to Hesha Vira, "Whilst the Common Desire may be schooled within normal circumstances, our challenge lies there."

They moved back towards the main focus of chaos, and Master Kanla shook her head. "Tanas! All female Masters approach our seventh two-week of pregnancy! Our babes clamour to be born ahead of their time! How may our Grand Work dysfunction to this extent? A Principle Face declares war upon us! Despite all Masters focusing together, we do not achieve efficacy!"

Tanas looked at the mother of Shuna-Shapta. Even within the Living System, she was clearly pregnant, although here it manifested as a tiny second face dwelling beneath her adult face. Though blank in expression, it possessed vital energy.

"This flaw magnifies as a tear," he shouted back. "Tatchlan rushes ahead to fortify itself. Because of our efforts, Hesha Vira is unable to destroy what generations of Masters built."

"She shall destroy herself! Blind Indatubangas perceives her as another agent of what thwarts and frustrates its crude existence! How may Hesha Vira not know this?"

"She is terrified. She does not understand herself or her place. We laid many burdens upon her without sufficient guidance. When she wakened, she became alarmed at the contradictions of her existence."

"What shall we do? This pulls all apart! We stand just equal to the blind Suvuka! Fresh members fortify their core group whilst we approach exhaustion. Their primal rage proves a match for us! How is it mindless chaos may overcome generational order with such ease?"

"We could attempt to turn Hesha Vira. We know the ultimate key to correcting errors manifesting within our Faces entails approaching them from behind, where their inner workings are evident," Master Tanas had to shout over the growing noise. "Stay!" he gestured to a new movement amongst the eleven other Faces. "Our Faces seek their own remedy!"

Humma, the fourth of the Principle Faces, now rested on one side of Hesha Vira. His long curving Face came to points at the top and bottom, his skin of red and yellow beads complimented his fiery sister Hesha Vira's flesh. On the other side, one of Master Tanas's patron Faces, Neferdush, arrived. Her long nose, signifying her powers of perception, hung far below her jaw.

"At last!" Master Kanla called out.

Naprahath, displaying a Complete's features, moved beside Humma on one side and Muramal, his eyes tight shut, moved to the open side of Neferdush. Each Face came to rest in their place, creating the linear sequence. Alatanda's huge broad Face stood at one end, and Hashahanu's small Face, composed of two faces either side of one head, at the other.

"We are indebted to our ancients for imparting such flexibility to them," Master Tanas said. "I have learned this is named the 'Line of Faces Formation.'"

"What is this 'Line?'" Master Kanla was interrupted by a series of loud cracks. The Faces spun and fell away from each other. Kanla and Tanas stood, their mouths wide open in shock. Voices from the other Masters echoed in consternation.

"Our Line failed!" Master Kanla exclaimed. Master Tanas continued to watch as the defeated Faces regained their equilibrium and hovered in scattered grouping either side of the defiant Hesha Vira. The Secondary Faces swirled about their Principle Faces as the angry soldiers issuing out of a disturbed Ketukku nest.

"What are we to do?" Master Kanla was near tears. "How did none anticipate this? Our Resplendent Work has come alive too soon! Our Majastas is not *ready*!"

Master Tanas turned to look at Kanla. "Despite their wisdom, the ancient Masters could not foresee this dilemma. Our Living Orb has to quicken prior to our Majastas emerging. Yet, a Majastas alone may master this turbulent landscape. This sudden and violent emergence has produced this unlooked-for result. None ever dreamt of Hesha Vira losing connection, but for Hesha Vira's shocking insolence, we would have maintained our Quickened System until Thakadush-Satwa had her Life Cake ceremony."

"Would the 'Cluster' or 'Wheel Formation,' such as we witnessed when they wakened within the presence of my daughter and our Majastas babe, be more robust than this Line?"

Master Tanas shook his head, "The Wheel Formation displayed their harmony. This opened her eyes and sparked Hesha Vira's rebellion. We shall not witness our Wheel again until the resolution of this matter."

Master Kanla looked in desperation at the deteriorating situation. "Our grandmothers and their mother's dreams come undone! What remains for us?"

Master Tanas pondered, "We must attempt a 'matching' of our Twelve Faces."

Master Kanla stared at him, "'Matching?' What may this mean? And what of this 'Line?' Where do these unfamiliar terms reside within our traditions?"

"Myself and others commissioned our Esteemed Librarians with many tasks at the onset of this crisis. We are now instructed on arcana once deemed reserved for the future. The Faces themselves would have revealed these formations and other secrets to our full Majastas. Alas! Even with Shuna-Shapta's aid, this is not yet possible. It appears our Uluvatu Masters fashioned our Principle Faces to one template to assume a series of 'formations' as required by rare circumstance. We may behold Alatanda presenting the broadest visage and Hashahanu the smallest; thus, our Twelve Faces are ordered according to their size to each other. We all know large Alatanda awoke first and small Hashahanu last."

He was forced to near shout, "Our Esteemed Librarians and Venerable Scholars have poured over our founding texts and many subsidiary annals long predating our Duamang Age. They now instruct us, prior to the Suvuka invasion, our grandmothers and their mothers 'matched' or 'stacked' our slumbering Faces within their order, from largest to smallest, one atop the other for a massive alignment. This Formation was referred to it as the 'Mountain of Faces.' The strength of this arrangement exceeds the Line, or another Formation known as the 'Arch' and would seal Hesha Vira to her brothers and sisters. Only then may they collectively dissuade her from her present course."

Master Kanla shook her head in amazement, "Why am I innocent of all this?"

"I shared your innocence of this aspect of the Faces and how they function, but one two-week ago. I have since learned of this and the other marshallings beside the Wheel or what our ancients referred to as the 'Spoke Formation.' Our ancients completed this 'Mountain' procedure to their satisfaction. Enacted for a different issue, those involved did not foreknow it being needed again until a future Majastas possessed our Grand Work. There has not been time to inform you of these findings. We have just witnessed our Faces attempting to rectify this of themselves by employing one of these Formations without a Majastas directing them."

"Our Majastas is not *ready*! Shuna-Shapta lies exhausted! Our babe clings to her as to a log bobbing upon the open ocean, and I fear for them both! We must not rouse them too soon. If their strength fails, how are we to accomplish this or any 'Formation' without them? Our knowledge and skill are thwarted by blind ignorance! For years we walked with ease between our sleeping seedlings. Now they burst forth, and we find ourselves within a blazing thicket!"

Master Tanas looked at the trembling Hesha Vira in the distance, "Our ancients accomplished this whilst our Faces slept. How are we to quieten them during this riot?"

A deep rumbling in Indatubangas interrupted them, as the Suvuka below gained momentum and pulled Hesha Vira toward them.

CHAPTER 53

Shuna-Shapta

Pictured: Primary Epoch icon for the Mountain of Faces Formation. Within Tatchlan the Faces fit neatly atop one another. This image ensures all are visible

Day 349, Two-Week Dolmel, the Hand, Thakadush Cluster in the city of Bhampay, later the same day.

Shuna-Shapta sat in a daze with Thakadush-Satwa curled in her lap. Both teetered on the brink of exhaustion on the raised dais within the large central Thakadush Cluster chamber. Her mother, Master Tanas, and several other Masters sat in a circle on the floor around the dais, overcome by their weariness. Their Living Instruments were locked inside their shells on either side. The numb Invocate Master Servants hardly noticed as members of Thakadush Cluster gently bid them rise so their sore and weary bodies could be once again coated in various unguents before settling them on fresh thick mats.

The cluster had gathered a set of twenty of their healthiest Nara Plants and their attendant Shesha creatures on their stands to encircle the dais and the surrounding Masters. Whenever a Nara fruit ripened, a Yellow Clad, and Orange Masked, Gatherer fed it to a waiting Shesha. When the creature had digested the fruit and emitted its new batch of Sheshenara Nectar, the Gatherer siphoned it off, combined it with a variety of other fortifying salves, and served it to the Masters. They drank without tasting or even knowing they drank. Of late, most Sheshenara Nectar went to Shuna-Shapta and the infant Majastas. The Gatherers of the cluster monitored the plants night and day. They harvested, fed and siphoned the Sheshenara by their own hands alone. The Masters, living on this diet, had seen their stays within the Living System lengthen during the past few days. It had significantly helped them fight their growing fatigue until now. The remainder of the chamber was filled by a portion of the cluster, taking turns in remaining in readiness to assist in any way they could.

Many hands reached out to rest on this circle of once vital Masters, assisting them to remain upright.

* * *

Shuna-Shapta snapped awake. She hovered over the surface of the Living Orb of Tatchlan. The surface churned with a dynamism she had not witnessed before. Despite their dilemma, it was clear a growing power and clarity possessed the Resplendent Work. She looked up at the horizon as a black shape approached her at speed. She immediately realized it was not a Secondary Face but the Principle Face of Alatanda. She could not say how, but she knew their relationship had changed. She realized this was because there was a face behind her own. The infant Majastas looked out through her eyes. Alatanda stopped before them, and his benign 'Black

Moon Face,' with his polished long blue lips and wide eyes, was no larger than Shuna-Shapta's head. Clouds of moisture rose from the surface of the Living Orb as Alatanda did something wondrous. He began to turn. Shuna-Shapta had long known that, except for specialized maintenance or at the utmost end of need, no Principle or Secondary Face suffered being beheld from behind.

To reveal their back face was to expose their inner workings. Shuna-Shapta had never witnessed this mystery and found its living intricacy hard to interpret, but in an instant, the configuration resolved into something entirely different. What now formed inside this 'black moon' was an impression of her own face, as with the Jezin impression on the outer cluster walls. Without thought, both Shuna-Shapta and Thakadush-Satwa reached out and took hold of what had become the glittering black mask of Alatanda and slowly drew it towards them. The mask fit onto Shuna-Shapta's face like a second skin. Her eyes looked through his, and her nostrils breathed through his. Through his eyes, they gained unimaginable depth and insight. Wearing the Bridge to all Faces as a mask, they knew what must be done.

* * *

"Of course!" Shuna-Shapta called out. The other Masters started and looked at her. She held her hands out before her face and brought them to her ears. A look of amazement and sudden peace washed over her. Master Tanas signalled Master Kanla not to say anything as they peered at her in fascination.

"Of course! Of course!" she shouted out.

Thakadush Cluster's usual cacophony beyond the central chamber came to a sudden halt. The rest of the hall quickly filled as all, including the weakened Masters, stood to view Shuna-Shapta and the baby. The dais was high enough; most could still see Shuna-Shapta's head and shoulders. Thakadush-Satwa had buried her face in Shuna-Shapta's belly, gripping her tight. All those present began to feel their insides trembling.

Shuna-Shapta laughed long before calling out, "Skarashing!" After a brief pause, she reached out her hands and drew them back to her ears. Her face went through an intense series of different expressions. The Masters and cluster mates watched in complete silence.

"Naprahath!" her voice now took on increasingly amplified qualities, as if several voices called. She repeated her gestures, and again her face transformed. She reached out again and said, "Come, Humma!"

Most of the Masters and Invocates gasped.

"What is she doing?" Master Kanla hissed, her face had gone pale, and her dots stood out in sharp relief in concern for her daughter. Master Tanas shook his head in amazement. "Wait," he said.

Shuna-Shapta brought her hands to her ears, and her face became radiant. With exaggerated care, she held out her arms. Her face became tender and solicitous as if calling a lover. "Hesha Vira, come to me."

Each jaw dropped, and eyes went wide as Shuna-Shapta's hands caressed the open air and drew them back to her face. Her expression became one of stillness and peace. She held her hands to her ears and did nothing but breathe. Finally, she put out her arms and smiled at the air, calling the name "Neferdush!"

"Majastas Be! Majastas Be! Shash! Shash! Shash!" Master Tanas whispered as tears began streaming down his face. He turned to Shuna-Shapta's mother, saying in a trembling voice, "She and Thakadush-Satwa form the 'Mountain of Faces!' They match them from largest to smallest, as our Majastas alone may, as 'Masks of Power.' They wear our Faces and access Tatchlan at the deepest level. She has brought peace to Hesha Vira and wakens and aligns them." He stopped and began to weep, his large frame shaking with emotion.

Master Kanla looked back at her daughter, who appeared to be slipping Neferdush over Hesha Vira and those behind, to her face. Shuna-Kanla looked at the baby. The child tried to bury herself in Shuna-Shapta's body. Master Kanla wondered how the baby could continue breathing; yet, she did.

"We are Servants this day," Tanas whispered beside her. Shuna-Kanla turned to look at him.

Shuna-Shapta called out, "Muramal!"

"She wears six of our Principle Faces as Masks," Tanas whispered.

"Muramal is the seventh. She shall wear them to achieve their final wakening and complete integration. Thereafter, when she enters our Resplendent Work, she shall invoke or call any or all at will. They shall stand within her reach, and she shall don each one, or any combination, suiting her purposes. She assumes the proportions of our Faces and shall stride across Tatchlan as her domain. Our Shapta . . . acts as our Majastas."

"Gavaduru!" Shuna-Shapta's voice had grown powerful and sounded like a small chorus as she reached out and brought the eighth Principal Face to rest on her face and overtop the others.

"Kava-Kura!" she called out and stuck out her tongue as the Face of Vital Delight did. Everyone laughed at the sight, easing the nearly unbearable tension of the cluster. Shuna-Shapta brought the ninth Face to hers and took several sharp breaths before crying out in sudden bliss. After a few calming breaths, she again reached out, calling out the Tenth Face's name, "Vashivonos!"

Sighs and murmurs rose among Thakadush Cluster. A few began to dance. The twelve Gatherers and their six attendants, living in two Circles of Eight within the cluster, approached on silent feet and began to move the Nara and Shesha back to a nearby wall. Others with exaggerated care moved the Living Instruments to join them. Members of Thakadush started to move closer to Shuna-Shapta and their Majastas baby. Masters Kanla and Tanas had their hands taken by children who had been sent to accompany them to a secondary platform set to the dais's right. Thick sets of mats were laid out for the Servants to sit and observe.

"Sukakap!" came the name of the eleventh Principle Face. Shuna-Shapta stood, her voice amplified. As Thakadush-Satwa clung to her, she began to bend and twist her body. Her face flowed through an endless series of expressions. Eleven personalities now shared her body with her, and each shifted to join the whole.

"Hashahanu!" She reached out her arms for the Twelfth and final Principle Face, composed of two heads attached at the back, one eye looking out and the other looking back upon a Wise Spider body. Once in place, Shuna-Shapta began to leap and shake her arms and legs. The cluster erupted in jumping and hooted their excitement. Shuna-Shapta began to sing out the opening lines of the chant to call a Living

Instrument. "Yom Sha! Yom Sha!" she cried, and the cluster called it back to her.

"Vuna Sana Ya!"

The cluster repeated the call.

"Wonal Chinnal Ya!

"Sosu Yaso Jas!

"Pana Musha Shay!

"Sen! Sen! Sen!

"Suv! Suv! Suv!

"Sha! Sha! Sha!" she completed the call. She paused, and the group slowed to watch her. She licked her lips and shook her hands and feet as a dancer. She filled her lungs and ran off the invocation in quick succession,

"Yom Sha! Yom Sha!

"Vuna Sana Ya!

"Wonal Chinnal Ya!

"Sosu Yaso Jas!

"Pana Musha Shay!

"Sen! Sen! Sen!

"Suv! Suv! Suv!

"Sha! Sha! Sha!"

The cluster began to echo it back, and when she finished, they continued to chant as they began to dance, the entire cluster swarmed to encircle and repeat the invocation. Shuna-Shapta grew quiet and held her arms out either side. As the cluster continued to move in a streaming circle and chant, Shuna-Shapta began to spin her arms outstretched. The baby buried her face in Shuna-Shapta's chest.

"We should return to Tatchlan," Kanla said, turning to Tanas, "She requires our assistance."

Tanas shook his head, "My strength ebbs. Shapta knows what to do, as do our united Faces. Hesha Vira has found peace. The roaring surface of Indatubangas shall grow calm. We must stand aside so our true Master may complete our task."

Mi-Yang, the second wife of Shuna-Shapta's Circle of Eight, approached the platform. "Mother Kanla, our Circle of Eight and the secondary Circles, shall surround Shapta."

Tanas nodded encouragement. The others sat mute in amazement. With some difficulty, Kanla got down, and the two women made their way through the boisterous cluster into the calm space surrounding Shuna-Shapta. She had stopped spinning and watched them approach.

"Ama," she whispered. Kanla kissed each of her wet cheeks.

"Ama, they separate and form the Wheel as I saw them at the birth of the one-hundredth Maja." She looked at the upturned face of Thakadush-Satwa. The baby reached up, and Shuna-Shapta brought her beside her face. The baby lay her tiny head on Shuna-Shapta's shoulder and fell asleep. The two women laughed at this. Shuna-Shapta found her knees yielding, and she sank back down on her mat, her mother beside her. Mi-Yang came and sat on her other side, and their six men formed a close circle. Shuna-Shapta's original Circle surrounded this group. In the shifting and jostling formed an interlacing of arms and legs to bring them into a secure and comforting whole enveloping her and the tiny Majastas. She fell into a deep sleep as the cluster continued to stomp their feet and sing.

CHAPTER 54

SINKIN

Day 353, east coast of Mushumafal Peninsula, Thermistal.

Two heads!" a voice rang out. It echoed off the hills, followed by the sounds of hundreds of Suvuka roused. "To the north!" The group galloped along the shore. When they arrived, they found another spotter standing on his hind legs and pointing out to sea. The panting herds strained to look across the turbulent waters. The tide was out, so they stepped on the newly exposed sand and rock, glistening and teeming with sea life left behind. Another voice confirmed the sighting, "Two heads!"

The black specs bobbing out in the distance grew in size. The group moved as one out to meet them. Hiratak and Morakav were hopeful.

"It should be them!" Morakav breathed close to his friend.

"They are late!" Hiratak fumed. "The entire wave should have returned! Soon the next wave will arrive!"

"You can guess what has delayed them," Morakav said.

They both began swimming out to meet them. As they approached, Hiratak and Morakav cried out in recognition. It was them! They turned back to allow the New Stags to complete their return swim. They found the bottom and stepped away enough to permit their New Stags to do the same. Sinkin and Setush found their footing and let out happy yelps and howls. They emerged and gave mighty shakes. While glad to see these two, many looked out on the waters for more.

"Come away," Hiratak said under his breath.

Sinkin and Setush came ashore. Both seniors noted their wide strides out of the water, remembering their own difficulty returning after their swim.

"Follow us," Hiratak said in a quiet voice. They loped back along the shore, reaching the spot where the two had begun their swim twenty days before. Hiratak led them back along the same path they had taken to enter the sea. The rest of the Durka and Makusk herds formed close around the New Stags. The remaining herds held back.

"The hills look different at sea," Setush breathlessly said to Morakav. "We thought we had lost our way. Your calls guided us."

The others led Sinkin and Setush to a pile of fruit and other dried food.

"This will ease your thirst," Morakav said. "There is no fresh water here. We will find the last few rivers exiting the Jaladanu Mountains. They will refresh you before we re-enter Kukernef Desert."

"Do not fear!" Hiratak answered their expressions at the naming of the desert. "There is no urgency to our journey. We need not enter the desert for many weeks. You will be rested and ready. The mountains move up this side of Mushumafal. They shield us more than on the western coast. We are far north already. Jabun Isthmus is closer than you know."

"Our pace will be set by you," Morakav said. "We may amble back if you wish."

They laughed, and the two New Stags began to attack the food. At last, Sinkin looked up from his feast.

"We cannot eat this mountain! Did you gather all this?"

"No," Hiratak said. "We all add to this pile for the returning Stags. It will grow until the last one returns. Many more come behind you. They will feed on it also."

While they ate, members of their herds turned to look back at the rest. Most stood looking out to sea. The spotters spread out along the shore and far beyond sight in each direction, watching for those coming in far from where they left.

"No others started when we did," Setush said. The herds turned back to look at them.

"We parted from the rest at Gramerem Round," Sinkin said. "They kept us there for six days."

"What?" Hiratak said. He looked at Morakav, "It was one day and night for us. They had a song about it."

"Did none returning tell you?" Sinkin asked.

"Custom says returning Stags are surrounded by their herds. They withdraw from those continuing to wait," Hiratak said. "Two did not survive the return swim." The others bent their heads. "This has added to the groups' distress. Among those returning are murmurs of novelties. We have lived on hope alone."

Sinkin bowed his head to the ground, "We regret our delay." Between them, Sinkin and Setush described their journey, including Gramerem Round. When Sinkin recounted the conversation he overheard between Keeper Nakuk and another Keeper, Hiratak fought to control his anger.

"Shameful! They forget their place! Those Keepers lose their way! They abandon the dignified and peaceful rituals? They replace them with madness?"

Morakav nodded, "It is true. Once you had left, we spoke of our ordeals to reach Pramath. Each related what we did.

We remember details differently, but we agreed on essentials. Your experience is like ours until you arrive at Gramerem. We all remember the same rites, the one thing you say are overthrown."

"The Keeper told me this was the original tradition," Sinkin said. "They revive it with Hesha Vira's return."

"What you describe sounds more like a melee," Morakav said.

"Black Dream Moss!" Hiratak near shouted. "These potent medicines are reserved for vital work. They are not for Stags recovering from the Four Paws!"

"Herdmaster," Setush said to Morakav, "they said the visions of Hesha Vira were known here. They said a new war had begun where each side contended for Hesha Vira. She sought us out. She wants us to pull her back to Anu."

Members of Durka and Makusk exchanged glances. "We had dreams," Morakav said. "Even our Hiratak here had one," he smiled at the other remaining expressionless. "Many had visions of her Face calling to them. Some of the others fell into trances. They said . . . they pulled in the black place."

"Those trances stopped?" Setush asked.

"Yes," answered Morakav. "What does it mean?"

Setush glanced at Sinkin, "From Gramerem, we ran toward the place of monuments." The others nodded in memory of the narrow corridor between the wall and the sea. "We slept on the way. We dreamt wonderful dreams. Neither of us understands them. The battle is over. Hesha Vira is altered. She now shines. She is larger and fuller. We do not know if Gramerem accomplished this. Her many limbs no longer seek us out."

"We began our swim," Sinkin continued. "The sea was gentle. The waves did not wash over us. Fish near swam into our mouths."

"I recall how exhausted we were on the way," Setush said. "After our swim, we had to scale the wall. This time, the sea pushed us. It seemed half as wide."

Sinkin nodded, "Gramerem Round will be silent. The rest will soon return," he gestured toward the ocean beyond their view.

"I also regret our delay," Setush declared. "Even so, I wish we had stayed an extra day. I must discover what happened at Gramerem."

"More fell in stupor. More died," Sinkin said in growing heat. "The rest stumbled until they fell. The Keepers' rants fell on a sea of closed ears."

"You do not know this!" Setush countered. The others sat in silence. "The rest may have pulled Her free! Now She sinks into Anu. Perhaps Her new fullness is a sign of freedom and victory."

"My friend, your summaries lack foundation," Sinkin replied. "Those to come will tell us if they recall anything." He turned to look at the rest, "I did not like how the Keepers acted. I would hear their reasons. I would listen to what other Keepers say. Keeper Datal of Avanchil would not do as Keeper Nakuk did."

Sinkin's words moved Hiratak. "My boy, you were so devoted to Her. You left Gramerem early despite your Keeper's wishes. Why did you abandon Her call? I thought you would give everything to Her."

Sinkin sat on his haunches and smiled at his Herdmaster. "We were blind," he began. "We were changed when we entered Her realm. We became monsters of the deep. Her realm is raw, pristine and unrefined. Wildness and vigour range free in unruly abundance. Her powerful limbs demanded we pull. I did, and all thought left me. The pulling overshadowed everything. She . . ." He understood more in the telling, "She robbed us of reflection."

"Her need was great!" Setush interjected. "She struggled in desperation. She called on those opposing our enemy."

"When has this been the way of Anu?" Sinkin countered. "She is unforgiving, yes. Yet, she sustains us when we meet her with open eyes! She waits for our bodies to return to her. Anu is impassive during our calamities. Anu never demanded sacrifice!" He looked at Hiratak, "Hesha Vira was native to this black ocean. She was not life entire. She dwelt there and possessed many powers. I think She grew out of life."

"What are you saying?" Setush demanded.

"I said I required distance to judge this large matter," Sinkin said.

"And what do you now see?" an angry Setush asked. "Do you suggest She is *not* Anu's Face? Do you now claim she is a deception of the enemy? Has she lied to us? Why would she do so? How is it you see all this? How is it the Keepers of Pramath remain blind?"

"I cannot answer your rush of questions. I continue to ponder what we saw and did not see."

"If we sank beneath Anu, we would be blind!" Setush declared. "All our other senses were alive! We felt the truth of our lives! It shouted in our ears! It filled our nostrils! Hesha Vira dwells in this 'ocean' of depth. Perhaps our valued 'sight' and 'insight' are of little worth there. Perhaps it is they separating us from a full life."

"'Perhaps' becomes your favoured word," Sinkin replied unmoved. "I do not dispute your observation. We may discover a profound truth. Our conceptions may hinder us from knowledge. Our ideas may block our living. What do you propose? Are we to live on Dream Moss? Will our lives be spent in blindness?"

"Black Dream Moss was not our only approach. We witnessed Her in Avanchil Round. When we ran She came with our honest labour. I had glimpses of Her during our return."

"Was she content?"

Setush hesitated, "Yes, She rose in front of me. She was larger and fuller. Her vision was clear. Her presence was defined."

"So we remain blind to what happened," Sinkin said. "Why did we pull until some died? Why did this struggle end? What was the outcome? Did we win or lose the battle?" He looked at Hiratak, "I was compelled to pull. A feral peace possessed me. The Keepers without meaning to opened my eyes. How did they come to such certainty? I saw Stags following the battle cry without question. I am not afraid to fight. I will know what I fight for."

"Yeeeaaaaoooo!" Setush shouted. "Battles are not won by philosophers! We will learn all in time. I will wait before drawing conclusions. Taaaoooo! I do not recognize you, Sinkin! First, you embrace this revelation. Now you throw it over! I am slower in my enthusiasm. I remain steadfast in my convictions once I come to them."

"I will place myself between our heroes," Morakav said. "Possessing such vigour after your swim reveals great power. Your last obligation is to regain your strength. For this, you must rest. We are here for many days. The others follow with their own news. Perhaps we will find some willing to share their versions of these events."

The new Stags bowed at this. Sinkin bent to pick one last piece of fruit while Setush moved with resolution away and made ready to sleep. The rest of Makusk Herd gathered around him. Morakav gave Hiratak one glance as he joined them. Durka Herd watched their young champion calmly pulverize and swallow his food.

CHAPTER 55

Seti

Day 363, Two-Week Twenty-One, Andura, the Ocean, outside the Red Ring harbour of Bhampay

Seti stood at the prow of the Yamagad. The Bhampaian harbourmaster, bedecked in ornate robes and ornaments, took temporary command at the wheel to guide the ship through the Inner Harbour's intricacies once they entered the Red Ring. The Yamagad tacked through the blustering winds toward the broad gap between the immense red walls where a series of high-water marks could be seen. Seti's exposed head and neck had a Nu burn, and his white robe was weathered from fourteen days at sea.

The Panchala so swiftly carried them Seti wondered if it was possible ever to defy her and travel east and south along this coast.

"The surf," he said to Hegev, "it sounds different."

"Yes," Hegev answered, "the ancients who built this Red Ring used marvellous craft to make it endure. Its true power lies in its ability to give with the surf and spring back. This produces the sound you hear termed the 'Red Ringing.'"

Seti listened to the distinct sound before asking, "So the name is for this sound, the wall's colour, and its shape? This 'Red Ring' runs around the city?"

"In a near-perfect circle," she said.

"This part is rooted deep beneath the ocean?"

"Very deep, it is said the walls spread out beneath the surface. Perhaps they are already below us! The land rises steeply at the shore and continues to rise inland gently. The wall maintains its height throughout, still high enough for sizeable carts to pass under its main gate on the far side. It is said there is no measurable difference in its height here to its height on land. I am told it rises near as high as this at the shore before diminishing as the land rises to meet it."

"Why not follow the contours of the land? Why go to the trouble of making its height uniform on land and sea?"

"There may be a practical reason for this," she gestured at it. "We are acquainted with Panchala's rare temper. One reason the city is so ancient is it has survived occasional calamities washing other coastal cities away. I believe the truth is pride and power made the Ring. There is no city like Bhampay, and this is one of many distinguishing features. It is also the official gateway to the state of Statos-Vey, and its capital, Upata-Shepsus. Its famed gate lies nine hundred and seventy-seven andas to the west and south of the city in the vast natural formation known as the 'Primary Mountain Circle.' This colossal arrangement is part of the Veradapandra Mountain range. These ancient mountains have been dramatically sculpted since prehistoric times to form a massive theatre of power. Over uncounted millennia, the peaks have been shorn down to create a flattened top running around the outside. Some speculate it was once the Mother of all Mountains on Anu. Then it was hollowed out in the centre to form the greatest of all enclosures. Before her falling out with her masters, Nallurakon dwelt there. Nebutan also lived and worked in Upata-Shepsus before she fled north. The core of the state is divided between this port and the capital. While Upata-Shepsus is the political hub of all Statos-Vey, Bhampay is the undisputed seat of commerce. In most-ancient times it also stood as its own imperial capital. The principal avenue, composed of broad Azure and Magna paving stones, is a direct highway from here to Upata-Shepsus, linking the mercantile and ruling hearts of the subcontinent. This highway bisects the centre of the Red Ring circle. It travels in a perfect line southwest, ending over one thousand, two-hundred andas away at the foot of what is named 'The Plateau' within the Primary Mountain Circle's heart. The flattened top of this towering megalith houses the ceremonial and governance complex of the empire with many administrative and other government structures surrounding the base. Either side of their 'Imperial Way' are some of the most densely populated lands on Anu. National dignity ensures they are well maintained. This power and assurance exude out of all here."

Seti looked at her in amazement, "This is where the Yin-Vinulan dynasty ruled?"

Hegev smiled and inclined her head, "A scholar indeed! Yes, their seat lay here, and they devised this Ring. Long after near all other traces of them vanished, it remains. I am sure more have been added to this massive edifice, but the Yin-Vinulan laid the foundations."

The ship passed through the yawning gap between the colossal red walls on either side.

"What is that?" Seti pointed at a folded network of cable netting fastened to the edge of the gap.

Hegev frowned at Seti, "It is their Wum Barrier."

"Their what?"

"How is it possible you sailed the seas all this time and never encountered a Wum?"

Seti shrugged, and his Adept laughed.

"I know of a sea creature you do not! In fairness, they are more prevalent in the Panchala than the colder waters of the Wakanda. A Wum is a being whose shell floats on the surface, while its immense long body trails the depths below. They emit powerful lights attracting their prey and may glow brightly at night. Their tendrils reach the seafloor and propel it forward while the shell is round and grows as the creature ages. Ancients are known to grow so large they are called 'floating islands.' They travel in colonies along both coasts of the Panchala and through the shallow waters of the Panchala further north. They can be a hazard to shipping. All southern ports here have these barriers. Had we travelled along Statos-Vey's Eastern coast, you likely would have seen many herds of them in the shallow waters. When a group is sighted, the barrier is drawn across. They are designed to thwart the packs of Wum from entering and causing unwitting mischief."

Seti smiled, "I am glad many wonders remain to be discovered."

They returned to examining the massive gap in the Red Ring. Figures moved on top of the wall, and as they passed through and looked back, stairways leading to various levels built into the wall could be seen. Faces came and went from numerous windows. Inside the vast harbour, another wall stood, as wide as the gap in the outer wall.

"Beyond it lies what they name the Inner Harbour," his Adept said. "There is a second harbour near the ring's southern wall," she pointed into the distance to their left. "It is called the Siana Harbour, extending down the southern side of the city to where the mouth of the River Siana empties. This river flows around the city within the Ring, with two branches dividing and emptying at both ends of the Inner Harbour. They name her 'encompassing Siana,' as she also flows through Bhampay in a network of canals spreading as veins across the city. This is my first visit, but all has been described many times in several books of my acquaintance."

Signs of a shimmering marvel appeared either side of this broad sea barrier. The ship turned to the left and moved parallel to the Inner Harbour's wall until its end. As they turned, the Inner Harbour and entire city beyond filled their eyes. Smoke rose in colourful and fragrant ribbons above what, for an instant, seemed a dream garden of fantastical mushrooms and ornamental plants. The sounds and smells helped solidify the reality. They looked at a vast population living in unimaginable splendour. Their eyes tried to focus on the riot of rich orange and burnt yellow structures. Shocking punctuations of fantastic constructions clothed in dark green and sumptuous purple vied with lush gardens and garish troupes of cousins in their thousands jumping from roof to roof. They saw many giant statues wrapped in a dazzling array of trailing banners, standing as tall as towers beside domes coated in iridescent patterns. This plush and effusive spectacle made the sky and sea grey in comparison. Small ships moved through the city on the many canals. The land rose in soft steps forming a gentle bowl revealing most of Bhampay to those in the harbour. The Red Ring bound all within a radiant wholeness.

"It is as the hide of a vast creature . . ." Seti said, his eyes wide and voice hushed. ". . . or a shimmering insect colony. Of the many cities I visited, none compare to this!"

Hegev shook her head, "This humiliates the attempts I read describing it."

"What is this?" Seti pointed up and to the left, where an abrupt rise of land stood. Atop this odd formation rose glittering edifices. It was sheer on the sides and slightly wider near the top. A profile of a ramp stretched far out from its base to the plateau. He saw tiny carts and other traffic on it.

"'The Tooth,'" Hegev answered. She smiled and looked at him.

"'The Tooth' . . . 'The Tooth' . . ." Seti frowned at the title before his eyes went wide, "Where the Yin-Vinulan emperors sat under their wide canopy?"

Hegev nodded, "There is no trace of their palace now. I read an author suggesting the 'Tooth' is what remains of an ancient mountain, perhaps even a northern orphan of the Veradapandra Mountain range far to the south. The Veradapandras have most of the 'Azure Stone,' to be found on Anu. This is a dense and distinguishing rock run through with precious minerals of Argent, Lapis and Cupric. As I mentioned, the capital, Upata-Shepsus, has a massive version of this 'tooth,' simply named The Plateau. It is purported to be of solid Azure Stone, within its circling mountains. That is where the Imperial Way you see begun here ends. It is roughly in the centre of the vast interior of the Primary Mountain Circle. This Plateau is where the seat of the current empire rises. Long before the

Yin-Vinulan Dynasty, the top of this formation was flattened and the entire hill modified. The unintended result being from most prospects the appearance of a giant tooth rooted in the ground. Like the Ring, the broad ramp leading to The Tooth is the other preserved legacy of this fabled dynasty. Although they built over an existing ramp, they did so on a scale unmatched. The core avenue leading to this Tooth from the Imperial Way is broad, allowing for large ceremonies to take place."

Seti and Hegev continued to take in the rest of the city and the shore curving inward toward a central outcropping of land, studded with constructions and bays for shipping. Many branching ways and small islands went far out into the Inner Harbour. Shipping of every description filled them. A second city existed offshore on this network of islands and piers connected by sturdy causeways. The noise level increased as they drew closer to this vibrant mass of ships and cargo loading and unloading. Creaking walking-wheels powered cranes lifting out and lowering cargo into ships. Figures crawled overall, and many carts and wagons hurried back and forth between the mainland and the vessels. A multitude of skiffs and other small craft swarmed the waterways between these lanes and islands. A Tatchlan creature known as a Ninusay Vine wrapped around the hull of one ship while an extended tendril latched onto a cart pulling it forward. Seti wondered how their caravel would fit down some of these narrow watery laneways, let alone the larger Jefaka. He could not believe these tiny craft did not sink each other in the bobbing fray.

Notwithstanding the setting, the surprising scents of cooking and incense predominated. He then realized this was the source of the multicoloured ribbons of smoke rising from the city. They were rivers of fragrance travelling up into the sky.

Seti turned to watch as the Bhampaian Harbourmaster began a complex series of turns to weave the Yamagad into this frenetic maze. The captain stood beside him, relieved not to be piloting the ship through this floating labyrinth. Soon enough, they were enveloped inside a quaking landscape of vast proportions. The city on land was lost amid the tall masts and harbour structures surrounding them. Enclosed by the bustling effort, Seti noted how the walls of buildings were fully coated in mosaics and many fanciful adornments. He marvelled at the ornamentations hanging from the corners of roofs. As a verdant jungle, no open space existed. There was no flat surface broader than a single brush stroke or mosaic tile, and no colour matched its neighbour on any side. A multitude of tiny bells sounded in the ocean breezes. A small orchestra performed somewhere employing drums and gongs amid the straining of ropes and the thud of crates on decks. Despite the ongoing commotion, a few found the time to tend elaborate gardens on the roofs of buildings, suggesting this was home to many working here.

They moved deep into one of the waterways between land bridges and, at a signal from the Harbour Master, deckhands threw their lines to those waiting onshore. Large numbers moved in either direction, towing ships to their final docks. The pullers wove their way with considerable skill around many obstacles. The ships were shunted to either side of the waterway according to their size and cargo. Those on board stopped to watch a procession of tall trees on a series of riding carts, their lush foliage bound and huge round sacks over their roots. The trees were loaded onto a vessel. Part of the deck had been removed so they could rest on the bottom.

"Seti," Hegev said, "the Yamagad will soon dock. Their cargo will be unloaded, and their agents will go into the city to begin securing what they will take home. What do you propose to do?"

"My business is on land," he said. "Please accompany me. I will seek out these Masters and request the return of my Memanu Knot. There is no reason to withhold it from me. I will be content to return and wait for the ship to depart, and we will begin our mission on Rho-Jashun."

"They will not detain you?"

Seti looked at the panorama of activity and did not answer at once. "When I am thus surrounded, all the tumult inside me rests. My wayward Menem cannot compete and so lay down and leave me in peace." He focused on his Adept. "I fall in and out of certainty. When I am sure I am strong and vital. Despite this, there is much I do not comprehend. I am driven in turn by innocence and certainty, as I am by Nu's presence and absence above us. My confidence tells me I must be here. My innocence tells me I have no notion what will happen," he gestured at the obscured city, "I performed a fearful dance around this place for many two-weeks.

Because of me, friends died in a storm, and the Suvuka near destroyed us."

"Seti! You are not responsible for the storm or where we landed! Emedin and I wanted to avoid this place for your sake. The burden of our decision rests on us. You made clear your desire to come here from the start."

Seti continued to gaze at the colourful melee filling his senses. "I must learn the steps leading to where we stand."

"You truly intend to speak to these masters?"

Seti nodded, "They alone can answer my questions."

"Seti, Nebutan asked many searching questions of these twisters of life. Their extensive replies are written down in her books. Their motivations are open to us."

Seti nodded, looking toward the city, "I would hear from them myself."

CHAPTER 56

SINKIN

Day 363, east coast of Mushumafal Peninsula, Thermistal.

For ten days, Sinkin and Setush rested. At last, waves of Suvuka Stags crowded the horizon and swam ashore within hours of each other. The pile of food was consumed down to the bare ground. News spread of six lost to the ocean. With the sad exception of these, the remainder had returned.

After many days apart, Durka and Makusk herds gathered at the news. Hiratak shook his head, "So many drowned!"

"Our New Stags spoke of the ease of the return swim," Morakav said.

"Perhaps rogue currents or sea predators attacked them."

The group lowered their heads at the loss. When they raised again, Sinkin spoke, "The stocks are gone. We should move on. I have long been ready. The desire to hear what these ones say has kept me."

"As have I," Setush said. "I will endure privations to hear them. I must learn what happened after we left."

Sinkin and Setush had seldom spoken to each other since their debate. Setush suffered more from the silence. "I will learn what I can," he said, turning and heading for shore.

The others watched him go. Sinkin sat back on his haunches, content for whatever news came. In a short time, Setush returned.

"They are leaving!" he gasped.

"Were they anxious or fearful?" Morakav asked.

"No, joyful. Like those exiting Gramerem Round before we entered."

Sinkin frowned, "Do not New Stags rest first?"

The adults nodded, "For at least a few days," Hiratak replied. "I never heard of so sudden a departure! It is foolish to travel this soon."

"It makes no sense," Morakav agreed. "They should at least sing and boast."

"Setush," Sinkin said, rising, "let us find one willing to talk. Perhaps bragging is to come. Herdmaster, I recommend you all remain. New Stags might be more frank with fellow New Stags."

"Yes, Sinkin," Hiratak said, his eyes glowing, "we will wait."

The two New Stags began to make their way back over the rocks and around the scrub. In the distance, they heard many voices calling out, "Hesha! Vira! Hesha! Vira!" They came out of the brush into the sea's open air. Still, none remained by the shore once crowded with anxious Suvuka scanning the horizon. They heard raised voices and made their way toward them.

"We witnessed wonders," came a voice through the brush, "Anu has opened! She revealed her Face! Diviners visions now fill our eyes."

As they came closer, they heard others speaking. "Hesha has long filled our Bard's dreams. Today She rises for all. We will be a nation of seers! She has opened this noble path. We enter Her realm. We learn our true qualities. We possess new depths. We will rebuild our herds."

Sinkin and Setush stopped to listen.

"Hesha follows us in the eyes of every creature," another voice said. "Her Face fills calm waters. She will renew our ancient ways. She will rebuild our original selves. She enobles our steps. She unifies our purpose."

"What are they saying?" Setush whispered to Sinkin. Sinkin frowned and shook his head. The herd moved away from them, and the New Stags continued north, seeking out more voices. After travelling several andas, they encountered a gathering by the shore. They kept to the trees.

"Hesha was rooted below," a black pelt said. "Anu gave birth to Her. She is a gift to us. We assisted in Her delivery. She now flows in the rivers. She rides the winds. Our paws brush Her Face. We travel deep into Anu. Through Her, we feel the roots of life."

Another deep black pelt stood on his hind legs and spoke. "Hesha was ripe for emerging. She has come in answer to our pleas. She will guide us. She sang many long songs. She whispered many secrets. We bring many declarations to the Suvuka."

A red pelt nodded and said, "This came in a vision. She brought wisdom to Pramath's Keepers. They are honoured servants of Anu's long-hidden Face. The Keepers openly show their inspiration."

"The Keepers!" Sinkin hissed to a frowning Setush.

"Through the Keepers we heard Her message!" A brown and gold pelt said, "Hesha offers us a way to peace. She frees us of rancour. We must accept our lives." Several New Stags stood by him. "Our defiance of the Tolku lacks focus. We waste our strength. We must learn patience. We live now. We wait for our vengeance."

Beyond the collective intake of breath, only the swelling ocean and the circling Krall were heard.

"They returned from a different island!" Setush whispered." "They say nothing of the Black Dream Moss or our blind struggle!"

"The Tolku believe they defeated us!" the black pelt shouted. "Sealing us in one place magnifies our might! Behind the Tolku's mountain walls, they brewed foul arts. Now we brew what will destroy them!"

Sinkin and Setush recalled Master Nakuk saying the same to them. This group also began to run along the coast away from them. Sinkin and Setush came out of their cover to watch their retreating backs in the craggy coastline ahead of them. They heard the movement of others in the brush moving north.

"We were to forge deep links," Sinkin said. "Yet, they remain strangers." They looked sadly at each other. "In the 'Song of Shushkup,' the hero abandoned his group," Setush said. "Shushkup met one after Pramath, here on the coast. We will always have each other, Sinkin." They touched noses before looking after those who had gone. "Many paths bend around the trees," Setush said. "Most do not follow the open shore."

Sinkin nodded, "We choose to avoid the sea after our near drowning!"

Sinkin and Setush moved back into the brush and found a series of wide pathways, similar to those along the southern coast through the tall grasses. They moved north, their steps hidden by the constant ocean winds. They searched in vain for small knots of herds around their returned Stags. Instead, they came on a lone Stag, lying on his side. He rose at once as they approached.

"Sinkin and Setush lifted one front leg, "Hail to you fellow Stag!" Setush said. "We arrived back from Pramath days ago. We would speak to you. I am Setush of Makusk Herd. This is Sinkin of Durka Herd. Both our herds are aligned to Chitikal Round."

The New Stag had a sand-coloured pelt. Splashes of yellow and orange ran through, and it had the familiar look of long emersion in saltwater.

"I am Visko of Kutur Herd," he said in a deep voice. "We run far to the north. We are aligned to the ruined mound called Dakast."

Sinkin and Setush were surprised to hear the name of the Round pulled down in ancient times when Hesha Vira first rose there. They thought him old for a New Stag as they bowed to him. Visko scrutinized them, "My tale confuses my herd. They go to listen to others. Why seek me out when many bray their news?"

"Because brayers have little to say," Sinkin replied. "They make up for it by repeating themselves. What we hear confuses us. It is customary to rest after the swim. Why do they leave?"

"I do not remember you." Visko began a rumbling chuckle, "I forget most of Gramerem. I do not know why they clamour to leave. My pelt is wet from the ocean. I will leave when I am ready. Some are more gifted with vision than others." He bent his head down to the ground, and Sinkin and Setush exchanged puzzled glances.

"The Black Moss," Visko said at last, "made me ill! I could not stop emptying myself!" He gave them a sour smile, "I woke under a tree. My eyes burned. My head ached. Those I came with were gone. I heard the moans and shouts over the wall. When the dams and cubs came, I took water but nothing more. They spoke in whispers. I heard many secrets."

Sinkin stepped closer and peered at Visko, "Secrets?"

Visko looked at him warily, "I lay sick, dream mixed with wakefulness. They spoke softly. I heard half of their words. A thick fog surrounds me. I kept my cubs in mind to endure it all. Others were also stricken." He looked at them, "You said you arrived days ago?"

Sinkin and Setush nodded. Visko looked at each of them in turn, "When?"

"We have seen ten dawns since we touched land," Setush said.

"So many?" Visko repeated in amazement, "You left before they finished. You left before they began!"

"Began?" Sinkin asked.

Visko grew angry and began pacing, "For a time, they thought me dying. I heard them repeating declarations over and over. The Keepers worked while the Stags glutted themselves on Moss. I heard the Keepers whispering to each other. One thing I heard clearly." He stopped and stared at them. At last, he nodded once and said, "They said Hesha granted them a gift. Their time had come to rebuild the old orders."

They stared at Visko before Sinkin turned to Setush, "Remember what Keeper Datal said? The Keepers are the highest of the old orders left to us." He turned back to Visko, "We met Keeper Datal at Avanchil Round. He said the Keepers struggled over matters once entrusted to the others. The old songs refer to our Priests. They are no more. The one herd of leadership remaining are the Keepers."

"Avanchil Round," Visko said, "I am told a mighty vision of Hesha Vira came there."

"We are witnesses," Setush said. "We saw the entire bowl transformed into her Face."

Visko nodded at the familiar description, "We had left Avanchil just ahead of this. The story found us on the eve of our little swim and absurd climb. I am not certain what it means."

"I am not sure Pramath's Keepers know," Sinkin said. "They use Hesha Vira's call to strengthen themselves. Our other Orders are no more. I overheard Keepers speak when they thought none listened. They said we were engaged in a battle to keep Hesha Vira from the Tolku. They felt the power of their words. They directed our collective force in Her realm, and now all has altered. Hesha Vira wears a sweet aspect. She sings and smiles. I also suspect they aspire to rebuild the old orders. Without understanding, they use Her to elevate their station."

Visko sat pondering this, "What of it?"

The other two stared at him in amazement.

"What of it?" he repeated. "I do not pretend to comprehend this, Hesha Vira. I would see the old orders restored. Fortifying our ancient ways with fresh visions is a good aim. This Keeper movement maybe what we need."

Setush shook himself with frustration, "What of the truth?"

Visko chuckled, "I am late getting to my Four Paws. Our herd ranges in the far north. We are close to the ruins of Dakast Round. If it stood, I would have gone there instead. Of necessity, I have had Stag duties for years. My cubs climb on, and fall off, my back. Some debate the value of this journey. We are less observant than you southerners. I came to please our ancients. This is why I am separate from most. I mean no disrespect, but you sound like fresh bucks."

His kind eyes examined Setush, "You ask of truth. We endure endless stories of our defeat. They are meant to feed our resentment. We drink rage and bitterness with our mother's milk. I see my cubs soured by it. What has this 'truth' accomplished? We exhaust ourselves running to this place! Why did we leave our herds? Why did we risk death, for you perhaps two years and us near three? Do you believe we will swim the Vettencore Passage? We spend ourselves on this absurd effort. Your interpretation of the Keepers' actions is correct. I welcome their initiative. The weight of the past breaks our backs. Our fictions delude us. It is time to let go."

"What fictions?" Sinkin asked.

"You southerners are so traditional. My grandfather laughed at the old sagas. He said they always left out our original crime."

Sinkin and Setush stared at Visko.

"My dear Stags! How did we come to this? What led to our present captivity? They did not invade us! We invaded them! Our arrogance in demanding all Anu brought us to this. Our precious eyes fooled us when we looked at their tiny bodies. Our grand Orders condemned any thought of studying them. They thought their patience a weakness. We permitted them to grow strong. When they struck back, we could not rise. Perhaps they might have invaded us. Until then, we would have filled our Thermistal. Instead, we stampeded toward our ruin! Fools believe the Suvuka possess all virtue. Those seeking power say the Tolku are filled with all vice. They beat us at our own game. We are powerless to stop them for now. It serves no purpose to brood. We must live our lives."

Sinkin and Setush were shocked at his words. For a time, there was silence between them.

"Are we to become pets of the enemy?" Setush asked.

"I have no clear notion what our future will be," Visko answered. "What I do see clearly is what obsessing on our past has done. Our enemy defeated us and pens us in. It is said some engage in hidden rituals. They possess weapons we cannot imagine. Yet, they are fools and will suffer for it."

"Why?" Sinkin asked.

"Why? Because we live! We had the sense to attempt to exterminate them. Only then would our dominance have been assured. They attempt to change us into Toboku or Tamku. I do not say we should forget. I welcome this call for patience. Several generations after our defeat, we roar and posture to no end. This must stop! One day their grip will loosen. They cannot hold us so tight forever. If we endure now, our time will come. The one thing the Tolku taught us is the power of waiting. Forget dreams of glory for yourselves. Our distant progeny will re-take our lands. Anu will only see one of us cover her in the end."

Sinkin and Setush frowned at him. "Visko," Sinkin began, "you approve of the Keeper's plan and welcome their message?"

"We must end this wasting mania. It weakens us and does nothing to them," he said. "Those young fools repeat what they were fed. Those mixing the buck's Black Dream Moss, and composing their litanies, know what they do. The Keepers do dream of power. They chart a new course. I embrace such a change. These silly visions of a Face of Anu are their best tool. They will inspire the majority with a unifying vision."

Sinkin and Setush sat pondering this. "I thank you for your insights," Sinkin said. "You give us much to contemplate. We plan to travel by the coast. When will you be leaving?"

Visko smiled and nodded, "Despite being surrounded by fog, I intend to move my herd soon. Let the others blaze our trail, we will manage well enough." He eyed him them, "Make no mistake, Full Stags! You determined your course across the desert. It is you who choose when you begin your trek home. Many herds make the return journey. Your herd and mine are suddenly left behind, so let us travel together. Where are the rest?"

"Back at a food pile," Setush said. "We could be here by tomorrow morning."

Visko nodded, "When my herd returns, I will say we wait for you. We will be out by the shore." He smiled, "I thank you two for finding me. We may have unravelled the mystery of Pramath and our future."

Sinkin and Setush bowed at this and began to make their way back. They had gone a short way when they heard splashing and roaring at the shore. They stopped and made their way on soft paws toward a clearing. There stood ten Stags dripping with seawater, shaking themselves and looking exhausted. Sinkin and Setush recognized the one standing as their leader.

"Follow me!" Keeper Nakuk called out. "We must get off the coast to avoid stragglers. Keeper paths cut through the mountains to Avanchil Round. You will soon bathe in mighty rivers. Cache-laden shelters wait for us. We must not rest long. We must relay our news without delay!"

The group followed Nakuk as they plunged into the thicket near where the two New Stags hid and continued west toward the mountains. Sinkin and Setush made their way to what stood as a clear pathway extending away from the coast into the dense jungle. It had swallowed any sound or sight of the Keepers. They stared in silence at the Keeper path before turning to run back to their herds. The roaring of the incoming tide could not compete with their racing thoughts.

CHAPTER 57

Shuna-Shapta

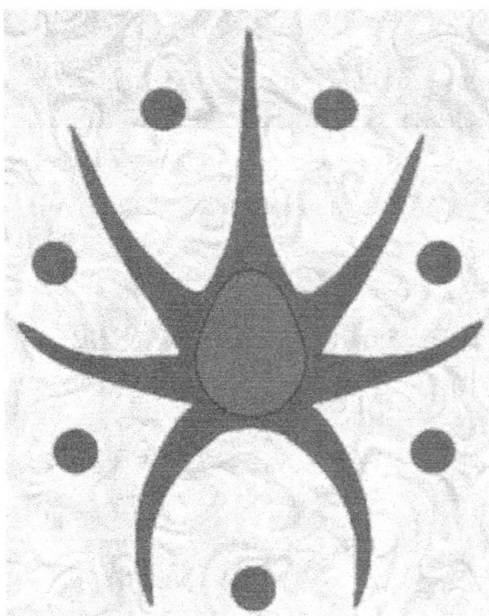

The Blue Star, symbol of Royalty

Day 366, Two-Week Twenty-One, Andura, the Ocean, Thakadush Cluster, city of Bhampay.

Shuna-Shapta carried the infant Thakadush-Satwa on her hip through the cluster compound. Surrounded by her founding circle, including her First and Second Ama, both now immensely 'round with child,' and her adult Invocate Circle of Eight. They formed a unified ring radiating out from her, the infant Majastas, and the two pregnant Amas. Either side of the core group walked two of Shuna-Shapta's three siblings, Shuna-Vovans, the next eldest girl and little Shuna-Samshep. They trotted around the inner four, one hand passing over Shuna-Shapta and Thakadush-Satwa, the other reaching out to the surrounding circle of adults.

The Majastas child enjoyed this and touched each hand as it passed over her. Together, these cluster mates advanced with Shuna-Shapta. The outer circle of adults, with deliberation, orbited around the Majastas as they walked. They stepped in unison and turned their bodies as they moved ever to look forward. A rolling cadence formed their dancing steps, suggesting this dynamic arrangement flowed with ease. While all were barefaced, their bodies were extensively painted.

They approached the antechamber where the newly titled 'Everlastingly Serving' Tanas, along with three guests, knelt on thick mats. Behind them stood three groups of seven figures, associated with the three kneeling guests. Everlastingly Serving Tanas wore a full, black Alatanda Mask, representing the first Face and the hub of the Twelve Faces. He had just conducted the three eminent Tatchlan Servants, each with their seven retainers, into Thakadush Cluster and now knelt just in front of them. These illustrious guests had just arrived from the capital, Upata-Shepsus.

The first on the left wore the life-and-death Mask of Sukakap, the eleventh Principal Face, representing Unflinching Truth. Her seven retainers stood immediately behind her, wearing simple masks and robes divided down the middle. Their painted masks and woven livery were matching. On the viewer's left side were effusive signs of life filling the eye, on the right side, a bare skeleton on a black ground.

The second wore Vashivonos, the bird Face of Necessity and tenth of the twelve Principal Faces. Her seven servants wore painted masks and woven robes appearing to be composed of blue and green feathers, with a fashioned design of two feathers spreading out from either side of their masks to meet over their heads.

The third wore a combination of Humma, the Face of Recollection, and Neferdush, the Face of Perception. Her seven attendants wore painted and woven depictions in the colours of the two Faces, on the viewer's left, Humma's orange and yellow, on the right, Neferdush's blue and purple. These three significant figures and their retinues exuded a mixture of potent aromas as the procession approached the gap between the antechamber and the rest of the cluster.

"Greetings to our Treasured Majastas and her Operant," Everlastingly Serving Tanas said, placing his head on the antechamber's exuberant sea life mosaic floor.

Shuna-Shapta smiled, "Greetings to our beloved Everlastingly Serving Tanas and most honoured guests," she replied in what all heard was an amplified voice.

Everlastingly Serving Tanas now rose and solemnly moved to Shuna-Shapta's right to be seated beyond the edge of the guest company filling the antechamber. With his back near the wall, he faced back across the archway separating the two chambers "This is Memnum-Cath," he indicated the kneeling official wearing the Face of Sukakap on the far left, "of the Adjudicator Bureau of our Chancellery, who serves within our Paramount Magistracies Office." The official raised both her palms facing out in greeting while her seven attendants smoothly prostrated themselves on the cool mosaic floor before rising again. "'We are helpless, bowed, stooping and humble' in the presence of our Majastas and Her Estimable Regent," Memnum-Cath declared in ringing tones. "With these poor words I would proffer my credentials," she brought out a tight-rolled document and bowed low as she pushed it out in front of her.

"This is Telmun-Pava of the Regions Bureau of our Grandee Secretariat, who serves the new station for the designation of 'Seats of Collective Districts,'" Tanas indicated the office-bearer in the middle, wearing the Mask of Vashivonos. She mirrored her colleague's gestures before declaring, "To our New Majastas and Her Regent, 'we stand in the attitude of expectancy and practice submissiveness unremittingly.'" Her seven retainers prostrated and rose. "With these meagre words, I would proffer my credentials," she added, mirroring Memnum-Cath's offering.

"And this is Acharum-Eita of the Census Bureau of our Enumerator Ministry, entrusted with the venerable institution of our Decennial Census." The dignitary on the right raised her palms, "'We stand within the fixed position of serving' to our Treasured Majastas and Regent Operant," as her company prostrated themselves. "With these poor words, I proffer my credentials," she added.

"All are on secondment from our capital to commence this immense transition," Everlastingly Serving Tanas said as mats were set out for the company of Thakadush-Satwa. Shuna-Shapta knelt in the middle facing directly across the short divide from Telmun-Pava of the Grandee Secretariat Ministry in her Vashivonos Mask. The remainder of her circles arranged themselves on a close half circle around her and the tiny Majastas.

Shuna-Shapta drew in their aromas before smiling, "Powerful Invocates all! In this alone, I may presume to instruct you, in all else, we are your humble pupils. As one who has also studied our Classics, I shall endeavour to approach your facility in weaving ancient texts into our formal discourse by saying, 'We shall prevail upon you to dispose of yourselves in easy postures.'

Gentle laughter filled the antechamber as the group relaxed. The three dignitaries removed their Masks of Office. Their attendants removed their clothes while retaining their simple masks before seating themselves. Everlastingly Serving Tanas also removed his mask and placed it on his lap. "Prior to our commencing our work, Honoured Regent," the venerably aged Memnum-Cath of the Paramount Magistracies Office said as she placed her Sukakap Mask on hooks attached to her robes, so it hung on her chest, "may we enquire as to the significance of your Circle's deportment about you and our Majastas?"

Several members of the two Circles chuckled, and the Majastas baby smiled. "Since we healed Hesha Vira," Shuna-Shapta said, "peace returned within our Magnificent Work. The strength once diverted to Hesha Vira now flows as it should. Roots animate and sprouts fill our horizon. Each modification has its source here," she pointed to where they sat. "Its manifestations blossom amongst us. What you witnessed, we now refer to as our 'Circle Walk.' You shall find other Circles of Thakadush Cluster begin to travel together thus. Our circles and cluster approach resonance. Whilst preferred within our cluster and for various ceremonies, other simpler forms develop for longer journeys outside."

Telmun-Pava, of the Regions Bureau of the Grandee Secretariat, perhaps in her early fifties, had also hung her Vashivonos Face and leaned forward at this, "I presume to offer the following observation, this appears a novel variation of most-ancient Nethuns and Alpanum rites described in primordial lore."

"Perchance," Shuna-Shapta said. "In this case, it also reflects the particular instance of those attending our Majastas and my scant self as Her designated Regent."

There was a pause before Acharum-Eita of the Census Bureau of the Enumerator Ministry stirred. While the youngest of the three, possibly in her mid-forties, her aromas presented both an advanced authority and kindly disposition. "Beloved Regent! In this fortunate two-week of Andura, at this pleasant hour of Nu Strides, now witnessing your treasured charge I know why 'all beings flock to Her!' As here in Bhampay, we within Upata-Shepsus, our capital of unifying dynasties, are but the surface foam of a deep ocean of generations dedicated to beholding this day! From the Third Unifying Dynasty of Yin-Vinulan, having its ancient seat here within your beloved city, through to the crown of our age just ending, our Muraharoma Dynasty, all emperors have quietly stated their correct place as stewards to the future crown of all unifications, seated upon your lap! Most of our Ministries were established by the first of all unifying dynasties, the most-ancient Funomanru. They were perfected by the second, the Buyanupithar, along with their vast and comprehensive legal codes. Be assured, Treasured Regent! We are a firm foundation and vital organism! Many of our numbers are also Invocates who have witnessed the wonders our Majastas has wrought within Tatchlan. We have witnessed the commencement of the Quickening with our own eyes. To these profound current events, we bring the collective wisdom and experience of generations of servants to this noble parade of dynasties. We are well ordered to carry forward our versions of the 'continuity of ages' in the service of our emerging Cluster-of-Clusters Nation!"

Telmun-Pava, of the Regions Bureau, nodded enthusiastically, "May your Majastas Cluster 'be visited by transports of happiness!' Our company includes both Esteemed Librarians and Venerable Scholars, well able to ensure the ancient conventions find new service for our Tolku.

History may look back upon this as the necessary way for the birth of our hopes to proceed. As with a sound delivery, the head has emerged prior to the rest of the body."

General laughter followed this comment before all were surprised by a lad running up to Shuna-Shapta. "Majastas Regent," a young man said approaching, "as per your forceful instruction, I immediately inform you the one you spoke of has entered our Companion Avenue. He wishes his knot returned."

Everlastingly Serving Tanas turned sharply to look at Shuna-Shapta, "The boy? The one making those declarations?"

"Our agents inform us he boarded another ship," Shuna-Shapta said, "It docked here three days past. He and his Menem Adept made enquiries alerting us to his presence. We shall meet at our Companion Pond." She turned to her youngest sister. "Samshep, go and fetch the Memanu Knot."

The young girl ran through the surrounding Circles back into the compound.

"Shapta?" Everlastingly Serving Tanas said, "You mean to speak with him? To what purpose?"

"We find each other intriguing," she replied.

Everlastingly Serving Tanas stared at her, "We study the development of this knot within our Resplendent Work. It did little during Hesha Vira's wanton disobedience, yet it remains a key focal point to those resisting us."

Samshep returned and gave her elder sister the knot. Shuna-Shapta passed the knot down to Thakadush-Satwa. Without hesitation, the babe stuck one end in her mouth. "This boy mixes many combustible elements," Shuna-Shapta said. "His madness hobbles his genius, whilst at the same time fuelling it."

Everlastingly Serving Tanas bowed, "You say he came for his knot? Does he believe it possesses power for him?"

Shuna-Shapta smiled and looked down at Thakadush-Satwa, engrossed in touching and licking the knot. "It has the power of a symbol. He plans to brandish it during his exaltations. Because he requires it, we shall meet."

Everlastingly Serving Tanas shook his head, "Is this wise? We may have a measure of understanding of his numerous conditions. This information led to the falling out between him and his captain, but do we begin to gage his evident strengths?"

"Everlastingly Serving and Estimable Regent," Memnum-Cath said. "May I presume to speak upon this matter?"

Shuna-Shapta nodded.

"We at the Adjudicator Bureau of our Chancellery Ministry have been informed of this wildling Sensitive. We Invocates have also examined this," she indicated the knot in Thakadush-Satwa's little hands, "knot's presence within Tatchlan. It has been agreed upon within Upata-Shepsus that gentle and patient domestication is the best course of action. Conducting our Majastas to him may be vital in ensuring this peaceably takes place at this moment of his choosing. Your most submissive servants and these attendants have all we need to commence preparations for our Emperor to travel here for his audience with our Majastas."

"Honoured Regent," Telmun-Pava said, leaning forward causing her Vashivonos Mask to gently swing on its hooks. "Our Grandee Secretariat Ministry shares this assessment. I would presume to encourage you to go forth at once to him. I would also make a verbal petition for one of each of our ministry's entourage to assume street clothing and quietly observe your conference with him. We each have amongst us those able to hear and recite with exactness each spoken word."

Shuna-Shapta quietly instructed the boy to retrieve simple long shirts for the three adults. "They are to attend us but hang back," she said. "We wish naught to disrupt what is to take place."

She stood and immediately gestured for all the others to remain seated. "Proceed with your preparations. We shall attend to this matter by presenting him our gift."

CHAPTER 58

Shuna-Shapta

Day 366, Two-Week Twenty-One, Andura, the Ocean, Companion Pond before Thakadush Cluster, city of Bhampay.

The tall lad and mature woman stepped onto the Companion Avenue. Either side, extensive renovations continued. What remained of private dwellings and blocks stood open, and many labourers piled debris in carts for removal. Each side of the avenue was cleared, the paving stones were pried up, and the ground levelled. Sturdy crates lay stacked in orderly formation behind each of the fish statues. Seti looked in a few opened ones to find them filled with tiny mosaic tiles in vivid hues. Troupes of Mayku and Asaku scurried over the roofs in every direction carrying messages across the bustling city. The two visitors stopped before the Companion Pond and watched the murky forms moving in it. Yellow hair covered the young man's round head as delicate moss, dominated by his large ears. Despite a series of recent Nu burns, compared to natives of the city, his pale peach skin with a minimum of beige spots marked him a northerner. Passersby noted his pale blue and grey eyes standing out on his pallid face, and how his body was curiously wrapped in a white robe.

Nearby, members of the Singing Bowl Guild sat in an open circle facing onto the Companion Avenue. The workers moved around them apparently without complaint. The Guild had begun sounding their burnished and etched bowls of varying widths and sizes. Each contained different levels of an intense-smelling liquid. They rubbed the rims and tapped out a complicated rhythm using a variety of elegant instruments. The resulting sweet notes and thrumming tones echoed off the sparkling fish statues and buildings beyond. Seti recalled the last time he heard such sounds when the Jefaka prepared to say goodbye to those not surviving the storm. A tall girl, wearing a simple green dress and her black hair worn up in a bun, approached the pair carrying a baby. Her skin's accents of dark half-circles travelled across her light copper skin. Her dark brown eyes, featuring a striking yellow radius around her wide pupils, focused on the boy. On either side of her walked two younger girls who were clearly her siblings, each wearing similar dresses and carrying lovely parasols. Behind them, three adult women in pale shirts followed one step behind. This group approached the pond on gentle feet. Notwithstanding what they knew of his mental state, there was no denying his singular presence. Shuna-Shapta came to stand on the other side of the pond to him.

"Look into our pond and call out the name 'Capecashwa,'" she smiled.

Seti looked at the clouded water, at her and back before calling, "Capecashwa!"

The pond waters remained unaltered. The numerous denizens rose and fell back into the gloom. A creature of vivid orange with green and black markings rose like a dream to the surface. It had extended side fins containing deep black and orange streaks along the veins. Its large liquid eyes regarded him before sinking back into his realm.

"He is older than I," Shuna-Shapta said in a soft voice watching after him. "As a child, I recall him as a little 'wiggler.' He has not done growing!" She frowned in thought before saying, "I invite you to try calling one other Companion. Call out 'Menthuhatha.'"

"Menthuhatha!"

The name banished the Companions. They sank away, leaving the surface blank. The water became agitated, and a series of vivid spikes rose out of the gloom. A fantastic creature of yellow scales and blue accents filled the surface of the pond. Its broad face turned to look at Seti. He was amazed at the sight of this fantastic creature. Shuna-Shapta and her companions smiled broadly at the watery beast.

"Our Companion Pond forms an underground network from the sea," Shuna-Shapta said. "Many places allow them to surface, and marvellous underground engineering allows the water to raise to this level. At this and other ponds they may be fed, but this Companion Pond is notable for historic reasons. Their wild relatives dwell within the deep. Generations raised and kept these. They teach us, and we teach them." As she spoke, Menthuhatha began to sink beyond sight, and many others lurked in the thick salt waters.

"Most shall respond to anyone. Menthuhatha and some others seldom come when called," Shuna-Shapta said, looking into Seti's eyes.

Hegev shifted and grew agitated. "What do you suggest? Because he can call a fish, he has powers you could use? You want to recruit him?"

Shuna-Shapta brought out the Memanu Knot. She gave it to Shuna-Samshep. The young girl walked around the rim of the pond to present it to Seti. He took it and made a face at the sticky texture of the knot.

"You came for this," Shuna-Shapta said. "We heard the tale of your offering and its return. A gift from the 'Glorious Swaying Ones' is a treasure."

Seti's hands ran over the knot. He eyed Shuna-Shapta and the baby staring at him. He focused on the infant with her dark amber eyes tending to cross toward each other.

"This child . . . " He looked at Thakadush-Satwa, "Is this baby what you hope for?"

Shuna-Shapta lost her composure for an instant as the eyes and aromas of her companions betrayed their surprise. Hegev also startled. His Adept looked first at Seti before gazing at the baby.

"A most profound Raw Sensitive!" Shuna-Shapta said as she smiled and looked down at her little charge.

"You and the child," Seti said, giving them an appraising look, "your faces are smooth!"

Shuna-Shapta frowned at him.

"Those possessed by your system have twisted faces in my eyes as if I walked through a ward filled with plague victims . . . but not you . . ." He continued to grip the knot as he leaned over the pond as if to examine them close. "The twisting is done for you. You possess a new face, distant from those remaining . . . what you would term 'raw.' You are a new creature distinct from our ancestors."

"Correct," Shuna-Shapta replied. "Each face here shall become 'smooth.' Your Sensitive eyes discern the sometimes awkward transition from the old to the new."

Seti pursed his lips and nodded. He rubbed the knot while looking into the Companion Pool. Several fish watched him back. "These fish," he gestured to the pond, "you said their wild relatives dwell in the sea?"

"Yes, though, an untrained eye would find little resemblance. These attained their perfection over generations."

Seti continued to watch their passive movements, "You plan this for us," he said, looking at her. "Their ancestors were unrefined, living in the open. These are 'improved' and live in a particular way in a place set aside for them. Were you to release them into the harbour, would they survive amongst their 'rude' relations?"

A group of nine laughing young women, most of them pregnant, walked to one side of the pond and stood oblivious to the discussion occurring at either side. They called out a series of names in turn, but not that of Menthuhatha. Each Companion rose when called, and they threw little morsels in for them. When done, they moved off, engaged in their own happy business.

"I may not say about our Companions," Shuna-Shapta said after they left. "I may speak of what shall occur as our Resplendent Work grows amongst us. Waste and stupidity shall dwindle and fall away. The screams sounding within this 'Kingdom of Pain' shall turn to a sweet, harmonious chorus. The needless suffering of 'death chasing life chasing death,' this absurd and pointless struggle, shall be channelled into a new society."

"I want no part of your 'new society!'" Seti raised his voice. "You venture too far! You go beyond reason in your presumption! Your ambition transcends hubris! You speak of 'needless suffering' while robbing us of what we hold most dear, our unique selves living as we choose. You are as those mocking sophisticates of the old capital of Thithanu, who laughed at all belief and attended plays where those attaining an afterlife chafed with boredom and overthrew their Gods. Despite our true faith not being thus lampooned, the noble Menem Priesthood still purged such shocking blasphemy. They knew what the populace wanted, a simple belief in a better world after death, ruled over by our supreme Untasha-Kabash."

"With respect," Shuna-Shapta said, "there is naught 'simple' about beliefs our bodies are prisons containing some immaterial aspect. To speak of all Anu as a putrid theatre of punishment suggests profound cognitive disquiet born within the midst of very dark and ignorant times. Most of your prophets, as with those speaking for say Achalam, the 'God of Four Bodies,' would now be diagnosed as suffering from a variety of brain ailments. As with all the other divinities satirized within that collection of plays known as the 'Everlasting Ennui,' fixed dogmas based upon what now appear to be wild delusions did not adapt to the fluid nature of life and the growth of society. The once prevalent Chelyakan faith was defeated by our distant grandmothers and their mothers growing cities and cultivating new cultures. Your 'noble' Menem priesthoods were themselves 'purged' by our common enemy, the Suvuka, during their terrible onslaught. Much of their senior hierarchy and civilization did not make it over the Mulungu Mountains to find sanctuary here upon Statos-Vey. They and their vast collections of Menem theology perished without a trace. I do not celebrate the loss of Thithanu, the 'World City.' I mourn for the suffering and death of its inhabitants and the destruction of history. I do not regret the breaking of the power of those craven priests and their endless persecutions. Unlikely though it may be, amongst those refugees reaching our grandmothers and their mothers here, were a few carrying copies of those satirical plays. They are still performed regularly as timeless comedies. If I may say so, given your background, I marvel at your education for even knowing of them."

Seti, gave her a mocking bow, "Our ship was notable for its extensive library, and my Adept is an excellent teacher. I could not begin my mission without understanding the extent of the Tolku's plight. While much was lost during the Suvuka Onslaught, more survived and new works have been added in Menem's honour. I presume you are aware of the writings of Nebutan?"

Hegev shook her head, but Seti appeared not to notice.

"My mother's generation were her contemporaries and knew her works well," Shuna-Shapta said. "Unlike many of her predecessors, she was regarded as neither deluded nor a simpleton. You do know she, and another critic from an earlier age known as Geltran, were indifferent to Menem or any religion." She looked at the baby in her arms, "I was just a few years older than this one when she died. Within that short span, her name has ceased being evoked here. Such is the fickle nature of fame with the passage of time and the arrival of new thoughts. What I do know is many of her dire warnings and predictions have failed to come to pass. All agree as to the quality of her work, but few now subscribe to her conclusions."

Seti had begun to twitch, and his eyes roved around them wildly. Hegev appeared distressed and tried to calm him while the silent ministry observers drew closer to observe him.

"It is clear to me," Seti raised his voice again, "that you have been raised in privilege and know little of the less fortunate's troubles. What of those lacking in your background and education? What of those whose desperation far outweighs their intellect? Are they to be deprived of their awe at their existence? Are they to be robbed of their comfort of eventual freedom from the muck of this life? Are they to be ridiculed for wishing to worship and give thanks for their deliverance?"

"Even the plays you mention spare the followers," Shuna-Shapta said in calming tones. "They mock bad ideas, not the credulity of the simple.

So many living within encompassing darkness has been the motivation for our Masters through the ages. They desired to rescue us from the horrors of our own making. Our general population has been subjected to each form of abuse from those purporting to be their saviours. They have been bent and twisted into terrible aberrations at their suzerain's bidding. You speak of those you have seen with 'twisted' faces. Whilst your Sensitive perceptions are profound, your understanding of what you perceive remains shallow. Your study is incomplete if you do not apprehend the sad procession of religions, leaving destruction and misery within their collective wake. The very worst appear to have used toxic notions of fear and shame to poison us against our bodies and natural inclinations. Self-Absorption was a universal malady. Self-Loathing seems the particular legacy of these absurd fortresses, composed of thin and empty air, demanding absolute obedience whilst providing no evidence of their existence."

"And what do you and your 'masters' provide them? All I see is the supreme form of abuse and manipulation. You reach in and change our very minds! You take the worst of the past and turn it into a science! Do you dare to accuse others of bending us into aberrations? In this, you are most certainly 'masters,' possessing terrible powers over us all. Even the Suvuka knew you were an offence to life. Their hatred for you is visceral! How can any of this be what the common population desire? What do you truly know of their needs and wants? All this," he gestured wildly around him, "is about your own power! You know nothing, and care nothing, for who the Tolku truly are!"

Shuna-Shapta smiled, "Throughout history and across our Skin of Anu this day, most wish for peace, order and good governance. They seek purpose, direction and fulfillment. They long to be honoured and cherished. Beyond these fundamentals, they adore beauty, grandeur, and majesty. When filled with satisfaction, the cancers of venomous ambition and vile greed die away. Naught is evil of itself until it grows beyond its proper bounds. Ambition is a pernicious deformation of personal esteem. Violence is its tool of choice. Greed is an obscene inflation of our basic need for sustenance. Theft is its primary action. We say those poisoned by these, and many other base impulses, are suffering from

'Self-Absorption.' This disorder harms both those possessed by it and the many victims surrounding them. Whilst few would genuinely dispute these observations, we alone possess the means to right the balance. This shall not destroy any vital aspect of ourselves, but change the proportions of each element to bring about a new harmony. You shall find a rich diversity of temperament and use within our Enclaves. Each member of our emerging clusters sparkles with their distinctive genius. What you shall not encounter is pride, avarice, greed, envy and a host of other plagues inspired by fear."

Shuna-Shapta paused. Seti said nothing, so she continued, "Your aunt counted herself among the ancient order of Water Mystics. These most-ancient Sensitives suffered through late prehistoric times when social and political violence abounded. From their deep observance of all life, they were amongst the first to speak out against Self-Absorption but possessed no tools to counter it. Thousands of years later, the Yin-Vinulan dynasty ruled an empire from this city. They enacted virtuous policy and enlightened governance just to be defeated by vile greed and venomous ambition leading to a series of ruinous civil wars."

She gestured around her, "Mystics and ethical philosophers had aroused this unifying dynasty and the rulers of other ancient royal houses. Their many well-meaning efforts were ever frustrated by failure. Their most magnificent creations, inspired by generosity and genius, were ever brought down by meanness and stupidity. This sad drama became a perennial theme of our history. Out of this fruitless effort and ineffectual struggle, our early Masters arose. They foresaw the ultimate solution to our dilemma and launched upon a plan taking hundreds of generations. 'Life must live with life' was their declaration. Their aim was for us to become the compassionate eyes of a balanced existence. Our Four Virtues of Majastas Life are 'Kindness,' 'Comfort,' 'Patience,' and 'Openness.' These aspects of 'Impartial Love and Caring' shall take the place of the current survival strategy of self-absorption and its litany of horrors."

"And what of those, in their perversity, refusing this general satiation?" Seti asked, gripping his knot. "It is true; you never concealed your plans. You broadcast them, and most on Statos-Vey welcome the news. I assure you this is not the case on Rho-Jashun. I also found many opposed to this ancient scheme on Avatay, an island inside your sphere of influence. I think it likely there are many such pockets, perhaps some closer than you think." He paused, "I stared into the eyes of a Suvuka! I have witnessed the elegance and perfection of what you would denigrate as 'raw' life. What you do subverts life's intention."

"And the noble 'intention' of crude and unrefined life? Blind survival forms its foundation. An agony-filled balance maintained by predation, infection and starvation upon one side and overproduction upon the other. It is an endless chain of mouths ever consuming and being consumed. Desperate survival may require such pitiless mechanisms, but they stand as an enemy to full living. This is the kernel of the issue playing out inside and outside of us." She leaned forward and looked into his eyes across the pond. "We heard of your encounter with our ancient enemy. We would have you tell us how you faced such a creature and lived."

"I danced," Seti answered.

"I welcome your explanation as to why this novel strategy worked."

Seti frowned, "Without warning, the giant rose over me. I had no hope of escape, and thought fled me. I began to dance to the creature's amazement. Something distracted it, and the beast fled, otherwise it would have tired soon and consumed me."

Shuna-Shapta gave him a respectful bow. "Your courage does you credit, but it was your imagination that saved you. You confounded the beast by cultural knowledge. We understand you performed a meditation exercise from the Menem tradition, itself the child of earlier customs. These creatures have their own rituals, including ceremonial dances. Your inspiration may prove vital to the work those upon Thermistal attempt with them. You provide living proof of the power of culture, the vital, living, cumulative environment we generate. With it, we weave a garment able to shield us from the excesses of raw life."

"'Culture?'" Seti shook his head and gestured, "Is this what we are surrounded by? This is a garish circus, an absurd and bizarre spectacle baring no resemblance to ordinary life. To my eyes, this is the height of artificiality and excess. The plants and animals here are not natural. They are creations of Tatchlan, as these 'Companions.' The southern cities, in particular this one, are at war with the surrounding countryside.

The 'cumulative environment' you generate is alien and offensive to those living outside it. You eat flat cakes but have no notion of what it is to grow and harvest Salarish. You may create a place where freaks and abnormality thrive, but beyond your Red Ring wall, they will die." He stood breathing hard after this tirade before frowning and looking down at his knot.

Shuna-Shapta smiled "So it may seem to you. As we speak, the refinements of this peak of civilization move well beyond our wall. I do not say the degree of specialization found here shall travel into the rude hinterland. Centres of power and their attendant concentrations of skill collect or generate specific areas of confluence. A new spring of life connections, breaking down the barriers and fear-inspired Self-Absorption, shall flow over the land. Within your lifetime, you shall witness the transformation. No matter where you go upon Anu's Flesh, you shall behold it."

She paused and noted how Seti's aroma began to alter, "You spoke of Salarish," she said quietly. "Those tall fields of your birth are not natural. Prehistory knew it as but one breed of grass amongst many covering the Marachla Plain. I am told the raw version had a very modest head of seeds. As earlier generations had done to perfect Charsha, the cereal crop best suited to our hot and wet climate, subsequent generations worked to improve Salarish. By unnatural means, these two crops eventually became the twin foundations of all our dishes. Any agricultural landscape is as 'artificial' as an urban one. The simple actions of a humble gardener are an imposition of mental culture upon thoughtless raw life. The arbitrary culling of some plants so that others may thrive is an act of benign imposition. Our Uluvatu Masters cultivated us with love for a better future."

Seti was beginning to lose the thread of what she said. He shook his head several times before opening one palm and staring at it. He began to shake, and his pale face went white. Hegev cried out as she grabbed the knot and threw it into the Companion Pond.

"You poisoned him!" She shrieked at Shuna-Shapta. Seti's knees began to buckle, and he held onto the rim of the pond, looking at Shuna-Shapta.

She shook her head and smiled at them, "He arrived poisoned. We begin to heal him."

Many of the Companions came to investigate the slowly submerging knot, nibbling at it as the juices of the Memanu spread over the surface.

CHAPTER 59

SINKIN

Secondary Epoch icon for the Ketukku mound

Day 399, jungle trails of southern Thermistal, hundreds of andas north of the Jabun Isthmus.

Sinkin, Setush and their new friend Visko danced in circles in the pouring rain. Durka, Makusk, and Visko's herd Kutur, numbering seven, also spun and shook in the welcome downpour.

"At last we rid ourselves of Kukernef Desert," Visko shouted out to the others' acclaim and shook himself hard. The rain began to fall in sheets, and the group of twenty-two Suvuka stood on their hind legs and allowed the torrent to buffet and cascade down their lean bodies. The three small herds had covered many hundreds of andas in the thirty-five days since they left the coast. They had passed by the desert and re-crossed the Jabun Isthmus on their way home. The rain let up, and they knew the little biters would soon return. They wallowed in pools of mud. Shortly after this they found a large Ketukku mound and began ripping it apart to feast on the millions of tiny insects. Together they reduced it to tiny broken pieces and lapped up enough for each of them to feel full.

"Will we return to Latatroos Shelter?" Sinkin called out as they sat and wiped themselves before licking each others fur to gain the final few defenders.

"Latatroos is north and far west of here," Morakav called out. "We are nearer the eastern coast. The trails are more level. The pathways are broad. They assist us in our speedy return."

Sinkin barked twice, "They were crooked and narrow to Avanchil by design?" Sinkin asked. The three herds began to laugh at the New Stags' expense.

"There was no malice in this," Hiratak said to the expressions on Sinkin and Setush's faces. "The run is a series of trials. With your triumph the way is made smooth. Now we must return you to your herds. They waited long for you. We see you alive. They do not. Our return home will take less than half the time."

"Sinkin," Morakav called out, "The next wave travels south. They fill those narrow pathways. There would be no room for us. Those starting their Four Paws remain ignorant of their ordeal's design. Brash New Stags cannot imprudently reveal what is to come. It also means we are not delayed in our return."

"Our one goal is ensuring bucks have their trials and return safely," Hiratak said.

"Long lines of Dams impatiently wait," Visko said, bumping Setush playfully. "Your new trial is siring the next generation. You must assume all adult duties. You will bring relief to the rest of the herd."

Hiratak nodded at this. He had come to have high regard for this late New Stag and valued his mature influence on Sinkin and Setush. "Visko is correct. This is the purpose of the Four Paws," Hiratak continued. "You left as cubs with modest roles. You return as Full Stags. You assume adult privileges and responsibilities. You are now full members of your herd."

Setush sat down, and the herds turned to him. He looked at the others and at Sinkin and Visko. "We run and run! Inside me, I do more running. The Four Paws forced me through many thickets. The path ahead is clear an I am lost." He looked at his own herd and asked, "What do we return to? The enemy remains unseen. I will join you. I will do my part. We saw many wonders and mysteries. They revealed the fate of our kind. How do we adapt to this larger life? Hesha Vira has revealed Herself. What does She intend? How will this Keeper movement affect us?"

Sinkin sat down beside Setush and nuzzled his ear playfully. "Our Paws Run left us with much to ponder. Those running ahead bring change. Pramath's Keepers will be in Avanchil. Keeper Datal will know their mission. Bucks travelling to Avanchil may hear new words. We will learn more. Our greatest challenge will be knowing what to embrace and what to reject."

Hiratak nodded, "Setush, I declared war on this Face. I fought Her presence among us. I near sacrificed my part of the run. I am not quick to embrace change. She had no place in my upbringing. I struggled learning of our Keeper's secret knowledge. This became my burden. Now . . ." He sat down in front of him and sighed, "She comes in my dreams like yours." Morakav and the others exchanged glances.

"She is benign and pleasant," Hiratak admitted, well aware of his surprising words. "My fear and distaste for her recede. I am accustomed to Her presence. I grow more peaceful at Her visage. I can accept Her positive influence. For one as old as I, change is difficult. Now I turn to embrace Her. I make this improbable adaptation. You will come to terms with these events."

Sinkin and Setush stared at Hiratak in amazement. Hiratak smiled, chuckled and laughed. Everyone laughed, and many tensions began to release.

"My dear comrade," Morakav came and playfully bumped Hiratak. "This reminds us of your courage! We welcomed Hesha Vira's visions.

We withheld speaking out of respect for you. A new root extends into Anu beneath us. Does it matter what the Keepers' plan is? This spreads beyond us. Their actions channel this new power. This is a worthy vision. It lifts us out of our bitterness."

"Setush," Visko said in a tentative voice, "you mention the enemy walking unseen among us."

Durka and Makusk herd tensed, Kutur Herd knew nothing of what Makusk Herd had revealed at Latatroos Shelter.

"We also heard rumours of altered herds," Visko said. "Do not give in to fear. Herdmaster Hiratak mentioned our gathering in larger numbers. Since our confinement, we have become spread out. Our vigour fades, and our numbers dwindle. We must examine our traditions. Our Danta, and other food beasts, also decline. We must refresh our stocks. Our gathering in larger numbers may prohibit the enemy sneaking among us."

As they pondered this, Sinkin stirred, "I hope I do not sound naïve," he looked at them, "I say this changes our future. Our Herdmasters say we ask new questions. We had new visions. The Keepers of Pramath Island possess a new purpose. Hesha Vira brings a new mission for ourselves and Anu." He looked at Setush's frown, "I know many questions remain! I am now at peace with them. These are large matters. We need time. Our paws will find Anu warm and gentle. I say this goes beyond a well-laid path. It is as when we swam back to shore. Anu tilts to send us home."

Setush smiled at his friend, "Perhaps Hesha Vira tilts Anu for us."

They laughed and began to run as the wind rose and stirred the jungle above them.

CHAPTER 60

Shuna-Shapta

Pictured: icon for Sheshenara

Day 444, Two-Week Twenty-Five, named Alatahanu – the 'Twelve Faces,' in the Master Enclave within the city of Bhampay at the start of the Twelve Faces Carnival.

Shuna-Shapta entered the Master Enclave, where she had spent most of her life. Since leaving for Thakadush Cluster over two hundred days before, she had not returned. She wandered through the complex, already bustling this early in the morning, to what had been her residence. She welcomed the familiar smells, sounds and sights of her childhood home. She made her way through the residence to a chamber rich in memory. Surrounded by peach-coloured walls and still holding conventional Masks of Office and Jubilation, sat a young man finishing a plate of steaming Charsha. Rich aromas followed familiar servants as they bobbed acknowledgement to her while carrying other emptied plates from the chamber.

"Greetings, Seti! Does our day of Alatahanu find you well?"

The boy smiled and set down his plate, "I enjoy 'fullness and fitness' Regent Shapta. Many thanks for your coming. Would you care to eat or drink?" He reached for the bell.

"With gratitude, I decline," she stood appraising him. "How long since we first met?"

"Is it over…one-hundred days?" Seti replied, beginning to rise as Shuna-Shapta gestured for him to sit. She came over to join him on the low bench facing the red and yellow lacquer screen. Through it could be seen various preparations for the annual Alatahanu Carnival.

Shuna-Shapta shook her head. "Our Companion Pond conversation took place within Two-Week Andura, making it some eighty days. I hear your hours here are full."

"Eighty?" Seti exclaimed, "I feel like five hundred days have passed! I have lived another lifetime in this brief span. I once feared doctors, but currently, I have extensive dealings with more 'Healers' and 'Soothers' than crew aboard the Jefaka."

Shuna-Shapta took the boy's hand. For the first time she noted the small markings on the underside of each of his fingers. His entire hand had lost some of its coarseness, and he had gained weight. His skin regained its colour after a recent shedding, and his lovely yellow hair assumed comely locks. "Have you benefited from these attentions?"

Seti sat back on the long bench and stared through the lovely screen, "If from birth you heard bells ever ringing in your ears, you accept it as normal. Should they stop, would you not be amazed?" He turned to look at her, "It is thus for me. An agitation has ever filled me," he shook his head in wonder. "This has largely ended. Whilst aiding in many ways, I remain mystified by how it began."

"How it began?"

"This 'ringing' was finally interrupted at the Companion Pond when we met. It was not sudden but just diminished as we spoke. Near the end, it dropped off, and I felt faint. Now it is gone. Gone! Much I now appreciate, but not this."

Shuna-Shapta nodded, "Majastas Salt."

Seti stared at her, and she smiled back, "To clarify, your Memanu Knot, coated with Majastas Salt, halted your 'bells.' You have learned more concerning our miraculous baby, Thakadush-Satwa. Our Resplendent Work chose not to follow our sober plans and produced a Majastas at once. Our Cluster-of-Clusters society hurries behind her, backward to our expectation. As a Majastas, she has many distinctive abilities, including linking those partaking of her fluids to herself and our Living System. She impudently licked and sucked upon your knot prior to your receiving it at our Companion Pond. Your skin absorbed her juices. We term this her 'salt.'"

"'Majastas Salt,'" Seti mused, "I recall my annoyance at, what I believed, a baby eating it."

They surprised each other by laughing in unison. Seti then began to muse. "So this 'Majastas Salt' forms the foundation of my new life. Salt is an effective cleanser," he looked at her hand holding his, "you are infused by it." They smiled at each other, "Thakadush-Satwa has touched me," Seti said. "I learn from those attending me, I arrived a tortured mass. I have found peace within true majesty, and so approach a new balance. I was bound in invisible chains and now find myself extended and opened in many ways. My head does not ache. Invisible weights no longer crush me. My endless chatter of voices is reduced to an occasional murmur. If my 'Menem' appear, their antics make me laugh. Many of these Soothing and Healing companions work with me each day to re-order myself."

He patted her hand, stood and walked over to the screen to examine it. He kept his back to her, "They employ methods I never associated with doctors. Forward, intimate, and assured in ways unknown back in my little spot amongst the Salarish. They oversee my body, altering each day. Your enclave has permitted me a portion of your former residence. Two women and five men attend me. We work for days and nights at a time. They use a variety of methods, and I perform unique tasks. Others join us, and we work together at length. They combine surprising actions and words. Elementary exercises reveal deep issues, intricate ceremonies simplify much, 'Vision Windows' open many dark rooms inside me." He pointed to a jumble of simple masks in a corner, "I did not appreciate the power of masks, nor how they could unleash inner truths as a bare face cannot. Employing these and many other amazing tools, they free me of bonds I did not know constrained me."

He turned to look at her, "So much fear! I carried and nurtured so much fear, engendering so much rage, feeding so much pride! I was a monster! Never in my life have this many, possessing such skills, devoted themselves to my welfare. Under their loving barrage, my body grows, and my sickness fades." He faltered and turned away from her.

Shuna-Shapta remained seated, listening to the emotion in his voice and scrutinizing the aroma coming off him. "Beyond employing masks, I remain innocent of these treatments," she said quietly. "Many skills converge here. They say you teach them more than they teach you. We have witnessed very few suffering from your state of health for many generations."

"This is in part due to Sheshenara," Seti said, turning to face her. "I have never known the like. Initially, I took just one drop a day. Now I have small doses, complimenting many other agents at each meal. They tell me these medicines aid me."

"Is this process hurried for you? I was assured you would not suffer pressure. Are you able to adjust to these innovations?"

Seti shook his head, "They have not rushed me. My body pushes me onward as if I stride down a hill growing ever steeper. My pace quickens with each step. When I pause, the pressure to continue grows strong. I feel a great weight," he indicated his pelvis, "growing and urging me ahead. As by a rope issuing from my navel, I am pulled to further depths."

Shuna-Shapta leaned forward, "Your life has changed! Your old self has fallen away. Without disturbing you, I have met a few of your healers here prior to this day. I spoke with two an hour ago. They praised your progress, yet said beyond speaking to me, you wished isolation this day. You do not wish to join our carnival? Has this work wearied you?"

"Regent and Operant, I am grateful for your concern," Seti said. "I have yet to decide how to mark this Alatahanu Day. I assure you we recess when I wish. I desired to speak to you quietly. I grow away from most former conventions, but a few linger. They introduce me to a way of life I had believed evil. I may no longer deny it paves the way to deep happiness and peace."

"Evil?"

Seti made a face and turned to look through the screen. Huge heads of several Principle Faces of Tatchlan could be seen bobbing down a distant avenue. He heard faint echoes of music and cheering accompanying the parade.

"I look with fresh eyes at my childhood," he continued to watch the distant celebrations. "It has now occurred to me we seldom touched each other. I recall hearing the phrase, 'Privation begets Self-Absorption.' Father told me just 'tapping hands' was dangerous. I have read how . . ." he turned and blushed.

"One of the Menem texts is titled the 'Zitapermas' after the author. He lived in northern Rho-Jashun long ago, perhaps a century before the Suvuka came. It has occurred to me our childhood and early life were similar." He shook his head sadly. "Zitapermas said the detained Menem inside him wakened and began to speak to him. Through this voice, he spoke to a Grand Menem, one of the four 'generals of the air,' named Vindaviran, known as 'The Teacher.' The utterances of this Vindaviran fill the works of Zitapermas. Regarding touch, The Teacher told him it enslaves us to Anu. He said it deludes us as to the truth of our genuine selves - being 'imprisoned' inside a 'sac of skin.'"

Despite herself, Shuna-Shapta frowned, recovered and nodded neutrally for him to continue.

"The Soothers better hide their expressions," Seti smiled at her, "but I begin to smell their true feelings on this. We have read several of these texts and speak of them at length. In a way, this continues what began aboard the Jefaka with my Adept, Hegev. I had begun to discover many inconsistencies in what I once believed to be immutable texts."

"Ah!" Shuna-Shapta said, "How fares Hegev? Does she play a part in what you do?"

"At first she stayed away and found lodging nearby. Later she came, and these Healers spoke to her. They say she did not suffer from my afflictions. We have spoken here of late, and I would presume to say she has found her own resolutions here." He paused at a new thought, "She also handled the knot, though less than I did. The Majastas Salt affected her also?"

"Yes," Shuna-Shapta replied. "One pat would suffice. As you say, our Majastas Salt would find a different situation inside her to yourself." She waited before saying, "I would hear more of your childhood taboos."

Seti nodded, "Restrictions surrounded us. I now realize we actually feared each other. I do not understand why this hateful state was established. We worked and had our meals together, but compared to here, we generally avoided contact and lived separately. Whilst I observe cluster mates having solitary walks and quiet moments, you remain within close proximity to each other. My Soothers and Healers wish to initiate me to this life and surround me. I begin to find deep tranquillity encompassed by this profusion of stroking."

"Shash!" Shuna-Shapta said, "I heard you mention your ripening sense of smell."

"I begin to appreciate the vital role of scent," Seti said. "My doctors use many ways to stimulate and challenge my ability to read aromas. They say my nose is 'growing.' I note how they confer by scent alone and wish to delve to their level."

"Shash! Shash!" Shuna-Shapta said. "Whilst reading another's Aroma Accord may reveal emotions, it may not replace speech." She then frowned, "I remain interested in what else you once believed 'evil' here. My life has been dedicated to bringing happiness and hope. I would never have imagined others saw it as evil."

Seti remained facing her, "My former thoughts retreat. Our Majastas Salt both cleanses and provides a balm to my entire self. Yet, eighty remarkable days cannot fully address fourteen difficult years." He cocked his head, "I have heard a saying, something on 'thin air' and 'loam.'"

"This resembles an ancient Master truism," Shuna-Shapta said. "Many link these two, I assume you refer to: 'The air is thin and empty, the loam is rich and full.'"

Seti came back to sit beside her, "Yes! You made a passing reference to it at the Companion Pond. I recall another . . . referring to the 'empty sky.' These phrases contain my struggle. I always loved the air and hated the soil. We bent and scraped in the fields, and I saw just dirt, filth and death in the black ground. I believed the Salarish rose to nobility as it grew away from its roots. As a child, I believed our cakes, coming from the seeds ripening high above us, were pure because they dwelt in the winds. Nothing stood between them and Nu. I suppose one short step separated such notions from believing Menem, pure creatures of light, brushed our Salarish as they passed by. I have come to terms with many self-deceptions, including my willful division of life and myself."

"What do you mean by 'willful division?'"

Seti sat back on the bench and pondered. Outside could be heard distant rhythms of many tiny street bands playing in different quarters of the city with voices raised in song and laughter.

"I grew up in fear," he began. "Unlike others, our families suffered no hostility. We were so poor and remote, no one thought us worth the trouble to raid. Despite this, we ever scanned the horizon, when we could see it, for signs of trouble. We listened for sounds of approach through the windswept fields. Within our walls, I cannot say I suffered abuse. I now admit to myself my mother, aunt and sisters did love me. Despite this, I ever felt . . . inadequate. I was the smallest and found tasks others mastered quickly challenging. Fear of failure, coupled with my first voices, let to my growing isolation. To compensate, I strove to be emphasized for supposed powers. I regret to say I longed to dominate them. Their laughter and good-natured mockery further fed my frustrations. My father and a few others clung to the Menem faith. They spoke of this life as a filthy stop on the way to shining Ranvartawan. I watched my mother and siblings smeared in mud for the rites and judged them polluted. Their ease with their own and other's flesh disturbed me. Then came the crushing weight on my chest, the pounding headaches and . . . the thundering voices. I had a shining vision of perfect forms of light and felt freed from my little life. I was now special! I was now important! In this way, I divided myself from others. I also divided myself into a polluted body encasing an imprisoned Menem."

Tears gathered in his eyes. "My illness chose to take the form of my father's simple faith. Their myths fed my delusions. I look back on what I became and find myself filled with revulsion. I told so many lies to my father, many others, and the most to myself. I must confirm, under the fine words and complex observances, the Menem faith was based on terrible fear and delusions. Its founding tenants speak of Anu as a prison. Our bodies served as 'disease-ridden cocoons.' Splendour belonged to death alone and the resulting freedom from forms. It was the ultimate escape from the challenges of living. Captain Emedin said religion captures vulnerable credulity, ties it to insanity and drags it to power. I can no longer deny the madness of Zitapermas or that I almost followed his delusional path. Unlike him, I now have enlightened companions assisting me in freeing myself from my folly."

Tears flowed freely down his cheeks, "I now pity Zitapermas! I realize how alike we were. I mourn his sad fate and wonder at how near I came to follow him. I look at his life with new eyes, revealing his contemporaries' ignorance and gullibility for their believing his every utterance. They saw his glowing presence not as a sign of his fevers, but of his Menem made manifest. Those who became his lieutenants saw him as a way to their own power. The tragedy of Zitapermas and others like him is they were surrounded by those who fed their illness. The sole difference between those benighted 'prophets' and myself is the quality of our friends. During our visits here, Hegev and I have spoken much of Zitapermas. She is ashamed of how her growing ambition came to guide her actions towards me. She even donned some of those masks and allowed herself to purge these terrible inclinations." He looked at the pile of masks and heaved a quaking sigh.

"Dear boy!" Shuna-Shapta exclaimed, taking his hands in hers. "You are bare-faced, yet this sounds as a primal mask speaking."

Seti nodded toward the pile of masks, "One of those sent me to this deep level. I have repeated this several times wearing him and others. I put his dire face on, looked in our mirror and plunged to a depth beyond deception. My terrible pain and rage have filled this chamber."

Seti drew slow breaths, and Shuna-Shapta continued to gently grip his hands.

"When we met at the Companion Pond," Seti began at last, "I said the Masters wished to rob us of our uniqueness. I hear Nebutan, the Sawlu Clan's anti-Tatchlan scholar who died over a decade ago, described the cluster ideal as destroying individual dignity. I note you step with ease outside your circle, showing no signs of distress. I know your brother freely travels to and from Thermistal to study the Suvuka. Open cluster structures allow movement within and between circles based on shifting desires and changing 'uses.' As you predicted at the Companion Pond, I observe a great diversity of personality amid these circles and see each cluster-mate has time alone. All my experiences agree that true majesty surrounds me. At the pond, you told me most Tolku wish peace and security over 'self-absorbed' ambition and greed. You said fear dwindles before satisfaction and abundance. These Menem warnings are disproved each day. This, complimenting my inner work, modifies me. Until this day, such wisdom and nobility were unimaginable to me."

"Come," Shuna-Shapta said as they stood. She drew him around the screen and onto the wide balcony where she and her little sister once spoke about her school trip. They went to the railing and looked past the enclave's roofs to the jubilant city beyond, down to the distant harbour.

"This city bears many Maja infants," Shuna-Shapta gestured to the distant glittering metropolis. "They perform powerful alchemy throughout Bhampay and all Statos-Vey. Employ your 'growing nose' to sense our health and vitality. True Clusters multiply! These splendorous babes infuse our city! Emerging Clusters encircle Thakadush, where all are born Maja."

Seti examined the jubilant vista as it continued to grow more animated before turning to Shuna-Shapta, "Why have you, and many others, done this for me? I could have left here and, like Zitapermas, led a crazed and short life having no impact on this beautiful world."

"Tatchlan wishes this for each Tolku of Anu," Shuna-Shapta found herself raising her voice over the celebrations. "We Servants may all be seen as 'Healers and Soothers' of our nation. You were mired and burdened more than most, and thus we were drawn to administer aid. You also possess gifts worthy of unfettered expression. We find joy and gain honour in leading you to your true self."

They stood for another moment. Without another word, they walked together through the enclave and out into the boisterous festival.

CHAPTER 61

Seti

Above: icon for Bhampay

New Year 1273, Day One, Two-Week One, Atra, the Bursting Flame, within the Inner Harbour of the city of Bhampay.

Captain Emedin stood to the harbourmaster's right as she guided the Jefaka through the maze of Bhampay's Inner Harbour. The ship passed into the tall shadows of the outer docking structures and the interlocking labyrinth of quays and wharves amidst the city's dense sounds and smells.

"The harbourmaster will not say," Emedin said quietly to Dine on her right, "but something stirs in the city. I have never seen the Inner Harbour this full, and most of these are not commercial craft."

Dine nodded but said nothing. Their relations were still quite strained since events on the island.

"She informs me due to our stay on Avatay, the usual inspection is deemed unnecessary," Emedin continued in a conversational tone.

"They already have what they want," Dine answered.

Before Emedin could answer, one of the crew called out, "Seti! I see Seti!"

Dine frowned at his captain, "Even with unforeseen delays; the Yamagad should have sailed out of here many two-weeks ago."

Emedin shrugged, "They are likely mistaken. If the masters had detained Seti, he could not meet us; otherwise, he is likely long gone."

Emedin and Dine watched the busy wharf on their right to follow the waving directional arms at the front of the ship.

"Dine!" Emedin exclaimed. "Look there! It *is* Seti!"

Seti's yellow hair fell in short golden locks, and he wore an oversized orange top, yellow wrapped pants, and thin green sandals typical in the city. Above his head was an elegant patterned parasol the same colour as his sandals. He waved at the approaching ship. Dine's face had lit up as he followed his Captain's pointing finger. As he examined the boy, his expression became ashen. In contrast, Emedin's tense expression relaxed, and she grinned as few of her crew had ever seen. Most on deck began to cheer and shout at Seti.

"You are grown, fat boy!" Emedin bellowed out across the ship, causing many of the crew to laugh and clap at him. Seti turned comic as he tried to hide his stomach with his parasol. Dine turned to look at the Captain.

"*This* is our Seti? It cannot be!" He moved forward to get a better look at him. "This accursed place has swallowed him, and you laugh and cheer?"

The Captain stepped away from the startled harbourmaster, puzzled by this sudden jubilation followed by contention. She cast them a sideways glance as they stood by the railing.

"Recall how he looked three years ago this day!" Emedin exclaimed. "A scrawny, filthy, lost little creature, his fevered head full of nonsense. He was a New Year's novelty you did not want onboard. This is a healthy and happy young lad. Is this not a cause for celebration?"

Dine shook his head, "Where is our *prophet*? This is but another sleek Bhampaian dandy! What of our *mission*? What of his voice raised in the cause of our clan?"

"Yoking our cause to madness dishonoured our clan! He was sick! Now he has received treatment."

"I fear for us all if one possessing his fire is quenched! Will we receive 'treatment?' Where is Hegev? How can they rob him of his dedication and vision?"

They could no longer see him where they stood but heard his voice. Crew members now began shouting down to him, and he answered back. Emedin turned back. "Is it a crime for a 'prophet' to bathe and feed himself?"

"Captain! His attire is a minor issue. His manner has changed! By his bearing, I see his restlessness and drive are gone!" Dine frowned as Seti now appeared below them on the starboard side in front of a raised platform. Two walking wheels were positioned on top of the platform, either side of an unloading crane. Most of the crew had moved to this side as a shorter figure in a dark uniform approached and spoke to Seti. "Is that young Master Mek?" Dine said.

Emedin screwed her face as she peered down at the second figure, "Well, he has grown." Mek-Piprith cast a glance at them while gesturing to Seti. As they watched, Mek-Piprith and Seti's intensive discussion turned into an argument. Emedin turned back to Dine. "I am going down."

She strode forward and called for a ladder as the ropes were caught by the waiting dockhands below. She descended and jumped onto the shore as Mek-Piprith and Seti turned to watch her approach. The two young men could not be more different. While shorter, the heir to Sawlu Clan stood stocky and robust. His square face had his father's hardness, along with a gravity Emedin had not seen in him before. These features and demeanour gave him the look of one ten years older than Seti instead of three to four. His piercing eyes, dark hair worn in a tight braid, and his father's strong jutting jaw were defining features. He was dressed in the black and green uniform of the Sawlu Clan, itself more formal than expected at the docks.

"For one hundred and twenty-four days I have been restrained from meeting this lad sending Jefaka to Thermistal!" he gestured at Seti as he strode toward Emedin. He appeared to be accompanied by a sizeable entourage, similarly attired, who stood poised nearby. "The authorities informed me of his arrival on Day 363 of last year but instructed me to wait on your arrival before we could conclude our business."

"Seti! Seti" a voice from the deck called out above.

"Hail to our Prophet Seti!" cried another.

"I need a dream read, Seti," this comment was followed by general laughter.

Mek-Piprith stared at the crew in amazement.

"Enough!" Emedin shouted. "Dine! Prepare to unload all cargo." Her First Officer nodded once up on deck and began barking orders as the crew rushed away to their duties. Jefaka came to rest with the platform and crane positioned amidships. The port crew freed the walking wheels and made the necessary fastenings to power the crane. Several carts stood in line behind the platform and were now brought forward to receive the cargo.

Mek-Piprith regarded the Captain before turning back to Seti. "You appear troubled at this display of devotion. I was given to understand before this you cultivated it." He began walking back toward him as he spoke, "You were their Storm Invocate and Dream Reader, both ancient if seldom employed shipping vocations. Then you became their prophet! Did you not plan to become a Menem General next, sweeping over Rho-Jashun?"

"I am the cause of their error," Seti answered in a small voice lost in the noise. He looked at Emedin. "Out of kindness," he raised his voice, "my captain took me aboard three years ago and attempted to educate me. I repaid her with trouble and disaster. My illness has brought sorrow and loss to this venture."

"That it has," Mek-Piprith said, looking at Emedin. "Despite these catastrophic errors in judgement on 'your' captain's part, we have more than salvaged Jefaka's situation. Given our enforced delay in interviewing you, we have conducted extensive negotiations with our clients here. Part of our leniency towards you comes from your powerful new associates here. They arranged for us to be granted an audience with a new class of patrons formerly beyond our reach. As a result, we have procured a precious cargo of luxury items."

He gestured at nearby crates, "These include two hundred Azure Stone cubes of the finest quality from a new mine in the southern Veradapandra Mountains. Each possesses such perfect densities as to be guaranteed to produce one hundred slices each! These cubes are filled with generous deposits of Argent and Lapis and an abundance of other gem-quality minerals coming on the market from the same mine. Along with these, we were able to purchase quantities of black Antimony and unfinished pieces of Ferrite, Cerium and Azel."

He looked around the assembled group, "Our metal crafters will produce many fine gems from them. Captain Emedin may be aware of my father's passion for Antimony. The usual exchange of our raw materials and produce for their rare elements, and finished goods are in our favour for once. Our Jefaka will return with more than quadruple value aboard. The profits from this unexpected boon offset both the cargo losses and will handsomely compensate the lost shipmates' families. It will also bring a smile to many wealthy and powerful faces back home. By this stroke of good fortune, your costly diversion is more than balanced out."

While the dock was more noisy than usual with all the traffic, it seemed to Emedin that Master Mek was speaking more for the surrounding group than for them. All his words and mannerisms were exaggerated as if he were on the stage.

"Your reprimand is misdirected," Emedin said, coming to stand beside Mek-Piprith. At Dine's direction, the crane began to creak to life and sent its cables down into the hold. The dock walkers set a slow pace on the crane's two wheels before the first cargo lift.

"I am finished with him and start on you," Mek-Piprith said, looking up at the Captain. "The regulations on bringing passengers aboard are clear."

"And are broken by each captain of my acquaintance," Emedin replied. "I recall your father finding a wife here many years ago."

"Wife?!" Mek-Piprith spat. He began to say more but forced himself to stop and took a long breath. "You more than most know captains foolish enough to deviate from their course always come to grief! You exceeded all other follies by sailing out into the open sea in an absurd attempt to avoid this city! You could have lost this ship, two year's worth of cargo, and her crew! Lives and cargo were lost!"

"We repeat what we already corresponded to each other," Emedin said. "You detail my errors and I our unique circumstances."

"Despite all our correspondence, I admit still being unprepared for the intensity of your crew's acclaim for this one," he gestured to Seti. "He bears none of the marks you described."

"Ah! I must agree and am happy for it! He is marvellously recovered since arriving here. Seti looks well and rested."

"I am improved," Seti ventured. "I submit to wise doctors, yet many other hands healed me within these past two-weeks. The voices, riot and delusions dissipate into the thin air. I regret my shameful manipulation. I used my bewildered state to aggrandize myself at your expense."

"No need for such words!" Emedin said, moving to embrace him. "Saying you are better is sufficient. I put us in the storm path, and the storm stole our crewmates and friends."

The first large crate rose above the deck. Other dockhands now turned the entire platform, so it swung over to the dock to be lowered into the waiting cart. Many began familiar work songs as they settled into their routines.

Mek-Piprith appeared distracted and several times looked down the pier in expectation of something. "What remains is the fact this boy turned you inside out," he near shouted over the noise as he turned back to ensure those on the ship heard him. "We will interview the entire crew on this to complete my report to father." He turned back and stepped closer to them, "From what I see, they will agree with your assessment and actions." He looked long at Seti, "Nothing mitigates the harm your claims and deeds caused our clan. None suggest you are responsible for those deaths or the loss of our property, yet you would not be welcome in Wazaratcha. I can assure you this radical message of yours would be poorly received there. I am tasked with informing you the entire council unanimously voted to bar your entry."

Dine had clambered down the ladder and approached. Behind him, the crew continued to work below decks. He approached as Seti bowed his head "I am not recovered and wish to stay within Bhampay where a new education begins for me. I may not return to Rho-Jashun for some time, if ever."

"Apostate!" Dine shouted. "Faithless and disloyal servant! Our Menem weep over your treachery! Generations will condemn your infidelity! You abandon us and lie down with the enemy! Slave!"

"Dine!" Emedin shouted. As the next crate rose above the deck, many crew rushed to look down at the shouting. The dockworkers also paused in their songs at the unusual commotion.

"Where is she?" Dine ranted, ignoring the captain. "Where is Hegev? She would not consent to this!" He gestured to his decorous clothing. "She found new life in your visions! Your uncompromising purity renewed her! Despite her years, she had travelled from the bitter 'Eastern Gate' of Kana-Moptu on her 'Warm Rewards.' She had such pride at the thought of returning and remaking Rho-Jashun. Now you make filth a virtue. Where have you abandoned her?"

The other members of the 'Suvuka Pact,' those accompanying their water-gathering trek through the night before Seti met the Suvuka, now began to climb down to join Dine.

"No harm has befallen her," Seti said in a calm voice. "When we heard our Jefaka had arrived, she planned to join me here. She shall arrive presently, and you may enquire as to her health yourself."

A tense silence filled the group standing before him. The clan officials and Captain also stood as witnesses to this anxious moment.

"Both of you!" Dine said at last. "We lost our Adept and our Prophet!" He turned and looked at the Suvuka Pact and the others. "He has deserted us! Our cause is lost!"

"Your cause was lost from the beginning!" The powerful voice of Emedin rang over them. "See past your sorry ambition and vainglorious dreams to your memories of our Nebutan! You dishonoured her memory by even considering using this boy's illness! She would have loathed you for what you tried to fashion out of his web of delusions! Have you forgotten her contempt for all credulity and superstition? Now he has finally received proper care. Are you blind to how happy and well our boy is? Do you not care about our Seti being whole and at peace?"

"I do, and I merit your condemnation the most."

Hegev stood more vital and calm than any remembered. She wore a multicoloured dress, and her hair gently caught the sea breeze.

"I congratulate you, Captain," she smiled and gave Emedin a short bow, "I had not thought it possible one voice could dominate the din here."

Emedin examined her for a time, "It comes with the position."

"How is this possible?" Dine exclaimed, looking at her. "We are destroyed when two so committed and devout are twisted in so short a time!"

"My friend," she stepped closer, and Dine backed away from her. "My friend," she continued, "I do not deny I am changed. Seti's transformation is more profound because his disorders varied so from his true nature. He is happy and at peace! When have you beheld him so?"

"The virtues of 'happiness' and 'peace' do not stand alone," Dine hissed at her. "When a complete abandonment of deep values couples them, they are signs of vice! I know friends who came to contrary positions from what they once held. The dramatic amending of views comes from many things, most important being the gentle passage of time. But this . . ." he gestured at her and Seti. "This is no natural modifying of perspective! This is a demonstration of two passionate advocates of freedom overwhelmed by the force they once swore to oppose. I loathe the sight of both of you! Perhaps we can do nothing to this power, but I will no longer deal with either of you. The Seti and Hegev I knew and loved are gone!"

He turned to Emedin and took a deep breath, "Captain, you have known me for a plain and simple man. It was an accident of circumstance that brought us together all those years ago under your patron. I say now you were far more the devotee of Nebutan than I. Many of her elevated musings flew over me. I was not alone in being discomforted by some of her teachings but saw hope for our historic cause in her influence. Perhaps this was ambition more than conviction. What I know is, for a time, I knew true devotion," He pointed at Seti. "I was possessed by a noble belief! An elevating faith fortified me! They provided me with joy and grandeur, such as I had never known. Now it is all gone. My inner Menem shrinks away and is extinguished." He turned and climbed back up onto the ship.

"The rest of you!" Mek-Piprith barked at the remaining members of the Suvuka Pact, "get back to work!" Confused, they turned and slowly followed Dine back up on deck. The second crate was now secured on the first cart and began to pull away as the dockworkers slowly returned to their songs. Mek-Piprith turned to Emedin and was about to speak when he spun around at the approach of a large, enclosed cart.

He turned to his entourage, "Continue supervising this," he gestured at the ship. He pointed at Emedin, Seti and Hegev, "You three will accompany me. We must speak in private."

He pulled the door open and jumped in, directing Hegev to be seated beside him on his left and Emedin across from him and Seti at her side. With the doors shut, the noise was significantly lessened. The windows patterned with artful depictions of interlocking flocks of birds so none could see in or out. The stationary cart had a lush interior of quality workmanship and carried a trace of a floral aroma.

The young man hung his head and held out a hand to forestall any enquiries. At last, he sat back and looked at Emedin across from him.

"Father is coming."

"Jine-Piprith?" Emedin exclaimed, "Coming here? Impossible! He swore he would never come back to the south, certainly not to this city."

"After Nebutan's death, I know." Master Mek's manner had entirely changed. All his bluster was gone, and in its place was uncertainty and resignation.

"Surely this is unnecessary! Apart from seeing my log, you and your father have everything you need for the enquiry."

"Oh, I have seen your log, or rather I have seen a facsimile of such professional-grade as would put our copyists to shame," Master Mek answered. "It was reviewed here and sent north. No doubt father has it by now." He leaned forward, "Do you find this at all curious?"

Emedin regarded him for a moment, "That you had received a copy of my log?" she paused, "No, on reflection, I suppose not. The Avatay Port Authority told me they were making a copy, as is standard practice. It was clear to me the Memanu Field incident had flagged the Jefaka. Certain events, including several intensive interviews, also suggested their keen interest. The master's hand was evident in many events on Avatay. I did not know how many copies were made or where they went."

Master Mek sat back, "I have been informed that multiple copies were made, including some now residing in Upata-Shepsus. They occupy reading tables of ministry officials you and I would never hope to be granted an audience with."

Emedin paused, finally answering, "Indeed?"

"Captain, we are swept up in larger events, and all we can do is stay afloat. Jefaka's voyage is both of no importance and extreme significance, to not only to this city but Statos-Vey and all of Anu. Before you left home and began The Circuit, our agents here began making reports of strange events in this city and the capital. They have only increased in the ensuing three years. While our lives changed without our knowledge on Day 163 of 1271, an additional decisive event occurred on Day 349 of Two-Week Dolmel of last year. Since then, all trends increase in frequency and continue to accelerate. There is no time to go into greater detail on this. Suffice it to say that the Duamang Age has ended, and the age of Tatchlan begun. It would have been imprudent of me to commit any of this to paper, so we finally discuss this rapidly changing circumstance."

Captain Emedin stared in silence at Master Mek.

"Emedin!" Mek-Piprith again leaned forward and began an urgent whisper causing the rest to lean in towards him. He pointed south as he spoke, "The 'Tooth' and the parade grounds before it teems with activity! Hundreds of temporary shelters are raised at speed. The air is filled with banners and ensigns! A third of all top officials from every ministry arrive from the capital!" He leaned in even further, "They prepare for the arrival of the Emperor!"

Captain Emedin sat back, "I do not understand! What import do such events have for us Master Mek? Surely the Emperor visits this, the commercial hub of Statos-Vey, many times each year. Why would your father feel the need to be in attendance? What do you mean by declaring the Duamang Age at an end? What happened two years ago on Day 163?"

Mek-Piprith sat back abruptly and appeared to struggle with his next words; finally, he threw up his hands and declared, "The Emperor comes to pay homage to the Majastas." He held up both hands to forestall questions before clapping them over his face while taking several deep breaths. He took his hands away and stared into space before he began to twist the end of his braid.

"Our Nebutan was mistaken!" he finally declared leaning in again. "Tatchlan did not come in a thousand small miraculous births, although those now take place each day throughout Bhampay, Upata-Shepsus and beyond. It is confirmed the supposed culmination of the Master's plan has come first."

He paused again and took another breath, "The Majastas was born here in 1271 on Foremost Day of Two-Week Paultesh, Day 163. Since her arrival, Tatchlan has blossomed in full in this city. You have just stepped off the Jefaka captain. A short walk will confirm this to you. Neither father nor myself can afford not to be here to protect Sawlu Clans' interests in what is certainly an epochal event."

He looked at each of them, "The four of us are from the north," he gestured to them all. "Three of us are from the Wazaratcha Archipelago. We are very far from our windswept home, subject to the deadly embrace of the Tharapura Ocean. You madam," he turned to Hegev on his left, "took the longest journey from our 'Eastern Gate.' Now we sit together, south of the equator, needing to hold on to what little we have during this tropical maelstrom."

He was now sweating profusely to the detriment of this uniform. "Notwithstanding my upbringing and the history of our clan, my father and I, who often disagree, are of one mind." He looked directly at Emedin, "Before he commenced his trip here, he sent a final dispatch. It arrived last night. In it, he asked me to say to you . . ." he pulled out a tube and shook out the rolled document inside. The scroll was thin and surprisingly long. He expertly unrolled the bottom and re-rolled the top until he reached near the end, "'Tell Emedin,' he says, "to recall the play we saw in our youth, 'Turms and Aivas,' where the vanquished foe Ermania gave a speech with the famous line 'we cannot fight the wind.'"

He looked up, and Emedin, whose face had become blank, nodded.

Master Mek continued to read, "Twelve hundred and seventy-three years ago the Tatchlan Master Duamang took the ancient horror of the Brangnam Plague and recast it into a servant only interested in the Suvuka. We should have then seen the futility of our cause. Tatchlan painlessly and silently struck down the Suvuka by making them barren. By making our wombs fertile, our ambition is undone by joy.' He goes on to say, 'The winds favour our gentle contention with the will of Panchala so we should make good time. Tell her she may arrive before me, but I will be there soon. Then we may speak at length on our future." Master Mek meticulously re-rolled the document and inserted it back into the tube while Captain Emedin sat in stunned silence. "He sails on one of our new sloops equipped for swift travel down the coast against Panchala's northward current. We expect him here tomorrow or the day after."

Captain Emedin pondered before finally saying, "Be all this as it may, what role do the Jefaka, my logs, and these two play in this?"

Master Mek laughed, "*These two*," he gestured at Hegev and Seti, "have already had an audience with the infant Majastas! They are on friendly terms with the Majastas Regent, herself an exceptional Master among her kind despite being younger than myself. Oh, and they now both reside in what is known here as a 'Master Enclave,' in the former residence quarters of the Shuna Cluster. The Majastas Regent's name is *Shuna*-Shapta. Seti has been receiving intensive treatments for the ailments you, and the island clinic, chronicled. His former Adept here has now joined his endeavour inside this residence. Despite having just a few other matters to attend to, the Majastas Regent has visited them on more than one occasion, having a great interest in Seti's progress. This personal interest of hers has signalled a general interest in every aspect of Seti's life. I have heard him referred to here as a 'powerful raw sensitive' worthy of extensive study."

"Captain," Seti turned to look at Emedin, "there is so much more to tell. Know I was innocent of much that has been said here until back on Two-Week Alatahanu, during Wellbeing Day, when I attended our Alatahanu Carnival here. Until then, complete seclusion enveloped me as I underwent intensive ministrations. This commenced immediately after Hegev and I arrived during Two-Week Andura. I have no involvement in these profound state affairs. Our Regent greeted us when we first arrived and has overseen my subsequent therapy. My healing began with our tiny Majastas herself and continues this day."

"You can see why father wishes close relations with Seti and Hegev, captain." He turned to look at them both, "Sawlu is your captain's employer and Wazaratcha is her home. We have no such hold over either of you. My briefings on your progress, coupled with my observations today, lead me to think it likely neither of you will hasten to return to our wintry home. I can see this lush place has far more to offer you both. A 'powerful sensitive' will no doubt have innumerable opportunities within these specialized Enclaves. If I may say so madam, you may have noted how the aged are treated with reverence here. If you can adapt to this climate, I would, in fact, recommend you remain here for a better future."

He bent his head, and the rest waited. "We would hope both of you will consider assisting us, in the memory of the land of your birth, and all those relations and friends still dwelling there. While your aspirations for your futures may have changed, I hope you retain some measure of affection and respect for your original homeland." Seti and Hegev looked at each other before both nodding to Master Mek. "We shall do what we can," Hegev answered.

The group then briefly lapsed into silence until all noticed Captain Emedin shaking her head in amazement.

"Captain," Hegev said, looking across at her. "You grapple with this all at once. We who have had near one-third of a year here to digest this are still struggling to encompass it all. Seti and I have both dealt with profound regret, have renounced much and embraced more. Our visage may be familiar, yet our inner selves have undergone a metamorphosis. You behold its benefits for Seti. Whilst my alterations are less apparent, I am grateful, even at my age, for many rectifications of my modest person.

I now see the tragic waste of others reaching my age burdened with such useless cargo."

After a brief pause, Master Mek stirred, "I must now take my leave. Father's instructions are clear that you three are going to the Master Enclave. Captain, your effects may be sent for at any time. You and the senior members of your crew are to commence your own sequestering there at once. My staff will see to this, and there will be no exceptions, including your disgruntled first officer. You are correct, Sawlu knows all it needs about your journey and Seti's impact on it. The interviews are a formality that will be dispensed with in short order before our real business begins. Eventually, all the crew will be relocated to the Enclave, where you will occupy the former residence of this new Regent's cluster. Despite being the senior Sawlu Clan representative in this city, there is no room to turn around in my quarters, so I will also be taking up temporary residence there. I am informed the layout will be unorthodox in our eyes and may require some adaptations. When father arrives, he will be immediately conducted to the Enclave and the future, not the past, will be the sole subject under discussion."

"Master Mek!" Captain Emedin said as the youth reached for the door. "I am speechless about much, but can say one thing. Your work and words this day does credit to your father and our clan!"

Young Master Mek managed to contain his emotions as he bowed to them all, opened the door, and stepped out of the cart. He swiftly instructed the driver, and, as the carriage jolted into life, his former brass voice could be heard receding into the general port racket.

The three rode in silence for a time before Seti stirred and turned to his former captain. "When we are settled, I shall show you a new skill I have acquired."

"What skill is this?"

Seti smiled, "How to *untie* knots."

CHAPTER 62

Sinkin

Pictured: Vettencore Passage icon

Day Forty-Eight, Two-Week Three, Topy - The Needle, Sursogra Round near the Vettencore Passage.

Over three years since their initial standing at the Vettencore Passage before Sinkin's Stag Run, Durka, Makusk and Kutur herds entered Sursogra Round. After their initial haste, they often rested during their return trip. Sinkin, Setush and Visko now led as they ran and bellowed for their celebratory Mesmerizing Run. Many gathered to watch, including those from Durka and Makusk Herds remaining behind. Kutur had a long way to go before reaching their homeland. The three New Stags returned to where their run began. They would roar, gesture and dance their defiance at the Vettencore Passage.

* * *

Shuna-Vurupta, the comely brother of Shuna-Shapta, climbed the stair toward the top of the eastern wall of the Vettencore Passage. This time he went alone to look over the Suvuka territories on the other side. He had returned home from his school trip to find all changed. His sister and the Majastas Babe were merged, and government officials of the most profound grade waited at the Companion Pond for an audience. She, 'Everlasting Servant' Tanas and many others showed a keen interest in his observations regarding the Tolku on Thermistal and their work on the Suvuka. Prior to his arrival, his elder sister had met a powerful Raw Sensitive, raised in the wilds of the north. Shuna-Vurupta was amazed to hear of his meeting a Suvuka and dancing before it. He had the youth demonstrate the dance to him several times and practiced it during his voyage back across the Panchala Sea.

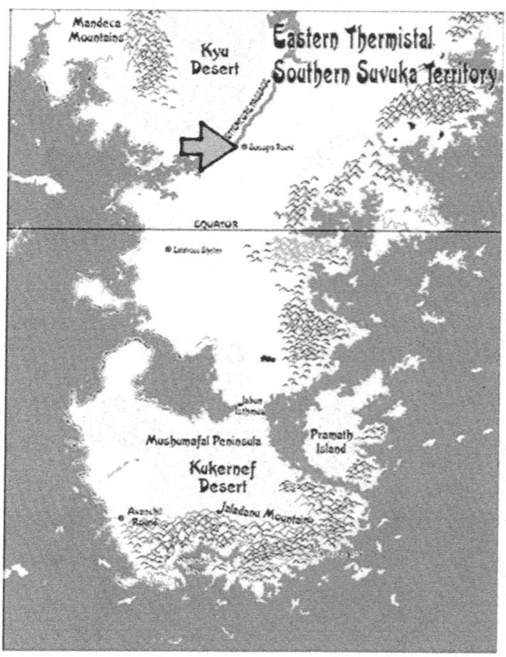

Many returned on a mission for the Servants to determine the depth of the Suvuka's identification with Hesha Vira. The local authorities processed this new information and tracked herd movements on the other side. Shuna-Vurupta re-visited several museums to study the reconstructed skeletons and other Suvuka artifacts and asked the curators questions. Authorities informed him of increased activity occurring near the observation post. He made the crossing from the Western Walls of the Vettencore Passage to the Eastern Wall at once. He had lain in the observation tunnel, buried within the wall having tiny openings for him to look through and watched the approaching group with a powerful viewing glass. He made his way along the lower level of the inner wall to where they could see him on top of the wall. The group of Suvuka, perhaps half an anda away, watched him. He counted twenty-two figures and presumed this a small herd, or portion of a pack, come to howl and posture at the wall. He prepared himself in haste in case they chose to leave after seeing him.

* * *

"Sinkin!" Setush whispered. "Is this it?"

Sinkin nodded in wonder. "They change their pelts! Its head is now dark!

"What is it doing here? How did it find you?"

Sinkin said nothing. The three New Stags and their attending herdmates stood looking at the tiny lone figure of the enemy. To their amazement, it began shifting from one of its hind paws to the other. It did this several times before raising and lowering its front limbs reflected in its back limbs' movements. Its thin torso twisted front and back and to each side, each movement ending in a gesture of one of the limbs.

"This is what it did?" Hiratak asked.

"This is what it did in front of me," Sinkin said. "Why? What does it mean? Is this a language?"

Visko came to stand beside Sinkin, "They are tiny! Their bodies and limbs are thin! Look at its head! How does this little neck hold its head up? Small wonder we underestimated them."

The Tolku continued to move its limbs and body rhythmically. Setush decided to try something and roared at the top of his lungs. The little figure froze before continuing its movements.

"I have not heard of this," Hiratak said, continuing to watch the creature. "There is no mention of this in the songs. The movements are deliberate, but to what end?"

"How could this creature track us?" Morakav said. He turned to Sinkin, "You found it on Mushumafal's southern shore. That is below the Jaladanu Mountains! They floated away on their cart. We never saw them again. We did not smell them once. We know their scent!" The other members of Makusk Herd nodded at this. "It is beyond belief this creature found you."

"While an amazing sight," Visko said, "this conforms to the descriptions. Is it the same one?"

Sinkin looked at Visko before looking back at the distant figure high on the smooth wall. "Yes. It is a juvenile. Do you agree, Herdmaster?"

Hiratak came forward and peered at the figure. "I do. Descriptions detail their different ages. This one is the equivalent of a young buck. The body will grow heavier. The limbs will thicken with age."

The little Tolku stopped and gazed at them. The three herds watched as the skin of the enemy turned red and yellow.

"What is this?" Hiratak said. "What is it doing?"

They looked to each other to confirm they witnessed the same sight.

* * *

Shuna-Vurupta could not believe it. The rude group of creatures, whose powerful odours he smelled from this distance, became transformed into one of the Principle Faces of Tatchlan! He looked into the living Face of Hesha Vira! The heads of the Suvuka studded Hesha Vira's Face, also looking at him. Suvuka heads punctuating one of the Principle Faces of Tatchlan was near impossible for him to comprehend. His sister and the Servants' predictions had come true! He began the second phase by lowering himself to a seated position and clapping his hands and chanting. "Hesha Vira! Hesha Vira!

Cold and burning do come nearer!
Wild and frightening, bold and brightening,
you who hold the chaos fighting!
Hesha Vira! Hesha Vira!
Tamer, calmer, and our fighter!
Flesh of flame and air a tangle,
on Kava-Kura's tongue, you dangle.
Hesha Vira! Hesha Vira!
Queen of horror, sage and hearer.
Be our Face that draws us nearer!
Hesha Vira! Hesha Vira!
Stoke your furnace, feed your flames,
remake all things, achieve all aims!
Hesha Vira! Hesha Vira! . . ."

He stopped the litany as Hesha Vira began to melt away, leaving the Suvuka. His instructions were to watch what happened next with care. One by one, they sat on their haunches, and Shuna-Vurupta held his breath.

* * *

The Suvuka comprehended one word, the Tolku uttered. This and his transformed flesh shocked and amazed them. With the ending of its rhythmic noise, it sat watching them.

"Perhaps," Setush began looking at Sinkin and Visko, "Hesha Vira rose as Anu's new champion. She has shown us favour. She demonstrates Her hold over our enemy."

Sinkin looked thoughtful, and Visko bewildered. "I had thought my head ached with questions already! This creature . . . squeaked Her name!" Visko looked at the others, "Does anyone doubt hearing this? The creature ill pronounced it - but said it. His flesh altered to Her colours!" The others nodded to him and each other. Visko frowned at the far-off shape seated on the wall. He looked at the other two New Stags, "You told me what the Keepers said. How they wanted you to 'rescue' Hesha Vira. You pulled on Her limbs to aid Her." Sinkin and Setush nodded.

"Something deep has happened! This has become a Face of Anu. She smiled on ancient bards, the mad and dreamers. She makes the Keepers of the Rounds quake." He stared at the little creature. It continued to watch them. "This is a revelation! I do not understand it. I am certain it is important."

"How are we to understand this?" Sinkin said. "I am also sure it said Hesha Vira's name. It said one of our words! What does its gibberish and slapping mean? This one's Face transformed into Hers. When its body took Her colours, I felt the murmur of Her realm."

"No!" Hiratak said. "You are mistaken to say so. This creature did not alter. We felt the presence of our Hesha Vira. We witnessed Anu transformed. This creature but reflected the surrounding glory. She compelled it to do homage to Her and to us. Setush is correct in this. Hesha Vira is Anu's gift to us. She is revealed to each herd. We must work to learn her language. We must read her signs. This twisted creature perverts Anu. It must not partake of her visage!"

Sinkin noted the fire in their eyes and remained silent. He frowned as he looked at the creature and kept his questions and doubts to himself. He confronted new loneliness. Surrounded by his herd and his friend Setush, he knew his busy thoughts separated him. The Sagas were suspect, and this new layer of religion over their old insecurity grew strong. Setush would ever look to him. Who would he look to? He turned back to the tiny figure and began to feel a new emotion. Instead of contempt and hatred, stirrings of warmth rose within him. What did this mean? While the rest argued and declared, he could not take his eyes off the little Tolku. He felt the urge to stand and dance, but dared not do so before the others.

* * *

Shuna-Vurupta heard the name Hesha Vira said in garbled fashion several times among the distant grunts and growls. While his dance was not answered, his mission was still complete. He continued to watch the animated vocalizations among the group. He was grateful for the land's steep incline leading down to the base of the smooth wall he sat on. From this distance, he saw how large most of them were. The wind came in gusts on top of the wall, and he shivered. Vurupta decided to perform the last act, despite having what he required and his fingers being numb. He took out a small flute delicately wrought of a juvenile Danta head horn. He had been told the Suvuka could not hear high notes. He began to play a childhood tune in the lower register. The gentle notes of the ancient 'Lay of Lasam,' customarily associated with elegant settings, now echoed across the wilderness. He worried the wind might carry his music away, but the group stopped as he played and stared at him. He stood as he continued playing. He chose to play the tune very slowly. As he played, he also moved his body to the deliberate rhythm of the song. He began to repeat the body and leg movements the northern boy had shown him. The creatures sat and watched him. He stopped and stood, looking at the group. In silence, they stared back at him. It was enough; he had laid the groundwork for future work. Shuna-Vurupta raised one hand to them, as Seti said he did on the ship. He forced himself to turn and descend the stairs. He walked a short way along the inner wall, squeezed into the Observation tunnel and crawled forward to observe.

* * *

The Suvuka sat, staring at the empty wall. Visko turned to Sinkin, "Did this mite also sing to you?"

Sinkin shook his head. "Beyond the usual bleating of prey, it made no such sound. I have never heard such a bird song, yet," he frowned at Sinkin, "there was something familiar about it."

"Take care!" Morakav growled. "Remember what our herd endured! They still wrap themselves in bewildering wiles. To my ears, this 'song' smelt of stealth and secret powers. Hesha Vira was not present. Whatever we just saw was meant to baffle and mystify us."

Hiratak gave his friend a warm glance before speaking. "Anu has ever favoured *us*! She rose up to meet *our* paws and smiled on *our* shepherding of her children. We were not always as we are now. The Bards tell of the infancy of our kind and how our bodies and minds have grown. Our history is filled with terrible conflict and great change. Now we witness this new Face of Anu named Hesha Vira. She is for us! She runs with us! Our enemy impudently attempted to enslave Her, as they have so many others. She broke free! She dominated that little thing! For all their powers, She possesses them at will! Do not be fooled by their wiles! They have disfigured themselves. They aspire to pollute Anu! We stand with Anu and Hesha Vira against them! We are the guardians of Anu. We will prevail! Hesha Vira now makes our hearts sing. She becomes the Face of our honour! What fortifies us is true! What elevates us is true! What comforts us is true!"

None noticed that Sinkin did not join the general roar in answer to this speech. Hiratak then reared up, his back to the enemy's monument, "Here you three began your Four Paws. Our repeated declaration seals your childhood. It opens your adult lives. We will reflect on this run for many years to come. Now we finish the run and return to our herds. These new visions will take long to seep in and remake us." With difficulty, he turned to face the wall on his hind legs and began the declaration.

"Behold our prison wall!"

"Yeeeaaaaoooo!" the rest called out.

"Behold our shame! Behold our defeat!"

"Taaaoooo! Tatal! Tatal! Tatal!" the others called.

"Behold the place our honour will return! Behold the place our vengeance will commence!"

"Vooooaaarrrrat! VAT! VAT! VAT!"

"Vooooaaarrrrat! VAT! VAT! VAT!"

Members of the three herds stood in a half-circle. They began to stamp their paws and bite their lips. They rolled their eyes, bared their fangs, raised their front paws bristling with sharpened talons. They swiped them in the air while extending their long tongues. Sinkin made the gestures with the rest but knew something profound had shifted inside him. He watched as all his herdmates embraced what comforted them over what was plain truth before their eyes and ears. This Tolku had been able to follow him back to the wall. It danced for him again! It did not arrogantly bray or stamp but sang and treaded artful steps. It even gave the same departing gesture of raising one limb. They were bonded by the same wondrous Face. Were he by himself, he might have tried to come closer and forge a new song and dance for them both. How could he ever leave this creature behind?

* * *

Shuna-Vurupta found tears forming in his eyes. The descriptions and illustrations he had studied paled witnessing this wall ritual. Two deep things came together for him. Within his body, he carried what the Servants in Bhampay call the 'Majastas Salt.' This referred to the infant Thakadush-Satwa's sweat. It had sunk into his skin, and he became a new source of it. His many charms paved the way for a wide dispersal since his return, ensuring the Majastas Salt now took root on Thermistal. As the modification grew among the Tolku here, he would find his place within this emerging Cluster-of-Clusters Society. Beyond this, he had a second deep aspiration. Shuna-Vurupta would become part of work more extensive than the Vettencore Passage itself to genuinely domesticate and harmonize the Suvuka with the Tolku.

Hesha Vira had already laid the foundation for them. From the impending Cluster-of-Clusters society on Thermistal, he would serve his glorious Shuna-Shapta and Majastas by devoting himself to this noblest conclusion to the Suvuka issue. The Suvuka and Tolku would be woven together into a single thread with a shared destiny. He recalled a line from his studies, 'There is no greater joy than to labour on what you did not begin, and others shall continue.' He had found his work and his place at last.

CHAPTER 63

Emedin

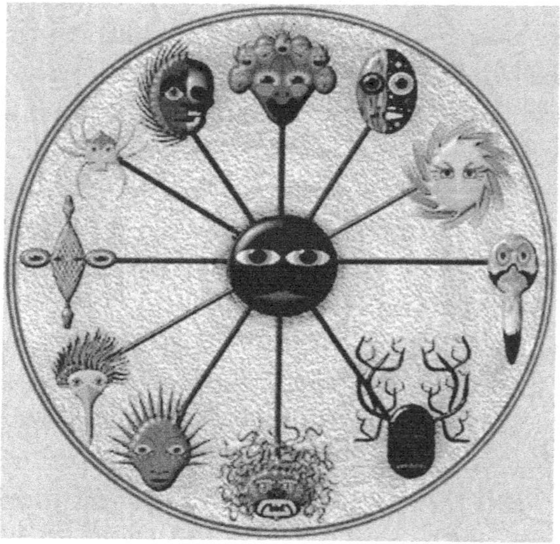

Day Fifty-Five, Two-Week Four, Ingeen, the Wheel, it is the Hesha Vira Festival in Bhampay.

For forty days Bhampay had been saturated by imperial splendour. His Imperial Highness had arrived on Day Five and left on Day 45 of the new year 1273. With great ceremony it had been declared that this year marked the final decade of the Duamang Age. It was now ten days since the Muraharoma Emperor had returned to Upata-Shepsus. The formal Sawlu Clan business was for now concluded and Everlastingly Serving Tanas and Captain Emedin, who had become fast friends, finally resolved to take a long-delayed journey together. They stepped out of the Master Enclave and into streets scoured by two days of heavy rains. These ancient avenues now sparkled and steamed under Nu's gentle Eye. The pair were a study in contrasts. Emedin was near a head taller than Tanas and was a pale, blond northerner. Tanas was comparatively square and stocky with his dark copper skin and black shining braids. Emedin wore the same hat with its broad rim she had purchased on Avatay Island, complimenting her flowing green top and blue leggings. Tanas had dispensed with alternating between ceremonial and formal attire for a similar type top in orange and yellow leggings. Both held elegant green parasols rich in floral patterning and featuring tiny bells at the end of each of their eight tips.

"I hear you, Dine, and Seti joined Hegev in completing her original quest to visit our intact Menem Shrine," Tanas said.

"Yes!" Emedin exclaimed as they strolled hand in hand. "Notwithstanding what has happened since she first arrived on Statos-Vey so many years ago, she was most gratified with the monument. Having it so close to Bhampay and in such pristine condition led to much delight and bemusement. She regaled us with stories of previous attempts to approach some of the others, often involving difficult negotiations through a sea of thickets. When she arrived, bruised and scratched, she was met by crumbling ruins choked with vines. We all came away with a sense of having caught a glimmer of the best intent of that tradition."

"All twenty of these sites and their surrounds should be restored and protected," Tanas answered shaking his head. "It is most unfortunate they have been neglected so long. Menem has a fraught legacy here on Statos-Vey. This land is filled with history, and its features fill each vale and dot each hill. These shrines were once significant gathering places and must be accorded the proper respect. To allow them to die of neglect would be most unwise of us."

"Seti was able to recite several lines from the Tarunachit as we examined the fresh-painted murals. His voice echoed along the curving walls, suggesting their design may have in part been to contain the sound of pilgrim's devotions. Dine was able to summon from memory an old Menem song I had not heard in forty years! Now we four are reconciled, it was a fit setting for us to complete our journey together. Soon, Dine and

I shall begin our journey home. As with the practice on Hegev's island, upon our return we shall be feted and regale many with the wonders we have seen."

Tanas stopped and looked up at Emedin. "What will you tell them?"

Emedin looked off into the distance, "There was a time when I thought myself a witness to historic events. I was eleven when Nebutan arrived and grew up to her lectures and debates. Through my early years on land I had served as a book binder before turning to teaching. I first met Dine in the Printer House where he was my supervisor. That was over thirty years ago! We took different paths, and each suffered our own set of reverses. In different ways we were also victims of larger events dashing our initial plans. As is not uncommon for an island nation, fate sent us both to the sea. By the time we met again our roles had reversed and I outranked him. Whilst siblings and childhood friends produced an excess of offspring, they stay in place. My return visits find them amidst their noisy brood unaware of the larger world and unchanged in their parochial views. Meanwhile I am transformed. My home floats upon the waves, where I have been filled with Anu's glory and horror. Seti is but the most recent chapter in the epic of my life."

"And now you witness a new company of wonders," Tanas said.

"Indeed! One being a giant! I knew they existed and had heard about the Emperor's stature but was not prepared for how large he was!"

"Giantism runs in the Imperial Family," Tanas answered.

"To see Him seated half way up the stairway of The Tooth, with Shuna-Shapta on his lap and Thakadush-Satwa on hers, eclipses all former marvels I have witnessed. Like the Emperor's magnified body, the canvass of all events extends beyond my view."

As they continued their stroll it became clear Bhampay was alive with frenetic activity. Instead of resting after so many ceremonies and festivals, a profound desire to remake itself appeared to possess the city. After a pause during the recent torrent, the sounds of construction once again echoed in all directions. Piles of debris dotted the streets. More came out of blocks and dwellings as they tried to navigate their way through the growing confusion. They passed a pile of doors, taken off their hinges and stacked as garbage by a common two-storey tenement. There they saw a child singing and dancing as he moved from one characteristically tall and narrow southern window to the next. Through these narrow slits they could see half of the eight separate sets of walls partitioning the narrow dwellings of the block had been removed on the main floor. Rough gaps in some of the back walls suggested plans for more windows. The alternating walls appeared half cut away to create an open space across the front half of the structure. The singing boy, joined by many more children, cavorted through this open front space, their high-pitched voices echoing from end to end. Between two of the half walls stood a group of buoyant adults laughing as they appeared to prepare the wall for plastering. A mild odour of sulphur exited the windows. Loud banging on the second floor suggested similar plans being enacted there.

"I fear they may bring the ceiling down on themselves," Emedin said.

Tanas pointed to a triangular medallion affixed on the outer wall in several places. "That signals the approval of the engineers of the Preeminent Works Ministry's Enhancement Bureau. This building would have been inspected and masters brought in for specialized structural work prior to these inhabitants taking on these tasks. I am told some in their enthusiasm have attempted to proceed without such permissions but one or more neighbours quickly correct them. I understand this is happening throughout the city, the fact there have been no injuries is a credit to our provincial ministries."

"So!" Emedin exclaimed looking around, "All at once Bhampay determines to abolish each barrier. This is yet another wonder to witness!"

They continued through the jubilant construction zone as the towering statues seen in the distance began to loom over them. They stood on tall pedestals ringing an open plaza. Emedin read off the inscriptions, such as Yin-Vinulan XII, the 'dwarf' and Yin-Vinulan XXIV, the 'dancer.' Their elegantly sculpted bodies were covered in glittering mosaics, their arms draped in fresh flowers and their legs wrapped in new scarves.

"How you Bhampaians love your ancient dynasty!" she exclaimed.

"They gave us much that endures and above all other unifying dynasties treasured beauty and art," Tanas answered. "The Suvuka robbed all Tolku of the legacy of that far larger capital of Thithanu, the 'World City,' on Rho-Jashun. Bhampay was spared that fate behind the

Mulungu Mountain's 'Impenetrable Barrier Region,' and connects us to much of great value in our treasured past. This is also the city that was the first to openly welcome the Masters and support their work, back when your Menem Priests persecuted our grandmothers and their mothers in Rho-Jashun."

"Aya! I beg you do not call them 'my priests!" Emedin laughed. "Our founder, the renegade Nallurakon, was a rebel against all priesthoods past and present. My ancestors knew well the follies of what to them were already 'ancient Menem priests' based in Thithanu before the Suvuka Onslaught ended them. As children our teachers taught us to condemned them for their corruption, their oppression, and their being far too enraptured with their own power."

"Ah! A most welcome correction! There are likely others in Bhampay knowing this distinction well. For all I have learned from your clan these past fleeting two-weeks, it is clear I remain innocent of much."

They continued to stroll out of the plaza and past another surrounded by statues of animals and other creatures standing beside those representing fantastic beings out of the epics. These figures were either painted vivid colours or wore brilliant adornments. Very little bare stone or metal was left on any of them. Many of the statues gestured in ways Emedin could not fathom and stood in absurd combinations. Were she not so eager to reach their destination she would have asked many questions about them. A chorus of near and distant banging and other sounds of construction echoed back and forth across a third open space

Patzku icon

Varku icon

they crossed as intricate flock formations of Krall performed maneuvers overhead. They stopped and watched as a group of six Varku, divided into two groups of three, carried two long poles across the third plaza of their journey. Their orange and red fur shone under Nu's gaze.

"I had quite forgotten," Emedin said watching them. "Long before we reached the Memanu Field, I recall seeing another branch of Cousin, the dark brown Patzku, employed in large groups in a farmer's field near the coast. I knew of the ancient's use of all Cousins here in the south, but had never clearly seen a group of near sixty working in such a co-ordinated manner with no attendants present. Had I not employed my glass to examine them during our swift passage I would not have believed it. I also thought I saw the occasional Varku up in the rigging of other ships during this trip here in the south, but was occupied or too far away to be certain. For the little ones to be present in the ropes is a common sight, but there have always been rumours of Varku tending to the sails of ships here."

"Our ancient grandmothers and their mothers first steps along the path to Tatchlan involved reaching out to all classes of our Cousins," Tanas answered. "You are accustomed to our little 'Tree Dwellers' running messages, but our larger 'Long Tail Troupes,' such as our Patzku and these Varku, and even our 'Massive Land Walkers,' have had an honoured place with our Masters for generations. These ones," he indicated the Varku as they stepped off the square in the distance and moved towards a group of waiting Tolku, "possess a pronounced presence within Tatchlan. Future generations shall likely witness their emergence as a wonder amongst us."

They exited the plaza and continued until finding extensive work on their intended roadway and moved off to the left side where an unaffected street progressed in the same direction. They heard groups of voices rising in unfamiliar song, accompanied by rhythmic clapping. They saw a large group performing a Circle Dance in another opened building interior. An elaborate puppet performance with huge figures wearing peculiar masks could be seen a few streets away. A new sound filled the background as a multitude of clapping and clicking sounds issued from many windows. Then, without warning, they approached the entrance to the Companion Avenue to their right.

"I have arrived," Emedin declared staring at the unmistakable shimmering fish statues. "I feel as if I have journeyed all my life to reach this place. How is it I have never been here before, yet my feet feel at home for the first time?"

As they turned to approach the avenue Emedin saw it was surrounded by recent construction. Six simple structures formed a half circle from the beginning to the end of the avenue on either side, for a total of twelve. Strangely silent crowds were moving through the avenue, obscuring the fronts of the right hand buildings. She saw the backs of the left set as from behind the two of them approached. Each structure was painted a different set of colours. On the left, the first structure was black, wearing radiant spots. The second was half black with the four moons painted on it. The other half was white, covered in speckles she assumed signified the elaborate patterns of stars visible during the day. The next was rich green overlaid in an elaborate pattern in lighter and darker shades and warm brown horizontal patterns. The roof had yellow spikes rising out of it. The quiet crowd was exiting and began to disburse into small groups, suddenly leaving the two of them alone at the entrance.

As they moved along the avenue, beyond the ancient fish statues, the fronts of the buildings revealed themselves as enclosures. Inside stood a face of similar dimensions and matching the colouration of its shelter. Something like an altar stood before the entrance of each one, similarly coloured to the occupant of the enclosure. Emedin looked down to see brilliant mosaics beneath the buildings. The residual grout used in their recent completion filled her nostrils. A radiating pattern repeating the dominant colours and symbols of each figure moved in toward the central avenue, retaining its original paving stones. It was worn and displaying deep cart ruts from many generations of use. The effect was of one large mosaic wheel with the avenue forming a central spoke, surrounded by the twelve buildings as fasteners for the spokes to the wheel.

"Behold the Twelve Faces of Tatchlan," Everlastingly Serving Tanas said.

"I have begun to dream of them," Emedin answered in hushed tones. "Some are tender and others daunting, but all possess such majesty!"

As Emedin and Tanas approached the Companion Pond they saw

Seti between it and a large round structure behind him. The walls had something growing over them punctuated by what appeared as face and hand designs. It gave the illusion of the building being alive. Seti knelt beside the Regent and her First and Second Amas holding their beautiful newborn girls, just thirty days old. They formed a circle around a tiny girl standing firmly in their midst. They all engaged in earnest conversation and Seti gestured several times to his head. As the two of them moved around the pond, casting a quick glance at the amazing aquatic creatures watching them, Seti had bowed. The baby stuck her fingers in her mouth and then pressed them to Seti's forehead. None showed any indication of wonder. Seti straightened and smiled at his old and new friend as they approached. In the short time since their last meeting, Seti had grown. His smooth and light skin suggested he had gone through yet another skin shedding. His face was rounder and at the same time more solid. His frame had filled and he was an even stronger and healthier a young man than Emedin had ever known. Emedin settled beside Seti, raised her palms to the two Amas, the tall and handsome young woman, and the tiny Majastas. The little girl was naked save for a pretty design painted on her face and chest. Emedin reached out her hand and the baby grasped one of her thick, calloused fingers.

"You must be our future," she smiled at the child.

The End

Book Two of the
Anu Awakes Series

Amarel
Mountain

About the Author

I live in Canada and my first sixty-five years have included extensive exploration, education, and reading along with travelling around the world. The early stirrings of this world within came in part from reading such fantasy and sci-fi classics as Tolkien's Lord of the Rings, Herbert's Dune series and Asimov's Foundation series. All this informs my personal Utopia Epic Fantasy series. Other aspects include being a member of the LGBTQ community and thus bringing subtle aspects of that part of my life into my work.